EARTHDAWN

FOURTH EDITION

GAME MASTER'S GUIDE

FASA GAMES INC. 2015

CREDITS

EARTHDAWN GAMEMASTER'S GUIDE
FOURTH EDITION

Line Developer: Josh Harrison
Fourth Edition Development: Josh Harrison, Morgan Weeks, R Scott Tilton
Additional Material: Brenton Binns, Bryan Little, David Marshall
Editing: Tiffany Ragland, Benjamin Plaga
Art Director: Jeff Laubenstein
Layout: Ian R Liddle
Interior Black and White Art: Janet Aulisio, Travis Hanson, Jeff Laubenstein, Eric Lofgren, Jeremy McHugh, Melanie Philippi, Nadine Schakel, Tony Szczudlo
Interior Color: Milivoj Ceran, Jeremy McHugh, Maik Schmidt, Karsten Schreures, Kosta Schleger
Cover Painting: Milivoj Ceran

Original Earthdawn Material (First through Third Editions): Carlton W Anderson, L Ross Babcock III, Eike-Christian Bertram, Randall N Bills, Steven J Black, Jennifer Brandes, Zach Bush, Robert C Charette, Loren Coleman, Robert Cruz, Kathleen E Czechowski, Carsten Damm, Tom Dowd, Nigel D Findley, Nicole Frein, Robert Fulford, Marc Gascoigne, Greg Gorden, Lars Gottlieb, Keith Graham, Josh Harrison, Attila Hatvagner, Lars Heitmann, Achim Held, Shane Lacy Hensley, Chris Hepler, Michael L Jacobs, Steve Kenson, Jay Krob, Christopher Kubasik, Robin D Laws, Sam Lewis, Jacques Marcotte, Angel Leigh McCoy, Michael A Mulvihill, Mike Nielson, Diane Piron-Gelman, Neal A Porter, Louis J Prosperi, Sean R Rhoades, Bradley Robins, Chris Ryan, Carl Sargent, James Sutton, John J Terra, Richard Tomasso, Allen Varney, Daniel Vitti, Jason U Wallace, Nicholas Warcholak, Jordan Weisman, Olav Wikan, Donovan Winch, Sam Witt, Teeuwynn Woodruff, Hank Woon

Playtesters: Michael S Allegro II, Brenton Binns, Leanne Binns, Doug Campbell, Megan Cherry, Matthew Croco, Jeff Davis, Mary Harrison, Cory Hurst-Thomas, Sam Kelly-Quattrocchi, James Kephart, Sarah Miller, Peter Plankis, Kyle Pritchard, Katja Reid, Sarah Richards, Karol Rybaltowski, Jason Schindler, James Summerton, Pierre Summerton, D J Zissen

Josh's Special Thanks: Ross Babcock, Lou Prosperi, Andrew Ragland, Todd Bogenrief, James Sutton, the Freedonian Engineering Corps, the online Earthdawn community, and the many people who have sat at my table at home and at cons.

Internet: www.fasagames.com
Contact: earthdawn@fasagames.com
Version: First Printing, January 2016

Earthdawn is a registered trademark of FASA Corporation. Barsaive, FASA and the FASA Logo are trademarks of FASA Corporation. Copyright © 1993-2015 FASA Corporation. Earthdawn and all associated trademarks and copyrights are used under license from FASA Corporation.

Published by FASA Games, Inc. All rights reserved.

KICKSTARTER CREDITS

Over 1,000 fans and supporters backed this project on Kickstarter. Special thanks goes out to each and every one of them. Your generosity made this book possible.

@JohnPatrickMCP
A Williams
A. Postlep
A. Quentin Murlin
A.G.
Aaron Alberg
Aaron Fleishman
Aaron Gottschalk
Aaron Reimer
Aaron Rollins
Aaron Scott
Aaron Smith
Aaron Weick
Aaron Wong
Adam Everman
Adam Longley
Adam Mock
Adam Rajski
Adam Reynolds
Adam Strong-Morse
Adam Waggenspack
Adrian Vinci
adumbratus
Aelfryc An'Aldar
Aidan Carr
Aktiv Ungdom Skellefteå
Alain Dame
Albert Ordonez
Albert Perrien II
Alex Bauer
Alex Manduley
Alex Pogue
Alex Robinson-Hamilton
Alexander J. Prewett
Alexander Sawyer
Alexander Schmidt
Alexandre MISSOTY
Alexis & Holly Edminster
Allan Prewett
Allen L Farr
Alosia Sellers

Amiel Kievit
Amy & Adam Roloson
Anarion Avemark
Anders Blom
Anders Nordberg
Andre Knappe
André Roy
Andrea "L2P" Urbani
Andrea Martinelli
Andreas Sewe
Andrew "Ranneko" Delaney
Andrew Chang
Andrew Curtis Quach
Andrew George
Andrew Graves
Andrew Kelsoe
Andrew Marshall
Andrew Moreton
Andrew Parent
Andrew 'Whitenoise' Rogers
Andrew Wojcik twitter handle
@ blackrobemage
Andy 'awmyhr' MyHR
Andy Cowen
Andy 'Jhandar' White
Angel Leigh McCoy
Angelo Pileggi
Anne Cross
Anonymous
Anthony Cordeiro
Anthony Enright
Anthony Popowski
Antonio Vincentelli
Antti Walhelm
Arnaud 'Mahar' Métais
Arthur McMahon
Arthur Vaccarino
Ash
Ashtar le Partagé
Ballard
Bapf

Bart Vanderstukken
Bastian Mueller
Bastien Daugas
ben hammer
Ben Hayes
Ben Messer
Ben Rosenblum
Benjamin Colecliffe
Benjamin Sperduto
Benoit
Benoit Devost
Benyi Grath Laszlo
Bevan Anderson
Bez Bezson
Bill Wilson
Björn Hansson
Bo Bjerregaard
Bob Huss
Bob Manasco
Bob Petrowski
Brad Blissett
Brad Decker
Brad Gunnels
Brad Smith
Bradford Moreland
Bradley Russo
Brandon Bradley
Brandon Bryan
Brandon D. Ove
Brandon Gillespie
Brandon Kaya
Brandon W. Bryant
Bren Rowe
Brennan M. O'Keefe
Brent Evans
Brent Selle
Brett Anderson
Brett Bowen
Brett Easterbrook
Brett Griggs
Brett Lea

Brian "Blorg Deathcheater" Stanley
brian allred
Brian Brown
Brian Hecht
Brian Hevlin
Brian J. Burke
Brian Sniffen
Brian Stiegler
Bruce Gray
Bruce Turner
Bryan A. Ellis
Bryan Graham
C C Magnus Gustavsson
C.Lowe
C. Ryan Smith
Caedric
Cameron Johnson
Cameron Mark Doyle
Carl Swienton
Carlos (Charlie) Martinez
Carlton Davis
Carode
Carsten Bärmann
Cédric Chardon
Chad Hoblitz
Chad Waterman
Chapel
Charles A. Wright
Charles Crowe
Charles Kubasta
Charles Myers
Charlie Collins
Che "UbiquitousRat" Webster
Chih-Hsien Wang
Chris & Andi Knight
Chris Bunch
Chris DiNote
Chris Edwards
Chris Fazio
Chris Heath

3

EARTHDAWN

Chris Kirby
Chris Rotllan
Chris Slazinski
Chris Snyder
Chris Thesing
Chris Thompson
Chris VonPickles
Chris W Mercer
Chris Wightman
Christian Wallraven
Christoph Flandorfer
Christophe "Dragrubis" H.
Christopher "SHAZAM" Prott
Christopher D. Mahoney
Christopher Mangum
Christopher Marks
Christopher Smith
Christopher W. Dolunt
Ciaran Conliffe
Claus Lütke
Conflict Games llc
Corey Lowenberg
Corey Owens
Cory
Coyotekin
Craig "Stevo" Stephenson
Craig Bonnes
Craig Cameron
Craig Dutton
Craig Wright
Crow Tomkus
Curt L. Koenig
D Sonderling
D.J. Cole
Dale Bragg
Dale R. Sines III
Damon E Jacobsen
Dan
Dan 'Berli' Brown
Dan Boice
Dan Derby
Dan Forinton
Dan Hiscutt
Dana "Odo" Flood
Daniel "Nameless1" Gaghan
Daniel Astermo
Daniel Fruchterman
Daniel Lanigan
Daniel Lopretto
Daniel Mooneyham
Daniel Nissman
Daniel Ofer
Daniel Pritchard

Daniel Scheppard
Danilo Alexandre Soares Takano
Danny Godin
Darren Buckley
Darryl Mott Jr - Gamer's Tavern
Darryl Smith
Dave Corner
Dave Perry
Dave Thomas
David "Quindrael" van Nederveen Meerkerk
David "Rockbender" Corcoran, Jr.
David Bendfield
David Bowers
David Chart
David Futterrer
David Gdula
David Grant Sinclair
David Hall
David Harrison
David Lucardie
David Mandeville
David Marshall
David Miller
David Morledge
David Orna-Ornstein
David Renard
David Stephenson
David Sutherland
David Vibbert
David Wiley Holton
David Wilson Brown
David Yellope
Dean Bailey
Dean Keith
DeAnna Ferguson
DeathBurst
Debbie Seale
Declan O'Connell
Dehove Gildas
Delano Lopez
Denis Laporte
Dennis Humm
Dennis Schieferdecker
Dennis Timm
Derek "Pineapple Steak" Swoyer
Devon Peterson
Devrim Turak
Di King
Dick Kingman

Dmitry Avramenko
Doc Smiley
Don Pierce
Donald Gadberry
Doubleclick
Doug Campbell
Douglas Reid
Douglas Snyder
Douglas W. Cunningham
Dr. Dustin Spencer, DNP
Dr. Jeremy Qualls
Drew (Andrew) South
Drew Pessarchick
Duncan Pickard
Dustin D Rippetoe
Dustin Headen
Dwayne MacKinnon
Ed
Ed Gibbs
Ed McW
Edward
Edward A. Ritsch
Eeeeka
Elaine Uy
Elijah Scheidemen
Emmanuel "Ketzol" LANDAIS
Empress Alaria Festryl
Eoin Burke
Epic RPG Blog
Eric Aili
Eric Bonnet
Eric C. Kiefer
Eric Coates
Eric Gunsolus
Eric Josue
Eric Lohmeier
Eric S.
Eric Schleuning
Eric Williamson
Erik Schmidt
Erik Singer
erik tenkar
Ernie Juan
Erwin Burema
Evan Odensky
F Steyert
Fabian Sasse
Fantask
Fawa
Filip 'Denadareth' Koza
Finn-Lë Gryndil
Florian
Florian 'Ghrik' Kohn

Florian Greß
Franck "Scorpinou" Mercier
François TRAUTMANN
Frank "Grayhawk" Huminski
Frédéri "Volk Kommissar
Friedrich" POCHARD
F-side Games
G. Hartman
Garabaldi Montrosse
Garren Keckley
Garvin Anders
Gary E.
Gaxx & Beth
Geoffrey BOYD
George DeBeck
Gérald Degryse
GhostBob
Gian Holland
Giuliano Matteo Carrara
Glen R. Taylor
Glenn Berry
Goblin Dung Studios, @
GoblinDung
Graeme Gregory
Graeme Rigg
Greg Qatsha
Gregoire Macqueron
Gregory C. Fellin
Gregory Frank
Griffin Mitchell
Grimagor
Gunnar Högberg
Guy Eliahu
Guy Nuyda
Guy Thompson
H. Th.
Håkon Gaut
Halvor Sæther Berge
Hamish Laws
HANATAKA Shinya
Harald Hellerud
Harold Reavley
Harris Gaiptman
Hauke Thomas
Hawk Haines
Heinrich Krebs
Henrik Augustsson
Howard and Melissa Bein
Hugo van der Velden
Hunter Goins
Ian Cox

4

EARTHDAWN

Ian Hughes
Ikalios
ivnin
J. Quincy Sperber
J.R. Riedel
Jack Gulick
Jacob, Natasha, Lilly Quinn, and Simon David Germany
Jacques Marcotte
Jade Meskill
jaime Robertson
James
James Buster
James Carl Scott
James L Buchanan
James McPherson
James Potter-Brown
James Van Horn
James Williams
James Wilson
Jamie Dannatt
Jan Jansen
Jan Lamely
Jan "Orci" Waller
Jared Graymayne
Jared Hunt
Jason Atkinson
Jason Blalock
Jason Buchstaber
Jason E Petrea
Jason Lund
Jason Marks
Jason Newell
Jason Reynolds
Jason Thompson
Jason Withrow
Jay Kominek
Jay Watson
Jayna Pavlin
Jean-Christophe Cubertafon
Jean-François Homehr
Jeff McAulay
Jeff McElroy
Jeff Painter
Jeff Robert
Jeff Roberts
Jeff Troutman
Jeffery Payne
Jennifer Short
Jenny Langley
Jeppe Hansen
Jer Leedy
Jere Manninen

Jeremiah L. Schwennen
Jeremiah Ramey
Jeremy Fox
Jeremy Kear
Jeremy Mettler
Jerry Ha
Jerry Jakobsson
Jerry Willing
Jesper Hallberg
Jesse Butler
Jessica Hammer
Jessica Lilith Darke
Jessica Roth
Jimmy Ringkvist
JL Couturier
Joe Lawrence
Joe Monti
Joe Russell
Joe Strainic
Joey Lawrence
Johan Fält
Johan Karlsson
Johannes "Stilgar" Horak // @Horak_J
Johannes Link
Johannes Rumpf
Johannes Stock
John "The Breaker" Bonar
John Auer
John Burroughs
John Constable
John D. Kennedy
John 'johnkzin' Rudd
John L. Foster
John P. Schloe
John Paul Ashenfelter
John Paul Pilny
John Scanlon
John W. Thompson
Johnny Burlin
Jon T. Folk
Jonas Schiött
Jonathan Barrette
Jonathan Beverley
Jonathan Karlsson
Jonathan Loyd
Jonathan Reichman
Jonathan Short
Jordi Rabionet
Jorgen Karlsson
Jose Fernandez
Jose Luis Porfirio
Jose Toledo

Josef Wegner
Josema "Yrdin" Romeo
Joseph "Chepe" Lockett
Joseph Budovec
Joseph Fong
Joseph Higgins
Joseph Manning
Joseph Pound
Josh Peters
Joshua "Za Monkey" Ramey
Joshua AE Fontany
Joshua Bursey
Joshua Krage
Joshua LH Burnett
Joshua M. A. Hackett
Joshua McQuinn
Joshua Wilson
Juho
Julien Guignard
Julien Pirou
Jun Suzuki
Justin Thyme
K Kuhn
K. Malycha
K. Scott Rowe
Kaelex
Karim Boivin
Karl the Good
Karl Kreutzer
Karl Larsson
Karl Thiebolt
Karol Rybaltowski
Karoly Kopataki
Kathi Petree (aka the Windling Ninja, Delena)
Kathy Czechowski
katre
Kay Arne Hjorthaug
Kees DeBruin
Keith '1tactician' Duggins
Keith Atkinson
Keith Minsinger
Keith Nelson
Keith Preston
Keith Z
Ken "Professor" Thronberry
Ken Brooks
Ken Marquetecken
Kenn "Kendricke" White
Kenneth Gatt
Kenneth Pepiton
Kerry Shatswell
Kevin Bronakoski

Kevin Flynn
Kevin Hislop
Kevin Knight
Kevin Mason
Kevin Moldenhauer
Kevin R. Czarnecki
Kevin Schantz
kevin shilling
Khalypm
Kimberley Garoni
Kingsley Lintz
Kjell-Runo Ärlebrant
Koen Robijn
KorzenRPG
Kris Kelly
KRWLL
Kyle Greene
Kyle Pritchard
Kyle Rimmer
Kyle Siemer
Lance Henricks
Larry Srutkowski
Lars Gottlieb
Lauren Watson
Leanne Hoffman
Lee DeBoer
Lee F. Foster
Lee Sims
Leo Tokarski
Lesley Mathieson Stratton
Lester Ward
Lily & Ted
Lindon Paxton
Living Worlds Games, LLC.
Liz Fife
Lorm
Lowell Francis
Lubos Comor
Luca Beltrami
Lucas Paynter
Lucy Soika
Ludwig Fiolka
Łukasz Wieloch
Luke Irwin
Luke Thompson
Lykos Vlk
Lyndon Martin
Mads Halling
Magnus Olsson
MakorDal
Makoto TAKADA
Malcus Dorroga
Malte Böhm

5

EARTHDAWN

Marc Bennett	Michael Alexis	Nathan Wiltse	Pelle Ulvegrip
Marc Bevan	Michael Baker	Nathaniel Bowers	Percy Dietz
Marc Novel	Michael 'Cyrion' Kirschbaum	Neil Coles	Persio Sposito
Marc-André Laurence	Michael F. Lowery	Nezgrath & Sheerar	Peter Dean
Marc-André Perreault	Michael F. Wagner	Nicholas A. Tan	Peter J Kaufmann III
Marcel Fuhrmann	Michael Feldhusen	Nicholas Edwards	Peter Jeaiem
Marceli	Michael Fienen	Nicholas Howard	Peter Mundt
Marcin Darmetko	Michael G Kinsley Jr	Nicholas Matzen	Peter Steketee
Marcin sirserafin Pindych	Michael G.	Nicholas Peterson	Peter Teismann
Marco Kosinski	Michael Garoni	Nicholas Zakhar	Petra Shaw
Marcus Arena	Michael Hellenbrecht	Nick Adams	Petri Wessman
Marcus Gschrey	Michael Hill	Nick Cawley	Phil Adler
Marcus Maniakes	Michael J. Burrage	Nick Ireland	Philip D'Hollander
Marcus Morgan	Michael McSwiney	Nico Pendzialek	Philip Stein
Marcus Sannig	Michael Mihallik	Nicolas Acosta	Philipp Schneider
Marie Godyn	Michael Olsen	no	Philippe Hamon
Mario Delfa Rodriguez	Michael R Harding	None	Piers Meynell
Mark "Dojo" Brown	Michael Richards	Notaure	Piotr Konieczny
Mark "Naron" Knights	Michael S Allegro II	NW Zachary	piruett.se
Mark Benfele	Michael Sprague	Obryn	PJ Rausch
Mark Buffington	Michael Staley	ol' Roger	Qali Va'Shen
Mark Pavlou	Michael T Dupler	Ole Thoenies	Quasi
Mark R James	Michael Trapp	Oliver Elias	Quincy James LoBue
Mark Tyler	michael venderdahl	Oliver Kasteleiner	R. Eric Reuss
Mark Watkins	Michał Kosmit Kosmala	Oliver Lind	R. J. Scott McKenzie
Markus Raab	Michelle Eggleston	One Sided Die	Rafal Zaniewski
Markus Schubert	Mickey	Orlean	Ralf Bleh
Markus Schwarz	Mikael Rydfalk	Otmar Rausch	Ralf Bretz
Markus Viklund	Mike Boaz	Otto Martin	Ralf Weustermann
Markus Watt	Mike Davies	Owen Milton	Rasmus Boldt Madsen
Martin Theiss	Mike Mekler	Owen Smith	Ray Chiang
Massin Christophe	Mike Smith	Pablo "Hersho" Domínguez	Ray Wisneski
Mathieu Lapierre	Mike Swiernik	Pablo Saldaña	Raymond Delbert Spencer
Matt "Psyce" Phillips	Mike Tidman	Parker Cestaric	RC <3 AIR
Matt Doidge	Mikhail Tsarev	Patrick Henschel	Remy Handler
Matt 'Fabio' Guyder	Mikko Kuosa	Patrick Martin	Ricardo Alvarez
Matt Harms	Mitch "Haematite" Christov	Patrick Myst	Richard Brown (White_Ghost)
Matt Hayes	Mock	Patrick Northedgers	Richard D Gillespie
Matt Hee	Mordom	Patrick Stalter	Richard Hewett
Matt Petruzzelli	Morgan Hazel	Paul	Richard Hirsch
Matt Rock	Morgan Weeks	Paul Aujla	Richard Hunt
Matt Waddilove	Morten Njaa	Paul Bachleda	Richard Mundy
Matthew C Snydrr	MSpekkio	Paul Clark	Rick Stringer
Matthew Croco	Muckpug	Paul E. Olson	Rik Stewart
Matthew Justin	NA	Paul F	Rikard Jespersen
Matthew Lanigan	Nadine Beu	Paul Hayes	RJ Stewart
Matthew Pennington	Nat Lanza	Paul Maloney	Rob Celada
Matthias Weeks	Nate Nieman	Paul Moore	Rob Little
Mattias Hansson	Nathan Callaway	Paul 'Ogrebear' Baker	Rob van Empel
Max Hollis	Nathan Deno	Paul R. Bahler	Robert "Moricon" Sanders
Max Larivee	Nathan Doyle	Paula González Muñoz	Robert Biskin
MaxMahem	Nathan Hill	Paweł Gołębiewski	Robert Dempsey
Meric Defen	Nathan Seidenberg	Paweł Szczubiał	Robert Edward Webb

EARTHDAWN

Robert Fulford
Robert Griffin
Robert James
Robert Loper
Robert Lyster
Robert Newman
Robert Van Natter
Robert Wilson
Roger Brasslett
Rolph de Ruiter
Ron Reamey
Ron Searcy
Ronald Edel
Ronald Mayrand
Ronald Strong
Ross Thompson
RpgAaron
Russell Hooper
Russell Hoyle
Russell Morris
Ruth Hyatt
Ryan Brooks
Ryan H.
Ryan Hart
Ryan Hinson
Ryan Moore
Ryan Wallace
S J Jennings
S. Wingate
Sage Brush
Saleem Halabi
Sascha Schneider
Scott B & Laura D
Scott Heystraten
Scott K. Ernest
Scott Krok
Scott Rick
Scott Sims
SE Weaver
Sean "Vhoghul" Gallagher
Sean Littlepage
Sean M Smith
Sean McAlister
Sean McPherson
Sebastian
Sebastian Wittler
Sebastian Wolfertz
Sebastien Chabot
Sebastien Doggwiller
Sebastien Houlgate
Sebastien Louvion
Sebők, András
Sequoyah Wright

Serge Billarant
Seth Fogarty
Seth Joseph Feierstein
Sethariel
Seumas Macdonald
sev
"Sexy Mike" Lawson
Shades of Vengeance
Shane B. Bauer
Shane Gaillard
Shane Mclean
Shard73
Shaun D. Burton
Shaun Hill
Shawn "Eidos" Thill
Shawn Campbell
Shawn Dritz
Shawn P
Shelby Abercrombie
Sichr
Sigurd Rubech Hartmeyer-Dinesen
Silvio Lopes
Simon `Vylesse' Jones
Simon Eccles
Simon Ward
Simon Withers
Sirius Pontifex
Skyland Games
Spyke Alexander & Majack
Stark
Stan Brown
Stark
Stefan Jargstorff
Stefan Ottillinger
Stefan Persson
Steffen Palme
Sten Lindgren
Stephan Allgeier
Stephan Bonetti
Stephan Hamat-Rains
Stephan Szabo
Stephen Holder
Stephen Marks
Stephen McKowen
Stephen Webb
Stephen Wilcoxon
Stephen Wroth
Sterling Brucks
Steve Burk
Steve Heydinger
Steve Hurovitz
Steve Jasper

Steve Klein
Steve Kramer
Steve Lord
Steve Sena
Steven Danielson
Steven Griffin
Steven Siddall
Steven Williams
Stoperssonn
Studio 2 Publishing
Sugihiro Imanishi
Sven
Sven "Ke'ronn" Torstrick
Sven Konietzko
Svend Andersen
SwiftOne
T.C. Seuret
Tam and Danks
tauli
tentacle
Teppo Pennanen
Thalion of Throal
The Arcology Podcast
The Mordak
The Tekwych
TheAIY
Theodore Thorp
Thomas Constantine IV
Thomas G Treptow
Thomas Holm
Thomas Langille
Thomas Maund
Thor Olavsrud
Tim Bogosh
Tim Cooper
Tim Martin
Tim Olker
Tim Partridge
Tim Skirvin
Tim Vandenberghe
Timothee Gautheron
Timothy Martin
Timothy Walsh
Timothy Walsh
Timothy Wolford
Tjal
Tobias Jaeger
Toby gilham
Todd Cavanaugh
Todd D. Degani
Todd Rigertas
Tom Smith
Tomas Juhlin

Tommaso Cho'Jin Gollini
Tony & Becky Glinka
Trace Moriarty
Travelers of the Thread
Travis Fauber
Travis Shelton
Trip Space-Parasite
Tristan Hendrick-Beattie
Trollune
Troy Lees
Tyler J Dean
Tyson D. Petty
Tyson Weise
Uriah Blatherwick
Vance Agte
Vaughan Cockell
Veronica & Ron Blessing
Victor "Hellmaster" Pérez
Vincent Arebalo
Vitamancer
Vojtech Pribyl
Wade Geer
Wade Jones
wadledo
Walter F. Croft
Wayne Seeger
Wayne Welgush
Wefra
Wendy & Nicholas Ream
Weston Clowney
Weston Harper
Whitt.
Will Sylwester
William Dunsford
William H.G. Johnson
William Metzler
William Staab
Wölfchen
WOoDY GamesMaster
wraith808
WTP
www.laguaridadeltrasgo.es
Wyldstar
Xavier Freycon
Y. K. Lee
Yachabus
Yann Herpe
Yvan Chatelier
Zabuni
Zach Bertram
Zalzator
Zoldar

7

TABLE OF CONTENTS

CREDITS 2

KICKSTARTER CREDITS 3

INTRODUCTION 11
How to Use This Book 12

WHAT HAS COME BEFORE 15
The Separation of Shosara 15
The Books of Harrow 16
A Foundation is Laid 17
Growing Theran Influence 18
Rites of Protection and Passage 19
Founding an Empire 20
The Scourge Approaches 22
The Long Night 24
Return to the Surface 25
A Changed World 27
The Theran Return 28
An Uneasy Peace 29
The Battle of Prajjor's Field 30
Rebirth of a Nation 32
The Harwood Incident 33
The Capture of the Triumph 35
The Fall of Vivane 36
Aftermath 38
An Uncertain Future 39

THE LAND AND ITS PEOPLE 41
Climate and Terrain 41
People and Politics 42
Culture and Tradition 43
On the Namegiver Races 46
Where People Live 52
The Kingdom of Throal 53
Major Cities and Powers 62

GAMEMASTERING 81
Ground Rules 81

Gamemastering Guidelines 85
Storytelling 89
Game Aids 93
Customizing Earthdawn 94

ADVENTURES AND CAMPAIGNS 99
Creating Adventures 99
Adventure Ideas 109
Creating Campaigns 111
Campaign Ideas 115
Loot 118
Awarding Legend Points 119

EXPLORATION AND TRAVEL 125
Traveling 125
Exploring Kaers and Citadels 131
Complications for Travel
and Exploration 134

ENCOUNTERS 139
Gamemaster Characters 139
Gamemaster Character Attitudes ... 142

CHALLENGES AND OBSTACLES 159
Creating Difficulty Numbers 159
Perception Tests 162
Barriers and Structures 164
Climbing 167
Drowning and Suffocation 168
Fire 170
Secret Doors 171
Poison 171
Traps 179
Curses 184
Disease 186
Fatigue and Injury 192

THREAD ITEMS 197
Overview of Thread Items 197

8

Introducing Thread Items	198	Ally Spirits	376
Key Knowledge	200	Elemental Spirits	383
Designing Thread Items	200	Invae Spirits	404
Thread Items	207		

CREATURES 245

Selecting Creatures for
Encounters 245
Creature Combat 248
Creature Entry Format 252
Creature Descriptions 254

SPIRITS 361

On Ally Spirits 361
On Elemental Spirits 363
On the Invae 364
On Tasked Spirits 365
Using Spirits in Adventures
and Campaigns 365
Strength Ratings 366
Named Spirits 367
Spirit Powers 369
Spirit Descriptions 375

DRAGONS 409

On the Nature and Ways of
Dragons 409
Using Dragons in Adventures
and Campaigns 420
Dragon Powers 424
Dragonlike Creatures 429
Dragons 435
Sample Dragons 444

HORRORS 451

On the Study of the Horrors 451
Using Horrors in Adventures
and Campaigns 454
Horror Powers 455
Horror Constructs 467
Minor Horrors 481

INDEX 502

INTRODUCTION

Magic can do a great deal, but there are rules, and the universe does not take kindly to them being broken.
•*Camryn Pattern-Weaver, addressing a new apprentice* •

When a group of people get together to play a roleplaying game, most of the players take on the role of a specific character that they continue from session to session. One player, however, does not play a fixed character. Instead, he (or she) changes characters multiple times during a session, taking on the role of any secondary, supporting, or antagonist characters needed to flesh out the story. In addition, they referee and manage the game's progress, keeping in mind and enforcing the game's rules. This player is the **gamemaster**.

The gamemaster is the arbiter of the game world. It is a demanding job, but ultimately a rewarding one. Where the other players in the game have a single character to keep track of and make decisions for, the gamemaster is responsible for everything else. They create the situations and scenarios the heroes find themselves in, determine what actions and goals the non-player characters have, sets the difficulty of the challenges the group faces, and helps determine whether any given task succeeds or fails. The gamemaster also acts as the eyes and ears of the players, describing what their characters see and feel. On top of this, they must keep in mind that the ultimate goal of a roleplaying game is to have fun as a group sharing in an exciting tale of danger and adventure.

While the **Earthdawn** *Player's Guide* lays out the rules for player characters, it focuses on rules that the players will use in the course of their adventures. This book includes rules and advice that will help the gamemaster bring those adventures to life, populating the world with people, places and things for the player characters to encounter and interact with. Shopkeepers and sages, towns and temples, heroes, Horrors, and magical treasures, all of these things, and advice on how to use them are included in this book.

HOW TO USE THIS BOOK

If you are new to the world of **Earthdawn**, you might be intimated by the massive tomes of rules. Don't worry, the **Earthdawn** game is pretty easy to learn, and you only need to be familiar with some of the rules to get started. The best advice we can give new players and gamemasters is this: only use the rules you need. Most roleplaying games are intended to be used in an ongoing campaign, and so the *Player's* and *Gamemaster's Guides* provide material that can be used to span years of play. As you become more familiar with the game and its rules, you can start including optional rules and material included in other **Earthdawn** sourcebooks.

While you might want to read the books from cover to cover, you don't need to memorize everything—it can be pretty tedious to work your way through page after page of creature descriptions and blocks of game statistics. Instead, try to familiarize yourself with where different information is located in this book. It is a reference book, and knowing how to find the information you're looking for is better than trying to cram it all into your head. The **Contents** and **Index** should make it easy to find the most common rules and references you will need.

This book is divided into three main sections. The first section covers the world of **Earthdawn**, focusing on the default setting of Barsaive. It looks at the history of the province, including recent events as well as those hundreds of years in the past. It also describes the people and places of Barsaive, including information about how they survived the Scourge.

The second part of the book focuses on the role of the gamemaster in **Earthdawn**, offering advice on how to manage the game, create adventures and encounters for your players, along with ideas and rules about different hazards they might encounter on their travels.

Finally, the third part of the book provides more specific resources for populating your game. It provides descriptions and game statistics for common animals and more fantastic creatures. Additional chapters focus on Dragons, Spirits, and of course the Horrors. This section also includes information on magical treasures, items that heroes find (or seek out) to help overcome the challenges they face. A number of example items are given, along with rules for creating your own unique treasures.

With the information in this book, you should be able to get your **Earthdawn** game up and running. Welcome aboard!

WHAT HAS COME BEFORE

The following are excerpts from "Kingdom and Empire", considered one of the definitive scholarly works of history in Barsaive. Our thanks to Lorekeeper Ensail's apprentice for providing the library with a copy of his master's magnum opus.
•*Thom Edrull, Master of the Great Library* •

There can be no disputing that Barsaive has been shaped by the events of the past, and the Scourge has perhaps had the most profound influence on the land and the Namegivers that live in it. But the Scourge is not all of history, and any understanding of Barsaive must look beyond that long night, into ancient decisions that echo into the present day.

THE SEPARATION OF SHOSARA

Centuries ago, long before the Scourge was even a shadow at the edge of our dreams, well before the Kingdom of Throal was founded, the Elven Court at Wyrm Wood stood as the center of culture and civilization. The Queen ruled from her seat on the Rose Throne, and even elves in distant lands looked to the Court for guidance in what it meant to be an elf.

The first hints of what would become the Schism appeared during the reign of Queen Dallia. The nation of Shosara on the shores of the Gwyn Sea needed ships more suited for the open ocean than traditional elven vessels. They looked instead to the designs used by the residents of the nearby city of Khistova.

What began as mild concern over the departure from tradition became a full-blown scandal when the Court learned that the Khistovans were human. The more traditionally minded viewed this as an unforgivable insult to the purity of the elven ways. The only recourse, they argued, was Separation—formally sundering Shosara's ties with the Court, and declaring them no longer true elves.

Before deciding what sanctions should be leveled against the Shosaran elves, Queen Dallia decided to travel to Shosara. Separation would be a fate worse than death, and she was not willing to impose such a severe punishment without first visiting the land and its people.

Unfortunately, the Queen's expedition met with tragedy. Not long after the Queen and her escort left the safety of Wyrm Wood, they were set upon by the great dragon Alamaise and killed. The reason for this is disputed to this day. Some tales claim it was driven by the bloodthirsty nature of dragons. Others hint the attack was punishment for some unspecified crime. The story told in the Elven Court is that Dallia was murdered for refusing to acknowledge Alamaise as the true ruler of Wyrm Wood.

15

> **Timeline**
> ~400 BT*: First record of settlement at what is now Vivane.
> ~100 BT: Elianar Messias banished from Wyrm Wood
> * Reference to years is based on the Throalic calendar. BT refers to years before the founding of Throal.

Whatever the reason for the attack, any hope of reconciliation between Shosara and the Elven Court was lost when Dallia's successor, Failla, claimed the Rose Throne two years later. A staunch traditionalist, in her eyes there was no excuse for Shosara tainting elven purity the way they did. Shosara was declared forever apart from the Court, and all elves were to sever ties with the nation immediately.

Not surprisingly, much turmoil resulted from Queen Failla's declaration, especially among those elves with ties to Shosara. The Queen held firm, punishing those who spoke out against her. One of the Court's most favored advisors, Elianar Messias, was banished from the Court for speaking out against the decision. Failla declared he might return when he "learned the value of heritage and a quiet tongue."

Decisions like these chart the course of nations.

THE BOOKS OF HARROW

Messias never returned to the Court. He travelled to a small monastery in the foothills of the Delaris Mountains dedicated to Mynbruje, the Passion of Knowledge. The scholars there had uncovered a trove of ancient books and scrolls and gleaned from the parts they were able to translate that they were written during a time when magic was dormant.

Included in the trove uncovered by the scholars was a set of six volumes, identical in style and size. Each had an unsettling rune inscribed in blood on its cover. Messias was convinced they contained powerful, and possibly dangerous, knowledge, and dedicated his life to translating their secrets.

Those secrets would, in the end, cost him his life.

Some years later, his fellow scholars found Messias on the floor of his chamber, wracked with pain and near death. His hands were burned and his face bloody; he had apparently dug his own eyes out and then cast them into the fire.

The mysterious books lay stacked on his desk. A note beside them, in Messias's hand, read:

> These are the Books of Harrow
> They are our doom and our salvation.
> Learn from them, or we all perish.

That night, six more scholars died horribly, killed by something stalking the corridors of the monastery. The next day, one of the surviving scholars, Kearos Navarim, accompanied by three others, set out with the Books of Harrow. Their destination was an island in the Selestrean Sea, far to the southwest, where Navarim was born. The island was a naturally occurring focus of magical energy, and the scholars hoped that energy would protect them as they continued Messias's work.

EARTHDAWN

> **Timeline**
> **~50 BT:** Elianar Messias is found dead with the Books of Harrow. Kearos Navarim founds Nehr'esham.
> **~1 TH:** Construction begins on the Eternal Library.
> **12 TH:** Thandos I, first king of Throal, mysteriously vanishes and is succeeded by his son Thandos II.

When they arrived at the island, they called their new home *Nehr'esham*, or "center of the mind" in the elven tongue. They dedicated themselves to unraveling the mysteries of the Books of Harrow, honoring the memory of Elianar Messias, who would become known as the Martyr Scholar.

A FOUNDATION IS LAID

As part of their efforts to translate the Books of Harrow, Navarim and the other scholars sent word to sages and magicians around the world. In addition to looking for help deciphering the Books, they were certain that similar tomes could be found surviving in other places. The island became a center for scholarship and learning as adepts and scholars of all kinds came together to assist in the Great Project. Nehr'esham grew quickly, drawing merchants and tradesmen.

As the collection of books and scrolls grew, the city's managers arranged for the construction of what would eventually be known as the Eternal Library. It would be a place dedicated to the study of ancient knowledge, magically warded and controlled for the safety of the tomes it contained, as well as those studying them.

Construction of the library continued for more than a hundred years. During that time, disturbing news filtered to the island from other parts of the world. In the human kingdom of Landis, wraithlike spirits stalked the night, turning men to violence. For the dwarfs of Scytha, every child born withered and died in its first month of life, throwing the kingdom into chaos. In many other places, nests of twisted, insect-like humanoids were found. In southern Barsaive, attempts to root out these creatures, called invae, resulted in the total destruction of the city of Emmerlich. To this day, none are certain how many were corrupted by these creatures, and how many were simply innocent victims caught up in the panic.

For Navarim and the other scholars of Nehr'esham, these events were portents of things to come. Jaron, a brilliant dwarf scholar and one of Navarim's main assistants, managed to complete a translation of the First Book of Harrow. The Book warned that the dark events taking place around the world heralded the coming of the Horrors.

The Horrors are powerful and terrible spirits from the darkest reaches of the netherworlds. As the earth's magical energy reaches its peak, the Horrors are able to cross into this world. The Horrors are twisted and beyond reason. Their only desire is to consume and destroy. Some feast on anything physical. Others prefer the flesh and blood of living creatures, while the most powerful and terrible feast on pain, fear, and other dark emotions.

The Horrors were coming, and little could be done to stop them.

Copies of the First Book of Harrow were sent to leaders throughout the known world in an effort to warn them of the coming danger. At first, few listened.

> **Timeline**
> **~100 TH:** Eternal Library completed. Jaron completes translation of First Book of Harrow. Early signs of Horrors recorded in Scytha, Landis, and elsewhere. The Invae Burnings.
> **~200 TH:** Kearos Navarim becomes First Elder of Thera. House K'tenshin founded.
> **212 TH:** Theran envoys first contact Landis with news of the coming Scourge.

The mission of Nehr'esham changed. Work to translate the remaining Books of Harrow continued, but now with the goal of finding a way to stop the Horrors, or at least craft some kind of defense against them. With this changed focus, the leaders of Nehr'esham gave their city a new Name: Thera, which means "foundation," reflecting the hope to provide a foundation for the salvation of the world.

GROWING THERAN INFLUENCE

While many nations initially disregarded the warnings of the First Book of Harrow, the city continued to grow as more and more people travelled there to study, trade, and live on the island. One unfortunate side effect of the rapid growth was the development of slavery as an institution.

Workers from other lands traveled to Thera to provide the labor needed to support the city. Demand led merchant houses to charge high rates for passage. As many of those traveling to the city were unable to pay their passage in advance, financial arrangements were made that indentured the workers to the merchant house as a way of paying off their debt. Over a few decades, the arrangements became more and more favorable for the merchants. Eventually, an indentured worker would never be able to actually pay off his debt, making him—and frequently his family as well—permanent property of the merchant house.

To administer the burgeoning city, leading citizens created a more formal government. They created a council of advisors and administrators known as The Twelve. While Navarim was still considered the leader, his advanced age and focus on his work with the Books of Harrow made his position mostly ceremonial. One of the first actions taken by the Twelve was establishment of a military force to protect Thera and its citizens from bandit and pirate raids.

Navarim cemented his legacy by founding the School of Shadows, the center of the effort to gather information about the coming Horrors and devising ways to defeat them. The research uncovered insights and understandings about the nature of magic that opened up remarkable abilities.

By manipulating the powerful energies contained in the True Elements, the Therans crafted buildings of stunning beauty, as well as airships enabling fast, reliable travel over long distances. Other discoveries included insights into magical warding and protection, healing, illusion and transformation magic, and knowledge of the netherworlds.

As the influence of Thera grew, the island nation forged trade alliances with cities and nations around the Selestrean Sea. Their reach eventually returned to Barsaive, where the Books of Harrow were found and the course of history set in motion. The area was rich in natural resources Thera needed to support its growing population and power. The initial envoys to Landis, Ustrect, Throal, and other powers in the

Timeline
220 TH: Thandos V of Throal dies without heir. A brief civil war erupts. Braza I becomes king and begins excavating Braza's Kingdom.
300 TH: Theran forces conquer Vivane.
309 TH: Construction begins on Sky Point.
341 TH: Kearos Navarim dies.
346 TH: Meach Vara Lingam unveils Rites of Protection and Passage.

region were welcomed, and the rulers happily made agreements with Thera to share in her growing wealth and influence.

RITES OF PROTECTION AND PASSAGE

Nearly four hundred years after founding Nehr'esham, Kearos Navarim died of old age. His body was preserved in amber and given a place of honor in the great plaza of Thera's citadel. Rumors indicated that Navarim worked to the very end trying to complete the Great Project.

The rumors proved true. Not long after Navarim's death, his successor, a human Named Meach Vara Lingam, revealed his final achievement, the Rites of Protection and Passage.

While little beyond a sharp blade and a strong will can defeat the Horrors, Navarim's four-volume work lays out a theoretical basis for protection from them. Because of their power and numbers, direct confrontation would prove suicidal. Only isolation could provide a true means of protection.

This isolation could be achieved by constructing great underground fortresses. Called kaers, these shelters used the living stone of the earth itself to protect against the physically powerful Horrors, as well as those who traveled through astral space. Cities could construct domes of True Earth, or woven from True Air or True Fire. Kaers could be built under the sea and reinforced with True Water. Additional protection could be woven into the kaer's defenses with wards and runes that could "trap" a Horror within the maze of the ward's construction.

The work concluded with a charge for the School of Shadows to put the theory presented in the Rites into practical use. It also recommended that work begin constructing kaers wherever possible, to prepare for the day when the Horrors would be so numerous as to make the surface uninhabitable. That time, Navarim warned, was about eight hundred years in the future.

Reaction to the Rites was mixed at best. Some disregarded its conclusions entirely, unable to believe in a threat so far in the future. Other people, especially those in areas that had been in areas subject to early indications of the Horrors, viewed the Rites with prophetic reverence.

The School of Shadows continued to develop the magical knowledge needed to construct the protective wards. They succeeded, but the knowledge was kept secret. Instead, the mercantile interests in the city and within The Twelve planned to use them as a way to extend Theran influence.

> **Timeline**
> **~405 TH:** Crystal Raiders attack a Shosaran trading vessel, sparking the Orichalcum Wars.
> **~440 TH:** Cara Fahd collapses after Cathon Grimeye causes a lava field to erupt during battle with Landis.
> **443 TH:** Battle of Sky Point and Theran Declaration of Empire.

FOUNDING AN EMPIRE

Despite the reluctance of many nations to take Navarim's warnings seriously, Thera did not wait. Its location at a nexus of magical energy, and the collected magical power and influence it had accumulated meant that it could very well act as a beacon to the Horrors. Construction of the island's defenses began, and the Therans began importing large quantities of the magical metal orichalcum.

Orichalcum is found when certain minerals interact in the presence of True Elements. Long valued by Elementalists and Weaponsmiths because it takes enchantment easily, it was usually considered a byproduct of efforts to mine True Earth. Nobody was sure why the Therans needed such large quantities of the material, but they were all too happy to provide it.

The value of the orichalcum trade drew all manner of merchants and profiteers, and with that came the attention of bandits and raiders. The Crystal Raiders, troll clans that lived in the Twilight Peaks of Barsaive, began attacking shipments of orichalcum, sometimes ranging as far as Shosara in their raids. Other bandits took inspiration as well, and lords and leaders of different powers seized the opportunity to attack or sabotage the shipments of their rivals.

This time in Barsaive is referred to as the Orichalcum Wars. Landis and Cara Fahd fought over territory rich in orichalcum and other True Elements, with the Kingdom of Ustrect joining in the conflict. The elves of Wyrm Wood fought with the dwarfs of Scytha, while Throal was beset with marauding tribes of orks. Nation turned against nation. Mercenaries sold their services and betrayed their employers for a fatter purse.

The Therans didn't concern themselves with the conflict as long as they got their shipments. Their own mining efforts continued, with their airships able to use refined techniques to mine True Air and True Fire from the skies over Death's Sea.

The Crystal Raiders were unable to resist the target presented by the Theran airships. They struck swiftly and often, disrupting mining operations across the region. Thera warned against interference with their vessels, and began arming their mining ships. The trolls continued their raids, leading Thera to start using military escorts. Even in the face of increased resistance, the trolls thumbed their noses at the Therans, using their ships' smaller size and greater maneuverability to their advantage.

The conflict was put to an end when the Therans revealed the true extent of their power. Early one morning a massive airship drifted towards the Twilight Peaks from the southwest. Unlike traditional airships, which bore some resemblance to waterborne vessels, this demonstration of Theran might was a massive stone fortress floating in midair. Nearly a thousand feet across, and propelled by raw magical power, the Therans called it a behemoth.

The troll clans did their best to mount a defense, but the behemoth was able to shrug off their attacks. The battle raged as the behemoth drew ever closer to the mountains. Once within range, the behemoth turned its attention to the villages on the mountain slopes. Siege engines rained rocks and massive arrows down on the trolls' homes and families. Fireballs and bolts of magical energy carved swaths of destruction across the landscape, while bound elementals took care of what little resistance was offered.

Stunned at the massacre, the Crystal Raiders surrendered. The clan leaders were taken back to Thera in chains, and their airships were destroyed. In what became known as the Battle of Sky Point, the Therans demonstrated their true power. They used the Battle to show what fate would befall those who interfere with their interests.

One hundred days after the Battle of Sky Point, Thom Edro, then Elder of Thera, issued the Proclamation of Empire. Barsaive was made a Theran province, and Edro promised protection for any who would swear fealty. To enforce its decrees, a permanent military force was stationed near the city of Vivane. The Declaration also established the city of Parlainth in northeastern Barsaive as the province's capital. It took time for the various powers in Barsaive to fall into line, but the might of the Theran Navy solidified their control.

The other piece of Theran dominance came from the knowledge developed by the School of Shadows. Only subjects of the Empire would be given access to the wards and runes needed to protect the kaers from the Horrors. In return for this protection, subject nations needed to provide the Empire with support in the form of orichalcum, money, and other resources.

Kern Fallo was installed as first Overlord of Barsaive. Fallo understood the need for local administration, and invited the dwarfs of Throal to assist in running the province. Caught between the Theran Navy and the need for the protective enchantments, the Kingdom agreed. They managed to mediate the effects of Theran occupation, defusing much of the tension that would have otherwise resulted. An added benefit of their role as provincial administrators was greater influence in the flow of trade across the land, resulting in the dwarf language becoming the common trading tongue in Barsaive.

> **Jaron and the Sphinx**
>
> When Thom Edro took the title of First Governor, many suspected it was only a matter of time before he gained enough support to declare himself Emperor.
>
> The famed scholar Jaron believed Edro was turning Thera into a mockery of its true purpose and spoke out against the First Governor at every opportunity. Each time he did so, one of Jaron's followers would disappear. Realizing it was only a matter of time before Edro had him eliminated, Jaron took action.
>
> Overnight, with the aid of three powerful earth spirits, Jaron constructed a massive statue in the park across from the First Governor's palace. The statue resembles a sphinx with its head bowed and eyes closed.
>
> At daybreak, Jaron addressed the assembled crowd, reminding them of the Martyr Scholar and Thera's purpose. The sphinx is intended to watch over the Empire and its governors, lest they succumb to the lure of power for its own sake.
>
> When he was done speaking, the three elementals surrounded Jaron carrying him into the body of the sphinx. The statue lifted its head and its eyes opened, glowing with a fierce blue light.
>
> The leader of Thera retains the title of First Governor. Despite efforts by generations of magicians, the Therans have been unable to unravel the mysteries of the sphinx, and are unsure what might happen if they try to manipulate or unmake it.

THE SCOURGE APPROACHES

While Thera dominated the lands around the Selestrean Sea and neighboring territories, they did not have absolute control. Many kingdoms and peoples searched for their own solution to the coming Horrors rather than submit to Theran authority.

Some petitioned dragons for aid. These powerful beings were keepers of magical secrets even the Therans did not know. It was also suggested that dragons, as long-lived creatures, might have even survived the prior invasion of the Horrors.

As a rule, dragons prefer to keep their secrets, and many of these requests were met with silence. A few dragons, however, agreed to share some of the methods involved in the creation of dragon lairs. This knowledge often came with a price, but as the invasion neared, and signs of the Horrors became more common, more and more people were willing to pay the price necessary for survival.

Thera was torn over what response, if any, they should have. Edro had no desire to antagonize the dragons. Even a behemoth would have a difficult time facing down the might of an enraged dragon. Unfortunately, merchant factions that most profited from the trade in Theran provinces brought enough pressure to bear that the Empire was forced to act.

Strikes were made against three dragons that were known to be sharing information. Two of the dragons were killed, their lairs looted and destroyed—though one of the Theran behemoths was also destroyed in the process. The third attack on the great dragon Icewing found only an empty lair with anything of value long removed. Convinced that their message had been delivered, Theran merchant guilds sat back and prepared to sell even more protective enchantments.

The retaliation was swift and definitive. One evening at sunset, residents of Great Thera were surprised to see a dragon perched atop the head of Jaron's Sphinx. While it flew away after a few minutes, twelve Theran citizens were found dead the next morning. Each had agitated for or profited from actions against the dragons. Over the course of the next two weeks, two more strikes resulted in the deaths of two dozen more Theran citizens.

Thom Edro issued notice through diplomatic channels: Therans were to leave the dragons alone. No further raids against dragons were to be authorized or carried out.

Another conflict developed in the Court at Wyrm Wood. Queen Alachia commanded that no elven nation, and no elf, take advantage of the Theran protective magic. Her Elementalists had developed an alternative, intending to weave the living trees of Wyrm Wood into a kaer that would shelter the Court during the Scourge.

Many elven scholars outside the Court disputed the efficacy of Alachia's plan. While the Theran proposals were not guaranteed protection, a wooden kaer—however much it might be reinforced with elven magic—had little chance of withstanding the physical punishment it was likely to endure.

Alachia threatened any elves who followed the Theran rites with Separation. Rather than galvanize the elven nations to stand together, the threat of the Horrors outweighed the desire to remain part of so-called true elven culture. Several elven nations refused to follow her decree, greatly weakening the Court's influence. In the end, Alachia did not follow through on her threat, as the action would have been meaningless in the face of such widespread opposition.

It is known that many families left Wyrm Wood during this time, leaving only Alachia's strongest supporters at the Court. Debate continues to this day as to whether those refugees left of their own free will, or were exiled as a result of speaking out against the queen. For her own part, Alachia decided to demonstrate her wisdom by constructing the Court's wooden kaer, confident that the wayward nations would come back to the fold after the Scourge was over.

Many different methods were developed to protect people from the coming invasion of the Horrors, the majority of them based on the Theran rites. The dwarfs of Throal hollowed out most of a mountain for their kaer. Other cities constructed fantastic citadels, inscribing every stone of the city walls with magical runes and raising protective domes crafted of True Elements.

The Theran provincial capital at Parlainth used what is arguably the most extreme method of isolation. The magicians of the city planned to cast a great ritual that would shift Parlainth into a pocket of the netherworlds. To further protect the city, the ritual was designed to remove the memory of the city from the mind of every living person in Barsaive. With no memory of the city, it would remain safe from the Horrors until the Scourge was over.

> **Timeline**
> **~900 TH:** Construction begins on the Halls of Throal.
> **950 TH:** Varulus I becomes king of Throal.
> **960 TH:** The Book of Tomorrow is commissioned.
> **997 TH:** A group of Throalic nobles known as The Fourteen are banished for plotting against Varulus I.

Thera's demand for slaves increased during these final decades. Many towns and villages, unable to acquire the resources to construct shelters of their own, sold themselves into Theran slavery for the chance that their descendants would survive. Some kingdoms bankrupted themselves and collapsed trying to protect their citizens.

THE LONG NIGHT

Historians place the beginning of the Scourge as the sealing of the Theran citadel. The dwarfs of Throal mark this year as 1008 TH, while the Therans count the year TE 565. As a center and focus of magical energy, the imperial seat was beset by Horrors sooner than the rest of the world. A final message was sent out before the protections were activated, wishing their subjects the best of luck.

The Theran Empire had largely been responsible for holding together the fraying threads of civilization in the years leading up to the Scourge. Within two decades, virtually all communication between kingdoms was cut off and people were left on their own. Horrors appeared with increasing frequency, with herds of mindless Horrors ravaging the lands, quickly becoming more than a match for local forces, even when supported by powerful adepts.

The dwarfs of Throal were not idle in the final decades before the Scourge. After centuries of administering the province, they knew that six hundred years of isolation could be as devastating to civilization as the Horrors. While the Therans planned for every aspect of physical survival, they did not account for cultural stagnation.

The dwarfs created The Book of Tomorrow. In it they recorded the history of Barsaive and the Theran Empire, along with legends and tales of the past. It also included a guide to the dwarf language and alphabet, so that children could be instructed to read and write a common tongue. The dwarfs provided instructions on common and useful crafts and skills, so that these abilities would not be lost. Finally, The Book of Tomorrow contained instructions on how to tell when the Scourge was over, and how to rebuild and reclaim the surface when that day came.

Copies of The Book of Tomorrow were distributed to every kaer and citadel that could be reached, and the dwarfs did what they could to keep their gates open and allow refugees into the kingdom. Finally, in the year 1050 TH, Throal sealed its kaer and prepared for the worst, as they had little doubt that some Horrors might have managed to enter the kingdom disguised as refugees. Their suspicions were proven correct; at least one battle against a powerful Horror took place in the early days after the kingdom was closed.

> **Timeline**
> **1008 TH:** Thera seals its citadel.
> **1032 TH:** The Raggok Incident in Throal gives the first indication of Passions being driven mad.
> **1045 TH:** Parlainth enacts the ritual that moves it to the pocket netherworld.
> **1049 TH:** Varulus I visits the Great Dragon Icewing.
> **1050 TH:** Throal seals its gates.

The years of the Scourge brought suffering and hardship, but the will to survive was strong, and people were comforted with the knowledge the Scourge would one day end. While they might never again see the sky, their descendants would reclaim the surface.

King Varulus II of Throal, himself a scholar and philosopher, combined common sense with imagination to drive discussion of the future world. Over many years scholars and philosophers, nobles and craftsmen, artists and laborers debated and discussed what an ideal society would look like.

The resulting document was the Council Compact of 1270 TH. It serves as a blueprint to the formation of a society for both the dwarf Kingdom and its neighbors, laying out individual rights, property rights, and the role of law in society.

Among the many notable aspects of the Council Compact is the stance it takes on slavery. After establishing that property rights are necessary for an orderly society, it asks whether people can be property. The conclusion drawn is that the body is the property of the soul that inhabits it, and involuntary servitude—slavery—grants control of the body to the slave owner without compensating the soul. It is, in essence, theft of the body from its rightful owner.

This philosophical foundation is just one example of how the Council Compact is a rigorously thought-out document intended to develop a fair, orderly society for the benefit of its citizens. Those who wrote the Compact decided that the world after the Scourge would be different than the one before.

RETURN TO THE SURFACE

For centuries the people of Barsaive hid in their shelters. The Book of Tomorrow described a ritual that allowed people to judge when the Scourge was over. A ball of True Earth is enchanted and suspended over a dish of True Water. As the strength of the world's magical energy wanes, the ball descends until it reaches the water and the two mix. At this point, the Horrors should have been forced to retreat to their native realms.

About four hundred years after the beginning of the Scourge—in the year 1415 TH—the ball stopped dropping about an inch above the water. For some reason, the magical aura of the world stabilized. Even today, a hundred years on, no one is sure why this has happened.

The Kingdom of Throal actually made the first tentative steps towards reclaiming the surface, sending the first scouting party outside the gates in 1409 TH. Dwarf scholars and magicians believed that the world's magical energy had dropped enough to force the more powerful Horrors to retreat. They also doubted the accuracy of

> **Timeline**
> **1057 TH:** The Horror Whisper is discovered in Throal and defeated through the efforts of several adepts.
> **1160 TH:** Varulus I dies at age 270. Varulus II takes the throne.
> **1262 TH:** The kaer in Wyrm Wood collapses. The elves enact the Ritual of Thorns.
> **1270 TH:** The Council Compact is completed.
> **1373 TH:** Varulus II dies at age 258. Varulus III takes the throne.
> **1409 TH:** First Throalic scouting party heads outside.

Theran predictions, suspecting the Therans may have given conservative estimates to their subject nations, planning to be the first to reclaim the surface.

The first scouting party was destroyed in hours. The dwarfs sent a party out each year after that, and none succeeded until 1412 TH, when Vaare Longfang returned with news that while some Horrors remained, there were far fewer and they were less active. The Kingdom planned a more extensive expedition to learn how extensively the Scourge had affected the surface. They outfitted an airship, Named the *Earthdawn*, and Longfang set forth in 1416 TH. The ship returned about a year later, having charted much of Barsaive. As suspected, most of the Horrors were gone.

The next year, the *Earthdawn* set out again. Its mission was to spread the word that the Scourge is over and it is safe to open the kaers. The mission was not particularly successful; of the twenty-one kaers visited by Longfang and her crew, only two opened their doors. The rest believed the expedition was a ploy by the Horrors.

The *Earthdawn* set forth one last time, intending to contact the largest kingdoms first. The airship disappeared, and the fate of its crew has never been learned. To this day stories are told where the haunted hull of the Earthdawn is seen drifting the skies over Barsaive, but these tales remain unverified.

Despite the loss of the *Earthdawn*, Varulus III opened the gates of Throal in the summer of 1420 TH. The residents were reluctant to return to the surface, afraid of Horrors that might still remain. Eventually, King Varulus offered a grant of land to any who chose to farm, mine, or otherwise make productive use of it. A few brave souls took advantage of the offer, and while a few were unfortunate enough to encounter isolated Horrors, many more thrived. This led to a rush of settlers reclaiming the surface.

Throalic merchant houses mounted expeditions to reestablish trade routes with nearby communities. Some kaers refused to open their doors, and some had been destroyed or otherwise failed. Many more opened their doors and welcomed the merchants. They were given a copy of the Council Compact and invited to join the new world.

The merchant companies and other envoys of the dwarf kingdom worked quickly, for they believed that if the Therans survived the Scourge, they would one day come to reclaim Barsaive.

A CHANGED WORLD

As more and more kaers opened and people worked to reclaim the surface, the true effects of the Scourge were discovered. While mountain ranges and major rivers remain much as they were before, other landmarks have changed or been destroyed. The wild animals and living creatures of the surface underwent changes as well.

While the changes resulting from the Scourge could fill a series of volumes on their own, there are two notable examples that best illustrate the kinds of losses caused by the Horrors.

The first is the fate of the Elven Court. About halfway through the Scourge, the wooden kaer of Wyrm Wood began to fail. The process was slow, but total collapse of the magical protections was inevitable. The magicians and scholars of the Court searched desperately for a solution; there was no time to construct underground shelters, nor did they have the resources of True Earth, Fire, or Air to reinforce the existing wards. Depression set in as the elves did their best to mend the breaks in the barriers and keep the Horrors at bay.

It is not recorded who first made the observation, but the more powerful and devious Horrors that broke through the kaer's defenses all but ignored elves who were already insane or in extreme pain. The Queen's advisors theorized that these Horrors needed to cause pain and madness themselves in order to feed. This idea planted the seed for the salvation of the Court; a salvation so terrible that some still question whether it would have been better for the elves to fall to the Horrors.

As the breaches in the Court's defenses threatened to take the kaer down completely, the plan was put in motion. The Court magicians performed a massive, twisted blood ritual that forced thorns to grow from within the bodies of the elves of Wyrm Wood. The thorns tore their skin, leaving the subject in constant, excruciating pain. While many elves died as a result of the Ritual of Thorns, those who survived learned to live with the pain, even coming to draw strength from it.

For the Horrors, the elven kaer no longer held anything of value. While attacks by more bestial Horrors continued through the remainder of the Scourge, they were easily dealt with. Those who fed on pain and suffering moved on, looking for other meals. Wyrm Wood became known as Blood Wood, and is a continuing reminder of the price some paid for survival. Queen Alachia still reigns, and the Blood Elves do not allow outsiders to enter the Wood. The Court still welcomes elves, but any who wish to remain within its borders must undergo the Ritual of Thorns.

The fate of Parlainth is the other notable cost of the Scourge. What we know today is the result of brave heroes who have ventured into the ruins of the Forgotten City. As you may recall, Parlainth sought shelter from the Scourge by retreating into a pocket of astral space and removing all memory of the city from the minds of those left behind.

The magicians of Parlainth left behind many clues that would lead to their return when the Scourge was over. Among them was an artifact called The Longing Ring, giving visions of the city to any who put it on, driving them to seek it out. By the time the mysteries of this magical item were unraveled and the city returned to the world, all of its inhabitants were dead and gone. Records that have been recovered since the city returned tell us that Horrors had infiltrated the city before the ritual was enacted,

> **Timeline**
> **1415 TH:** Elemental clocks stop moving for some unknown reason, indicating the magic level has stabilized.
> **1418 TH:** The *Earthdawn* vanishes without a trace during its second voyage.
> **1420 TH:** Throal opens its gates.
> **~1430 TH:** The city of Urupa is founded.
> **1449 TH:** Theran forces return to Barsaive, resulting in the First Theran War.

and the citizens ended up trapping themselves with the very things they were trying to escape. The Horrors apparently took great pleasure in prolonging the suffering of the people of Parlainth.

To this day, dark and terrible things stalk the ruin, but many adepts and adventurers brave the haunted streets in search of forgotten treasure and knowledge.

THE THERAN RETURN

The Therans did not return to Barsaive as quickly as Throal feared. Reports indicate that the first Theran vessels did not return until 1449 TH, nearly thirty years after Throal opened its gates. It is believed that Thera likely lowered its wards around the same time as the dwarf Kingdom. Whether the delay in returning to Barsaive was because they believed their subject nations were still sheltered in their kaers, or because they were still working to recover from the Scourge, is unknown.

Regardless, these years gave the dwarfs time to spread the ideals of the Council Compact, and the people of Barsaive time to live free of the Empire's control. Theran emissaries received little welcome and, not prepared for anything except respect and subservience, threatened violence if their demands were not met. In response a troop of locals set fire to three Theran airships anchored near Vivane and killed the crews.

First Governor Nikodus appointed Fallan Pavelis as Overlord of Barsaive, ordering him to assert Theran supremacy in the province. Pavelis began a campaign of reprisals. Theran vessels carried out slaving raids on isolated villages. Theran soldiers attacked towns and collected "forgotten tribute." Mercenaries harassed merchant caravans, and tribal leaders that spoke out against Thera were assassinated and replaced with leaders more favorable to the Theran cause.

The people of Barsaive looked to Throal for help. The principles of the Council Compact all but declared open rebellion, surely the dwarfs would stand up to the Empire? While the dwarf Kingdom believed that the Therans must be stopped, they did not have the strength to face down Theran forces.

Varulus III sent messengers to the various rulers and powers of Barsaive, stating that Barsaive must stand together as free people, or fall back under Theran oppression. While his words brought hope to the beleaguered people, the reality of Theran forces acting with impunity forestalled any serious resistance.

This situation might have continued to this day, if not for the First Governor. Nikodus received a copy of the Council Compact and was infuriated by its contents. He dispatched a message to Overlord Pavelis, stating that the logic of commerce and property laws contained in the Council Compact indicated that every man, woman, and child in Barsaive owes their life to Thera, and as First Governor it is his duty to

> **Timeline**
> **1452 TH:** Parlainth discovered by Garlthik One-Eye and J'role the Honorable Thief.
> **1458 TH:** First Theran War ends as Theran forces retreat to Sky Point.
> **1474 TH:** Neden, only child of Varulus III, born.
> **1484 TH:** The Death Rebellion. The Theran Nethermancer Mordom abducts Prince Neden. He is rescued by J'role and healed by the Great Dragon Mountainshadow.
> **1485 TH:** The troll Torgak and his associates begin clearing the southeastern corner of Parlainth to be used as a base of operations.

collect on this blood debt. Nikodus ordered Overlord Pavelis to begin the systematic destruction of all Barsaivian cities not vital to Theran mercantile interests, beginning with the Kingdom of Throal.

The First Governor supplied troops from other parts of the Theran Empire, and Pavelis fielded one of the largest armadas ever assembled. The intention was a demonstration of raw power to remind the province of Theran superiority.

Fortunately, loyalists within the Overlord's palace in Sky Point intercepted the message and sent copies across the province. With the First Governor's arrogance in full view, anger overcame fear. The people of Barsaive committed themselves to their freedom.

As the armada moved into the heart of the province, other powers came to Throal's aid. The Crystal Raiders, remembering the Battle of Sky Point centuries earlier, harassed Theran shipping lanes. T'skrang river captains ran blockades and intercepted supplies. Ork cavalry and elven archers assaulted caravans and melted back into the wilds. Windling Scouts and Thieves infiltrated Theran camps to commit sabotage and gather intelligence.

Before the siege was over, half of the Theran armada was lost. With supplies dwindling and no sign of relief, the Therans retreated. The First Theran War ended in a victory for the people of Barsaive.

AN UNEASY PEACE

In the wake of the defeat outside Throal, the Therans withdrew to Vivane and Sky Point. While they still considered Barsaive part of the Empire, they turned their attention to restoring control over other territories. Subsequent Overgovernors of Barsaive took a more subtle approach, gathering intelligence on the dwarf Kingdom and using their agents to destabilize Throalic interests outside the direct influence of the Kingdom.

In time, political change in Thera brought change to the state of affairs in Barsaive. In 1497 TH, First Governor Nikodus was succeeded by the obsidiman Kanidris. As hard and inflexible as the stone he resembles, he was frustrated by the lack of progress in bringing Barsaive to heel. The dwarfs had been given too much time to strengthen their influence, and there was no Theran military presence to remind the people where the true power lay.

Vivane and Sky Point were too far removed to serve as an adequate base of operations. Kanidris authorized a plan that would establish a fortress in the heart of Barsaive. An ancient behemoth scheduled for retirement, the *Triumph*, was refit by

EARTHDAWN

> **Timeline**
> **1491 TH:** Haven officially founded with Torgak as de facto mayor.
> **1502 TH:** Battle of Sejanus between House Ishkarat and House Syrtis stops Ishkarat expansion at Lake Vors.
> **1507 TH:** Varulus III travels the pilgrimage route for an audience with the Prophetess. The meeting ends with Varulus flying into an uncharacteristic rage.

Theran magicians. Accompanied by a small fleet of airships and the Theran Eighth Legion under the command of General Nikar Carinci, the *Triumph* traveled to the heart of Barsaive. In 1509 TH, it landed atop the Ayodhya Liferock on the shores of Lake Ban. Imperial magicians used ritual magic to draw on the elemental power of the liferock to strengthen the walls of the fortress. They also removed the elemental air from the behemoth's hull, using it to weave a protective dome.

Ayodhya was chosen for several reasons. In addition to the magical power that could be drawn from the Liferock, it commanded a strong position on central Barsaive. The Liferock also holds a great deal of spiritual significance, as it marks the beginning of a traditional t'skrang pilgrimage route. Seizing control of the site was intended to be an intimidating and demoralizing symbol of Theran superiority.

It was successful. The arrival of the *Triumph* and a Theran army sent a shockwave through the province. The Kingdom of Throal, along with their allies in the t'skrang *aropagoi* V'strimon and Syrtis started making plans in anticipation of Theran aggression. Other powers in Barsaive watched closely, hoping to strike a balance between the independence they had enjoyed for decades, and the desire to not antagonize the Therans.

The *Triumph's* presence galvanized opposition to Theran rule. The obsidiman Omasu, owner and head of the Overland Trading Company, is a member of the Ayodhya brotherhood. While he had previously avoided involvement in politics, he was unable to ignore the insult the *Triumph* represented. Omasu devoted his considerable wealth and influence to build a resistance force—the Liferock Rebellion.

THE BATTLE OF PRAJJOR'S FIELD

The same year the *Triumph* landed, Throal suffered another blow. King Varulus III, who had ruled the kingdom for over a hundred years, was found murdered in his chambers. Rumors had circulated for some time that the king had been ill, and over recent years his son and heir, Prince Neden, had been assuming more responsibility.

In Neden's grief-stricken state, he perceived the recent arrival of the *Triumph* and his father's murder as no coincidence. Within days of his coronation, and against the advice of his advisors, the new king prepared his forces for an attack on the behemoth.

General Carinci had no desire to start a war with Throal—at least, not yet. His forces were still settling in, and supply lines with the Theran Empire were still being established. He did his best to convince Neden that Thera played no part in his father's death, but Neden would not listen. In the end, Carinci was given little choice. Part of his mission was to demonstrate the might of the Theran military, and if the young king was foolish enough to pick a fight, Carinci was willing to oblige.

EARTHDAWN

> **Timeline**
> **1509 TH:** The *Triumph* lands at Ayodhya. Varulus III killed. Neden becomes king and leads an attack on the *Triumph*. Cara Fahd declares its sovereignty.
> **1512 TH:** The Harwood Incident. Neden writes the *Harwood Declaration* and distributes it across Barsaive.

The two-day battle took place on the plains north of Ayodhya known as Prajjor's Field. It was a disaster for the Throalic forces, who suffered significant losses. During the battle, Theran agents managed to provide proof to Neden of the party responsible for Varulus's death. The Denairastas clan, rulers of the city of Iopos, had killed the late king and framed the Therans for the assassination. Their goal was to push the two sides into open conflict, weakening them both and shifting the balance of power in Barsaive more in Iopan favor.

Despite the losses at Prajjor's Field and the revelation that Thera was not behind his father's death, Neden started Throal down the path of military expansion. He pushed for more spending on mercenaries and airships, and used the contacts and influence the kingdom had accumulated to back operations against Theran interests. This extended to a purge of suspected Theran and Denairastas agents in the kingdom as well as the ostensibly independent Bartertown outside the kingdom's gates. Tensions between Throal and its neighbor, already rocky, became even more strained.

The political climate in Throal itself became divided into two broad groups. The first supported war with Thera, both to try and reclaim pride lost as a result of Prajjor's Field, and to maintain the independence that Barsaive had enjoyed for decades. The second group sought to reconcile with Thera, seeking some kind of accommodation that would allow them to continue doing business without worrying about the uncertainty that comes with open military conflict.

REBIRTH OF A NATION

In the months after the Battle of Prajjor's Field, a series of letters arrived in Barsaive. Called the Seeds of Nation, they provided a manifesto for ork pride and also called on them to rebuild their nation, lost since the end of the Orichalcum Wars. Orks across the province, from scorchers to city-dwellers, were caught up in the dream of Cara Fahd.

The author of the letters was Krathis Gron, a descendent of the legendary hero Hrak Gron, known for leading the orks from slavery in the distant past. Blessed by the Passions, Krathis became the living embodiment of the ork people's love of freedom. After many years in Cathay preparing for her task, she returned to Barsaive and began preaching her dream of a new ork nation.

Inspired by Krathis Gron's message, orks across Barsaive began a migration to the lands that were once the domain of Cara Fahd. In a few months they united under Krathis's leadership along the southern edge of the Delaris Mountains. When Theran and Throalic forces clashed at Claw Ridge, thousands of ork warriors appeared on the surrounding hills. At the head of the ork army, Krathis Gron declared the sovereignty of Cara Fahd.

Heavily outnumbered, the forces of Thera and Throal were disarmed and forced to retreat, carrying the news back to their leaders. While opposition to slavery makes

CALLING THE POWER — JEREMY MCHUGH

EARTHDAWN

TILLONUK, SEEKER OF SHADOWS — KOSTJA SCHLEGER

EARTHDAWN

LOOTING THE TOMB · KARSTEN SCHREURS

EARTHDAWN

HEROES, LEGENDS AND FOES

MILIVOJ ĆERAN

EARTHDAWN

DANGER AND DISCOVERY — MILIVOJ CERAN

EARTHDAWN

SKYPOINT IN RUINS
MAIK SCHMIDT

EARTHDAWN

DESCENT INTO KAER PALLIX   KOSTJA SCHLEGER

EARTHDAWN

BARSASIVE MAP — MAIK SCHMIDT

Cara Fahd and Throal natural allies against the Theran Empire, and relations between the dwarf kingdom and the ork nation were friendly, Krathis made it clear she and her advisors would not stand for other powers meddling in their affairs.

Over the next several years, Krathis did her best to lead the orks. Despite the Passions inspired fervor that drove the rebirth of the nation, the reality of daily governance was a more tedious affair. The long-standing rivalries of the different tribes were not so easily set aside, and the cultural conflicts between the nomadic scorchers and the city-dwelling orks caused their own problems. Nation building, especially among those who have gone for a long time without a structure beyond their individual tribe, is a difficult prospect.

Other matters made life difficult for the new nation. The lands of Cara Fahd had gone largely unoccupied for centuries even before the Scourge, and there was no infrastructure left from the old nation to support the sudden population growth. Additionally, Cara Fahd's proximity to Sky Point and the city of Vivane made conflicts with the Therans common. Finally, the human communities in the remains of Landis, Cara Fahd's traditional rival, did not take kindly to the new arrivals, and skirmishes along the border were a frequent occurrence. It is likely that both Thera and Iopos provided support to the humans to help destabilize the situation.

Despite the problems, the return of the ork nation had a noticeable effect on the balance of power in Barsaive. Where previously the Therans would have needed to account for a mercenary cavalry or two coming to Throal's aid, they now had to factor in the combined strength of an ork nation.

THE HARWOOD INCIDENT

After the rebirth of Cara Fahd, the situation in Barsaive stabilized into a new status quo. Thera continued to expand its influence in the province, while Throal did its best to hinder the Empire's operations and build towards an alliance that could stand against the Theran forces.

King Neden's efforts were complicated by a few factors. As a Warrior adept, he preferred direct action to the wheeling and dealing required for successful diplomacy. Also, there were many prominent nobles in Throal that preferred reconciliation to rebellion. Ideals are well and good, but the practical reality was a Theran fortress in central Barsaive. These voices in the halls of Throal had some support from other normal Throalic citizens, as many lost friends or family as a result of Prajjor's Field.

Another complication facing Neden's efforts was the presence of the Denairastas clan. Long seen as a minor player in Barsaive, the revelation that they had manipulated events to force Thera and Throal into conflict indicated they were a problem that could not be ignored. Iopos had long been a reclusive and unfriendly city to outsiders. Information on this new enemy was needed, and so resources—already weakened by the losses suffered that Prajjor's Field—were divided.

Fortunately, the Liferock Rebellion aided Throalic operations against the Therans. Recognizing that the Dwarf Kingdom represented the best hope for driving the Therans from Ayodhya, Omasu provided intelligence and logistical support to Throalic agents in southern and central Barsaive.

All parties spent the next three years preparing for a conflict they knew was coming. As with many things in history, the event that triggered the conflict took a shape none of them could anticipate.

A Theran patrol encountered a Throalic merchant caravan on the plains north of the *Triumph*. A running battle broke out between the caravan guards and the Therans, and moved from the open plains to the nearby town of Harwood—one of many unremarkable settlements that dot the plains between the Coil River and Servos Jungle. When the sun rose the next day, half the town was in ruins and dozens lay dead. The surviving members of the caravan were hauled back to the *Triumph* in chains.

The exact cause of the conflict was never determined. The Therans claimed they were pursuing a fugitive wanted for crimes against the Empire, and the caravan was sheltering him. The merchant house responsible for the caravan stated that the officer in charge of the Theran patrol—known in the area for strong-arming locals into paying tribute—pushed things too far and the caravan was merely defending itself from an aggressor.

Some survivors of the incident told of a group of adepts that got involved, causing events to spiral out of control as they did. These adepts have never been identified. Whether they were acting to keep the residents of Harwood safe, were actually agents of the Denairastas taking advantage of the situation, or had some other personal reason to get involved is unknown.

Whatever the truth of the situation, news of the incident spread across Barsaive over the next few weeks. There was much debate in Throal. The factions more interested in appeasement pointed out that the merchant family backing the caravan was notorious for using their operations as a cover for anti-Theran agitation, doing quite a bit of business with the Overland Trading Company, another known front for rebellion. More than likely they did something to provoke the Therans.

Those more inclined toward opposition to the Theran presence in Barsaive pointed out that merchants do business with a lot of different groups and individuals. Without real evidence of wrongdoing, what right did the Therans have to interfere with the flow of trade? If the Therans were interested in a positive relationship, why were they seizing and detaining Throalic citizens without involving the crown or other diplomatic channels?

King Neden saw the Harwood incident as the perfect opportunity to push for a greater alliance of powers in Barsaive. With the aid of his closest advisors and philosophers from the Great Library, he wrote the Harwood Declaration. This document stated Thera still clearly viewed Barsaive and its inhabitants as their personal property, and continuing to tolerate their presence at Ayodhya only encouraged further abuses. The people of Barsaive must unite and drive the Therans from Barsaive if they were to have any hope of long-term freedom.

Copies of the Harwood Declaration were sent across the province, and it was not long before it fell into Theran hands. General Carinci had become frustrated with the continued sabotage and espionage since he arrived in the province, and was getting increased pressure from the First Governor to bring the province to heel.

Thera made the first move by sending a cohort north from the *Triumph*. The soldiers set up camp just outside Bartertown, and dispatched a smaller armed force to the gates of Throal with a message. The message stated that despite recent difficulties, Thera still valued the dwarf kingdom as a tribute state, and to demonstrate their loyalty, its citizens should turn Neden over to Theran authority, to be placed on trial for supporting insurgence against the Empire. Not turning him over would be considered a declaration of war.

Historians are not clear on why Thera took this initial approach. Given the results of the battle at Prajjor's Field, the most likely explanation is Carinci believed the threat of open war with the Empire would prompt a coup by Theran loyalists in the dwarf kingdom. This would save the Empire the trouble of a protracted siege.

General Rancyrus carried Throal's response, backed by 500 troops. The kingdom would not accept Theran authority over the rightful ruler of an independent nation. If the Therans wished to push the matter, that would be in their hands.

The Therans withdrew, but that night a fire swept through Bartertown, destroying nearly a quarter of the city and costing hundreds of lives. Some speculate Theran agents started the fire as retaliation for Throal's response. Others claim the Denairastas were trying to take advantage of the unrest, and some lay the blame on Throal itself to push Bartertown into accepting annexation by the kingdom, or eliminate the city as a haven for those opposed to Throal and its antagonism of the Empire.

THE CAPTURE OF THE TRIUMPH

King Neden knew the Therans would have to respond, and that Barsaive's best chance for victory was to take the fight to the Therans. Calling on alliances he had built over the prior years, a campaign of harassment was launched against the *Triumph*. Crystal Raider moots ambushed and intercepted Theran supply vessels in the air, while t'skrang riverboats blockaded supplies on the river.

While the harassment of Theran supply lines was taking place, Throalic forces set forth from the kingdom, supported by several airships and ork mercenary cavalry. Despite Neden's requests for assistance from other powers in Barsaive, most offered little material support. Surprisingly, Queen Alachia of Blood Wood sent a contingent of soldiers to assist in the attack on the behemoth.

Unlike the disastrous battle of Prajjor's Field, where Neden acted rashly and without adequate planning, the strategy for taking the behemoth was sound. T'skrang warships bombarded the walls of the fortress, while Throalic air forces acted as escort to the ground troops. While the Therans were distracted by attacks from two sides, several captured Theran mining vessels approached, pursued by Crystal Raider drakkars. This ruse was intended to sneak several elite adept groups inside the protective dome of elemental air.

The ruse worked. Once inside the behemoth, the adepts struck, disrupting Theran troops manning the walls and managing to lower the protective dome. They also inspired the slaves at the stronghold to rise up against the Therans.

Caught off guard and outnumbered, General Carinci called for the retreat. He set out in one of the Theran airships stationed at the *Triumph*, and the ground troops withdrew, leaving the *Triumph* in the hands of the alliance.

Shockingly, as the Therans withdrew, a troop of Blood Elves hidden in a woodland called Willow Grove ambushed and slaughtered the infantry, almost to the man. No reason has ever been provided for the massacre. The Blood Elf soldiers indicated that they were following their Queen's orders, and Alachia herself never provided an explanation. The Blood Elves returned to their homeland after the *Triumph* was captured, and took no further part in the war.

As one of the few surviving members of the Ayodhya Liferock, the *Triumph* was granted to Omasu, who began using it as a way station for the Overland Trading Company. He also invited magicians and scholars from across Barsaive to help heal the damage to his Liferock

THE FALL OF VIVANE

Despite the success of the plan to capture the *Triumph*, it was only the first piece of Neden's plan. There was still a Theran military presence in southwestern Barsaive, and unless the alliance pushed its advantage, the garrison at Sky Point would get reinforcements from Great Thera. The airship fleet transported Throalic ground forces and cavalry to the plains northwest of Vivane, where approximately two thousand cavalry from Cara Fahd joined them.

The success at *Triumph* also prompted support from some powers in the province previously reluctant to do so. The city of Jerris sent a small force supported by a pair of airships. More of the Crystal Raider clans contributed vessels. Because of their location far from the front, Urupa didn't send troops, but did provide support by funding a mercenary company. To everyone's great surprise, the Great Dragon Vasdenjas joined the fleet as well, accompanied by three smaller dragons.

While Theran forces were caught off guard by the attack on the *Triumph*, they were prepared for the arrival of the Barsaivian army at Sky Point. All available Theran forces had been recalled to defend the fortress.

As the armies assembled, disaster struck the city of Vivane. At Stormhead, located a few days travel north of the city, a mysterious and dangerous cloud had hovered for decades—at least since the days of the Scourge. The area was generally avoided. While rich in true elements, the cloud sheltered Horrors that would attack those who strayed too close.

For some unknown reason, the Horror cloud moved, heading toward the city of Vivane. Destruction followed in the cloud's wake as it rained acid, and winged Horrors attacked any in its path. Three days after it set forth, it arrived at Vivane and came to a stop over the city, effectively cutting it off from the outside world.

The reason the cloud moved is still debated to this day. Some have claimed that the combined suffering of the slaves and Barsaivian underclass in Vivane proved too rich a meal for the Horrors within the cloud. Most serious magical scholars discount this idea, instead suggesting the Therans were activating a powerful but untested magical defense for the coming battle, which drew the cloud as a moth to a flame. Another idea points to the presence of dragons at the battle, and that they were somehow responsible, perhaps taking advantage of the dispute to strike at their rivals.

Whatever the reason, Stormhead caused significant damage to Vivane, and thousands of lives were lost during the time it stayed over the city.

At Sky Point the bulk of the fighting took place in the skies. The larger Throalic airships and captured Theran vessels bombarded the fortress's defensive towers while the dragons and smaller Crystal Raider vessels worked to intercept and disable Theran airships.

On the ground, the fighting was more limited. Theran troops stationed in Vrontok, the settlement below Sky Point, clashed with Throalic infantry. The bulk of the cavalry from Cara Fahd corralled Theran reinforcements from nearby outposts.

The Therans deployed a new weapon in defense of Sky Point, one that combined and focused the powers of multiple magicians into a single blast of raw magical energy more powerful than a conventional fire cannon. While it fired infrequently, it was used to devastating effect, crippling any larger vessels it struck, and smaller airships like drakkars were destroyed.

King Neden directed and led the fighting from aboard the galleon *King's Justice*. When the danger presented by the Theran weapon became clear he directed the armada to focus on disabling the device. A strike force of elite adepts slipped through the chaos of the battle and landed a drakkar near the weapon.

A few moments later, a massive wave of magical energy ripped through the area. Nearby airships were disabled for a few brief moments, sending them careening in random directions. Adepts and magicians were likewise briefly incapacitated with crippling pain. The Horror cloud over Vivane, easily visible from the skies near Sky Point, broke into several smaller pieces and began drifting away.

The Theran weapon exploded, sending out several blasts of magical energy at once. Several airships, both Theran and alliance, were damaged by these blasts. One of them struck Vasdenjas, caught off guard as he tried to navigate the sudden chaos of multiple out of control airships. It is also possible the effects of the magical detonation distracted the Great Dragon. Vasdenjas was either killed outright by the blast, or knocked unconscious and died when he struck the ground hundreds of feet below.

In the wake of the magical explosion, the Therans changed tactics. The kila *Ascendancy* retreated to the southwest, presumably carrying Overgovernor Kypros and other Theran officers and officials. The remainder of the Theran fleet turned its attention to the *King's Justice*, hoping to prevent pursuit by threatening the alliance flagship. The Barsaivian fleet did its best, but the effect of the magical explosion, coupled with damage from the Therans, crippled the Justice, sending it toward the ground.

It is not known whether the next events were commanded by King Neden, taken by the helmsman on his own, or the result of simple chance. As the *King's Justice* descended, it steered towards one of Sky Point's support pillars. The collision rattled the platform and massive cracks appeared in the side of the pillar. The Crystal Raiders turned their attention to the damage, bombarding the column with cannon fire as the *Justice* crashed into Vrontok. The trolls also fired on the other pillars, looking to weaken them as well.

The damage caused by the *King's Justice*, coupled with the assault by the Crystal Raiders, shattered the support structure inside the targeted pillars. With a mighty groan the platform shuddered, shifted, and began to lean. The additional stress on the other pillars caused them to buckle as well. The platform of Sky Point dropped eight hundred feet onto the town below, burying thousands, and the Justice, under tons of rubble.

With the collapse of Sky Point, the battle was over. The remaining Theran vessels and troops retreated, leaving the battlefield in the hands of the alliance. As the Barsaivian forces regrouped, dozens of dragons appeared in the skies overhead. The dragons, which included individuals later identified as Icewing, Mountainshadow, and other Great Dragons, performed an elaborate flight over the corpse of Vasdenjas. Any who approached the body were warned away by the dragons, and the Throalic infantry established a perimeter and honor guard to keep the dragon's body from being disturbed. About one week after the battle, Mountainshadow descended on the corpse and burned it to ash with his fire.

The surviving Crystal Raiders returned to the Twilight Peaks, and the forces of Cara Fahd returned to their nation as well. The Throalic forces stayed longer, digging through the remains of Sky Point and helping with relief efforts in Vivane. Despite efforts to uncover the wreck of *King's Justice*, King Neden's body was never found.

AFTERMATH

Neden's death caused political problems in the dwarf kingdom. The late king had no recognized heir, and the Avalus family line ended with him. While there was the requisite period of mourning, it was not long before the noble houses in Throal began jockeying for position and looking to place their desired candidate on the throne.

To resolve this crisis of succession, the courtiers to the royal court—representatives of the various noble houses in Throal—convened to decide on a new king. The last time this had occurred was nearly four hundred years before the Scourge, when House Avalus assumed the throne.

As with many aspects of dwarf politics in recent years, the courtiers were roughly divided into two groups. Those who had been ardent supporters of Varulus and Neden had the victories at *Triumph* and Sky Point to strengthen their cause. Unfortunately, the kingdom had suffered significant military losses in the war, and there are few who do not have a friend or family member injured or killed. The more conservative faction used these losses as a reason to push for a more cautious approach. While they could not dispute the results of Neden's campaign, they argued Throal should take time to recover from the war.

The leading candidates supported by the conservative faction were Lomron of House Garsun and Selenda of House Ueraven. The reformist faction supported Tholon of House Elcomi and Beracia of House Byril'ah. The debate was heated, taking months to resolve. The lack of monarch on the throne drove unrest and rumor in the kingdom's population, including rumors that Neden actually survived the battle, and that Varulus had a second, illegitimate child.

The unrest in Throal reduced their presence in Barsaive, and Iopos took advantage of this to expand their influence. The Denairastas had been helping the city of Jerris research the ash blowing in from the Wastes, and possible ways to reduce or eliminate its effect. When it became clear that Throal was in no position to interfere, Iopos sent an occupation force, and seized control of the city.

When news of the occupation reached Throal, it nearly sparked a civil war. The

> **Timeline**
> **1514 TH:** Civil unrest in Throal as the question of succession is debated. Iopan forces seize control of Jerris.
> **1515 TH:** Kovar is selected as new king of Throal.
> **1517 TH:** Present day.

reformists argued the kingdom had an obligation to aid and support those who helped in the war with Thera, accusing the conservatives of failing to meet those obligations. The conservatives argued that however well intentioned the desire to aid and support the rest of Barsaive might be, Throal was in no position to march into another war, and must heal its own wounds.

In the end, a compromise was reached. House Maksei, a noble line with a rather unremarkable history, were chosen as the new rulers. The head of the house, Kovar, was a middle-aged dwarf who by all accounts never aspired to anything more than a comfortable retirement. Suddenly thrust into a position of prominence, he has had difficulty adjusting to his new role and significance in the kingdom, even four years after his coronation.

There is some speculation about what back room deal was struck to bring Kovar to the throne, but after nearly a year of uncertainty, most of the kingdom is happy for some semblance of normalcy.

AN UNCERTAIN FUTURE

The years since the Scourge have brought many changes. The Theran Empire returned and was driven out of Barsaive. One royal line in Throal has faded and a new one risen to prominence. A long dead nation has been reborn, and another extends its influence.

The Therans may have withdrawn to lick their wounds, but they still have an interest in the province. Theran agents and ambassadors do the bidding of the First Governor, hoping to rebuild influence damaged in the wake of the war.

Throal, while triumphant, is likewise wounded. The cost of war was high, and there are many dwarfs that would prefer the kingdom tend to its own affairs, even as others in Barsaive look to them for leadership in this new era. If Throal steps away from their responsibility, who knows what power will step up to fill that void?

The Denairastas, long considered a minor power in a distant corner of Barsaive, certainly appear to be willing. Their methods of assassination, deception, and manipulation, however, would indicate a free Barsaive in the tradition of the Council Compact is not what they have in mind.

And of course, the scars left by the Scourge are deep. Horrors still lurk in the shadows, ready to trap the unwary. While many have retreated, there is still enough magic in the world for some to remain, and no indication this age of magic will end. Kingdoms and Empires may rise and fall, but the Horrors are, apparently, eternal, and patient.

Perhaps now, more than ever, the world needs the light of heroes to guide the way forward.

EARTHDAWN

THE LAND AND ITS PEOPLE

The trolls raid the dwarfs. The dwarfs dislike the elves. The elves have no patience with humans. The humans war with each other. But everyone hates the Therans.
• Old Barsaivian proverb •

The land of Barsaive is broad and varied. Grasslands, jungles, mountains, and wastelands can all be found within its borders. The people that live in Barsaive are just as varied. From the urbane and cosmopolitan dwarfs of Throal to the gregarious t'skrang merchant princes of the Serpent River and the fierce yet honorable highland trolls, the Namegiver races all look to put the legacy of the Scourge behind them, and build a new future for themselves and their families.

The previous chapter, **What Has Come Before**, presented a look at past events that shaped the story of Barsaive from the perspective of characters in that setting. This chapter looks at the present day, and offers some glimpses into the possible future, but from a more objective point of view useful to gamemasters.

CLIMATE AND TERRAIN

Barsaive does not have specific borders. It is generally agreed the province ends at the Blood Wood to the north, the Wastes to the west, Death's Sea to the south and the Aras Sea to the east. Within those boundaries are over a million square miles of land, much of it unexplored. It takes weeks to cross the province, even on horseback.

The terrain in Barsaive varies from open plains and grasslands to lush jungle and forest, along with rocky highlands and mountains. In addition, many areas suffer from the effects of the Scourge, even decades past. Most notable of these is the Badlands in southern Barsaive, one of the province's most fertile areas before the Scourge. It is now a dry and barren wasteland home to Horrors and other vicious creatures.

The climate in Barsaive is generally temperate with ample rainfall, with more arid southwestern regions in the vicinity of Death's Sea. The temperature is generally cooler during the first half of the year, though outside of the higher mountain peaks it rarely gets cold enough for snow and ice. There is some debate about the reason for the climate and weather patterns. Some believe the rapid return and success of forests and other plant growth resulted from the influence of the Passions or some other magic, while others believe that Death's Sea—a massive source of heat—keeps the province from getting too cool.

Numerous rivers and waterways can be found across Barsaive, nearly all of which are part of the Serpent River system. The Serpent is a massive river that enters the province in the northwestern corner, makes its way east past the Blood Wood before turning south to dive into the canyon between the Throal and Caucavic mountains, then sweeps westward once more before draining into the Mist Swamps and Death's Sea.

The Serpent's largest tributary is the Coil River, which flows from the southern slopes of the Throal and Tylon mountain ranges, joins the Serpent at Lake Ban, and then continues southeast to drain into the Aras Sea, the large salt water body that forms Barsaive's eastern border. The Serpent and Coil River valleys feed much of the province's farmland, and is currently the source of the most fertile terrain available.

PEOPLE AND POLITICS

Barsaive is a diverse land, with many different Namegiver races living together. While some communities and regions are dominated by one race or another, there is a significant amount of integration. While discrimination exists, it is primarily cultural in nature, rather than driven by antipathy for different Namegiver races.

For example, the so-called "scorcher" tribes are predominantly orks, but other Namegiver races can be counted among their number as well. The Halls of Throal are heavily populated by dwarfs, but humans, elves, orks, and other races also live and work there.

Before the Scourge, cultural differences between races were more significant, and settlements were more likely to be segregated and dominated by a particular cultural group. The Scourge changed that. Neighboring villages banded together to construct a kaer, or people would travel to a nearby city to help construct its citadel. Four hundred years of living in close quarters blurred the lines that divided people. Neighbors are neighbors, whether they have pointed ears, wings, or tusks and horns.

Smaller settlements in Barsaive are usually autonomous, though it is not unusual for a town or village to have ties with a larger community nearby. These smaller hamlets and villages often have little in the way of formal government. They are frequently led by an elder or other respected citizen, sometimes advised by other members of the community. Larger towns will often be led by a council with varying degrees of involvement by the citizens. Larger cities often follow a similar pattern, but exert a greater influence on the surrounding area out of a need for resources.

While Throal is a monarchy, it is something of an exception. Kingdoms and noble titles were more common before the Scourge, but have not really returned. Many powers that had noble families and royal lines suffered during the Orichalcum Wars. Those that managed to weather that storm fell victim to the Scourge; their kaers and citadels were a more desirable target for Horror infiltration, or their bloodlines were thinned through centuries of isolation.

The Influence of Throal

A significant factor in the overall political culture of Barsaive is the Kingdom of Throal, largely as a result of the Book of Tomorrow. While it was not intended to spread Throalic influence, the Book was a product of dwarf culture, and the culture of many kaers shifted in favor of the dwarfs over the centuries. However, Varulus III chose not to take advantage of the subtle influence of Throalic culture on many of Barsaive's kaers.

The royal line of Throal had a long term plan—influenced by the Great Dragon Icewing—that encouraged diplomacy rather than military conquest. The Kingdom presented itself as an ally rather than an obstacle to rebuilding, reinforcing Throal's status in the province as a benevolent power. When the Theran Empire returned to lay claim to Barsaive through force of arms, the dwarfs of Throal stood in proxy for the rest of the province in opposition.

Unfortunately, after the Second Theran War, the ascension of King Kovar to the throne, and Throal's withdrawal from the provincial stage, the Kingdom's influence has waned. The long view, which served Throal well during the Scourge and the years after, has been lost. The strength of Throal is the strength of Barsaive, at least symbolically, and in the eyes of many Barsaivians the Kingdom has turned its back on the very people it inspired.

The Influence of Thera

While Theran influence has been greatly reduced in recent years, the Empire still maintains a network of agents and informers in the province. The First Governor and the Heavenherds consider Barsaive an important asset. The history of Thera is intricately bound to Barsaive, and those of a mystic persuasion theorize that difficulties in other parts of the Empire result from Thera's True Pattern being weakened by the lack of solid control of the province.

Whatever the truth behind these theories, recent history indicates that military conquest is not the ideal way to restore Theran primacy. In addition, there are multiple powers in Barsaive that have an interest in watching for Imperial activity. Throal does not maintain any formal diplomatic ties with Thera, though several noble houses have trading contacts that reach back to the Empire. Likewise, Cara Fahd watches for signs of Theran activity within its borders, and Iopan Holders of Trust keep watch for Theran agents.

Theran influence is currently strongest in the remains of Landis, where they agitate the humans along the borders of Cara Fahd to disrupt ork activities. They also maintain connections with the t'skrang house K'tenshin, though the *aropagoi* has seen its power diminish in the wake of the war. Throalic intelligence has also started to receive reports of mercenary companies in Theran employ patrolling and protecting remote towns and villages. If true, this could indicate a new direction for Theran activity in the province, building influence in places where Throal has withdrawn its support.

One thing remains certain: the Therans were driven out, but not defeated. While their military presence is reduced, they did not achieve their position in the world by accepting defeat. If the people of Barsaive wish to remain free, they need to be vigilant. It may take years, but the Therans are likely to return.

CULTURE AND TRADITION

While Barsaive is a vast and diverse area, there are some aspects of culture that are broadly observed. Some of these are the result of Throalic influence, while others have their roots much farther back in history.

The Throalic Calendar

The Kingdom of Throal divides the year into twelve months with thirty days each. The first of each month falls on or near the start of a new lunar cycle. The months are Strassa, Veltom, Charassa, Rua, Mawag, Gahmil, Raquas, Sollus, Riag, Teayu, Borrum, and Doddul. Halfway through the year, between the months of Gahmail and Raquas, Throal sets aside five days called Earthtime to celebrate the tradition of dwarf life underground.

The dwarf calendar is used in many parts of Barsaive, and it is not uncommon for Earthtime to be a festival time of some sort, though the exact traditions can very from place to place. Some use this time to celebrate the bounty of the Passions, others throw a harvest festival, and in some places it is a somber occasion to remember the dark times of the Scourge and those lost to it.

The Throalic calendar marks its years from the founding of Throal. According to this calendar, the current year is 1517 TH.

The Theran Calendar

The calendar used by the Theran Empire sees little use in Barsaive, but records found in Theran ruins might use that calendar. The Empire uses a calendar based on the solar cycle, divided into a five-day week. Theran dating convention marks the week followed by the day: for example, tenth week, third day, written as 10/3. Thera uses the same names for months as Throal, but they do not start or end at the same time. This can cause some confusion for those dealing with cross-cultural information. The Imperial calendar marks its year based on the founding of Thera, and the current year is 1077 TE.

Name-Day Feasts

An almost universal tradition in Barsaive is the Name-day feast. Naming is significant magic in the world of **Earthdawn**, and performing a ritual reinforces this magic. In many places the ceremony is held within the first week of the child's life, but other places delay the Naming until later. Communities that practice this delayed tradition often do so because of a higher rate of infant mortality, preferring to wait until the risk of death has passed its highest point.

Smaller communities often have a specific place set aside for the ceremony. The specifics of the ritual vary widely, often involving symbolism important to the community in question.

In one example, the ritual space is a small shack with no windows and a door facing east. The parents enter before sunrise, and the room is dark. A candle is lit, representing the light of life the child is bringing to into the world. The parents speak of their hopes for the child, telling a tale that highlights the virtues they hope the child will embody. To close out the ceremony, the parents speak the child's Name, and the door is opened to let dawn's light in.

In another version of the ritual the parents spend three days meditating on the Name they will select. The Name contains some part to honor a grandparent or other notable forbear. The parents bring the child to the ritual site, a glade on the outskirts of the village, and announce the Name before the assembled community. Three witnesses, chosen by the parents, repeat the Name and vow to protect and guide the child to adulthood. A piece of fruit is then shared between the parents and witnesses, symbolizing the new life shared between the ritual's participants.

Whatever the details in a particular community, the ritual is usually followed by a celebration or feast in which the entire community takes part.

Worship of the Passions

Spiritual life in Barsaive revolves around the Passions, mysterious beings that are seen as the embodiment of the universe's life force. Twelve Passions are recognized, though only nine are visibly honored. Three of the Passions fell victim to the Scourge and became twisted mockeries of their original selves.

There is extensive debate about the true nature of the Passions. Most believe they are given form by the collective thoughts and wishes of Namegivers acting on the magical nature of the world. A few theories look at the corruption of the Mad Passions as a sign that they are independent beings. Of course this raises the question of why these powerful entities choose to nurture and promote aspects of Namegiver life and society.

Most people in Barsaive interact with the Passions through Questors, individuals that choose to pursue a life devoted to the ideals of a particular Passion. Questors wield magical power like adepts and magicians, but their powers are related to the ideals of their patron. In addition, where the powers of an adept are the result of an internal philosophical dedication, a quester's powers are granted, and may diminish or be taken away if the Questor's devotion weakens.

Throalic as the Common Tongue

Throalic, a dialect of the dwarf racial language, is the common tongue in Barsaive. This came about in part because of the Kingdom's role as provincial administrators for the Theran Empire before the Scourge. In addition, Throalic caravans and merchants dominated trade in the province, and so their language became the language of commerce, establishing standards of measurement, money, and negotiation.

The other key piece of Throal's linguistic dominance in Barsaive was the Book of Tomorrow. Originally developed as a record of Throalic lexicon and grammar, it was expanded to include the history of Barsaive and Thera, information on ways to survive the Scourge, and legends and tales to remind people of the surface and inspire them to not give up hope.

Throal did what it could to distribute copies of the book as widely as possible. Since the book was written in Throalic, it included lessons on reading, writing, and speaking the language. As the years passed the stories contained in the Book of Tomorrow were told and retold, taking on a deep significance for the Namegivers hiding in the kaers. It told them of a world lost, and a world their descendants would one day reclaim. These tales were viewed with reverence, as was the language that carried these memories of the surface. In some kaers, the Book of Tomorrow was one of the few written works available.

All of these factors magnified the use of Throalic tongue across Barsaive. When the Scourge ended, the kaers opened, and the myriad isolated communities came into contact with each other, they found they shared a common language, making it that much easier to rebuild.

Other Languages

Despite the dominance of Throalic as a common tongue, other languages still see use in Barsaive. Some kaers did not receive a copy of the Book of Tomorrow, and so whatever language the residents spoke was maintained over the Scourge. Linguistic drift over the centuries has resulted in multiple dialects derived from older racial languages. These dialects are most frequently found in isolated pockets of Barsaive, in places that see few travelers.

Some parts of Barsaive are under the influence of powers that prefer their own language over Throalic. For example, the city of Iopos and the nearby villages and towns primarily speak a dialect of the human racial language. In Cara Fahd the primary language is or'zet, the modern dialect of the older ork language. Sperethiel is spoken in the Blood Wood and other elf enclaves, while the windlings of Glenwood Deep still speak their own native language. In places like this it is often still possible to find Namegivers that speak Throalic, especially among those who deal with travelers.

In southwestern Barsaive, Theran is still spoken, though it has fallen out of favor in the years since the War. During Theran control of Barsaive before the Scourge, Theran was spoken more frequently. In other parts of Barsaive dialects of the Theran language can be heard in isolated places, like the dialects of other languages.

Fortunately, the magic available to many adepts can make it possible for adventurers to communicate, whether their travels take them to isolated corners of Barsaive or lands beyond.

ON THE NAMEGIVER RACES

There are eight Namegiver races commonly encountered in Barsaive: dwarfs, elves, humans, obsidimen, orks, trolls, t'skrang, and windlings. Dragons are also counted among the Namegivers, though they are rarely encountered, even by adventurers. In the *Player's Guide* we provided a physical description of each race. Here we will provide some insight into the customs of each Namegiver culture, from their own point of view.

Dwarfs

Rulf Gadden, craftsman

When most folks think of dwarfs, they think of Throal. That's not a bad thing, mind, as nearly half the dwarfs In Barsaive live in the Kingdom. But that leaves half of us outside the Kingdom in villages, towns, and cities. Even when you take out the dwarfs in the Kingdom, we still almost end up as the most numerous Namegivers in Barsaive.

What this means is that you'll find dwarfs just about anywhere, involved in just about anything. There are some places where other Namegivers have more influence. For instance, the t'skrang own the lakes and rivers, but dwarfs help unload the riverboats, and dwarf merchants have the contacts to get the goods inland. The orks may hold sway in Cara Fahd, but our smiths help shoe their horses and arm their soldiers.

It's a dwarf's nature to make things. It doesn't matter what it is. Some of us make plows, others make swords. Some build houses, others build companies. Some forge iron, others forge kingdoms. Dwarf scholars build bodies of knowledge. We take pride in making things, and pride in things well-made—doesn't matter if it's dwarf work or not. We make good neighbors, since we know that many pairs of hands make work easier.

Now, don't go thinking that just because Throal is a dwarf kingdom that we all look to it for guidance. We provincials are proud of the Kingdom and what its done for Barsaive, but I tell you true, some dwarfs out here don't trust the kingdom so much. Given what's happened since the War, I can't say I blame them. Used to be you could look to a patrol from the Kingdom for aid. Nowadays, you don't see so many patrols, and the ones you do see tend to be focused on doing something else.

Of course, I don't go thinking that we've been abandoned, the way some folk do. Throal has its own interests, and it's going to tend them. Sometimes you need to clean up your own house, right? Even if the Kingdom itself isn't leading the way, we dwarfs will keep building, putting the shattered bits of the world back together.

Elves

Alliana Wintersbreath, Scout adept

The Blood Wood. Never mind how many elves chose not to follow the Court in their folly. It always comes back to the Wood.

It was a tragedy. A living reminder how the Horrors have destroyed so much beauty and value in the world.

Elves have old traditions and old ways. Yes, they hearken back to Wyrm Wood and the ancient seat of our culture. But like the trees themselves, we have grown and spread and adapted to the places we live. And unlike the Blood Elves, who close their minds as well as their borders, we live side by side with our neighbors, whatever Namegiver line they hail from.

Though—much as we might like to deny it—almost every elf feels the pull of the Wood at one time or another. Like a willful horse tugs at the bit, it tugs at your heart. Some answer that call. Most return to their homes and lives, wiser for the experience. A few... well, it's not my place to ask how madness takes root.

I heard the call. I could see it in my dreams. Looking over a rippling sea of green. The sound of the leaves in the wind. The smell of dirt and growth and life itself.

I answered. Two week's journey on foot, living on what I was able to forage and catch. Then one day I crested a hill and saw the Wood, just a few miles away.

Just as I had seen it in my dreams. Green. Greener than... anything. The wind was in my face, and while I know it's impossible, I could hear the leaves. Whispering.

Hungry.

I never got any closer.

I know there are some who hope to redeem our kin, reclaim the Wood. They're welcome to their dreams. Perhaps one day they will even succeed—though I doubt it will happen while Alachia remains on the Rose Throne.

The past is there to be remembered, learned from, but it's best we blaze our own trail.

Humans

Baer Portrail, merchant

We used to have a kingdom of our own, but that was ages ago. It was torn down. Burned to ash in a squabble over… who even remembers? Of course, some see what the orks have done, ask themselves why we don't do the same. Reclaim the ancient homeland of our people.

Lot of nonsense if you ask me. And a lot more work than necessary. Why go to all that work to build something when there are plenty of places where it's already built? I admit, sometimes the dwarfs have their noses stuck in the air, but overall they're not so bad. They certainly don't have anything against folk willing to work alongside them.

My granddad came out of the kaers. He wasn't much more than a boy at the time, but he loved telling tales of those early years, and the lessons they brought out of their hole in the ground. In the end, he'd say, we all want the same things: roof over your head, food in your belly. Doesn't matter if you've got round ears or pointed, wings or scales, everybody's the same. Neighbors are neighbors.

You can't assume things about folks just because of what they look like. But here's what I'll say about us humans. We're the best neighbors you're likely to have. You can find us anywhere, doing just about anything that needs doing.

Sure, there's humans out there that are rogues and bandits. Ones that will take advantage of you, manipulate you, look out for themselves. But you can find dwarfs, or orks, or even obsidimen doing the same.

Like my granddad used to say, you treat your neighbor right. You get through the dark times by working together, keeping an eye on each other. The dwarf kingdom did that. Not so much anymore. It's a shame.

Maybe those folk talking about a human kingdom aren't so full of nonsense after all. Maybe they're remembering the lessons of the Scourge, and stepping up to be a good neighbor when somebody else is falling short.

Obsidimen
Kayalna, Elementalist

All living things have the elements inside them, and that includes Namegivers. We all have different amounts of each, which is what makes the different races the way they are. For example, t'skrang are more heavily influenced by water, windlings by air, and orks by fire. My people, the obsidimen, are more heavily influenced by earth.

We are born from the living heart of the stone itself. As stone endures, we endure. Slow. Stable. Deliberate. All of these describe us. We are not easily moved, but when our fury is roused we are a boulder tumbling down the mountain.

Where the lives of other Namegivers pass like a summer rain, we witness the turn of the seasons, watch the passage of years, feel the deep thrum of the world's heartbeat. Our memory is not recorded in delicate scratchings on parchment; as each brother returns to the stone his knowledge joins the whole. We are one spirit, seeking to explore and understand this creation in which we find ourselves.

You other Namegivers fascinate us, with your ties to fire, water, and air. Your childhood and growth and energy. You build, and tear down, and build again. The march of time pushes on you so strongly, you seldom stop to contemplate the mix of fragile beauty and enduring strength that is the world. It is lovely, and it is a shame that you get only the barest glimpse of it during your brief lives.

Orks
Dazz Halftooth, city guard

Listen my friend, the dwarf kingdom may act like they're the champions of freedom, but we still remember the days before the Scourge. Sure, they helped boot the Therans out, but they used to be Theran lapdogs. When they got a chance to sit at the top of the heap? They didn't want to share that power.

We orks are the champions of freedom. Every true ork has the song of Blork—the Passion the dwarfs call Lochost—in his heart. This song goes back to our earliest days. We were slaves, crushed under the yoke and whips of other Namegivers. Hrak Gron was the first to hear the song of Blork, and sang it to his people. The song spread, and the orks rose and claimed their freedom. Bought it with blood and steel.

Those first free orks built Cara Fahd. The threat of the Scourge and the Orichalcum Wars brought our nation to her knees, and her people were scattered. We thought our land lost and the song of Blork was little more than a distant echo.

Krathis Gron, daughter of the Passions, descendant of the great Hrak Gron, reminded us of the song, rekindled gahad's fire. She showed us that while we were no longer called slaves, we were still shackled, living by the rules and traditions of other Namegivers. She reminded us of who we were, and who we should be. She restored our land.

Now we live as orks are meant to live. In our own land. By our own laws. With our own traditions. Our lives burn brightly but briefly, so we seize life by the throat, and laugh at Death.

We face the other Namegivers as equals, not subjects. The Therans did not respect that, and paid the price. Throal, Iopos, and anybody else that would seek dominion over the free orks of Cara Fahd would do well to remember that.

> I am proud of the achievements of my kin in Cara Fahd. But I must admit I don't understand their need to belittle those of us who chose not to follow Krathis Gron. Many of us have built lives and families in other parts of Barsaive, and call other Namegivers friends and neighbors. I wish them well, but hope they recognize there is more than one way to live!
> *Ranneth the Glib, Troubadour*

Trolls

Norkala Ironwing, caravan master

There are a lot of misconceptions about trolls. Other Namegivers think that because we're big and strong, we're clumsy and dull-witted. While there are trolls who are less graceful, or less intelligent than others, we show the same variety you find among orks, humans, or t'skrang.

Trolls can seem clumsy to other folk. Much of that is because of our size. Most Namegiver homes, furniture, and tools aren't really made to accommodate us. Using a sword that isn't suited to your hand can make you look a bit of a fool, and trying to navigate the close quarters of a shop built for smaller folk... well, there's a reason for the expression "troll in a potter's shop."

Because of the way most of Namegiver society isn't really made for us, we build our own villages, or an enclave within a larger town or city. This means that other folk don't interact with us as much as they otherwise might and learn how their view of us is a bit skewed. A troll jeweler is just as capable of delicate filigree as any dwarf craftsman, and our Troubadours and poets can stir the soul as well as any elf minstrel!

About the only other folk who recognize our position are the obsidimen, who share the troubles of a world not really built for them. It's part of the reason we respect and honor them.

Another incorrect assumption about trolls is that we are all warriors and raiders, prone to violence at a moment's notice. This is because of the highland moots, the Crystal Raiders. They live in harsh lands, and their culture is harsh as a result. Raiding lowland settlements, as well as each other, is the only way many of them are able to survive, and complex rules have developed around the practice.

This is where the aspects of troll honor come from, in all of its bizarre and contradictory forms. Don't be mistaken, lowland trolls consider honor a virtue, we just recognize that different people have different approaches to life, and it doesn't make sense to needlessly impose our philosophy on others. Think on it, would a Questor of Mynbruje find fault with the ways of a devotee of Lochost?

Never mind, that's a bad example. The point is, we lowland trolls generally focus on acting with honor and integrity in our personal lives and business dealings. If another Namegiver wishes to do otherwise, that's between him and the Passions. Meeting every perceived slight to honor with an attempt to remove the offender's nethers results in more violence, and isn't really the best thing for everyone, if you know what I mean.

T'skrang

Sho'vall Wavedancer Syrtis, deckhand

We are children of the river. Her currents are the lifeblood of our *nialls*, carrying goods to settlements up and down the Serpent, enriching our home. While a t'skrang may wander from the shores of our mother, she is never far from our heart and we always return.

Life is a struggle, but that doesn't mean we need to face it with fear or restraint. We face the challenges of life with a song in our hearts. Our lives are devoted to *jik'harra*, or 'brave passion.' Some consider this mere bravado, and think we t'skrang are braggarts and show-offs, but there is much more to it than that.

To us, how one performs an action is as important as the action itself. Our boasts and displays show the universe that we will not submit to despair, and that fear will not rule us. What better way to show the Horrors they did not succeed than to laugh at the trials we face in our day to day lives? We survived the Scourge!

Do not think that because we approach life with joy and laughter that we do not take things seriously. Life is precious, and not to be wasted. When pirates attack a riverboat, all the crew comes to her defense. After all, lost cargo means less profit, and our friends and loved ones back home might suffer as a result. If the crew drives off the attackers, they celebrate victory and share tales of their valor. If they fail, they are remembered by the Passions for facing the danger with bravery.

Other Namegivers could learn a lesson from us. The river flows where it will, and cares little for your desire. The wise read the currents, steer for the best course through the rapids, and enjoy the ride!

Windlings

Jaena Thistle, potter

Of course we see things differently! You big folk are limited to stomping around on the ground, while we have the freedom of the skies. Few can truly understand what a difference that makes. Air Sailors, maybe. We are blessed by the Passions with an awareness few can match, and recognize there is more that one way to view an issue.

What we lack in size and strength, we make up with wit and speed. We also adapt to our circumstances. We don't hold on to something for the sake of tradition. We watch and learn, and are willing to change when we see something better. Why limit yourself to one path, when there are so many to choose from? We'll try anything at least once, reveling in the experience of something new.

Some people compare this daring to the bravado of the t'skrang. In some ways they are not wrong, but it seems to me the river folk put too much emphasis on success, where windlings focus on what we learn from the experience. There is no shame in failure, it is another lesson learned!

Only death is a misfortune. There are not many of us, and each life lost is tragic. We also have few children, making each life lost even more keenly felt. All Namegivers love their offspring, but to us a child is potential made flesh. They see with new eyes, and bring a new perspective into the world. They are embraced and raised by the community. Anything, creature or Namegiver, that threatens the life of one of our children will find that our ferocity is far out of proportion to our size.

WHERE PEOPLE LIVE

The lands of Barsaive can be divided into three basic regions. The first is the Kingdom of Throal and its underground Inner Cities. The second is the lowlands, which includes most of the province's grasslands, forests, and jungles as well as the Serpent River and all of Barsaive's major cities. The final region is the highlands, which includes the mountains and plateaus.

The exact population in Barsaive is unknown, as there has been no comprehensive census since the Scourge. Most scholars believe that about one-third of Barsaive's population lives in Throal and the Inner Cities; about half the population lives in the lowlands, about half of them in the major cities; and the remaining sixth in the highlands.

Hundreds of villages and small towns can be found across Barsaive. Many of these are isolated, with only limited interest in the affairs of their neighbors. In a continuing legacy of the Scourge, trust is difficult to earn in these places. Strangers in areas off the beaten path are rare, and could be raiders or other folk with bad intent, including those potentially affected by a Horror's influence.

Most smaller settlements rely on subsistence farming, growing crops and raising livestock to keep themselves and their community alive. Surplus is put away for lean times, though fortunately the temperate climate and long growing season makes lean times relatively rare in the lowlands.

Even those places within a couple day's travel of a trade route tend to keep to themselves, with only a small handful of people dealing with the outside world; perhaps a contact in a merchant company or similar arrangement. Since travel is generally dangerous, it is rare, and the vast majority of Namegivers in Barsaive will be born, live, and die without seeing more than a few miles around their home.

In contrast, villages and towns located on a major trade route or within a day's travel of a major city tend to be more open and accomodating to travelers. These settlements often help provide food and other raw materials to craftsmen and traders in the city, and usually take on a cultural flavor similar to the nearby city. In addition, the increased reliance on trade means these places will have a wider variety of goods and services to offer travelers.

T'skrang River Towns

The settlements of the t'skrang deserve special attention. Dozens line the banks of the Serpent River and its tributaries, and even the smaller ones are more cosmopolitan than villages in other parts of Barsaive. This is due, in large part, to the Serpent River serving as the most significant trade route in the province, and the influence of the Great Houses, or *aropagoi*, in coordinating and managing the affairs of the settlements along their stretch of the river.

The center of t'skrang village life is the *niall*, literally translated as "foundation." A niall is an extended family of anywhere from twenty to sixty individuals, with a village made up of anywhere from four to twenty *nialls*. Each foundation is led by its eldest female, called the *lahala*, and each village is led by a council made up of the *lahalas* of each foundation. T'skrang society is matriarchal, with the male entering the female's covenant upon marriage.

While the council manages the day-to-day affairs of the village, meetings are held about once a month, and all residents over the age of 15 have some say in making decisions that affect the entire village. These meetings often reflect the nature of t'skrang culture: energetic, loud, and full of action. Impassioned speakers will often try and shout down their rivals, and it is not uncommon for scuffles or duels to break out between rivals.

T'skrang build large domes partially submerged in the water, and connect a village's domes with underground tunnels. The interior walls and ceiling of the domes ares often covered with nets and ropes, as t'skrang love to climb and swing. The domes themselves tend towards an open floor plan, with communal living space a common feature. Each foundation has its own dome, laid out around a much larger central dome that serves as the focus of village life. Smaller domes that serve different purposes are a common feature of large villages.

In some villages, the domes are completely submerged and access to the village is through towers that reach up above the surface of the river. They serve as a place for docking riverboats, and allow for the circulation of fresh air down into the underwater homes. From the shore, these towers may resemble little more than large, flat-topped rocks, but wealthier settlements may decorate these features with elaborate designs, and even set up battlements with fire cannon or other siege engines to defend access to the village.

In addition to these more mundane defenses, a series of barriers crafted of elemental water limit access to the towers. Called *refselenika*, or refs, they lie just below the river's surface. Residents of the settlement are able to navigate the maze presented by these defenses, but visitors need guidance, or risk having their hull damaged by the refs. If necessary the barriers can be lowered so that ships can pass without needing to navigate the maze, but raising and lowering the refs takes several minutes, and is not done lightly. If hostile forces are able to approach and seize a tower, they gain access to the entire village, and options for escape can be limited.

THE KINGDOM OF THROAL

A general overview of the Kingdom of Throal was provided in the *Player's Guide*, p. 487. This section will explore some of that information in more depth, describe some important personalities and organizations in Throal.

Bartertown

Located just outside the gates of Throal, Bartertown is not technically part of the Kingdom. Its politics and culture are, however, strongly tied to Throal, if defined mainly in their opposition. The city is a sprawling, ramshackle collection of buidlings that are home to roughly forty thousand Namegivers.

Bartertown was originally established as a trading post by merchants who wanted to take advantage of dwarf trading policy, but did not want to be subject to Throalic law or taxation. Over the years, the temporary huts and stalls gave rise to more permanent structures, though even those were cobbled together from available resources, and even though it has been in place for decades, Bartertown gives a strong impression of a shanty town.

Bartertown has one main road, wide enough for three wagons or large carts to pass, which runs down the center of the city towards the gates of Throal. Off this main thoroughfare are about twenty narrower streets called 'lanes,' named after goods sold by an early settler; for example Cloak Lane, Boot Lane, or Sword Lane. Between these lanes are countless alleys, only some of which are named (usually for a prominent early resident).

Because of the haphazard nature of Bartertown's construction, there are no real districts or any sense of urban planning. Houses and businesses are not numbered, and locations are usually referred to by the nearest cross street. For example, the offices of Magistrate Clystone are at "Hatchet and the Road", which means it lies near the intersection of the Royal Road (the main road through the city), and Hatchet Lane. Navigating the city can be daunting to newcomers, and the unwary traveler can find themselves in a dangerous situation if they end up in the wrong neighborhood.

Bartertown is not truly lawless, but it stands in stark contrast to the order found in Throal. As the city was founded by those looking to avoid Throalic taxation and rule, the culture of Bartertown has a strong independent streak, and most of those with some degree of power use it for their own benefit and protection rather than to better the city as a whole.

The city is ruled by Magistrate Clystone. On paper he serves at the behest of the Council of Merchants, but the balance of power shifted many years ago. Laws in Bartertown are by decree, and can be invoked or revoked at any time. Clystone is an Illusionist, though he has not seriously practiced his Discipline for many years. He has a force of armed tax collectors called *buundavim* that carry out his decrees. They are the closest thing the city has to a police force, but they are largely a band of corrupt thugs enforcing the whim of their master.

Those that complain too loudly about Clystone's policies, or get on his bad side in one way or another are likely to find themselves visited by his agents in the middle of the night. Clystone has amassed a great deal of personal power by using a not insignificant portion of the taxes he collects to buy the loyalty of his soldiers, and is not against making examples of those who would challenge his position at the top of the city's power structure.

Given Bartertown's history as a haven for tax avoidance, it should come as no surprise that a thriving black market exists, with a number of gangs operating in a manner similar to Clystone's tax collectors. Indeed, the only real difference is one of the gangs happens to have badges of office. Protection, racketeering, and smuggling are common, with alliances forming and shattering on a regular basis. The underworld of Bartertown is largely dominated by a human troubadour Named Shadowswift. He is a public figure and outspoken supporter of Clystone's policies, because he could not have gotten where he is without them. He has connections to many of the criminal gangs in the city, managing their affairs through intermediaries and taking his cut of the profits.

A long standing question when it comes to Bartertown is whether it will be annexed by Throal. At the moment, independence remains the city's official policy, as Clystone knows that if the dwarfs were to exert their influence his personal power would be in serious jeopardy. There are growing voices, however, that are calling for a stronger alliance with the Kingdom and the safety that would afford. For now, at least, the dwarfs are content to maintain the status quo, but if the barely organized chaos of Bartertown were to start cutting into the profits of any noble houses, that could change.

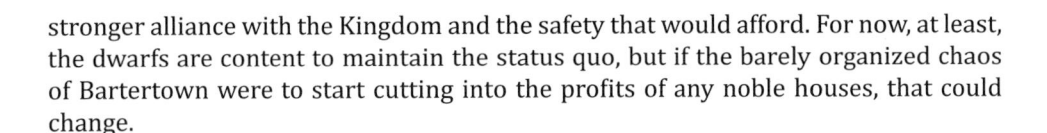

The Great Fire

Shortly before the Second Theran War, a large fire tore through Bartertown, destroying almost a quarter of the city and taking hundreds of lives. There are many rumors about the cause of the fire, but given its timing in relation to the hostilities between Throal and Thera, most believe it was the result of Theran agents trying to destabilize the situation outside the Kingdom and give Throal a more pressing problem to deal with.

The truth of the matter is the fire was part of an assassination attempt on Clystone by one of his rivals from the Council of Merchants. The magistrate's offices were originally a little bit farther from the Kingdom at the intersection of Butter Lane and the Road, not far from where the fire began. The rival realized that the presence of Theran troops and the tensions between the Kingdom and the Empire would provide the perfect cover. The fire was started as a distraction and a way to cover up the assassination if successful.

The Gates of Throal and Grand Bazaar

Entry into the Kingdom of Throal is through the gates, three enormous archways, each a hundred yards wide and a hundred yards high. Each arch can be blocked by a pair of three-yard thick double doors made of magically reinforced stone and wooden planks enhanced with kernels of elemental earth and wood, set in an iron frame laced with orichalcum.

The doors have not been closed since the Kingdom opened after the Scourge. They even remained open during the siege during the First Theran War. The doors can only be closed through the use of a spell known to a select group of high ranking Throalic magicians, or the use of dozens of thundra beasts chained to each door.

The gates are watched by thirty-six guards, twelve at each arch. Their only job is to present a strong face to visitors to the Kingdom, with no obligation to challenge travelers as the Grand Bazaar just beyond the gates is open to all.

The Bazaar itself is housed in a massive cavern about a mile across. It is a monument to the order and power of merchant life in Throal, standing in stark contrast to the barely organized chaos of Bartertown. The Bazaar hosts hundreds of merchants, organized into multiple districts dedicated to different goods and services.

All merchants must be licensed and officials of the crown keep a watchful eye to make sure that unauthorized vendors are shut down and fined. Royal guards patrol the area to keep the peace, investigate crimes, and apprehend thieves. Merchants who deal in exotic or expensive goods often employ private guards for additional protection.

Nearly anything can be found in the Grand Bazaar: carpets, furnishings, household goods, clothing, food both raw and prepared, jewelry and perfumes, works of art, mounts, pets, beasts of burden, weapons and armor, potions, blood charms, even thread items. The services of fortunetellers, scribes, and troubadours can also be found.

Because of Throal's stance on slavery, slaves cannot be purchased in the Grand Bazaar. Attempts to circumvent this restriction, for example making arrangements in the Bazaar for a transaction that takes place outside the kingdom, will result in the offender being arrested and exiled. In addition, any slaves brought into the kingdom are freed, and the owner escorted outside the gates.

The Halls of Throal

The Halls of Throal are the tunnels and passages of the original kaer, built before the kingdom was sealed for the Scourge. Constructed in a style best suited for dwarfs, the nine tunnels radiate out from the Grand Bazaar not unlike spokes from the hub of a wheel. Each tunnel entrance is protected by eight guards, whose job it is to watch for those exiled from the kingdom, as well as provide support to large-scale disturbances in the Bazaar.

Three of the halls are named for prior monarchs, three after heroic founders of the kingdom, two after great playwrights, and one for Upandal, the Passion of building and construction. From left to right as they branch of the Bazaar the halls are Tav, Thandos, Ulutur, Jothan, Donalicus, Bazrata, Bodal, Garaham, and Upandal.

The halls are more than mere passages, averaging about thirty feet wide with a ceiling of about fifteen feet, though the tunnels widen and narrow as they wind their way into the depths of the mountains. Each hall is dozens of miles long, and would take days to travel from end to end. Cross passages connect different halls so that residents can move from place to place without needing to travel all the way back to the Bazaar. Unfortunately, there is little to distinguish the cross passages from the normal halls, and it is all too easy for a traveler to get lost.

The halls and cross passages are lined with residences, workshops, and other businesses. The walls are decorated with scenes depicting Throalic history, as well as other artwork. The quality and upkeep of the art is a good indicator of the fortunes of the neighborhood: poor areas will have painted scenes, while wealthier areas will have elaborate mosaics with bright patterns and semi-precious stones. Houses and storefronts are not numbered, instead the various art pieces are used as landmarks. Since some scenes are very popular, this can result in even more confusion to travelers trying to find a location.

When the kaer was being constructed, the places closest to the gates were the least desirable, as they would be the first to fall if the gates were breached, and the wealthiest areas are those farthest from the Grand Bazaar. This arrangement is rather inconvenient now, as the offices and estates of the wealthy noble and merchant houses are farther away from the Grand Bazaar and the outside world.

The halls can be divided into three general areas. The *dahnat*, the poorest and most run-down area, a haven for beggars and others that have fallen on hard times. Fortunately, this part of the kingdom is not very large, given the overall population, with no more than about 5,000 Namegivers. The typical residence is a fifteen by forty foot rectangle attached to the main hall at one of the narrow ends. They are often crowded, with sometimes as many as fifteen or twenty members of an extended family living in that space with the barest of amenities.

Guard patrols in the *dahnat* are infrequent during the day, and it can take almost ten minutes for a patrol to respond to trouble. Later in the day, as activity in the bars and taverns increases, patrols increase as well in order to try and head off trouble before it starts.

Class Warfare

Having the *dahnat* as the first thing visitors encounter after passing through the Grand Bazaar has not made the noble and merchant families favorably disposed towards these neighborhoods. Since the ascension of Kovar I efforts have been made to move the poor to places where they can be more easily ignored, such as the inner cities. This is often done by increasing rents and fining those who don't maintain the outside of their homes.

Public support for these efforts are driven by propaganda that paints the problems of the *dahnat* as an influx of other Namegiver races, especially orks, humans, and trolls. This causes a bit of tension in these neighborhoods, and despite the rumors of rampant crime and corruption, many of the people in the dahnat are proud, self-reliant sorts who came to Throal looking for a better life for themselves and their families.

The second and largest part of the Halls is the *wedshel*. This is where the vast majority of ordinary dwarfs reside. Houses are larger, typically about forty by fifty feet, with five or six rooms. Most homes will house three generations, with a reception room, dining hall, kitchen, and a family room where most leisure time is spent. The family sleeps together in a common area, and an ancient and treasured verse of dwarf poetry reads, "To hear the snores of one's grandparents is the most perfect bliss."

The *wedshel* is well patrolled, with guards usually arriving at the scene of a disturbance in less than five minutes. Residents are likely to intervene if they see a crime being committed, though if adepts are involved they will give them a wide berth and wait for the guards.

The wealthiest part of the Halls are the Estates, the manor houses and offices of the wealthy merchant and noble families that make up the kingdom's social and political elite. The manors are often two stories, with dozens of rooms for the family, as well as housing for servants and guards. Unlike the dwarfs in the *dahnat* and *wedshel*, the rich sleep in their own rooms. This is generally seen as a bit decadent, and perhaps part of the reason why the rich seem a bit cold and selfish.

The manors also include a large ballroom or banquet hall where the family will host parties, salons, and presentations by notable artists. Many business dealings are negotiated at these affairs. Most manors also have a respectable library, as Throalic culture believes in the importance of education and knowledge.

The manors are heavily patrolled, not only by Royal Guard units, but also by private forces and bodyguards hired by the families. Guards will be on the scene as soon as trouble starts (if not before), and will often get reinforcements every minute or so if a disturbance is not quickly put to rest. These reinforcements often include adepts in the employ of the noble families.

The Inner Kingdom

Beyond the northern end of the Halls of Jothan and Donalicus are the chambers of the Inner Kingdom, containing the Royal Auditorium, the Great Library, the offices of various government agencies like the Chancellery and His Majesty's Exploratory Force, and the private chambers of the royal family. Some of these locations are connected with a network of secret passages known only to a trusted few.

The Royal Auditorium can seat nearly 4,000 Namegivers, and plays host to a wide variety of events. Lectures, amateur and professional dramatic productions, educational presentations, pageants, debates, demonstrations of combat or magical prowess, performances by troubadours or other musical acts, and any number of other displays can be found there. Some of these are free and open to the public, others might require admission. It is rare for the auditorium to be full—an event that draws 2,000 attendants is considered a rousing success.

The Great Library is one of the largest collections of knowledge in Barsaive, and the breadth and depth of information available to those willing to spend the time is rivaled by few other places in the world—most notably the Eternal Library of Thera. The collection is extensively indexed and cross-referenced, but there is no catalog available to the general public. Access to material is by request, with the researcher naming the subject of their query to the archivists, who search the index for appropriate tomes and scrolls. If the subject of inquiry is deemed to be dangerous, approval must be granted by the Master of the Hall of Records.

The Royal Chambers are where the king and his family live and conduct business. It is defended at all times by forty Royal Guard as well as a team of eight high-Circle adepts in possession of powerful magical items. In addition, the main door is protected by a powerful magical ward that can be activated on a moment's notice by the captain of these elite guards. Entry into the court is by invitation only. Those attempting to enter without such an invitation are subdued and arrested. Punishment can range from fines to exile and even execution, depending on the intent of the offender.

Master of the Hall of Records

The current Master of the Hall of Records is Thom Edrull, who took the position after Merrox, the previous Master, stepped down. Edrull is greedy and self-important, and secured the position despite not having as much experience as some other senior archivists. Speculation is rife in scholarly circles about how Edrull managed this feat. The truth is a combination of bribery, blackmail, and back room dealing among the courtiers to end up as the primary recommendation to the post.

Despite Edrull's desire for personal enrichment, there are still enough honest apprentice and associate archivists that corruption and favoritism have not overtaken the scholarship performed there. Still, characters that are investigating unusual or potentially dangerous knowledge are likely to come to Edrull's attention, and he or one of his lackeys will try to get extra money from them—despite this being against the royal charter for the Library.

Merrox is retired, though he still pursues some personal research projects. He was heavily involved in the debates that raged in the time between Neden's death and Kovar's ascension, and the stresses of that time, along with the loss of Varulus and Neden in a short period of time, led him to retire. He has heard the rumors of how Edrull's tenure as Master is resulting in graft and corruption, but does not place much stock in it. He still wields a great deal of influence, and while his support is difficult to gain, if earned it can make a notable difference.

The Inner Cities

After the Scourge, King Varulus III wanted to open Throal to all manner of Namegivers, and commissioned the construction of the Inner Cities. These places were built to be more suitable to other Namegiver races, but a significant number of Throalic dwarfs moved to these caverns as well in order to reduce overcrowding in the original Halls.

Each city is laid out roughly the same, with a large circular plaza in the center, and ten major avenues radiating out like spokes of a wheel. The plaza is used as a communal place for the city's residents to gather for celebrations, performances, and other public business. At one end of the plaza is the estate of the city's baron, which also contains government offices. The area around the plaza serves as a public market or bazaar, where merchants, vendors, and other tradesmen can set up shop. A park surrounds this central area, dividing it from the main bulk of the city. The park is decorated with elaborate sculptures of plant life, enchanted with illusion magic to look and smell authentic. In a few places real plants are grown and sustained by the light of the enormous light quartz crystals set in the cavern's ceiling.

Seven of the Inner Cities have been completed: Bethabal, Hustane, Oshane, Tirtaga, Valvria, Wishon, and Yistaine. Each city is ruled by a baron appointed by the King. The position is for life, unless removed by the King, but not hereditary. One has been appointed since Kovar's ascension, one was replaced by Neden shortly before the war, and the rest were appointed by Varulus III.

Two more cities, Raithabal and Thurdane, were planned but construction on them ended shortly after Varulus III's death and as yet have not been resumed. Raithabal's cavern has been excavated and the city inside has been partially completed, while

Thurdane's cavern has been partially excavated with little work on the city having been done.

The fate of these cities has been a frequent and contentious issue in Throal, and it is rare for a week to pass without some sort of discussion or demonstration. The issue has become even more pronounced in recent years, as both caverns have become

The Barons

Bethabal: Baroness Dajag Treaty-Keeper. She is an ork, and popular with the residents of the city. Her appointment by Varulus III was controversial, as she was originally a liaison from Terath's Chargers, an ork mercenary cavalry. Of all the barons, she is the one the more conservative old guard would like to see removed. Thus far they have been unsuccessful in their efforts.

Hustane: Baroness Divuna Divinicus. She is a member of Hose Moberl, one of the more conservative houses in Throal. She is, however, something of a black sheep in the family and was a vocal supporter of Varulus III and Neden's reforms. She is a devoted ruler, and has done her best to keep the recent troubles in the Kingdom from affecting her city too severely.

Oshane: Baroness Marruth. She served as chancellor to the former baron, and used that position to effectively run the city from behind the scenes. During the succession debate, she managed to shift much of the blame for city's corruption to the former baron, and not long after Kovar was crowned she was awarded the position. She has continued to use the city's treasury to finance her own lifestyle and enrich her relatives.

Tirtaga: Baroness Aurbach. In some ways, the opposite of her counterpart in Oshane. She was the former chancellor for the city, whose baron drove Tirtaga's treasury deeply into debt through lavish parties. She is a dedicated, if humorless, human who brought the waste to the attention of the crown and was given the position by Neden. She is still struggling to bring the city's finances under control.

Valvria: Baron Mardek Silkback. An ambitious ork, Mardek is a consummate Throalic political insider. While he was a vocal supporter of Varulus and Neden's reforms, he is also fairly well respected by the more conservative noble families. Despite outward appearances, he has little respect for the Kingdom's traditions, and would like nothing more than to bring the system down from the inside and be elevated to ruler himself. He has an extensive network of informants, and probably knows more about the political realities in Throal than anyone. The unrest surrounding Neden's death and Kovar's ascension gave him the opportunity to further insinuate himself into royal politics.

Wishon: Baron Clifberz IV. This fretful and energetic dwarf is an excellent administrator, and is more personally involved in the day to day operations of his city than any of the other barons. His family is the closest thing to a dynasty that can be found in the Inner Cities, as they have been barons of Wishon since it was first opened to settlement. A staunch loyalist, the stress surrounding Kovar's ascension have caused him some health problems. Despite his doctor's orders, he continues to put in long hours in the city's offices.

> *Yistaine:* Baroness Skaave. Granddaughter of Vaare Longfang, who captained the *Earthdawn*, Skaave is a Troubadour and Wizard, and the only adept currently serving as baron. She is also a devoted follower of the Passions, and more interested in mysticism than politics. Fortunately, Yistaine is a city that seems plagued with omens and mysterious happenings. These events date back to the city's construction, when the partial skeleton of a dragon was found fused into the rock while the cavern was being excavated.

havens for malcontents, smugglers, and those looking to avoid notice for one reason or another. Patrols are infrequent at best, and rarely have any kind of effect on illicit activities.

Greenhouses and Mines

The final areas of the Kingdom are also the deepest. The Crystal Greenhouses were the food source for the massive kaer. An improvement on Theran designs, these growing chambers are the most impressive found in Barsaive. Each greenhouse covers about 1800 square yards, and was capable of providing food for about 2,500 people through specially crafted light quartz crystals.

The greenhouses still see use, though much of the Kingdom's food supply is imported. Fruits and vegetables grown in the artificial conditions of the greenhouses do not have the same richness of flavor as ones grown on the surface, and many residents of Throal are willing to pay extra for the superior product.

These days the primary plant grown in the greenhouses are stoveplants, a hybrid created before the Scourge. These plants consist mainly of a tall, woody stem that burns slowly and gives off little smoke. These plants are excellent at providing heat and light to the underground environment without overly polluting the air.

Security in the greenhouses was very tight during the Scourge, but since Throal opened it has lessened considerably. Visitors are welcome, and in addition to the farmers and questors of Jaspree that tend the crops, lovers and other folk looking to meet away from prying eyes can be encountered.

Beyond the greenhouses are the mines. The roots of the Throal mountains contain a wealth of minerals including gold, silver, iron, even the occasional vein of orichalcum or True Earth. Countless miles of tunnels snake their way back and forth, the result of generations of dwarfs seeking their fortune in the depths. Some of the older areas are now abandoned, their veins tapped out. There are rumors that these places now serve as lairs for subterranean creatures, or meeting places for secret societies or cults devoted to Mad Passions or Horrors.

In contrast to the more ordered nature of Throalic society, the mines are a frontier, policed either by the miners themselves, or by mercenaries brought in by mine owners. Official patrols are rare, and often only in response to serious unrest. Politics in the mines are dominated by the Miner's Guild, and control of the guild often swings back and forth between workers and owners, depending on whose fortunes are on the rise.

MAJOR CITIES AND POWERS

Barsaive contains a few notable cities, and is home to some major powers. This section provides an overview of these urban centers, including their culture and government, along with any notable secrets.

Blood Wood

While not technically a part of Barsaive, Blood Wood has had a profound effect on the area, and one that continues to this day. The Martyr Scholar originally hailed from the Wood, and it is one of the oldest cultures in the world.

The Wood has been strongly isolationist since the Scourge. Elves that wish to visit are welcome, but any who wish to stay for more than a brief time must have a sponsor from within the Court, and are required to undergo the Ritual of Thorns, becoming Blood Elves. Other Namegiver races are unwelcome at best, and any unauthorized visitors that are found are either escorted to the boundaries, or taken prisoner and held in the cells under Alachia's Palace.

Alachia has been queen since before the Scourge, and is as beautiful today as when she took the throne. She is a Master-level Troubadour, in addition to being an accomplished Elementalist and Illusionist. Beyond her abilities as an adept, she is an expert politician, well practiced in playing the varying factions of the Elven Court against each other. Nothing happens in the Wood that she does not eventually learn about, and she has an extensive network of contacts and informants in Barsaive and other parts of the world.

> **Secrets of the Blood Wood: Alachia**
>
> Despite her centuries on the throne of the Wood, Alachia has not aged, which has led to rumors that she is one of the Great Elves—elves whose lifespan is far longer than normal. She has done her best to end this speculation, but it is accurate. Alachia is one of the oldest living beings on the planet, and is rivaled only by the Great Dragons in terms of her knowledge and experience. Her magical power is far greater than even her closest advisors believe, and include abilities that date back to the last age of magic.

Beneath the queen's authority are a group of eight advisors called *consortis*, chosen from the high ranks of the *ranelles*—the noble houses of the Wood. *Consortis* do not serve any fixed term, and can be appointed or dismissed as Alachia sees fit. To an outsider, she seems to change *consortis* at random, with no reason. In truth, she uses the position—and the chance of losing it—to maintain the balance of power among the *ranelles*, ensuring that no power bloc can develop to challenge her position.

The queen also appoints blood warders and exolashers. Blood warders are the queen's advisors on magical matters, and are ultimately responsible for the safety of the Wood. They serve for life, unless they voluntarily step down. Few have done so. The warders developed the Ritual of Thorns, and continue to research the effects the Ritual has had on the Wood.

Secrets of the Blood Wood: Ritual of Thorns

One of the Wood's most closely guarded secrets is the true nature of the Ritual of Thorns and its effects; only Alachia and her blood warders know the whole truth. In addition to the physical changes imposed on the Blood Elves, the Ritual also reNamed the Wood, altering its True Pattern in ways intended to keep out the Horrors. The Ritual is an ongoing effect, powered by the blood provided by the elves of the Wood.

While the Ritual did save the Court from being destroyed by the Horrors, it came at great cost. The heart of the wood is displaying signs of corruption, and thus far the blood warders have been unable to determine the cause, or a way to reverse it. The best solution would likely to be an end to the Ritual, but the patterns of the Blood Wood and the elves are so entangled through centuries of blood magic, no one can predict what the result would be.

Alachia's pride and fear are also obstacles to ending the ritual. While she would like to see the Ritual ended so the Court can resume its rightful place as the center of elven culture, she fears what the effect of ending the ritual could cost the Court. She also refuses to publicly acknowledge that the Ritual might have been a mistake, as it might weaken her authority.

The exolashers are Alachia's personal guard, and are also responsible for the security of the palace and its residents. They are all highly trained adepts, primarily following the martial Disciplines of Archer, Warrior, Swordmaster, and Beastmaster. They are fiercely loyal to Alachia, and willing to defend her with their lives.

Seekers of the Heart

The Seekers of the Heart were founded by Monus Byre, an elf from outside the Wood who traveled there and was appalled at what she found. Over the years she has gathered a large following devoted to redeeming the Wood and restoring it to its former glory. The cult counts both normal and blood elves among its membership, as well as a few members of other Namegiver races, mainly humans and windlings.

The focus of the cult's activities are the acorns of Oak Heart, the ancient tree that lies at the heart of the Wood. These acorns are imbued with the magic of the great tree, and ones that were gathered before the Ritual of Thorns might still contain echoes of the Wood's original True Pattern. Monus believes that if all the uncorrupted acorns are gathered and planted in the heart of the Wood, it will heal the corruption and end the Ritual.

Alachia has forbidden the Seekers access to the Wood, and views them as dangerous renegades.

Cara Fahd

The ork nation of Cara Fahd is still a new power player in the lands of Barsaive, and while they played a significant role in the attacks on Vivane and Sky Point, have thus far been focused on maintaining their own sovereignty.

The nation is ruled by High Chief Krathis Gron. A descendant of the legendary hero Hrak Gron, she was born a slave. She escaped, and was inspired by the Passions to rebuild Cara Fahd. After spending years studying in Cathay, she returned to Barsaive, traveling the land and spreading the dream of the orks reclaiming their lost homeland.

While Krathis is, effectively, the highest authority in the Cara Fahd, she is a humble leader. She does her best to honor the traditions that orks have followed for centuries, while at the same time taking inspiration from finer aspects of philosophical thought from elsewhere in Barsaive.

She is advised by four chiefs, each of whom has led their tribe for years. These chiefs have a history of not getting along, but they are all devoted to the vision of a new Cara Fahd, and their disagreements and personal history have not led to open conflict.

The primary issue that Krathis deals with is balancing the relationships between the various tribes that have chosen to join the nation. Despite the shared idea of a unified people, the orks that have spent generations living as nomadic tribes are finding it difficult to put aside old rivalries and work together. The situation is improving, but slowly.

The primary political division in Cara Fahd is the tribe. Any tribe with more than 500 members can petition Krathis and her council for territory rights. Within their territory, they have ultimate authority and are responsible for keeping the peace. Given the history of raiding and banditry of some tribes, some areas of Cara Fahd are more dangerous to travelers than others.

Cara Fahd boasts few cities. Claw Ridge is the largest permanent settlement, and contains *Wurchaz*, the fortress where Krathis lives and conducts business. Many city orks—those who were not part of a nomadic tribe—live here, and have their own traditions, often adapted from other Namegiver cultures. Just as there is tension between the various tribes, there is also tension between the traditional and city orks. Krathis and her people do their best to promote understanding, but ork tempers can run hot, and progress is slow.

The other major city is Gevosht, built and managed by Rejruk's Foxes, a tribe native to the lands of Cara Fahd. When their traditional grazing lands were granted to other tribes, the Foxes shifted their efforts to trade and construction, understanding that if Cara Fahd was to survive and thrive as a power in Barsaive, they would need to do more than carry on the traditions of nomadic tribal life. In contrast to the haphazard piecemeal construction of Claw Ridge, Gevosht is a more orderly settlement, its streets straight and paved with cobbles, clear signage, and straightforward, serviceable buildings.

With the Theran presence largely driven from southwestern Barsaive, the biggest threat to Cara Fahd are its relations with the settlements along the border with what used to be Landis. The lost human kingdom was a traditional rival of Cara Fahd, and in some parts of Cara Fahd the tribes displaced the other Namegivers that were living there. Many of these refugees have settled along the Greenheart River, which marks the border of Cara Fahd, and cause trouble by raiding into ork territory.

Fortunately, that part of Cara Fahd is still heavily overgrown with jungle, and few tribes claim territory in the area. It is mostly populated by logging camps, harvesting lumber to feed the growth of Claw Ridge and other settlements springing up in other parts of the nation. The jungles also hide ruins dating to the time of old Cara Fahd, and many adepts search the area for the kingdom's forgotten lore and treasure.

Echoes of the Empire

In the wake of the defeat at Vivane and Sky Point, some Theran troops made their way to the jungles along the border between Cara Fahd and Landis. While they have limited official support from the Empire, they do their best to incite the refugees and destabilize the ork nation.

Krathis is aware of the Theran presence, but thus far has been unable to do much about it. Her attention is still primarily focused on managing the internal affairs of Cara Fahd, working to forge the various tribes into a single people. She has agents that watch the area and pass along intelligence, and if a serious threat is developing Krathis will most likely send a team of adepts to deal with the issue.

Crystal Raiders

While not particularly numerous, the trollmoots of Barsaive have had a significant effect on the province. Nine major moots are recognized, with six in the Twilight Peaks, two in the Delaris Mountains, and the last in the Scol Mountains. Lesser clans and moots can be found in other parts of Barsaive, but thus far have played a minor role in Barsiavian affairs.

The various moots share many similarities. Each survives mainly through raiding caravans and settlements, as well as rival moots. They value honor and personal valor, believing—at least generally—that things belong to those who can keep them.

At the same time, each moot has its own traditions and interpretations of honor and valor. In addition, while the moots are traditionally rivals, there is a complex network of alliances, oaths, and honor debts that make interactions between the moots difficult to unravel. While the Second Theran War did result in nearly all the major moots contributing to some extent, in general they have fallen back into their old habits and patterns.

The *Blackfang* moot claims the southern ridge of the western Twilight Peaks as their territory. In the years leading up to the war their fortunes were fading. They had previously raided into Cara Fahd and Landis, but the resurgence of the ork nation cut into the success of their raids. The years after the war have seen some return to their former glory, however, as the reduced Theran presence allows them to range a bit further south into the plains around Vivane and the ruins of Sky Point.

The *Bloodlore* moot claims the northern ridge of the western Twilight Peaks. As their Name implies, they are a fierce collection of tribes, raiding and making war on their neighbors as they wish. They have no true allies among the other moots, and any agreements they make last only as long as it benefits them. They view lowlanders with contempt, and it was only through the promise of vengeance on the Therans they were persuaded to take part in the assault on Sky Point.

Secrets of the Bloodlores

The former chieftain of the Bloodlore moot, Charok Bonecracker Bloodlore, survived the assault on Sky Point, but sustained an injury that left him open to challenge for the moot's leadership. The new chieftain, Prokkuav Tornflesh Firefang, has been chief for about two years, and is a powerful questor of Raggok in addition to a Sky Raider. He is bitter at the success and honor afforded the former chieftain, and his patron is pushing him to act on these feelings. Prokkuav is currently working on a plan to lead the Bloodlores in an ambitious raid on a major population center. This could result in disaster for the Bloodlores, but cause a lot of collateral damage in the process.

The *Firescale* moot lives in the Scol Mountains in northern Barsiave. While they raid from airships, they also raid from the backs of large animals similar to thundra beasts. Unlike the other moots in Barsaive, they have extended their influence to lowland communities in their territory and do not rely exclusively on raiding for survival. They have allied with Iopos and House Ishkarat of the t'skrang, and no doubt will play a role in any plans the Denairastas clan has for Barsaive. Other than than these alliances, the Firescales are at best unfriendly to outsiders and many rumors have them killing outsiders on sight.

The *Ironmonger* moot claims the northern ridge of the central Twilight Peaks, closest to the former troll kingdom of Ustrect. They take their name from their expertise with crafting metal artifacts and weapons, often eschewing traditional crystal weaponry in favor of iron and steel. There is some strife within the moot, as a cult known as the Raisers of Ustrect has formed around the desire to restore the ancient troll kingdom to its previous glory, much like the orks have restored Cara Fahd. The Ironmonger chieftain has done his best to reduce the influence of this cult, but its members frequently travel to the troll ruins in search of forgotten treasures and lore.

Secrets of the Ironmongers

Unbeknownst to anyone—even members of the Raisers of Ustrect—their leader and several other members of the cult have been marked by a Horror Named Ago'astia. The crystal entity has been patient and slowly expanding its influence within the cult. It has started using its powers to infiltrate the dreams of its victims, pushing them to bring more trolls to the ruins it inhabits. Its long-term goals are unclear, but it most likely hopes to eventually take over the moot for its own purposes.

The *Rockhorn* moot lives in the eastern portion of the Delaris Mountains. Their territory oversees several key passes between Cara Fahd and the rest of Barsaive, and take advantage of this in their raids. They are one of the most spiritually focused moots in Barsaive, having a close relationship with many obsidiman brotherhoods in the Delaris Mountains, and even shared resources for the construction of their kaers before the Scourge. In the years since the Second Theran War, their raiding has decreased.

The *Skyseer* moot inhabits the western reaches of the Delaris Mountains, and raids into the lands around Jerris and the Liaj Jungle. According to legend, the moot is cursed. Before the Scourge the moot ransacked the monastery where Elianar Messias found the Books of Harrow, believing more tomes of valuable lore could be found there. The last questor cursed them to forever seek what they could not find, and while the Skyseers have been able to survive, they have been unable to find anything of significant value in their territory.

The *Stoneclaw* moot lives in the easternmost spur of the Twilight Peaks. While other moots have individuals from other Namegiver races (usually captured in raids), the Stoneclaws have a full dwarf clan. This influence has led them to adopt many dwarf customs and manners. These new habits have drawn the ire of the other moots, believing them weak for emulating lowland culture. As a result, the Stoneclaws are raided more often than other moots. Traditionally, the Stoneclaws have been Throal's closest allies among the Crystal Raiders, but the years since Kovar's ascension have seen that support wane.

The *Swiftwind* moot claims the territory just west of the Stoneclaws. They are the finest shipwrights among the various troll moots, and also have some of the most accomplished enchanters in Barsaive. Their territory borders the Gray Forest, a large woodland sheltered in the Twilight Peaks that is one of the main sources of wood for drakkars crafted by moots that border the region. Just after the Scourge, the moots agreed to share the wood. Unfortunately, skirmishes are becoming more common, and it may only be a matter of time before it breaks out into a more full-scale conflict.

The *Thundersky* moot also claims territory adjacent to the Gray Forest. Their home includes the highest peaks in the Twilight Peaks, and the isolation and difficult conditions have led them to be fierce raiders. They raid other moots more often than they raid lowland settlements and caravans, believing their neighbors are more worthy of their skills. While the Bloodlores are perhaps the fiercest hand to hand combatants among the Crystal Raiders, the Thundersky are unmatched when it comes to raids against other airships.

Great Dragons

While the Great Dragons publicly claim a policy of non-interference when it comes to Barsaivian affairs, they have been shaping events in the province from behind the scenes for centuries. They are beings of significant power, knowledge, and ability, and are among the oldest living things in Barsaive. There are four Great Dragons that are commonly known in Barsaive, with three others that are less well known.

Draconic nature has led to a formal and highly ritualized society to control and suppress the natural instincts of these apex predators. They are fiercely territorial, and outside of a few notable exceptions, do not welcome other Namegivers. At best, an intruder will be disabled and escorted out of the dragon's territory. At worst, they will be eaten.

> **The Dragon's Secret War Effort**
> While Vasdenjas was the only dragon that visibly contributed to the assault on Sky Point, the other Great Dragons were also involved. They performed a powerful ritual that moved Stormhead towards the city of Vivane in order to cut off any potential reinforcements to Sky Point. The destruction and loss of life caused by this ritual were, to the dragons, worth the victory. Keep this in mind when dealing with dragons, even the ones that appear friendly.

Aban is the youngest Great Dragon in Barsaive, the only one not born during the Age of Dragons, instead hatching very early in the current magical age. She claims the Mist Swamps as her territory, and brooks no intrusion from other Namegivers. She is one of the largest dragons in Barsaive, but the physical descriptions of her do not agree on color. It appears that whether through natural ability or concealing magic, she can change her color to blend into the environment she calls home. Her primary goal is the protection of the Mist Swamps, and the legendary city of Yrns Morgath that it conceals. Many explorers have sought the ruins, only to be chased away by Aban or her servants.

Dvilgaynon is a Great Dragon from distant Cathay. She traveled with Krathis Gron to Cara Fahd, and takes on the appearance of a human magician. She leads a small group of other magicians from Cathay that act as advisors to Krathis with regard to magical matters. Other than Krathis and the other Great Dragons, none are aware that Dvilgaynon is actually a dragon. She aided in the ritual the dragons performed that drew Stormhead to Vivane.

Earthroot is another Cathay dragon, living deep under the Throal Moutains. His existence is somewhat legendary, as few have actually encountered him. His primary servants are the Pale Ones, subterranean t'skrang that he sheltered during the Scourge. He has aided Icewing in support of Throal, but his influence has been much more subtle over the years. He guards a powerful magical artifact called the White Tree, which is tied in some unknown way to the fate of dragon-kind.

Icewing is one of the better known Great Dragons. He lairs in Mount Vapor, one of the highest peaks in the Throal Mountains. He has an extensive network of servants and agents, rivaled only by that of his brother, Mountainshadow. He is known to have aided Throal both before and after the Scourge. He provided Varulus I with the potion that would extend his life and those of his descendants, maintaining a strong continuity of rule. He is also known to entertain visitors. If a petitioner travels to his lair and brings a suitable gift, Icewing will answer questions or provide information.

Mountainshadow is Icewing's brother, and the other Great Dragon known for involvement in the affairs of lesser Namegivers. Unlike his brother, he does not welcome visitors to his lair in the Dragon Mountains, but his network of servants and informants is extensive, and he will often manipulate events to provide aid to those

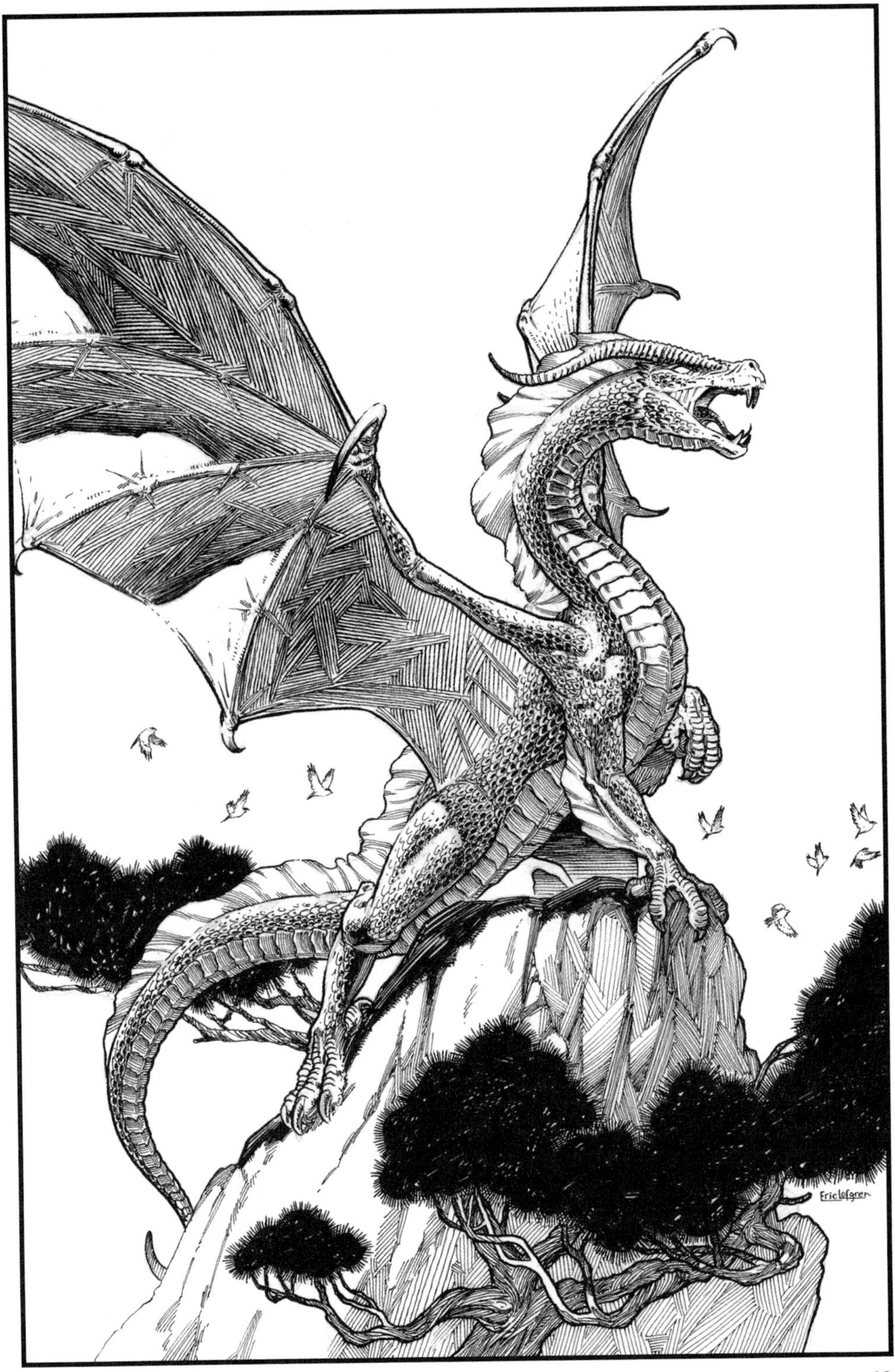
Eric Lofgren

who happen to be furthering his goals. Often times those he provides aid to are never aware of their patron's true identity.

Usun claims dominion over the Liaj Jungle, and is the most isolationist of the Great Dragons in Barsaive. He firmly believes that dragons should rule as they did in the past, and rankles at the way the other dragons manipulate events from behind the scenes. He is a fighter and hunter, with little taste for diplomacy. His jungle lair reflects this attitude, being home to some of the most ferocious beasts in Barsaive.

Vestrivan is a draconic tragedy, rumored but seldom seen. He was brother to Vasdenjas, and as interested in lore and knowledge as the late Master of Secrets. Unfortunately, his quest for knowledge proved to be his downfall. He has been marked and corrupted by a Horror known as the Despoiler of the Land, and when he appears destruction and suffering follow in his wake. Some of the other Great Dragons suspect it might be possible to redeem the corrupted dragon, but his draconic might combined with the powers of the Horror would make it difficult even for Great Dragons to face him and escape unscathed.

Haven

While not a true power in the political sense, Haven is a notable settlement. Located on the outskirts of the ruins of Parlainth, it serves as a base of operations for adventures exploring the Forgotten City.

It is led by the troll Torgak, a Warrior adept who first cleared out a portion of the ruins for use as a permanent base of operations. He maintains a group of deputies to help keep the peace and fight off incursions from the ruins. For the most part, Namegivers who don't cause trouble will have little trouble from Torgak.

Torgak and the other early settlers of Haven have made a decent living catering to the needs of adventurers seeking their fortune in the ruins. They have managed to maintain their position without much effort, as there is not much in the way of permanent population. Adventurers seeking their fortune seldom stay around for more than two or three years. Most are killed, or move on after striking it rich or failing to find anything of value.

There have been some recent shifts in Haven. Torgak and the other founders are getting on in years, and the permanent population has been slowly but steadily growing. While as yet there is no discussion of more formal government, long-term residents and power players are all looking at ways to turn the situation in Haven to their advantage.

Given the treasures and secrets still to be found in the former Theran capitol, control and influence in Haven is on the minds of most of the powers of Barsaive.

Iopos

The isolated city of Iopos represents the greatest current threat to the people of Barsaive. The powerful Denairastas clan rose to prominence shortly before the Scourge and solidified their control by helping thwart any breaches to the citadel. By the time the Long Night came to an end, the family ruled the city with an iron hand.

The family is currently led by the ancient Uhl Denairastas. Uhl has no children of his own, but he had several siblings (all long dead) who had children and grandchildren.

Uhl plays this extensive family tree of nieces and nephews against each other, each seeking the favor of the family patriarch in hopes of being named his successor. As yet, Uhl has not decided on an heir, and it is likely that his passing will be followed by a significant amount of backstabbing and jockeying for rulership of the city.

> **Secrets of the Denairastas**
> The Denairastas are dragon-kin, descendants of a pairing between a dragon and another Namegiver. The Great Dragons of the world have long prohibited the creation of dragon-kin, but one of their number disregarded this edict and sired the line. For this crime he was cast out of dragon society, and now works behind the scenes to show up the hypocrisy of his fellows.
>
> It was only with the death of Varulus III the Great Dragons of Barsaive learned the extent to which the Outcast was manipulating events in Barsaive. Their long standing conflict with Thera blinded them to the danger posed by the Denairastas, and they spent the years since gathering what intelligence they could and preparing to defend their interests from this new threat.
>
> Thus far, only the Denairastas and the other Great Dragons of Barsaive are aware of the family's legacy.

The residents of Iopos view the Denairastas—especially Uhl—as living legends, worshipping them with an almost religious fervor. Tales of their exploits during and after the Scourge are a popular source of entertainment in the city. In most major cities in Barsaive, the Throalic tradition of debate has taken enough hold that questioning the policies or decisions of the city's leaders is commonplace, but that is not the case in Iopos.

Devotion to the Denairastas is mandatory. Even visitors to the city are required to swear allegiance to the family. Those who express displeasure or question the perfect rule of the Denairastas end up arrested and exiled at best. Perhaps most disturbing is that unlike many places subject to tyrannical rule, the residents of Iopos seem genuinely happy with their lot, rather than making the necessary statements in public but grumbling in secret.

Order in Iopos is maintained by the Holders of Trust, a combination of official guard, and secret police. There are three branches operating in the Holders, and all have sworn oaths of loyalty sealed in blood.

The first, the Copper Branch, are the rank and file informants and operate mainly within the city, but some agents of this branch travel to other parts of Barsaive and pass information back to their superiors. It is the presence of the Copper Branch that contributes to the nature of life in Iopos. In theory, anyone can be a member of the Copper Branch, and they are quick to investigate and pass along rumors of treasonous behavior, with a notoriously wide definition of what that might entail.

The second branch, the Silver Branch, are perhaps the most visible representatives of the Denairastas. These individuals patrol the city, clad in shining mail and ready for any sort of trouble they might encounter. All are highly trained combatants, and many of them are adepts. They enforce city law and administer justice. Minor crimes are subject to fines and lashes from the Silver Branch, and significant crimes carry a death sentence. This harsh justice system results in a clean and orderly city, making Iopos one of the more beautiful cities in Barsaive.

The final branch is the Gold Branch. All highly trained adepts, these are the operatives that pursue and further the plans of the Denairastas clan throughout Barsaive. Nearly all members of the extended family are members of the Gold Branch, and these agents have carried out assassinations and other plots to further Uhl's goal to control the province.

Iopos has extensive influence in northwestern Barsaive, including close ties with the t'skrang House Ishkarat and the Firescale moot in the Scol Mountains. They will use whatever means to achieve their goals.

Jerris

Located on the western edge of Barsaive, Jerris is geographically isolated from the rest of Barsaive. To the west lie the Wastes, an area devastated by the Scouge, becoming blasted and ashen. To the east stands the Liaj Jungle, a largely unexplored wilderness claimed by the Great Dragon Usun.

Before the Scourge, Jerris was a wealthy merchant power. Its location served as a gateway to the lands that are now the Wastes, connecting Barsaive with lands to the west. In addition to trade, the city had a robust airship construction industry.

Despite a couple of close calls during the Scourge, Jerris managed to survive, but its fortunes have fallen from its pre-Scourge days. The city is still the major provider for airships in Barsaive, but it has fallen behind with regard to its power as a trading hub.

In addition to the money brought in through the city's airship trade, the city also benefits from adepts and other adventurers seeking their fortune in the Wastes. Many lost kaers and forgotten treasures can be found by daring explorers, though the difficulty of surviving the Wastes makes such expeditions a difficult way to make a living. The possibility of riches and potential discovery of forgotten lore, however, means plenty of adepts are willing to try.

In addition to providing inspiration to adventurers, the Wastes also pose a problem. The prevailing winds carry smoky ash from the Wastes over the city. While Jerris does its best to clean up the residue, the atmosphere is perpetually gray and gloomy. Sunlight is rare, and visitors report that everything is tinged with a bitter flavor.

Researchers have done their best to study the ash, but have yet to reach any conclusions. It contains traces of corruption, similar to that left by Horrors, and the condition of the Poison Forest right on the border of the Wastes indicates the ash has a negative effect on living things. But other than the general gloomy and brooding mood in the city, there are no obvious ill effects suffered by the residents of Jerris.

Many believe Jerris to be cursed in some way, and that a Horror or Horrors stalk the streets at night, invisible to those living there because of the ash. It is certainly true that the city suffers from a higher than normal amount of unusual and disturbing events. Namegivers go missing without a trace, and there have been more than a few cases where someone is found dead, torn apart by claws or something similar, with no evidence or eyewitnesses.

Since the War, Jerris has fallen under the influence of the Denairastas. For many years Iopan scholars have been in the city, researching the ash and offering assistance to the city government. After a number of shipwrights were found dead, Iopos offered to help magistrate Byth Vesten investigate the deaths. Within a few months Iopan troops were moved in to help keep the peace. Now, the magistrate is little more than a puppet.

There had already been pressure on the city's shipwrights to cut back on selling airships to powers and trade companies outside Jerris. The magistrate's office has brought significant political and financial pressure to bear on the guild, resulting in commissions being delayed or cancelled, and the resources going to build ships for Jerris—which are at this point effectively ships for Iopos.

Conquering Jerris

The takeover of Jerris had been in the works for some time, the Denairastas were just looking for the right moment to put it into action. The unrest in Throal after the War was the perfect opportunity. Iopan agents assassinated a few key individuals, and once they got close to the magistrate, gained influence over him through blood magic. Only the Denairastas know this detail.

Kratas

Located at the base of a mesa in the foothills of the Tylon Mountains in central Barsaive, the so-called City of Thieves is the remains of a citadel that fell during the Scourge. In the early years after the Scourge, explorers sought riches in the ruins only to determine it was easier to get rich raiding the surrounding area.

As various bandit gangs carved out bits of territory in the city, word spread that Kratas was a good place for those unable to toe the line in other places. As more thieves, smugglers, and scoundrels made the ruins their base of operations, a complex network of rivalry, alliance, and betrayal became the order of the day. Given the somewhat desperate nature of life in Kratas, the city drew merchants and others willing to risk their life to make money off the residents.

After his involvement with the discovery of Parlainth, the legendary ork Thief Garlthik One-Eye arrived in the city, expecting a peaceful retirement. Unfortunately, his reputation as a Thief and the wealth he had amassed over the years made him a target. He formed his own gang, the Force of the Eye, and used them to make it clear he was not to be trifled with.

Today, Kratas remains largely lawless and independent minded, with Garlthik and his gang the closest thing the city has to government. His men protect the non-criminal elements, ensuring that food and other supplies make it into the city without significant interruption. Other gangs are more or less free to operate as they wish, provided they don't cross Garlthik or his operations.

Kratas is the black market hub of Barsaive. Given sufficient time and money, just about anything can be obtained there. While Garlthik does all he can to prohibit the sale of slaves, even those can be found with the right contacts. In addition to illicit goods, mercenaries, assassins, and spies can be hired for the right price, and information is as much a black market good as anything else.

The biggest challenge to Garlthik's control of the city is Brocher's Brood, a gang led by Vistrosh, an exiled Blood Elf. While technically banned from Kratas, they operate in defiance of Garlthik's decree and actively engage in the slave trade. Every so often members of the Force of the Eye will raid places where the Brood is rumored to be hiding, and occasionally they will take some members into custody. As yet, Vistrosh has been very successful at avoiding capture.

Secrets of Kratas: Vistrosh and the Songbirds

Vistrosh's exile is only a cover. He is actually the head of Alachia's information network, called the Songbirds. He often sends letters back to the Court beseeching the Queen for clemency, containing coded reports on affairs and activities around the province. His operations as leader of Brocher's Brood are more to maintain contacts and gather information than any serious attempt to overthrow Garlthik's control of the city. Indeed, Vistrosh believes that Garthik is probably the best thing for the city right now, as he keeps the worst elements in check, but leaves enough freedom for information to pass through the city.

Travar

One of Barsaive's oldest settlements, Travar predates the founding of House K'tenshin and even the Naming of Barsaive itself. The city weathered the Scourge, as well as the political upheaval in the years since. Travar has traditionally remained neutral in the conflicts between Throal and Thera, but since the end of the Second Theran War, many eyes have been drawn to the white walls of the city and its wealth.

The city is ruled by a triumvirate of magistrates, determined through an annual tournament called the Founding. Prospective candidates sponsor teams of adepts to compete, and the winners earn seats. Competition is fierce, and successful candidates can be very generous to those they sponsor.

> **The importance of the Founding**
> Those who win the Founding gain a significant amount of power in the city. As a result, foreign agents have begun spending more and more money to try and influence the results, attempting to get favorable voices on the council, or possibly even puppets.

The magistrate's council arbitrates trade disputes between the trading houses in the city, and can have great influence over the fortunes of individual merchants. While the council itself maintains a neutral stance, individual merchants and trading houses act in their own interest. Many still maintain trading ties with Thera that began before the Scourge, and some have given shelter to Therans displaced by the War. Tensions between them and those with anti-Imperial sympathies have increased as a result.

Related to this, the issue of slavery is hotly contested in Travar, and clashes between followers of Dis and Lochost have become more common. The council does its best to keep the peace, and thus far has been able to keep a lid on the worst violence, but it may only be a matter of time before the dispute erupts into more severe and damaging conflict.

Trade with Jerris has dwindled in the wake of that city's control by the Denairastas, and long standing collaboration on airship design has been canceled. The death of King Neden and the reduced Throalic patrols in Barsaive have resulted in additional losses from increased banditry.

Travar had never maintained a formal standing army, relying on its neutrality to avoid conflict with other political and military powers. Outcry from local merchants over losses suffered in the wake of the War, however, has forced the council to take action. A new division of the city watch called the Road Wardens has been founded to patrol and maintain routes in the area around Travar.

For the first time in centuries the city is projecting military power outside its walls. This is likely to result in more direct conflict with other nations, especially House K'tenshin, who have traditionally controlled the settlements along the Byrose River.

For now, the greatest outside challenge faced by the city is the spread of the Badlands. This corrupted land has been slowly but steadily expanding towards Travar's western edge for decades. A group of Questors of Jaspree have been searching for a way to halt, if not reverse, the damage done to the area, but thus far they have been unsuccessful. As the taint grows closer, residents have begun reporting terrible dreams. These recurring nightmares are almost identical, despite there being no apparent connection between the afflicted.

Despite recent troubles, Travar still prospers. The debate about the city's role in the future of Barsaive continues, and the citizens may find themselves unwillingly thrust into greater political prominence. For now, Travar remains Chorrolis's city, ultimately focused on commerce and trade.

T'skrang Aropagoi

The t'skrang of the Serpent River are organized into six large covenants called aropagoi, or Great Houses. While independent villages remain, as do some independent riverboat crews, most t'skrang settlements are connected with one of these trading companies. Each aropagoi claims part of the Serpent River network as their territory. While it is possible to find a particular house's riverboats anywhere on the Serpent, rivalries and disputes can make trade in another aropagoi's territory challenging.

House Ishkarat controls the north reach of the Serpent. They are strongly allied with Iopos, and maintain strong control over their territory. While they allow riverboats to trade in the north reach, they exact high tolls and any who refuse or try to avoid the tolls are attacked.

There is tension between the House Ishkarat and House Syrtis. In the years after the Scourge, Ishkarat expanded control into Lake Vors, and area that had previously been controlled by House Syrtis. After a bloody conflict between the two aropagoi over a fortress in the lake, House Syrtis was forced to withdraw, leaving Lake Vors and its territory in Ishkarat hands.

House Syrtis controls this mid reach of the Serpent, from Lake Ban up to the disputed territory near Lake Vors. An old and powerful aropagoi, they are based out of the Cliff City, which is built into the walls of the Lalai Gorge between the Throal and Caucavic mountain ranges. Their fortunes have fallen somewhat in recent years, partly through the conflict with House Ishkarat. To try and prevent further encroachment, House Syrtis has formed an alliance with the Blood Elves, sharing support of Eidolon, a fortress where the Mothingale River flows out of Blood Wood.

House V'strimon claims the Coil River, the largest tributary of the Serpent. They have been a staunch ally of Throal since the first Theran War, and their warships played an important role in the assault on Triumph. They are currently the most prosperous aropagoi in the Serpent River valley, largely as a result of their alliance and trade connections with Throal and Urupa.

House K'tenshin's domain is the south reach of the Serpent, but their fortunes have been falling. They allied with Thera during the first Theran War and lost standing, then allied with them again when the Triumph landed. The Theran defeat has forced even more concessions from them. The aropagoi maintains ties with Thera, as a number of t'skrang from the Theran House Carinci were inducted into the aropagoi before the war, but material support has reduced greatly over the past few years.

> **K'tenshin After the War**
>
> Pride has been the biggest stumbling block for House K'tenshin in the years since the Second Theran War. The defeat has been rankling the Shivalahala K'tenshin, and she has been looking for ways to help reclaim the House's prominence in Barsaivian trade.
>
> The Denairastas have become aware of this desire, and have started covert overtures of support. The combined might of the Ishkarat and K'tenshin could put enough pressure on the other aropagoi to draw allies away from Throal, which further supports Iopan plans for provincial control.

House T'kambras is the newest aropagoi, having been formally recognized in the aftermath of the Second War. They include settlements along the tributaries of the south reach on the edges of K'tenshin control, and while small have been gaining influence at the expense of House K'tenshin. They do not follow the traditional structure of an aropagoi, lacking a shivalahala. Instead, they are a council of captains, primarily led by Jedaiyen Westhrall. In another unusual break from t'skrang tradition, the covenant has also accepted membership from some Scavian barges, who aided T'kambras against the K'tenshin before the Second War.

While *House Henghyoke* has been operating for years, little is known about this mysterious pirate federation. They have no known allies, and attack riverboats and settlements up and down the Serpent and its tributaries. They are more commonly sighted in the lower reaches, leading some to speculate they are based out of the Servos Jungle, but the truth remains elusive. Attempts to learn more are complicated by the fact that all Henghyoke t'skrang are mute, not even crying out when injured. This condition seems tied to the silver collar worn by each member of the House. Attempts to remove the collar result in the wearer suffering from catatonia, berserk rage, and even death.

Urupa

Less than a hundred years old, Urupa was founded by the survivors of seven kaers that banded together for protection shortly after the Scourge. Located at the base of high cliffs about a mile from where the Coil River flows into the Aras Sea, the city is a natural gateway for trade to the lands south and east of Barsaive.

The city is divided into nine sectors. Seven are named after the kaers the city's founders hailed from, and are still mainly settled by descendants of those kaers. In addition to the city's administrative offices, the central sector hosts three large temples to the Passions. Each temple is devoted primarily to a single Passion, with two smaller shrines. The largest temple is dedicate to Chorrolis, with shrines to Astendar and Floranuus. The other two temples are similar, if smaller, and devoted to Mynbruje (with shrines to Upandal and Lochost), and Garlen (with shrines to Thystonius and Jaspree).

Within the plaza formed by the temples are magnificent gardens, the centerpiece of which is the Blue Rose. This winding vine of thorny branches and blue rose blossoms was salvaged from Liandrill, one of the founding kaers. Its fragrance is said to provide clarity and insight, and if a Horror-marked individual gets too close, the flowers are supposed to glow with a cold blue light.

This final neighborhood is the Visitor's Quarter, established in the early days of the city when strangers were less trusted. Many inns, hostelries, and offices of most notable trading companies can be found here, as well as four embassies. The embassies for the Kingdom of Throal and the Theran Empire face each other across a plaza, and are frequently being worked on as each power tries to outdo the visual impact of the other. House V'strimon has an embassy on the water's edge with a flooded courtyard that will have one of the aropagoi's warships at the dock if it isn't patrolling the lower reaches of the Coil River.

The last embassy belongs to the so-called People from Across the Aras Sea. The building is a grim, square fortress with a single entrance and few windows. A mysterious and secretive people, only a handful of outsiders have been inside. Their ships bring goods from distant lands, but no one is sure where the People's home nation is.

Mysteries Across the Sea

The secrecy of People from Across the Aras Sea has caused the council some concern. Despite changes in recent years that have made Urupa more open to foreigners, that openness has not been reciprocated. Fellidra Jer has been quietly recruiting adepts to find information about the People and their goals.

The city is ruled by a council, with one representative elected from each of the seven founding neighborhoods. The council elects a Chief Councilor, who acts as the day to day executive in charge of the city. The Chief Councilor is Fellidra Jer, a human who has held the position for over a decade. She has been a popular and successful leader, balancing the city's anti-foreigner concerns with the growth brought on by burgeoning trade.

While Urupa's position as a major trading hub has brought the city a lot of attention, Fellidra was able to navigate the conflict between Throal and Thera with much success. The city did not offer military support to the War, though the council quietly supported Throal, and several Urupan trading companies provided logistical support.

Vivane

Before the Second Theran War, Vivane was the primary base of operations for Imperial activity in Barsaive. In many ways the city was the antithesis of the philosophies put forward by Throal in the decades after the Scourge. It hosted a significant slave market, and was significantly segregated between the wealthy Theran merchant class and an underclass of poor Barsaivians.

The War changed that. Most significantly, the population of the city has dropped. Many of the wealthiest Therans and their personal households were evacuated when it became clear that the Barsaivian alliance was on course to attack Theran interests in the area. More fled when Stormhead moved on the city, and thousands died in the destruction caused by the Horror storm.

The aftereffects of the storm, and the magical shockwave that disrupted it, still linger. Outbreaks of undead were common in the first few months after the battle as bodies were animated by fluctuating magical energy. The frequency of these events has declined, but packs of ghouls and cadaver men can still be encountered in the basements and catacombs of Vivane.

Astral space has, not surprisingly, been severely damaged by the magical assaults on the city. Spells and magical abilities used in the city can occasionally go awry, with unpredictable effects, striking the wrong target, or even completely failing to work. Some researchers and scholars work to try and understand the phenomenon, but the realities of life in Vivane complicate their efforts.

Shortly after the War, the head of the Barsaivian Resistance in Vivane, Tribas Koar, organized a citizen's council, with the goal of establishing a more egalitarian society free of Theran tyranny. Koar had hoped that Throal would help the city recover and rebuild, but those wishes never bore fruit due to Neden's death and the subsequent political struggle in the dwarf kingdom.

The lack of support led to fighting over limited resources, and the Council shattered into squabbling factions over the need to survive. A brief, bloody civil war swept over Vivane, which was only made worse by the mystical problems and undead incursions from the undercity.

Secrets of Vivane: Koar's Fate

Tribas Koar vanished during the strife. None in Vivane know his whereabouts, many believe that he was killed by one of his rivals. He managed to survive, however, and relocated to Landis. There he works to root out the pockets of Theran agents and build support to return to Vivane and make another attempt at his vision.

Some took the opportunity to turn the tables on Theran survivors who were not wealthy or important enough to leave. Others blamed the resistance for their support of Throal and the lack of aid from the dwarf kingdom. Most residents simply took their frustrations out on each other.

After about two years of strife a new leader, Maxil Korrida, emerged, backed by a strong militia force. He claims to have been a follower of Koar and cell leader in the Resistance, but because of how they operated, these claims cannot be verified. His methods run counter to Koar's high-minded rhetoric of equality and self determination, ruling the city as a despot. While Maxil speaks of returning safety and civility to life in Vivane, and life in the city is more peaceful than before, he is swift to stifle dissent and root out those who would challenge his position.

EARTHDAWN

GAMEMASTERING

Are Namegivers free to choose our path, or is our future written in the stars, dictated by some great spirit at the heart of creation?
•*Zabrak the Blind Sage* •

The gamemaster manages the game, and makes sure everyone follows the same ground rules and interpretations. They create the encounters and challenges the player characters will face, and rewards them for overcoming those challenges and achieving their goals. It isn't an easy job, but many gamemasters find it a rewarding and satisfying one.

The information in this chapter mostly benefits the gamemaster, but players may find it interesting as well. After playing for a while, the gamemaster and another player may want to trade places; the gamemaster becomes a player and creates his own character, and the player takes on the responsibilities of the gamemaster.

Before we reveal the specific methods and tactics for running an **Earthdawn** game, we want to offer some general advice for running **Earthdawn**, or any roleplaying game for that matter. Remembering these few ideas can make running the game a lot easier, but as with all the rules in this book and the *Player's Guide*, treat the following as guidelines, not gospel.

GROUND RULES

All roleplaying games have rules. Without them, it would be difficult to consistently determine whether a character succeeds at a given action, or the consequences of failure. The rules are what distinguish a roleplaying game from more free-form storytelling, and help ensure that all of the participants are playing the same game. But in addition to the rules specific to each game, roleplaying games tend to share the following ground rules.

Gamemaster's Authority

Because the gamemaster has accepted the responsibility of running the game, he ultimately has the right to determine what works and what doesn't. We've done our best to come up with rules to cover most situations that will come up, but there will be events or circumstances that aren't explicitly covered by the rules. Don't worry about it—when this happens, make a decision and move on.

At some point during the game, a player will inevitably disagree with a decision made by the gamemaster. This doesn't need to be a big deal, but if the players are uncomfortable with a decision, it is generally better to discuss it after the game session ends, or before the next game session. Stopping in the middle of play to discuss the rules interrupts the flow of the action and makes it difficult to resume play at the same level.

It also makes more sense to discuss rules disagreements after everyone has had a chance to calm down—explaining how the device that killed a character works may not make much of an impression on a player who just lost Barsaive's most legendary obsidiman Illusionist.

However, a gamemaster's increased authority comes with greater responsibility. The gamemaster must keep track of events in the game, and there can be a lot to keep track of. For example, if a character wants to visit the marketplace to purchase new equipment, the player must tell the gamemaster what his character intends to do. He cannot simply say, *"I went to the marketplace and bought some new equipment."* The gamemaster may simply reply, *"No, you didn't,"* and his decision stands whether the player likes it or not.

Keep in mind that the gamemaster's authority does not exist to allow the gamemaster to micromanage each player's character, or to ignore actions that throw off his plans. It simply prompts players to inform the gamemaster of any actions they want their characters to take. After all, the gamemaster cannot keep track of events unless he knows they are occurring. The gamemaster should approach his role as a director or facilitator, rather than a tyrant.

Make it Fun

Roleplaying games are first and foremost a form of entertainment. We play games to get together with some friends and have a good time. It can be easy in the heat of the moment to forget that you are playing the game to enjoy yourself. Some players pout when the adventure doesn't go the way they want it to. Some players get mad when their characters are injured or killed.

If at some point you discover that you are no longer having fun playing **Earthdawn**, then you have our permission to stop. Talk it over with the rest of the players, and try to figure out why you are no longer enjoying yourselves. Maybe you just need a break. There's no harm in stopping a game session early to go out for pizza. Or maybe you're tired of gamemastering, and want to try playing instead. As well as giving another player the chance to be the gamemaster, this gives you a chance to learn what it's like on the other side of the table.

On the Nature of Rules

The world of **Earthdawn** is fictional—and the rules and mechanics reflect that fictional universe. The mechanics are abstract guidelines for a character's actions, including combat, magic, and even social interactions. We take real world concepts and abstract them into game mechanics, but the rules of a game cannot take into account all conditions or factors affecting a given situation, and certain rules are there to make the game fun and entertaining rather than to reflect how things would work in reality.

We guarantee that different people playing **Earthdawn**, whether player or gamemaster, will read the same rule in this book and interpret it in different ways. Hundreds of individual abilities create a lot of rules to keep track of, and different interpretations will arise. For example, a player might declare that his character intends to resolve a situation using a talent that the gamemaster considers inappropriate to the task at hand. The talent description doesn't say that you can do that with the talent, but it also doesn't say you can't. Who's right?

In most cases, the gamemaster decides how the rule works. As a rule of thumb, the rules describe what your character can do, rather than what he cannot, and so in the example above, the gamemaster's interpretation of the rule would be correct.

We've tried to deal individually with most of the rules that we feel may pose problems, but we can't anticipate every possible question. We recommend resolving disputes over rule interpretations as they arise, on a case-by-case basis. Because of the vast array of possibilities presented in these rules, no single rule of thumb covers everything, and what works for one group may not work for another.

Changing the Rules

The gamemaster is in control. If a particular game mechanic doesn't fit your style of play or doesn't make sense to you, feel free to come up with something else you think works better. The rules are there to help tell good stories—if the rules get in the way of the story, ignore them. Getting bogged down in rules disputes is counterproductive—it is important to keep the plot moving, so be encouraged to improvise things on the spot.

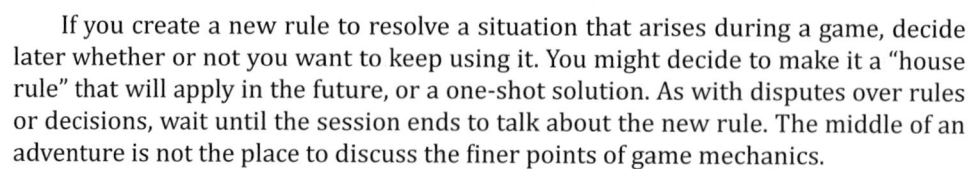

If you create a new rule to resolve a situation that arises during a game, decide later whether or not you want to keep using it. You might decide to make it a "house rule" that will apply in the future, or a one-shot solution. As with disputes over rules or decisions, wait until the session ends to talk about the new rule. The middle of an adventure is not the place to discuss the finer points of game mechanics.

If you do change the rules, make sure everyone knows the new version. Gamemasters and players need to follow the same rules so that everyone works with the same set of assumptions.

When Not to Use the Dice

The dice can bring an element of chance and uncertainty to the game, but it shouldn't be the only way you resolve things. Only use Action tests when the situation demands it. Sometimes it is better to roleplay a situation and work out what works best for the story instead of rolling the dice to randomly determine the outcome. For many actions, the outcome is obvious and no rolls are needed. Simply provide a description of the outcome of a character's action—go for the most dramatic, most amusing, or most appropriate result and move on.

Play Fair

Needless to say, everyone playing the game should play fair. Players should be honest (and good-natured) about lousy dice rolls, and admit it when a character falls unconscious. The gamemaster is the only one allowed to ignore his own die rolls, but only when the rules get in the way of fun (see **Death and Earthdawn**, p.87, for some additional advice).

Remember that the players and gamemaster know far more about what is happening than the characters. A player might know good tactics to use against a certain creature, or have read a sourcebook that reveals some secrets about a significant character, but he should avoid having his character take actions based on that information if the character doesn't have it. Likewise, the gamemaster knows the player characters' skills, weapons, spells, and so on, but the band of ork scorchers waiting in ambush on the edge of the forest should not.

Allowing gamemaster characters to respond to the player characters and make plans based on the gamemaster's knowledge is unfair to players, and can make for a frustrating game.

Mistakes

Everyone makes mistakes. As you play the game, you may misinterpret how we intended some of the rules to work. By using the rules, playing the game, and comparing notes with other players and gamemasters, you may discover these mistakes. Don't agonize over mix-ups, but do explain the mistake to the players, especially if changing the use of a rule drastically affects the game universe or mechanics as your players know them.

Mistakes don't have to be a big deal. If you make a mistake, don't waste your time trying to figure out how it happened. Just admit the error, apologize to the players, and correct it if you can.

GAMEMASTERING GUIDELINES

The world of **Earthdawn** is an exciting place filled with dangers and plenty of opportunity for adventure. Whether fighting a Horror, running a campaign against the Denairastas, protecting a merchant caravan from marauding ork scorchers, or rescuing a t'skrang lahala from the clutches of a mad questor—the player characters are the heroes.

An **Earthdawn** game session should challenge the players' wits, and the gamemaster should reward good roleplaying. The following guidelines will help you run a challenging, exciting game.

Be Aware!

The gamemaster has a lot to keep in mind when running a game—the major events of an adventure or campaign, the current flow of the story, and all the details that make the world come alive. You must listen to what the players say and keep track of both the player and gamemaster characters: their whereabouts, their plans, and so on. Organizing all this information is a good idea, and it helps to keep a pad handy for jotting down notes as the adventure moves along.

When you assemble a group of players, you should get a feel for their interests so that you can tailor adventures to appeal to them. A gamemaster who creates adventures solely for his own enjoyment may find that his adventures flop. In many cases it's a good idea for the group to make characters together and use that time to discuss what they want out of the game. Don't expect complexity and depth at first. The players probably know less about the game universe than you, and may only have vague ideas about what they want to do.

Once they get a few adventures under their belts, and their characters' stories take shape, the players will gradually develop better-defined goals and ideas. Rather than just looking for treasure, taking on a Horror, or dealing with the Blood Elves, they may want to hunt down a particular enemy, find a lost love, take revenge on a troll moot that did them dirty, or find a specific teacher or special piece of equipment. The gamemaster can and should build his players' ideas about and goals for their characters into major themes in his adventures.

Encourage the players to flesh out their characters' backstory, including background on their family and friends. In addition to using other sources, the gamemaster can draw on those histories to develop adventures that get everyone involved.

Taking notes about events in each game session will help you keep important information straight and consistent. Whether you keep these notes in a notebook or binder, a computer file or online resource like a wiki, this information can help make your campaigns and adventures deeper and more complex. You will create recurring allies and enemies, and the events in your game will change the world of **Earthdawn**. The world will be dynamic because of the characters in your group, not simply because we publish a sourcebook or adventure.

Players might perceive the game differently than the gamemaster, and knowing their perspective and interests will also help keep the adventure running. Adventure logs are a great tool to recap past events at the start of a session (see the **Building**

Your Legend chapter in the *Player's Guide*), can serve as a way for the players to develop their characters' personalities and goals outside of the game session, and give you insight into what they feel is important.

Be Knowledgeable!

The gamemaster should be familiar with the whole game. This does not mean memorizing every rule in the books, but you should familiarize yourself with them so you can find a rule quickly when you need to. You should also have a solid working knowledge of the basic game mechanics, and the most common situations that come up in play.

Keep a written outline of the adventure handy for reference. Experienced gamemasters often improvise as the story unfolds, but gamemasters working through their first adventures often find it easier to think the story through in advance and keep the plot relatively simple. This also helps gamemasters avoid those momentum-killing moments when the characters come face to face with a monstrous Horror, and the gamemaster says, *"Um—I just had it right here."*

Be Realistic!

Remember that the gamemaster characters are people with their own needs, hopes, fears, and desires. If you give gamemaster characters lives and personalities, the stories become more memorable for everyone involved, and can gain more depth

In the same way, play creatures as real creatures. Most animals do not kill for pleasure, they fight when they need to eat, protect their young, or save their hides. Most creatures live where they can find food and shelter—so your player characters shouldn't run into a flock of harpies unless there is a good reason for them to be there.

While the world of **Earthdawn** is filled with magic, and magic can present a certain level of mystery, you should be consistent in the way magic works, and the way you present it in your game. Magic in **Earthdawn** tends to follow certain rules, and while there may be strange edge cases or exceptions, your players might get frustrated if they can't rely on certain things holding true within the fictional reality of the game world.

Be Flexible!

As the gamemaster, you have a unique responsibility to make the adventure exciting, keep the players involved and hold the story on track. In describing the world, try to answer all the players' questions about what the characters see, hear, touch, smell, and taste.

If a player wants to do something not explicitly covered in the rules, don't refuse to allow it on principle—this will make the game less exciting. Instead, try to find a creative way to resolve the action. Decide what talent, skill, or Attribute applies to the situation and whether his chances are good, indifferent, or terrible.

Don't reveal the precise Difficulty Number, just indicate whether the intended action or move is possible and how tough it might be to pull off. This way, the players can set their characters' own limitations based on their experiences with past failures.

To keep the players connected to the action, ask "What do you do?" each time you describe a new scene or event. By describing what they want their characters to do, the players help shape the story and add to their own enjoyment. If the players wander from your planned story, you can try to nudge them back in the right direction, but keep it subtle. A good gamemaster guides the players, he does not tell them what to do. Players forced into situations they are trying to avoid are likely to end up resenting the gamemaster for not letting them play out the adventure their way.

Players will come up with their own ideas to solve a problem—and every once in a while, there will be one that wrecks your carefully laid-out plans. That doesn't have to be a bad thing. If the player characters act in a way you didn't consider, go with the flow and see where it leads—the results could be rewarding. Adjusting your plans to account for the players' unexpected actions not only lets the players help shape the story, but can give inspiration for future events and further plot lines.

Be Tough, But Kind!

Challenge the players. Give them obstacles and threats they can't defeat with one hand tied behind their backs. If the player characters haven't worked for their rewards, then they haven't really earned them. For example, two orks armed with short swords would not be the only guards at a city's gate, and few Horrors retreat from battle after taking just a single Wound.

Once you become comfortable with the way the rules work, and the capabilities of the player characters, you can fine-tune the "threat level" of your adventures. In a really rough adventure, the player characters should succeed by the skin of their teeth, and may not achieve all their goals exactly as they intended. However, the gamemaster shouldn't make the adventure so tough that only one or two characters survive. The gamemaster needs to challenge the players, not overwhelm them.

A gamemaster can kill off a character anytime. You can throw enormous risks at the group until their luck runs out. That's a cheap victory—the gamemaster has a lot of power, and should use it responsibly. Gamemasters who measure their success in dead characters frequently find themselves without players. In general, it is better to be too easy on the characters than too rough.

If the player characters get in over their heads, remember that bad guys like to take prisoners. Prisoners can be made to talk. Prisoners make great hostages. Prisoners can draw a ransom to enrich their captors. Most important, prisoners may escape and live to fight another day. Villains in adventure fiction like to gloat, and they can make stupid choices; if villains were smart enough to kill off the heroes at the first opportunity, then most adventure stories would be a lot shorter.

Death and Earthdawn

Death is a touchy subject in any roleplaying game. It's not much fun to lose a character you have invested time and energy into. In **Earthdawn**, characters can die before they figure out what is happening. Despite all the special rules designed to guard against dying, and despite the advantages of magic, sometimes characters will die during an adventure.

Some groups set ground rules about death in their game, preferring to have it as something that is only "on the table" when the stakes are high enough, and hate the idea of senseless death. Other groups like a greater sense of danger that comes with regularly having their character's lives on the line. Individual players can have different feelings about this, and it is a good idea to have a discussion about this aspect of the game when you're planning your campaign.

The same can be said for supporting characters, especially close friends and family of the characters. While putting friends or family in danger is a common way get a character motivated, it can just as easily become a bad cliché if you are frequently killing player character allies. Stories of players who create characters with no family or friends so they can't be exploited by the gamemaster are all too common in the roleplaying game community.

Sometimes, despite the best efforts to avoid senseless death, a string of bad rolls will put a character six feet under. If necessary, you can cheat to keep characters alive. If a character did everything right and it was just the dice gods were not smiling. the character need not die. Knock the character out! Break one of his limbs! Whatever! Don't let a well-developed character die just because the player rolled a 4 when he needed a 5. The gamemaster can (and generally should) decide that such a character survives long enough to get medical aid.

This can also be applied to gamemaster characters. If a villain you spent hours designing gets hit by a lucky blow, bury the body under a collapsing building or make it suffer some other disaster that *"no one could possibly survive."* Then bring the villain back a few months later, ready to wreak revenge against the player characters. Remember, if you didn't find the body, he isn't necessarily dead.

At the end of the day, death should have meaning. **Earthdawn** is a game about heroes. Tales are not generally told about how a character drowned in a river—unless it was while saving the life of a child. The main characters in your story probably should not die at the hand of a random thug in an alley, but facing down a Horror that is threatening a village.

STORYTELLING

Roleplaying games are a form of storytelling, but with a few differences from traditional forms. In a novel, for example, the author creates all the characters, the setting, and the plot. He knows how the story will end, and what the consequences will be. He decides every word the characters say, and what actions they take in service of the story.

In contrast, no one person creates every element of the story in a roleplaying adventure. The gamemaster determines the setting, outlines the situation, and creates supporting characters and antagonists. The other players create the main protagonists, and decide how they react to the encounters and situations they face. They decide what their characters say and do, while the gamemaster makes those decisions for the supporting characters. The story unfolds through the shared efforts of the players and the gamemaster.

While no individual has total control of the events of the game, and the story that results, the gamemaster is responsible for controlling the pacing, and deciding how events develop and circumstances change as the player characters get involved. It can be helpful for a gamemaster to be familiar the basics of storytelling: creating setting, characters, plot, and so on. A good adventure provides the player characters with objectives, motivation, and challenges to overcome. Fleshing out your adventures with elements like theme, mood, foreshadowing, and other more advanced techniques can make your shared story, and the overall experience of your game, more enjoyable and memorable for everyone involved.

Roleplaying

To help bring your game to life, you should try to roleplay gamemaster characters as fully as a player roleplays his character. While this can mean keeping track of a lot of characters, the effort is worthwhile. To make things easier, start by fleshing out the key characters in your adventure; for example, the village elder who asks the heroes for help, or the Theran officer in command of a patrol that is hunting them.

When developing a character, take a look at the suggestions for personality traits in the **Creating Characters** chapter of the **Earthdawn** *Player's Guide*. Choosing a couple of notable traits for a gamemaster character can help solidify them in your mind. Combine this with a distinctive look, mannerism, or pattern of speech to help make them pop. Make sure you keep notes, either ahead of time, or jot some down as the player characters interact with them.

It might seem a bit intimidating to portray dozens of characters, and try to make them each distinct, but there's no need to go overboard. You don't need award-winning acting for every gamemaster character, and you don't need to prepare pages of backstory. Being prepared is a good thing, but don't go overboard.

Pacing

Have you read a story that dragged on with no clear end in sight? How about one that barely gave you time to catch a breath from constant action? These are examples of pacing. Pacing is important, but it can be difficult to judge the best pacing for each adventure and your group.

A good way to pace your adventures is to follow your players' lead. Try to get a sense of the players' mood. Are they bored, or do they need a break in the action? For example, if the group is preparing for a long journey and they spend the first three hours of the session buying supplies, some players may get restless. You can pick up the pace by having a minor incident distract the characters; a fight between two farmers could draw the characters out of the various shops they were visiting and into the street. The gamemaster could take that opportunity to announce that all purchases have been made and ask what the characters intend to do next.

On the other hand, if your adventure feels like one fight after another, and the characters are injured and on the run, the players may need a break in the action to let their characters heal some damage or plan their next action.

Pacing can also help emphasize other storytelling elements. For example, an adventure with a creepy, dark atmosphere works well if run at a slow, steady pace. An adventure whose theme is action or heroism might work best when run at a more lively pace.

Secrecy

Many situations in an **Earthdawn** game benefit from a bit of secrecy. Simply announcing a Difficulty Number for a particular test tells the players an important piece of information. One way to avoid revealing secrets in such a case is to have the player roll the appropriate dice for the test and announce the results. Without disclosing the Difficulty Number, the gamemaster then determines if the test is successful and describes what happens.

Sometimes, even asking a player to make a dice roll can give things away. If you only ask for a Perception test when the characters are about to trigger a trap or ambush, the players will figure out that connection and know what to expect the next time you ask for the test. If you occasionally ask players to roll dice for no reason at all. Nod sagely at the results, or say *"Huh, I thought so."* This can keep your players guessing.

It's also a good idea to avoid too much detail when describing important people or things. A wealth of detail can tip off the players that you spent a lot of time designing it. This can result in them expecting something before you are ready to reveal it.

For example, if you introduce three gamemaster characters, one of whom is the main villain and the other two are just henchmen, avoid saying, "You meet three fighters from the troll clan. The one on the left is wearing expensive, well-made clothes and an opal ring on his left ring finger, and is carrying a large battle-axe. The other two? Oh, uh, they're obviously fighters, too." This kind of description immediately tells the characters to watch out for the troll on the left. Either describe all three in relative detail, not revealing which character to watch, or introduce all three as "troll fighters; you've seen one, you've seen them all," and let the players ask for more information.

Drama

Drama can be an effective tool to bring your players into the world of **Earthdawn**. The stories told in roleplaying games tend to be dramatic. Tales of heroes and danger are the very stuff of drama (or even melodrama). Don't be afraid to describe scenes to your players dramatically, or to dramatize when roleplaying your gamemaster characters. When a character offers his help to someone in need, don't just say, *"I'll help."* Instead, have the character say, *"Fear not, I shall aid you in this time of need."* It may sound corny, but dramatic roleplaying gives your characters personality.

Remember, the first ground rule of roleplaying is to have fun. As a gamemaster, one of your most important responsibilities is to entertain your players. If all your characters sound the same, then the players will begin to think they are the same, and that can lead to boredom.

Advanced Techniques

Authors and filmmakers often use other techniques for enhancing or reinforcing the theme, mood, or tone of their stories. These can be adapted for use in a roleplaying game, and the ones most commonly used are *foreshadowing*, *dreams*, and *the tale*.

These techniques can be difficult to use effectively, especially the first time. If you try to foreshadow events and discover that you were too subtle, or gave the story away by being too obvious, don't give up! Try to figure our what didn't work and learn from the experience. This will develop your skills and better prepare you to try again.

Foreshadowing

Foreshadowing is when an event early in the story hints at a similar, more important event later on. For example, the heroes may enter a town at the beginning of an adventure and see a child who has trapped and is torturing a small animal. The child isn't particularly cruel, he just doesn't know any better. It may occur to the characters that perhaps the child is imitating something he's seen or heard about, or is subconsciously acting out something his conscious mind has suppressed.

That event can foreshadow the climax of the adventure, when the heroes discover that a slaver recently raided the town and made off with a few of the townsfolk. When the heroes track him down and break into his stronghold, they find he is torturing his captives for information about a nearby ruin. The encounter with the small child foreshadows the heroes discovering the slaver torturing his captives.

Dreams

Dreams are a classic storytelling technique, often used in television shows and movies. Dreams can be used as a form of foreshadowing (see above), or to give the characters insight into a current or upcoming situation. Dreams let the player (and character) know that an event or situation is important.

Exactly how you use the dream to present information is another matter. Dreams may be sent by the Passions, exposure to powerful and mysterious magic, or come from more sinister sources. The dream's message may be obvious, such as an accurate enactment of an upcoming event in the adventure. A dream may send a more subtle message, providing obscure clues that hint vaguely at the true situation through a metaphor or by wrapping symbolism around an event in a character's life.

The Tale

Oral tradition is rich in the world of **Earthdawn**. Stories and legends were passed down through the generations spent hiding within the kaers and citadels. A gamemaster character sharing a tale or story can be an effective way to involve the characters in the adventure and provide the background for the story at the same time. The tale could be the legend of a long-lost magical treasure, the story of a town ravaged by a Horror that has yet to be defeated, or any number of other stories. The tale is a convenient way to tailor an adventure to your group's interests and the player characters' lives.

The players and their characters can also use the tale. The world's strong oral tradition of tales and legends should encourage adventurers to share the stories of their adventures with the people they meet throughout Barsaive. Characters may tell their stories to prove their credentials, as payment for lodging, food, or other supplies or favors, or simply to entertain the locals. And of course, the more people who know of them, the more their legend will spread.

Some players may simply say "We tell our story while we're in town" or something to that effect. Other players may be willing to tell the story out loud with the drama appropriate to a heroic saga. As the gamemaster you know what happened in the previous adventures, but you may not have heard the players' version of events. If they tell other characters the story as they remember it, you learn about events from their perspective and their view of the adventure's outcome—or at least the version they choose to tell strangers. This can be important if you want to build future adventures on the events of a past adventure. When the player characters tell their tale, you learn what the characters know (or remember) and can base your adventure on that information. Of course, what the player characters know may not represent the whole truth.

An adventure journal kept by the players (see **Group Journals** in the **Earthdawn Player's Guide**) can also fill this roles. Whether it is kept in an actual bound journal, loose pages in a binder, or updated on a website or wiki page, the information the players keep track of can help get them more invested in their characters and adventures, while at the same time providing you with a record of what they remember and felt was important. Some game masters encourage this behavior by awarding Legend Points to players that contribute to the group's journal.

If you keep careful records of everything that happens during an adventure, you will probably know what information the characters have and what they don't. But by hearing the players tell the tale of the adventure, you'll find out how they remember the adventure, and that's what's important. This knowledge allows you to build on their perception of the world, which in turn helps you maintain the illusion that the world is real.

GAME AIDS

To help the game run smoothly, gamemasters can use several strategies to keep track of story lines, gamemaster characters, combat, treasures, and the myriad other things that go into an adventure. The following describes the most useful aids in running a game.

Displays

Visual aids are one of the most useful game aids a gamemaster can have. They allow the players to see exactly where they are at any point during the adventure, helping settle the inevitable (and distracting) arguments about who is standing where, who got hit by the spell or falling rocks, and so on. Sketch the area on a big pad of paper or white board, or use plastic mats made for gaming with feature hexagonal or square grids. To show the placement of characters, enemies, creatures, and so on, use counters or metal miniatures. These add a lot of atmospheric detail and are small enough that you don't need an auditorium to display a battle.

Handouts

Players love handouts and props. When possible, try to create handouts to give the players something tangible to handle. If the characters find a letter, don't just read it to them, have it printed or written out for them to read themselves. If they need to solve a puzzle to open a kaer's vault, give them a drawing of what they see.

While handouts are cool, they should be relevant to the game in some way. For example, the price list of a trading post only enhances the mood of an adventure if the characters have to do business at the post. Handouts are sometimes the perfect way to present hidden clues. The trading post's price list could feature an item that you want the players to purchase, or contain a secret message intended for a "special" customer.

Maps

Maps are powerful tools. A map of the area where the adventure takes place, even just a simple sketch with shapes showing landmarks, can be critical when running a game. Try using two maps: one for the players that shows the explored area that everyone knows, and a private map that shows the locations of all those secret places the characters may discover. As the group discovers these secret locations, they can add them to the "public knowledge" map.

Maps of smaller places in which certain events take place (buildings, neighborhoods, and so on) are also helpful. Draw them or borrow them from elsewhere. Some publishers sell sets of maps and floor plans suitable for any fantasy game. Don't be afraid to re-use them—just as in the real world, many buildings in **Earthdawn** have similar floor plans. Heck, if you've seen one cheap inn, you've seen them all.

Gamemaster Character Files

Information on generic gamemaster characters, or the major characters in a specific adventure can also help a great deal. Use a card file, notebook, computer database, or any other system that works for you to store profiles for supporters, family members, lovers, people with special skills or talents (magicians, merchants, sages), or any other character likely to play recurring roles in adventures. Easy access to these characters lets you portray recurring characters consistently, and occasionally throw your players plausible left curves and helps keep the game moving.

If published profiles keep showing up as characters or opponents again and again, players eventually become familiar enough with the bad guys' stats to defeat them regularly, so creating your own variations on such character profiles pays off for your game.

Assistants

There is a lot to keep track of when running and managing a game. To help reduce the workload, you can ask your players for help. For example, one of the players can keep track of everyone's Initiative during combat—the "Initiative Master" would be in charge of organizing each combat round by asking for and announcing each player's (and the gamemaster's) turns and keep track of the duration of magical effects.

One or more players can take the role of non-vital gamemaster characters in scenes where their own characters aren't present. For example, if the group's Thief is caught by the town watch, the gamemaster can have the other players take the role of the watchmen—doing so helps keep everyone involved in the game, and takes some of the pressure off since you don't have to play all the gamemaster characters yourself. Beside offering a change of pace, it can add flavor to the setting and is a lot of fun. Along the same lines, a player whose character is dead or unconscious can take over creatures or characters on the other side during combat.

CUSTOMIZING EARTHDAWN

Every **Earthdawn** game is unique. The rules and information about the world that we publish are a starting point. From there, presenting the world to your players in an interesting and appropriate way is up to you. We have a few suggestions for how to use the various aspects of the world of **Earthdawn** to make it your own.

One thing to keep in mind: we have a firm idea of how the world of **Earthdawn** works and how it will develop. We plan to publish **Earthdawn** material according to that vision. Material in one of our future products may contradict something you've developed on your own or changed in your game. You must decide how to resolve such contradictions, since we can only consider our version of the universe for purposes of continuity and other issues in our products.

You can decide which ideas you like from your version and the published information and integrate both worlds into your next unique adventure or campaign. We don't think that is a problem, and neither should you. You can ignore what we've written or take it and change it to make it the game you want to play—the way the world of **Earthdawn** comes to life for you and your players is up to you. While we don't expect you to completely rewrite the rules, you are invited to tweak them here and there so that the game plays the way you like. **Earthdawn** will become your own world as a result.

Creatures and Horrors

If you don't like the creature or Horror descriptions we provide, feel free to change them and their game statistics. Keep in mind, however, that the Legend Point Awards for the creatures are based on their game statistics and abilities. If you change the statistics, review the ratio of the creature's power to the size of the Legend Point Award. The *Earthdawn Companion* contains information on how to do that.

The least risky thing to change about creatures and Horrors is their activity cycle and habitats. If it suits your adventure for a wormskull to be found in a wet, marshy swamp, then that's where it should be. We don't mind. What we publish serves as the starting point; the base from which the rest of the game grows. It's up to you to aid that growth.

Treasure

We encourage you to customize magical treasures. Even the treasures provided in this book present only about half the information you need to use them in your adventure or campaign — you must supply the remainder of the information. This includes specifics like Research Knowledge. The open framework we present for magical treasures allows you to take what we provide and fill in the details to best suit your group and adventures. Perhaps more than any other area, customizing magical treasure and the stories you build around them make **Earthdawn** your game. The **Thread Items** chapter (p.197) covers all you need to know about developing and customizing magical treasure.

Setting

We present information about the current state of affairs in Barsaive in this book. This represents the starting point for this edition of **Earthdawn**, and may differ from information provided in prior editions of the game.

If you don't like something we introduce here, or in a later book, feel free to ignore or change it to suit the needs of your game. While the influence of the Theran Empire has been reduced, you may want to keep them as a force to be reckoned with. Rather than pulling back to deal with internal conflicts, the Kingdom of Throal might be shifting to a more expansionist mode, showing a larger military presence in the farther corners of Barsaive.

Feel free to add to what we have here. Barsaive covers a lot of area, and we only present the broadest strokes in this book. In addition to the larger cities and powers, there are numerous smaller towns, and more villages and settlements than could be fleshed out in a library of sourcebooks. Bands of scorchers, cults and secret societies, not to mention the Horrors and their minions still threaten the lives of everyday people.

From the shores of the Aras Sea to the borders of the Wastes, from the ruins of Parlainth to the trading halls of Travar, Barsaive is a land ripe for adventure. Use what you want, and make the rest your own. Perhaps you will become ambitious, and explore how people in another part of the world dealt with the Scourge and its aftermath. We've provided the tools, it's up to you how you use them.

Tone and Mood

We will look at this more in depth in the **Adventures and Campaigns** chapter, but there are many ways to approach the game, with different moods to suit your style and goals..

Earthdawn can be a game of heroic fantasy, where the characters strive to reclaim the world from the evils of the Horrors and the others that threaten it. **Earthdawn** can be a world of discovery and wonder, where the characters recover lore and artifacts lost to time, surprised and amazed by each new discovery. This **Earthdawn** is full of unexplored lands and hidden secrets—some of which offer knowledge, others danger.

Earthdawn may also be a dark, injured world where the characters continually discover the scars the Horrors left on the world through their own efforts and through those corrupted by the Scourge. This darker mood can be easily related to a Horror theme, where people use whatever means necessary to protect themselves from the Horrors without regard for the consequences.

Choosing a specific mood and tone for your game is another way to make your **Earthdawn** unique. You can even vary the mood from adventure to adventure, with feelings of darkness and corruption while the group uncovers an evil cult in the alleys of Urupa, followed by a more lighthearted adventure competing with rival adventurers in pursuit of a king's ransom in treasure.

Blood Magic

Blood magic can be one of the more disturbing elements of the world of **Earthdawn**, depending on how you decide to use it. The blood charms and blood oaths in the *Player's Guide* represent powerful forces in the game. You should recognize that blood magic is one of the after-effects of the Scourge, and as such is inherently dangerous.

People turned to blood magic in an attempt to protect themselves from the Horrors before the Scourge. Though its use has diminished in the years since the Scourge, blood magic still has a strong presence in Barsaive. Many people consider blood magic a constant reminder of the days of the Scourge, a time that most people would prefer to forget, and many people are wary of this magic, if not outright shunning it.

Goods and Services

The **Goods and Services** chapter in the *Player's Guide* offers some guidelines for assigning Availability ratings to equipment and services in Barsaive. Availability provides another area in which you can customize your game. By making different goods and services more or less easy to obtain, you are altering the world to match your vision.

You may decide that blood charms are available, but only on the black market at outrageous prices. Perhaps you think that magical healing aids should be readily available nearly everywhere in Barsaive. Certain weapons and armor may only be available in certain marketplaces, or be sold only by traveling peddlers. These and other choices further define your game and make it different from others.

Player Ideas

One of your best sources of ideas for customizing your **Earthdawn** game will be your players. As they grow more comfortable with the game, they will be able to tell you what they want and don't want. Experienced players typically have ideas about specific items, rules, talents, and spells. Asking for this input may result in more information than you actually want or need! However, it lets you know how they would like to see the game tailored, and lets you know what type of game they want to play. If you create a campaign with a dark, gritty mood, but they tell you they want heroic fantasy, you may want to reevaluate your approach.

Giving the players what they want is likely to result in them staying with your game longer, and everyone will have a better time playing. However it ultimately falls to you, as the gamemaster, to decide how your game will be played. We don't suggest that you alienate your players by insisting that everything be done your way, but they should also be willing to compromise and try something different. After all, that's why you picked up a new game in the first place—because it offered something different.

Remember, having fun is the reason you chose to play **Earthdawn** in the first place.

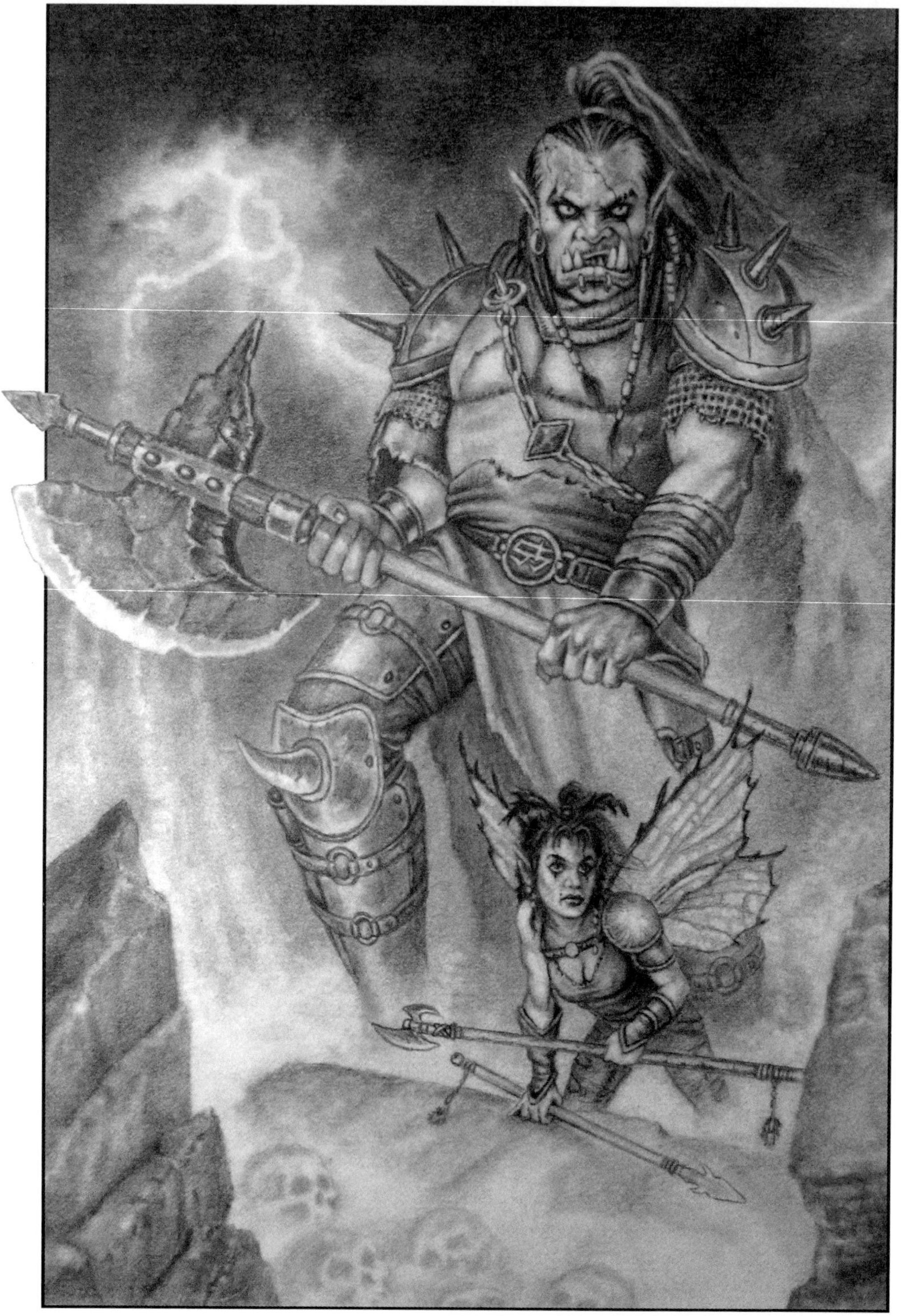

EARTHDAWN

ADVENTURES AND CAMPAIGNS

Adventure is long stretches of tedious discomfort punctuated by moments of fear, pain, and blood. Isn't it funny how the Troubadours leave out those kind of details?
•Palaemon, Warrior of the Crimson Star •

The people of Barsaive live in an exciting, dangerous time filled with opportunity for adventure. For player characters, journeying into danger and triumphing over it is a calling that can't be denied. Whether searching for a forgotten kaer, guarding an embattled prince against enemies, or confronting a Horror, the player characters prove themselves the heroes of this age. Gamemasters should create adventures that challenge their players' wits as well as their characters' swords and spells, and should reward good roleplaying as generously as lucky dice-rolling.

This chapter provides information for gamemasters on different approaches they can use for their adventures. Gamemasters may use themes, subplots, storytelling, roleplaying, and other techniques to create, change, or enhance adventures and campaigns. The techniques defined below provide examples of their use. This chapter also offers suggestions for creating and maintaining an ongoing **Earthdawn** campaign and guidelines for making your **Earthdawn** game unique. Finally, it provides guidelines for rewards that characters can earn in the course of their adventures, from the physical wealth of treasure and loot, to the intangible rewards of experience represented by Legend Points.

CREATING ADVENTURES

While experience is by far the best way to learn how to write a good adventure, the following suggestions and tips may help you take care of certain vital story elements. The main elements of an adventure include the adventure background, a plot synopsis, objectives, motivations, and opposition. Though these represent the most important elements of a good story, a good adventure also includes other elements such as atmosphere, mood, conflicts and challenges, themes, subplots, and storytelling.

Adventure Background

The *adventure background* describes the story up to the point where the player characters get involved, and often hints at what can happen after that.

Plot Synopsis

The *plot synopsis* lays out the potential series of events in the adventure, and describes the scenes and locations that can appear during the course of the story. It describes the most likely path that player characters might take through the adventure, and the actions that supporting and gamemaster characters are likely to take in response to player character actions.

The scope of the plot synopsis can vary depending on the scale of the adventure. For a small-scale story that involves a single villain in a small town it might only be a couple of paragraphs. For an adventure that involves the characters in a province-wide conspiracy, or a conflict between multiple factions, it can be more involved.

One thing that should be kept in mind with the plot synopsis is an idea of what will happen if the player characters do not get involved, or don't take action in certain ways.

Objectives

The most basic **objective** of every player character in an adventure is usually survival. Beyond that, the group often accepts a specific task: find a lost artifact, rescue a kidnap victim, pay off a debt, kill or capture a villain, or foil a villain's plan.

The final objective may differ from the original one. It isn't unusual for a group to change its goal mid-adventure. For example, the initial goal might be to escort a diplomat to a meeting with an ork clan, until the leader of the clan is found dead, with evidence pointing to the diplomat. The group may then decide on a new objective: solve the murder to clear their client.

When developing an adventure, keep track of the group's objectives and give characters a chance to meet them. Offer them assignments or let them find clues that reveal new objectives. Characters who accomplish their objectives earn Legend Points, so fulfilling objectives is an important aspect of the game.

Using Published Adventures

Many gamemasters will try and play **Earthdawn** by running published adventures as written. Keep in mind that published adventures that provide the appropriate challenge for every group of player characters are a myth. Some groups are simply more powerful than others. Therefore, you may need to adjust the game statistics and capabilities of an adventure's opposition to provide your players with an appropriate challenge.

You will find a lot of adventures available in printed or electronic format from publishers of other fantasy games. Even though they may not have been written for **Earthdawn**, they are likely to contain good ideas which can be easily converted into an **Earthdawn** story. All you need to do is use them as blueprints to develop adventures of your own.

If a story works well except for a problem here and there, modify the plot or events to make the adventure a better one. Come up with game statistics for the characters and creatures contained in that adventure and replace the names and locations with **Earthdawn**-specific ones.

This works with many fantasy adventures. We want you to keep your eyes open for new, original material. **FASA Games** is not the only source of ideas for **Earthdawn**.

It also helps to come up with objectives for important gamemaster characters in the adventure. Conflict, which often lies at the heart of storytelling, frequently arises from people having objectives that work at cross-purposes. What is the villain trying to accomplish, and how does that objective conflict with the objectives of the player characters?

Motivation

Put simply, motivation asks the question, "Why is the character doing this?" This applies to both player and gamemaster characters. People usually do things for a reason, often to achieve a personal goal of some kind, and so motivation ties into objectives. When developing an adventure, you should come up with reasons for the player characters to become involved. Sometimes this is as simple as having somebody hire them for a job, but having other motivations can bring more life to your game.

If your group doesn't bite at an offer, you should examine the group's motivations. Talk with the players about why they don't want to tackle the adventure. Does it seem too dangerous? Does it offer too little reward? Characters often prefer payment in kind to silver. Magicians may want teachers or supplies, all adepts need training at some point, and so on. If the premise of the adventure bores the players silly, it may be better to scrap the game in favor of a bull session on the kinds of adventures the players want their characters to get involved in.

The more information players give the gamemaster about their characters' lives, beliefs, and psychology, the more material the gamemaster can work with to build motivation into the adventures. As the players get more involved in the game, their characters will acquire friends, enemies, and obligations, and probably develop quirks. All these factors make good motivators for the adventurers, and the gamemaster should keep them in mind.

Opposition

Most adventures involve opposition, and the world of **Earthdawn** provides many choices. In some adventures, the opposition may be as impersonal as an impenetrable forest, a curmudgeonly innkeeper, or an obscure magical effect. These obstacles may have nothing to do with the adventurers' goals, they exist to make their lives difficult. In other adventures, the group may need to face and defeat a personal enemy in order to achieve their objectives.

Opposition from individuals or small groups roughly equal in size and power to the adventuring group can get personal very quickly, and a good enemy can become a valuable resource for the gamemaster. Depending on how their encounters went, such a foe may repeatedly oppose the group to get revenge. A personal enemy can turn adventures into a series of duels between the player characters and their relentless foe, building up to a final showdown. The enemy may show up in unrelated adventures, just to strike at his rivals any way he can.

Gamemasters may find the following descriptions of typical opposition useful. This list is by no means exhaustive, and lists only the biggest threats. Creatures, ork scorcher tribes, and trollmoots make for good opposition, while dwarf merchant houses or t'skrang aropagoi can provide a challenge that is more socio-political in nature.

The Horrors

The most obvious and probably most frequent opposition in **Earthdawn** are the Horrors. These dreadful, other-dimensional beings ravaged the world during the Scourge, and many remained behind after the world's magic ebbed. Though most Horrors have a bestial shape and nature, they possess great intelligence and cunning. They create schemes, lure victims into danger, and perpetrate a multitude of evil acts. The Horrors know no bounds.

Tragically, a number of people have felt the Horrors' touch and some have succumbed to these corrupt masters. These foul folk act toward ends no one understands, and often their seemingly innocent behavior lures adventurers to their doom.

The Theran Empire

Though the influence of the Therans has been greatly reduced in recent years, they still exert some influence in Barsaive. While they no longer control their former strongholds of Sky Point and Triumph, the Empire desires to regain control of the wayward province. Spies and agents of the Therans work undercover to gather intelligence for their masters, and rather than military conquest, seek to manipulate the political landscape to their ends.

The Mad Passions

Though your player characters would stand no chance against the Mad Passions themselves, they may meet and battle questors of the Mad Passions who work toward wicked ends. The questors of Dis, Raggok, and Vestrial willingly use whatever methods necessary to promote worship and promote the ideals of their patron Passions. Though not common, some questors of the Mad Passions serve Horrors. Some of these individuals have been corrupted by a Horror, and some simply follow their own misguided ambitions.

Atmosphere and Mood

The atmosphere of an adventure goes beyond its physical setting to include such elements as the attitudes of gamemaster characters, their actions, and the impression or feeling the characters receive from their environment. The atmosphere of an adventure taking place during the day in a big city should be different than the atmosphere of an adventure set at night in the Badlands.

In addition to the atmosphere evoked by a particular setting, an adventure should also have an overall feel or mood. Is the adventure a light-hearted journey or a dark tale of evil and corruption? By defining the mood of an adventure, it can help you come up with scenes and encounters to contribute to the emotional impression it should leave on the characters.

Atmosphere and mood complement each other. For example, if the adventure is the tale of a village's corruption into sacrificing its own to a Horror, the overall atmosphere should be dark and gloomy with a touch of despair. Mood also relates closely to an adventure's theme.

Conflicts and Challenges

Good adventures present the characters with conflicts other than combat. Conflicts can be emotional, intellectual, moral, or ethical. Using non-combat conflict in your adventures forces your players to think carefully about their characters' actions.

For example, one conflict may revolve around the heroes being manipulated by a servitor of a Horror. The heroes start out believing that their noble goal is to destroy an evil questor of Vestrial, but when they encounter the questor, they discover that he has been fighting to prevent a Horror from devastating a nearby town. By the time the characters realize they've been duped by their employer, they must choose between two evils.

Think about different ways conflicts can be resolved. In the above example, the characters can resolve the conflict in at least two ways. If they let the questor live, they allow him to continue his activities in the name of the Mad Passion Vestrial. If they kill the questor, they must deal with the Horror threatening the town. The way a group resolves a conflict will often have consequences that lead to further adventures.

An adventure may offer several conflicts and resolutions. If an adventure takes several game sessions to complete, each session should have a goal, which may be the resolution to one or more conflicts. A conflict does not always need a resolution, though players may find too many loose ends frustrating. Try to strike a balance between conflicts that can be resolved, continuing plotlines, and situations that simply offer no satisfactory conclusion.

Good adventures challenge the characters in different ways. Some challenges take the form of an opposing gamemaster character or creature. Another adventure may require the characters to solve a puzzle of some sort, presenting an intellectual challenge rather than a physical one.

Sometimes, the environment itself can be the adventure's challenge. An adventure set in the Blood Wood is more challenging than one set in a mundane forest. After all, most forests do not have patrols of thorn men and blood elves looking for trespassers.

Theme

A theme is a high-level idea or concept that the adventure focuses on. For example, if an adventure centers on the activities of a ring of Theran spies working in the city-state of Travar, the theme might be intrigue. If the characters become involved in one trollmoot's revenge against a rival moot, the adventure's theme might be vengeance.

Not all adventures need themes. The purpose of an adventure may be simply to get the characters from one place to another in an interesting way. For example, the courier job the characters are hired for may actually be a straightforward pickup and delivery, with no betrayal or double-cross awaiting the characters at the end.

Gamemasters use mood, atmosphere, and conflicts to support the adventure's theme by creating specific elements or events that emphasize the theme in different ways. For a theme of intrigue, the gamemaster might emphasize elements of mystery and distrust, with encounters that take place in shadowed alleys and challenges that are solved through indirect means.

Betrayal, vengeance, intrigue, and heroism all make suitable themes for adventures in **Earthdawn**, and you are sure to come up with others. As an illustration of one use of a theme, consider the commonly used theme of conflict with the Horrors.

Horror Theme

In this example, Horror does not refer to the horror genre. It refers to the creatures from astral space that ravaged the world of **Earthdawn** during the Scourge. The Horror theme is a way of exploring one of the reasons heroes adventure in **Earthdawn**. These themes are usually complex enough to weave the plot of an adventure or tie together a series of adventures.

An adventure with a Horror theme may be one of the best ways to initiate the players into the world of **Earthdawn**. Historically, the Horrors affected most of Barsaive by ravaging the land and its people. While Theran magic provided some protection, it was ineffective against some Horrors, and some communities found themselves forced to create new forms of protection, either to save themselves or to protect the rest of the world from the threat they faced.

These protections sometimes took forms that required the people to take actions as bad as or worse than those the Horrors perpetrated—the fate of Blood Wood being just one example. After the Scourge, some communities sought to leave those events in the past or to somehow redeem their actions, while others—in the name of safety—continue their darker practices to this day.

When first putting the game together, the gamemaster may decide to provide a common history for the player characters by placing them all in the same kaer or citadel, then creating or allowing the players to invent the history and events of that hiding place. The adventure would begin as the characters emerge into the world, and the theme might revolve around their efforts to cleanse themselves of the actions they took against the Horrors while in the kaer, or if nothing untoward happened during their time of hiding, to help free other people from the influence of the Horrors.

A storyline exploring this theme as described above could take the following shape.

1. The community isolates itself in an effort to protect itself from the Horrors. This isolation is not always physical; the Ritual of Thorns used by the elves of Blood Wood to fend off the Horrors is simply another form of isolation. In fact, many uses of blood magic in the days before the Scourge represented similar attempts at isolation.

2. The community emerges from their self-imposed isolation when certain signs indicate that the Horrors are gone or less powerful than before. In most cases, this means simply emerging from kaers and citadels. But sometimes the isolation affected a community as deeply as the Horrors themselves, and the physical emergence became only the first step to truly rejoining the world.
3. The community realizes that the isolation they believed would protect them has, in fact, corrupted their community on a deep level. At this point characters may realize that the means did not justify the ends.
4. The characters begin their efforts to recover what they once were, to redeem their actions, to grow beyond the damage done. Success in these efforts may take unexpected forms—redemption may involve more than performing ever-greater heroics.

Another way to approach the Horror theme could be to begin the adventure when the characters emerge from the kaer, when they recognize the consequences of what they have done, or as they begin their quest for redemption. Rather than creating an elaborate history at this point, you may simply give the characters a mission or other compelling reason to leave the kaer, then reveal the story behind their flight bit by bit as the adventure unfolds or allow the players to make up their characters' history. The gamemaster may set up their isolation as another type of protection from a Horror rather than the more common retreat to a kaer or citadel. The characters could still move through the same four stages: isolation, emergence, realization, and redemption; the focus would simply be slightly different.

The Horror Theme can even be used as the overall theme of a campaign, with different adventures dealing with each of the four stages. The Horror theme may also tie together a campaign through a series of subplots woven in and through the main stories and adventures.

Subplots

Subplots are secondary stories, and are often used to serve as a counterpoint or provide emphasis to the main story. Subplots can provide comic relief or serve as a device to accomplish something in the main story of the adventure. For example, a subplot could center on a young child who follows the heroes around the city during an adventure and manages to be in the way at inopportune times. The child may have nothing to do with the story and just a harmless annoyance, or he may turn out to be the son of the Nethermancer the characters are trying to find.

Subplots can help establish mood and atmosphere, or emphasize the theme of an adventure. For example, if the adventure's theme is vengeance, then a subplot about a gamemaster character from a past adventure seeking revenge against one of the players' characters would serve to support the overall theme.

Fleshing Out the Story

Once you've outlined the basic building blocks of your adventure, you need to bring it to life by adding color, creating gamemaster characters to fit various situations that may come up. Working out how much to tell the characters about what's really going on, and figuring out what kind of time limits the characters are working with can help shape the pacing and tone of the adventure. Details like these can help turn your story outline into an exciting adventure.

Adding Color

A good roleplaying adventure engages the players' imaginations. A good skill to develop is coming up with imaginative descriptions that engage as many senses as possible. Players need to see the scenery, hear the thunk of an arrow striking a tree near their heads, feel the chill of a wind blowing through a snowy mountain pass. Describing the odor of a particular place or the texture of the ground can help convey atmosphere to your players.

For example, describing the Blood Wood as "a big forest that is almost always dark and gloomy," doesn't create the same feeling as, "the dark woods stretch for miles in all directions. Twisted trees and plants make it seem like the entire forest is writhing. The ground under your feet is soft, each step making a faint squelch, and that normal smell of growing things is mixed with the iron tang of blood." The first description describes the setting, but fails to evoke much of the feeling of the second.

A rich description is not the only way to add color, the way you present it can help as well. Speaking slowly and quietly as the group explores a forgotten kaer can emphasize the emptiness and increase the tension the players feel. When a pack of ghouls comes surging out of a side tunnel, you can shift to speaking more quickly and use a louder volume to convey the change in circumstances and feelings. Look at other media like books, movies, and television shows to see how they use different visual, auditory, and narrative cues to convey atmosphere, mood, and tone.

Make gamemaster characters as colorful as possible. Many gamemasters act out their characters, complete with different accents or voices. It can often help to borrow attitudes or speaking styles from movies, television, or other sources. Don't be afraid to overact or ham it up! If you want to portray a Troubadour like Keith Richards, got for it!

Props can add a tangible, realistic feel to your game. If the characters find a message outlining the plans of a ring of slavers, don't just read it to them, write it up before the session and hand it to them. If they find a treasure map, give them a handout that shows the map and the information it contains. There are many sources offering advice on easy ways to create interesting props and handouts for your game.

As the gamemaster, you set the overall tone of the game, and the amount of effort you put in to adding color to your game can rub off on your players. Players should try to create a distinct character and stay in it. Your adventures can include subplots that bring different aspects of the player characters into the story. Does the Troubadour have a love life? Do they want one? How does the Warrior spend his time when not fighting Horrors? Does the Wizard have a favorite research project? Some players love creating and portraying these secondary aspects of their characters, while others are more reluctant. Don't force your players to do more than they are comfortable with; it's better to lead by example and show how much fun roleplaying can be by having fun yourself.

Masterminds and Equalizers

When populating your adventures with gamemaster characters, there are two special types that can be used flesh out your story.

Masterminds can add complexity to an adventure, and provide the foundation for a story arc that spans multiple adventures in a campaign. Consider whether an adventure, even a small one, could be part of some larger plan or conspiracy. The mastermind is the individual—or organization—behind the plot. Drop clues for the player characters that hint at larger things in motion behind the scenes. Even if the main plot of a particular adventure doesn't have anything to do with it, these sorts of detail can give your game the feeling of a being part of a larger world.

Sometimes characters can get into more trouble than they can handle on their own. *Equalizers* can be a way for you to bail them out. An equalizer can be a friendly person in an otherwise hostile town, an itinerant Warrior, or the henchman of an enemy that turns to their side. It can be helpful to have some pre-generated characters available, and plans for how you can introduce them to an adventure to tip the balance in favor of the player characters if necessary.

An equalizer can also fill in for a missing character in a pinch. If the player of the group's Wizard is sick and unable to show up, the group could be in serious trouble. In this case, you could bring a friendly gamemaster character to work with the group.

One thing to be wary of when using equalizers: do not let them overshadow the player characters! It can sometimes be tempting to have a gamemaster character come on the scene and solve problems for your group. But gamemaster characters should support the story, not dominate it. Equalizers should be used with care—nothing spoils a game faster than the dreaded "pet NPC" that steals the spotlight from the player characters.

Preparation Time

When the group has an objective, the players will want time to prepare. Some players will want to spend as much time preparing as possible, and it seems like a tough job they could easily spend an entire game session getting ready. Don't let them.

Heroes rarely book their adventures ahead of time. Many times, they are answering a call of distress or some other urgent matter. While you should allow the group some time to prepare, you should set some limits to keep the momentum going. Unless your players enjoy the process of researching, and you've planned for them to do so, feel free to have a supporter or other gamemaster character provide important information.

Feel free to compress the amount of time preparations take in session. There is no need to play out the interactions with every vendor and barkeep if the group is stocking up on normal supplies. If there is more specialized gear they are looking for, use the availability rules in the **Goods and Services** chapter of the *Player's Guide* to determine whether they can obtain the desired equipment. Of course, if your group is the sort that enjoys extensive roleplaying, you can indulge them, but make sure that everybody is on board, and keep an eye out for boredom, If you get the feeling that momentum is flagging, you can ask for any final preparations and move on with your adventure.

Ideally, you should give the group time to prepare, but don't let them keep the story from moving forward. It can be helpful to impose some sort of time limit or deadline. After all, unless they get moving, the cult could complete their ritual and summon the Horror! You can turn up the heat in other ways as well—give them a pressing reason to get out of town. Perhaps a rival group is after the same treasure, and they want to make sure they get there first. Whatever the reason, make the players want to move forward, but not feel like you're rushing them.

Along the same lines, you want to give the characters enough time between adventures for them to accomplish their personal goals. As they get more experienced, they will need time to meditate and advance their talent ranks, train to advance in Circle, study and research the magical treasures they recover, and many other personal goals. This is more an issue of time management in a campaign, but it is also an aspect of preparation time.

Integrating New Player Characters

Few gaming groups are willing to start a new campaign to add a new player or player character. But when a new player wants to join the game, or a new player character needs to join the group because a character retired or died, the group must find a way to integrate the character into the existing story.

Fortunately, there are many ways to use existing features of your campaign to introduce a new player character. One of the simplest is through known ally—a friendly gamemaster character can introduce the new character to the group and recommend they work together. The first adventure for the new group member can feature interesting surprises, because he will probably be unfamiliar with the group's talents, skills, methods, personalities, and vice versa.

Another more involved way to introduce a new character is to develop an adventure or story that introduces them through shared goals. Perhaps the new character was investigating a problem and their path coincides with the main group. For example, the main group could be pursuing the leader of a Horror cult, and the new character is searching for a friend or family member that has been captured (or is a member of) the same cult. After working together to achieve their objective, the new character can choose to travel with her new friends.

One other thing to consider when introducing new characters is handling different levels of player and character experience. If your game has been running for several months and the player characters have reached Sixth Circle, it can be difficult to bring in a new character at First Circle. Challenges that threaten the more experienced characters could crush the new one. At the same time, a player that is new to **Earthdawn** could be overwhelmed by the number of talents and abilities available to an experienced adept.

It can be difficult to strike a balance, but the nature of character advancement in **Earthdawn** means that a lower Circle character will advance more quickly than a higher one, and the advancement process will help less experienced players get a better handle on the **Earthdawn** game.

ADVENTURE IDEAS

The world of **Earthdawn** is full of adventuring opportunities. Given the size of Barsaive and the conflicts between its citizens, there are many different stories that can be told.

To keep you from being overwhelmed by the possibilities, we present some of the major setting elements from **Earthdawn** and suggest a few adventure ideas for each.

Horrors

The Horrors represent one of the most obvious sources of adventures in **Earthdawn**. Characters can battle the Horrors that remain, or work to fix the damage left by the Scourge. Many Horrors still dominate towns and villages, feeding off their captives' fears and other strong emotions. Adventures and campaigns centered on the Horror theme usually fall into this category.

Therans

Though their influence in Barsaive is greatly diminished since the conclusion of the war, the Theran Empire still has a presence in the province. Theran agents and spies can be found throughout the province and work to subvert local governments, laying the groundwork for their eventual return. The Therans have particular interest in Parlainth, their former provincial capital, as well as other major cities and powers.

Passions and Questors

The people of Barsaive look to the Passions for spiritual support. Because of their central role in peoples' lives, the Passions can serve as inspiration for many adventures. In particular, the questors of the Passions can make for good stories. Most questors believe that serving their patron Passion is the most important goal in life, and many would fight to the death to do so. Imagine the potential clash between questors of the same Passion pursuing similar goals but with different methods, or questors of different Passions coming into conflict over conflicting goals.

The Mad Passions and their questors present other adventure possibilities. The Mad Passions work to destroy the other Passions, giving no thought to the consequences. The result of a battle between the questors of a Mad Passion and the questors of any other Passion could be devastating. The questors of Mad Passions also work to further the dark and twisted goals of their patron, making them a threat to the health and well-being of innocents across Barsaive.

Denairastas

While the Theran Empire's influence has waned somewhat, the Denairastas clan of Iopos have been working hard to expand their influence. It is known that they have strong ties to the t'skrang House Ishkarat, as well as the Firescale moot in the Scol Mountains. Agents of the Denairastas can be found in many places across the province, working to bring other communities under their control, and undermine support for Throal and Thera. They can also serve as a rival for groups searching for lost treasures or lore, with the Iopans looking to secure the items or information for their ruling family.

Exploring Legends

Another important element of **Earthdawn** are the legends of the world before and after the Scourge. As the characters travel across Barsaive, they will learn of heroes, treasures, Horrors, and other monsters. These make excellent sources of adventures for your game. Share legends that will intrigue the characters and pique their curiosity, then use those legends to spark new adventures. For example, share the legend of the Crystal Spear, rumored to still lie within a kaer in the Badlands. The legend could serve as the focus of an adventure in which the heroes explore the Badlands and discover what lies within its borders.

Exploring Kaers and Citadels

Kaers and citadels dot the landscape of Barsaive. Most have been abandoned, though some remain inhabited, whether by people unwilling to believe that the Scourge has ended, or by those who have been corrupted by the Horrors. Kaers and citadels make great locations for an adventure, often to recover what was left behind. Kaers and citadels are also a frequent setting for an adventure or campaign with a Horror theme.

Mapping Barsaive

Barsaive changed significantly during the Scourge. Many towns, villages, and cities were completely destroyed and others relocated to escape the Horrors. Most of the natural terrain remains as it was, but even some geographic features have been dramatically changed.

As a result, large parts of Barsaive remain unexplored. As a change of pace from battle, some person or organization may hire the characters to map an area of Barsaive. This could lead the characters to uncover a forgotten city from before the Scourge, or simply afford them the satisfaction of a job well done.

Treasures

Much like adventures that focus on legends, you can base adventures on the magical treasures that player characters recover. The stories of magical items contain the history of the people of Barsaive, and that history is key to unlocking the item's power. The need to discover this information makes magic items a practical foundation for adventures and campaigns. Characters will often need to travel in order to discover the details of an item's past, and these travels can lead to any number of additional adventures.

Communities

In addition to kaers and citadels, numerous cities, towns, and villages dot the landscape and provide almost endless possibilities for adventures. Adventures set in or near communities can involve thievery, political intrigue, the Horror theme, and so on.

Several of the major cities of Barsaive are briefly described in this book and in the *Player's Guide*, but these only represent those known to the Kingdom of Throal. Many communities of various sizes wait to be rediscovered.

CREATING CAMPAIGNS

A campaign is a series of linked adventures featuring the same player characters, with the same players and gamemaster. A campaign offers several advantages, and the world of **Earthdawn** is designed to be played in this way. Over the course of a campaign, the characters grow more capable and powerful, and can become heroes of legend.

While many situations and elements in the **Earthdawn** setting work well for individual adventures, many of the underlying political and magical themes lend themselves well to being used as the background or foundation for a longer series of stories. For example, the Theran Empire's efforts to reclaim Barsaive for their own is a complex story, and one that really can't be explored with a single adventure. Another possibility is the investigation into the history of a legendary treasure—the potential of these items is better spread across a series of stories, allowing the characters to grow into the power of these treasures.

By the most common definition, a campaign may be nothing more than a series of unrelated adventures, only connected because the same characters appear in them.

However, you might find that it is more fun and rewarding to plot a more complex story that takes months of game time to resolve. For example, you might want the characters to track down and kill a powerful Horror with a legendary magical weapon. Rather than creating a single adventure where the characters find the weapon and kill the Horror, you can break the story up into several steps, each of which is a separate adventure, that taken together form a larger story arc—a campaign.

> The characters learn that a village was corrupted by a Horror, and set themselves the goal of tracking it down to destroy it. They start by seeking out the counsel of a sage, last known to be doing research at a retreat near the Wastes. The sage advises them that a prophecy states the Horror can only be defeated by Kestrel, a sword belonging to a noble family from the lost Kingdom of Landis. The group then travels to Landis and becomes involved in the struggles of different groups to rebuild the area. They find that the last known heir to the family traveled to seek the advice of the Great Dragon Mountainshadow before Landis fell to the Horrors, and his sword may be part of the dragon's hoard. Mountainshadow does indeed have the sword, but before he will give it to the characters wants an item in return—another magical treaure that must be retrieved from the vaults of Parlainth. Agents of the Theran Empire and Denairastas are also seeking this treasure, and so the group must retrieve it and return to Mountainshadow, then unlock the secrets of the magical sword in order to defeat the Horror.

Campaign Elements

An **Earthdawn** campaign can be as simple as running a series of adventures one after another, all featuring the same player characters. However, recurring player or gamemaster characters may not be enough to make an interesting connection between the stories in each adventure. Subplots, motivation, objectives, and opposition all serve as excellent techniques for creating an interesting, engaging campaign.

Subplots

You can use subplots to create continuity over several adventures to make a campaign. Secondary to the main story, subplots relate adventures to one another through a minor storyline, character, or series of events. Subplots can hint at upcoming adventures or refer to past events.

For example, in one adventure you might set the stage for an upcoming story by incorporating one or two scenes that relate to future events. When you run the new adventure, the characters (and players) will already be familiar with the present situation. Continuity through subplots helps maintain the illusion that the game world is a living place that changes over time.

In the earlier example, instead of simply setting the characters down in the village where the Horror lived, you might begin the campaign by enlisting the characters' help to rid a village of a Horror. In the first adventure, the characters travel to that village, staying at more than one inn on the way. At each resting place they hear a tale or a snippet of information about Mountainshadow. Later, when they discover that they must deal with the dragon to reach their goal, they already have some helpful information about this formidable character.

Subplots may also occur in a more haphazard fashion, though this use of the technique requires more complex planning. The gamemaster creates several apparently unrelated and unimportant events that the characters either witness or take part in during one or more adventures. The end of the adventure fails to reveal whether or not these events held any importance; the players may forget they even happened. In fact, these apparently unrelated and unimportant events form the basis of an adventure you plan to run in the near future.

When you get ready to run the adventure based on the subplot, review your notes on the events you used to hint at the new adventure and be sure to refer to those events during the adventure. The characters and players will have an 'aha!' moment as everything suddenly makes sense, and once again you present the game world as a real place where people and situations change and grow.

Objectives

Most campaigns benefit from a planned objective. This is certainly true of a campaign built by expanding on one storyline, as in the example above. However, a campaign objective could be more abstract in nature. For example, a legitimate campaign objective may be to explore Barsaive and free it from the remaining Horrors. As long as each adventure in a campaign has a clear objective, you may not need a focused campaign objective. But building an objective into your campaign can help focus the campaign and help you create a foundation on which to build adventures.

Motivation

Campaigns can also benefit from an overriding motivation. The campaign motivation is usually the overall reason that the characters continue their adventures. They may want to free the world from the Horrors, or spread the legends of the heroes of the world, or build their own legends. The motivation for a campaign may also be more practical, and share the motivation of a particular adventure. The characters may want to track down and rescue a person captured by slavers, seek knowledge of a specific race or place, or be determined to solve the puzzle of a family heirloom.

Tying your campaign motivation to the motivations of your player characters can help focus the momentum of your game. Players who feel that their personal goals are being achieved are likely to come back for more.

Opposition

Ongoing campaigns can also benefit from large-scale or powerful opposition, characterized by an enemy too large to handle in one or two adventures. The foe may continue to oppose the characters over a long period of time, such as the leader of a cult devoted to a Mad Passion, a powerful Horror that consistently evades destruction, or agents of the Denairastas clan.

A long-term campaign centered on a specific opponent can have the characters develop strong personal motives for defeating the antagonist, and adventures can look at opportunities to undermine the villain's power. For example, seeking out one or more of that opponent's Pattern Items, defeating or imprisoning the villain's supporters, or building a larger alliance to bring the enemy to justice.

Continuity and Change

Campaigns should be dynamic and change over time. Some changes are the direct result of the characters' actions; you must be prepared to incorporate these changes into your version of the setting, and alter your story to fit the new circumstances. For example, if an important gamemaster character dies unexpectedly in one adventure, he should not show up in a later adventure no matter how vital he is to your plans… unless you manipulated events so that the characters did not find a body.

Dead characters suddenly coming back to life is an extreme example of a lack of continuity, but one that is iconic—the afterlife having a 'revolving door' in comic books is but one example. While you should strive to be consistent, minor continuity gaffes are possible. With everything that can occur during a campaign, it is easy to lose track of details, and you shouldn't be too worried about it.

There are many ways you can show players that the world of **Earthdawn** is one that changes. A friendly gamemaster character may grow older, become sick, or experience a change of heart about some issue in the campaign. You can show changes in the setting by sharing news of places the characters have never been, or present rumors that change over time.

If the characters decide not to pursue a particular adventure for some reason, decide what the consequences of their inaction might be. Another group of heroes might have dealt with the problem, or perhaps the situation grew worse without the timely intervention of a group of adepts.

Another thing to keep in mind is that the player characters will change over time as they earn Legend Points and learn more and better abilities. Your campaign will need to adapt to this growth. As you and the players become more familiar with the rules, the obstacles faced by the group may need to become more complex to challenge their greater ability.

Just as player characters become more experienced and powerful over time, their rivals and enemies should as well. The Nethermancer the group defeated in an earlier adventure could return to gain vengeance on the adepts who defeated him, or perhaps he teams up with another gamemaster character to achieve one of his personal goals. Just as player characters can develop effective tactics and tricks using their abilities, other characters can as well, presenting varied challenges over the course of a campaign.

Another way your game may change over time will be the characters (and players) learning more about the world of **Earthdawn** and how that world works. As you create adventures that deal with the various elements of the game, the players and their characters will learn and remember more about the world, and that knowledge will show in the way they play the game. This particular change is a natural one, and should be welcome; part of the excitement of all roleplaying games is discovering and exploring a new world.

Greater familiarity with the rules of the game and the game world allows both players and gamemaster to use those rules and that knowledge more creatively and with greater complexity.

CAMPAIGN IDEAS

The following are some ideas for different campaigns that can be run in **Earthdawn**. Gamemasters are encouraged to expand or even mix and match these ideas to create a challenging and entertaining game.

Caravan Campaign

Merchants transport goods from one part of Barsaive to another, and hope to do so quickly and safely enough to ensure a profit. The hazards of the wild and the demand for new trade routes gives adventurers a ready-made source of employment, and an excuse to explore the wilderness.

The campaign can begin with a wealthy merchant or trading house hiring the characters to explore a new route, or provide protection for a caravan. In addition to the various hazards of travel in Barsaive, the characters could face opposition from rival trading companies, agents of Thera or Iopos, or the influence of Horrors or Mad Passions in towns and villages along the route.

Another possible avenue for this campaign to explore is for the characters to establish and build their own merchant company, perhaps as a way to finance their other expeditions, or to secure a future for themselves or their families. As their company gains power and influence, they could draw the attention of powerful figures looking to use the company and its influence to further their own ends.

Delving Campaign

Another way to use Barsaive's unique history to flavor campaigns is based on exploring ruined kaers and citadels. Adepts and explorers might investigate ruined kaers in search of information, artifacts and stories thought lost during the Scourge. Adepts can aid scholars and historians, such as those of the Great Library of Throal, in recovering these lost secrets. Ruined kaers might also hold valuable magical knowledge, such as spells created by long-dead magicians or Key Knowledges of various thread items and magical treasures that characters discovered in previous adventures.

When the setting includes extensive ruins like the Forgotten City of Parlainth, the group might develop or be part of a "delvers' guild"—explorers and adepts who work together to explore, map, and loot the local ruins. Such groups might harass adepts who are not members of their organizations. This situation already exists in Parlainth, where the Loyal Order of Delvers and the Association of Unaffiliated Explorers compete with one another to snatch the spoils of the Forgotten City's ruins. Similarly, characters may find themselves competing with other independent groups over the same ruins.

Exploration Campaign

The Scourge altered much of Barsaive beyond recognition, and many areas of the province remain unknown and unexplored. Many kingdoms and factions are interested in learning about these regions for the secrets and treasures they may contain or simply to expand their own knowledge. His Majesty's Exploratory Force is one example of an organization that employs adepts to explore Barsaive's distant wilds.

An exploration campaign gives characters the opportunity to travel to places no Namegiver has visited since before the Scourge. Characters are likely to discover lost kaers and ancient ruins, new trade routes and potential trade partners, isolated civilizations and other unfamiliar dangers. The Kingdom of Throal frequently uses their explorers as special agents. Other parties might do the same, thus providing a convenient way to involve player characters in Barsaive's political intrigues.

Kaer Campaign

This type of campaign typically begins inside a kaer that is still sealed from the outside world. The player characters are residents of the kaer, and are unsure whether the Scourge is over. For one reason or another, circumstances require the kaer to open, and the player characters are the ones chosen to go out and see if it is safe for the rest of the community to emerge.

The characters will know very little about the condition of the outside world—all they will have are the legends and tales from their kaer, information that is centuries out of date at best. As they emerge and explore the new world, the characters will be in for some surprises, including the dramatic changes wrought by the Scourge, the conflict between Throal and Thera, and experiencing things that had previously been bedtime stories. How would somebody who has spent their entire life in a cave, however large and comfortable, react to the vast expanse of a blue sky, or the fury of a thunderstorm?

The kaer campaign can provide a great way to introduce new players to the world of **Earthdawn**. There is no need to overwhelm your players with masses of setting background, and the players can experience the wonder of exploring a new world alongside their characters.

Military Campaign

In this type of campaign, the characters are part of a military organization, such as the Arm of Troal, a Theran legion, an ork scorcher band or cavalry, a riverboat crew on the Serpent River, even a drakkar or airship crew. The objective of such a campaign is usually straightforward and involves doing whatever the government, house, tribe, or trollmoot needs the characters to do. The characters could potentially serve as spies or scouts rather than in large-scale conflicts, or as a group suited for special operations.

Military campaigns focus on the warring factions of Barsaive, and usually involves a lot of combat. The gamemaster determines the assignments the characters have to follow, so he usually doesn't have to worry about motivation. The players, on the other hand, trade their freedom—but have the chance to become legendary war heroes, and may even advance to commanding their own troops.

Political Campaign

In contrast to the military campaign, political campaigns focus on diplomacy and negotiation rather than fighting. The characters can be involved in the day-to-day running of a particular government as court or council members, advisors, nobles, or influential merchants. When necessary they use their adept powers to negotiate with emissaries from other kingdoms or fight off threats to their land and population from within and from without.

The political campaign can take a number of forms. On the smaller end of the scale, the players form the ruling body of a small town or village. As the community grows, scorchers may threaten to become a constant threat requiring the characters to find allies for protection. On a larger scale, the characters might be involved in running a great city like Urupa or Travar, or advisors to the king in Throal.

The strength of a political campaign often relies on gamemaster characters, and frequently has more complex plots and motivations, with the player characters needing to navigate perils of intrigue and conflicting needs and agendas of the people in their communities.

Restoration Campaign

In many parts of Barsaive the Scourge left damage that has yet to be healed. Many different groups of Namegivers seek to restore wholeness to the land and its people. Questors of Jaspree and Garlen, the Seekers of the Heart, even groups like the Grim Legion fight to cleanse the taint of the Horros from the land forever. Corrupted places like the Badlands, the Wastes, and the Poison Forest are all good sites for the work of would-be restorers.

Characters in a restoration campaign may have the backing of a patron or a living legend cult, or may be working on their own. They will face powerful opponents—like Horrors or Namegivers who prefer the status quo. A restoration campaign that focuses on curing the corruption of Barsaive's people rather than the land might involve members of secret societies or cults, who might also make good patrons.

Player characters in such campaigns are likely to come into conflict with organizations like the Hand of Corruption, the Keys of Death, or the Elven Court of Blood Wood.

LOOT

During the course of an adventure, characters will discover many opportunities for gathering loot and often grab those opportunities with both hands. Loot may be money taken from fallen enemies, precious objects found in a creature's lair, pieces of a creature brought back as trophies, even magical or legendary items.

Earthdawn loot comes in two distinct varieties: **loot worth money** and **treasure**.

Loot Worth Money

Ancient gold coins, precious gems, artwork that can be sold, or silver pieces snatched from a dragon's hoard all qualify as loot worth money. Gold and silver coins can be gathered from dead opponents and used right away, while other treasures must be converted to cash. The gamemaster ultimately decides the amount of potential loot available in any given adventure. He must tailor the amount of money or other loot the characters find or acquire to the type of game he wants to run.

Unless your intention is to run a game where the player characters are just scraping by, it is recommended that you not be stingy with monetary rewards. If you look at the suggested costs for Circle advancement (*Player's Guide*, p. 454), the player characters will need to be bringing in enough money to cover those expenses, in addition to other training costs, living expenses, repairing or replacing damaged gear, and the like.

Another way for characters to acquire money in **Earthdawn** is for them to be hired for a job. A town, organization, or individual might offer payment in return for services. In addition, once they have some experience, they can potentially earn money training younger adepts. There is quite a bit of risk involved with the adventurer's life. If the financial reward isn't there, why would an adept keep doing it?

A somewhat less orthodox way of earning money from adventuring is to sell equipment that belonged to defeated opponents. This can cause problems for the unwary; local authorities are not likely to look kindly on those who leave town for a couple days and come back loaded down with second-hand equipment. Of course, some places in Barsaive—most notably the so-called City of Thieves, Kratas—look upon the resale of 'gently used' equipment as an important part of the local economy.

Treasure

In addition to monetary rewards, adventurers in **Earthdawn** can find treasures that have greater value than their potential worth in gold or silver. This can include journals or histories recovered from a forgotten kaer, magical treasure, even bits and pieces of powerful or dangerous creatures the adept has defeated.

Magical treasure includes thread items, as well as more common magical items that might come in handy in the course of an adventurer's career. The value of a thread item comes from the power it can grant. Stories abound of heroes slaying Horrors with magical weapons, or protected by armor of legendary strength. An adept who takes the time to learn about a thread item's history, and invest the energy necessary to bond it to his pattern will be able to face greater challenges.

It is also common for heroes in stories to take a trophy as proof they have defeated a powerful creature. Sometimes these bits and pieces can serve as useful materials for enchanters and alchemists, and other times they serve simply as a measure of an adventurer's prowess. Some of the opponents included in the **Creatures** chapter, p. 245, will have parts that can be harvested for various purposes.

Because of the way thread items, trophies from fallen enemies, and similar sorts of non-monetary treasure can enhance the reputation of an adept, this category of loot awards Legend Points to characters that claim them (see **Gathering Magical Treasure**, p. 122)

AWARDING LEGEND POINTS

The characters in a role-playing campaign are not static. They learn, gain experience, power, and knowledge. In the **Earthdawn** game this development is done through the use of Legend Points. Players spend Legend Points to increase their character's Attribute values, talent and skill ranks, permanent magical threads, and so on.

The gamemaster awards Legend Points at the end of each game session based on four elements: achieving goals, conflicts and obstacles, acquiring treasure, and individual deeds and roleplaying. The number of Legend Points earned for each category is based on how well the characters fulfill its requirements.

The Legend Points awarded for a particular category are referred to as a Legend Award.

Assigning Legend Awards

The Legend Award Table provides guidelines for determining how many Legend Points should be given for each of the four categories. Based on the character's circle, the award for each category should fall within the range given in the Legend Award column. For example, a Second Circle character should receive from 100 to 300 Legend Points for each Legend Award. The last column gives the range of total Legend Points characters could earn for all four categories in a single session.

Completing Goals

Most adventures have an overall objective, but only the most basic goals can be realized in a single game session. More frequently, there will be intermediate steps the group must complete before the overall story is resolved.

When developing an adventure for the group, the gamemaster should look at the events and see if there are any minor objectives that must be completed before the

Legend Award Table

Circle	Legend Award	Total Legend Per Session
1	25-75 (50)	100-300 (200)
2	100-300 (200)	400-1,200 (800)
3	200-500 (350)	800-2,000 (1,400)
4	250-700 (475)	1,400-3,000 (2,200)
5	500-1,500 (1,000)	2,000-6,000 (4,000)
6	900-2,500 (1,700)	3,600-10,000 (6,800)
7	1,500-5,000 (3,250)	6,000-20,000 (13,000)
8	2,500-7,000 (4,750)	10,000-28,000 (19,000)
9	5,000-14,500 (9,750)	20,000-58,000 (39,000)
10	8,500-26,000 (17,250)	34,000-104,000 (69,000)
11	15,500-46,500 (31,000)	62,000-186,000 (124,000)
12	23,000-69,000 (46,000)	92,000-276,000 (184,000)
13	42,500-127,500 (85,000)	170,000-510,000 (340,000)
14	77,500-232,500 (155,000)	310,000-930,000 (620,000)
15	120,000-360,000 (240,000)	480,000-1,440,000 (960,000)

overall problem in the adventure can be resolved. These goals can take one or more scenes to resolve, and are frequently achieved at or near the end of the game session. They are sometimes called *session goals*.

Session goals can be simple objectives, for example:

- Reach Travar
- Contact the guild representative in Jerris
- Discover the ruin in the Servos Jungle
- Uncover the identity of an assassin

When characters achieve a goal, they earn a Legend Award. Simple goals, or goals that are achieved quickly, should get an award on the lower end of the suggested range, while more difficult goals should offer higher awards.

Achieving an adventure goal also earns a Legend Award. As these represent major milestones in the overall campaign, achieving an adventure goal should earn a large Legend Award, as much as double the normal award for achieving a goal.

EARTHDAWN

Conflicts and Obstacles

Conflicts are what hinder the characters on the path to achieving their goals. This often involves defeating creatures or other opponents, but also involves other obstacles that hinder or block their progress. Each game session should involve one or more conflicts or obstacles for the characters to encounter while they pursue their goal, whether that involves capturing the thief that stole a magician's grimoire, finding their way through a corridor full of traps, or navigating the politics of a guild rivalry to learn important information.

The Legend Award for defeating foes, solving puzzles, or otherwise overcoming obstacles should be based on how many, and how difficult the challenges were. The more numerous and difficult the challenges, the higher the award should be.

While creatures and other Namegivers often present an obstacle to overcome, defeating the challenge they present doesn't always mean killing them in cold blood. Stealth, persuasion, and other methods that allow the characters to achieve success without bloodshed still overcome the obstacle, and should receive a Legend Award. Random butchery against creatures or gamemaster characters that were never intended as opponents should not be rewarded.

Many of the creatures and opponents included in this book and in other **Earthdawn** products include a measure of how much of a challenge they are likely to present, and can help you select appropriate opponents for the characters to face in the course of their adventures.

Gathering Magical Treasure

A common motivation for explorers to go diving into kaers is the potential for wealth. Even when money isn't the main motivation, adepts often find themselves carrying bags of loot on the way home. There are some treasures, however, whose value isn't measured in gold or silver, but in the tale that accompanies them or the fame it might bring.

People expect heroes to acquire unusual items during the course of their travels: bits of nasty monsters, items recovered from forgotten ruins, magical talismans, or gems snatched from a dragon's hoard. These rare and special treasures award Legend Points, as they often demonstrate proof of the character's deeds and enhance their reputation in some way.

An adventure should generally provide some treasures of this sort. Silver and gold looted from the bodies of a bandit gang wouldn't earn this award, but perhaps their leader had a distinctive cloak, or a fancy blade he was known for. The item would serve as evidence of the group's achievement, and would have a story to go along with it.

Unlike the Legend Awards for goals and challenges, this award is generally only given per adventure, rather than per session. Qualifying items should generally be tied to the resolution of the adventure's main plot, whether a trophy taken from a defeated foe, magical items recovered from the base of a Horror cult, or unusual treasures recovered from a kaer's vault. If an interesting story can be told about the item, or it somehow represents the adventure in a symbolic or thematic way, it is a good candidate for consideration under this award.

Individual Deeds and Roleplaying

Some players really dive into the role of their characters, going above and beyond to entertain the rest of the group. Others have a knack for finding creative ways to solve problems. Sometimes a player comes up with the right line at the right time, or performs a feat of derring-do. These moments can make a game extraordinary, creating stories that will be remembered for years.

To reward and encourage this sort of behavior, the gamemaster should award Legend Points. Unlike the other categories, which are shared among all members of the group, awards for deeds and roleplaying are given to individuals. The amount of the award and the frequency they are given out can vary. As a general guideline, giving out awards for deeds and roleplaying should be based on the way the group normally approaches the game, as well as the degree of involvement and immersion the individual players display.

Gamemasters may also give characters this award when a player remains true to their character's personality traits, even—or especially—if this puts the character at risk. Staying in character only when it is safe misses part of the point of roleplaying.

Customizing Legend Awards

As with many of the other aspects of the **Earthdawn** game, these are guidelines and suggestions, and you should feel free to modify or adapt them as you see fit. Adjust the awards to suit your play style; you may want to award more points for achieving goals, and fewer for fighting enemies, or perhaps you want to be more generous with the individual roleplaying awards.

In general, a character should earn between 2 and 5 Legend Awards per session. Earning a full five awards should not be a frequent occurrence—it should only happen when the group achieves an adventure goal, and the player does especially well in contributing to the group's success and fun.

The numbers presented in the Legend Award Table were designed to provide a reasonable scale for character development. If your group doesn't play very frequently, you may want to award more Legend Points so that it doesn't feel like progress is stalling. On the other hand, if the group meets more frequently, giving smaller awards may keep the power of the game from getting out of control, and make advancement feel more special.

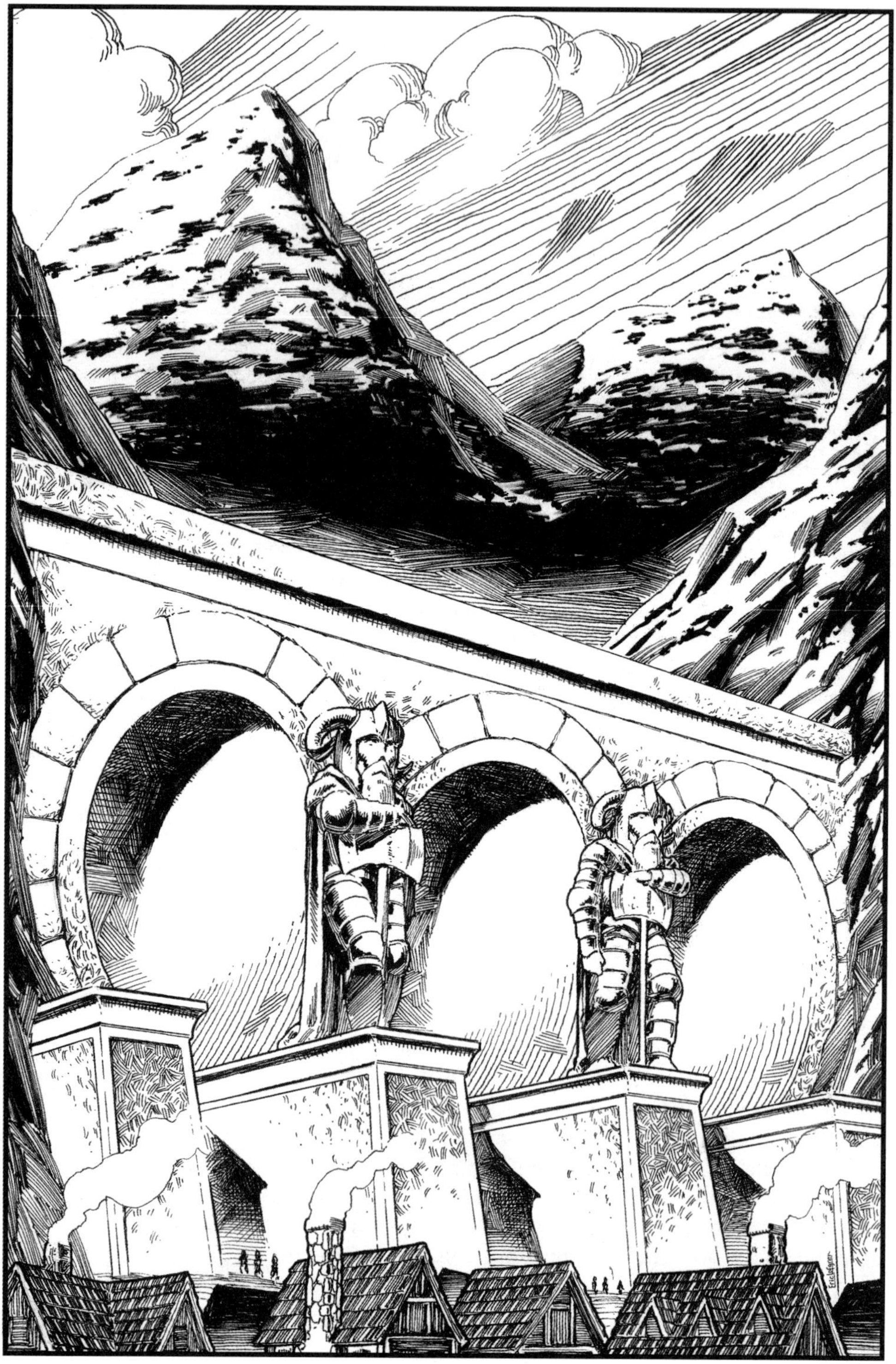

EXPLORATION AND TRAVEL

I will never forget the first time I saw the gates of Throal. A mile-wide gaping maw in the side of a mountain, looming over the homes and hovels of Bartertown like a merchant picking diamonds out of pile of gravel.
•Magistrate Clystone•

The Scourge may be over, but the lands of Barsaive are vast and contain many unexplored and wild places. Travel between cities and towns can be dangerous and time consuming. Adepts often find themselves needing to wander off the primary trails and paths to uncover lost ruins or seek out the lairs of Horrors and other dangerous creatures.

This chapter includes rules and information on travel and exploration, along with guidelines for hazards and complications that may come into play when characters venture into the wild and untamed corners of the world.

TRAVELING

Player characters in **Earthdawn** will spend many days traveling from place to place. Population centers are spread out, often requiring long journeys simply to get from one place to the next. Most travel is overland, either on foot or mounted. Travel by riverboat is possible in some places, and for those who can afford it (or have suitable need) airships can greatly reduce travel time.

Travel time is usually measured in days. Most maps made in Barsaive (and in most published **Earthdawn** products) contain scales for determining distance, and typical travel rates are provided in the Travel Rate Table. You can determine how long a trip will take by dividing the distance by the rate. For example, a 150 mile journey would take about six days if traveling on foot, but only a little over three days if mounted.

The information provided in the Travel Rate Table assumes the characters travel for eight hours a day, with stops to rest and eat. In addition, even characters that are traveling well-known routes should check their location; the wilds of Barsaive do not have paved roads and divided highways. Characters can push themselves and travel for more than eight hours a day, but there are consequences (see **Fatigue and Injury**, p.192), especially for those with mounts or beasts of burden. A careless traveler can push a mount until it drops from exhaustion, leaving them stranded. Some adepts—Cavalrymen in particular—have magic that can help mitigate the effects of exhaustion, but they don't replace the need for appropriate rest.

In contrast to most overland travel, riverboats and airships can travel for more than the standard eight hours by having a larger crew that takes shifts. Naturally these modes of transportation cost more to pay the additional crew members required for shift work, and an airship or riverboat that is short-handed will have their travel times suffer. Assuming a sufficient crew, riverboats and airships can travel almost indefinitely, only stopping to repair, take on supplies, or make deliveries.

Overland Travel

Most travel in Barsaive is over land, either on foot or mounted. Travelers on foot can cover roughly 25 miles per day, assuming eight hours travel, with occasional rest and food breaks. The rough terrain throughout most of Barsaive precludes any faster travel, and terrain can also play a factor; heavy forest or jungle, broken, or mountainous terrain can cut travel time to half or a third of normal distances.

Mounted characters can cover about 45 miles per day, again assuming eight hours travel with appropriate breaks. Terrain can potentially have more of an effect on the distance a character can travel, depending on the mount involved and the conditions—a mount well-suited to the terrain can help mitigate the effects.

Characters occasionally travel with a merchant or trader caravan, whether as hired guards or fellow travelers (there is safety in numbers, after all). Since most caravans and merchants are loaded down with heavy loads, they do not travel as far as a more lightly encumbered group would be. Merchant caravans generally cover about 30 miles per day when mounted, or 20 miles per day on foot.

Travel Rate Table

Method of Travel	Travel Rate
Airship	300 miles*
Caravan (foot)	20 miles
Caravan (mounted)	30 miles
Namegiver (foot)	25 miles
Namegiver (mounted)	45 miles
Riverboat	100 miles*

* 16 hours of travel instead of 8

Safe Areas

Even more than a hundred years after the end of the Scourge, much of Barsaive remains uncharted wilderness, and only the areas right around major cities and established trading routes are considered safe. Straying off the beaten path can prove hazardous to travelers. Multiple small towns and villages will surround the area around major cities within a 15-20 mile radius, and supply the city with food and other resources, often in exchange for protection or other benefits (like trade agreements). This proximity makes travel between the community and the city fairly easy, and there will likely be well-traveled roads with patrols. Even then, it is possible for a forgotten kaer or ruined settlement to lurk nearby, providing haven to bandits, cultists, or worse.

The major trade routes in Barsaive connect major cities and larger settlements on the Serpent River. Most caravans employ seasoned guards (adepts or otherwise), because while the major routes are considered safe, the potential dangers increase the farther you travel from a major city. Nearly all of the major trade routes cross stretches of wilderness, and it isn't unusual for a route to shift as reports filter back about dangerous creatures or other hazards encountered along the way.

If anything, the dangers of travel in Barsaive have increased in the wake of the Second Theran War. Before the War, the Kingdom of Throal supported patrols along the major trade routes to make sure they were safe for merchants and travelers, but also to gain intelligence about what the Therans might have been up to. The cost of the War—especially in manpower—has meant that patrols have been pulled closer to home, and more concern has been given to the protection of Throalic interests over those of Barsaive as a whole.

Wilderness

The life of an adventurer will often take them to places away from the major cities and well-traveled routes. Whether pursuing an enemy agent, seeking a forgotten kaer, or tracking down a Horror in its lair, the heroes of Barsaive must cross wide plains, scale mountains, or navigate dense forest and jungle. In the course of these travels, they need to find sufficient water, food, and shelter.

Most of the time a group of adventurers will carry rations and water with them, but sometimes mishap or poor planning requires them to live off the land for a time before they get back to civilization. The Wilderness Survival talent or skill can allow characters to find food, water, and shelter while in the wilderness.

Countless villages and small settlements dot the wilderness of Barsaive. Most of these communities survive by farming, and have little contact with the world outside of their immediate surroundings. They can be a valuable source of information about the local area, but many of them have little trust for outsiders, and more than a few tales are known that involve such places harboring cultists or followers of a Mad Passion, vindictive spirit, or even a Horror.

Encounters While Traveling

Adventurers may have a variety of encounters during their travels. In addition to the possibility of other travelers, they may notice or encounter wild animals, natural hazards like a river that needs to be forded, a steep hill that could suffer a rockslide, even ruined or abandoned settlements that could shelter a friendly hermit or dangerous creature.

The gamemaster can liven up a road trip by including encounters like these. Ask the characters to make Perception tests to see if they notice things of interest, using the guidelines found under **Perception Tests**, p. 162. Several Disciplines—notably Scouts and Archers—have talents or abilities that enhance their perception and ability to notice things that are unusual or otherwise out of place.

Encounters don't always have to involve danger to the travelers. Perhaps the group finds an uninhabited ruin to take shelter for the night, or they watch from a distance as a pack of wolves takes down an elk or other large herbivore. They might meet a group of Questors in search of a site dedicated to their patron Passion.

When adding encounters to your game sessions, try and think about where the encounter is taking place, and what role it serves. In addition to dangers of life and limb, encounters can help flesh out the world, provide hints to a current problem the characters are facing, offer future adventure hooks or tease upcoming events that might prove useful later on, or even just shake things up from time to time.

Because of the nearly limitless variety of encounters that are possible in the lands of Barsaive, there is no one way to resolve them. Some encounters can be resolved with diplomacy and words, others might require the characters to make tests to overcome an obstacle, while others might involve combat. The gamemaster's job is to facilitate, describing events and the results of the tests and choices made, based on the circumstances and the people involved.

Avoiding Attention

If, when traveling through the wilderness, a group of characters is not making any special efforts to avoid notice, the Difficulty Number for patrols, creatures, or other characters to notice them is the lowest Dexterity Step of all characters in the group, modified for visibility and other factors.

When approaching areas prone to conflict, known for being unfriendly to outsiders, or for any number of other reasons, travelers may wish to avoid notice. Moving through an area unobtrusively will reduce the chance the group will draw unwanted attention, at the expense of taking more time. Travel time is doubled, but the Difficulty Number for spotting the group increases to the highest Dexterity Step in the group (with appropriate modifiers).

Despite the extra time involved, player characters may well find this benefit desirable. The gamemaster should consider such factors when determining if anyone spots the adventurers.

Social Interaction

Player characters will meet all sorts of other Namegivers during their travels, from fellow travelers and local villagers to bandits and raiders. While combat sometimes results from these meetings, fighting isn't the only way for itinerant heroes to deal with other people.

Negotiation, intrigue, political maneuvering, and other forms of social interaction can provide a different sort of challenge. While gamemasters can use these as the basis of adventures or campaigns in civilized settings like the Kingdom of Throal, visitors will need to navigate the social waters of small towns and villages in the hinterlands.

The rules for social interaction provided later in this chapter can offer useful guidelines for encounters with gamemaster characters on the road. While not intended as a replacement for good roleplaying, they can help guide how different gamemaster characters might react to player character actions, as well as providing a framework for resolving social conflicts between player and gamemaster characters.

Greeting Rituals

While the Scourge is a distant memory for most of Barsaive, there are many who remain wary of lingering Horrors. Isolated villages are more likely to be cautious of strangers and travelers, and are more likely to require that visitors use their Artisan skills to demonstrate they are free of Horror taint.

While the efficacy of these tests may be debated, adventurers and other travelers in the hinterlands are well-advised to be ready to perform these rituals for potential hosts. There are many different ways these rituals can be performed, and some communities will have a special building on the outskirts where the ritual takes place. It is not unusual for the village leader to perform a test as well, showing the community is likewise free from taint.

A character using an Artisan test as part of a greeting ritual makes the test against a Difficulty Number of 5, as a method of **Making an Impression** (p.144). Success will improve the attitude of those witnessing the test by one degree, while a failure lowers their attitude, and may result in people refusing the character entry in to the village, believing the character to be Horror-touched.

Larger communities, especially those that see more trade and travel from other parts of Barsaive, are less likely to require an elaborate ritual, but it is not unheard of for some places to require a basic display in front of an authority of some kind.

River Travel

The Serpent River and its tributaries are a massive network of waterways that connects distant parts of Barsaive. If travelers need to cover a long distance, it is common to book passage by riverboat to a port near the destination. This can save time, and reduce exposure to some of the dangers normally associated with travel in the wilderness.

Passage on a t'skrang riverboat costs an average of 5 silver pieces per traveler per day, though rates can vary, with captains haggling to set the final price. Most riverboats require payment in advance, though some may allow partial payment with the balance due on arrival. Passage for mounts can be negotiated as well, for an added cost. For typical mounts, this also runs an average of 5 silver per mount per day, but this can vary even more than normal passenger prices, depending on the size of the mount in question and how much cargo space might need to be given up to accommodate the animal.

Player characters who lack the funds might be able to work off part of the price of their passage, negotiated with the captain and based on their skills. An inexperienced sailor might be able to cover half their costs in this way, while more experienced sailors can command higher fees.

T'skrang riverboats are the primary mode of travel on the Serpent River system, and typically cover about 100 miles per day, stopping occasionally to pick up and drop off passengers and cargo. Passage might also be available on cargo barges run by dwarf trading houses or similar interests, but they are typically slower—covering 40 to 60 miles a day on average—and less willing to take on passengers.

Pirates and privateers are the most common hazard on the Serpent River system, especially in areas more isolated from the larger ports of the t'skrang aropagoi. Characters helping fight off these dangers will often find part of their passage refunded by a grateful captain.

Airship Travel

While airships can be found in Barsaive, it is the least common method of travel. Several dozen airships exist in the province, but most of them are either military craft, who rarely take on paying passengers, or ships that belong to the crystal raider clans of the Twilight Peaks. Merchant airships exist, but the vessels are expensive, owned by the largest and wealthiest trading companies.

Despite the difficulties of arranging passage on an airship, there is no faster way to rapidly cross large distances in Barsaive. An airship typically covers about 300 miles per day of travel, turning an overland journey of weeks into a matter of days, with the added benefit of avoiding difficult terrain.

Given the value of an airship, most captains are reluctant to have large groups of armed strangers on board their vessels. Fares typically start at 20 silver pieces per person per day, and go up from there. Most airships are not designed for passenger comfort, and so cramped quarters are common, with only the barest of amenities available. In addition, cargo space is at a premium, and so travelers looking to bring more than basic luggage will find themselves paying for it; trunks or other large pieces of luggage might cost an extra 10 silver pieces or more to bring along. Mounts are an especially expensive prospect, with animals costing 50 silver pieces per day or more, with the possibility that a captain will refuse to carry mounts the size of a thundra beast.

Some captains are wiling to take on experienced Air Sailors or Sky Raiders as crew for a voyage, though the two Disciplines typically do not get along. Likewise, skilled navigators might find a way to work off part of their fare. Other adepts and adventurers are typically only able to work off passage on Crystal Raider vessels, and then usually only by taking part in raids. Travelers are advised to be very careful when negotiating with captains of raiding vessels.

Outside of extraordinary circumstances, merchant vessels will not go out of their way to drop off passengers. Most captains prefer to deliver passengers to their planned destination, though they may be persuaded to drop off passengers at a location along their planned route.

The most common hazard of traveling by airship is an encounter with crystal raiders. These troll clans tend to stay near their homes in the Twilight Peaks, but their raids can lead them to locations 500 miles away or more. The withdrawal of the Theran Empire from Triumph and Vivane means their presence has diminished, but slaver airships can still occasionally be encountered in south western Barsaive. Other threats include encounters with storm or tempest spirits, wyverns and other territorial dragon kin, or even flying Horrors.

Underground Travel

Whether exploring a ruined kaer, spelunking in search of True Earth, or taking shelter in a convenient cave during a storm, most player characters will find themselves underground at least once in their life. Underground travel offers a different slate of problems and experiences for adventurers to deal with.

Movement underground is usually slower than movement on the surface. Travel is almost always on foot; the ceilings in most tunnels and caves are too low for a mounted character to pass comfortably, and most mounts are uncomfortable with the darkness and close quarters found in natural caves. Some kaers will have some areas that allow mounted travel, but it isn't something explorers can rely on.

Navigation underground can also pose a problem, as there are fewer options for getting from one place to another. Outside of powerful magic that allows them to move significant amounts of stone and earth, characters must follow existing tunnels and paths. These naturally occurring roads seldom take the most direct route. Under the best conditions characters might be able to travel as much as half to three-quarters of their surface movement rate—about 10 to 15 miles of travel per day.

The environment can prove to be one of the more annoying obstacles characters might encounter. Tunnels are frequently narrow, with loose stone and dirt. Characters who aren't careful can easy trip and fall. Tunnels might also slope up or down, providing an additional level of difficulty. A gamemaster might require Dexterity tests to pass these kinds of obstacles, with failure resulting in a minor injury (see p. 193), or damage if the slope is steep enough.

EXPLORING KAERS AND CITADELS

Since the Scourge, most kaers have opened. Their residents settled nearby towns and villages, and may use the empty kaer for storage or shelter from severe weather and other dangers. Likewise, many citadels have dismantled or removed their magical protections and have returned to use as fortresses and strongholds. As discussed above, adventurers should be aware that the inhabitants of these places are likely to distrust or fear them simply for being strangers, especially in the more isolated hinterlands of Barsaive. While the Scourge is becoming a fading memory, the habits and traditions of generations of fear are hard to shake off.

Even so long after the Scourge, some kaers and citadels remain sealed. Their inhabitants might be dead, victim to disaster, plague, or Horror. Others might still have living Namegivers, either unaware the Scourge has ended, or collapsed into a more primitive state of raw survival, like the bands of cave trolls that can be found in many mountainous areas.

It is these still sealed kaers that most often draw adventurers. Tales of forgotten treasure are as common as flowers in the field, and more than one youth has been drawn to the life of an adept with thoughts of discovering a lost cache of wealth. Some loosely affiliated guilds of adventurers have formed with a more altruistic goal, seeking to find kaers with living residents and helping them reclaim a life on the surface. Even if there aren't piles of gold and silver to be found, the history and knowledge that can be recovered from these places can be a treasure greater than mere coin.

Unfortunately, the discovery and exploration of forgotten kaers is not without its dangers. Horrors are physically and magically powerful, and so the traps and wards designed to deter and destroy them will pose a challenge to even the most experienced kaer delvers. If the defenses were breached, the ruined citadel may have become a lair for Horrors or other dangerous creatures. Even less exotic creatures like stingers, brithan, or shadowmants would defend their home from intruders.

If adventurers discover a kaer with its seals and wards intact, just figuring out how to get inside can be a challenge. The wards and rituals used to seal most kaers involved powerful and unique spells—often Twelfth Circle or higher—and dispelling them can be very difficult. A magician must typically spend some time studying the wards with their Patterncraft talents, often supplemented with astral study, to have a chance of deactivating the defenses. There will often be multiple layers of wards, so penetrating a sealed kaer can be a time consuming process.

Most kaers and citadels also had multiple layers of physical traps to injure or kill Horrors or other creatures that managed to get past the magical protections. Large blades, collapsing tunnels, pits, and more are commonly encountered, and have resulted in injury or death for many explorers. In some cases, these traps might have succumbed to the passage of time, or been triggered by prior visitors, whether wild animal, Namegiver, or Horror. See **Traps**, p. 179, for more information on how traps are handled in the **Earthdawn** game.

One advantage to exploring kaers, in relation to exploring natural cave systems, is that kaers were designed to be a place for Namegivers to live for an extended period of time. Once past the wards and traps, much of a kaer's passages and chambers will be comfortable for most Namegivers. There may still be danger from cave-ins, or the collapse of a decrepit building, but coming across an impassable chasm or similar obstacle is much less common.

Kaer Design

There isn't any one way for a kaer to be designed. The circumstances of its construction and the people who planned to live there can have a significant influence on its layout and construction. For example, a kaer that was primarily for windlings is likely to take more advantage of vertical space, and be a lot more claustrophobic for larger Namegivers. A kaer built as an expansion of an existing mine will have a different plan than one built from scratch. The shelter intended for a village of a couple hundred Namegivers will differ from one made for a town of a couple thousand.

When designing a kaer for an adventure, there are some things to remember. Kaers and citadels were intended to be a self-sufficient home for hundreds, if not thousands, of Namegivers over the course of centuries. The environment of the kaer can be used to help tell the story. Living things need food and water to survive. While magic can help with this, you still need to consider how the residents of a kaer lived and survived in their shelters.

What did they eat? There would probably be a significant space in the kaer devoted to growing crops. Elementalist magic would be invaluable—allowing plants to grow away from the sun. Meat would be supplied by animals the residents brought into the kaer with them, but depending on the kaer, meat might have been an infrequent treat, as livestock would be expected to survive the centuries underground along with their Namegiver keepers, and animals need to be fed as well. Problems with food supply doomed many kaers, subjecting their residents to starvation or worse.

Water is an even more important consideration. Many kaers were built around a natural spring, but a source of water that extends outside the kaer's wards is a path that Horrors could exploit. Some kaers were able to work out an agreement with—or bind—a water elemental. Water sources were likely to be well guarded, and might include ritual spells or magic items that purify the water. A tainted water supply could wipe out a kaer faster than a problem with food.

Waste disposal is another issue that would need to be addressed. In most cases, manure and similar biological waste would be used to fertilize the plants that were the kaer's main food supply. When people died, many kaers would have some kind of ritual destruction of the corpse to protect against the danger of the dead being animated by a Horror.

Population control is another issue that would need to be considered. During the construction of the kaer, was population growth taken into account? This goes for livestock and other animals as well as Namegivers. What did the residents do when the kaer became crowded? Was it possible for them to excavate new living chambers? How did that affect the integrity of the kaer's wards? Did the kaer practice some sort of population control through restricting the number of children a family could have? How were these practices enforced? What sort of balance could be found between the need for children to ensure the survival of the kaer, and keeping the population from getting out of control and outstripping the available resources?

What about social and legal aspects? What sort of justice system would be in place to handle disputes, or deal with individuals who were causing trouble? Given the general need for everybody to chip in to ensure survival, perhaps punishment would involve assigning people to less desirable jobs rather than imprisonment (where they would drain resources without contributing anything). What about repeat offenders? Would execution be an acceptable punishment? What about some sort of banishment—condemning the convicted to whatever fate awaited them outside the kaer's protection?

Ultimately, the success or failure of a kaer would depend on available resources, and how they prepared and managed those resources. While many failed kaers were the work of the Horrors, just as many—if not more—were doomed as a result of poor planning or unforeseen circumstance.

COMPLICATIONS FOR TRAVEL AND EXPLORATION

Any traveler—merchant or adventurer—who ventures outside the relative safety of the larger towns and cities of Barsaive will need to deal with the risks involved, especially if traveling overland. While most can anticipate the danger posed by bandits, creatures, or even Horrors, it is often the impersonal aspects of nature that will catch explorers off guard. Characters in **Earthdawn** will often need their wits and skills simply to survive the wilds of Barsaive.

Survival

Whether mounted or on foot, traveling from place to place takes time, and adventurers should bring sufficient food and water, or make plans on how they can acquire these basic necessities during their journeys. Adepts will sometimes have the luxury of planning an expedition, but circumstances might require them to set out in a hurry.

The Wilderness Survival talent (*Player's Guide*, p. 179) covers a character's ability to survive in the wild. Some areas are difficult to survive, and even more experienced explorers are hesitant to venture into them without preparation. The system is intentionally abstract, allowing the larger picture of survival to be resolved with a few dice rolls. The consequences of failure, however, could be significant.

The degree to which the gamemaster invokes the need for characters to live off the land will depend on the theme and focus of the campaign. Even If the minutia of foraging for food and water don't appeal to you, long overland travel is not an easy thing. People who treat nature casually are the ones most likely to fall victim to its dangers. Even the modern world has stories of people who went up against nature and lost.

Weather

In addition to food and water, shelter from the elements—especially bad weather—is an important part of survival in the wilderness. While the overall climate in Barsaive is temperate, it can still get cold at night and at higher altitudes. Rainstorms and other severe weather events can also pose a challenge.

Frequently, weather can be used as a way of setting tone and mood, or to introduce complications to the story. Approaching a ruined citadel has a very different feel on a clear, warm day than under cold, foggy conditions where visibility is limited and details are scarce. A thunder storm might spook horses, or cause flash floods that could force travelers to take shelter.

In extreme cases, characters encountering weather they aren't prepared for could be devastated. Getting soaked in a downpour could result in hypothermia. Mountain expeditions will need to be prepared for the cold and altitude. Frostbite could cause the loss of fingers, toes, or other exposed extremities.

If you want weather to have more of a mechanical impact on characters in your game, some suggestions can be found under **Fatigue and Injury**, p. 192.

Visibility

When crossing the plains on a clear, sunny day, visibility is rarely a concern—characters will usually be able to see hazards in plenty of time to prepare for them. But how far can they see at night? What about the darkness of a cave or abandoned kaer, or during a torrential downpour?

On a clear day a character might be able to see the Throal Mountains from over a hundred miles away, simply by virtue of their size, but details would be very hard to make out at that distance. Generally speaking, characters must be closer to what they are looking at in order to discern any helpful details.

In clear weather during normal daylight hours, a person or object must be within about 750 yards in order to be seen. Beyond that, details blur and lose distinction. Within medium range—about 200 yards—a character can determine the identity of a person he knows, or enough detail to determine the race or type of creature being observed. More specific details generally require the target to be within close range—20 to 30 yards of the character. Ranges in this case refer to visibility, and do not have any connection to the ranges of missile weapons described in the *Player's Guide*.

Prevailing conditions like weather and darkness can influence effective visibility. The **Visibility Table** provides suggestions for determining effective visibility under different conditions.

When using the guidelines provided by the Visibility Table, use the lowest applicable values. Characters in heavy fog will not see any farther at night than they would during the day. The table also suggests ranges for the natural darkness of night, which will have the moon or starts providing some kind of illumination. Characters within a cave or kaer must cope with more complete darkness. Without a light source, a character in these circumstances will be subject to the penalties for darkness described under **Situation Modifiers** in the *Player's Guide*, p. 386.

Visibility Table

Condition	Short	Medium	Long
Daylight	25	200	750
Dawn/Dusk	15	125	500
Light Fog	10	75	250
Heavy Fog	2	5	10
Light Rain	15	175	350
Heavy Rain	10	50	100
Night, full moon	5	60	200
Moonless night	5	15	30

Typical light sources include campfires, torches, and lanterns. The Light Source Table suggests the effective range of light provided by different sources. The gamemaster can extrapolate the effect of other light sources based on these examples.

EARTHDAWN

The range provided indicates the effective visibility where no darkness penalty applies. Characters can see up to twice the distance indicated on the table, but suffer the penalty for partial darkness (*Player's Guide*, p. 387) unless they possess Low-Light vision or a similar ability.

Light Source Table

Source	Radius
Candle	2 yards
Torch	5 yards
Campfire	10 yards
Lantern	10 yards
Light Quartz	5 yards

Getting Lost

The province of Barsaive has large areas that are sparsely populated. Outside of major cities and trade routes the land is largely uncharted. It can be difficult for people familiar with today's world of satellite imagery and GPS to really get a sense of what this means. Rather than being an in-depth survey of a particular place, maps are more commonly used to help travelers get from one place to another, typically by providing helpful landmarks. The larger the area covered by the map, the less detail it is likely to have.

While celestial navigation is known and practiced in Barsaive, it isn't as precise as people might like, especially when it requires accurate charts to be truly useful. There also hasn't been a comprehensive geographic survey of the province, just as there hasn't been a real census. There have been efforts to try and chart the province in more detail, but such expeditions are time consuming, and therefore expensive. Those who might try to rely on older maps can run into trouble because of the changes wrought by the Scourge.

All of these factors mean that characters who stray off the beaten path run the risk of getting lost. Even when traveling a relatively well-known route, circumstances could lead travelers astray. A stretch of bad weather could affect the accuracy of navigational readings, a river could have changed course, or the trail could lead through an area recently claimed by hostile ork scorchers, requiring a detour.

While getting lost does not usually pose a threat on its own, it can complicate an already difficult overland journey. It could lead travelers into an area inhabited by dangerous creatures, whether wild animals, Horrors, or hostile spirits. Supplies could run short, putting the expedition at risk of starvation or worse. And perhaps even more significantly, the travelers might truly be on their own. Away from major trade routes, they might go for days without encountering other Namegivers, and those they might encounter are less apt to be friendly.

All of this said, the gamemaster should use getting lost sparingly. While playing out the minutia of daily survival might be an interesting aspect to an adventure, it rarely carries any kind of long-term enjoyment. Instead, getting lost should serve to advance some aspect of the story, whether to get the characters to a particular place, or reinforce a thematic aspect of the adventure. One thing to keep in mind—as with any technique—is that players might start to feel manipulated if you use it too much.

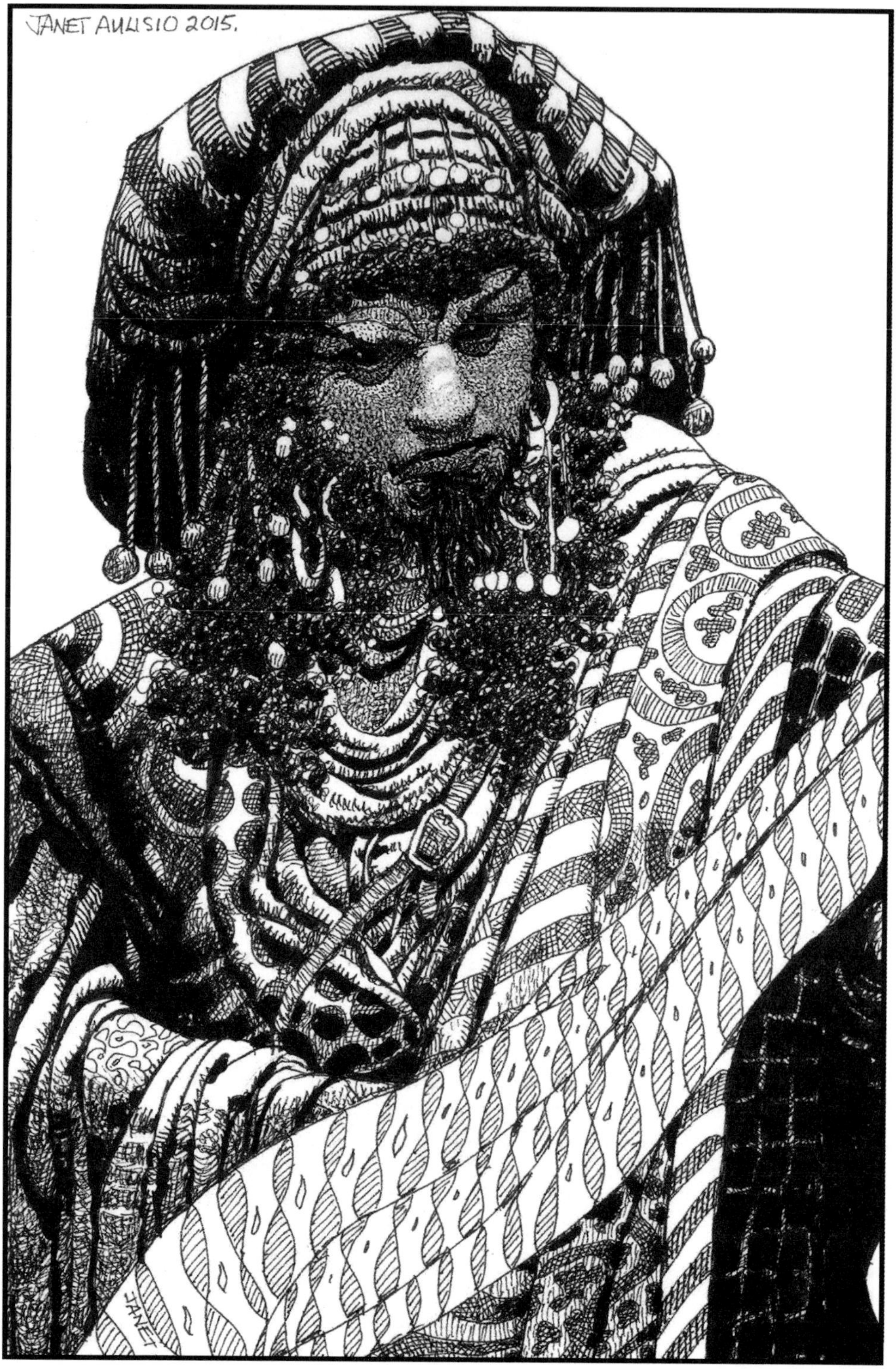
JANET AULISIO 2015.
JANET

ENCOUNTERS

Many thanks for driving off those scorchers! Can I interest you in these fine fire moth silks from the outskirts of the Liaj jungle? Deeply discounted, of course!
•*Comta Relb, itinerant trader* •

Adepts wandering the lands of Barsaive are not doing so in a vacuum. In the course of their adventures they will encounter the other beings that inhabit the world of **Earthdawn**. These meetings will range from friendly tavern keepers to rival treasure hunters, inscrutable dragons to powerful Horrors.

While swordplay is a common event in the life of an adventurer, an encounter does not automatically mean a fight will break out. While there are extensive rules for combat in the game, many Disciplines are suited to less violent means of conflict resolution. There will be many times characters will need to talk with the people they meet on their travels. This section provides guidelines and rules for creating gamemaster characters and handling these non-combat interactions.

GAMEMASTER CHARACTERS

In a role-playing game, the player characters are the protagonists. They are the main characters, but they are not the only characters in the game. Everybody else—the stable boy at the roadside inn, the general of the Throalic army, the corrupted Nethermancer leading a Horror cult, and all the others—are supporting characters referred to as gamemaster characters. Namegivers aren't the only beings that fall into that category. Dragons, Horrors, spirits, even animals the characters encounter in the wild are gamemaster characters.

In addition to coming up with the setting and events for the game, the gamemaster needs to populate the game with gamemaster characters. Without them, there isn't much for player characters to do. There are no townsfolk to save, no villains to thwart, no Horrors to slay. Coming up with a variety of gamemaster characters can be daunting. Fortunately, there are some convenient tricks and shortcuts that can make the gamemaster's life easier.

First, don't feel like you need to be completely original. Many creative works take ideas from other sources and mix them together to create something new. Take inspiration from books, movies, or television shows and dress them up a little differently.

Second, don't take on more work than you need to. If the character in question is not likely to be involved in combat, you don't need to come up with all of their attributes, talents, skills, and other game statistics. A physical description and a few notes on their personality are probably all that is needed.

Third, while a richly developed character can be a fantastic addition to the game, it is often better to start broad and add depth as needed. This relates to the previous point about not making more work for yourself than necessary. Choose one or two defining traits—whether physical, mental, or social—and hang the characterization on them. Play up stereotypes, or break them. Perhaps the t'skrang ship captain is gloomy instead of energetic, or the obsidiman Warrior has a fascination with delicate windling bone sculpture.

Finally, perhaps the most important thing when it comes to gamemaster characters is to remember that they are not the main protagonists. While some might end up with a significant supporting role in the game, they should not overshadow the player characters. There are countless stories of games that fell apart because the gamemaster had a "pet NPC" that turned the player characters into little more than glorified sidekicks.

Creating Gamemaster Characters

Gamemaster characters can be created in much the same way as player characters; you assign Attribute values, derive the relevant characteristics, assign talent and skill ranks, give them equipment, and flesh out the character's personality and goals. Examples of this type of character can be found in **Earthdawn** products, and is most often used for characters that player characters are likely to interact with in significant ways, for example an opponent or enemy the heroes will face in combat.

However, because every game of **Earthdawn** is different, we often include only basic information for gamemaster characters in our products. This is usually done for characters that are less likely to be a target for talents and other abilities, and it also allows individual gamemasters to flesh out details appropriate for their game. In this case, the information will usually be presented in the following format:

- **Name:** This is the name of the character.
- **Discipline** or **Occupation** and **Tier:** This provides the character's Discipline (for adepts) or profession (for non-adepts), along with their experience level (Novice, Journeyman, etc.).
- **Attributes:** The character's basic attribute Steps (not values).

From this point, additional details are up to the gamemaster to fill in as appropriate. While you can consult the Characteristics Table in the *Player's Guide* to figure out specific attribute values based on the provided Steps, and determine the appropriate characteristics, and go through a kind of character creation process, there is a more abstract way that requires less advance preparation.

The Step Number Conversion Table provides a range of values for different characteristics based on the associated Attribute Step. If you need a characteristic value for a character you only have basic information on, look up the Step Number on the table and choose a value from the range provided.

Step Number Conversion Table

Step Number	Defense Rating	Mystic Armor	Unc. Rating	Death Rating	Wound Threshold
2	2-3	0	2-6	4-8	3-4
3	3-4	0-1	8-12	11-15	4-5
4	5-6	1	14-18	18-22	6-7
5	6-7	2	20-24	25-29	7-8
6	8-9	2-3	26-30	32-36	9-10
7	9-10	3	32-36	39-43	10-11
8	11-12	3-4	38-42	46-50	12-13
9	12-13	4	44-48	53-57	13-14
10	14-15	5	50-54	60-64	15-16
11	15-16	5-6	56-60	67-71	16-17

If you need to make a test for a character, you can add a Step modifier to the appropriate Attribute based on the character's tier. Novice characters will typically add +1 to +4, Journeyman characters +5 to +8, Warden characters +9 to +12, and Master characters +13 to +15. These modifiers should be the ones used for tests involving the gamemaster character's primary focus. For secondary skills and abilities, use modifiers based on the next lower tier, or just have the character make an unmodified Attribute test.

Leanne is running a game, and introduces a non-adept Journeyman guard captain Named Bryant. He is provided a Dexterity Step of 6 and Willpower of Step of 5. If Leanne wants to make a test relating to Bryant's status as a guard captain—for example, melee weapons—she can roll a Step 12 test; Dexterity Step 6 with a +6 Step modifier for being a Journeyman-tier character. Helping fly an airship, on the other hand, is not in Bryant's expected area of expertise. He does work in Jerris, however, and has picked up some of the basics. In this case, Leanne chooses to make a Step 7 test; Willpower Step 5 with a +2 Step modifier.

Adept characters have additional special abilities that provide bonuses to these basic characteristic values—most notably increasing their Defense Ratings. Generally speaking, modifiers to Defense Ratings will be half the Step bonus provided to the adept's tests. For example, a Novice Troubadour will have +1 or +2 added to an appropriate Defense Rating or Ratings, while a Journeyman would have +3 or +4.

GAMEMASTER CHARACTER ATTITUDES

Each gamemaster character has their own personality, desires, and goals. Every one of them will react to player characters based on these aspects. As gamemaster, you may give your characters a detailed personality, but with the number of characters you will be dealing with, it can be overwhelming. As a shorthand way of dealing with social interaction between player characters and gamemaster characters, **Earthdawn** uses a mechanic called **Attitude**.

Attitude helps determine how easy it is for a player character to influence, persuade, or deceive a gamemaster character. While it can provide a handy guideline for roleplaying character interactions, it is also frequently used in conjunction with magical talents and abilities that target a character's Social Defense.

There are seven attitudes that gamemaster character might have: Awestruck, Loyal, Friendly, Neutral, Unfriendly, Hostile, and Enemy. A gamemaster character may hold different attitudes toward different people. For example, a servant might be Loyal to his employer, but Hostile to a player character Thief breaking into his home. In general, you only need to keep track of gamemaster character attitudes towards the player characters, though other significant attitudes might come into play. A player character will likely have a hard time convincing the Loyal servant to betray his master, especially without the aid of magic!

Certain talents and other social mechanics may shift a gamemaster character's attitude, or only work on certain attitudes. In any rules text relating to attitudes, an attitude is "better" if it is closer to Awestruck than the current attitude, and it is "worse" if it lies closer to Enemy. Therefore, an attitude of "Friendly or better" means Friendly, Loyal, or Awestruck, while "Neutral or worse" means Neutral, Unfriendly, Hostile, or Enemy.

Awestruck characters think the player character is the most wonderful person in the world. They may view the player character as a hero, worship the ground the player character walks on, or be madly in love. Awestruck characters willingly make great sacrifices to please the object of their worship, frequently taking risks with no thought to the consequences, even at risk of their own life.

Loyal characters as a devoted ally or close friend, convinced of the player character's worth. Loyal characters may look up to or otherwise admire the player character, devote themselves to the same cause, or serve faithfully as a long-time employee. They tend to look out for the player character's best interests, though they expect their loyalty to be returned or rewarded. They may wait patiently if this doesn't happen right away, as long as they consider the player character's actions and behavior worthy of their loyalty. They may take great risks on behalf of the player character, and is unlikely to betray them.

Friendly characters enjoy the company of the player character, and value them as a person. This attitude covers positive relationships formed over time, whether that is a friendship, an employer and trusted employee, or characters who share some sort of common bond, for example a group of t'skrang in an otherwise all-dwarf part of Throal. Friendly characters expect their friendship to be returned over the short term as well as the long term.

They will readily do small favors—as long as those favors are eventually returned—but convincing them to take considerable risk is difficult unless they also stand to gain.

Neutral characters take a "live-and-let-live" attitude towards the player character. The gamemaster character won't go out of their way to accommodate them, but will typically speak up or step in if they see somebody not taking the same approach. Neutral characters include neighbors, merchants, or anybody else that would be considered an acquaintance. They might help a player character with an obvious, immediate problem—fighting off an attack by a gang of thugs, for example—but they may not intervene if they think the player character caused the problem, or deserves it in some other way. They can be persuaded to occasionally do small favors, but are unlikely to take risks without the promise of significant reward.

Unfriendly characters are out for themselves, and typically take a "live-and-let-die" attitude towards a player character. Greedy merchants and suspicious guards are examples of Unfriendly gamemaster characters. They will take advantage of a player character without openly causing harm, and will have no qualms about deceiving him. The gamemaster character may be polite, and may even act friendly to gain the player character's trust. Persuading them to do even small favors is difficult at best, and they will do their best to get out of any commitments to the player character.

Hostile characters will not hesitate to harm the player character if the opportunity presents itself. Examples of Hostile characters include thieves and other criminals, rival adventuring groups, and many creatures in the wild—especially if they are hungry or threatened. Like Unfriendly characters, hostile gamemaster characters may feign friendship to gain the player character's trust, but many don't bother with such pretense. Convincing a Hostile character to take any kind of action that would benefit the player character is almost impossible.

Enemy characters harbor a personal vendetta against the player character. While they might pretend to be friendly, in most cases the best they can manage is chilly politeness. An Enemy will take any opportunity to harm the player character, and often will make plans that involve disrupting their life in significant ways. They cannot be convinced to do any kind of favor for the player character, and the only risks they will take are ones that would lead to the player character suffering as a result.

Social Interactions

There will be times when player characters need to interact in non-violent ways with gamemaster characters. Whether persuading a librarian to give them access to the restricted archives, haggling over the cost of supplies, or interviewing a witness to a crime, not all problems can be solved by waving a sword or slinging fireballs. There are two main ways to resolve these kinds of interactions, roleplaying and Interaction tests.

Each method has strengths, weaknesses, and pitfalls that gamesters should be aware of. Depending on the situation, one method may be more appropriate than the other, though in most circumstances a mix of the two methods is most appropriate.

Roleplaying

Roleplaying is perhaps the most common way to resolve interactions with gamemaster characters. That's why they are called roleplaying games, after all! The players describe their characters' actions and what they say, and the gamemaster does the same for the gamemaster characters. This continues until the scene is resolved. The degree to which dice rolling and mechanics come into play depends on the goals of the characters involved in the scene.

When you are roleplaying interactions, put yourself in the character's shoes. What do you want? What are you willing to do to get it? Is there anything you won't do? What does the other character want? Does that conflict with what you want? Is there a compromise that might work out to your mutual benefit?

When roleplaying, try to keep the gamemaster character's attitude in mind. As you will see in the rules for Interaction tests, attitude can have a significant effect on how easy it is for a player character to persuade, deceive, or intimidate a gamemaster character.

The strength of a pure roleplaying approach is that it does remove the uncertainty that dice can bring. It also can play out a little faster; a few words of dialogue, a couple of descriptions and you're on to other things.

Unfortunately, there are weaknesses to this approach as well. It can often give an advantage to players that are more quick-witted, whether their character is or not. Eschewing die rolls in social conflicts also reduces or removes the effectiveness of talents and abilities dedicated to interaction tests, which affects certain Disciplines more than others.

Interaction Tests

There are times where no amount of roleplaying will resolve an impasse between player and gamemaster characters. When this happens, the conflict can be resolved through the use of an **Interaction** test.

Five different Interaction tests are described here: Making an Impression, Deceit, Insight, Intimidation, and Favors. Most social interactions in **Earthdawn** will fall under one of these categories. The character makes a Charisma test against the target's Social Defense. The number of successes required usually depends on the target character's attitude towards the player character.

If a character has a talent or skill appropriate to a situation that calls for an Interaction test, they may use the talent or skill. The effect of some talents, spells, or other abilities might provide a bonus to Interaction tests. In most cases, the rules for the relevant talent or effect supersedes the rules provided here.

Making an Impression

Sometimes when meeting a gamemaster character, a player will want to make a good impression on them. This interaction does not work on gamemaster characters who are already Awestruck, Loyal, or are Enemies of the character.

To make an impression, the character makes an Interaction test against the target character's Social Defense. A successful test improves the target's attitude one degree—for example, a Neutral character becomes Friendly. A Rule of One result worsens the target's attitude by one degree—for example, an Unfriendly character becomes Hostile.

The effect of the impression normally lasts for one day, but it may wear off. Any openly hostile act against the impressed target will end the effect. The impression might also fade if the player character interacts with the impressed target in a manner worse than the gamemaster character's adjusted attitude (for example, Neutral or worse if the target is Friendly), as determined by the gamemaster. The target makes a Willpower test against the player character's Social Defense. If the target scores at least as many successes as the player character made on their Interaction test, the effect of the impression ends.

Kira Makes an Impression on an Unfriendly merchant in a town her group is visiting. She makes a Charisma test against the merchant's Social Defense of 7 and rolls an 11, scoring one success and shifting the merchant's attitude to Neutral.

Later that evening, she is gambling at a local tavern with the merchant and a couple of other gamemaster characters. She decides to cheat, and unfortunately gets caught. The gamemaster decides this counts as an Unfriendly act, and rolls to see if the positive impression Kira left goes away. The merchant rolls a 9 on a Willpower test, matching Kira's Social Defense and scoring one success. Because the merchant scored as many successes as Kira, his attitude reverts to Unfriendly. Kira is going to have a little bit harder time talking her way out of this one.

Deceit

Sometimes a player character will want to convince a gamemaster character of something that isn't true. This can be a difficult situation to adjudicate purely through roleplaying, because the gamemaster knows the truth of the situation. It is possible to make a ruling based on how convincing the false information is, coupled with what the gamemaster character might already know, but people can often be convinced of the most ridiculous things.

Deceit through Interaction tests covers everything from "little white lies" to the deepest sorts of personal betrayal. In order to deceive a target, the characters must be able to speak to and understand each other. The effects of a successful deception will last until presented with evidence that contradict the deceit. There are three different types of deception, with varying degrees of difficulty.

Exaggeration is stretching the truth, or changing the details of the story—usually to make it more impressive. An example would be describing a fight with fifteen bandits, when in truth there were only eight. Any kind of change to the details, while still maintaining the overall truth of the matter—whether overstating or understating the reality—falls under exaggeration. The character makes an Interaction test against the target's Social Defense. If successful, the target believes the exaggeration.

Fabrication is an outright lie. The story, or important parts of the story, have no basis in reality, For example, describing an attack by bandits when no attack actually took place, or saying you didn't take the queen's necklace when you did. To tell a fabrication, the character makes an Interaction test against the target's Social Defense. With a single success, the target is inclined to believe the lie, but the character needs to come up with other reasons for the story to be believed, which might require an additional Interaction test. With two or more successes, the target believes the lie to be the truth.

Half-truths reveal a part of the truth, but withholds some vital information. The character is telling the truth, but is trying to mislead the target. For example, telling the town guard you didn't see anything at the scene of a crime, when you actually heard the cries of the victim. The character makes an Interaction test against the target's Social Defense. If successful, the target believes the character's story.

Insight

When a character wants to get a read on another character, or try and determine whether they are being deceived, they use this kind of Interaction test. If successful, the character gains information that might provide useful information with regard to current or future social interactions. There are two main uses for insight.

Basic Emotions can be determined with a successful Interaction test against the target's Social Defense. The character is able to detect surface feelings like anger, love, fear, hunger, or nervousness.

Detecting Deception is the other main use for insight. The character must be able to observe the target as he speaks in order to pick up on the subtle clues and body language that might indicate the target is not being honest. The character makes an Interaction test against the target's Social Defense. If the target is attempting to deceive the character, the character must achieve more successes on his test to detect the deception than the target scored on their Interaction test to deceive the character. If the target's features are obscured by a mask or helmet, then the character must score an additional success in order to overcome the difficulty.

Silar is infiltrating the headquarters of a cult to find information on their plans. He is making his way down the corridor towards the cult leader's quarters when he encounters one of the higher ranking cult members. Silar wants to keep the cult from learning his group is on to them, and decides to try and talk his way out of the problem.

He tells the cult member that he is a new initiate, and has been asked to deliver a message to the leader. Silar is wearing a set of initiate's robes, so the gamemaster decides this is a half-truth rather than an outright fabrication. Silar makes a Charisma test against the cult member's Social Defense of 8 and rolls a 10, scoring a single success. The cultist is suspicious, since acolytes really aren't supposed to be in this part of the complex, so the gamemaster decides he will make an Insight test to see if Silar is lying.

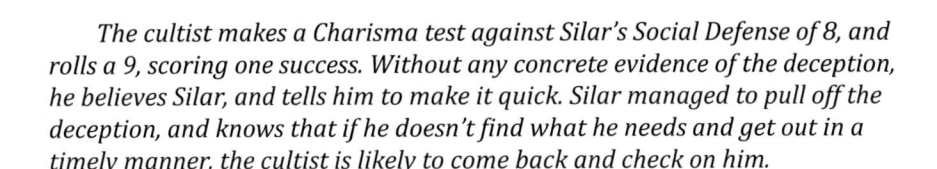

The cultist makes a Charisma test against Silar's Social Defense of 8, and rolls a 9, scoring one success. Without any concrete evidence of the deception, he believes Silar, and tells him to make it quick. Silar managed to pull off the deception, and knows that if he doesn't find what he needs and get out in a timely manner, the cultist is likely to come back and check on him.

If the target is attempting an outright fabrication (see **Deceit**, p. 145), then the character detects the deception if they score at least the same number of successes, rather than needing more.

Generally speaking, this use of insight will only be used by gamemaster characters that have a reason to suspect the target might not be honest, or when they have an Unfriendly or worse attitude towards the target character.

Intimidation

Some social interactions are intended to force a target to take a course of action through fear, whether that is the threat of physical harm or other negative consequences like losing a job, or getting in trouble with an authority figure. These interactions fall under the category of Intimidation.

Generally, a character may only attempt to intimidate a target that can successfully communicate with, and that is within line of sight. In some cases, the gamemaster may allow non-verbal intimidation, but those attempts should be more difficult.

Intimidation works best against targets that have a reason to fear the character (or fear the consequences the character could cause), and that hold negative attitudes towards the character. If a character uses intimidation on a target that has a Neutral or better attitude towards them, their attitude shifts one degree worse.

Stopping an action uses Intimidation to order another character to not perform an action, or to do nothing. For example, a player character could order a gamemaster character, "Don't touch that," or "Leave her alone!" A single success on the Interaction test means the target will follow the instructions for one round. With three or more successes, the target will refrain from the forbidden action for as long as the character remains in sight. This type of intimidation cannot be used to prevent a character from performing an action they have no control over; you could not order a person to stop breathing.

Forcing an action uses Intimidation to try and make the target character perform a particular task they would otherwise not do. Examples include leading the way into a dangerous cave or providing information they are trying to keep secret. This is more difficult because the target needs to be convinced that the character's threat is more dangerous than the requested action, so two successes are required on the Interaction test. An intimidated character stops performing the requested action as soon as they are out of the intimidator's sight.

Interaction Success Table

Type of Interaction Test	Required Successes
Deceit:	
Exaggeration	1+
Fabrication	2+
Half-Truth	1+
Insight:	
Detect basic emotion	1+
Detect deception	2+*
Detect deception when features obscured	3+
Intimidation:	
Do nothing	1+
Take action	2+
Make an Impression:	
Improve target's attitude by one level	1+
Worsen target's attitude by one level	Rule of One

* If actively being deceived, the character must score more successes than the deceiving character scored on their Interaction test to deceive.

Favors

When a player character is trying to convince another character to take an action, whether through logical argument, flattery, appeals to friendship or other forms of persuasion, they are trying to have the target do them a favor. Favors take on many forms. A shopkeeper might provide free or reduced costs on goods, an innkeeper might provide information, a guard might look the other way and let the character slip away. Essentially, a favor is any grant of time, money, or resources that benefits another character.

This type of Interaction test is best used on characters who have a Neutral or better Attitude towards the player character. The target's attitude determines how difficult it is to persuade him to do the favor, as shown on the Favor Success Table.

Small favors include things like holding your place in line, buying a round of drinks, or bringing food or water to your cell. As a general rule, a small favor will not endanger a character, or take more than about 30 minutes of time or effort to perform. They will typically not cost a character more than 5 silver, a few hours' wages, or 1 percent of his cash on hand (whichever is largest).

Favor Success Table

Target Attitude	Small Favor	Large Favor
Awestruck	Automatic	1 Success
Loyal	1 Success	2 Successes
Friendly	2 Successes	3 Successes
Neutral	3 Successes	4 Successes
Unfriendly	4 Successes	NA

Large favors include giving loans (which must be repaid in a timely manner), giving a character a place to stay for a few days, delivering a package or message to a questionable neighborhood, and so on. As a general rule, a large favor will not require more than 8 hours of time or extra effort, though it may pose some risk to the character providing the favor, though only Loyal and Awestruck characters will agree to obviously dangerous favors. A large favor should not cost a character more than a day's wages or 3 percent of his total savings. A loan could be larger depending on the terms of repayment, but typically will not exceed a week's earnings or 15 percent of the target's total savings.

Economy of Favors

Favors help make the world go round, greasing the wheels of society. Most people expect favors to be returned in kind, but their Attitude can influence how closely they keep track of what they might be owed, and how long they will wait.

Friendly characters might be willing to let the occasional small favor go unpaid, but will keep track of large favors and will rarely extend a second large favor without the first favor having been paid back. Loyal characters are more forgiving of small favors, and may extend two or three large favors before expecting repayment. Awestruck characters generally consider small favors a privilege to provide and don't keep track of them at all, and are more generous with their large favors.

Unfriendly characters might be persuaded to perform small favors, but only if it is to their advantage. Hostile or Enemy characters will not provide favors at all, except in truly extraordinary circumstances.

Characters may help persuade a target to provide a favor by offering a specific favor in return. This allows a character to make an additional Interaction test, hoping to accumulate sufficient total successes on the rolls to meet the required threshold. If the character offers to perform their favor first (effectively putting the target in favor debt), they earn one free success for a small favor, and two free successes for a large favor, which is then added to the results of their Interaction test to determine total successes.

The Favor Payback Table shows the amount of time a character will typically wait for a favor to be repaid, based on their attitude towards the character that owes them the favor. If the favor has not been repaid within the indicated timeframe, the character's attitude drops one level. If there are extenuating circumstances—for example the player character has been traveling for some time and not had a chance to repay the favor—they can restore the lost level of attitude by paying back the favor at first opportunity.

Favor Payback Table

Target Attitude	Small Favor	Large Favor
Awestruck	Never	1 year
Loyal	1 year	1 month
Friendly	1 month	1 week
Neutral	1 week	1 day
Unfriendly	1 day	NA

Using Interaction Tests

Interaction tests can provide a useful mechanic for determining how successfully player characters influence and persuade gamemaster characters in different kinds of social situations. They are not intended as a replacement for roleplaying, but should be used to enhance or influence the progress of a roleplaying scene. In this section we are going to address a number of different ways Interaction tests can be used, and some common pitfalls to watch out for.

In general, Interaction tests will be used by player characters interacting with gamemaster characters. They can be used on player characters, but there are some potential issues to be aware of. Players do not usually like having control of their character taken out of their hands. Having your troll Warrior intimidated into backing down from a fight as a result of a die roll can be a disheartening experience.

On the other hand, social mechanics are like any other mechanic in the game. If you rely purely on roleplaying to resolve social conflicts, then the characters whose talents and abilities take advantage of those mechanics are not being given their chance to shine. Just as the Warrior has to roll to hit things with his sword, or the Elementalist needs to follow the mechanics for weaving spell threads, the Troubadour should be given the opportunity to dazzle the crowds with his social prowess.

Another potential drawback of downplaying the mechanics around social interactions is the potential of turning Charisma into a "dump stat". Should a player who is naturally charismatic and quick witted be able to take advantage of that, despite his ork Archer having a below-average Charisma score? What about a player who is more withdrawn and introverted in real life? They might be at a disadvantage if they couldn't take advantage of their t'skrang Swordsmaster's outgoing nature and high Charisma score.

There are a couple of primary ways to integrate Interaction tests and social mechanics into your roleplaying. The first is to have the characters roll the appropriate Interaction tests, and allow the flow of the scene to be informed by the result of the test. When player characters first interact with a gamemaster character, have them

Make an Impression (see page 144), using appropriate talents when available. This helps determine the gamemaster character's attitude going into the scene, and attitude is everything. Resolving a conflict with a Friendly character is much easier than one with a Neutral or Unfriendly character.

The other major approach is to call for Interaction tests at particular moments, perhaps offering a bonus (or penalty) to the roll based on the roleplaying up to that moment. This can help balance out the natural social advantages that players might have. A good speech will give a bonus, but a socially awkward character will still be likely to have a hard time inspiring troops to follow him. Likewise, a player that isn't as affable in person gets the advantage of a high Charisma Step, or appropriate talents or skills.

The degree to which gamemaster characters can use Interaction tests to influence player characters will depend on the group. It is strongly recommended that—outside of magical talents or spells—that no kind of social interaction forces a player character to take a particular action. You can use interaction tests to inform a scene and provide information to the player, or better yet use the result of an Interaction test to inform the roleplaying in a scene. You may remind the player that their low Social Defense means they are more likely to be taken in by a con man or swayed by a charismatic individual. You might even award them bonus roleplaying Legend Points for staying true to their character. Ultimately, however, the decision about whether a character is affected by the social wiles of a gamemaster character should be left in their hands.

The cautions about the gamemaster using Interaction tests to influence player character actions goes double for player characters attempting to use Interaction tests against other player characters. There is a certain expectation of a gamemaster taking a mildly antagonistic stance towards the player characters, but one player trying to usurp control of a fellow player's character is a recipe for resentment and hurt feelings. For some groups it can work, but often requires trust from everyone, and discussion of the limits involved.

At the gamemaster's discretion, he may choose to apply appropriate bonuses or penalties to interaction tests based on circumstances. For example, a battle-scarred troll Warrior might be granted a bonus to intimidate a gamemaster character with threats of violence. He may also choose to use an Attribute other than Charisma if particularly suited to the scene. If the troll threatens a gamemaster character by picking him up, the gamemaster might choose to have the troll's player use Strength instead.

Example of Interaction Tests in Play

Doug is playing the t'skrang Swordmaster Landal, and Mary is playing the windling Beastmaster Girr. They have been hired to investigate the disappearance of a dwarf girl. Her father thinks she was abducted by the son of a rival merchant, when she has actually run away to marry him. Their inquiries have led them to a tavern where some of the young man's friends are known to pass the time. They know where the couple has run off to, but are reluctant to share that information with those they believe are the merchant's lackeys.

Gamemaster: You enter the tavern. On the left side of the main room is a low bar, behind which several small casks are on stands, probably filled with ale or beer. A set of shelves next to the casks has a few bottles of wine or other spirits, along with a number of wooden and metal tankards. The floor is wooden planks, covered with an inch or so of dried straw. Several low rectangular tables with benches take up the rest of the room, which is lit with lanterns hanging from the rafters.

Doug: How many people are here?

Gamemaster: There's an older dwarf standing behind the bar, who looked up when you came in. A pair of humans are at the table nearest the door, and the table in the far corner has half a dozen young dwarfs playing some kind of dice game.

Mary: Those must be the ones we're looking for. I take off from Landal's shoulder and fly over to the table with the dwarfs.

Doug: Landal will follow, and see if I can get in on the game. [As Landal] Greetings my friends, is there room for another?

Gamemaster: Give me an interaction test to make an impression.

Doug: I want to use my First Impression talent to try and get in good with them. [Rolls] I scored a twelve.

Lacking a reason otherwise, the gamemaster decides the dwarfs started as Neutral toward the adepts. The result of Landal's First Impression test scored one success against the dwarfs' Social Defense of 8, shifting their attitude to Friendly.

Gamemaster: The dwarfs shoot you a look, and one of them gives you a shrewd smile. [As dwarf] As long as your silver is good.

Doug: As I sit down I call over to the bartender, ordering an ale. I take some silver out of my belt pouch and stack it on the table in front of me.

Mary: As Landal gets settled into the game, I fly over to the bar and see if they have any keesris.

Gamemaster: [as bartender] Sorry, don't have any of that. Closest thing I have is a spice wine from the Aras shores.

Mary: I'll take it! I pay for my drink and Landal's, then fly over and perch on the rafters and watch the game.

Gamemaster: How do you approach the game? Are you going to keep it friendly? Cheat to win? Intentionally lose?

Doug: I'll keep It friendly to start with, make some small talk to put them at ease.

Gamemaster: You play for a few minutes, breaking about even. The small talk eventually shifts. [As dwarf] What brings you this far from the docks?

Doug: [as Landal] Funny you should ask. We're actually looking for someone. A dwarf by the Name of Harnott. We were told he comes here frequently.

Mary: Do they react when his name is mentioned?

Gamemaster: They certainly do. The apparent leader of the group narrows his eyes. [As dwarf] Why are you asking?

Doug: [as Landal] Rumor has it he might know where Rinalla Steelshank is.

Gamemaster: The dwarf replies with some hostility. [As dwarf] You working for old man Steelshank?

Doug: [as Landal] Her father did ask us to look for her. He's concerned for her safety and just wants to make sure she's all right.

Mary: Kind of laying it on thick, aren't you Doug?

Gamemaster: I agree. These dwarfs are well aware of the bad blood between Steelshank and Harnott's father. Give me an interaction test for deceit.

Doug: [rolls] 5. Looks like they probably don't buy it.

Gamemaster: Not in the slightest. [As dwarf] You seem a decent sort, but you can go back and tell Steelshank to get stuffed. Even if we knew where Harnott was—which we don't—we wouldn't tell you.

Mary: Do I think he's telling the truth about Harnott?

Gamemaster: Give me an insight test.

Mary: [rolls] Sweet! That's a 10, followed by [rolls again] a 6, for a total of 16.

Gamemaster: He totally knows where Harnott is.

Mary: Enough of the soft approach then. I drop down from the rafters onto the table, and grab the dwarf by the ear, twisting it. [As Girr] I think you do know, and I think you'll tell us.

Gamemaster: The coins rattle on the table, some of them falling on the floor. The dwarf cries out in pain.

Doug: What are the others doing?

Gamemaster: The other dwarfs are caught off guard by Girr's sudden assault. The humans at the other table are noticeably not paying attention, and the bartender has stopped wiping a mug and is watching you closely. Girr, give me an intimidation test.

Mary: [rolls] Only an 8.

Girr's roll of 8 is only one success against the dwarf's Social Defense of 8; not enough to force him to take an action. But the gamemaster decides it is enough to stop anybody else from acting.

Gamemaster: It doesn't look like anybody is taking any hostile action towards you at the moment, but the dwarf isn't talking.

Doug: Time to try and salvage the situation. I pick up my silver and as I speak I start stacking the coins in front of him. [As Landal] Now Girr, I'm sure our friend here is more than willing to be reasonable. There's no need for this to get ugly.

Mary: [As Girr] He's ugly.

Doug: I snort and continue stacking coins. [As Landal] What say you friend? Do us a favor, keep these coins... and your ear.

Mary: I give his ear a twist for emphasis.

Girr's intimidation is an unfriendly act at best, and drops the dwarf's attitude back to Neutral. However the gamemaster decides that Landal's offer to pay up front for the information they want will buy a small favor, and decides the dwarf will talk without needing another roll.

Gamemaster: [As dwarf] Ow! Okay! Harnott and Rinalla are hiding out at Astendar's shrine outside the west gate.

Doug: [As Landal] Thank you, friend. You can let him go, Girr.

Mary: I let go of the dwarf's ear and down the rest of my wine. [As Girr] Let's get going. The night is still young.

Gamemaster: Landal, you end up down twenty silver. Where to next?

Doug: The shrine, I guess, though it doesn't seem like the place you would take your kidnapping victim. I think there is more going on here than Steelshank is letting on.

Thus the scene is resolved. The adepts could probably have beaten the answer out of the dwarfs, but town guards tend to frown on those who go busting up a tavern. In the end they got what they wanted—the information, and the dwarf avoided getting beaten up, and made a little extra money as well. The gamemaster handled the scene with a combination of roleplaying and Interaction tests. Not every interaction needed to be handled with die rolls, but the overall shape of the scene was guided by the gamemaster character attitudes and the actions of the player characters.

Wild Animals and Creatures

A common hazard for adventurers in the world of **Earthdawn** is encountering the wild animals and other creatures that inhabit the wild and isolated parts of the land. While sometimes these encounters provide little more than background color and fill in the scenery, others are potentially dangerous. Some wild animals will attack to protect their young, others to defend their territory or food supply; only rarely will a creature attack without provocation. There is usually some reason for the behavior, whether hunger, illness or even the influence of a Horror.

On the one hand, this relative simplicity of intent makes creatures and wild animals easier to deal with. On the other, you can't really negotiate with an animal the way you can with a Namegiver opponent, and most socially based talents and abilities do not work on them.

That said, you can still use the Attitude mechanic when it comes to wild animals and creatures. The Beastmaster and Cavalryman Disciplines both have talents that interact with animals and creatures, influencing their attitude and the way they react to player characters, or requiring the adept to have developed a Loyal relationship with an animal or creature to make it an animal companion, opening up even more options.

As a general rule, wild animals and creatures start with a default attitude of Unfriendly. How they react to player characters at that point depends on what the environment is, and what is motivating the creature at that point. Most interactions will boil down to the simple question of "fight or flight." Would the creature consider the characters to be a predator? Potential prey? A rival or threat of another kind?

Wild animals and creatures rarely fight "to the death" without significant motivation. They will often flee when encountering strong resistance, especially if they suffer Wounds or significant damage. The gamemaster is encouraged to keep this in mind when running encounters with these denizens of the world of **Earthdawn**.

Also keep in mind that in many cases, the characters will be encountering these creatures in their native habitat, which can give the creature an advantage when it comes to remaining unnoticed. As with Namegiver travelers, noticing a creature when traveling in the wilderness requires a successful Perception test against the creature's Dexterity Step, modified based on the terrain and conditions. Wild animals often have camouflage or other abilities that make them more difficult to notice. When applicable, these will be noted among the creature's powers and abilities.

If a fight does break out between characters and wild animals, the creature might use some basic tactics and take advantage of certain combat options (see page 382 in the *Player's Guide*). Predators might attempt to strike gain surprise by striking from ambush, and then Attacking to Knockdown their prey. A mother defending her young might use the Aggressive Attack option, and other creatures might use charging or swooping attacks as appropriate. A pack of wolves may not have the intelligence of human bandits, but they do have a level of cunning and survival instincts that serve them well in wild places.

At its most basic level, encounters with wild animals and creatures should not result in a toe-to-toe battle. Just as with more intelligent opponents, gamemasters should do their best to make encounters interesting and challenging for their players.

Creatures and Interaction Tests

At the gamemaster's discretion, certain kinds of Interaction tests may be applied to encounters with wild animals and creatures. A character might Make an Impression to demonstrate they are not a threat, shifting a creature's attitude one degree in their favor. They might use Insight to get a sense of the creature's feelings and attitude, or Intimidation to force the creature into backing down or running away. Certain creatures might have their own behaviors or powers that work in a similar way to Interaction tests.

When using Interaction tests on wild animals, the gamemaster may require the character to have some kind of relevant knowledge or skill relating to the animal and its behavior. For example, the character might first need to succeed at a Wild Animals test in order to recognize the creature's behavior and the best way to handle it. Creative use of certain talents or skills might provide additional insight and allow characters to travel the wilderness without needing to slaughter everything they encounter.

Animal Training and Animal Companions

Cavalryman and Beastmaster adepts have a closer relationship with animals and creatures than other Disciplines, and several of their talents are intended to build on and take advantage of that relationship. The Animal Bond and Animal Training talents (*Player's Guide*, p. 125 and 127), along with their equivalent skills, allow characters the ability to develop a rapport with an animal and eventually train the animal as an animal companion.

Keep an eye on the number of animal companions that characters acquire—especially Beastmaster adepts. An animal companion is not just a piece of equipment, it is a living creature with needs and desires and should be treated with care and respect. They need food, water, shelter, and affection from their companion, and failure to provide these things can have negative consequences.

Neglected animals will become more demanding, perhaps bothering the character for food or attention at inconvenient times. Neglect will also reduce the companion's attitude toward the character, making them less willing to do as the character asks. If seriously neglected—or outright mistreated—the animal may run away from its former friend.

The gamemaster should remind the player of the responsibility involved in caring for an animal companion, and the time required to maintain that bond, as well as any specialized training the animal may require. Animal companions can add a bit of color and enrich a campaign, but they should be handled with care.

At the gamemaster's discretion, characters might be able to develop a Loyal relationship with domesticated animals like dogs, cats, or horses purely through interactions, removing the need for the Animal Bond talent or skill. Developing this kind of relationship with a wild animal or magical creature, however, should always require the use of the appropriate talent or skill, requiring a character to spend time developing the relationship and teaching the animal to respect the trainer.

EARTHDAWN

Horrors

In contrast to wild animals and magical creatures native to Barsaive and the other lands of **Earthdawn**, Horrors, as well as their minions and constructs, often deliberately attack for no significant reason. Horrors enjoy causing pain and suffering, and will frequently take any available opportunity to do so.

The more bestial and unintelligent Horrors, as well as most Horror constructs and undead minions, will typically fight to the death. This is part of the reason why these opponents are so feared; they cannot be reasoned with, and lack any kind of independent will or desire to do anything beyond their urge to cause pain and destruction.

While intelligent Horrors can be reasoned with, adventurers who might consider such a course of action are reminded that intelligent Horrors are notorious for using subtle means to draw out the pain and agony of their victims. There are many tales and legends of Namegivers who thought they came out on top in a deal with a Horror, only to find themselves sorely mistaken.

Horrors are almost invariably Hostile to Namegivers and other living beings. While they may occasionally present a friendly face, their interactions are almost always full of doublespeak and deception. Their ultimate intent is to lead their prey down a path of emotional and physical pain in order to satisfy whatever urges drive them. Insight is typically the only Interaction test that will be of any use, though the power and cunning of these powerful opponents makes it very difficult to see through their lies and discern their true motivation.

More information on using Horrors as opponents in your game is provided in the **Horrors** chapter, p. 451.

Earthdawn

CHALLENGES AND OBSTACLES

Horrors aren't the only danger out there in the wild. I lost my ear to frostbite in the Dragon Mountains, a rusty blade trap in Parlainth nearly took my leg, and the Galloping Lung-Rot I caught in the sewers of Kratas almost killed me.
• *Nerala Ravensong, former agent of Throal* •

The heroes of **Earthdawn** pit their skills and courage against supernatural creatures and Horrors on a regular basis and confront their fears as a matter of course. Adepts explore abandoned kaers and forgotten citadels, face ork scorchers and crystal raiders, and fight to protect their world from the Horrors that remain. They strive to reclaim their world from the ravages of the Horrors and the tyranny of powers like the Theran Empire. As characters explore the world of **Earthdawn**, they will also face dangers that bear no relation to the plotting or malice of villains and creatures. Sometimes just surviving is a challenge.

This chapter starts off by offering general guidelines on creating Difficulty Numbers, and then moves on to more specific rules for the everyday perils of adventuring, including climbing, traps, poison, diseases, curses, and so on. If you find dealing with all the situations outlined in this chapter bewildering, use the examples and guidelines presented until you feel more confident of your own judgment. These rules should help you run your adventure, not get in your way.

Keep in mind that you are still responsible for choosing the exact Difficulty Numbers required and determining how successfully a character performs various actions. No matter what a player may desire as an outcome for his character, the gamemaster always has the final say.

CREATING DIFFICULTY NUMBERS

Difficulty Numbers are often determined by an opponent's characteristics or abilities. Sometimes a character wants to perform an action or task that does not involve another being, or does not otherwise offer an obvious value for a Difficulty Number. This section explains general guidelines on creating Difficulty Numbers for these situations.

Behind the Numbers

In the Step System, the Step Number also indicates the average result the dice will produce for that Step, factoring in the possibility of Bonus Dice. For example, a Step 9 (D8+D6) will, on average, roll a 9. This means that against a Difficulty Number of 9, a Step 9 will succeed about half the time, and the larger the difference between the Difficulty Number and the Step, the greater the chance of success (or failure).

This fact, combined with the Success Level mechanic—where you get an additional success for every five points you exceed the Difficulty Number—makes calculating Difficulty Numbers on the fly a fairly easy task. The examples given in this section and elsewhere in the **Earthdawn** rules are based on the statistics underlying the mechanics and assumptions about the relative skill and ability levels characters are likely to have.

Who Can Do It?

The key to creating Difficulty Numbers is deciding what type of person would normally perform the task being attempted. Might an ordinary person take this action? Would a low level of skill be enough to succeed? Is it a task that only a highly skilled practitioner would dare try? This system sets up five levels of expertise: Ordinary, Novice, Journeyman, Warden, and Master. Note that while these classes correlate to the status levels of adepts, they also apply to non-adepts.

An *Ordinary* character has no special skill or talent with which to perform the task.

A *Novice* character possesses some skill or talent suited for the task, though not at an outstanding level. Novices include those characters with beginning and average skills (Rank 1–4) and adepts from First to Fourth Circle.

A *Journeyman* character is a seasoned veteran who knows the ropes and has climbed more than his share. Tasks that seem almost inconceivable for an Ordinary character, a Journeyman character considers merely difficult. The Journeyman category includes characters with above-average skills (Rank 5–8) and adepts from Fifth to Eighth Circle.

A *Warden* character enjoys a reputation as one of the best in his field, maybe even in the history of his field. His prowess has made him famous, and others in his area of expertise think highly of his ability. The Warden category includes characters with high-level skills (Rank 9–10) and adepts from Ninth to Twelfth Circle.

Difficulty Number Table

Acting Character	Easy	Average	Hard	Very Hard	Heroic
Ordinary	1-2	3-5	6-9	10-12	13-15
Novice	1-2	3-7	8-12	13-16	17-20
Journeyman	3-6	7-12	13-18	19-22	23-27
Warden	6-8	12-16	18-24	25-29	30-35
Master	8-11	17-20	25-28	29-34	35-41

A *Master* character is legendary. Ordinary people know tales of his deeds, and tell them in awestruck whispers around the fire. He is an example of the best that is, was, and will be. Tasks that he accomplishes with ease are the stuff of dreams to mundane characters. The Master category includes adepts from Thirteenth to Fifteenth Circle.

Task Difficulty

After you determine the class of character that would normally perform a task, you decide how hard that task would be for the character actually attempting it: Easy, Average, Hard, Very Hard, or Heroic. The Difficulty Number Table lists the five classes of characters in the Acting Character column and the levels of Difficulty in the row across the top of the table. Each entry gives a range of Difficulty Numbers appropriate for a given class of character and Difficulty level.

> *Roona the Troubadour is visiting the Great Library to research a lost kaer, rumored to be the location of a magic sword destined to slay a Horror. She knows the Horror is looking for the sword as well, and may have agents in the library doing their own research. In order to keep the information from the Horror, and find the sword first, she needs to keep the true nature of her research a secret.*
>
> *The gamemaster decides that the research would normally be an average task for a Journeyman researcher, but Roona's need for secrecy and speed pushes it up to a hard task. Reading across the Journeyman row to the Hard column, the Difficulty Number range is 13-18.*

Choosing the Difficulty Number

Choose the Difficulty Number that you think fits the situation from the range given. Assigning a Difficulty Number is an art, not a science. Your most important job is to choose a reasonable number quickly. Making a task too easy (or too hard) might cause a small ripple in the game, but agonizing over the Difficulty Number can stop your game dead in its tracks.

Choose a number that seems reasonable, explain your reasoning if appropriate, and have the player roll the dice. It's okay to make mistakes—even the most experienced gamemasters can have an off day.

Adjusting Difficulty Numbers

While the rules in this chapter present recommended Difficulty Numbers for various tasks and obstacles, they are not set in stone. You have tools available to adjust the difficulty of a given task. You can use modifiers that affect a player's Action test (see **Bonuses and Penalties** in the **Game Concepts** chapter of the *Player's Guide*). You can adjust the Difficulty Number directly, or require additional result levels.

Modifiers vs. Difficulty Numbers

Although minor, there is a difference between applying a modifier to a test and modifying the Difficulty Number directly. How do you decide what is best in a given situation? As a general rule, apply a modifier to the test if the effect is temporary, and modify the Difficulty Number if the effect is permanent.

Result Levels

As a third option, you can also require additional success levels to affect the difficulty of a given task. To do this, determine the Difficulty Number of the task under normal (Average) circumstances, and then require additional successes based on how hard (or easy) you want the task to be. For example, if you want the task to be Hard, the character would need an extra success. A Heroic task would require three extra successes. An easy task would succeed if the test were no more than 5 under the base Difficulty Number.

The Disguise skill uses the test result to set the Difficulty Number to see through the disguise, but requires the use of make-up, costuming, and the like to use. If a character is quickly putting together a disguise to look like a castle guard, and has less than ideal materials, the gamemaster might allow the test, but may apply a penalty because of the circumstances.

If the character tries to use the disguise to move around the castle grounds, and another guard sees him across the yard in dim light, the gamemaster might require the guard to score an extra success against the Difficulty Number to spot the disguise.

Climbing a rocky cliff normally requires a test against a Difficulty Number of 9. If the cliff is next to a waterfall, so the rocks are slick with moisture and moss, the gamemaster might increase the Difficulty Number for Climbing tests to 12, making it harder to scale the cliff.

PERCEPTION TESTS

In **Earthdawn**, much of what happens during an adventure depends on what the player characters notice around them. The fate of the characters may hinge on them spotting an ambush, opening a vault might rely on finding and deciphering clues, or the scent of a creature or person could provide insight into the identity of an assassin.

When the gamemaster wants to determine if characters notice something, he can ask for a Perception test. The Difficulty Number for the test depends on the object of the test. For example, noticing an ambush usually uses the hiding character's Dexterity Step as the Difficulty Number. A Perception test to spot a trap uses the Detection Difficulty of the trap.

Perception Difficulty Table

Situation	Typical Difficulty
Hidden target	Target's Dexterity Step
Locate trap	Trap Detection Difficulty
Spot secret door	8+
Notice clues	5+
Notice anything unusual about surroundings	6

The Perception Difficulty Table lists common situations that require Perception tests along with the Difficulty Number for those tests. These are guidelines; the gamemaster should adjust these numbers up or down to fit the circumstances at hand.

Using Perception Tests

Perception tests can be used in a number of ways. One way is to determine whether characters notice something that is hidden or concealed, like bandits waiting to spring an ambush. Another use is to find out how successful a search of a room or other area is. Some gamemasters use Perception tests to determine which character notices something, rather than whether a character notices it.

Regardless of the reason for the test, characters use their Perception Step to make Perception tests, unless they have a talent or skill appropriate for the task.

A group of adventurers is exploring the entrance to a kaer. There is a trap in the tunnel, and the gamemaster wants to see if they notice it. He asks the group to make a Perception test. Most of the characters use their Perception Step, but the Thief uses his Awareness talent, because his ability to disarm traps allows him to use Awareness to notice them.

Sometimes the gamemaster wants to keep the result of a Perception test hidden from a player. This is usually done when the character is deliberately looking for something—like a trap or secret door—and the result of the roll could indicate whether there is something there to find. If the player get a high result on the test, and is told he doesn't find anything, he can be fairly sure there isn't anything to find. If he doesn't know the result, an air of mystery and doubt can be maintained.

While Perception tests can be a useful tool, it is important not to become overly reliant on them. This is especially true when it comes to finding or noticing clues or unraveling mysteries. Few things can be as frustrating as an adventure grinding to a halt because a bad run of Perception tests means the heroes lack the information they need to proceed.

There are a couple of ways to approach this problem. A common trick is to use the Perception test to determine which character finds a clue, as opposed to whether a character finds it; the gamemaster has all the players roll, and reveals the clue to the one that rolls highest. Another tactic is to provide many more clues than you think necessary. While this could make a mystery or puzzle much easier to solve if the dice are hot, it also means players are a lot less likely to be frustrated by a few poor results.

Perception Test Success Levels

Success levels are another tool that can be used with Perception tests. Much like the amount of detail a character recalls from a Knowledge test (see **Knowledge Skills**, p. 188 of the *Player's Guide*), the result can determine not just what a character notices with a Perception test, but the amount of detail and additional information that is provided.

For example, if a group is walking into a situation where they might be ambushed, a single success on a Perception test will indicate to a character that something is wrong—enough to put them on their guard and possibly avoid being surprised. Additional successes might provide information on the nature of the danger, the number of attackers hiding in the underbrush, or even (with three or more successes) give enough warning that the group as a whole is given a chance to avoid surprise.

Perception Test Modifiers

Not all Perception tests are as clear-cut as the examples given on the Perception Difficulty Table. Many different factors can affect a character's ability to notice something, including environmental conditions, or distracting sights or sounds. The Perception Modifiers Table suggests possible modifiers a gamemaster can apply to the Difficulty Number, making it harder (or easier) for characters to succeed on a given test.

BARRIERS AND STRUCTURES

There will often be times during an adventure where characters will find themselves on one side of a wall or locked door and need to get to the other. Without a key or other easy way of getting past the barrier, the characters will need to use force.

The rules for destroying a barrier are similar to the one used in combat, with a few notable differences. Attempts to destroy a barrier must generally be made with

Perception Modifiers Table

Condition	Difficulty Modifier	Condition	Difficulty Modifier
Sight:		People talking nearby	+2
Dusk/dawn	+2	Boisterous talking/singing	+3
Darkness:*		Combat/battle noise	+4
Partial	+1	Sound lower pitched than background noise	+2
Full	+2	Sound higher pitched than background noise	-2
Light rain	+1	Sound has steady rhythm contrasting with background noise	-2
Heavy rain	+3	Listener has heard sound before and recognizes it	-2
Target concealed:		Only audible sound	-3
		Smell:	
Partial	+2	Obvious odor	-2
Full	+4	Other odors present	+2
Target same color as surroundings	+3	**Touch:**	
Target contrasts with surroundings	-3	Extreme temperature	-3
Target uniquely shaped compared to surroundings	-2	Perceiver is wearing gloves	+3
Viewer knows what to look for	-2	**Taste:**	
Sound:		Taste is obvious	-3
Background noise:		Perceiver has a cold	+3
Soft background noise	+1		

*In addition to relevant test penalties (see **Situation Modifiers**, p. 386 of the *Player's Guide*).

melee or unarmed attacks. Trying to break through a wall by firing arrows at it isn't likely to do much good, and unless a spell is designed to affect the material a barrier is made of, it won't have any effect.

The character does not usually need to make an Attack test against a barrier. This does mean that many of the talents and abilities that enhance Attack tests will not provide any benefit against a barrier. The character makes a Damage test, and reduces the result by the barrier's **Physical Armor** rating. Since there is no Attack test, and the barrier doesn't have a Defense rating, extra successes do not apply a bonus to damage against barriers.

Once the amount of damage a barrier has sustained equals or exceeds its **Death Rating**, then the barrier has been effectively destroyed, opening a space that allows a human-sized (or similar) character to pass through. At gamemaster's discretion, larger or smaller characters like trolls or windlings might need more or less of the barrier destroyed in order to pass through. In general, the space created by destroying a barrier is about one yard wide, two yards high, and one yard deep. Thicker walls and barriers can be treated as multiple layers that need to be broken through.

The Barrier Rating Table suggests Physical Armor and Death Ratings for common building materials. The gamemaster should use these as the basis for determining similar ratings for other materials.

Barrier Rating Table

Barrier Material	Death Rating	Physical Armor
Blood Ivy	15	3
Cave or Natural Wall	150	30
Wood (up to 2 inches thick)	20	7
Wood (more than 2 inches thick)	30	9
Stone Wall (mortared)	45	12
Stone Block	85	20

Simplifying Barriers

Rather than deal with specific Death Ratings, breaking through a barrier can be abstracted by requiring that the character accumulate a certain number of successes with Strength or Damage tests, using the Physical Armor as the base Difficulty Number.

The number of successes should be based on what the character is trying to achieve. Getting through a locked door doesn't require the character to destroy the door, only cause enough damage to break the lock, so only one success might be required. Completely removing the door so the doorway is clear would require more destruction, and therefore three (or more) successes.

CLIMBING

Whether climbing mountains, exploring caves, or delving into an abandoned kaer, adventurers will sometimes find themselves needing to clamber to safety. These rules apply whenever a character decides (or is forced to) climb up or down vertical surfaces.

The character makes a Climbing test against a Difficulty Number based on the type of surface. The Climbing Difficulty Table suggests Difficulty Numbers for common obstacles the gamemaster may use as a guide.

Climbing uses a character's Standard Action each round spent climbing, but a character does not need to make a test each round (see below for the exception of **Climbing in Combat**). A test should be made at the beginning of the climb, and additional checks should generally only be made when the surface condition changes. For example, if the characters want to get inside a fortress, and decide to get in by scaling the bluff it stands on then climb the wall, they would make one test to scale the cliff, and a second when they start climbing the wall.

Climbing characters move up or down 2 yards per round, plus 1 yard per extra success on the Climbing test. This rate can be divided into the total distance to determine how long the climb takes.

Climbing Difficulty Table

Surface	Difficulty
Tree	5
Pole	7
Rocky Cliff	9
Wall	12
Sheer Surface	15
Distance (Choose highest)	
20+ yards	+1 DN
50+ yards	+2 DN
100+ yards	+3 DN
Each additional 100 yards	+1 DN

Silar is trying to scale a 20-yard cliff with a DN of 10, and succeeds on the Climbing test with a result of 13. He doesn't score any extra successes, so climbs 2 yards per round. The total climb takes him ten rounds (20 divided by 3 is 10).

Climbing Gear

A character using ropes and pitons, or other suitable climbing gear, gains a +4 bonus on their Climbing test.

Failing a Climbing Test

If a character fails a Climbing test, he fails to make any progress, and may fall. If the result misses the Difficulty Number by 5 or more, he falls and suffers damage (see below). If the character is using appropriate climbing gear (ropes, pitons, etc.), then he only falls if the test result misses the Difficulty Number of 10 or more.

Falling Damage

When heroes spend a lot of time climbing cliffs, scaling walls, or exploring caves, it is inevitable that at some point they will fall. When gravity takes hold, use the Falling Damage Table to determine how much damage a character suffers. Armor does not reduce the damage from falling. The number in parentheses following the Damage Step indicates the number of Damage tests that need to be made.

Mica has unfortunately been knocked overboard during a battle on an airship. He falls 110 yards, and so the gamemaster makes four Step 30/2D20+2D6 Damage tests to determine how much damage he takes, without his armor reducing the result. The dwarf is apt to have a long recovery—if he even survives.

Climbing in Combat

Trying to climb in a combat situation adds an additional layer of difficulty. Rather than making a single test to climb the entire surface, a character makes a Climbing test each round, moving up or down 2 yards, plus 1 yard per extra success on the climbing test.

If a character fails a Knockdown test while climbing, they fall and suffer damage based on the distance (see above). At gamemaster's discretion, a character may make a Climbing test in place of the normal Knockdown test to avoid being knocked down while climbing.

Falling Damage Table

Distance Fallen	Damage Step
2-3 yards	5
4-6 yards	10
7-10 yards	15
11-20 yards	20 (2)
21-30 yards	25 (2)
31-50 yards	25 (3)
51-100 yards	30 (3)
101-150 yards	30 (4)
151-200 yards	35 (4)
201+ yards	35 (5)

Creatures and Climbing

Some creatures are natural climbers, able to scale surfaces as easily as others travel on the ground. They generally do not need to make Climbing tests as described here, their climbing speed is based on the Movement Rate given in their description.

DROWNING AND SUFFOCATION

The Serpent River and its tributaries are important to trade and travel in Barsaive, and there are countless smaller bodies of water. In the life of an adventurer, water travel almost inevitably leads to somebody getting wet. Most characters find the Swimming skill (see the *Player's Guide*, p. 201) useful, but even the best swimmer can find it difficult to stay afloat when weighed down with armor.

A character who is underwater can hold his breath for a number of rounds equal to his Toughness Step. T'skrang possess rudimentary gills that allow them to breathe underwater for a number of minutes equal to their Toughness Step. Once a character runs out of breath, he starts to take damage from drowning.

The gamemaster makes a Damage test each round. In the first round, the character takes Step 4 damage, and each subsequent round the Damage Step increases by +2 until the character is rescued, reaches the surface, or dies. Armor does not reduce the damage suffered from drowning. A drowning character may try to reach the surface by making a Swimming test, but the Difficulty Number for the test is increased by the step of the most recent drowning Damage Step.

Suffocation

There are other circumstances where characters might suffer from lack of air. For example, while exploring a cave system they might encounter a pocket of stale air or even poisonous gas. The effects may not be as severe as with drowning, but it can still cause problems. After being exposed to the stale air for a number of rounds equal to their Toughness Step, a character suffers Step 2/D4-1 damage, with no reduction for armor. Each subsequent round, the damage Step increases by +1. While suffering from suffocation, a character is considered Harried and their Movement Rate is halved.

Holding Your Breath

A character can hold their breath to try and avoid poison gas or similar hazards, but it can be difficult to overcome the body's instinct to breathe. Once suffocation damage begins, a character that is voluntarily holding their breath must make a Willpower (5) or Toughness (5) test. If successful, they continue holding their breath, if they fail they take a breath. They do not take suffocation damage the next round, but may suffer the ill effects of whatever they were trying to avoid. The Difficulty Number for the Willpower or Toughness test increases by +1 for each round they continue to hold their breath.

The character can begin to hold their breath again, but the accumulated modifiers to the Damage Step do not immediately reset. Instead they drop by one for every additional round the character breathes normally.

Mica is trying to climb out of a cave where the air is heavily tainted with sulfurous fumes. To try and avoid the damage the poisonous air will cause, he decides to hold his breath. He has a Toughness Step of 6, so he can hold his breath for 6 rounds. On the fourth round of suffocation, he suffers Step 5 Damage (Step 2 for the first round + 3 for rounds 2, 3, and 4) and needs to make a Toughness (8) test (Step 5 for the first round, +3).

He fails the Toughness test with a result of 6. He takes a breath and suffers damage from the bad air. If he holds his breath right away, the suffocation Damage Step and the Difficulty Number to keep holding his breath stay at Step 5, and DN 8 respectively.

If instead he spends another round without holding his breath, the damage lowers to Step 4, and the Difficulty Number to hold his breath lowers to 7.

Some spells or abilities might cause suffocation as a secondary effect. In that case, use the rules provided with the spell or ability rather than these rules.

FIRE

Fire is a wonderful tool. Unfortunately, the same qualities that make it useful also make it dangerous. While magic can help with the potential danger, fire is a volatile and dangerous element. Raiders often set fire to a village to sow panic and confusion, and adventurers are likely to encounter fireball-flinging magicians, elemental spirits, or other creatures with an affinity for flame. This section provides guidelines for how much damage fire can inflict.

The size of a fire determines how much damage it causes. The Fire Damage Table suggests Damage Steps for fires of different sizes. Like other tables in this chapter, this list is not exhaustive; it simply provides guidelines for the gamemaster.

Smaller fires like a torch or campfire must be touched to cause damage. The damage is dealt each round the character remains in contact with the flame. Larger fires, like a burning house, can harm a character that happens to be nearby, just from the high temperature. Each round a character is adjacent to a fire of this kind—within 2 yards—he takes damage. At the gamemaster's discretion, the Damage Step may be reduced based on how far away the fire is. For example, the Damage Step could be reduced by -2 for each additional 2 yards between the character and the flames.

Fire Damage Table

Size of Fire	Damage Step
Torch	4 (touch)
Campfire (Small)	6 (touch)
Campfire (Large)	8 (touch)
House Fire	10
Forest Fire	12

Physical Armor normally provides protection from fire damage, but the gamemaster may decide that a character exposed to an especially large or fierce fire, or who has touched a fire with an unprotected body part, may not receive the protection his armor would normally provide. Magical abilities that specifically ward against heat and fire should always work to protect the character.

An unlit torch is treated as a club if used as a melee weapon. If the torch is lit, it causes damage based on the fire instead. At gamemaster's discretion, attacks may extinguish a lit torch depending on the circumstances.

Brighton is exploring a ruined kaer, carrying a torch to help him see. A ghoul rushes at him out of the dark, and the Troubadour swings the torch to ward off the undead attacker. If Brighton hits the ghoul, the lit torch will do Step 10 damage (Brighton's Strength Step of 6 + Step 4 = 10).

Dara is having a rough day. She has rescued one of her friends from the clutches of a mad Wizard, but the magician's pet lightning lizard set the tower ablaze with a stray bolt. As the Sky Raider makes her way down from the upper floors of the tower, the gamemaster decides that the growing fire causes Step 10 Damage each round that Dara and her friend are exposed to it. Dara's player hopes there aren't more surprises waiting that might delay their escape.

SECRET DOORS

Secret doors and hidden passages are a staple of adventure fiction. They often lead to areas used as hiding places or treasure rooms. Some kaers and citadels would have a bolthole or panic room through a secret door where they could retreat in the event the kaer was breached. A cult dedicated to one of the Mad Passions might have their shrine behind a hidden door. A blacksmith might secure his lock box in a concealed space under the floor.

A character trying to find a secret door makes a Perception test against a Difficulty Number based on how well the door is hidden (see **Creating Difficulty Numbers**, p. 159 and **Perception Tests**, p. 162). The gamemaster should modify the number based on the circumstances and how extensively the characters are searching. Since the point of a secret door is to remain hidden, it shouldn't be too easy to find!

Finding out there is a secret door might only be the first step. Opening it might be another matter. The gamemaster should decide how a secret door opens when he decides the purpose of the door and how well it is concealed. One secret door might open when pushed against, another might slide into a slot in the wall, while a third could require manipulating some kind of mechanism—like the classic "switch disguised as a book on a shelf." Secret doors might also be locked and/or trapped, depending on its purpose.

POISON

Characters can be exposed to poisonous substances in many different ways. Some creatures have venomous bite or sting attacks, and cults, assassins, or rogues may use poison as a weapon. A weapon coated with poison usually requires a Wound in order to affect the target, while some poisons work when ingested, and others work simply by contact.

Poison Resistance Tests

When a character is exposed to a poison, whether through a Wound, ingestion, or contact, he makes a Toughness test against the poison's Effect Step (see below). If successful, the character resists the poison and it has no effect. If the test fails, the gamemaster makes an Effect test for the poison, and the character is affected based on the type of poison.

If a poison affects a character for more than a single round (based on its duration and interval, see below), he may make a Toughness test each time the poison would affect him to see if he resists. A poison stops affecting a character once he has resisted it, but the damage or other penalties the character has suffered may take some time to go away.

In game terms, poisons are described with four characteristics: effect, onset time, interval, and duration.

Effect

Different poisons can have different effects. Most commonly, a poison directly inflicts damage, others paralyze, sicken, or kill their victims. A poison's strength is measured with a Step Number. This is used to determine the effect on the target, and to measure how well the poison resists attempts to reduce its effects with magical or mundane treatment.

Damage

Most poisons simply cause damage rather than imposing some other disadvantage on the character. The result of the Effect test is the number of Damage Points the victim takes. Armor does not normally provide any protection against poison, but there may be magical effects that provide some defense from damaging poisons.

Paralysis

When a paralytic poison affects a character, the Effect test is compared to the victim's Toughness step. For each success, the character suffers a -2 penalty to all action tests. If the total penalty equals or exceeds the character's Strength Step, the character is fully paralyzed and cannot move. They fall down and are unable to make any action tests (other than Resistance tests) until the penalty has been reduced.

Debilitation

Like with a paralytic poison, the Effect test is compared to the victim's Toughness, and he suffers a -2 test penalty for each success. However, a debilitating poison creates a more adverse effect on its target, and usually has a longer duration and interval. If the penalty from a debilitating poison equals or exceeds the victim's Toughness Step, the character is bedridden, and may not make action tests (other than Resistance tests) until the penalty has been reduced.

Death

Fast acting, truly deadly poisons are rare. For most wild creatures, their venom mainly serves as a way to survive. A predator might have a paralytic poison to keep prey from struggling while it feeds, while another animal might have a debilitating poison coating its skin to dissuade predators from eating it.

Most so-called deadly poisons generally kill through large amounts of damage, but even paralytic or debilitating poisons may cause death. They could paralyze a victim's heart or ability to breathe, or cause internal organs to shut down resulting in death.

If a paralytic or debilitating poison indicates it can cause death, the character dies if the total penalty from the poison equals their total STR+TOU Steps for paralytic poisons, or twice their TOU Step for debilitating poisons.

> *Kira has been injected by a Horror construct's deadly paralytic poison. She has a Strength Step of 4 and a Toughness Step of 6. She becomes fully paralyzed once the poison has inflicted a -4 or greater penalty to her tests, and if the penalty reaches -10 (4+6=10), she dies.*

Onset Time

Onset time describes how quickly a poison affects a character. Many poisons affect the character upon exposure. Others take longer to affect a character; for example, a debilitating poison may have an onset time of several hours, or even days.

Interval

Interval describes how frequently the poison affects a victim. The interval is represented by two values: a number and a time. The number indicates how many Effect tests the gamemaster makes for the poison, and the time represents how frequently the tests are made. For example, a poison with an interval of 4/5 minutes, a total of four Effect tests are made, with five minutes between each subsequent test. The victim may make a Resistance test each time they would be affected by the poison.

Duration

Duration indicates how long the poison affects the character's system. For damaging poisons, the duration is "until healed" as the damage stays until recovered normally (see Recovering From Poison below). Paralytic and debilitating poisons may last for hours, days, or even longer. Once the duration has expired for these poisons, any penalties they have imposed no longer apply. Unfortunately, death caused by a poison is permanent—outside of magic that would otherwise bring a character back to life.

Recovering From Poison

If a poison causes damage, the character recovers through their Recovery tests, as they do with any other damage (see **Recovering from Damage**, p. 380, in the **Earthdawn** *Player's Guide*). Penalties imposed by a paralytic or debilitating poison go away after the poison's duration ends. If the character wishes, they may make a Recovery test against the poison's Effect Step, reducing the penalty by 2 per success. Using a Recovery test in this way is subject to the normal limits of using Recovery tests, but does not heal any damage.

> *Kira managed to avoid death from the Horror construct's poison, but she is suffering a -6 penalty. After her companions kill the construct, they help Kira drink a healing potion. She spends a Recovery test and scores two successes against the poison's Effect Step of 8, reducing the penalty to -2 while the poison's duration lasts.*

If a character is killed by a deadly paralytic or debilitating poison, Last Chance Salves and similar recovery magic can still bring them back to life. Any Recovery tests allowed by the method are made, but do not heal damage. Instead, the character must accumulate at least two successes against the poison's Step to return to life. If the character is able to make multiple Recovery tests, these successes may be accumulated over multiple tests.

If the character achieves the required successes, they are brought back to life, and the total penalty is reduced based on the total number of successes scored. Any remaining effects from the poison must be treated and recovered from by normal means.

Unless otherwise noted in the poison's description, no further resistance tests are needed. It is assumed the healing magic stops the progression. The duration period for natural recovery is counted from the time the character was restored to life.

Antidotes and Poultices

Fortunately for adventurers, remedies exist to counter the effects of many poisons. There are two main ways these are delivered; antidotes and poultices.

Antidotes typically stop the progression of a poison, keeping it from continuing to harm the character. The character continues to make Resistance tests to shake off the poison, but no Effect tests are made while the antidote is in effect. Any damage or penalties suffered before the administration of the antidote remain and are recovered normally. In addition, once the antidote's duration ends, the poison may continue to affect the character unless he has succeeded on a Resistance test.

Poison Table

Poison Type	Effect Step	Onset Time Interval	Duration
Damage	6-9	Rounds	Until Healed
Paralysis	7-10	Rounds	Hours
Debilitating	8-11	Minutes/Hours	Days/Weeks

A *poultice* is usually administered while a poison is affecting a character, and while it doesn't stop the poison from affecting the character or remove any damage or penalties already suffered, it typically grants a bonus to any Resistance tests made to shake off the poison, and while in effect also grants its bonus to Recovery tests made to heal damage or reduce the penalty caused by a poison.

Poison Descriptions

Namegivers have an unfortunate tendency to turn things into weapons. Whether driven by the lethal experiments of the ill intentioned, or the thoughtless curiosity of scholars and naturalists, many medicinal herbs and other substances in nature have been turned into dangerous or deadly poisons. Fortunately, despite the many different poisons known, only a few see regular use. Some examples are described below. This list is not exhaustive; it is only intended to provide guidelines for a gamemaster to deal with poison in his game.

Black Brine
Type: Debilitation
Onset Time: 2 rounds
Duration: 2 hours
Effect Step: 8
Interval: 3/2 rounds

Black brine is extracted from the shelgar fish native to Lake Vors. A dark oil that smells strongly of salted fish, it is most commonly used on the tips of weapons, but may also be ingested. The t'skrang of House Ishkarat often dip their arrowheads and dagger blades in black brine, and rumors say that many secret societies use it to advance their goals. The toxin causes muscle weakness and a painful stiffness in the tendons, making it difficult to move quickly or perform any feats of strength such as fighting or running.

Black Mercy
Type: Paralysis
Onset Time: Instant
Duration: 6 hours
Effect Step: 8
Interval: 4/1 round

This poison comes from the black mercy flower. In the wild, the flower's pollen attracts animals, which soon die; their decomposing bodies enrich the soil around the plant. When ingested or inhaled, black mercy induces a sense of euphoria and vivid hallucinations in which the victim imagines his fondest wishes granted. While under the poison's influence, the victim is unaware of the world around him. If he is given regular doses—for example, by lingering near the plant to keep breathing the pollen—he will eventually die from starvation or thirst. A single dose, however, wears off in a matter of hours with no lasting effect.

Elfbane
Type: Debilitating (Deadly)
Onset Time: 1 hour
Duration: Permanent
Effect Step: 9
Interval: 6/1 hour

This poison is derived from a rare flower that grows in the northern reaches of Barsaive, near the Blood Wood. The blossoms are pale blue with three petals, each roughly the size of a human's thumb. When boiled and distilled, the flowers produce a bitter-smelling liquid that can be mixed with wine or spread on the edges of weapons. Elfbane causes wracking joint pain, muscle spasms, and eventual death. Even if the victim isn't killed, the effects can take some time to fade (the only way to remove the penalties caused by this poison are through the use of Recovery tests as described under **Recovering from Poisons**, p. 173).

For some reason, this poison only affects elves. According to legend, bitter feelings plagued the Elven Court during the Separation before the Scourge. Many of the elves cast out by Queen Alachia were so heartsick at leaving Wyrm Wood that they preferred to die, and took their own lives. Elfbane is said to grow where these exiles spilled their blood, and to this day the blossoms carry the pain they felt.

Eyebite
Type: Special (see text) **Effect Step:** 8
Onset Time: 3 rounds **Interval:** 3/1 round
Duration: 4 hours

The corak shrub is a hardy plant that grows in and around Barsaive's mountain ranges. When its roots are boiled, they produce a greasy, dark liquid called eyebite. It must be ingested, and its bitter, burnt taste is usually disguised in spiced dishes or savory sauces, and only a few drops are needed to affect most Namegivers.

Eyebite causes the victim's pupils to contract so tightly that they appear to vanish, resulting in temporary blindness. The Effect test result is compared to the victim's Toughness, and each success imposes a -2 penalty to sight-based Perception tests. The drug wears off after a few hours and the victim's eyesight returns. Eyebite is sometimes administered to imprisoned magicians and adepts to prevent them from using spells and talents that require clear vision.

Fireleaf
Type: Damage **Effect Step:** 7
Onset Time: 1 round **Interval:** 4/1 round
Duration: Until healed

This creeping vine grows at ground level, and bears small, dark, glossy, arrow-shaped leaves that some say resemble tongues of dark flame. The leaves produce colorless oil that severely irritates the skin, causing a red, itching rash similar to a mild burn. Though uncomfortable, the rash is largely harmless.

When collected and distilled, fireleaf oil can cause more serious blistering and scarring where they touch bare skin. The pain and itching of fireleaf can be relieved with soothing poultices of aloe and mist blossoms, both of which help to keep down swelling and promote swift healing.

Hemlock
Type: Debilitating (Deadly) **Effect Step:** 9
Onset Time: 10 minutes **Interval:** 4/10 minutes
Duration: 12 hours

The juices of this fleshy plant are a deadly poison. When consumed, they cause nausea, chills, convulsions, and eventually death. Victims of hemlock poisoning often feel cold and lethargic when the toxin begins to work. Hemlock grows in cool, damp places and is most prevalent along the Serpent River and its tributaries.

Keesra
Type: Paralysis (see text) **Effect Step:** 8
Onset Time: Instant **Interval:** 4/1 round
Duration: 8 hours

Keesra is made by windlings from the same berries that they use for keesris wine. The poison is soporific, putting victims into a deep sleep. They awaken several hours later with splitting headaches and other symptoms that resemble a severe hangover.

The poison is absorbed through the skin. Windling hunters typically soak their nets in keesra to take down dangerous creatures or other enemies.

Laésal
Type: Paralysis (see text) **Effect Step:** 10
Onset Time: 5 rounds **Interval:** 5/3 rounds
Duration: 6 hours

The laésal tree is native to the Blood Wood, and bears a fruit that resembles a gold-colored cherry. The fruit is sweet and produces feelings of mild euphoria. The fleshy red center of the fruit is filled with small, dark seeds, which can be ground into a powder that dissolves easily in food or liquids.

When consumed, laésal powder causes the victim to fall into a deep sleep for a brief time; when he wakes, he has forgotten the experiences of the past several hours. There is no known way for a victim to recover these lost memories. Laésal is often used by the Blood Warders of Alachia's court when removing intruders from the Blood Wood.

Night Pollen
Type: Damage **Effect Step:** 8
Onset Time: 1 round **Interval:** 3/1 round
Duration: Until healed

This fine, gray powder is the pollen of a night-blooming moon creeper that grows throughout the Servos Jungle. Inhaling night pollen causes irritation of the throat and lungs, severe coughing and shortness of breath. Victims of this poison may suffocate, but most recover soon after exposure. Many tribes in the Servos use night pollen as a weapon, blowing it from hollow tubes into the faces of their enemies.

Padendra
Type: Paralysis (Deadly) **Effect Step:** 10
Onset Time: 2 rounds **Interval:** 5/2 rounds
Duration: 4 hours

Padendra may be injected or ingested, and is the only fatal poison known to be used by windlings in Barsaive. It causes nausea and paralyzes muscles with painful cramps. In many cases, the paralysis causes the victim to stop breathing and suffocate. If the victim manages to survive, the paralysis wears off after a few hours with no lasting ill effect.

Windlings carefully guard the secret of padendra's production, and never use it lightly. Some scholars believe that the poison comes from the same insect that produces the less deadly whadrya venom.

Poison Gas
Type: Damage
Onset Time: 1 round
Duration: Until healed
Effect Step: 5
Interval: See text/1 round

This is an example of poisonous or toxic air characters might encounter while exploring underground caverns. Unlike most poisons, the damage continues as long as the character is exposed to the gas. The damage can be avoided by the character holding his breath, or by leaving the affected area. See **Drowning and Suffocation**, p. 168, for rules and effects on a character holding his breath.

Remis Berries
Type: Debilitating (Deadly)
Onset Time: 2 hours
Duration: 24 hours
Effect Step: 8
Interval: 5/1 hour

When the small white berries of the remis bush are ripe, they can be pressed to yield a tangy, milky juice. If ingested, it leads to painful muscle cramps, internal bleeding, and death.

The potion is commonly called "whiteberry wine," and mockingly called "mother's milk" in some circles. It is commonly sold in Kratas, and can be found in black markets around Barsaive.

Shadowmant Venom
Type: Damage
Onset Time: Instant
Duration: Until healed
Effect Step: 10
Interval: 10/1 round

The shadowmant is a flying subterranean animal that resembles a cross between a bat and a manta ray. It is a familiar hazard to adventurers and explorers of old ruins and forgotten kaers. Its venom is highly toxic when mingled with a victim's blood, and is so virulent that it can kill almost any Namegiver in minutes.

Shadowmant venom is a popular poison for coating spear points and sword blades. Fortunately, the dangers involved in acquiring the venom keep this toxin expensive and rare. Many would-be collectors wind up falling victim to their desired prize in the dark caves the creatures haunt.

Whadrya Venom
Type: Paralysis
Onset Time: Instant
Duration: 1 hour
Effect Step: 9
Interval: 3/2 rounds

Whadrya venom is derived from the natural venom of a common wasp. The venom causes temporary paralysis when injected. Windlings often use it to tip arrows or blowgun darts. The substance must be handled carefully, as even small amounts can affect the user if they are accidentally exposed.

Witherfang Venom
Type: Debilitating (see text) **Effect Step:** 9
Onset Time: Instant **Interval:** 4/2 rounds
Duration: Permanent

The witherfang serpent is found in and around the Blood Wood. Unlike most venomous snakes, the witherfang's venom is injected through a stinger on its tail. The thin, clear liquid it produces can be harvested and kept for up to a year in an airtight container without losing much potency.

The venom must enter the victim's bloodstream through a cut in the skin. It causes severe weakness and muscle pain, but only in the affected area. The affected limb withers and weakens until it becomes useless. The penalty from the poison only affects tests made with the affected limb. Apart from healing magic, no known antidote for witherfang venom exists. Many believe that Archers among the blood elves harvest witherfang venom to coat their arrowheads.

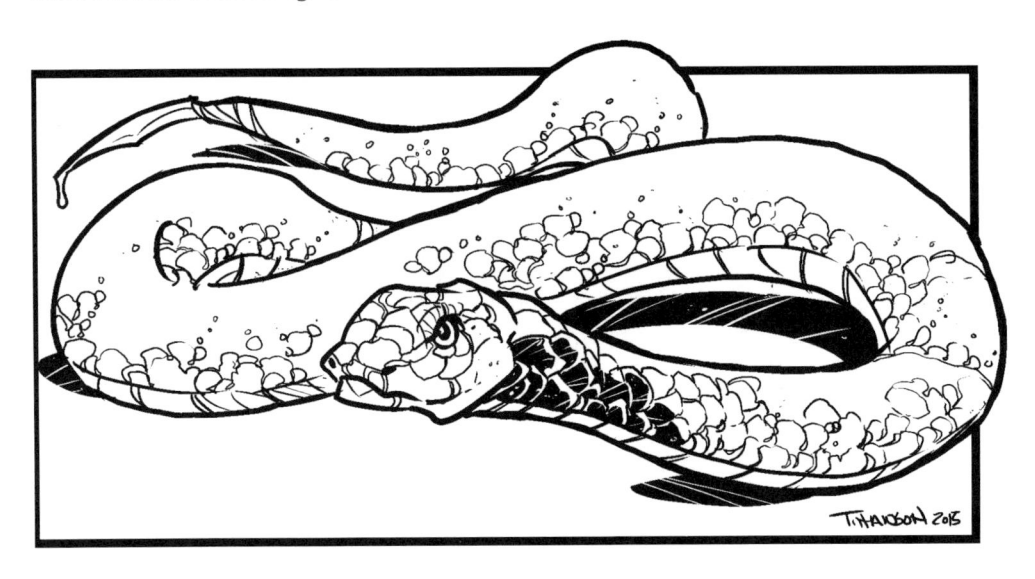

TRAPS

For almost as long as Namegivers have been in existence, they have devised ways to protect themselves and their possessions. Traps come in a wide variety of sizes and styles: from the poisoned needle hidden in the lock of a chest, a concealed pit to capture animals, or a rigged cave-in to protect the entrance to a kaer or citadel. Those who built the kaers before the Scourge constructed elaborate and deadly traps they hoped would keep the Horrors from breaking into their shelter.

Characters in **Earthdawn** are likely to encounter traps as they explore the world, especially if their adventures take them to kaers and citadels that remain sealed. In addition, there are other obstacles that are handled in the same way as traps, but are not man-made. For example a natural cave-in, or pocket of explosive gas encountered while exploring underground. The guidelines presented here for traps should be used when you have a natural or mechanical hazard that could catch the characters off guard and cause harm.

Traps in the **Earthdawn** game are described with the following game statistics:

Detection

Detection represents the Difficulty Number for a character to notice or sense a trap with a Perception (or appropriate talent) test. Traps typically start with a Detection of 5, though some traps are more cleverly concealed, and others are so obvious that they are essentially saying, "This thing is trapped. Why don't you go somewhere else?" Magical traps typically have a higher Detection than physical traps.

Disarm

This represents the Difficulty Number for a character's Disarm Trap test. If the character does not have the appropriate talent or skill, the best they can do is try to avoid triggering the trap. In this case, the character must succeed at a Dexterity test (for mechanical traps) or Perception test (for magical traps) against the Disarm Difficulty.

Mechanical traps typically have a Disarm Difficulty of 7 to 9. Magical traps start at Disarm Difficulty of 8 and go up from there. The Disarm value also acts as the appropriate Defense Rating for talents, spells, or other abilities that target the trap.

Initiative

A trap's Initiative rating measures how quickly the trap activates. When a trap is triggered, the gamemaster makes an Initiative test using Initiative rating as the Step. Any character that would be affected by the trap also makes an Initiative test; characters who achieve a higher result have a chance to act and possibly avoid the trap. This is the only way to avoid a trap's effect once it is triggered.

Mechanical traps have an Initiative rating of 8 to 10. Magical traps usually have a higher Initiative.

Trigger

This describes the mechanism or action that triggers the trap. Stepping on a pressure plate, lifting the lid of a chest, and opening a door are common examples of trigger conditions for mechanical traps. Characters using talents or spells within a certain range may trigger magical traps.

Effect

This entry describes the type and amount of damage the trap inflicts. Some traps restrain their targets, others may mark them with a magical stain, or put a spell on the character that takes effect after a delay. A trap may have any effect conjured by the imagination and resources of the character building the trap. If the trap causes damage, this entry will indicate its Damage Step. For example, the effect of a simple pit trap might be only Damage Step 4 from falling, while a trap designed to smash an intruder with a falling rock could have a Damage Step 10 or more.

Trap Descriptions

Several example traps are presented here. Feel free to use these as a starting point to develop traps of your own.

Blade Trap

Blade traps feature one or more sharp blades meant to slit a victim's throat or cut him across his legs. In old ruins or kaers the blades may be centuries old and rusted or corroded. These rusty blades might cause infected Wounds or be weakened with age and do less damage than a clean, new blade. While there are many different styles of blade trap, an example is provided here.

Detection: 7   **Disarm:** 9
Initiative: 17/D12+2D8
Trigger: Pressure plate
Effect: A large blade springs from the wall, causing Step 13/D12+D10 damage, with Physical Armor providing protection. The blade is old and corroded. If armor prevents the blade from causing damage, it shatters. If the blade causes a Wound there is a chance that blood poisoning sets in. Treat this as a poison with the following characteristics (see **Poison**, p. 171 for more information):

Type: Debilitating   **Step Number:** 7
Onset Time: 48 hours   **Interval:** 4/12 hours
Duration: 4 days

If blood poisoning sets in, the Wound will not heal until the character has resisted the poison, the duration has passed, or it is cured by magic.

Cave-In Trap

At best, cave-ins impede progress by blocking the way ahead. At worst, they trap characters under tons of dirt and stone. This trap can be natural, the result of damage to a cave or tunnel ceiling or wall, or it might be man-made, constructed as a way to damage invaders and block access.

Detection: 8 **Disarm:** See text
Initiative: 10
Trigger: A collision or loud noise.
Effect: The ceiling collapses, causing Step 16/DD12+D8+D6 damage to characters trapped in the fall, reduced by Physical Armor.

Natural cave-in traps generally can't be disarmed, as they are the result of structural weaknesses in the area, though clever use of magic or the service of elemental spirits could prevent the trap from being triggered. A man made cave-in trap, on the other hand, would have a pressure plate, tripwire, or the like and can be disarmed in the same way as other mechanical traps.

In addition to causing damage, cave-ins can also trap characters underground by blocking their way out of a cave or mine or burying them in rocks. To dig themselves out, characters must make a Strength test each round against a Difficulty Number based on the difficulty of moving the fallen rock aside without triggering a second collapse (usually 5 to 7). If the characters have talents, spells, or other abilities appropriate for digging out, the gamemaster may allow those in place of the Strength tests at his discretion. It takes an average of 10 accumulated Successes to dig out.

At gamemaster's discretion, a Rule of One result on the Strength test could trigger a secondary collapse, causing Step 7/D12 damage to any digging characters, and adding an additional success to the total needed to dig free.

Dart Trap

Dart traps are commonly used to protect chests, cabinets, and the like. In this example, three spring-loaded darts are launched at the victim. The darts are often coated with damaging poisons (see **Poison**, p.171).

Detection: 15 **Disarm:** 8
Initiative: 13/D12+D10
Trigger: Opening the box lid.
Effect: The darts strike the victim, each causing Step 6/D10 damage, with Physical Armor providing protection. If the victim takes any damage, the **Shadowmant Venom** (see p. 178) that coats them takes effect.

Explosive Gas Trap

This is a naturally occurring trap usually encountered while exploring underground. Many natural gases are flammable and could ignite or explode when exposed to open flame.

Detection: 10 **Disarm:** See text
Initiative: 7/D12
Trigger: Exposure to open flame.
Effect: The gas explodes, causing Step 15/D12+2D6 damage to all characters within the area of effect, reduced by Physical Armor. The explosion typically covers a 10-yard radius area, but could be larger depending on the concentration of gas. If characters detect explosive gas, they can attempt to douse all fire sources before accidentally triggering an explosion. To do so, each character carrying a fire source must make an Initiative test against the Initiative result of the gas. If successful, the

character manages to douse his flame in time. If one or more of the tests fail, the gas ignites and causes the damage listed.

Kaer Ward

Wards are magical traps designed to prevent access to a location by injuring or hindering intruders. They were often the primary means of protection for wealthier kaers and citadels, and were designed to deter intrusion by powerful Horrors. As a result, they pose a serious danger to the unwary explorer. Fortunately, these wards were not usually concealed or hidden.

Detection: 5 **Disarm:** 19
Initiative: 30/2D20+2D6
Trigger: The gamemaster makes a Step 17/D12+2D8 Spellcasting test against the Mystic Defense of any character within 2 yards of the ward. If successful, the ward is triggered.
Effect: The trap casts a sustained damaging spell against the victim, causing Step 23/D20+2D10 damage per round for ten rounds, with Mystic Armor providing protection.

Mantrap

When triggered, serrated metal jaws spring up and grip the victim's leg, causing damage and preventing the victim from moving until released. This example has been concealed with illusion magic, making it difficult to detect.

Detection: 16 **Disarm:** 12
Initiative: 13/D12+D10
Trigger: A pressure plate.
Effect: Jaws spring shut on the victim's leg, causing Step 20/D20+D8+D6 damage, with Physical Armor providing protection. The victim is also held in place; until freed, he may not move and is considered Harried (see **Situation Modifiers** in the *Player's Guide*, p 386). In some cases, a mantrap may be poisoned, adding to the victim's misery.

The victim can be freed by prying open the metal jaws with a Strength (12) test. If more than one person is attempting to free the victim, add their Strength Steps together to determine the Step rolled on the Strength test.

Pit Trap

One of the simpler and more common traps, it consists of a pit hidden by a false floor or illusion magic. The victim suffers damage from falling, and this example has stakes at the bottom to cause additional damage.

Detection: 7 **Disarm:** 7
Initiative: 10/2D8
Trigger: A trip wire.
Effect: A 3-yard by 3-yard section of floor drops away, dumping anyone in the affected area into a 6-yard-deep pit. The fall causes Step 10/2D8 damage (see Falling Damage, p. 167), and the character is impaled on D4 stakes. Each stake causes an additional Step 12/2D10 damage, with Physical Armor providing protection.

Spike Trap

Similar to blade traps, a spike trap consists of sharpened metal or wooden stakes hidden in the gaps between stones and released through a powerful spring. They are commonly found in ruined citadels and kaers. While an individual spike typically causes less damage than a larger blade, they are typically grouped together and are harder to detect.

Detection: 15   **Disarm:** 15
Initiative: 25/D20+2D12
Trigger: A pressure plate.
Effect: Six spikes shoot out from cracks in the walls, striking the victim who tripped the trap with incredible force. The spikes cause Step 18/D12+D10+D8 damage, with Physical Armor providing protection. If the victim receives a Wound, he is impaled on the spikes and is consider Knocked Down (see **Situation Modifiers** in the **Earthdawn** Player's Guide, p. 386). Other characters may attempt to ease the victim off the spikes with a Dexterity (15) test. If successful, the victim is safely removed, otherwise the victim remains impaled and suffers an additional Step 6/D10 damage, with no protection from armor. If multiple characters are attempting to free the victim, add their Dexterity Steps together to determine the Step rolled on the Dexterity test.

Once triggered, the trap blocks passage along the corridor. To proceed, characters must move the spikes out of the way. This may be done with a successful Disarm Trap test, a Strength (15) test, or some other suitable method, such as breaking the spikes, at the gamemaster's discretion

Ward Trap

Like the kaer ward, this magical trap is designed to keep people from entering certain areas. Magicians often set wards to detect and ignore certain beings—for example, the ward's creator—and to trigger only if an unauthorized person attempts to pass the ward. A Nethermancer created this example, but there are as many different types of wards as there are magicians to create them.

Detection: 10   **Disarm:** 12
Initiative: 30/2D20+2D6
Trigger: When an unauthorized character passes through the warded doorway, the gamemaster makes a Step 15/D12+2D6 Spellcasting test against his Mystic Defense. If successful, the ward's spell effect is triggered
Effect: The victim is targeted by the Bone Shatter spell (see the **Earthdawn** Player's Guide, p. 334). Unlike the normal version of the spell, only one target may be affected. The spell is considered to have a Willpower Step of 10 for determining the Effect Step.

CURSES

A curse is a negative magical effect attached to an item or place, which affects a character that comes into contact with it. The effects of a curse can vary widely. One curse might cause a penalty to a character's actions, another could create a lasting effect similar to a disease, while a third might cause misfortune to follow in the victim's wake, giving the character a reputation as a jinx or bearer of ill omen.

The gamemaster is free to create the specific nature and effect of curses, but we recommend you keep in mind the following guidelines.

Becoming Cursed

There are many ways in which an item or place can become cursed. The most common way is for the item or place to be exposed to the corrupting magical nature of the Horrors. The influence of a Mad Passion or one of their questors can result in a curse, or an item could be cursed through a random magical mishap during its creation.

The details of how a curse came about could be an element in the background of an adventure, and influence the nature of the curse. For example, a corrupt Nethermancer might have summoned a Horror to destroy a village that exiled him, and now the village has become cursed to inflict a wasting sickness on all who enter it. Many people in Barsaive believe that the Blood Elves are actually the victims of a powerful curse.

There are three general types of curses that can affect characters in **Earthdawn**: minor curses, major curses, and Horror curses.

Minor Curses

The effects of a *minor* curse should handicap a character, but not threaten his life. This can range from a small (–1 to –3) penalty to a character's tests, affecting the character with the equivalent effect of a weak debilitating poison (see **Poison**, p.123), or even requiring extra successes on certain actions. Minor curses are most often associated with magical items rather than places.

Major Curses

The effects of *major* curses should seriously impair a character, and in extreme cases might even threaten his life. For example, a character might have one (or more) of his Attribute Steps lowered; if his Strength were reduced, his blows would not cause as much damage. Perhaps the curse results in a runic scar that causes other characters to fear the victim, resulting in penalties to Interaction tests, or negatively shifting the Attitude of gamemaster characters (see **Interaction Tests**, p. 144).

Major curses can be associated with items or places; the curse lasts at least as long as the character remains in contact with the cursed item or place. Sometimes the effects will last beyond the initial exposure, and affected characters must appeal to a powerful magician to help free them from the curse.

Horror Curses

Horror curses represent the most powerful and dangerous curses in **Earthdawn**. A Horror-cursed place or item functions much like a Horror Mark (see p. 462). It establishes a link between a Horror and an item or place, allowing the Horror to use its powers against anyone exposed to the item or place. Fortunately, the strength of a

Horror's powers are often reduced when used through a cursed item. A good rule of thumb is to apply a -5 or -10 penalty to the power's Step.

However, the dangers posed by a Horror curse go beyond the ability of the Horror to use its powers against an unsuspecting victim. Their desire to inflict pain and suffering prompts many Horrors to use their influence carefully, hoping to keep potential victims from entirely abandoning an item or place. Some Horrors use a curse to gradually corrupt a victim by making them assist in spreading the Horror's influence.

The potential effects of a Horror curse are limited only by the gamemaster's imagination, keeping in mind the Horror's motivations. Simple death is usually too direct, and doesn't result in the same degree of satisfaction as an extended ordeal of emotional pain and suffering. There are many stories in Barsaive of Namegivers that have been the victim of long-term Horror curses, and the most notorious cursed items often start off providing some kind of benefit to the user, only revealing the true cost—and connection to the Horror—once the victim has become dependent on it.

Horror curses are often used as the focus of a longer story or campaign arc, as frequently the only way to break these kinds of curses is to kill the Horror causing it. There are rumors that powerful magic—perhaps known by dragons, or powerful, reclusive adepts or questors—may be able to remove a Horror's influence, but as with many things related to the Horrors, the truth is uncertain.

Curse Effects

A curse's strength is measured by its Step. When a character comes into contact with a cursed item or place, the gamemaster makes a test using the Curse Step against the character's Mystic Defense. The Curse Table summarizes the suggested Step Numbers for each curse type. The gamemaster should use this table as a guideline; each curse is unique, and no two will necessarily affect a character in the same way.

Curse Table

Curse Type	Step Number
Minor	7-8
Major	9-15
Horror	Horror's Spellcasting Step

Though you may create any effect for a curse, the curse should work within the adventure. Avoid making the effects of the curse overwhelmingly powerful. Remember that curses are meant to challenge and hinder the player characters, and should be carefully thought out.

DISEASE

Disease has been a part of life since life began. While some illnesses vanished during the Scourge, others have appeared to take their place. The diagnoses and treatment of disease remains a difficult and challenging art, even with magic to make things easier, because so much knowledge was lost during the Scourge.

Diseases in **Earthdawn** work like poisons. Each disease has an onset time, an Effect Step, an interval, and a duration. See Poison, p.171, for more information on these terms.

While some diseases run their course and the victim recovers, others are chronic. Chronic diseases continue to affect a character until cured, represented by the character resisting the disease at some point. In many cases, this requires medical or magical intervention.

Methods of Exposure

Namegivers usually contract illnesses by consuming tainted food or drink, or through contact with someone who is infected. In some cases, a character can be exposed by breathing the air near an infected person, or through the bite of infected animals or insects. Some environments, like jungles and swamps, are especially disease prone, and explorers could find themselves exposed to exotic and unusual illnesses.

When a character is exposed to a disease, they make a Toughness test against the disease's Effect Step. If successful, the character resists the disease. If the test fails, the character falls ill, and starts to suffer the effects of the disease once the onset time has passed.

Many diseases display initial symptoms during their onset time, which might allow a knowledgeable character to diagnose and treat an oncoming illness. Others give no indication that the character is infected until they have come down with a full case. As with poison, the character may make additional Toughness tests to try and shake off the illness as it progresses.

Disease Treatments

Diseases can be treated with the Physician skill, various medicines, and magic. The rules and guidelines in this book do not get into the details of different remedies and their efficacy against particular diseases. The gamemaster is encouraged to develop these details in their own games, keeping in mind that these kinds of details should be used to enhance a story, rather than drag down the game in minutia.

To keep things simple, remedies should work like the Cure Disease and Halt Illness potions (see **Healing Aids** in the **Earthdawn** *Player's Guide*, p. 422), either providing a bonus to Toughness tests made to resist the disease, or halting the progression of an illness. Generally, the effectiveness of medicines should not be more powerful than magical healing, which could potentially cure a disease completely.

Example Diseases

The diseases listed below provide rules for using them in your games. Many additional diseases exist in Barsaive, however, along with plagues and illnesses spawned by curses, Horrors, and magic gone wrong. Feel free to invent new and insidious diseases to inflict on your players as they explore Barsaive. Generally speaking, a disease should provide some obstacle or limitation for a character to overcome, rather than simply laying him flat on his back for a week of game time. Playing sick for a whole game isn't much fun.

Following are descriptions of several diseases and treatments known to healers in most regions of Barsaive.

Bone Plague

Type: Debilitation
Onset Time: 3-4 days
Duration: 4-5 weeks
Effect Step: 8
Interval: 3/1 week

Bone plague begins with a mild fever, a feeling of listlessness, and pains in the joints. Over the course of a few days, the victim becomes progressively more fatigued, and his joints turn rubbery. In serious cases, the victim's joints and bones become so weak that they no longer function as they should; he cannot stand, walk, hold onto things, or lift so much as a feather.

The illness itself is not fatal and passes within a few weeks even if left untreated. However, the weakness and paralysis that it causes can do great harm if the victim is far from help when the disease takes hold. There are cases where bone plague swept through a small village, striking down everyone virtually at once. With no able-bodied persons to help the sufferers eat and drink, many poor victims starved to death.

While the effect of Bone Plague is treated like a debilitating poison, the penalty only applies to tests made for physical actions. Recovery from bone plague requires a week's rest and hearty food to fully regain their strength. Increased appetite is a sure sign that the disease is departing.

Death's Caress

Type: Debilitation (Deadly)
Onset Time: 3–6 hours
Duration: 4–5 days
Effect Step: 10
Interval: 4/1 day

Known as fire plague in some areas of Barsaive, Death's Caress is the most deadly and virulent plague known in Barsaive. The disease brings high fever, sweating, chills, and painful muscle cramps. Victims become extremely sensitive to touch, smell, sound, and light, and are most comfortable in a darkened and quiet room.

If the illness is left untreated, the fever burns the victim up from the inside until no more moisture remains in his body. Many victims see visions of Death's fiery kingdom while afflicted by this plague, and some scholars speculate that Death created the disease to avenge his imprisonment.

Places where outbreaks of Death's caress are known to have occurred are shunned by the wise, to prevent infection. Infection can spread through food and water, or from exposure to infected people—the blood and other bodily fluids are especially dangerous. The bodies and clothing of victims are usually burned.

There is no known cure for Death's caress, save for powerful healing magic. Certain methods of treatment offer comfort to the sufferer and may even give him strength enough to hold on to life while the illness runs its course—but this happens rarely. Most victims of Death's caress succumb within days of first displaying the symptoms. The principal treatment is to bring the fever down, using cool water or even ice (if it can be had).

As with deadly debilitating poisons, the victim dies if the total penalty equals twice the victim's Toughness Step. A character who fails his tests to overcome this illness is likely to die without powerful magical healing.

Horrorfever

Type: Special (see text)
Onset Time: 20 days
Duration: Chronic
Effect Step: 12
Interval: Chronic/20 days

This fever earned its name because the victim experiences nightmares and terrors while the illness is active. Despite the name, flies and other biting insects spread this disease, not by Horrors.

Twenty days after infection, the victim is overcome with horrifying dreams and night terrors. For every success on the disease's Effect test, the active period lasts for 12 hours. After the active period ends, the affected character makes a Toughness test to resist the illness. If successful, he has shaken off the fever. If he fails, the active phase returns in 20 days. This continues until the character is cured,

While the disease is active, the character is unable to get a full night's rest and does not regain Recovery tests. In addition, he suffers a -6 penalty to his tests, and finds sustained mental effort almost impossible. Once the active phase ends, the character recovers from the effects after a full night's rest.

Lung-Rot

Type: Debilitation (Deadly)
Onset Time: 1–4 months
Duration: Chronic
Effect Step: 7
Interval: Chronic/1 month

This disease, sometimes called galloping lung-rot, is usually contracted in cold and damp regions. It takes a few months to manifest, with the incubation period marked by congestion and coughing, labored breathing, and a mild fever. While the illness's slow progression usually allows for successful diagnoses and treatment, the disease is fatal if left untreated for too long. Victims of an extended bout of lung-rot can suffer from shortness of breath and weakened constitution for the rest of their lives.

When lung-rot affects a victim, the maximum penalty applied per Effect test is -2, regardless of the Effect test success level. The penalty only applies to tests made for physical actions. If the disease progresses to the point where the penalty equals or exceeds the victim's Toughness Step, his lungs become scarred and he permanently reduces his Dexterity, Strength, and Toughness values by -3 each. As with other deadly debilitating poisons and diseases, if the accumulated penalty equals or exceeds double the victim's Toughness Step, he dies.

Treatment for lung-rot usually involves boiling the leaves of certain plants, with the victim breathing in the steam. The steam relieves congestion and eases breathing. The most popular plant for this treatment is Rianna's Fan, which grows in clusters around trees and decaying stumps. The plant has broad, fan-shaped leaves, said to share the same dark green as the legendary elf healer's eyes.

Quaking Fever

Type: Debilitation
Onset Time: 1–3 days
Duration: 7–10 days
Effect Step: 6
Interval: 4/2 days

Quaking fever is usually contracted in marshy and swampy areas with standing and stagnant water. Symptoms include fever, trembling limbs, sore nose and throat, along with a wet cough. The disease is not contagious, so exposure to infected victims poses no danger.

While no specific cure is known, the disease is not fatal unless to victim is already severely weakened in some other way. The symptoms typically persist for about a week, with many common treatments helping alleviate the coughing fits and nasal congestion.

Smiling Death
Type: Debilitation (Deadly)   **Effect Step:** 8
Onset Time: 1 week   **Interval:** 4/3 days
Duration: 2 weeks

This strange disease can be caught from tainted water or from contact with an infected person; even breathing the air too near a victim may result in infection. The marks of smiling death include headaches, blurred vision, high fever, sweating, and muscle cramps severe enough to incapacitate the patient.

As the disease progresses, victims suffer from facial grimaces and respiratory spasms that resemble smiling and faint laughter. In the most serious cases, victims lapse into unconsciousness and die. Healing magic can cure smiling death even after the patient has lapsed into unconsciousness, provided the healer is powerful enough and the patient has been unconscious for no more than two days.

Stenchfoot
Type: Debilitation   **Effect Step:** 7
Onset Time: 1–4 days   **Interval:** 4/48 hours (see text)
Duration: 1–2 weeks (see text)

This grisly disease is an unfortunately common danger to careless explorers, as it is most often contracted by walking in boggy ground and picking up parasites through the feet. This disease causes flesh to rot, with blood poisoning eventually setting in. It typically affects lower extremities first, but the infection can spread anywhere once contracted.

Once contracted, the interval is 48 hours while the character is in jungle or swamp conditions, but if a character escapes to a cool, dry environment the interval period extends to 1 week. The penalties inflicted by the disease only affect a character's Toughness and Charisma tests. If the cumulative penalty equals or exceeds the victim's Toughness Step, the character loses an extremity. The extremity lost is usually the one where the disease first manifested, but could be any part of the body: for example a foot, an ear, the nose, or a hand.

The effects of losing an extremity are left to the gamemaster, but some results are obvious. For example, a character that loses a hand will be unable to use a bow, and will likely have a hard time using a shield strapped to his forearm (perhaps resulting in a reduction to the shield's Physical Defense bonus). Cosmetic losses (ears or nose) could result in a penalty to Charisma or Interaction tests where appearance might matter, while the loss of a foot could result in penalties to a character's movement rate or Dexterity value.

The penalties inflicted by the disease go away after the disease is cured, but the loss of body parts is permanent outside of powerful healing magic.

Walking Fever
Type: Death (See text) **Effect Step:** 8
Onset Time: 1–2 days **Interval:** 3/1 week
Duration: 3 weeks

Scholars debate whether Walking Fever is a true disease or not, but healers still treat it, concerned more with saving lives than intellectual exercise. The illness is contracted through exposure to the spores of the darkbloom fungus, which grows in damp caves and dark forests where sunlight doesn't reach.

Anyone who breathes in the spores and fails the initial Toughness test develops a sore throat, headaches, and a mild fever. The fever progresses until the victim falls unconscious, then after a day or two they awaken, making their second Toughness test to resist the disease. If successful, they have shaken off the infection and recover in a few days. If this second test fails, the fever continues and the victim develops sensitivity to bright light.

After a week under the effects of the second stage of the infection, the victim makes a third and final Toughness test. If this test fails, the victim succumbs to the final stage of infection. They seek shelter in a dark, dank place, and the air around them becomes heavy with darkbloom spores. For the next ten to fourteen days, anybody that comes near the victim risks infection. At the end of that time, the victim dies and his body becomes host to new sprouts of fungus.

Unlike other diseases, Walking Fever does not inflict penalties on the victim, and so the gamemaster does not make Effect tests for the disease. While they may be restless and uncomfortable, the victim is able to act normally until they fail the final Toughness test, at which point the influence of the fungus drives them to take shelter as described above.

Yellow Jig
Type: Special (see text) **Effect Step:** 8
Onset Time: 2–4 days **Interval:** 14/2 days
Duration: 2–4 weeks

Yellow jig can be caught from tainted water or by touching an infected victim. The disease causes a slight yellowing of the victim's skin, the whites of the eyes, and underside of the tongue. Within a few days of these initial signs, the victim experiences weakness and trembling limbs, and sometimes suffers from random fits of jerky, uncontrollable muscle spasms, as if engaged in some macabre dance.

The disease itself is not fatal, though some have died from accidents caused by convulsions at the wrong moment. A popular tale mentions a hero from before the Scourge who broke his neck falling down a flight of stairs when spasms struck him. Yellow jig commonly passes within two to four weeks, during which time various potions and elixirs can be used to ease the spasms and provide the patient with much-needed rest.

If the character does not resist the disease when an interval passes, the Effect test determines the intensity of the symptoms. A single success causes a -2 penalty to the character's tests, two successes cause a -4 test penalty, and 3 or more successes cause a -4 test penalty, and the victim will suffer 1-4 convulsive episodes, each lasting 2-12 combat rounds. During a convulsive episode, roll an Effect test for the disease against a Difficulty Nmber equal to the victim's Strength Step. If successful, the victim is considered Knocked Down and unable to act until the episode passes.

FATIGUE AND INJURY

The rules for damage in **Earthdawn** are intended to reflect injuries inflicted in combat with creatures, Horrors, and other enemies. They aren't designed to reflect the fatigue and injuries that can occur with travel through the wilds of Barsaive. This section includes rules and guidelines for fatigue and other non-combat injuries. They are presented here for groups that wish to include more detail in their explorations.

Fatigue

The distances given in the **Exploration and Travel** chapter (p. 125) assume that characters travel for about 8 hours per day, take sufficient rest breaks do not push themselves (or their mounts) too hard. Unfortunately, the need sometimes arises for adventurers to push beyond their normal limits. After all, the cultists aren't going to delay their ritual because the heroes are four days' travel away instead of three!

Sometimes called a forced march, characters must make a Toughness (7) test for every two hours—or fraction thereof—beyond the standard 8-hour travel time. If the test fails, the character begins to suffer fatigue. Each failed test results in a cumulative -1 penalty to the character's tests, including future tests to resist fatigue. For example, if a character traveled for 11 hours, they would need to make two tests, and if they failed both tests they would start suffering a -2 penalty to their tests.

To recover from the penalties associated with fatigue, the character must rest. Namegivers normally require eight hours of rest a night. For every four hours beyond this, the fatigue penalty is reduced by one. Using the prior example, if the character was able to get an extra four hours of rest, the penalty would drop from -2 to -1. During this time a character cannot partake in any strenuous activities, and is considered to be injured for the purposes of increasing talent ranks and skills (see **Building Your Legend** in the *Player's Guide*, p. 445), as well as restricting any other activity that requires the character to be uninjured.

Brief exertions, such as fighting off bandits attacking the camp, do not interrupt this rest unless the combat lasts for more than 15 to 20 minutes. Other activities may be allowed at the gamemaster's discretion, but any kind of extended physical or mental work, such as hunting or foraging, doing research in a library, long distance travel (on foot or mounted) should be restricted.

Another way characters might suffer from fatigue is if they do not get enough rest at night, even if they aren't pushing themselves during the day. As mentioned previously, Namegivers generally require 8 hours of sleep a night. If a character is not able to get enough sleep, they may also suffer fatigue penalties. For every two hours of sleep missed, the character must make Toughness tests as described above, suffering a cumulative -1 penalty for every failed test. In addition, characters who get less than four hours of sleep do not refresh their allotment of Recovery tests the next day.

When traveling in the wilderness, most adventuring groups will set up camp to rest for ten hours (or more) so that watches can be set and still have all of the characters in the group get sufficient sleep. A character who is asleep for four hours, on watch for two, and asleep for another four (or similar arrangements) is still getting enough sleep for the purposes of these rules.

Injuries

There are a number of minor injuries or illnesses that characters can suffer as a result of traveling in the wilderness: twisted or sprained ankles, sunburn, blisters, food poisoning, and more. An exhaustive list of these afflictions and their possible effects is beyond the scope of these rules. They are best used as flavor to help enhance the mood or tone of your game, or to enrich the magic-rich fantasy setting with a dash of the mundane.

In general, minor injuries or illnesses should apply a -1 penalty to tests made with certain Attributes. For example, a character that gets caught in a rainstorm or similar severe weather might catch a cold if they aren't prepared for it—whether by having appropriate gear, or changing into dry clothes and warming up at the first opportunity. The cold could sap the character's energy, resulting in a -1 penalty to tests made with some or all of their physical Attributes, or perhaps the congestion and stuffy nose results in a penalty to Perception tests.

The amount of time that a character is affected by an injury can vary, but usually lasts between two days and a week. They should not limit healing of normal damage or Wounds, though injuries that penalize Toughness may affect Recovery tests. After the appropriate amount of time, the injury and its associated penalty are cleared after a full night's sleep and the character's morning Recovery test. This test will still heal damage or a Wound as applicable (see **Recovering from Injury** in the *Player's Guide*, p. 380).

Minor injuries may also be treated with magical healing aids, like booster or healing potions. The healing aid removes the character's need to wait and also eliminates any penalty associated with the injury. As with Recovery tests that heal injuries, a healing aid used in this way still heals damage or Wounds.

Advanced Rules for Injuries

For groups that want to introduce more mechanical effects for injuries resulting from environmental conditions, we offer these suggestions. These are far from exhaustive, and are recommended only for groups interested in that level of detail.

Dehydration

Assuming he doesn't get involved in strenuous activity, a human sized Namegiver requires at least one quart of water per day. For each day that a character doesn't get enough water, he takes 3 Damage from dehydration, with no reduction for armor. He also suffers a penalty to all tests equal to the number of days he has gone without enough water.

The gamemaster should increase the damage and associated penalties based on prevailing conditions, any strenuous activity the character might perform, and the amount of water available. Without any water at all, most Namegivers are not able to survive more than about three days.

Exposure and Frostbite

For every half hour a character is exposed to extreme cold without adequate protection, he suffers Step 4/D6 damage, with no reduction from armor. The Step may increase for exceptionally harsh conditions at gamemaster discretion. If any single Damage test for exposure to cold causes a Wound, the character suffers frostbite, incurring a -1 penalty to Dexterity and/or Strength tests, depending on the affected body part. If left untreated, the frozen flesh could begin to rot and become infected, which should be treated like a disease similar to Stenchfoot (see

p. 190), but affecting Dexterity and/or Strength. If the penalties get too severe, the limb in question might be lost.

Heat Exposure

The intense heat that can be found in the area around Death's Sea, or near underground volcanoes or steam vents might damage characters without adequate protection. For each hour of exposure, characters will suffer Step 4/D6 damage, with no reduction from armor. The intense heat also increases the risk of dehydration, and tires characters more easily. Strain costs are doubled, and characters suffer a -1 penalty to Fatigue tests. If a character is wearing armor that imposes an Initiative penalty, the character takes strain equal to that penalty for every hour of exposure, and for every minute spent fighting.

High Altitudes

Characters that are not acclimated to high altitudes become tired more easily. All Strain costs are doubled, and characters also suffer a -1 penalty to fatigue tests in high mountain regions. Highland trolls are typically used to dealing with high altitudes, and at the gamemaster's discretion Air Sailors and Sky Raiders might also be acclimated, depending on their experience.

Starvation

Characters can go longer without food than they can without water, but starvation is still dangerous. The penalties for starvation are the same as for dehydration, but accumulate every three days instead of every day. For example, a character that has been without food for 6 days suffers 6 Damage and suffers a -2 penalty. As with dehydration, this assumes the character is getting some food, just not enough. Without any food at all, most Namegivers will not survive more than about three weeks.

EARTHDAWN

THREAD ITEMS

You can keep the gold and gemstones. The greatest treasure here is Tercel, Blade of the House of Elcor.
•*Dimos, Warrior of the Inheritors of Landis* •

There are many different magical items within the world of **Earthdawn**. These fantastical treasures are divided into three categories: common magic items, pattern items, and thread items. Common magic items include a wide variety of items to fulfill just as many functions. This category includes blood magic charms and healing aids, in addition to a multitude of other items. They are referred to as common because they can be found throughout Barsaive and purchased as a simple (though possibly expensive) transaction. Even the smallest of hamlets will have access to common magic items and they can be used by anyone.

The magic of pattern items and thread items is part of the fabric of reality and can only be accessed by adepts. Pattern items are a part of the true pattern of a greater true pattern, either a location or a person, while thread items have their own true pattern. Both require knowledge of the pattern to weave a thread to it. This process is discussed in more detail in the *Player's Guide*, p. 220.

Pattern items and thread items will be integral to every game. They give players access to power and can help drive the story forward. The search for these items and their Key Knowledges will help reveal the rich history of the setting and campaign, and create a greater connection between players and the world.

This chapter focuses on thread items in your game. How to use pattern items and thread items in your campaign, creating thread items for your campaign, and examples of thread items which can be used as written, or adapted to your campaign.

OVERVIEW OF THREAD ITEMS

Thread items are grouped into tiers, which determine their base power: Novice, Journeyman, Warden, and Master. Within each category is a subset of Legendary items.

Novice thread items are the most common and weakest thread items. They are comparatively easy to create, particularly since there are a variety of pre-made patterns to follow. These designs are tried and true methods, effectively recipes for creating thread items. In general they perform a specific function and do not have any special abilities.

197

Journeyman thread items are naturally more complex and more powerful than their Novice brethren. There are some which follow designs, though these are much less common. These designs were more common before the Scourge when magic levels were greater. The reduction in magic and loss of knowledge has conspired to make these less common in the contemporary era. Many of the thread items of this tier have special abilities and possibility a variety of functions.

Warden thread items are generally considered the limit of what can normally be crafted. Designs for these items were rare prior to the Scourge and are virtually unheard of afterwards. When created, these items are almost always unique and require a great deal of planning, effort, and talent to create. It is extremely unusual for a thread item of this tier to not possess a special ability of some kind.

Master thread items represent the apex of power for magical items. The few crafted items of this tier represent the magnum opus from a master of their craft. It is unlikely an adept will ever create a Master tier thread item, let alone more than one.

Legendary thread items can be of any tier and each is unique. What all have in common is their legend has been created or extended by deeds associated with their use. These thread items can be crafted and then increase in power through the actions of their user, or have a true pattern spontaneously generate.

Spell matrix objects are thread items, but are handled differently. In magical terms, they exist somewhere between common magic items and other thread items. The spell matrix they contain is the only ability they can have. The Standard Matrix version of these thread items can be found for sale in most major cities. Those containing an Enhanced Matrix are significantly less common, while Shared Matrix objects are virtually unheard of for sale.

INTRODUCING THREAD ITEMS

Given the power that thread items grant, players are going to want them. This is a good thing and can be used to the advantage of the story. The primary way thread items are gained is as a result of an adventure. They can be found during the course of the adventure (for example, found while exploring a ruined kaer), given as a reward for an adventure or deed (for example, a village gifts the players with a thread item of their founder for saving them from an invae cult), or the purpose of the adventure (for example, after extensive research and following rumors, the characters find the legendary Purifier).

In general, thread items are not be available for purchase (spell matrix objects are the exception). Before the Scourge this was not the case, but as magic levels have dropped, the time and effort involved in crafting even a Novice tier thread item means having them as a part of general wares is prohibitive. Also, adepts tend to be very picky about their thread items. It is possible to commission a thread item, though this should involve a significant cost in addition to adventuring for all of the components required to create the item. This cost should include things beyond mere pieces of silver.

More commonly available are designs for thread items. These describe a tried and true way to create a specific thread item. The resulting item is effectively the same as all other thread items created from the same design, with the appropriately different information for Key Knowledges. Designs from before the Scourge, when the magic levels were higher, may not be perfectly replicable and require some modification to be used in the current era. The design can also be changed to produce slightly different effects. This topic is discussed in greater detail in the *Earthdawn Companion*.

It is generally best to introduce specific thread items with a purpose. This purpose can be as simple as giving a particular character an iconic thread item they will enjoy using, providing a specific tool for defeating a foe or resolving a plot, using the thread item to further the plot, reveal back story, or expand the history of the setting, or any combination of these. The important concept is to use thread items that have been selected for this purpose. They can be from the example items provided (perhaps modified to suit the needs of the campaign), or crafted specifically for the purpose.

When introducing thread items, here are some suggestions worth keeping in mind. First, you don't need to make every item a powerful, legendary thread item to make it special. Even Novice tier thread items should have their own story and distinctive appearance. By the same token, not all thread items should be at the low end. One benefit to the Key Knowledge system is powerful thread items can be handed out early in the game without an adverse impact on game play. The more powerful ranks require advancement and discovering information controlled by the gamemaster. This is discussed in greater detail in the next section.

There can be a temptation to only introduce thread items that provide impressive, unique effects. Having a couple thread items for each character like this is good; it makes the character distinct and provides a strong image of them. However, there is a danger in too many such effects. The more effects available, the more likely there will be unintended consequences from combining effects. If you encounter this situation, it is best to discuss the problem with the group as a whole and come to a resolution together. Another problem is that providing so many powers can dilute the flavor of the adept and create the feeling they are simply a vessel for the their thread items. In addition, too many abilities can be overwhelming and **Earthdawn** already provides quite a few abilities through each Discipline.

Some groups will be inclined to craft their own thread items, and some players may have some very specific desires. It may be useful to ask each player about what they want in terms of thread items. Getting this information up front and updating it periodically throughout the campaign can help to prevent a mismatch of expectations. For example, if an Archer wants to have a war bow custom made by the group's Weaponsmith, but a thread bow is introduced based on the misconception they want a magic bow, this can create an uncomfortable sense of obligation from the player to use the bow, or perhaps a key plot is missed because it is not pursued and the part of the setting it introduces is lost.

Similarly, some players may be very interested in legendary thread items. These can be introduced in two ways: they can be found as is (e.g. Purifier), or they can be generated by player actions. The latter situation is the one of most interest because it further connects the players and their characters to the setting through their deeds. Legendary items can turn a previously mundane item into a thread item, or they can expand the power of an existing thread item by turning it into a legendary item if it wasn't already. When spontaneously generating a thread item, it is best to keep the initial parameters to those suggested in the Creating Thread Items section. Additional thread ranks can always be added by additional legendary deeds.

KEY KNOWLEDGE

When a thread item is introduced into a game, it needs to have its Key Knowledges established. This is an opportunity to chart the direction of the group in a unique fashion. Each Key Knowledge can serve as the objective of an adventure and take the characters to specific locations. These adventures can also serve many different purposes beyond just the Key Knowledges.

Key Knowledges can be used to expand the background of the setting, creating a rich history for the characters to explore. It can also be used to introduce connections from history to the current era, as their exploration reveals information that is relevant to their activities. These adventures can also take the characters to areas that expand the plot in ways not directly related to the Key Knowledge, but are relevant to the campaign as a whole. They can even be to put the players in the right location for a cool scene. Do you want them swashbuckling on an airship slowly crashing into Death's Sea as they look for a particular island among the clenkas? Have their search lead them to an abandoned hut on the island that holds the last known living space of a famous Elementalist.

Finding Key Knowledges requires effort on the part of the characters seeking the knowledge. They should not get something for nothing, though the Name of the thread item should generally not be a trial, unless it is a Name of significance to the campaign. For example, a character should have to undertake a journey of some distance to find a tome that has the information he seeks, rather than merely walking to the nearest collection of books and flipping through the pages for a few minutes. Once he arrives at his destination, he might also have to persuade the caretaker of the collection to allow him to look through the tome. To accomplish that, he may have to agree to do a favor.

The character must not only learn the Key Knowledge, but also understand how it fits into the history of the item. This is generally accomplished through the search for the Key Knowledge and considered to be a part of the journey, rather than a separate accomplishment. Specifically, this is to prevent a character from simply asking someone for the answer. For example, if a character must learn the Name of the jungle that produced the wood used to create a staff, it isn't enough for him to guess the name of the jungle, even if he manages to guess correctly. The character may research different kinds of wood to pinpoint the type used to make the staff, in the process learning about where different types of trees grow, and then discovering important stands or forests of those trees. Through this process, he will understand the significance of the wood used to make the staff.

DESIGNING THREAD ITEMS

Threaded magic items are an integral part of the world of **Earthdawn** and many of the theories of its magical world cover threaded items as well as they cover people or spells. They have a Name, a True Pattern, Key Knowledges, and Pattern Knowledge. They are magically alive and by that differ from mundane objects. In addition, many are as much a focus of legends and tales as daring heroes and horrific villains.

The guidelines presented here enable players and gamemasters to more easily design thread items for use in their game. While it is possible to create a thread item by simply assigning it Key Knowledges and effects, players and gamemasters may benefit from a general guideline when player characters craft threaded items of their own, and gamemasters may benefit from having insight into how typical, official threaded items are designed to maintain a balance between thread items used in their game.

To design a thread item for use in the game (as opposed to creating, crafting, or enchanting an item as a player character as part of the game), the player or gamemaster determines what tier of thread item is created. Skilled player character enchanters can refer to the **Enchanting** chapter in the *Earthdawn Companion* to determine how far their enchanting abilities go. The design process contains three parts:

- Item description
- Item characteristics
- Thread rank properties

There is no right place to start designing a thread item. For example, it is fine to start with a particular effect, then assign a tier as appropriate. or decide how the thread item should fit in the story, then determining the mechanics to fit those details.

Item Description

A thread item's description not only includes how it looks, but also how it fits into the world. Someone invested a great deal of time and effort into creating it, or it was shaped by legendary deeds. In the former case, the creator may have wanted it to be a work of art on its own or at least distinctive in some way—though deliberately choosing a mundane appearance is also valid. The form and appearance of the item also tend to indicate what kind of effects it has.

Legendary thread items that were spontaneously created tend to have mundane appearances. These were functional before they were magical. It isn't uncommon for them to bear the marks of the adventures and seem worn, but still effective. Others may be restored to pristine condition by the process of gaining a true pattern.

Example thread items presented in this and other books will often deliberately leave out details important for Key Knowledges. This is so the thread item may be more easily adapted to a particular game. The answer for the Key Knowledge is whatever will best fit in the campaign.

A threaded item usually retains many of the properties of its normal counterpart, including size and weight, unless an effect specifically changes these details. Depending on the game, it may be considered default for thread items to resize to fit their owner as necessary. Others may assign this only to particular thread items, or not include it at all.

Item Characteristics

To determine an item's characteristics, refer to the **Thread Item Characteristics Table**. An item's characteristics, as opposed to its Key Knowledges and effects, are raw numbers that are easily assigned, and most of them remain constant once the item is used in the game. They do not change after the item is created.

Thread Item Characteristics Table

Tier	Rank Limit	Mystic Defense
Novice	4	8-12
Journeyman	6	10-14
Warden	8	12-16
Master	10	14-18

Tier determines the amount of Legend Points a character has to spend to weave the individual Thread Ranks. These correlate to the cost for increasing talent ranks. For example, the first thread rank of a Journeyman tier thread item costs as many Legend Points to weave to as learning Rank 1 Journeyman talent (200 Legend Points), the second thread rank costs as many Legend Points as increasing that talent to Rank 2 (300 Legend Points), and so on.

Rank Limit is a gauge of the overall power a thread item has to offer—the more ranks, the more effects an item has and higher ranks tend to have more powerful effects. This limit is the maximum number of thread ranks for the different tiers of thread items. Thread items can deviate from this number, both up and down, but the increased costs associated with increased tiers comes from the access to a greater number of thread ranks. Increasing the number of thread ranks is recommended only for legendary items.

Mystic Defense notes the raw magical power of a thread item. A high Mystic Defense makes it harder to target the thread item, for better or worse. This means it will be more difficult to learn about the item's Key Knowledges and for an opponent to specifically target it with effects. The range provided is typical for an item of the tier. It is rare, but not unheard of, for an item to be outside of the range.

Another characteristic all thread items have is **Maximum Threads**, which is the number of characters that can weave a thread to the item without dislodging any existing threads. Even if more than one character can attach a thread to an item, only characters touching or using the item benefit from it. If an item already has the maximum number of threads woven to it and a character attaches a new thread, the thread of the lowest Thread Rank is replaced. The maximum number of threads is not influenced by tier, but by function. It is typically 1 or 2, but if an item is supposed to be used by a group of characters, increase it.

Thread Rank Properties

This section discusses the elements that make up each thread rank, specifically Key Knowledges, Deeds, and the effects granted to the user.

Thread items that have been crafted tend to have Key Knowledges related to the creator, materials, and circumstances related to their creation. Novice tier thread items tend to only have the Name of the thread item and Name of the creator. More powerful (higher tier) thread items have additional information due to the increased effort and care that went into the creation of the item. These Key Knowledges are generally at least at every odd thread rank. The Rank One Key Knowledge is almost always the item's Name.

Instead of a Key Knowledge, an item can also feature a Deed; this tends to be at higher Thread Ranks, although Deeds are more commonly found on Legendary items. A Deed on a non-legendary thread item often requires the item's user to repeat a step in the production process, such as adding more material or ornamentation to the item to fuel its magic, or bind it to him in some fashion. Items created for a specific purpose may require Deed related to this purpose.

A Key Knowledge or Deed at every odd thread rank is a guideline and can always be modified to suit the needs of the game. It is recommended to add additional Key Knowledge requirements, rather than reduce them. This will help control the rate at which characters gain power and allow greater use of Key Knowledges to further the story. Increasing the Key Knowledge requirements too much may slow down other aspects of the game, as characters spend an increasing amount of time researching Key Knowledges and potentially not interacting with the plot or engaging in adventure.

Effects listed at a Rank indicate a new power, ability, bonus, or replaces a previous one. For example, weaving a thread to Thread Rank Three of the Bracers of Aras (p. 208) replaces the previous +1 bonus to the wearer's Physical Defense; the bonuses are not added together to provide a +3 bonus. Thread Rank Effects for some items do not convey bonuses, but change their characteristics and properties. Most often, this concerns armor and weapons. A weapon with a Damage Step of 5 which increases its damage as a Thread Rank Effect does not generally gain "a +1 bonus to Damage tests," but "becomes Damage Step 6." It is treated as a weapon with a Damage Step of 6 for all intents and purposes now, and abilities and effects that use a weapon's Damage Step use this new Step of 6 when interacting with the item.

Some Thread Ranks provide a bonus to a character's rank in a talent (but never skill), for example, "+1 rank to Avoid Blow". If the character does not know the talent in question, he now knows it at the indicated rank, but cannot increase its rank by spending Legend Points, nor can he spend karma when using it. If he knows the talent, the thread item increases the effective rank, but does not affect his natural rank for improving the talent with Legend Points.

Girr has Claw Shape at rank 3 and Feral Bracers at Thread Rank 2, this gives her an effective Claw Shape rank of 4. However, if she wants to increase her Claw Shape, she spends the necessary Legend Points to purchase rank 4. This raises her effectve Claw Shape rank to 5.

Talent ranks provided by thread items do not count towards meeting any requirements, such as Circle advancement.

Some Thread Rank effects allow the owner of the item to cast a spell. This spell is considered to be cast from a Standard Matrix (which is part of the item's design, but unless otherwise noted cannot be attuned to another spell). Threads usually need not be woven, the wielder takes Strain instead, with a base cost of 1 Strain, +1 for each thread required. Many items provide the wielder with the means to cast the spell using his Perception Step only if he does not know the Spellcasting talent. He uses his own Willpower or Willforce to determine the spell's effect unless otherwise noted.

Examples for the effects available when a thread is woven to a specific rank are found in the lists below, one effect is assigned to every rank the item has. Not all effects can be assigned to every thread rank. While most effects can be assigned to any rank, the more powerful effects can only be assigned to higher thread ranks, which means they are not available on all types of items.

Effects Available for All Thread Ranks:

- Add +1 to a weapon's Damage Step.
- Add +1 to Physical or Mystic Armor Rating.
- Reduce Initiative Penalty by 1.
- Add +1 to Physical, Mystic, or Social Defense.
- Add a +1 rank to a talent, or to Thread Weaving tests.
- Add a +1 bonus to a test type (unarmed damage, ranged attacks, Charisma tests, Climbing tests, Initiative tests, etc.).
- Increase short range and long range by 25% each.
- A Standard Matrix of rank equal to the thread rank (only one spell matrix per item and not recommended for Novice tier items).
- A special effect affecting the item's usability, visual appearance, or other properties not directly related to another effect option (a magically collapsible quarterstaff, an anvil weighing only 3 pounds, a piece of clothing perfectly fitting any wearer). Inconsequential abilities may be part of another effect.
- A special ability similar to a spell up to Second Circle that costs 1 Strain to use.

Effects Available from Rank Five Upwards:
- A special ability similar to a spell of up to Fourth Circle that costs 2 Strain to use.
- Add +1 Recovery test per day.
- Add +2 to an Attribute value.
- Add a +3 bonus to a test type (unarmed damage, ranged attacks, Charisma tests, Climbing tests, Initiative tests, etc.) for 1 Strain per use.
- Add a +2 bonus to a characteristic (Defense, Wound Threshold) for several rounds for 1 Strain per use.
- Add a +2 bonus to a test type against a very specific type of target or for a very specific type of action.
- An Enhanced Matrix with significant limitations (only one spell matrix per item).

Effects Available from Rank Seven Upwards:
- Two effects available at all ranks, or one effect available at all ranks with double the bonus.
- A special ability similar to a spell of up to Sixth Circle that costs 3 Strain to use.
- An Enhanced Matrix with no restrictions (only one spell matrix per item).

Special effects (those beyond a simple, numerical improvement) frequently give a thread item its unique character. The potential problems with having these on every item were discussed previously (see **Introducing Thread Items**, p. 198). For thread items that do possess these unique abilities, it is recommended for them to be prominently featured. If there is a particular talent that the effect requires, previous effects should provide at least moderate access to this talent. This is to ensure any adept who possesses the thread item will be able to use it and give a boost to those who already have access to the talent. Additional effects can be included at later thread ranks that build on the previous effect.

When designing the effects of thread items, it is also important to be aware of stacking the available effects for one potentially unbalancing result. For example, a thread item might theoretically provide a +1 bonus to Initiative tests on the first four thread ranks, and then a +3 bonus to Initiative tests for Strain at thread ranks five and six, for an overall +10 bonus to Initiative tests for 2 Strain. While some gamemasters may be fine with this, others may not. It is also suggested to limit more powerful and interesting effects to thread ranks five and later, unless they are critical to the function of the item. This puts them out of range for typical Novice tier items and makes the higher costs associated with those higher thread ranks worth it. Of course, these are guidelines and suggestions. The only right answer is the one that works for a given group.

Legendary Thread Items

Every legendary thread item has an event that transforms a mundane or minor magical item into something greater. This is usually a deed of some significance, one worthy of being told in song and saga, resulting in a noteworthy change to the world (interacting with and affecting the world rather than just taking place in it). The interaction allows the item to develop a True Pattern of its own.

Transforming existing thread items into legendary items is more likely to spontaneously happen than creating a new thread item, as they already have the magical potential. This act expands the item's power by adding additional Thread Ranks. However, it could change the Name of the thread item and turn it into something entirely different. Events that cause an item to become a thread item usually need to be of a greater magnitude than those that expand the thread ranks.

The events that lead to legendary thread ranks are generally deeds that result in a notable Legend Point award (even if not awarded individually), or cause powerful opposition or obstacles to be overcome. There is no rule as to what exactly constitutes an event worthy of developing legendary thread ranks. Each case is unique and magical interactions with the world are poorly understood and can seem to be fickle. It is up to each gamemaster and group to decide how they want to handle the generation of legendary thread ranks. Below are some guidelines that may offer some assistance and a place to start.

Some legendary thread ranks are developed in an instant, when the arrow pierces the eye of a Horror, while others are formed over decades and the result of a life's work. Realistically, the former are going to be more relevant to the immediate needs of the group and the latter will generally already be a part of the setting. Player characters can develop legendary thread items through investment over a long time.

For example, a player character may tend to his fellows' injuries after every conflict with the same physician's kit. After being used in a defining moment to save a life and avert a war, the investment over time combined with the event cause it to become a legendary thread item.

Legendary thread ranks may also develop some time after an event that was important, but not considered worthy at the time. As the ramifications from the event and the legends surrounding it grow, this can cause an item closely associated with it to develop legendary thread ranks.

After its creation, a legendary thread item still has the potential to gain additional Thread Ranks and associated Key Knowledges. Additional Thread Ranks are added under circumstances similar to those which allow an item to become legendary in the first place: by the item taking part in legendary events, usually by someone who has a thread woven to the item performing noteworthy deeds with it.

Once an event noteworthy enough occurs, the item develops at least one additional thread rank. This rank has a Key Knowledge or Deed related to the event, and the effect of the new rank is often connected to the event as well. While one new thread rank is the minimum, it is recommended two thread ranks be added. The first new thread rank should hold a Key Knowledge, while the second new Rank does not require a Key Knowledge. The use of paired ranks paces the research and other aspects of weaving threads to the item so it does not become too long-winded in the game.

When added to a thread item, legendary thread ranks are simply added on top of the existing ranks. This does not cause any threads to be lost as the True Pattern expands. It does not automatically increase the rank of the woven thread either; the expansion of the True Pattern needs to be studied and Legend Points spent in the usual way.

If a pattern item becomes a thread item (either through the artifice of item creation, or more commonly through legendary deeds), the general rule is it is no longer a pattern item as it now has a True Pattern of its own. Any threads woven to the pattern item are lost as it gains a Name and True Pattern. There are exceptions to this, but they should be rare and not the norm.

Once an item develops into a legendary thread item, the character discovers the item has developed magical properties instinctively after handling the item for some time. He needs to confirm this by examining the item astrally. He still must learn the Test Knowledge for the item's thread ranks per standard rules.

Since the item has developed due to his actions, he does not need to learn any Key Knowledges: his own legend is interwoven with the item and he has witnessed any noteworthy event. Any Deeds required by a thread rank may be considered already completed by the character at the gamemaster's discretion.

THREAD ITEMS

This section describes thread items, some of which are unique creations, while others gained their magic through legendary deed, and some are common patterns that are popular to craft and can even be purchased. In the latter case, it is rarely a matter of walking into a store and browsing the wares, as even the most basic thread item is a great labor to craft. Nor is the price usually settled only in silver coin.

For an explanation of the game information presented in this section, see **Item Characteristics**, p. 202.

Band of the Elements
Maximum Threads: 2
Mystic Defense: 10 **Tier:** Journeyman

These metal bands come in a variety of different styles and are designed to be worn on the upper arm. The bands are adorned with five stones, each different and infused with one of the true elements. They are given by Warrior brotherhoods to those who have shown qualities that brotherhood prizes. This is most commonly done within their ranks, but it is not unheard of for outsiders to bear these gifts.

Thread Rank One
Key Knowledge: The owner must learn the Name of the band.
Effect: The owner gains +1 rank to Wood Skin.

Thread Rank Two
Effect: The owner gains +1 rank to Air Dance.

Thread Rank Three
Key Knowledge: The owner must learn the Name of the creator of the band.
Effect: The owner gains +1 rank to Waterfall Slam.

Thread Rank Four
Effect: The owner gains +1 rank to Earth Skin.

Thread Rank Five
Key Knowledge: The owner must learn which where the stones and their true elements were harvested.
Effect: The owner gains +1 rank to Fire Heal.

Thread Rank Six
Effect: The owner gains +1 rank to Durability.

Bracers of Aras
Maximum Threads: 3
Mystic Defense: 12 **Tier:** Journeyman

Bracers of Aras are made of flexible, silvery metal that wraps around the wrists and forearms of the owner. The flexibility is a result of the elemental water that has been forged into the bracers. The elemental water pieces used in the crafting of the bracers resemble aquamarine gems, each piece approximately one inch across. These arm bands are made from metals found only in mines located along the shore of the Aras Sea, and are encrusted with pieces of elemental water. The color of the elemental water gems constantly changes, oscillating with a swirling effect across the spectrum from deep aqua to bright blue.

Thread Rank One
Key Knowledge: The owner must learn the Name of the bracers.
Effect: The owner gains +1 to Physical Defense.

Thread Rank Two
Effect: The owner gains +1 to Mystic Defense.

Thread Rank Three
Key Knowledge: The owner must learn the Name of the mine from which came the metals used to create the bracers.
Effect: The owner gains +2 to Physical Defense.

Thread Rank Four
Effect: The owner gains +2 to Mystic Defense.

Thread Rank Five
Key Knowledge: The creators of the Bracers of Aras formed the gems from a mixture of elemental air and water. The ratio of water to air varies for each set of bracers. The owner must learn the ratio of water to air used to create the bracers he wears.
Effect: For 1 Strain, the owner gains a +3 bonus to Swimming tests.

Thread Rank Six
Effect: For 2 Strain, the owner may breathe underwater for 10 minutes.

Bracers of Obsidiman Strength
Maximum Threads: 2
Mystic Defense: 12 **Tier:** Journeyman

These bracers are shaped from stone and will form perfectly to the owner once a thread is attached. Usually, they are both made from a single stone and are functional in appearance. Some will have small decorations in the form of metal inlay or carvings. While they are termed "obsidiman strength", obsidimen can benefit from them and are generally believed to be the originators of these items.

Thread Rank One
Key Knowledge: The owner must learn the Name of the bracers.
Effect: For 1 Strain, the owner gains a +3 bonus to any Strength-based test, except Damage or Knockdown tests.

Thread Rank Two
Effect: The owner gains a +1 bonus to close combat Damage tests.

Thread Rank Three
Key Knowledge: The owner must learn the Name of the creator of the bracers.
Effect: For 1 Strain, the owner gains a +6 bonus to any Strength-based test, except Damage or Knockdown tests.

Thread Rank Four
Effect: The owner gains a +2 bonus to close combat Damage tests.

Thread Rank Five
Key Knowledge: The owner must learn where the stones and their true elements were harvested.
Effect: The owner gains the ability to wield weapons one size larger than normal. For example, a human could wield a Size 4 weapon in one hand, or up to a Size 7 weapon in two hands. If the owner wishes, the magic of the bracers can increase the Size and Damage Step of a melee weapon they are wielding by one. For example, a broadsword (Size 3, Damage 5) can be increased to the equivalent of a troll sword (Size 4, Damage 6).

Thread Rank Six
Effect: The owner gains +2 to their Strength attribute value.

Conspicuous Smuggler
Maximum Threads: 2
Mystic Defense: 14 **Tier:** Journeyman

This set of alligator hide armor is covered with buckles, pouches, and places to store, hang, or hide nearly anything. Soft and supple, water beads easily from the surface and never truly gets wet. It has clearly been well loved and taken care of over the years. A few bright patches of color make it stand out in any setting. Without a thread attached, the item is treated as normal hide armor.

Thread Rank One
Key Knowledge: The owner must learn the Name of the armor.
Effect: The owner gains +1 rank to Conceal Object.

Thread Rank Two
Effect: The armor no longer has an Initiative penalty.

Thread Rank Three
Key Knowledge: The owner must learn the Name of the armor's first owner
Effect: The owner gains +2 ranks to Conceal Object.

Thread Rank Four
Effect: The armor is Mystic Armor 2.

Thread Rank Five
Key Knowledge: The owner must learn the details of the first owner's most famous smuggling adventure.
Effect: For 1 Strain, the owner may alter the appearance of the armor for 10 minutes, gaining +3 ranks to Disguise Self. The owner may continually extend the time limit by 10 more minutes for 1 Strain each.

Thread Rank Six
Effect: The armor is Physical Armor 6.

Elemental Long Spear
Maximum Threads: 2
Mystic Defense: 12 **Tier:** Journeyman

These six- to eight-foot long wooden spears incorporate each of the five True Elements. The shafts are woven with True Wood, the hollow cores are filled with True Air, and the spears' metal tips are woven with True Earth. Each spear is then soaked in liquid rich in True Water and hardened in flames fueled by True Fire. The spears float in water. With no threads attached, they have the same characteristics as a normal long spear.

Thread Rank One
Key Knowledge: The owner must learn the Name of the spear.
Effect: The spear is Damage Step 6. It becomes immune to damage from fire and from the effects of spells or abilities that damage it. This latter property also keeps the spear from splintering when leveled against an opponent when making Charging Attacks.

Thread Rank Two
Effect: The owner gains a +1 bonus to Initiative tests.

Thread Rank Three
Key Knowledge: The owner must learn the Name of the spear's creator.
Effect: The owner gains +1 rank to Wound Balance. The spear becomes extremely resilient; tremendous force can bend, but not break, it. Even the strength of a dragon twisting the spear in its talons cannot harm the spear.

Thread Rank Four
Effect: The spear is Damage Step 7.

Thread Rank Five
Key Knowledge: The owner must learn what type of wood the spear haft is constructed from and where it was grown.
Effect: The tip of the spear can become glowing, red-hot. For 1 Strain, the owner rolls a bonus Step 4/D6 Flame die on the next Damage test.

Thread Rank Six
Effect: The spear is Damage Step 8.

Espagra Boots
Maximum Threads: 2
Mystic Defense: 12   **Tier:** Journeyman

These fine boots are made from the hides of espagra. Because of their origin, espagra boots are usually bright blue, interwoven with brown leather. The espagra scales also give the boots a brilliant luster, a trademark of espagra-skin products. Similar in appearance to espagra cloaks and saddles, these boots are often worn by those whose work requires stealth, secrecy, or great agility.

While worn most often by thieves and rogues seeking an advantage of stealth and secrecy, legends claim Theran soldiers and mercenaries wore this type of boots in the years before the Scourge. These legends contradict stories that say these boots were first made in the city of Kratas, commissioned by the legendary ork Thief, Garlthik One-Eye.

Thread Rank One
Key Knowledge: The owner must learn the Name of the boots.
Effect: The owner gains +1 rank to Avoid Blow.

Thread Rank Two
Effect: The owner gains +1 rank to Stealthy Stride.

Thread Rank Three
Key Knowledge: The owner must learn the Name of the creator of the boots.
Effect: The owner gains +2 ranks to Avoid Blow.

Thread Rank Four
Effect: The owner gains +2 ranks to Stealthy Stride.

Thread Rank Five
Key Knowledge: The owner must learn the number of espagra hides used to create the boots.
Effect: For 1 Strain, the owner gains +3 ranks to Great Leap for one test.

Thread Rank Six
Effect: For 2 Strain per round, the owner gains the ability to fly at Movement Rate 10. He may spend additional Strain, adding +2 to this Movement Rate for every 1 Strain. This ability cannot be combined with talents or skills allowing increased movement. After the owner stops using this ability, he may not use it again that day.

Espagra Saddle
Maximum Threads: 2
Mystic Defense: 10 **Tier:** Journeyman

These saddles are constructed using a combination of the hide and scales of the flying, dragon-like predators known as espagra. The shimmering blue espagra scales give these saddles a beautiful luster that makes them immediately recognizable. The hanging flaps of an espagra saddle are made entirely of the creatures' hide. One saddle typically requires three to seven hides to make.

Cavalrymen and others who depend upon their mounts covet these saddles. Legend says Guyak Jorann used the first espagra saddle, but these saddles were probably being stitched and enchanted centuries before the ork hero was born.

Thread Rank One
Key Knowledge: The owner must learn the Name of the saddle.
Effect: The mount gains +1 to Physical Armor.

Thread Rank Two
Effect: The mount gains +1 to Physical Defense.

Thread Rank Three
Key Knowledge: The owner must learn the Name of the creator of the saddle.
Effect: The owner gains +1 to Physical Armor while mounted in the saddle.

Thread Rank Four
Effect: The owner gains +1 to Physical Defense while mounted in the saddle.

Thread Rank Five
Key Knowledge: The rider must learn how many espagra hides the maker used to create the saddle.
Effect: The mount may gain +2 to Movement Rate at the owner's choice.

Thread Rank Six
Effect: Either the owner or his mount (owner's choice) gains an additional Recovery test each day.

Faerie Mail
Maximum Threads: 2
Mystic Defense: 14 **Tier:** Journeyman

Faerie mail is very high-quality armor made of fine links. Because the links of this armor may be as small as one-half the size of normal chain mail, suits of faerie mail fit the owners better. Faerie mail varies in color: most are the steel-gray of typical armor, but some suits have a bronze color or a color similar to that of orichalcum. Without a thread attached, it has the same characteristics as normal chain mail.

Thread Rank One
Key Knowledge: The owner must learn the Name of the armor.
Effect: The armor has an Initiative Penalty of 2.

Thread Rank Two
Effect: The armor has Mystic Armor 1.

Thread Rank Three
Key Knowledge: The owner must find out what type of faerie creature or enchanted beast gave its blood for the armor.
Effect: The armor has an Initiative Penalty of 1.

Thread Rank Four
Effect: The armor has Mystic Armor 2.

Thread Rank Five
Key Knowledge: The owner must learn the Name of the individual who created the armor.
Effect: The armor has no Initiative Penalty.

Thread Rank Six
Effect: The armor has Mystic Armor 3.

Fastoon's Very Impressive Staff
Maximum Threads: 1
Mystic Defense: 14 **Tier:** Journeyman

Fastoon's Very Impressive Staff is made of black and white wood, perfectly fit together to form an intricate, interlacing design. It is adorned with an impressive collection of bones and feathers, braided with a variety of different leathers. The shaft is carved with a variety of runes which translate to affirmations of how very impressive is Fastoon.

Thread Rank One
Key Knowledge: The owner must learn the Name of the staff.
Effect: The staff holds a Standard Matrix of rank equal to the thread rank.

Thread Rank Two
Effect: The owner gains +1 rank to Spellcasting.

Thread Rank Three
Key Knowledge: The owner must learn what the runic carvings on the staff say and where Fastoon called home.
Deed: The owner must carve a new, sincere affirmation of how very impressive is Fastoon on the staff in the same style of runes.
Effect: The owner gains +1 to Physical Defense.

Thread Rank Four
Effect: The owner gains +1 rank to Willforce.

Thread Rank Five
Key Knowledge: The owner must learn where the wood used to craft the staff was harvested from.
Effect: The owner gains +2 ranks to Spellcasting.

Thread Rank Six
Effect: The owner gains +2 ranks to Willforce.

Feral Bracers
Maximum Threads: 2
Mystic Defense: 10 **Tier:** Journeyman

These rugged, leather bracers are quite popular with Beastmasters who can acquire them. Most are simple affairs; thick leather with only a little beadwork or tooling as decoration, but others can get quite elaborate with metal inlays and precious stones. All share prominent markings that suggest the bracers were gashed by claws.

Thread Rank One
Key Knowledge: The owner must learn the Name of the bracers.
Effect: The owner gains +1 rank to Unarmed Combat.

Thread Rank Two
Effect: The owner gains +1 rank to Claw Shape.

Thread Rank Three
Key Knowledge: The owner must learn the Name of the creator of the bracers.
Effect: The owner gains +2 ranks to Claw Shape.

Thread Rank Four
Effect: The owner gains +1 to Physical Defense.

Thread Rank Five
Key Knowledge: The owner must learn from what creature the leather used for the bracers came and where the creature was killed.
Effect: The owner gains +3 ranks to Claw Shape.

Thread Rank Six
Effect: For 1 Strain, the owner may gain a +3 bonus to Damage tests against an opponent who is Blindsided or Surprised.

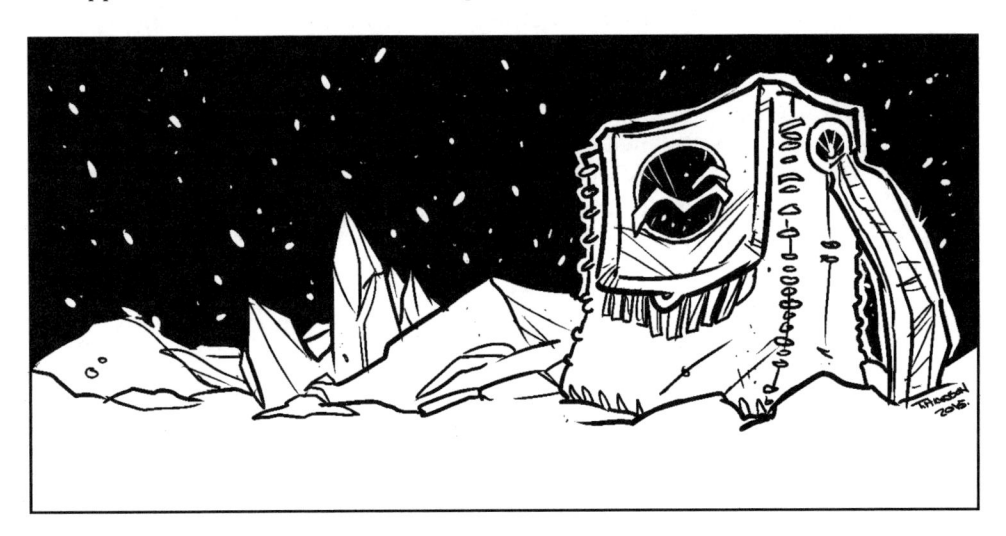

Frost Pouch
Maximum Threads: 2
Mystic Defense: 10 **Tier:** Journeyman

These are small pouches, usually 3 by 5 inches in size and made of white or blue cloth. The pouches always feel cool to the touch. Water elementals are essential for making a frost pouch.

Thread Rank One
Key Knowledge: The owner must learn the pouch's Name.

Effect: The owner may draw frost from the pouch a number of times per day equal to the thread rank. For 1 Strain, the owner may sprinkle frost into water, purifying it by casting Purify Water (*Player's Guide*, p. 274) as a Standard action. The owner uses either Spellcasting or PER + thread rank as the Step for the test.

Thread Rank Two
Effect: For 1 Strain, the owner may use frost to shield themselves from extreme heat by sprinkling frost on themselves and casting Resist Element (Fire) (*Player's Guide*, p. 274) as a Standard action. The owner uses either Spellcasting or PER + thread rank as the Step for the test. The duration of the effect is based on the thread rank.

Thread Rank Three
Key Knowledge: The frost in the pouch originally came from mountain snow or glacier ice. The owner must learn the Name of the mountain or glacier.
Deed: Return to the mountain or glacier of origin and fill the pouch with snow or ice.
Effect: For 1 Strain, the owner may use the frost to dangerously chill a weapon as a Simple action. The next Damage test made with the affected weapon gains a bonus Step 4/D6 Frost Die.

Thread Rank Four
Effect: For 1 Strain, the owner may toss frost in the area as a Standard action, creating a Chilling Circle as per the spell (*Player's Guide*, p. 323). The owner uses either Spellcasting or PER + thread rank as the Step for the test. The duration and Effect Step are based on the thread rank.

Thread Rank Five
Key Knowledge: The owner must learn the Name of the water elemental who lent its power to the pouch.
Effect: For 1 Strain, the owner may blow the frost along the surface of the ground as a Standard action, creating an Icy Surface as the spell (*Player's Guide*, p. 276). The owner uses either Spellcasting to PER + thread rank as the Step for the test. The duration is based on the thread rank.

Thread Rank Six
Effect: For 2 Strain, the owner may rain frost on the area as a Standard action. A chill wind will pick up the frost and create a Blizzard Sphere as per the spell (*Player's Guide*, p. 281). The owner uses either Spellcasting or PER + thread rank as the Step for the test. The duration is based on the thread rank.

Kranguk's Interjection
Maximum Threads: 2
Mystic Defense: 10 **Tier:** Journeyman

Kranguk was a wise and just troll. He led his moot fairly, listened, and took on all who came before him. There was little he loved more than a lively discussion. Something he did love more was a lively fight.

This large metal helm is intricately decorated with pastoral, hunting, and battle scenes. It is adorned with two massive antlers, one broken in half and the other having seen better days. Really, the whole helm has seen better days; the forehead and nosepiece are badly dented and mangled, and any attempt to fix this will find the damage soon returned, often at the owner's expense. Upon weaving a thread, the helm will automatically adjust to the size of the owner.

Thread Rank One
Key Knowledge: The owner must learn the Name of the helm.
Effect: The owner gains +1 rank to Swift Kick when used to head butt. The owner may explicitly use the Swift Kick talent to deliver a head butt. Forge Weapon can be used on the helm to increase the damage done by the head butt.

Thread Rank Two
Effect: The owner gains +2 ranks to Swift Kick when used to head butt.

Thread Rank Three
Key Knowledge: The owner must learn the Name of Kranguk's trollmoot.
Effect: The owner gains +3 ranks to Swift Kick when used to head butt.

Thread Rank Four
Effect: The owner gains a +2 bonus to any social tests to impress or intimidate through sheer strength or toughness.

Thread Rank Five
Deed: The owner must win the approval of Kranguk's trollmoot.
Effect: The owner gains +2 to Damage tests resulting from a head butt.

Thread Rank Six
Effect: The owner gains +4 to Damage tests resulting from a head butt.

Lightning-Bolt Earring
Maximum Threads: 2
Mystic Defense: 12 **Tier:** Journeyman

Lightning-bolt earrings are intricate pieces of silver jewelry, shaped like forked lightning, studded with small white, blue, and purple gems, and attached to the owner's ear by a short chain of delicate links. Crafting lightning-bolt earrings requires great skill and concentration, so magicians and jewelers often work together to produce these highly desired treasures.

Thread Rank One
Key Knowledge: The owner must learn the Name of the earring.
Effect: The owner gains +1 rank to Avoid Blow. The earring glows momentarily when used.

Thread Rank Two
Effect: The owner gains a +1 bonus to Initiative tests.

Thread Rank Three
Key Knowledge: The owner must learn the Name(s) of the creator(s) of the earring.
Effect: The owner gains +1 to Physical Defense.

Thread Rank Four
Effect: The owner gains a +2 to Avoid Blow.

Thread Rank Five
Key Knowledge: The owner must learn the composition of the earring: the number and type of the gems, and also the relative amounts of silver and gems used in the earrings construction.
Effect: The owner gains a +2 bonus to Initiative tests.

Thread Rank Six
Effect: For 2 Strain, the owner may use Avoid Blow against a spell with a touch range, or which is visible (e.g. Earth Darts, Ephemeral Bolt, and Razor Orb).

Metal Inquisitor
Maximum Threads: 1
Mystic Defense: 14 **Tier:** Journeyman

This item is a gleaming metal skullcap that fits perfectly to the skull of the owner once a thread has been woven. It forms a widow's peak on the owner's forehead and follows the approximate hairline (or where one would be) around the rest of his skull. As the thread woven increases in rank, ghostly images can be seen moving across the surface, often reflecting the mood of the owner. They are most prominent for aggressive moods and thoughts.

Thread Rank One
Key Knowledge: The owner must learn the Name of the skullcap.
Effect: The owner gains +1 to Mystic Defense.

Thread Rank Two
Effect: The owner gains +1 rank to Steel Thought.

Thread Rank Three
Key Knowledge: The owner must learn the Name of the first owner.
Effect: The owner gains +1 to Social Defense.

Thread Rank Four
Effect: The owner gains +2 ranks to Steel Thought.

Thread Rank Five
Key Knowledge: The owner must learn what fate befell the first owner.
Effect: For 1 Strain, the owner gains +3 ranks to Steely Stare for one test.

Thread Rank Six
Effect: For 1 Strain, the owner gains a +3 bonus to a test made to determine if someone is lying.

Mirror
Maximum Threads: 1
Mystic Defense: 12 **Tier:** Journeyman

The ironwood buckler called Mirror sports a dull iron plate in its center, a reinforcing rim of bronze, and espagra-leather hand straps. The Weaponsmith who forged this buckler, Vsthrix, a t'skrang Weaponsmith, created it as a companion piece to the broadsword Named Smoke. Without a thread attached to it, Mirror is a normal buckler.

Thread Rank One
Key Knowledge: The owner must learn the Name of the shield.
Effect: The shield is +1 Mystic Defense.

Thread Rank Two
Effect: The shield is +2 Physical Defense.

Thread Rank Three
Key Knowledge: The owner must learn that the Name of the shield's creator.
Effect: The shield is +2 Mystic Defense.

Thread Rank Four
Effect: The shield is +3 Physical Defense.

Thread Rank Five
Deed: The owner must locate the sword Smoke and attach a thread to it.
Effect: The shield gains the Blinding Reflection ability. For 1 Strain, the iron plate brightens and any opponent who can see the shield is distracted by light gleaming off the metal. The owner gains a +3 bonus to his next Attack test against an adjacent opponent. If the sword Smoke is ever lost, the owner cannot use the Blinding Reflection ability until the sword is recovered.

Thread Rank Six
Effect: The shield is +3 Mystic Defense.

Naga-Scale Brooch
Maximum Threads: 2
Mystic Defense: 12 **Tier:** Journeyman

These brooches are made from the scales of a naga. Nagas are territorial creatures; their homes are very important to them. Naga-scale brooches can be made only with scales willingly donated by a naga. Each brooch is Named after the naga from whom its scale came. Nagas only give their scales to those who are neither ensnared by their entrancing powers, nor repulsed by their unnatural looks. Each brooch is crafted from a single naga scale, set into a gold or silver backing which is often engraved with a serpent motif. The scale changes color to blend with the owner's clothing. Any other piece of jewelry containing a naga scale will exhibit the same magical effect. Such jewelry reputedly gives the owner some of the naga's power to entrance those who observe it.

Thread Rank One
Key Knowledge: The owner must learn the Name of the brooch.
Effect: The owner gains +1 to Interaction tests.

Thread Rank Two
Effect: The owner gains +1 to Social Defense.

Thread Rank Three
Key Knowledge: The owner must learn the Name of the person who obtained the scale and created the brooch.
Effect: The owner gains +2 to Interaction tests.

Thread Rank Four
Effect: The owner gains +2 to Social Defense.

Thread Rank Five
Key Knowledge: The owner must learn where the naga who supplied the scales for the brooch lived.
Effect: The owner gains +1 rank to Hypnotize.

Thread Rank Six
Effect: The owner gains +2 ranks to Hypnotize.

Nioku's Bow
Maximum Threads: 2
Mystic Defense: 18 **Tier:** Master

Nioku was a troll Archer, a hero of an earlier time known for making arrowheads from the bones of slain enemies among other things. She is one of the very few heroes who could truthfully claim to have killed a dragon in one-on-one combat.

Legends tell of a long-running competition between Nioku and an elf Archer Named Talondel. Talondel had been corrupted by a Horror, though he did not fall under its control. He and Nioku crossed paths and competed in feats of archery, which always ended in a tie, for more than seven years. Nioku finally defeated Talondel, who was shortly thereafter captured and held in rune chains in a dwarf prison. Several months after she defeated Talondel, Nioku uncovered the lair of a Horror which had been terrorizing Sky Raiders, including members of her trollmoot. Nioku could not defeat the Horror's magic because the creature knew too much about her. Soon after her failed attack, the Horror ravaged another Sky Raider camp, killing Nioku's uncle and younger brother.

Nioku traveled to the dwarf prison where Talondel lay chained and asked the elf to slay the Horror who was killing her kinsmen. In exchange, she would convince the dwarfs to pardon the elf. Talondel laughed at her proposal, asking how he could kill a Horror Nioku and her mighty bow had not been able to touch. Nioku swore a blood oath and offered Talondel her bow to use against the Horror, and to keep if he killed it. Impressed by her willing sacrifice, Talondel accepted the offer. The power of the oath somehow allowed Talondel to use the bow while it still drew power from Nioku's thread.

Talondel slew the Horror and then disappeared. Nearly fourteen months later he returned and gave the bow back to Nioku, saying from this day forward he must use his own magic. As Nioku touched her bow, it began to glow, then became translucent with a silvery sheen.

Nioku's Bow is a larger than average elven warbow, made of dark oak with small grooves along its sides lined with fine red crystal. The bowstring is made of catgut lined with True Air. With no threads attached it is a normal elven warbow.

Thread Rank One
Key Knowledge: The owner must learn the Name of the bow.
Effect: The bow is Damage Step 6.

Thread Rank Two
Effect: The range of the bow is 2-60 (short range) and 61-120 (long range).

Thread Rank Three
Key Knowledge: The owner must learn the Name of one of Nioku's enemies.
Deed: The owner must carve twelve arrowheads from the bones of one of his enemies.
Effect: The bow is Damage Step 7.

Thread Rank Four
Effect: The owner gains a +1 bonus to Attack tests made with the bow.

Thread Rank Five
Key Knowledge: The owner must learn the Name of the first person killed by the bow.
Effect: The bow is Damage Step 8

Thread Rank Six
Effect: The range of the bow is 2-72 (short range) and 73-144 (long range).

Thread Rank Seven
Key Knowledge: The owner must learn the Name of Nioku's elf Archer competitor and their legend together.
Deed: The owner must give the bow to a previously defeated enemy. The enemy will perform a Deed with the bow, and is then entitled to keep the bow. Whether or not the enemy ever returns the bow is up to him. The owner may not accompany the other character, nor send anyone else along with him, either to help or keep an eye on the enemy; the former enemy is on his own. The bow continues to draw power from the owner's thread.
Effect: The owner gains a +2 bonus to Attack tests made with the bow and a +2 bonus to his Willpower tests when resisting the effects of spells or other magical effects.

Thread Rank Eight
Effect: The bow is Damage Step 10.

Thread Rank Nine
Key Knowledge: The owner must learn the Name of the Horror Talondel killed using Nioku's Bow.
Effect: The bow becomes translucent and silvery like a silver-speckled moonbeam. The owner gains a +3 bonus to Attack tests made with the bow and it is Damage Step 11.

Thread Rank Ten
Effect: The owner gains a +4 bonus to Attack tests made with the bow and it is Damage Step 12.

Oratory Necklace
Maximum Threads: 2
Mystic Defense: 10 **Tier:** Journeyman

Oratory necklaces are strings of eight to twelve semi-precious stones such as turquoise or tourmaline. Each stone measures roughly half an inch in diameter. The stones of most oratory necklaces vary wildly in color, making each necklace unique. When the abilities of a necklace are in use, some of the stones glitter. As Thread Rank increases, the sparkles grow brighter and a pattern may emerge.

The creator of an oratory necklace usually uses silver and semi-precious stones to make this magical item, though only five of the stones are magically active. The owner must attach his thread to one of those five stones.

Thread Rank One
Key Knowledge: The owner must learn the Name of the necklace.
Effect: The owner gains a +1 bonus to Interaction tests.

Thread Rank Two
Effect: The owner gains +1 to Social Defense.

Thread Rank Three
Key Knowledge: The owner must learn the Name of the creator of the necklace.
Effect: The owner gains a +2 bonus to Interaction tests.

Thread Rank Four
Effect: The owner gains +2 to Social Defense.

Thread Rank Five
Key Knowledge: The owner must learn the Name of the location the stones were mined.
Effect: Crowds react to the owner as if their Attitude were one degree more favorable.

Thread Rank Six
Effect: The owner gains +2 to their Charisma attribute value.

Orichalcum Shield
Maximum Threads: 1
Mystic Defense: 16 **Tier:** Warden

Similar in size and shape to crystal raider shields, orichalcum shields are made of orichalcum-lined wooden and metal plates. Crafting these shields requires the combined efforts of a Weaponsmith and an Elementalist. With no threads attached, an orichalcum shield is +3/+3 with an Initiative Penalty of 3. Orichalcum shields are extremely powerful, but so expensive to make they have reportedly been traded for entire airships.

Thread Rank One
Key Knowledge: The owner must learn the Name of the shield.
Effect: The shield is Mystic Defense +4.

Thread Rank Two
Effect: The shield is Physical Defense +4.

Thread Rank Three
Key Knowledge: The owner must learn the Names of both the Weaponsmith and Elementalist who created the shield.
Effect: The shield is Mystic Defense +5.

Thread Rank Four
Effect: The shield is Physical Defense +5.

Thread Rank Five
Key Knowledge: The owner must learn the Name of the place where the shield was created.
Effect: The Initiative Penalty is 2.

Thread Rank Six
Effect: The Initiative Penalty is 1.

Thread Rank Seven
Key Knowledge: The owner must learn either where the orichalcum was mined, or where the true elements used in the creation of the orichalcum were gathered.
Effect: The owner gains +1 to Physical Armor and +1 to Mystic Armor.

Thread Rank Eight
Effect: The owner gains +2 to Physical Armor and +2 to Mystic Armor.

Poison Ivy
Maximum Threads: 2
Mystic Defense: 14 **Tier:** Warden

Poison Ivy is a set of fernweave armor. If allowed to go dormant, the armor will appear to die off and be reduced to a single seed. It will not awaken until a thread is woven. When a thread is woven, the seed will burst open with vines that entangle the future owner and grow into a suit of armor. The plants composing the armor change each morning with the rising sun based on the prevailing flora of the area. In urban settings, it will align itself with the nearest rural environment, underground it appears as lichens and fungi, while in desolate areas, it takes the form of whatever plant life could possibly survive.

Once a thread is attached to the armor, it draws all sustenance from the magical connection and does not require the enchantment to be renewed as normal fernweave. As the thread rank increases, the armor becomes more reactive to the surroundings and the moods of its owner, even growing and adapting to help intercept attacks.

Thread Rank One
Key Knowledge: The owner must learn the Name of the armor.
Effect: The armor is Physical Armor 3 and Mystic Armor 3.

Thread Rank Two
Effect: The armor is Mystic Armor 4.

Thread Rank Three
Key Knowledge: The owner must learn the Name of the armor's creator.
Effect: The armor is Physical Armor 4.

Thread Rank Four
Effect: The owner gains +1 rank to Stealthy Stride.

Thread Rank Five
Key Knowledge: The owner must learn from where the materials used to create the armor were gathered.
Effect: For 1 Strain, the owner can cause the armor to perfectly match the environment, even looking like cave walls, or whitewash. This gives the owner a +3 bonus to all Stealthy Stride or other concealment related tests for 10 minutes.

Thread Rank Six
Effect: The armor takes on a slick, oily sheen. For 1 Strain, the owner may wipe a weapon on the armor as a Simple action to poison it for his next attack this round. The poison is equivalent to Shadowmant venom (see p. 178) with a Step equal to the Thread Rank.

Thread Rank Seven
Deed: The owner must visit the location where the materials were gathered and enchantment performed in Poison Wood.
Effect: The armor is Physical Armor 5 and Mystic Armor 5.

Thread Rank Eight
Effect: The armor will grow thorns in reaction to attacks. The owner may spend 1 Strain to inflict the poison on any successful unarmed attack against him. For 1 additional Strain, the owner may increase the Step of the poison by +3.

Purifier
Maximum Threads: 2
Mystic Defense: 18 **Tier:** Master

Purifier was created at the direction of King Varulus I of Throal when the Horrors first began to enter the world, and was used by many heroes of pre-Scourge Barsaive. According to legend, a powerful Wizard cast a spell on the sword to make it look old and rusted.

Purifier appears as a worn, rusty broadsword, damaged from several years' use. Carved along the blade's flat side are runes bearing the symbols of the Kingdom of Throal and of King Varulus I. With no thread woven to it, Purifier has the same characteristics as a normal broadsword, but is only Damage Step 2 (from the rust).

Before a character can weave any threads to Purifier, he must first remove the spell that changes its appearance. The spell resists any attempts to dispel it as if it were an Eleventh Circle spell. Once the spell is removed, the character can weave threads to the sword. If Purifier ever has no threads attached, the illusion returns.

Thread Rank One
Key Knowledge: The owner must learn the Name of the sword.
Effect: The sword can be wielded by anyone, regardless of size or strength and is Damage Step 6.

Thread Rank Two
Effect: The sword is Damage Step 7.

Thread Rank Three
Key Knowledge: The owner must learn the Names of the Weaponsmiths who created the sword.
Effect: The sword is Damage Step 8.

Thread Rank Four
Effect: The sword is Damage Step 9.

Thread Rank Five
Key Knowledge: The owner must learn the Name of the first owner of the sword.
Effect: When used against Horrors, the blade glows red-hot and the owner gains a +2 bonus to Damage tests against Horrors and Horror constructs.

Thread Rank Six
Effect: The owner gains a +4 bonus to Damage tests against Horrors and Horror constructs.

Thread Rank Seven
Key Knowledge: The owner must learn the Name of the magician who cast the illusion on the sword.
Effect: The owner gains the power Corruption's Brand and can use it as a Standard action. He can detect those who have been corrupted by a Horror. For 5 Strain, the owner places the searing hot blade on the target makes the higher of a Spellcasting test or PER + thread rank against the Horror's Mystic Defense. If the test succeeds, the owner is alerted to the Horror's corruption by searing the skin of the target, causing 5 points of damage that cannot be reduced and leaving a distinctive mark. If unsuccessful or there is no corruption, the heat does not affect the target.

Thread Rank Eight
Effect: The owner gains a +8 bonus to Damage tests against Horrors and Horror constructs.

Thread Rank Nine
Deed: The owner must Wound a Horror using the sword.
Effect: The owner gains the power Corruption's Price, which allows the owner to deal a devastating strike to a Horror. As a Free action the owner may take blood magic damage that can never be healed up to the thread rank. The blade becomes searing hot and the bonus to Damage tests against Horrors and Horror constructs is added again for each additional point of blood magic damage taken (e.g. 1 blood magic damage increases the bonus to +16, and 3 blood magic damage increases the bonus to +32). If at least 1 damage point from a successful attack is inflicted, the Horror or Horror Construct automatically takes a Wound for every point of blood magic damage. The attack can still inflict the normal Wound from damage.

Thread Rank Ten
Effect: The sword is Damage Step 10 and the owner gains a +10 bonus to Damage tests against Horrors and Horror constructs

Rapier of Wit
Maximum Threads: 2
Mystic Defense: 12 **Tier:** Warden

If legends are to be believed, the queen of windlings has held an annual Swordmaster tournament at her palace since the end of the Scourge, in mockery of a tournament held annually in Blood Wood. The winner is said to receive a special threaded windling sword, tapering to a point so thin it can split a hair with a thrust. Either this story is true or it is the fabrication of the finest Weaponsmith among windlings, if not all Namegivers, for the purpose of being left alone to work in peace. Without a thread attached to it, the weapon is a windling sword.

Thread Rank One
Key Knowledge: The owner must learn the Name of the sword.
Effect: The sword is Damage Step is 4 and any windling can wield it, regardless of their Strength.

Thread Rank Two
Effect: The owner gains +1 rank to Taunt.

Thread Rank Three
Key Knowledge: The owner must learn the Name of the weapon's creator.
Effect: The weapon is now Damage Step 5.

Thread Rank Four
Effect: The owner gains +2 ranks to Taunt.

Thread Rank Five
Deed: The owner must learn a skill or talent that conveys knowledge of weapon design or construction.
Effect: The weapon is now Damage Step 6.

Thread Rank Six
Effect: For 1 Strain, the owner gains +3 ranks to Distract for one test.

Thread Rank Seven
Deed: The owner must publicly show up or humiliate a victor of the tournament held in Blood Wood.
Effect: The sword now inflicts +3 damage points for each additional success on the Attack test.

Thread Rank Eight
Effect: The weapon is now Damage Step 8.

Savage Hides
Maximum Threads: 2
Mystic Defense: 14 **Tier:** Journeyman (Warden)

Savage hides are enchanted hide armor, usually using bear, brithan, or skeorx hides. The beast's head acts as a helmet, the paws as gloves that cover the top of the hand. Only the best pieces of hide are chosen for the enchantment, and usually an extremely large and dangerous specimen provides the material. Savage hides are common among tribes living in the hinterlands, whether in the mountains, steppes, or jungles. They are often made for war chiefs and exceptional hunters. The Journeyman version of this armor has six thread ranks, but some exceptional examples are Warden tier with eight. Without a thread attached, savage hides are normal hide armor.

Thread Rank One
Key Knowledge: The owner must learn the Name of the armor.
Effect: The armor is Physical Armor 6.

Thread Rank Two
Effect: The owner gains +1 rank to Wilderness Survival.

Thread Rank Three
Key Knowledge: The owner must learn the Name of the tribe that is the source of the armor.
Effect: The armor is Mystic Armor 2.

Thread Rank Four
Effect: The armor no longer has an Initiative Penalty.

Thread Rank Five
Key Knowledge: The owner must learn the tale of the hunt for the animal that provided the hide.
Effect: The owner gains +1 rank to Tracking and the claws on the hide's paws can be used as weapons in unarmed combat; their Damage Step is 3. The claws may not be improved with Forge Weapon.

Thread Rank Six
Effect: The owner gains +1 rank to Awareness.

Thread Rank Seven
Deed: The owner must single-handedly hunt and kill an animal of the type that provided its hide for the armor.
Effect: The owner gains +2 ranks to Tracking and +2 ranks to Wilderness Survival.

Thread Rank Eight
Effect: The armor is Physical Armor 7 and Mystic Armor 3.

Seven League Striders
Maximum Threads: 2
Mystic Defense: 12 **Tier:** Novice (Journeyman)

These boots come in a variety of styles, but always share certain traits: they are always tall, at least to the knees, and made of shiny, black leather. When a thread is woven, they will form perfectly to the owner. Some of these boots are more powerful than others, in which case their Mystic Defense is 14, Tier is Journeyman, and have six thread ranks. Novice tier boots only have four thread ranks.

Thread Rank One
Key Knowledge: The owner must learn the Name of the boots.
Effect: The owner gains +2 to Movement Rate.

Thread Rank Two
Effect: The owner gains +1 to Physical Defense.

Thread Rank Three
Key Knowledge: The owner must learn the Name of the creator of the boots.
Effect: The owner gains +4 to Movement Rate.

Thread Rank Four
Effect: The owner gains +2 to Physical Defense.

Thread Rank Five
Key Knowledge: The owner must learn from what creature(s) the leather for the boots came.
Effect: For 1 Strain, the owner gains a +3 bonus to a Great Leap test.

Thread Rank Six
Effect: The owner gains +2 to their Dexterity attribute value.

Silvered Shield
Maximum Threads: 2
Mystic Defense: 16 **Tier:** Warden

A silvered shield is typically a footman's shield. Crafted from elementally charged earth, the shield gains some of its power from an earth elemental. Silvered Shields have fine silver lines decorating their edges, making them appear of more than average worth. Many of these shields have sigils and designs outlined in silver. With no threads woven to it, the shield has the same characteristics as a normal footman's shield.

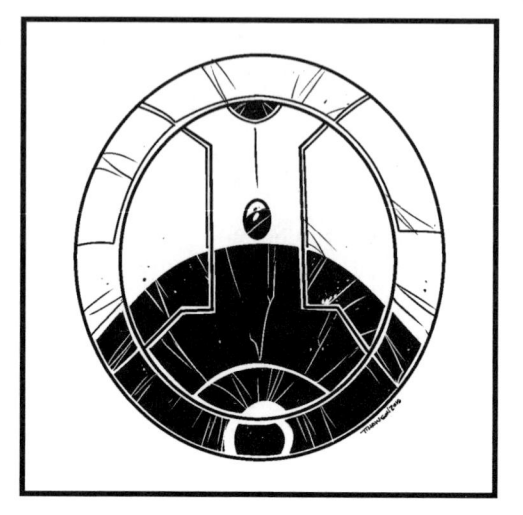

Thread Rank One
Key Knowledge: The owner must learn the Name of the shield.
Effect: The shield is Mystic Defense +1.

Thread Rank Two
Effect: The owner gains +1 rank to Steel Thought.

Thread Rank Three
Key Knowledge: The owner must learn the Name of the shield's creator.
Effect: The shield is Mystic Defense +2.

Thread Rank Four
Effect: The owner gains +2 ranks to Steel Thought.

Thread Rank Five
Key Knowledge: The owner must determine the source of the elemental earth used in the creation of the shield.
Effect: The owner gains the power Spell Riposte and may use it as a Free action. For 2 Strain, once per turn after achieving 2 successes on a Steel Thought test against a spell targeting the owner, the spell is directed back at the caster. Use the original Spellcasting test result to determine if the spell affects the caster.

Thread Rank Six
Effect: The owner gains +3 ranks to Steel Thought

Thread Rank Seven
Key Knowledge: The owner must learn the Name of the earth elemental who helped create the shield.
Effect: The shield is Physical Defense +3 and Mystic Defense +3.

Thread Rank Eight
Effect: The owner gains +1 to Mystic Armor and +4 ranks to Steel Thought.

Smoke
Maximum Threads: 1
Mystic Defense: 14 **Tier:** Journeyman

The broadsword called Smoke features a hilt wrapped in espagra leather and a smoky-gray steel blade with a ruby-studded fuller. The Weaponsmith who made this sword, Vsthrix, a t'skrang Weaponsmith, created it as a companion piece to a buckler Named Mirror. Without a thread woven to it, Smoke is a normal broadsword.

Thread Rank One
Key Knowledge: The owner must learn the Name of the sword.
Effect: The sword is Damage Step 6.

Thread Rank Two
Effect: The owner gains a +1 bonus to Attack tests with the sword.

Thread Rank Three
Key Knowledge: The owner must learn the Name of the sword's creator.
Effect: The sword is Damage Step 7.

Thread Rank Four
Effect: The owner gains a +2 bonus to Attack tests with the sword.

Thread Rank Five
Deed: The owner must locate Mirror and attach a thread to it.
Effect: The owner gains the power Mystic Strike and may use it as a Simple action. For 3 Strain, the sword blade becomes insubstantial for the next Attack test and Mystic Armor provides protection instead of Physical Armor. If the buckler Mirror is ever lost the sword loses the Mystic Strike ability until the shield is recovered.

Thread Rank Six
Effect: The sword is Damage Step 8.

Spell Matrix Object
Maximum Threads: 1
Mystic Defense: See text   **Tier:** See text

Spell matrix objects are simple thread items that contain a spell matrix. There are four different kinds, one for each of the different matrix types available to magicians. They can take any form, but most commonly are small and easily carried, like a ring, necklace, or piece of clothing.

When a thread is woven to a spell matrix object, it activates the matrix contained inside, which has the same rank as the thread woven to it. Once active, the matrix is treated in the same way as the character's other spell matrices. For more information on spell matrix objects, see the *Player's Guide*, p. 260.

Only Standard Matrix Objects can typically be found for sale, and even that is rare. Magicians that use matrix objects typically create their own. Market prices are at gamemaster's discretion, but typically start at 500 silver and increase from there.

All matrix items have only one Key Knowledge, the item's Name, that must be learned before the thread can be woven.

Standard Matrix Object
Mystic Defense: 8   **Tier:** Novice

Enhanced Matrix Object
Mystic Defense: 10   **Tier:** Journeyman

Armored Matrix Object
Mystic Defense: 12   **Tier:** Warden

Share Matrix Object
Mystic Defense: 14   **Tier:** Master

Spell Sword
Maximum Threads: 1
Mystic Defense: 14   **Tier:** Journeyman (Warden)

Spell swords come in differing styles and sizes, though most are broadswords. The elemental earth and air used to forge these swords mark the flat sides of their blades with an unusual swirled appearance. With no threads woven to it, the sword has the same characteristics as a normal broadsword. When a thread is attached, the swirls on the blade move slowly. As the Thread Rank increases, they begin to appear as a tempest on the blade.

The people of Barsaive no longer possess the art of making spell swords, though rumors say that the Therans have revived the art. These broadswords are created from a delicate mix of forged steel, elemental earth and elemental air. Some swords crafted near the height of the magic cycle are notable for their power. These swords are Warden tier and have eight ranks instead of six, which Journeyman swords possess.

Thread Rank One
Key Knowledge: The owner must learn the Name of the sword.
Effect: The sword holds a Standard Matrix of Rank equal to the Thread Rank.

Thread Rank Two
Effect: The sword is Damage Step 6.

Thread Rank Three
Key Knowledge: The owner must learn the Name of the creator of the sword.
Effect: The owner gains a +1 bonus to Spellcasting and Effect tests for the spell in the sword's spell matrix.

Thread Rank Four
Effect: The owner gains +1 to Attack tests with the sword.

Thread Rank Five
Key Knowledge: The owner must learn the exact composition of the magical elements used to create the sword.
Effect: The owner gains a +2 bonus to Spellcasting and Effect tests for the spell in the sword's spell matrix.

Thread Rank Six
Effect: The weapon is Damage Step 7.

Thread Rank Seven
Deed: The owner must decide on an appropriate Deed to perform using the blade (GM's discretion), publicly declare his intention of performing the Deed, and actually succeed at performing the declared Deed.
Effect: For 2 Strain, the owner may declare a Spell Strike. The owner makes an Attack test with the sword and if successful may cast the spell within the sword as a Free Action as long as no threads are required to be woven. This is in addition to the sword's normal damage.

Thread Rank Eight
Effect: The spell matrix is now an Enhanced Matrix.

Spike Bomb
Maximum Threads: 2
Mystic Defense: 14 **Tier:** Journeyman

Spike bombs were originally invented to help in construction and demolition. As the Scourge approached, they were adapted to help battle Horrors once it was discovered their safety features did not protect Horrors from their effects. The bombs are small, four-inch-diameter, metal balls covered with magical symbols. These symbols are usually arcane markings of no particular significance. Spike bombs were first invented by the t'skrang alchemist Vreesfyr, but the technique eventually spread throughout Barsaive.

Thread Rank One
Key Knowledge: The owner must learn the Name of the bomb.
Effect: The owner may place or throw the bomb onto a surface as a Standard action, causing a controlled explosion as soon as no living creatures are within a one-yard radius. The owner makes a WIL+6 test as the Damage test. Barriers do not reduce this damage, but Physical Armor does provide protection. Horrors and Horror constructs do not count as living creatures and will be affected by this. The throwing range is that of a throwing dagger. For 1 Strain, the owner may immediately reform the bomb in his hand. Tests to throw the bomb use the greater of the owner's Throwing Weapons or DEX + Thread Rank.

Thread Rank Two
Effect: The Damage Step is now WIL+8.

Thread Rank Three
Key Knowledge: The owner must learn the Name of the bomb's creator..
Effect: The owner may now divide the spike bomb into smaller bomblets and throw them as a Standard action to cause a great deal of minor damage. While not dangerous to living creatures, they will wreak havoc on nearby objects, scenery, and structures. The owner may create a number of bomblets equal to twice the thread rank and each bomblet creates a two-yard radius area of difficult terrain within throwing range. All characters within the difficult terrain have their movement halved and are Harried (*Player's Guide*, p. 388)

Thread Rank Four
Effect: The Damage Step is now WIL+10

Thread Rank Five
Key Knowledge: The owner must learn the meaning of the arcane symbols on the bomb, and if they have any significance.
Effect: The owner can delay the effects of the bomb and bomblets, activating them as a Simple action at a time of their choosing. The character can create a second bomb that can be thrown or placed, but only one bomb can be used per Standard action.

Thread Rank Six
Effect: The Damage Step is now WIL+12.

Talisman Statue
Maximum Threads: 2
Mystic Defense: 14 **Tier:** Journeyman

Talisman statues are small statuettes, usually 3 to 4 inches tall, fashioned from stone, wood, or clay; some rare statues measure up to 7 inches tall. Their creators usually carve intricate runes into talisman statues; some creators make their statues more valuable by embedding small gems into the statuette's eyes.

Talisman statues can enhance the magical abilities of spellcasters. The owner must wear the statuette in order to benefit from its power (many owners wear their talisman statues around their necks, on leather thongs or metal chains).

Thread Rank One
Key Knowledge: The owner must learn the Name of the statue.
Effect: The statue contains a Standard Matrix of rank equal to the thread rank.

Thread Rank Two
Effect: The owner gains +1 rank to Spellcasting.

Thread Rank Three
Key Knowledge: The owner must learn the Name of the statue's creator.
Effect: The owner gains a +1 bonus to Thread Weaving tests.

Thread Rank Four
Effect: The owner gains +2 ranks to Spellcasting

Thread Rank Five
Key Knowledge: The owner must learn the Name of the mountain, forest, or mine from which the material used to create the talisman statue originated.
Effect: The owner gains a +2 bonus to Thread Weaving tests.

Thread Rank Six
Deed: The owner must bind the statue to the part of his pattern that holds his spellcasting abilities. This takes an hour-long ritual requiring a successful Thread Weaving (16) test. Completing the ritual causes 1 point of blood magic damage that can only be healed a year and a day after the owner no longer has a thread attached to the statue.
Effect: The owner gains a +1 bonus to his Karma Step when using Karma to enhance Spellcasting, Effect, or Thread Weaving tests.

Thorn Bow

Maximum Threads: 2
Mystic Defense: 12
Tier: Journeyman

Thorn bows are magical elven warbows whose wooden shafts sprout thorns similar to those the blood elves themselves bear. These weapons are crafted by Queen Alachia's blood warders for use by her elite archers among the exolashers, her personal guard. Each of these bows was originally crafted for a specific member of the exolashers and has been passed down through the ranks over the years. A total of 25 thorn bows exist in the Blood Wood, and exolashers have been known to go to extreme lengths to protect them. Without a thread attached, they behave as normal elven warbows.

Thread Rank One
Key Knowledge: The owner must learn the Name of the bow.
Effect: The bow is Damage Step 6.

Thread Rank Two
Effect: The owner gains +1 to Attack tests with the bow.

Thread Rank Three
Key Knowledge: The owner must learn the Name of the individual for whom the bow was originally crafted.
Effect: The bow is Damage Step 7.

Thread Rank Four
Effect: The owner gains +2 to Attack tests with the bow.

Thread Rank Five
Key Knowledge: The owner must learn the Name of who crafted the bow and the date it was given to its first owner.
Effect: The owner gains the power Thorn Arrow and may use it as a Standard action. Each day, the owner may pluck up to 10 thorns from the shaft of the bow for 1 Strain each. Removing a thorn is a Simple action. When removed, the thorn grows into a thorn arrow that only the owner may use. Thorn arrows sprout backwards pointing thorns while in flight and any target struck by a thorn arrows takes an additional Step 4/D6 damage when the arrow is removed. No armor

protects against this damage. Any thorn arrows remaining when the bow regrows its thorns each day will revert to mundane thorns.

Thread Rank Six
Effect: The bow causes bleeding Wounds. When the owner Wounds a target with an arrow fired from the bow (including from removing a thorn arrow), the target suffers 2 points of damage per round until they make a Recovery test or have their Wound bound or treated (e.g. Cold Purify or Physician). The effects of bleeding Wounds are cumulative; a character with 2 bleeding Wounds from the bow would suffer 4 points of damage per round. Undead, spirits, and other creatures that do not bleed are not affected by this power.

Thorn Man Spear
Maximum Threads: 1
Mystic Defense: 12 **Tier:** Journeyman

These are the spears wielded by the thorn men who guard the Blood Wood. Though the size and shape of these spears is unremarkable, thorn men spears sprout wicked thorns up and down their lengths, which make them more dangerous than usual. Unless the owner is immune to the effects (like thorn men or blood elves), the thorns cause 1 damage point each round the spear is used. No armor protects against this damage.

When wielded by thorn men, the spears are used as if the thorn man had a thread woven to it. When used by others, the damage is based on the Thread Rank woven to the spear. The same ritual used to create thorn men creates these spears. They can only be obtained by slaying a thorn man.

Over the years, a number of these spears have been acquired by members of the exolashers and Blood Warders of Blood Wood, who use them as thread weapons.

Thread Rank One
Key Knowledge: The owner must learn the Name of the spear.
Effect: The spear is Damage Step 6.

Thread Rank Two
Effect: The owner gains +1 to Attack tests with the spear.

Thread Rank Three
Key Knowledge: The owner must learn the Name of the spear's creator.
Effect: The spear is Damage Step 7. The owner no longer takes damage from the thorns protecting the spear's haft.

Thread Rank Four
Effect: The spear is Damage Step 8.

Thread Rank Five
Key Knowledge: The owner must learn the Name of the tree from which the wood for the spear was harvested.
Effect: The owner gains the power Entangling Thorns and may use it as a Free action. For 2 Strain, the owner may cause thorny vines to grow from the haft and entangle the target. On a successful attack with the spear, the target is Harried until the end of the next turn.

Thread Rank Six
Effect: The owner gains +2 to Attack tests with the spear.

Thread Axe
Maximum Threads: 2
Mystic Defense: 8   **Tier:** Novice

These Scythan axes come in a small selection of styles, though they are almost all works of art in addition to their function as a weapon. Each is an opportunity for the creator to display their talents and vision. Without a thread attached, the axe is treated as a normal Scythan axe.

Thread Rank One
Key Knowledge: The owner must learn the Name of the axe.
Effect: The axe is Damage Step 6.

Thread Rank Two
Effect: The axe is Damage Step 7.

Thread Rank Three
Key Knowledge: The owner must learn the Name of the creator of the axe.
Effect: The axe is Damage Step 8.

Thread Rank Four
Effect: The owner gains +1 rank to Durability.

Thread Crystal Ringlet
Maximum Threads: 2
Mystic Defense: 10   **Tier:** Novice

These sets of crystal ringlet come in a small selection of styles, though they are almost all works of art in addition to their function as a weapon. Each is an opportunity for the creator to display their talents and vision.

Thread Rank One
Key Knowledge: The owner must learn the Name of the armor.
Effect: The armor is Physical Armor 5.

Thread Rank Two
Effect: The armor is Mystic Armor 5.

Thread Rank Three
Key Knowledge: The owner must learn the Name of the creator of the armor.
Effect: The armor is Physical Armor 6.

Thread Rank Four
Effect: The armor is Mystic Armor 6.

Thread Sword
Maximum Threads: 2
Mystic Defense: 8 **Tier:** Novice

These broadswords come in a variety of styles, though they are almost all works of art in addition to their function as a weapon. Each is an opportunity for the creator to display their talents and vision. Without a thread attached, the sword is treated as a normal broadsword.

Thread Rank One
Key Knowledge: The owner must learn the Name of the sword.
Effect: The sword is now Damage Step 6.

Thread Rank Two
Effect: The owner gains +1 to Attack tests with the sword.

Thread Rank Three
Key Knowledge: The owner must learn the Name of the creator of the sword.
Effect: The sword is Damage Step 7.

Thread Rank Four
Effect: The owner gains +2 to Attack tests with the sword.

Thread Wand
Maximum Threads: 2
Mystic Defense: 12 **Tier:** Novice

These wands come in a wide variety of styles, ranging from 8 to 18 inches, though they are almost all works of art. Each is an opportunity for the creator to display their talents and vision.

Thread Rank One
Key Knowledge: The owner must learn the Name of the wand.
Effect: The owner gains +1 rank to Spellcasting.

Thread Rank Two
Effect: The owner gains +1 to Thread Weaving tests.

Thread Rank Three
Key Knowledge: The owner must learn the Name of the creator of the wand.
Effect: The owner gains +2 ranks to Spellcasting.

Thread Rank Four
Effect: The owner gains +2 to Thread Weaving tests.

Thread Warbow
Maximum Threads: 2
Mystic Defense: 8   **Tier:** Novice

These elf war bows come in a small selection of styles, though they are almost all works of art in addition to their function as a weapon. Each is an opportunity for the creator to display their talents and vision. Without a thread attached, the bow is treated as a normal elven war bow.

Thread Rank One
Key Knowledge: The owner must learn the Name of the bow.
Effect: The bow is Damage Step 6.

Thread Rank Two
Effect: The owner gains +1 to Attack tests with the bow.

Thread Rank Three
Key Knowledge: The owner must learn the Name of the creator of the bow.
Effect: The bow is Damage Step 7.

Thread Rank Four
Effect: The owner gains +2 to Attack tests with the bow.

Threaded Instruments
Maximum Threads: 3
Mystic Defense: 8   **Tier:** Novice

Threaded instruments are popular among Troubadours, and come in a wide variety of different styles, though most commonly are lutes, small harps, and other stringed instruments. They are often beautiful works of art, even without their magical enhancement. Without a thread attached, they behave as normal instruments of their type.

Thread Rank One
Key Knowledge: The owner must learn the Name of the instrument.
Effect: The owner gains +1 rank to Emotion Song.

Thread Rank Two
Effect: The owner gains +1 rank to Impressive Display.

Thread Rank Three
Key Knowledge: The owner must learn the Name of the creator of the instrument.
Effect: The owner adds +1 to Social Defense.

Thread Rank Four
Effect: The owner gains a +1 bonus to Interaction tests.

Unrequited Wave
Maximum Threads: 2
Mystic Defense: 12 **Tier:** Journeyman

Before the Scourge when Barsaive was broken, there was an obsidiman who loved that which he could never have. He would stare longingly at the waters of the Aras and the Serpent, the waves lapping at his feet, but he would always be a Namegiver of Earth and never truly know the kiss of water.

As a testament to his love, he crafted a weapon of both worlds. It appears as a blue crystal two-handed sword. The blade is shaped to look like a torrent of water. The stone hilt has carvings in t'skrang, while the blade has carvings in obsidiman. When immersed in water the blade almost disappears, only a shimmer betraying its presence.

Thread Rank One
Key Knowledge: The owner must learn the Name of the sword.
Effect: For 1 Strain, the owner may reform the weapon into other melee weapons, totaling size 6 as a Simple action. Any bonuses from Forge Weapon or Damage bonuses from thread ranks apply equally to all subdivided weapons.

Thread Rank Two
Effect: The sword is Damage Step 9.

Thread Rank Three
Key Knowledge: The owner must learn the Name of the weapon's creator.
Effect: The owner gains +1 to Attack tests with the weapon.

Thread Rank Four
Effect: The sword is Damage Step 10.

Thread Rank Five
Key Knowledge: The owner must learn the Name of the obsidiman who created the weapon.
Effect: The total size of the weapon may be up to 7. The weapon can be reformed from any distance as a Free action, as long as the owner has at least one piece of it (e.g. a dagger formed from the larger weapon).

Thread Rank Six
Effect: The weapon gains +2 Damage Steps.

War Helm of Landis
Maximum Threads: 2
Mystic Defense: 12   **Tier:** Journeyman

The War Helm of Landis is a metal helmet adorned with the symbol of the ancient human kingdom of Landis. Mages and Weaponsmiths worked together to provide this protection to important military commanders of the kingdom of Landis. Many of these helmets were lost in the battles against the mindless ravagers who were the forerunners of the Horrors and marked the beginning of the Scourge. The helm has a faceplate that can swing down or up, depending on whether the owner wants to protect his face or simply wants to see well.

Thread Rank One
Key Knowledge: The owner must learn the Name of the helmet.
Deed: The owner must polish and repair the helmet. Replacing the unit insignia on the helmet reactivates its magic.
Effect: The owner gains +1 to Physical Armor.

Thread Rank Two
Effect: The owner gains +1 to Social Defense.

Thread Rank Three
Key Knowledge: The owner must find out what military unit was under the command of the helmet's original owner.
Effect: The owner gains +1 to Mystic Defense.

Thread Rank Four
Effect: The owner gains +2 to Physical Armor.

Thread Rank Five
Deed: The owner must lead troops to victory in battle. The owner's leadership must be a factor in the reason for the victory.
Effect: The owner gains +2 to Interaction tests.

Thread Rank Six
Effect: The owner gains +2 to Social Defense.

Wyvernskin Robe
Maximum Threads: 3
Mystic Defense: 14   **Tier:** Journeyman

These robes are made of several wyvern skins sewn together. As wyverns vary in color from deep red to bright green to muddy brown, the robes often have a patchwork appearance. Those that are arranged in a particularly eye-catching fashion are considered suitable attire for even the highest court functions. With no threads attached, a wyvernskin robe provides the same protection as an espagra scale cloak:

3 Physical Armor and 1 Mystic Armor with no Initiative penalty. The robe may not be worn with other armor.

Thread Rank One
Key Knowledge: The owner must learn the Name of the robe.
Effect: The robe is Physical Armor 4.

Thread Rank Two
Effect: The robe is Mystic Armor 2.

Thread Rank Three
Key Knowledge: The owner must learn the Name of the group of heroes who defeated the wyverns from whose skin the robe was crafted.
Effect: The robe is Physical Armor 5.

Thread Rank Four
Effect: The robe is Mystic Armor 3.

Thread Rank Five
Key Knowledge: The owner must learn the Name of the creator of the robe.
Effect: The owner gains a wyvern-like ferocity and can imitate a wyvern's screeching roar. For 1 Strain, the owner gains +3 ranks to Battle Shout for one round.

Thread Rank Six
Effect: The owner gains +1 to Initiative tests.

EARTHDAWN

CREATURES

Namegivers have the unfortunate habit of forgetting they share the land with other living things.
• Alisa, Questor of Jaspree •

A wide variety of creatures, from the mundane to the magical, populate the lands of **Earthdawn**. Some inhabit the isolated and wild corners of Barsaive, posing danger to the unwary traveler, while others live alongside Namegivers. This chapter provides a selection of creatures to challenge the player characters in your game.

SELECTING CREATURES FOR ENCOUNTERS

Player characters can encounter creatures almost anywhere in Barsaive, even in larger towns and cities. Just as in our world, however, the different creatures living in the world of **Earthdawn** have different habitats and environments they prefer, and an ecological niche they inhabit. For example, a crocodile is unlikely to thrive in the dry and ashen lands of the Wastes, and the heat-loving firebird is probably not going to be found in the snowy peaks of the Throal Mountains. On the other hand, undead and Horror-tainted creatures can make their home in any number of places.

When selecting creatures for encounters in your game, a good general rule to follow is for the creature to have some kind of connection to the adventure, rather than occurring at random. The connection need not tie directly into the main plot; it could be a thematic or environmental connection. A group seeking the ruins of a kaer serving as a Horror's lair might encounter creatures suffering from the effects of astral taint. Explorers investigating the edges of the Liaj Jungle might be more likely to run into more aggressive or dangerous creatures, representing the type of habitat the Great Dragon Usun encourages in his domain.

Another factor to keep in mind when selecting creatures for encounters is the level of challenge they will provide the player characters in your group. This is what the **Challenge** value provided in the creature descriptions can be used for. A group of five First Circle characters will have a pretty hard time facing off against a half dozen cave trolls, while a party of eight Seventh Circle characters would handle a pair of hell hounds without breakage a sweat.

A creature's Challenge value is intended as a guideline. Because each adept, and each group, has different strengths and weaknesses the challenge an individual creature can pose can vary significantly. For example, a creature with a high Physical Defense but a low Mystic Defense might pose more of a challenge to a Warrior than a Wizard, or a wild animal could be a pushover for a Beastmaster. As you become more familiar with the strengths and weaknesses of the player characters in your game, you will get a better handle on the level of challenge posed by different creatures.

The number of creatures to include in an encounter also depends on the abilities of the player characters in your game. While the descriptions provided in these pages suggest the number of creatures that normally live or travel together, the gamemaster should take the capabilities and power of the group. For example, ghouls might travel in packs of twenty-five to thirty individuals, but only more powerful characters will be able to survive that kind of onslaught. In general, if the Challenge value of a creature equals the average Circle of your player character group, then having the same number of creatures as player characters is a good starting point for a balanced encounter. If the Challenge value is lower than the average Circle, then more creatures can be included to challenge the characters, and a single more powerful creature might provide a suitable challenge for a group of adepts.

Balancing Encounters

There is no hard and fast rule to gauge the challenge of an encounter, but there are some tools which can be used to help determine the difficulty. By looking at the Step Numbers and Defense Ratings for the participants in an encounter, the gamemaster can determine how much of a challenge it is likely to present.

Start by determining the average Defense Ratings for each side of a conflict by adding up each Defense Rating (Physical, Mystic, and Social) and dividing by the number of characters, rounding up. Compare this value to the appropriate Attack Step for the other side. If the Step number is equal to the appropriate Defense Rating, then the opponent has an even chance of successfully using the attack on the target. If the numbers are not even, then the advantage lies with the higher value, and the greater the difference, the more significant the advantage is.

A player character group has four characters: An Archer (PD 10, MD 8, SD 6), an Elementalist (PD 7, MD 10, SD 6), A Scout (PD 9, MD 7, SD 7), and a Warrior (PD 8, MD 7, SD 5). A harpy uses Step 9 for its physical attacks, which is the same as the group's average Physical Defense of 9 (10+9+8+7=34, 34 divided by 4 is 8.5, rounded up to 9). The group has no advantage or disadvantage when it comes to the harpy's physical attacks. However, the harpy also has the Taunt power at Step 12, which is higher than the group's average Social Defense of 6 (6+6+7+5=24, 24 divided by 4 is 6). This gives the harpy a significant edge when using this power against this group of characters.

Another aspect to take into account is the potential damage each side can do to the other. Take the average Damage Step of one side and subtract the appropriate Armor value (Physical or Mystic) of their opponents. This will give you the average amount of damage a successful attack will deal. If you divide that into the Unconsciousness and Death Ratings of the player characters, you can get a sense of how many successful attacks are needed to incapacitate the character. Comparing the average damage to a character's Wound Threshold can also provide a useful measure of how well the character can withstand the damage they would be suffering.

> *Continuing with the previous example, a harpy does Step 10 damage with their claws. If the player characters have an average Physical Armor of 4, then the harpy will do an average of 6 damage with each successful attack. Given the harpy has an even chance of successfully hitting the characters (on average) the harpies pose a physical threat to these player characters, but not a significant one.*

By knowing the strengths and weaknesses of the player characters in your game, and comparing that to potential creatures and opponents, you can create more balanced encounters for your game. Determine which side holds the advantage by comparing each of these parameters:

- Characters' Attack vs. Opponents' Defense
- Opponents' Attack vs. Characters' Defense
- Characters' Damage potential vs. Opponents' Damage resistance
- Opponents' Damage potential vs. Characters' Damage resistance

In some cases, you might need to make a comparison more than once; for example, compare physical attack and damage potential separate from magical or mystic attack and damage potential. In each comparison, the side with the advantage is the side with the higher value, and whichever side has the most advantages will, in general, have the overall advantage in the encounter.

Do not forget the characters' access to spells and talents that boost their abilities.

As adepts increase in circle, their access to karma increases as does the number of abilities on which they may spend it.

Creatures considered too challenging for the characters can have their difficulty adjusted. Novice tier creatures should have all Defenses, Attack Steps (including Creature Power), and Damage Steps reduced by one. Journeyman creatures should additionally have Armor values reduced by one.

At this point, the gamemaster can modify the circumstances to shift the balance. There are many different ways to accomplish this, including increasing or decreasing the number of opponents, adding special circumstances that might favor one side over another, or modifying expectations for the encounter.

> *While the physical advantage in the example encounter is about even, the harpies have a significant advantage when using their social attack (Taunt) against the characters. They also have the ability to fly, which could give them a tactical advantage.*
>
> *The gamemaster can use this knowledge to shape how the harpies behave during the encounter. The harpies will stay at range and soften up their targets with taunts and curses, and then direct physical attacks against the opponent who appears to be most affected by their other abilities.*
>
> *Another way the gamemaster could modify the encounter to provide balance is to bring a different creature into the encounter, one who poses more of*

a physical challenge to the group. In this case, the harpies weaken the prey so the tougher creature has an easier time with the kill, and the harpies scavenge what is left.

Alternately, the gamemaster might decide rather than serving as an encounter designed primarily for combat, the harpies present a different sort of obstacle. Perhaps they have some information the group needs to uncover, through roleplaying, or their presence highlights something about the area the group is exploring.

Balancing encounters is more art than science. Comparing different characteristics and Step Numbers can serve as a good starting point, but many other factors can come into play. Encounters do not usually take place in a featureless blank arena, and creatures are likely to use whatever advantage they can to come out ahead.

Creature Behavior

Outside of the Horrors and their corrupted minions, creatures rarely attack because they are "evil". They will usually attack only when hungry or threatened in some way, such as defending their young, territory, or a source of food. It is rare for creatures to fight to the death unless they are defending their young, or under some kind of magical or supernatural influence. Even the hungriest predator is likely to retreat in the face of strong resistance, especially if their life is threatened as a result.

A good general rule to follow is most creatures will retreat if they suffer a Wound, or if they take cumulative damage equal to about half of their Unconsciousness Rating. Characters with knowledge of wild animals and their behavior would be familiar with this concept, and so a creature which doesn't follow it might indicate something unusual is going on, whether that is the presence of young, illness, starvation, or magical influence of some kind.

Even more intelligent enemies are likely to think of their own survival, unless they have strong motivations. Whether creature or Namegiver, a character's Attitude (see p. 142) can influence their willingness to keep fighting. The more negative the opponent's attitude towards the player characters, the less likely they are to surrender or flee. As with many other aspects of managing encounters and interactions with creatures and gamemaster characters, there are no hard and fast rules. Instead, differing circumstances are likely to play a role in a creature's decision to keep fighting.

CREATURE COMBAT

General rules for combat are provided in the *Player's Guide*, starting on page 371. Provided here are special rules which apply to creatures in combat.

Multiple Actions

Some creatures are able to make more than one Standard action per round, which is indicated under the "Actions" entry of their characteristics. Unless otherwise noted, a creature with multiple Standard actions may only use one Standard action to move, allowing them to move double their normal movement rate in a round; the same limit applies to player characters.

A creature with multiple actions is able to attack multiple times, but certain types of attacks are limited, depending on the creature and the nature of the attack. General rules are provided later in this section, with exceptions being included in the descriptions of specific creatures.

Most creature powers require the use of an action, but some powers are effects of another ability which requires an action. For example, the fiery breath of a hell hound requires the creature to use a Standard action to make a Creature Power test, with the breath weapon power being used as the Effect test. Any exceptions or special rules will be included in the description of the creature's power.

Creature Attacks

Some creatures have more than one way to attack a target, and will generally use the most effective means available. If a creature has multiple actions, it can divide its attacks up as it wishes, subject to the limits provided here and any exceptions listed in the creature's description.

The following text provides rules for the most common forms of creature attacks. Unless noted otherwise, each of these attacks requires the creature to use one of its actions in a given round.

Bite Attacks

While attacks with claws are more common, most creatures are able to attack with their teeth as well. Unless a creature's description indicates otherwise, it may only make one bite attack per round, even if it has multiple actions. This limit applies to any other attacks using a bite, as described below.

Claw and Other Attacks

Since most creatures have claws, this type of attack is the most commonly used. Most creatures will use one or both of their forelimbs, clawing and raking their target. The number of claw attacks a creature can make will be indicated as part of the description. A creature with only one claw attack may use both forelimbs to attack, but for game purposes it is resolved as a single attack. Attacks using other appendages (e.g. a tail) are handled in the same fashion as claw attacks with any special rules as noted for the creature.

Disease

Some creatures carry a disease which can affect their victim. In most cases, the disease is transmitted through a bite, and is a secondary effect of the creature's attack. Some creatures, like the plague lizard or harpy, are disease carriers and characters may be exposed to the disease through simple proximity. The information provided in the game statistics provides the relevant information for resolving the effect of the disease on the victim. See Disease, p. 186, for more information.

Poison

Some creatures overcome their prey with venom instead of physical damage. Like disease, poison is usually a secondary effect or combat option of another attack. The creature can choose whether to inject its poison on an attack, but must cause damage in order to do so. Unless otherwise noted in the creature description, a Wound is not required to affect a target with poison. The statistics provided in the creature description give the appropriate game information for resolving the effects of the poison. See Poison, p. 171, for more information.

Combat Options for Creatures and Opponents

Some of the combat options available to player characters can be used by creatures. The specific rules regarding the different combat options are provided in the *Player's Guide*, starting on page 382. The commonly used options are provided here with information to reflect how or why a creature might use them.

Aggressive Attack: Creatures who are wounded, dying, or defending their young will often use this option. Some predators might take advantage of this option on their initial attack to kill or disable their prey more quickly.

Attacking to Knockdown: Knocking down a target allows a creature to expose them to more effective attacks. Some creature attacks, including pouncing and charging, have this option already built into their mechanics.

Called Shot: Any creature that wishes to attack a particular location on a target's body can use this option.

Defensive Stance: Creatures who are wounded and attempting to retreat may take advantage of this option.

Splitting Movement: This option is most commonly used by flying creatures for swooping attacks, but any creature may use it for hit and run style tactics.

Creature Powers

Many creatures in the world of **Earthdawn** have magical abilities. As a general rule, most magical powers require a test to take effect, either a direct test using the Step of the power, or a Creature Power test with the power serving as an Effect test.

Some powers or abilities are common to a wide variety of creatures. To save space the rules for those powers are listed below, with only the power name and Step listed in the creature description. Sometimes a creature will have additional notes modifying the base power in some way. Other creatures have unique powers, and those rules are provided with the creature.

Ambush: When attacking from surprise, the creature gains a bonus to its Initiative, Attack, and Damage tests equal to their Step in this ability. This power cannot be combined with Surprise Strike.

Charge: The creature may move up to twice its Movement and make a single attack. If the creature moves more than its base Movement, it gains a bonus to its Attack and Damage tests equal to the Step of this ability. This ability may not be used when the creature has a rider.

Climbing: Creatures with a climbing speed do not have an associated Climbing skill due to their natural ability.

Creature Power: This ablity is used to make Attack tests with other magical powers. The description will indicate what powers it is used with for that creature.

Dive: The creature may move up to twice its flying Movement and make a single attack. If the creature moves more than its base flying Movement, it gains a bonus to its Attack and Damage tests equal to the Step of this ability. This ability may not be used when the creature has a rider.

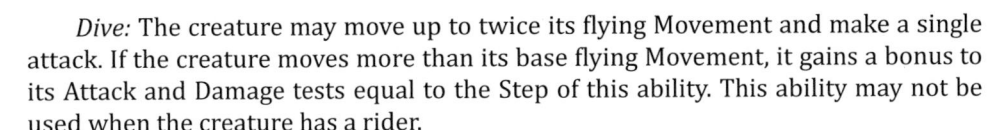

Enhanced Sense: This ability grants the creature various improved senses. A parenthetical number is the bonus granted to any Awareness tests using the associated sense, or any other abilities listed in the description. Adepts with the Borrow Sense talent may target these senses individually, gaining all associated bonuses to a particular sense. The basic use of Borrow Sense may only target hearing, sight, smell, taste, and touch. Senses listed as [Other] require more powerful magic to be targeted.

Fury: Instead of suffering penalties, Wounds grant this creature a bonus to tests. Once the creature has more Wounds than indicated by the Step of this ability, the bonuses are lost and the creature suffers normal penalties for Wounds.

Great Leap: A creature may leap a distance in yards equal to this rank as a part of their normal movement. The distance is divided between the horizontal and vertical distance leaped.

Hardened Armor: Bonus damage resulting from additional successes on Attack tests is reduced by one per success. Typically, this means that instead of +2 damage per additional success, the attacker only gets +1 damage per additional success.

Resist Pain: The creature ignores penalties for Wounds equal to the Step of this ability. For example, a creature with Resist Pain (2) ignores the penalties from the first two Wounds suffered.

Swimming: Most non-flying creatures have an innate ability to swim. If the Swimming skill is necessary and no swim Movement is listed, assume an Action Step of Dexterity Step +2.

Swooping Attack: The creature may split its flying Movement (*Player's Guide*, p. 386) and not suffer any test penalties, or spend Strain.

Willful: Talents and abilities used to dominate, control, tame or train the creature require additional successes equal to the Step of this ability.

Special Maneuvers

Some creatures have a special maneuvers section. These are ways either the creature or their opponent may spend additional successes instead of gaining the standard additional damage. Opponents may only use these with physical attacks (not using spells). It will be noted in the description if there are any further restrictions on the kind of attacks which must be used for the special maneuver. Characters may learn of these options through successful Creature Analysis Creature Lore, or other appropriate skills as determined by the gamemaster.

The **Called Shot** combat option may be used to specify a special maneuver. On a successful attack, the character gains an additional success from the called shot, which must be applied to the special maneuver. Any further additional successes applied to the same special maneuver are counted twice.

Gamemasters are encouraged to apply their own special maneuvers based on creatures and circumstances.

Common Maneuvers

Clip the Wing: The attacker may spend two additional successes from an Attack test to remove the creature's ability to fly until the end of the next round. If the attack causes a Wound, the creature cannot fly until the Wound is healed. If the creature is in flight, it falls and suffers falling damage for half the distance fallen.

Crack the Shell: The attacker may spend extra successes from physical attacks (not spells) to reduce the creature's Physical Armor by 1 per success spent. This reduction takes place after damage is assessed, and lasts until the end of combat.

Defang: The opponent may spend additional successes to affect the creature's ability to use its poison. Each success spent reduces the Poison's Step by 2. If the attack causes a Wound, the creature cannot use its Poison power at all until the Wound is healed.

Enrage: An opponent may spend additional successes from an Attack test to give a -1 penalty to the creature's Attack tests and Physical Defense until the end of the next round. Multiple successes may be spent for a cumulative effect.

Grab and Bite: The creature may spend an additional success from an Attack test to automatically grapple an opponent. Grappled opponents automatically take bite damage each round until the grapple is broken.

Hamstring: The creature may spend an additional success from an Attack test to halve the opponent's Movement until the end of the next round. If the attack causes a Wound, the penalty lasts until the Wound is healed.

Overrun: The creature may spend an additional success from an Attack test to force an opponent with a lower Strength Step to make a Knockdown test against a DN equal to the Attack test result.

Pounce: If the creature reaches its opponent with a leap and the opponent isn't too much larger, the creature may spend an additional success from the Attack test to force the opponent to make a Knockdown test against a DN equal to the Attack test result.

Provoke: The attacker may spend two additional successes from an Attack test to enrage the creature and guarantee he will be the sole target of the creature's next set of attacks. Only the most recent application of this maneuver has any effect.

Pry Loose: The attacker may spend additional successes from an Attack test to allow a grappled ally to immediately make an escape attempt with a +2 bonus per success spent on this maneuver.

Squeeze the Life: The creature may spend two additional successes from an Attack test to automatically grapple an opponent. Grappled opponents automatically take claw damage each round until the grapple is broken.

CREATURE ENTRY FORMAT

Unless otherwise noted, the game statistics provided in this chapter describe an "average" example of each type of creature. This section explains the format in which the statistics are presented.

Each creature entry starts with some opening text that includes a physical description of the creature, along with details about habitat, behaviors, natural defenses, and any other interesting or relevant information. This is followed by the creature's game statistics, and rules for resolving the use of the creature's powers and abilities, presented in the following format:

Challenge: This entry is a rough guideline to the creature's power level. It represents what Circle adept would find the creature a fair challenge in a one-on-one fight. This is not a precise measurement, as different groups will find different challenges more or less difficult. Some creatures will require more than one adept working together in order to provide a fair challenge, which will be noted in the description. See **Selecting Creatures for Encounters**, p. 245, for a more in-depth examination of how to use this value when selecting creatures for your games.

Attributes: Each creature is given a Step number for the following Attributes: Dexterity (DEX), Strength (STR), Toughness (TOU), Perception (PER), Willpower (WIL), and Charisma (CHA). When making Attribute tests for the creature, use the appropriate dice for the given Step.

Initiative: The Step number used when the creature makes an Initiative test.

Physical Defense: The creature's Physical Defense.

Mystic Defense: The creature's Mystic Defense.

Social Defense: The creature's Social Defense. Some powers and abilities may require the character to be able to communicate with the creature.

Unconsciousness: The creature's Unconsciousness Rating. If the creature cannot be knocked unconscious, this value will be given as "NA".

Death Rating: The creature's Death Rating, with any applicable Durability factored into the total.

Physical Armor: The creature's natural Physical Armor rating. In most cases, this represents the natural hide, tough skin, thick fur, or some other covering. Some humanoid creatures may be able to wear armor.

Mystic Armor: The creature's Mystic Armor rating.

Knockdown: The Step number used when the creature makes a Knockdown test. If the entry is given as "Immune" then the creature cannot be knocked down.

Wound Threshold: The creature's Wound Threshold. If the entry is given as "None" then the creature cannot suffer from Wounds.

Movement: The creature's movement rate, given in yards per round. Any special forms of movement are provided in this entry as well. Unless otherwise noted in the creature's description, creature movement works like movement for player characters, including the need to use a Standard action to move up to double their Movement.

Recovery Tests: The number of Recovery Tests the creature has.

Actions: The number of Standard actions the creature may make each round. Also provided as part of this entry is the basic attack types the creature can use, along with the Step number used for the attack. The Damage step of the attack is provided in parentheses after the Attack step. For example, a creature with Bite 11 (17) can attack with a bite, using Step 11 for the Attack test, and Step 17 for the Damage test. Some creatures have multiple attack types they can use, but each attack requires the use of a Standard action.

Powers: This entry lists the creature's powers and special abilities. If the power shares the name of a talent or skill, it usually works the same way. Any special rules or notes about the creature's powers will be included here.

Spells: A list of spells the creature knows and is able to cast. Unless otherwise noted, the spells work as described in the **Earthdawn** *Player's Guide*, including the need to weave any relevant threads.

Special Maneuvers: This entry lists special options, which may be employed by the creature, or employed against the creature by applying additional successes from physical attacks (not spells). Successes used in this way may not be used for increased damage.

Loot: This entry lists any valuable items the creature may carry, including money, equipment, or body parts that may be of value. If any of the loot is worth Legend Points, it will be noted here as well (see **Awarding Legend Points**, p. 119).

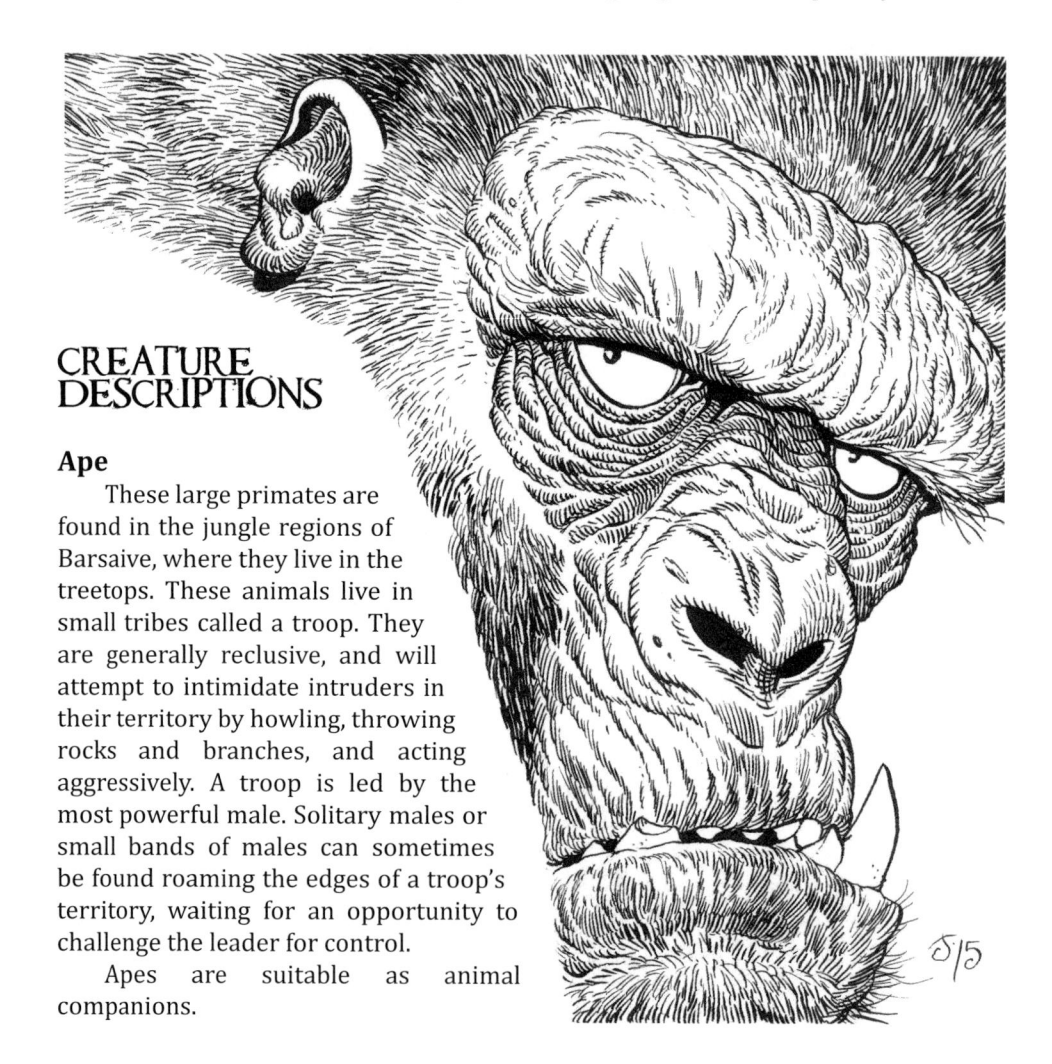

CREATURE DESCRIPTIONS

Ape

These large primates are found in the jungle regions of Barsaive, where they live in the treetops. These animals live in small tribes called a troop. They are generally reclusive, and will attempt to intimidate intruders in their territory by howling, throwing rocks and branches, and acting aggressively. A troop is led by the most powerful male. Solitary males or small bands of males can sometimes be found roaming the edges of a troop's territory, waiting for an opportunity to challenge the leader for control.

Apes are suitable as animal companions.

Challenge: Novice (Second Circle)

DEX:	7	Initiative:	7	Unconsciousness:	28
STR:	8	Physical Defense:	9	Death Rating:	34
TOU:	6	Mystic Defense:	8	Wound Threshold:	9
PER:	5	Social Defense:	9	Knockdown:	10
WIL:	5	Physical Armor:	3	Recovery Tests:	2
CHA:	4	Mystic Armor:	2		

Movement: 12 (Climb 12)
Actions: 1; Unarmed 11 (12), Bite 11 (13), Thrown 8 (10)
Powers:
Enhanced Sense [Smell] (2)
Great Leap (6)

Silverback Ape

The leader of a troop of apes, the silverback male is a fearsome and powerful opponent. He will defend his troop with naked aggression, attempting to intimidate intruders with roars, posturing, throwing large rocks, or branches. When a member of his troop is directly attacked, he will quickly leap to attack the most threatening opponent, and will not flee unless its troop has already escaped.

Silverback apes are suitable as animal companions.

Challenge: Novice (Third Circle)

DEX:	7	Initiative:	9	Unconsciousness:	36
STR:	10	Physical Defense:	10	Death Rating:	43
TOU:	7	Mystic Defense:	9	Wound Threshold:	10
PER:	5	Social Defense:	11	Knockdown:	12
WIL:	5	Physical Armor:	4	Recovery Tests:	2
CHA:	5	Mystic Armor:	2		

Movement: 12 (Climb 12)
Actions: 1; Unarmed 12 (13), Bite 12 (14), Thrown 8 (12)
Powers:
Battle Shout (8): As the skill, *Player's Guide*, p. 131.
Enhanced Sense [Smell] (2)
Great Leap (8)
Willful (1)

Special Maneuvers:
Opening (Silverback Ape): The silverback ape may spend additional successes from an Attack test against an opponent affected by their **Battle Shout** to give other apes a +1 bonus per success spent to Attack tests against the opponent until the end of the next round.

Basilisk

A basilisk looks like a cross between a garden snake and a four-foot-long lizard. These creatures are usually colored in gray or brown tones, with no distinguishing features save for gray, rooster-like combs atop their heads and large eyes glowing with a fierce white light. The light inflicts terrible damage to any living being in its path. During the day, sunlight obscures the basilisk's eye light. The basilisk hunts by night, crawling out of its cave at twilight. Unlike most creatures, basilisks sleep with their eyes open, lighting up their small caves as if with a hundred candles.

The basilisk is a deadly predator, able to cause damage far out of proportion to its size. If a basilisk encounters anything hostile, it tries to kill its opponent, and can usually succeed. If it can't kill its target, either because the target is too tough or the light in the area weakens its deadly gaze, it usually flees. If necessary it can bite a target, but it prefers not to use this mode of attack unless cornered.

For many centuries, magicians and scholars puzzled over how basilisks reproduce. A creature that can kill anything it looks at can hardly be expected to mate in any normal way and would most likely kill any young it managed to spawn. The answer to this puzzle is the basilisk does not mate, but splits. Every so often in a basilisk's life, its tail begins to grow thicker and takes on the appearance of a second head. After several weeks, both heads look exactly the same, and the creature splits in half. The two halves begin to grow new tails, and within days there are two basilisks instead of one.

Some scholars claim the basilisk resembles the cockatrice—others believe basilisks and dragons are related. Some magicians and scholars have sought to determine the source of the basilisk's deadly gaze, perhaps seeking to harness the magic for their own ends. Most of these efforts result in painful failure.

Challenge: Journeyman (Sixth Circle)

DEX:	6	**Initiative:**	6	**Unconsciousness:**	48
STR:	6	**Physical Defense:**	11	**Death Rating:**	54
TOU:	6	**Mystic Defense:**	14	**Wound Threshold:**	9
PER:	7	**Social Defense:**	9	**Knockdown:**	Immune
WIL:	7	**Physical Armor:**	10	**Recovery Tests:**	2
CHA:	4	**Mystic Armor:**	6		

Movement: 8
Actions: 1; Bite 12 (12)
Powers:

Creature Power (18, Killing Glare, Standard)
Killing Glare (27): The basilisk's eyes shine in a 45-degree cone in front of the creature. The range of the effect depends on the ambient light in the area. In direct sunlight it can only affect targets within 4 yards, in twilight the glare harms targets within 10 yards, and in complete darkness the range extends to 20 yards. To use this power the basilisk makes a Creature Power test, comparing it to the Mystic Defense of all targets within the area of effect. If successful, the Killing Glare Step is used to determine damage, reduced by the target's Mystic Armor.

Special Maneuvers:
Go For the Eyes! (Opponent): The attacker may use two additional successes on an attack test to inflict Partial Blindness on the basilisk until the end of the next round. In addition to the normal penalties, this reduces the **Killing Glare** Step by 10. If the damage causes a Wound, the blindness lasts until the Wound is healed. A basilisk

suffering from this twice cannot use Killing Glare as long as the effect of both maneuvers lasts.
Loot: Two eyes worth 200 silver each (worth Legend Points).

Bat, Messenger

Messenger bats are slightly larger than windlings, with monkey-like faces and long fingers at the ends of their wings. They are usually brown, gray, or black and are found primarily in Cara Fahd's jungles, where native orks have tamed and trained them for years. The bats eat insects, small mice and lizards, and do not attack Namegiver-sized creatures.

The bats can navigate perfectly, using magical direction sensing organs in their heads, scent cues and a faultless memory for flying to any given location. If a messenger bat is ordered to fly to a place it has previously been, even as an infant, the bat will be able to get there. For this reason, messenger bats are often used in Cara Fahd to deliver message stones and documents between towns, though communicating with the animal frequently requires a Beastmaster. Critical information isn't usually sent by messenger bat, as the animals are slow-witted, and easily distracted. When attacked, they try to flee unless cornered, in which case they flap their wings in the attacker's face and bite in an attempt to distract him.

Messenger bats are suitable as animal companions.

Challenge: Novice (First Circle)

DEX:	8	**Initiative:**	9	**Unconsciousness:**	14
STR:	3	**Physical Defense:**	14	**Death Rating:**	17
TOU:	3	**Mystic Defense:**	12	**Wound Threshold:**	4
PER:	8	**Social Defense:**	7	**Knockdown:**	3
WIL:	3	**Physical Armor:**	2	**Recovery Tests:**	1
CHA:	3	**Mystic Armor:**	2		

Movement: 2 (Flying 16)
Actions: 1; Bite 9 (4)
Powers:
Enhanced Sense [Hearing] (2)
Enhanced Sense [Other] (4): The magical organ in their head gives messenger bats incredible ability to sense and locate targets, even in complete darkness, and ignore darkness penalties. Add a +4 bonus to any tests made to detect a hidden or concealed target within 150 yards.
Enhanced Sense [Smell] (2)
Stealthy Stride (10)
Special Maneuvers:
Clip the Wing (Opponent)
Loot: Direction sensing organ worth 20 silver pieces.

Bat, Shrieker

The shrieker bat resembles its smaller cousins, but at full extension, its leathery wings span 4 feet. It also has larger eyes and smaller ears. Unlike other bats, the shrieker bat does not navigate by sound but by sight. Instead, it produces a painfully irritating cry, worse than sharp talons on metal. The shrieker bat uses its cry to paralyze its prey, most often birds and rodents. The shriek affects any animal within hearing range. The shriek can also affect inanimate objects. Glassware, pottery, and other objects made of similar materials may well shatter into slivers when near the shrieker bat's cry.

This creature is quite dangerous when hunting; its dull black fur makes it almost impossible to see in the dark, and its high-pitched cry is beyond the ability of the Namegiver races to hear—only the rush of its wings gives its presence away. Unlike other bats, the shrieker bat also flies in daylight, most often to protect its nest from harm, but a ravenous bat will also hunt in sunlight if it must.

Once the bat paralyzes its prey, it lands on its victim and begins to tear out great chunks of flesh with its sharp claws and teeth. Travelers unlucky enough to fall victim to a shrieker bat had best hope his companions are close enough to drive off the beast. However, these bats usually travel in packs—defeating them should prove a challenge for even the most experienced heroes.

Shrieker bats are suitable as animal companions.

Challenge: Novice (Third Circle)

DEX:	7	**Initiative:**	8	**Unconsciousness:**	30
STR:	4	**Physical Defense:**	13	**Death Rating:**	35
TOU:	5	**Mystic Defense:**	10	**Wound Threshold:**	7
PER:	5	**Social Defense:**	8	**Knockdown:**	4
WIL:	4	**Physical Armor:**	4	**Recovery Tests:**	2
CHA:	3	**Mystic Armor:**	3		

Movement: 2 (Flying 16)
Actions: 1; Bite 10 (9)
Powers:
Enhanced Sense [Hearing] (4)
Enhanced Sense [Sight]: Low-Light Vision
Willful (2)
Stealthy Stride (9)
Sonic Shriek (12): By using a Standard action, the bat can use its piercing cry to strongly affect the sense of balance of any target within 10 yards. It makes a Sonic Shriek test against the target's Mystic Defense. If successful, the victim is knocked down for one round per success. If the Sonic Shriek test result scores three or more successes against the Mystic Defense of any fragile or brittle objects within range, the object shatters. This can affect glassware, pottery, even gemstones and crystal.
Surprise Strike (5): As the skill, *Player's Guide*, p. 172.
Special Maneuvers:
Clip the Wing (Opponent)
Dizzying Cry (Shrieker Bat, Sonic Shriek): The shrieker bat may spend an additional success from a **Sonic Shriek** test to cause an opponent to be Blindsided (*Player's Guide*, p. 386) for the duration as well.

Bear

Bears are forest and mountain dwelling omnivores who are usually not dangerous unless an unwary traveler enters their lair, or threatens their cubs. Bears usually permit travelers to pass through their territory, unless the trespassers pose an obvious threat to the animal's food supply.

Common bears are relatively docile. They are most often encountered near settlements. Near larger unwalled settlements, they are often found raiding refuse piles and farmlands. They are not very aggressive and will generally flee if wounded, except in the case of a mother defending her cubs. However, if backed into a corner, they become quite dangerous.

Bears are suitable as animal companions.

Challenge: Novice (Third Circle)

DEX:	5	Initiative:	5	Unconsciousness:	30
STR:	8	Physical Defense:	8	Death Rating:	36
TOU:	8	Mystic Defense:	5	Wound Threshold:	10
PER:	3	Social Defense:	7	Knockdown:	9
WIL:	5	Physical Armor:	5	Recovery Tests:	2
CHA:	3	Mystic Armor:	0		

Movement: 14 (Climb 8)
Actions: 1; Bite: 10 (17), Claws: 10 (15)
Powers:
Enhanced Sense [Smell] (2)
Fury (2)
Special Maneuvers:
Grab and Bite (Bear, Claws)
Pry Loose (Opponent, Close Combat)
Provoke (Opponent, Close Combat)

Great Bear

This is a larger and more aggressive version of the common bear. When these creatures rear back on their hind legs, they tower a head above a troll. They live in higher mountain ranges far from settled areas. They are extremely protective of their territory and will attack any creature they consider an intruder.

Great bears are suitable as animal companions.

Challenge: Novice (Fourth Circle)

DEX:	5	Initiative:	5	Unconsciousness:	53
STR:	11	Physical Defense:	7	Death Rating:	64
TOU:	11	Mystic Defense:	9	Wound Threshold:	16
PER:	3	Social Defense:	11	Knockdown:	15
WIL:	5	Physical Armor:	7	Recovery Tests:	4
CHA:	3	Mystic Armor:	3		

Movement: 14
Actions: 1; Bite: 11 (19), Claws: 11 (17)

Powers:
Battle Shout (12): As the skill, *Player's Guide*, p. 131.
Enhanced Sense [Smell] (2)
Fury (2)
Willful (1)

Combat Options:
Grab and Bite (Great Bear, Claws)
Pry Loose (Opponent, Close Combat)
Provoke (Opponent, Close Combat)

Behemoth

Sometimes called "swamp thundras," these giant beasts have attained near-mythical status among Cara Fahd's Cavalrymen. Physically, they resemble thundra beasts with dragon-like necks and tails and shorter horns. Males stand ten feet high at the shoulder, average twenty-five feet in length, and weigh about fifteen tons. Behemoths grow throughout their lives, and females live about twice as long as males on average, so it is possible to find older behemoths in excess of sixty feet in length.

Behemoths are slow, shy, and secretive, supporting their bulk in the waters of the swamps in southwest Cara Fahd. Though generally docile, they may attack by stomping or goring if threatened. They require a lot of food, so a herd usually consists of a female, three to five males, and two or three half-grown young. The numbers provided here are for a typical adult male.

Behemoths are suitable as animal companions.

Challenge: Journeyman (Eighth Circle)

DEX:	5	Initiative:	5	Unconsciousness:	91
STR:	17	Physical Defense:	13	Death Rating:	108
TOU:	17	Mystic Defense:	16	Wound Threshold:	25
PER:	4	Social Defense:	17	Knockdown:	21
WIL:	10	Physical Armor:	10	Recovery Tests:	6
CHA:	3	Mystic Armor:	5		

Movement: 16
Actions: 2; Horns: 21 (27), Tail: 21 (23), Trample: 21 (25)
Powers:
Enhanced Sense [Hearing] (2)
Enhanced Sense [Smell] (2)
Willful (2)
Resist Pain (2)
Special Maneuvers:
Provoke (Opponent, Close Combat)
Overrun (Behemoth, Trample)
Tail Sweep (Behemoth, Tail): The behemoth may spend additional successes from an Attack test using its tail to throw its human-sized or smaller opponent. Each success spent in this way throws the opponent 2 yards and the opponent treats this distance as falling (see **Falling Damage**, p. 167)

Blood Bee

Blood bees resemble two-foot-long wasps with an accordion-like sac flapping from their thoraxes. When attacking, the bee flies backward, strikes its prey with the sticky sac, then flies forward. The forward motion extrudes a hollow spine from within the sac, which punctures the victim's skin and drains his blood. Once filled, the bag becomes heavy enough for the bee to pull free. The laden insect then flies back to its nest to feast on the victim's blood.

Blood bees typically gather in swarms of several dozen individuals.

Challenge: Novice (First Circle)

DEX:	7	Initiative:	7	Unconsciousness:	14
STR:	2	Physical Defense:	10	Death Rating:	17
TOU:	3	Mystic Defense:	9	Wound Threshold:	4
PER:	5	Social Defense:	7	Knockdown:	2
WIL:	4	Physical Armor:	3	Recovery Tests:	1
CHA:	2	Mystic Armor:	1		

Movement: 2 (Flying 12)
Actions: 1; Stinger 9 (10)
Powers:
Blood Veins (5): Once latched onto a target, the victim suffers Step 5 damage each round, with no reduction for armor. The bee is removed automatically if Knocked Down.

Vulnerability to Salt: A blood bee's sac is terribly susceptible to salt. If a blood bee touches salt, it takes Step 6 damage, with no reduction from armor. A character covered in salt will enrage blood bees, but the buzzing swarms rarely gather the courage to attack him.

Special Maneuvers:

Blood Sucker (Blood Bee): The blood bee may spend an additional success on an attack to latch onto the target and use Blood Veins.

Clip the Wing (Opponent)

Pull the Stinger (Opponent): The attacker may spend an additional success on an attack test to remove a blood bee using Blood Veins on a target.

Blood Raven

Blood ravens can be distinguished from normal ravens by their larger size and reddish legs. Individually, blood ravens pose little threat to Namegivers. However, they most often appear in flocks of dozens of birds. Blood ravens are intelligent, with sharp eyesight and the ability to see astral space as well. For these reasons blood ravens are highly sought after by magicians, and blood elves often take blood ravens as familiars.

Blood ravens are suitable as animal companions.

Challenge: Novice (First Circle)

DEX:	7	Initiative:	11	Unconsciousness:	14
STR:	2	Physical Defense:	11	Death Rating:	17
TOU:	3	Mystic Defense:	10	Wound Threshold:	4
PER:	7	Social Defense:	10	Knockdown:	2
WIL:	6	Physical Armor:	1	Recovery Tests:	1
CHA:	5	Mystic Armor:	2		

Movement: 2 (Flying 18)

Actions: 1; Bite 10 (6)

Powers:

Enhanced Sense [Other] (3): Astral Sight, as the talent, *Player's Guide*, p. 129.

Enhanced Sense [Sight] (2)

Special Maneuvers:

Clip the Wing (Opponent)

Eye Gouge (Blood Raven): The creature may spend two additional successes on an attack test to inflict Partial Blindness on an opponent for two rounds. If the target is affected by this ability again in the same conflict, it inflicts Full Blindness. If the damage causes a Wound, the blindness penalty lasts until the Wound is healed.

Boar

Wild boars are hunted throughout Barsaive and their meat is a staple in many woodland settlements. A single male leads and protects each boar pack, attacking all threats to the pack with a pair of wicked tusks that can cause ragged and bleeding wounds. A boar often directs its first attack by charging at the nearest character or animal posing a threat, and frequently uses the Aggressive Attack combat option (*Player's Guide*, p. 382).

Boars are suitable as animal companions.

Challenge: Novice (Second Circle)

DEX:	6	Initiative:	6	Unconsciousness:	31
STR:	7	Physical Defense:	9	Death Rating:	38
TOU:	7	Mystic Defense:	8	Wound Threshold:	10
PER:	4	Social Defense:	7	Knockdown:	11
WIL:	5	Physical Armor:	5	Recovery Tests:	2
CHA:	3	Mystic Armor:	3		

Movement: 14
Actions: 1; Tusks: 10 (12)
Powers:
Charge (5)
Enhanced Sense [Hearing] (2)
Enhanced Sense [Smell] (2)
Fury (2)
Willful (1)
Special Maneuvers:
Provoke (Opponent, Close Combat)
Goring Charge (Boar, Charge): The boar may spend an additional success to cause a Knockdown test against the target. The Difficulty Number is the Attack test result.
Loot: Tusks worth 3D6 silver pieces (worth Legend Points).

Bog Gob

Bog gobs are squat, ugly, wicked creatures with glowing yellow eyes set in mottled-gray heads. Their bodies resemble a crude mannequin made of mud, standing four to five feet tall, and weighing about two hundred pounds. The same magic holding their mud-colored, bipedal bodies together also acts as resilient natural armor. They gather in groups numbering from ten to as many as sixty members. According to legends, these creatures came to Barsaive from faraway swamps in the lands to the north.

Bog gobs often attack simply to injure victims. These creatures almost always leave survivors, though larger groups of bog gobs leave fewer survivors. Scholars and sages have puzzled over this behavior; with the most popular hypothesis being bog gobs leave survivors because they enjoy the resulting tales. Powers that specifically target or affect animals or creatures do not affect bog gobs, leading some to speculate they might be some degenerate form of Namegiver.

Challenge: Second Circle

DEX:	5	**Initiative:**	5	**Unconsciousness:**	34
STR:	6	**Physical Defense:**	7	**Death Rating:**	42
TOU:	8	**Mystic Defense:**	8	**Wound Threshold:**	12
PER:	4	**Social Defense:**	12	**Knockdown:**	8
WIL:	5	**Physical Armor:**	5	**Recovery Tests:**	3
CHA:	3	**Mystic Armor:**	2		

Movement: 10
Actions: 1; Half-spear 9 (10)
Powers:
Sticky Body (7): When a bog gob's body comes into contact with another character or item, the bog gob makes a Sticky Body test against the target's Mystic Defense. If successful, the target is stuck fast. The target is Harried (*Player's Guide*, p. 388), but the bog gob may act freely. The target may use a Standard action to make a Strength (7) test to try and break free. A single target may be affected by multiple bog gobs, suffering from Overwhelmed penalties as appropriate. If four or more bog gobs are stuck to a single target, the victim starts to suffocate, taking 1 point of damage per round until freed (no armor protects from this damage).

Special Maneuvers:
No-stick Strike (Opponent): The attacker may use two additional successes to prevent their weapon from being stuck in the bog gob despite coming into contact with it.
Pry Loose (Opponent, Close Combat)
Loot: Half-spear (Size 3, Damage Step 4), 1d10 silver pieces.

Brithan

Dwarf hunters have described the brithan as a cross between a bear and an elemental having a bad day. The animal's eyes are flecked with luminescent specks, their bodies are covered with shaggy, deep brown or blue-black fur, and their large heads sport a pair of curving horns.

Brithans are territorial and will stand on their hind legs and roar a challenge to anything entering their domain. If a single character answers the challenge, the brithan enters into ritual combat with him, and the two fight until one submits.

A brithan will submit after taking a Wound. The submissive state will last for about three days, after which the creature tends to forget who beat him. If the character submits to the brithan, the character and his companions must leave the creature's territory, moving at least a half-mile away, the brithan will enter into a frenzy and pursue them. If the brithan encounters the character within the three-day period, it will attack to kill in frenzy.

Brithans are suitable as animal companions.

Challenge: Journeyman (Fifth Circle)

DEX:	5	Initiative:	5	Unconsciousness:	61
STR:	12	Physical Defense:	10	Death Rating:	73
TOU:	12	Mystic Defense:	13	Wound Threshold:	18
PER:	4	Social Defense:	9	Knockdown:	16
WIL:	7	Physical Armor:	8	Recovery Tests:	4
CHA:	3	Mystic Armor:	5		

Movement: 12
Actions: 2; Bite: 14 (20), Claw: 15 (18)
Powers:
Battle Shout (12): As the skill, *Player's Guide*, p. 131.
Enhanced Sense [Smell] (2)
Frenzy: If more than one character attacks a brithan, the animal fights back savagely, gaining an additional Action and a +4 bonus to Attack and Damage tests.
Fury (2)
Willful (1)
Special Maneuvers:
Grab and Bite (Brithan, Claws)
Enrage (Opponent) Using this maneuver will cause the brithan to frenzy.
Pry Loose (Opponent, Close Combat)
Provoke (Opponent, Close Combat)

Cat

Common, domesticated house cats are found in almost all towns and cities of Barsaive. They are often kept as pets by Namegivers of all races. Cats are virtually harmless to Namegivers, but they are useful for keeping buildings free of mice and rats.

A cat will not attack a Namegiver unless cornered, and even then it will only attack until it has a chance to escape. Cats have an innate sense of astral space.

Cats are suitable as animal companions.

Challenge: Novice (First Circle)

DEX:	7	Initiative:	9	Unconsciousness:	11
STR:	2	Physical Defense:	10	Death Rating:	13
TOU:	2	Mystic Defense:	9	Wound Threshold:	3
PER:	6	Social Defense:	8	Knockdown:	6
WIL:	5	Physical Armor:	0	Recovery Tests:	1
CHA:	5	Mystic Armor:	1		

Movement: 14
Actions: 1; Bite 9 (4), Claws: 9 (3)
Powers:
Climbing (11): As the skill, *Player's Guide*, p. 134.
Enhanced Sense [Hearing] (2)
Enhanced Sense [Other] (1): Astral Sight, as the talent, *Player's Guide*, p. 129.
Enhanced Sense [Sight]: Low Light Vision

Great Leap (2)
Stealthy Stride (10): As the skill, *Player's Guide*, p. 170.
Special Maneuvers:
Pounce (Cat)

Cave Crab

The cave crab lives in the Delaris Mountains, which ring the southern region of the terrible and corrupted Wastes. Unlike its ocean-born brethren, the cave crab possesses four legs and two pincers instead of six legs and pincers. A thick armored shell encases its entire boneless body, including its unnaturally slim legs. The shell is as strong as iron and as light as wood—almost impossible to pierce.

The crab's horrible pincers, each more than 4 feet long, are strong and sharp enough to slice a thick tree trunk or any nearby obsidiman neatly in half. The underside of each claw is sharp also, enabling the crab to slash at its opponent or close its great pincers on a convenient limb. The crab lives in the many caves throughout the Delaris peaks, where it can hide in the cool shade during the day. It leaves the cave at night to hunt—these creatures eat everything from tree branches to horses to people.

Dragons find the cave crab absolutely delicious. Any dragon who has tasted the flesh of a cave crab at least once will usually risk anything to eat any other cave crab it encounters.

Challenge: Journeyman (Eighth Circle)

DEX:	6	**Initiative:**	10	**Unconsciousness:**	87
STR:	16	**Physical Defense:**	10	**Death Rating:**	101
TOU:	16	**Mystic Defense:**	15	**Wound Threshold:**	7
PER:	4	**Social Defense:**	10	**Knockdown:**	17
WIL:	7	**Physical Armor:**	18	**Recovery Tests:**	5
CHA:	3	**Mystic Armor:**	11		
Movement:	14				

Actions: 2; Bite: 18 (20), Claws x2: 20 (25)

Powers:
Hardened Armor
Special Maneuvers:
Armor Cutter (Cave Crab): The cave crab may spend additional successes to instead reduce an opponent's Physical Armor by 1 per success. This may not destroy thread armor.
Crack the Shell (Opponent)
Pry Loose (Opponent, Close Combat)
Squeeze the Life (Cave Crab, Claw)
Loot: Intact shell, for which armorers will pay up to 300 silver pieces (worth Legend Points). Large pieces of shell may fetch lower prices, at the gamemaster's discretion.

Cave Troll

Cave trolls are descended from tribes of trolls who took to the deep places of the Earth when the Horrors came. Their isolation from the rest of the world led to cultural stagnation, and in some cases, degeneration among these tribes. Elemental magic has raised the strength of these cave trolls beyond civilized trolls, however, and in recent years they have emerged from their tunnels to explore the world above. Rude, and often violent, the cave trolls' habit of mixing trade with raiding has made them unwelcome visitors in most of Barsaive.

Cave trolls use large stone weapons called cave axes, little more than crude stone axes bolstered with the cave troll's innate elemental magic. Cave trolls take offense at anyone other than a fellow cave troll using one of their axes. Their Attitude towards the wielder and his obvious companions is lowered by one degree for Interaction tests (see **Attitudes**, p. 142).

Challenge: Journeyman (Fifth Circle)

DEX:	6	**Initiative:**	5	**Unconsciousness:**	49
STR:	13	**Physical Defense:**	13	**Death Rating:**	57
TOU:	8	**Mystic Defense:**	13	**Wound Threshold:**	12
PER:	4	**Social Defense:**	8	**Knockdown:**	15
WIL:	7	**Physical Armor:**	6	**Recovery Tests:**	3
CHA:	3	**Mystic Armor:**	3		

Movement: 14
Actions: 2; Cave Axe 14 (21)
Powers:
Enhanced Sense [Sight]: Heat Sight
Fury (2)
Special Maneuvers:
Provoke (Opponent, Close Combat)
Equipment: Cave Axe (Size 6, Damage Step 8, worth 50 silver), Hide Armor.

Chakta Bird

Chakta birds resemble large ravens with red-tipped wings and gold-flecked feathers. These social animals usually travel in flocks of five to ten birds, and can use their limited telepathy to communicate with intelligent beings within 25 yards. They often approach travelers to share news of the air (or road) ahead, an example of the "civilized" behavior prompting some scholars to speculate about their origins. Chakta birds are courteous animals and expect courtesy in return. Any rude behavior or omission of simple road courtesies, such as sharing of bread or hunting catch, proper introductions, or offering of places at a fire, enrages chakta birds.

When angered, chakta birds will attack the offending character. They attack by swarming around their target, cawing and screeching, and telepathically assaulting their target. This attack can incapacitate the target, and once the target is incapacitated, the flock swoops in to physically attack.

The offending character may be able to placate the birds by offering a suitable apology, which requires successful Interaction test against the bird's Social Defense.

Challenge: Novice (Third Circle)

DEX:	8	**Initiative:**	12	**Unconsciousness:**	27
STR:	3	**Physical Defense:**	12	**Death Rating:**	31
TOU:	4	**Mystic Defense:**	12	**Wound Threshold:**	6
PER:	7	**Social Defense:**	11	**Knockdown:**	3
WIL:	7	**Physical Armor:**	1	**Recovery Tests:**	1
CHA:	7	**Mystic Armor:**	4		

Movement: 2 (Flying 18)
Actions: 1; Bite 12 (10)
Powers:
Enhanced Sense [Sight] (2)
Mental Assault (12): When a flock of chakra birds is swarming a target, their telepathic assault can distract or even incapacitate a target. As a Standard action, the bird makes a Mental Assault test against the target's Mystic Defense. Chakta birds may combine their efforts; each additional chakta bird adds +2 Steps to the Mental Assault test (there is still only one test). Each success gives the target a -1 penalty to all tests for as long as the mental assault continues. If the total penalty equals or exceeds the target's Willpower Step, he is incapacitated and unable to defend himself.
Special Maneuvers:
Clip the Wing (Opponent)

Changeling

These Horror-tainted windlings, called changelings by those few who have encountered them and survived, live only in the Scytha Mountains near the eastern edge of the Blood Wood, although there are rumors of at least two other places where they have appeared. Changelings retained the same size as windlings, but with a terribly distorted shape. Their faces are bulbous and hairless, their teeth elongated, and their hands tipped with nails so long and wicked they look more like claws. Their legs have joined together to become an armored, wormlike tail. Once-healthy flesh is tinted a murky blue, resembling the color of corpses. Only their thin, fragile wings have remained the same.

The Horrors granted the changelings a terrible ability, one allowing them to reshape living bones. A fragmentary account of these creatures in the Great Library says the bones also strengthen the kaer walls and serve as a powerful defense against intruders. At a changeling's command, the bones turn into wicked spikes, making it almost impossible to enter without getting cut to ribbons.

Changelings are completely corrupted. They cannot be redeemed, and have very little in common with their untainted brothers. In physical combat, they are relatively weak. They often carry a bone they can reshape into a weapon if their magical abilities fail them, but their bone-shaping power is their true weapon. Changelings maintain a semblance of the eager, childlike curiosity windlings are known for, but twisted as a result of their corruption. If time allows, they take the time to reshape each of a victim's limbs, inflicting extreme pain, before killing him.

Challenge: Journeyman (Sixth Circle)

DEX:	9	**Initiative:**	13	**Unconsciousness:**	45
STR:	4	**Physical Defense:**	17	**Death Rating:**	50
TOU:	5	**Mystic Defense:**	17	**Wound Threshold:**	7
PER:	8	**Social Defense:**	15	**Knockdown:**	4
WIL:	6	**Physical Armor:**	4	**Recovery Tests:**	2
CHA:	7	**Mystic Armor:**	8		

Movement: 4 (Flying 16)
Actions: 1; Bone Weapon 14 (7)
Powers:
Creature Power (16, Bone Shaping, Standard)
Bone Shaping (18): The changeling twists and shapes the bones of a target within 10 yards, causing a great deal of pain. It makes a Creature Power test against the target's Mystic Defense. If successful, the Bone Shaping Step is used to determine damage, reduced by Mystic Armor. At gamemaster's discretion, Wounds caused by this power might cause permanent penalties. Affected bones maintain their new shape, even after the damage is healed. Powerful healing magic might be able to correct the problem, or victims could subject themselves to further use of this power.
Enhanced Sense [Other] (5): Astral Sight, as the talent, *Player's Guide*, p. 129.
Special Maneuvers:
Clip the Wing (Opponent)
Return the Favor (Opponent, Steel Thought): The opponent may spend two additional successes on a Steel Thought test against a Creature Power test to turn the power against the changeling, using the changeling's original result. Knowledge of this special maneuver is exceedingly rare.
Skull Folding (Changeling, Creature Power): Changelings can use Bone Shaping to fold the victim's skull backwards into the brain. The changeling may spend two additional successes from a Creature Power test to inflict +10 damage, instead of the normal +4, and cause an automatic Wound. This is in addition to a Wound that may result from damage dealt.
Loot: Sculpted bone weapon (Size 1, Damage Step 3). A changeling kaer may contain eerie, yet beautiful bone sculptures each worth 1,000 silver pieces or more.

Cheetah

The cheetah is a long-legged and swift running cat, with black spots, yellowish-brown fur, and non-retractable claws. These creatures are most likely to be encountered in plains regions near Barsaive's forests.

Unlike other cats this size, a cheetah's high speed is what makes it a threat. They surprise their prey by quickly covering any intervening ground, often before a herd (or group of travelers) realizes what hit them. Cheetahs prefer hit and run tactics, and prefer to flee rather than get involved in a direct fight.

Cheetahs are acceptable as animal companions.

Challenge: Novice (Second Circle)

DEX:	8	**Initiative:**	12	**Unconsciousness:**	20
STR:	6	**Physical Defense:**	12	**Death Rating:**	24
TOU:	5	**Mystic Defense:**	9	**Wound Threshold:**	7
PER:	6	**Social Defense:**	7	**Knockdown:**	10
WIL:	5	**Physical Armor:**	3	**Recovery Tests:**	2
CHA:	5	**Mystic Armor:**	1		

Movement: 20
Actions: 1; Bite: 12 (10); Claws: 13 (9)
Powers:
Charge (5)
Enhanced Sense [Hearing] (2)
Enhanced Sense [Sight]: Low-Light Vision
Great Leap (8)
Stealthy Stride (11): As the skill, *Player's Guide*, p. 170.
Special Maneuvers:
Pounce (Cheetah)
Dash: The cheetah may move up to three times its Movement on a charge.

Cockatrice

This large earth-bound bird appears to be half rooster and half lizard. Some claim it bears a passing resemblance to the basilisk. Unlike the basilisk, which looks more like a lizard, the cockatrice shows more of a bird in its appearance. Approximately 6 feet in length, its body is covered with many-hued feathers, with scaly legs and tail. The feathers are rough enough to draw blood from a human's, elf's, or dwarf's fragile skin. The cockatrice prefers wide plains such as those near Parlainth and Iopos, but they have also been spotted in the Badlands near Travar and the Scytha Mountains.

A cockatrice's short, stubby wings are useless for flying, but can help the creatures double or even triple the distance they can jump. A cockatrice's mouth is a perfect blending of a chicken's beak and a lizard's jaws, and though its legs look like a lizard's, the knee joint bends backward like a bird's. The cockatrice's only reptilian feature is its snake-like tail, which is often half the length of the entire creature.

Though deadly, cockatrices fight like cowards, attacking from behind. If a cockatrice is met head on, it will do everything it can to get behind its target. It hunts by sneaking up on its victims, carefully placing its feet to make no sound, then tries to leap onto the victim's back, biting and clawing. Tiny hooked barbs grow all over its tail, able to pierce the victim's skin and inject a paralytic poison. The poison will immobilize a victim and leave it entirely at the creature's mercy. These hooks grow so fast if a cockatrice cannot leave them in some hapless foe's hide, it must scrape its tail against a tree or rock every two days or so to remove them and give fresh barbs ample room to emerge.

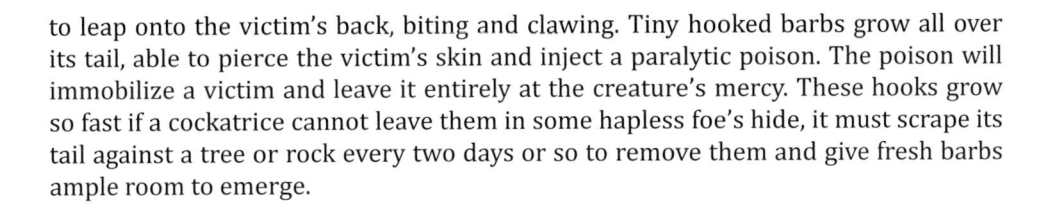

Challenge: Novice (Fourth Circle)

DEX:	7	**Initiative:**	9	**Unconsciousness:**	41
STR:	6	**Physical Defense:**	12	**Death Rating:**	48
TOU:	7	**Mystic Defense:**	11	**Wound Threshold:**	11
PER:	6	**Social Defense:**	8	**Knockdown:**	6
WIL:	6	**Physical Armor:**	4	**Recovery Tests:**	2
CHA:	4	**Mystic Armor:**	2		

Movement: 10
Actions: 1; Claws 14 (12), Tail 13 (13, Poison)
Powers:
Great Leap (10)
Poison (10): If the cockatrice manages to damage a target with its tail, it injects a paralytic poison. The poison is Step 10 [Onset: 1 round, Interval: 5/1 round, Duration:10 rounds]. See **Poison**, p. 71 for more information.
Stealthy Stride (9): As the skill, *Player's Guide*, p. 170.
Special Maneuvers:
Back Attack (Cockatrice, Claws): The cockatrice may spend two additional successes from an Attack test to land on the opponent's back. The opponent must succeed at a Knockdown test with a difficulty equal to the Attack test or be knocked down.
Defang (Opponent, Close Combat):
Loot: Feathers worth D6×10 silver pieces, blood worth 5D6×10 silver pieces, and 2d6 venomous barbs worth 10 silver pieces each (all worth Legend Points).

Crakbill

Crakbills are five-foot tall carnivorous birds with necks extending to just over half their height, weighing about 75 pounds. They travel in gaggles of 3 to 18 birds. Though crakbills have skulls and body and leg bones, their necks contain no vertebrae. Instead, a crakbill's neck is a thin tube of interwoven muscle. A flexible spiral of magical material that looks like burnished copper connects the skull to the body and reinforces the neck muscles.

The crakbill's most potent weapon is its paralyzing breath, which the bird spews in an orange, gaseous stream against a victim. The creatures usually charge past their victim, splitting their movement (*Player's Guide*, p. 386), breathing as they run past. These attacks continue until at least one or two victims succumb, and then the birds move in for the kill. They use their heavy bills like stone hatchets, cracking open the skulls their prey to feast on the brains.

The crakbill's breath stains skin and cloth orange. The stains are difficult to remove, requiring either vigorous scrubbing, or washing in vinegar or alcohol.

Challenge: Novice (Fourth Circle)

DEX:	7	Initiative:	7	Unconsciousness:	35
STR:	7	Physical Defense:	12	Death Rating:	40
TOU:	5	Mystic Defense:	12	Wound Threshold:	7
PER:	4	Social Defense:	7	Knockdown:	9
WIL:	7	Physical Armor:	4	Recovery Tests:	2
CHA:	3	Mystic Armor:	4		

Movement: 16
Actions: 1; Beak: 12 (14)
Powers:
Creature Power (11, Standard, Paralyzing Breath)
Paralyzing Breath (15): The crakbill breathes a stream of noxious orange mist at its target. It makes a Creature Power test against the target's Mystic Defense. If successful, the Paralyzing Breath Step determines damage, reduced by Mystic Armor. If the damage causes a Wound, the victim is automatically Knocked Down and paralyzed. The victim may break the paralysis by making a Willpower (10) test.
Special Maneuvers:
Armor Cutter (Crakbill): The crakbill may spend additional successes to instead reduce the target's Physical Armor by 1 per success. This may not destroy thread armor.
Stifle (Opponent): A character may spend two additional successes to prevent a crakbill from using Paralyzing Breath until the end of the next round. If the damage causes a Wound, the crakbill may not use Paralyzing Breath until the Wound is healed.
Loot: Neck cord worth D6×10 silver pieces (worth Legend Points)

Crocodile

This large reptile is approximately twelve to fourteen feet long, and possesses sharp teeth and powerful jaws. It is found in the numerous river and marshland areas of Barsaive, although they are most prevalent in the rivers of the Servos Jungle. When in the water they are difficult to discern from floating wood or other detritus. They are not especially territorial, and seeing several crocodiles at a good feeding ground is common.

Crocodiles are ambush predators. They lie in wait just below the surface of the water, usually near a muddy bank, with only its eyes and nostrils showing. When prey gets within reach, they surge out of the water and attack. If it fails to catch prey on the first attempt, it will often slink return to the water to escape and wait for a new opportunity.

Crocodiles are suitable as an animal companion.

Challenge: Novice (Third Circle)

DEX:	6	Initiative:	6	Unconsciousness:	36
STR:	7	Physical Defense:	11	Death Rating:	43
TOU:	7	Mystic Defense:	8	Wound Threshold:	10
PER:	4	Social Defense:	8	Knockdown:	11
WIL:	8	Physical Armor:	7	Recovery Tests:	2
CHA:	3	Mystic Armor:	3		

Movement: 8 (Swim 8)
Actions: 1; Bite 11 (16)
Powers:
Ambush (5)
Awareness (8): As the skill, *Player's Guide*, p. 129.
Semi-Aquatic: Crocodiles can hold their breath for 30 minutes before drowning.
Stealthy Stride (12)
Special Maneuvers:
Grab and Bite (Crocodile)
Death Roll (Crocodile): The crocodile may spend two additional successes from an Attack test to inflict Bite and Hold and force it and its opponent to make a Strength test. If the crocodile succeeds, it drags its prey below the water where it rolls the victim against the bottom, causing Step 7 Damage; no armor protects against this damage. This damage is in addition to continuing damage from the crocodile's bite.
Pry Loose (Opponent, Close Combat)
Loot: Skin worth 5d10 silver pieces.

Crojen

Crojen are deadly predators who hunt in packs of five to ten males and females in the Servos and Liaj jungles. Small black tigers resembling panther cubs even when fully grown, crojen are roughly two feet long and one foot tall at the shoulder. Their tails add another foot to their body length, though adventurers who have come into contact with them swear these creatures are larger.

Crojen patiently stalk their prey for days if necessary, using both normal vision and their innate astral sight, making it difficult to elude them. Despite their small size, they are fierce and tenacious predators, and their ferocious claw and bite attacks pose a serious danger, even against larger prey.

Crojen are suitable as animal companions.

Challenge: Journeyman (Fifth Circle)

DEX:	10	**Initiative:**	14	**Unconsciousness:**	43
STR:	7	**Physical Defense:**	16	**Death Rating:**	49
TOU:	6	**Mystic Defense:**	11	**Wound Threshold:**	9
PER:	7	**Social Defense:**	9	**Knockdown:**	11
WIL:	6	**Physical Armor:**	6	**Recovery Tests:**	2
CHA:	6	**Mystic Armor:**	3		

Movement: 16
Actions: 2; Bite: 20 (14), Claws x2: 20 (12)
Powers:
Climbing (14): As the skill, *Player's Guide*, p. 134.
Enhanced Sense [Hearing] (2)
Enhanced Sense [Other] (3): Astral Sight, as the talent, *Player's Guide*, p. 129.
Enhanced Sense [Sight]: Low-Light Vision
Frenzy: A crojen that gets a taste of blood may enter frenzy. After making a successful attack, the crojen must make a Willpower (5) test. If the test fails, the crojen gains an

additional action. A frenzying crojen will not break off its attack; the only way to stop it is to knock it unconscious or kill it.
Great Leap (10)
Willful (2)
Stealthy Stride (13): As the skill, *Player's Guide*, p. 170.
Surprise Strike (5): As the skill, *Player's Guide*, p. 172. Crojen do not use this power while in frenzy.
Special Maneuvers:
Cat Fight (Opponent, Avoid Blow): An opponent may spend an additional success from an Avoid Blow test against a crojen in Frenzy to lure the crojen into combat with another, adjacent crojen.
Enrage (Opponent): This maneuver also penalizes the crojen's Willpower test to resist frenzy.
Pounce (Crojen)

Death Moth

This repulsive insect, which some call the nocturnal headhunter, resembles the harmless moon moth. It grows to a length of two feet or so, with a wingspan of five feet, and possesses similar coloring. Most death moths are dark blue to dull black, though there are tales of lilac-colored ones in remote parts of Barsaive. Like all insects, the death moth has six legs which end in hooked claws and two sets of wings.

While the moon moth is harmless, the death moth can kill. The only visible difference between them is a horrible, leering face peering from the death moth's underbelly, as if a Horror had tattooed its image on the moth's underside. Close examination reveals this image is natural coloring—but most people who encounter the things are far too terrified to inspect them. From any distance greater than a few feet away, the death moth looks like the bodiless head of a madman floating through the air—a sight to send even the boldest adventurer into screaming fits.

The death moth bears a long barbed stinger at the end of its belly. The venom inside this stinger is potent enough to paralyze almost any victim. Those with a strong constitution can fight the paralysis, but even they usually succumb to the venom's second effect—the victim forgets the past four hours of his life, including encountering the moth.

The death moth attacks other living things because it must lay its eggs in a living host. The eggs live in the venom and enter the host when he or she or it is stung. The death moth prefers large animals such as cattle or horses, but willingly uses Namegivers. It most often stings its victims in the shoulders and back, laying its eggs in the muscles. Within two weeks the infesting larvae completely consume their host's internal organs. Once the insects reach a length of six inches, they eat their way out of the host's body in search of a nearby tree or house to climb, in whose branches or eaves they cocoon. Upon leaving the cocoon as adult death moths, they must mate and find a host for their eggs within two weeks, and then they die.

Challenge: Novice (Fourth Circle)

DEX:	7	**Initiative:**	7	**Unconsciousness:**	32
STR:	4	**Physical Defense:**	12	**Death Rating:**	36
TOU:	4	**Mystic Defense:**	10	**Wound Threshold:**	6
PER:	4	**Social Defense:**	8	**Knockdown:**	4
WIL:	4	**Physical Armor:**	5	**Recovery Tests:**	1
CHA:	3	**Mystic Armor:**	3		

Movement: 2 (Flying 14)
Actions: 1; Stinger 12 (12, Poison)
Powers:
Enhanced Sense [Hearing] (4)
Grim Visage (12): As a Standard action, the death moth shows the grim visage on its belly and makes a Grim Visage test against the target's Mystic Defense. The victim is crippled with fear for one round per success. They are Blindsided (*Player's Guide*, p. 386) and their Movement is reduced to 0 while affected.
Larvae: If a moth lays eggs in a victim, the larvae grow rapidly. After a week they begin to feed on the victim's internal organs, causing Step 8 Damage each day and imposing a -2 penalty to all tests made by the victim. Diagnosing the infection requires a successful Physician (8) test, and treatment requires another Physician test or appropriate healing magic.
Poison (10): If a death moth inflicts damage with its stinger, it injects paralytic venom. The poison is Step 10 [Onset: 1 round, Interval: 4/1 round, Duration: 15 minutes]. If the victim succumbs, the death moth lays its eggs in their body. The venom also causes memory loss; the victim does not remember the encounter with the moth or the previous four hours or so.
Stealthy Stride (11): As the skill, *Player's Guide*, p. 170.
Special Maneuvers:
Clip the Wing (Opponent)

Defang (Opponent)
Loot: Two wings, highly prized for clothing, worth 200 silver pieces each (worth Legend Points)

Demiwraith

Demiwraiths are an unusual type of animated dead. Not true undead, such as ghouls or cadaver men, these creatures are the result of a malevolent spirit possessing a victim during the long years of the Scourge. Some of these spirits could not separate from their host when the host died, and became demiwraiths. Demiwraiths animate the dead flesh imprisoning them, and revel in destroying the living. A black, foggy astral substance often shrouds a demiwraith's body, giving these beings an appearance similar to a true wraith.

Even though they are unable to return there, a demiwraith's touch carries the chill of the netherworlds. This touch can freeze their victim in place, making them easy prey for these hateful beings.

Challenge: Journeyman (Fifth Circle)

DEX:	7	**Initiative:**	9	**Unconsciousness:**	46
STR:	7	**Physical Defense:**	13	**Death Rating:**	53
TOU:	7	**Mystic Defense:**	15	**Wound Threshold:**	10
PER:	6	**Social Defense:**	12	**Knockdown:**	9
WIL:	8	**Physical Armor:**	3	**Recovery Tests:**	2
CHA:	6	**Mystic Armor:**	6		

Movement: 12
Actions: 2; Claws 14 (14)
Powers:
Chilling Touch (15): The demiwrath makes a Chilling Touch test against the target's Mystic Defense. If successful, the vctim is frozen in place for 1 round per success. They take 1 damage each round they are frozen, with no protection from armor.
Resistance: Because they are not true undead, demiwraiths gain a +5 bonus to their Mystic Defense and Mystic Armor against spells or powers specifically designed to target undead.
Special Maneuvers:
Grave Danger (Demiwraith): The demiwrath may spend additional successes on an Attack test to use Chilling Touch on the opponent. Each additional success beyond the first increases the damage by 1 and adds +2 Steps to Chilling Touch.
Loot: D4 small gems, each worth D12×10 silver pieces, or a total of 5D6×10 silver pieces (worth Legend Points)

Dog

Like cats, dogs are found in almost all populated areas of Barsaive, since they are often kept as pets by Namegivers of all races. Dogs can be trained for all kind of things, but are most frequently used as guardians.

Guard Dog

Guard dogs are trained to guard a house or an area. They bark at anyone who enters their territory and will attack if the intruder persists.

Guard dogs are suitable as animal companions.

Challenge: Novice (First Circle)

DEX:	5	Initiative:	7	Unconsciousness:	20
STR:	6	Physical Defense:	8	Death Rating:	25
TOU:	5	Mystic Defense:	8	Wound Threshold:	7
PER:	6	Social Defense:	8	Knockdown:	10
WIL:	4	Physical Armor:	3	Recovery Tests:	2
CHA:	5	Mystic Armor:	2		

Movement: 12
Actions: 1; Bite 9 (10)
Powers:
Awareness (10): As the skill, *Player's Guide*, p. 129.
Battle Shout (6): As the skill, *Player's Guide*, p. 131.
Enhanced Sense [Hearing] (2)
Enhanced Sense [Smell] (2): Tracking.

Hunting Dog

Dogs trained for hunting are used to hunt and track down other animals and creatures. They usually try to help their masters in the hunt, but can bring down the prey if ordered to do so.

Hunting dogs are suitable as animal companions.

Challenge: Novice (First Circle)

DEX:	5	Initiative:	5	Unconsciousness:	17
STR:	5	Physical Defense:	8	Death Rating:	21
TOU:	4	Mystic Defense:	8	Wound Threshold:	6
PER:	6	Social Defense:	6	Knockdown:	9
WIL:	3	Physical Armor:	1	Recovery Tests:	1
CHA:	3	Mystic Armor:	1		

Movement: 14
Actions: 1; Bite 8 (9)
Powers:
Awareness (8): As the skill, *Player's Guide*, p. 129.
Enhanced Sense [Hearing] (2)
Enhanced Sense [Smell] (4): Tracking.
Tracking (8): As the skill, *Player's Guide*, p. 175.

War Dog

These dogs are a rare breed, as they need careful training. Bred for aggression, the animals are trained for war and attack to kill on command. Often outfitted with armor to protect them in combat, they are fierce and bred for war.

War dogs are suitable as animal companions.

Challenge: Novice (Second Circle)

DEX:	5	Initiative:	7	Unconsciousness:	28
STR:	6	Physical Defense:	9	Death Rating:	34
TOU:	6	Mystic Defense:	8	Wound Threshold:	9
PER:	5	Social Defense:	8	Knockdown:	10
WIL:	4	Physical Armor:	5	Recovery Tests:	2
CHA:	4	Mystic Armor:	2		

Movement: 14
Actions: 1; Bite 11 (12)
Powers:
Enhanced Sense [Hearing] (2)
Enhanced Sense [Smell] (2): Tracking
Tracking (6): As the skill, *Player's Guide*, p. 175.
Equipment: Leather armor (3/0)

Dyre

The dyre eats grasses, travels in herds, and appears to pose little danger to adventurers, but anyone foolish enough to think the dyre a placid, docile creature should think twice. The slightest annoyance triggers a killing frenzy in these huge animals, a trait valued by many ork cavalries. A Cavalryman bonded with a dyre will happily guide his mount's ferocious wave of destruction while spearing enemies with his long lance.

The dyre resembles a cross between a bear and a bull. Like a bear, the dyre has squat, stubby legs and a short tail. Its head looks like a bull's, only wider, with sharply curving horns. It stands about twelve feet at the shoulder, is covered in long, matted brown fur, and its back rises sharply in the middle as if humped. The beast has hardly any neck at all, holding its head so low to the ground only its back-hump shows over the top of the high plains grass.

A herd of wild dyres numbers about forty animals—mostly females, half-grown males, and young. A herd has only one adult male, who has the sole privilege of mating with the females. Once a young dyre reaches maturity, the herd leader challenges him and usually forces him out. After a few years on his own, the hardened young male often returns to the pack to challenge the leader—those not strengthened by their solitary ordeal die. Most returning males are more than a match for the leader, and so often win the fight to become the new herd leader. Mating season comes only once every two years, and so very few herd leaders mate more than once or twice with the females before being deposed.

When approached by a predator, the dyres gather into a huge circle with the young at the center. The females stand on the outside of the circle to hold off attackers. Most predators lack the strength necessary to take down a healthy adult, and won't risk getting crushed by the dyres' hooves or speared with their wicked horns for the slight chance of bringing down a young animal.

Dyres are suitable as mounts for dwarfs, elves, humans, obsidimen, orks, t'skrang, and trolls, and as animal companions.

Challenge: Novice (Fourth Circle)

DEX:	4	Initiative:	4	Unconsciousness:	59
STR:	12	Physical Defense:	9	Death Rating:	72
TOU:	13	Mystic Defense:	9	Wound Threshold:	19
PER:	5	Social Defense:	12	Knockdown:	16
WIL:	6	Physical Armor:	6	Recovery Tests:	4
CHA:	4	Mystic Armor:	3		

Movement: 16
Actions: 1; Horns 11 (18), Trample 11 (16)
Powers:
Beast of Burden: When used as a mount, the dyre effectively has 2 less Strength for the purposes of a charging attack.
Charge (5)
Enhanced Sense [Smell] (2)
Resist Pain (2)
Special Maneuvers:
Horn Sweep (Dyre, Horns): The dyre may spend additional successes from an Attack test to throw its approximately human-sized or smaller opponent. Each success spent in this way throws the opponent 2 yards and the opponent treats this distance as falling (see **Falling Damage**, p. 167).
Overrun (Dyre, Trample)
Provoke (Opponent, Close Combat)

Eagle

Eagles are large birds of prey, characterized by a powerful, hooked bill, broad wings; and strong, soaring flight. Eagles can be found almost everywhere in Barsaive, hunting for food in the air and on the ground.

Eagles are suitable as animal companions.

Challenge: Novice (Second Circle)

DEX:	7	Initiative:	11	Unconsciousness:	22
STR:	4	Physical Defense:	10	Death Rating:	26
TOU:	4	Mystic Defense:	9	Wound Threshold:	6
PER:	6	Social Defense:	8	Knockdown:	4
WIL:	4	Physical Armor:	0	Recovery Tests:	1
CHA:	4	Mystic Armor:	1		

Movement: 2 (Flying 20)
Actions: 1; Claws 14 (12)
Powers:
Dive (5)
Enhanced Sense [Sight] (4): Eagles do not suffer penalties from distance to vision-based Awareness tests.

Willful (1)
Swooping Attack: The eagle may split its movement (*Player's Guide*, p. 386) and not suffer any penalty, and does not spend Strain.
Special Maneuvers:
Clip the Wing (Opponent)

Earth Q'wril

This furred creature resembles a mole with a scaly tail and bird-like beak. About as long as a human's forearm, the earth q'wril looks harmless, and in truth these beasts pose no threat to anything save a few plants. The earth q'wril feeds on roots, berries, and fruit, but a rare few have developed a taste for meat.

The earth q'wril can move through the earth as easily as a fish through water. The beak dribbles a thin fluid, which acts as a lubricant and has a magical property that somehow thins the soil, allowing the beast to pass through all but the hardest clay and stone. Most earth q'wril travel just a few feet below the earth's surface, though they can move as far below ground as they desire.

The earth q'wril's senses are abnormally sharp. When combined with its prowess at hurling itself out of the earth with great force, the subterranean beast can find the fruit on which it lives. The earth q'wril can burst several feet from the ground to seize objects, bounding into the boughs of an oak to graze on its leaves or plucking a tasty apple from an exposed branch. It can even spear small animals, leaping into them like a tiny furred javelin. The surface disturbance caused by the earth q'wril's subterranean movement ceases just before it leaps because the animal is sinking deeper into the soil to get a longer run at the surface.

The earth q'wril is a social animal, often moving in groups of twenty or more. A pod of earth q'wril cresting above the fields or weaving around the trunks of trees below a forest floor is one of Barsaive's most fascinating sights, though most farmers would not agree, as a large pod can devastate a field in a few days. In areas plagued by earth q'wril, the working folk build stone corrals around their fields with high palisades to keep the creatures from burrowing in or leaping over the top. Farms in these areas can resemble intricate mazes or daunting fortifications, all to stop the depredations of a creature smaller than a dog.

Villages plagued by the earth q'wril rarely seek to exterminate the animals, having learned from bitter experience they will only lose lives in the process. The creatures burst suddenly through the earth at high speed and use their deadly beaks to stab their attackers through even the heaviest armor. Elves prize these beaks as arrowheads, and windlings use them as spear tips when they can get them.

Earth q'wril are suitable as animal companions.

Challenge: Novice (First Circle)

DEX:	6	Initiative:	8	Unconsciousness:	11
STR:	2	Physical Defense:	8	Death Rating:	13
TOU:	2	Mystic Defense:	8	Wound Threshold:	3
PER:	6	Social Defense:	6	Knockdown:	6
WIL:	3	Physical Armor:	2	Recovery Tests:	1
CHA:	4	Mystic Armor:	1		

Movement: 10 (Burrow 10)
Actions: 1, Bite 11 (7)
Powers:
Ambush (5)
Enhanced Sense [Other] (4): The earth q'wril is able to know the location of a target within 10 yards, even if it can't see. It makes a Perception test with a +4 Step bonus against the target's Mystic Defense. If successful, the earth q'wril knows the target's location and does not suffer penalties for darkness or cover (*Player's Guide*, p. 386).
Great Leap (4): Earth q'wrils usually use this power when coming up from underground.
Stealthy Stride (8): As the skill, *Player's Guide*, p. 170.

Special Maneuvers:
Armor Cutter (Earth Q'wril): The earth q'wril may spend additional successes to instead reduce an opponent's Physical Armor by 1 per success. This may not destroy thread armor.
Loot: Triangular beak worth 25 silver pieces (worth Legend Points).

Elephant

These large, long-nosed herbivorous mammals are often trained to serve as mounts in the provinces of Creana, Indrisa, and Thera. Elephants are often used as beasts of burden for transporting goods. In Barsaive, elephants are typically found in the plains and forested regions. If provoked, elephants tend to gore their victims before trampling them.

Elephants are suitable as mounts for elves, humans, obsidimen, orks, t'skrang, and trolls, and as animal companions.

Challenge: Novice (Fourth Circle)

DEX:	5	Initiative:	5	Unconsciousness:	53
STR:	10	Physical Defense:	8	Death Rating:	64
TOU:	11	Mystic Defense:	12	Wound Threshold:	16
PER:	6	Social Defense:	9	Knockdown:	14
WIL:	6	Physical Armor:	5	Recovery Tests:	4
CHA:	5	Mystic Armor:	4		

Movement: 16
Actions: 1; Trample: 10 (14), Tusks: 10 (16)
Powers:
Charge (5)
Enhanced Sense [Hearing] (2)
Enhanced Sense [Smell] (2)

Resist Pain (2)
Special Maneuvers:
Overrun (Elephant, Trample)
Provoke (Opponent, Close Combat)
Loot: Tusks worth 2D6×10 silver pieces.

Espagra

The espagra is a flying predator with a wingspan up to twelve feet. They resemble a small dragon with an iguana-like head, colored a brilliant shade of blue. While they are quick and agile flyers, espagra prefer to swoop down on an enemy, knock him down, and continue the struggle on the ground.

Espagra scales exude elemental air magic, adding luster and brilliance, making the creature shimmer in a way many find appealing. Master tailors often make clothes using espagra scales (for example, the espagra-scale cloak, *Player's Guide*, p.413). Such clothes look richer than other fine garments, even those decorated with precious jewels.

Espagra are suitable as animal companions.

Challenge: Journeyman (Sixth Circle)

DEX:	9	**Initiative:**	15	**Unconsciousness:**	54
STR:	6	**Physical Defense:**	16	**Death Rating:**	62
TOU:	8	**Mystic Defense:**	15	**Wound Threshold:**	12
PER:	7	**Social Defense:**	11	**Knockdown:**	10
WIL:	10	**Physical Armor:**	5	**Recovery Tests:**	3
CHA:	6	**Mystic Armor:**	6		

Movement: 10 (Flying 16)
Actions: 3; Bite: 15 (14), Claws x2: 16 (13), Tail: 17 (12)
Powers:
Dive (10)
Resist Pain (2)

Willful (1)
Special Maneuvers:
Clip the Wing (Opponent)
Power Dive (Espagra): Following an attack using Dive, the espagra may spend an additional success to cause a Knockdown test against the target. The Difficulty Number is the Attack test result.
Loot: Skin worth D20×10 silver pieces (worth Legend Points).

Falcon

Falcons are small birds of prey, characterized by long, pointed, and powerful wings, and capable of swift flight. Falcons can be found almost everywhere in Barsaive, hunting for prey. These birds are typically trained for hunting.

Falcons are suitable as animal companions.

Challenge: Novice (First Circle)

DEX:	7	Initiative:	12	Unconsciousness:	14
STR:	3	Physical Defense:	10	Death Rating:	17
TOU:	3	Mystic Defense:	9	Wound Threshold:	4
PER:	7	Social Defense:	6	Knockdown:	3
WIL:	4	Physical Armor:	0	Recovery Tests:	1
CHA:	4	Mystic Armor:	1		

Movement: 2 (Flying 22)
Actions: 1; Claws: 14 (9)
Powers:
Dive (5)
Enhanced Sense [Sight] (4): Falcons do not suffer penalties from distance to vision-based Awareness tests.
Swooping Attack: The falcon may split its movement (*Player's Guide*, p. 386) without penalty, and does not spend Strain.
Special Maneuvers:
Clip the Wing (Opponent)

Felux

The felux looks like a lion, but with eyes almost the size of a human's hand. A night hunter, the felux uses its eyes to catch its prey. The felux is one of the few cases in which a change induced by magic helped a creature to survive instead of destroying it.

The felux stalks its prey in deadly silence, then throws a beam of light brighter than a thousand moons from its eyes. The glare blindsides the unfortunate victim; the felux gives a quick flick of its sharp claws and its erstwhile quarry becomes a tasty dinner. If necessary, the felux can also attack by causing its eye light to flicker at an amazing speed. Those who gaze at the flashing light fall to the ground, racked with spasms. More than a few people find this method of crippling an enemy extremely useful, and several magicians have been known to develop spells duplicating this effect.

A felux can also be trained, though they do not feel the same loyalty or warmth toward their masters as a dog or a house cat. They can be managed only if caught as kittens and trained from their earliest weeks. Catching a kitten is nearly impossible, unless the guarding mother has been killed. There are rumors of mercenaries who use trained feluxes for night work and ambushes. Once their targets enter a certain area, they command the feluxes to use their flickering eye light. Anything within the light falls to the ground in an uncontrollable fit.

The guards of Stoneforge Keep use feluxes as guard animals and walk around the walls of the castle with them. On command, each felux gazes out across the surrounding lands. Anything anywhere near the Keep might as well try to hide in broad daylight; the felux will certainly see it and flash its eye light to incapacitate would-be intruders. For an unknown reason, the felux's eye light terrifies the Horrors, and some accounts tell of a few adventuring bands which have used these creatures to explore forgotten kaers.

Felux are suitable as animal companions.

Challenge: Journeyman (Sixth Circle)

DEX:	9	Initiative:	13	Unconsciousness:	48
STR:	8	Physical Defense:	16	Death Rating:	54
TOU:	6	Mystic Defense:	12	Wound Threshold:	9
PER:	6	Social Defense:	12	Knockdown:	12
WIL:	6	Physical Armor:	5	Recovery Tests:	2
CHA:	5	Mystic Armor:	6		

Movement: 16
Actions: 2; Bite: 18 (15), Claws: x2 19 (14)
Powers:
Blinding Glare (16): This magical eye light creates a cone of steady light extending to 30 yards. As a Standard action, the felux may focus on a single target and make a Blinding Glare test against the target's Mystic Defense. If successful, the target is Blindsided until the end of the next round. Additional successes may be spent to extend this effect by one round each.
Climbing (13): As the skill, *Player's Guide*, p. 134.
Enhanced Sense [Other] (6): Astral Sight, as the talent, *Player's Guide*, p. 129.
Enhanced Sense [Sight]: Low-Light Vision
Great Leap (8)
Stealthy Stride (12): As the skill, *Player's Guide*, p. 170.
Willful (1)
Surprise Strike (5): As the skill, *Player's Guide*, p. 172.
Special Maneuvers:
Go For the Eyes! (Opponent): The attacker may use two additional successes on an attack test to inflict Partial Blindness on the felux until the end of the next round. In addition to the normal penalties, this reduces the Blinding Glare Step by 8. If the damage causes a Wound, the blindness lasts until the Wound is healed. A felux suffering from this twice cannot use Blinding Glare as long as the effect of both maneuvers lasts.

Induce Seizures (Felux, Blinding Glare): The felux may spend two additional successes from a Blinding Glare test to rapidly strobe its Blinding Glare power. This causes the target to be Knocked Down for the duration of the effect. The target may attempt to resist this effect each turn with a Willpower (10) test.
Pounce (Felux)
Loot: Two extremely delicate eyes, worth 300 silver pieces each (worth Legend Points).

Firebird

The firebird is a beautiful creature. Soaring in the air above the molten lava of the Death's Sea, it is one of many living creatures inhabiting the unusual environment. The firebird is closely related to the fire eagle, with a wingspan of about 10 feet, but its feathers change color depending on its surroundings.

Like most creatures of Death's Sea, the firebird can tolerate the intense heat of the lava without burning, but the firebird does not really care for such temperatures. When gliding over the lava in search of food, its feathers change to a burnished silver color to reflect the heat back down to the sea. Other color changes help it hide from predators; the firebird can change color to match the reddish lava flows or the dark brown of a lava stone island, depending on its needs.

When mating, the male hunts down a large creature as a gift for the female, and then the couple feasts on the carcass. The female then lays about two dozen eggs, each the size of a human's fist. Almost all of the eggs and hatchlings are eaten by other predators within a year, the large clutch of eggs ensures enough offspring will live to adulthood.

Because of their ties with Death's Sea, magicians and enchanters often pay handsome sums for firebird eggs, feathers, and even hatchlings in order to extract elemental fire.

Firebirds are suitable as animal companions.

Challenge: Journeyman (Seventh Circle)

DEX:	8	**Initiative:**	8	**Unconsciousness:**	35
STR:	4	**Physical Defense:**	11	**Death Rating:**	40
TOU:	5	**Mystic Defense:**	6	**Wound Threshold:**	8
PER:	4	**Social Defense:**	8	**Knockdown:**	4
WIL:	5	**Physical Armor:**	2	**Recovery Tests:**	
CHA:	6	**Mystic Armor:**	2		

Movement: 4 (Flying 18)
Actions: 2; Bite: 11 (6); Claws x2: 11 (5)
Powers:
Dive (10)
Burning Aura (10): The firebird turns its feathers dull black to absorb the heat from Death's Sea. When this power is in effect, all creatures within 6 yards of the firebird take Step 10 damage per round from the intense heat. Clothing, sails, and other easily flammable objects usually burst into flame when exposed to this power.

Color Change: When the firebird changes to dull black it gains the Burning Aura ability. When it turns silver, it gainst Stealthy Stride.
Enhanced Sense [Sight] (2)
Immune to Fire: The firebird suffers no damage from mundane fire attacks, and gains +20 Physical and Mystic Armor against magical or elemental fire.
Stealthy Stride (12): As the skill, *Player's Guide*, p. 170.
Swooping Attack: The firebird may split its movement (*Player's Guide*, p. 386) without penalty, and does not spend Strain..
Special Maneuvers:
Clip the Wing (Opponent)
Enrage (Opponent)
Loot: Feathers worth D6×10 silver pieces, eggs worth 3D6×10 silver pieces, and hatchlings worth 300 silver pieces each (all worth Legend Points).

Gargoyle

Like obsidimen, gargoyles are creatures of elemental earth and stone. However, these creatures are the results of a magical experiment gone wrong long before the Scourge. Their exact origins have been forgotten, but gargoyles are found in many parts of Barsaive. Gargoyles stand about 5 feet 6 inches tall and weigh an impressive 900 pounds. Their heads are elongated and distorted. Their hands end in long claws they use to rake opponents, often in fly-by attacks.

Though they gather in groups of six to ten gargoyles, similar to lion prides, gargoyles are not social creatures. Individual gargoyles sometimes leave the pride for months, wandering the skies alone or in pairs. Because many of these wandering gargoyles are staking a claim to new territory, they act more aggressively than full prides. Occasionally an entire pride of gargoyles migrates, for unknown reasons.

Challenge: Journeyman (Seventh Circle)

DEX:	7	**Initiative:**	7	**Unconsciousness:**	83
STR:	16	**Physical Defense:**	14	**Death Rating:**	99
TOU:	16	**Mystic Defense:**	16	**Wound Threshold:**	24
PER:	4	**Social Defense:**	14	**Knockdown:**	18
WIL:	10	**Physical Armor:**	10	**Recovery Tests:**	5
CHA:	4	**Mystic Armor:**	10		

Movement: 10 (Flying 16)
Actions: 2; Claws x2: 12 (20)
Powers:
Hardened Armor
Resist Pain (4)
Swooping Attack: The gargoyle may split its movement (*Player's Guide*, p. 386) without penalty, and does not spend Strain.
Special Maneuvers:
Clip the Wing (Opponent)
Crack the Shell (Opponent)
Loot: Horns worth 5D6×10 silver pieces (worth Legend Points).

Gate Hound

The gate hound resembles a giant dog or wolf, often standing 6 feet tall at the shoulder. Stocky and thick-muscled, they are covered in dull red fur that seems to soak up the light. Their eyes glow with a fierce white light. They have huge jaws crammed full of sharp teeth, and hunt in packs large enough to bring down almost any living creature—eight to ten hounds at least, sometimes more.

The gate hound is the result of Namegivers meddling with Nature. In the years before the Scourge, many magicians searched for ways to protect people from the Horrors. The sensible ones built the kaers and citadels. A few mages attempted to lower the magic levels around their city of Chasteyn so the Horrors would never arrive there. Halting the natural cycle of magic is far beyond the ability of any magician in Barsaive, however, so the magicians sought to create a creature who could drain magic. Their experiments failed to produce the desired result. They produced the gate hound instead, a creature with a limited ability to drain magic and an enormous appetite for warm flesh.

Gate hounds can drain magic, though nowhere near as well as their creators hoped. They store magical energy drained from another creature in an organ just below their thick, ugly necks. The drain is short-lived, wearing off within a few seconds. Gate hounds can only use this ability on another creature. While they are drawn to magic-rich places, they are unable to drain magic from an area.

Gate hounds attack by biting, or raking their victim with their powerful claws. Their favorite tactic is to clamp their jaws down on a target and shake them back and forth.

Some secret animosity exists between Horrors and gate hounds; even intelligent Horrors known for savoring their prey's slow death over many years will not hesitate to destroy a gate hound quickly. Some sages speculate gate hounds really enjoy the "flavor" of Horror magic, and Horrors find the magic draining ability of a gate hound painful to endure.

More than a few magicians—spiritual descendants of the fools who created these beasts—have attempted to harness the power of the gate hounds. Thus far, all have failed. One rumor tells of a magician who tried to use a hound's magic-draining organ to lower the level of magic around his house. He failed and drained his own magical ability, somehow managing to make the effect permanent.

Gate hounds are suitable as animal companions.

Challenge: Journeyman (Fifth Circle)

DEX:	7	**Initiative:**	9	**Unconsciousness:**	49
STR:	8	**Physical Defense:**	10	**Death Rating:**	57
TOU:	8	**Mystic Defense:**	12	**Wound Threshold:**	12
PER:	8	**Social Defense:**	7	**Knockdown:**	12
WIL:	6	**Physical Armor:**	4	**Recovery Tests:**	3
CHA:	4	**Mystic Armor:**	10		
Movement:	12				

Actions: 2; Bite: 14 (18), Claws: 14 (14)

Powers:
Enhanced Sense [Hearing] (2)
Enhanced Sense [Smell] (2): Tracking
Magic Drain (15): As a Standard action, the gate hound makes a Magic Drain test, comparing the result against the Mystic Defense of each target within 30 yards. Each success reduces the rank of the target's magical abilities (including talents and relevant creature powers) by 1 until the end of the next round.
Willful (1)
Tracking (8): As the skill, *Player's Guide*, p. 175.
Special Maneuvers:
Grab and Bite (Gate Hound, Bite)
Drain Stopper (Opponent): The attacker may spend two additional successes on an Attack test to strike the gate hound's magic draining organ and remove the Magic Drain power until the end of the next round. If the attack causes a Wound, the gate hound cannot use Magic Drain until the Wound is healed.
Pry Loose (Opponent, Close Combat)
Loot: Magic-draining organ worth 500 silver pieces (worth Legend Points).

Genhis

The adult genhis is a placid, faintly foolish-looking grass eater that resembles a large cow. It travels in herds, though only in small ones. Surprisingly, this gentle, slow-thinking creature destroyed every village and town in the ancient troll Kingdom of Ustrect.

In some areas of Barsaive genhis are used as meat animals. The prudent among genhis herders rid themselves of their herds every 10 years, if not more often, for it is almost impossible to tell which of the cow-like adults is a pregnant female. The young take a decade or so to grow large and strong enough to survive outside the womb. It's when they emerge from the womb the trouble begins, as young genhis are ravenously hungry beasts who raze everything in their path in a frenzied search for food.

A pregnant genhis carries her young in a large, tough, sack-shaped membrane. Without the membrane to restrain them, the horrible little beasts would swiftly eat their way out of their mother's body. Before giving birth, the mother looks for the perfect spot to deliver her young. She prefers forests, farms, or other places with plenty and varied food for her ravenous babies—trees, birds, deer, cattle, horses, crops, people, everything. After choosing the birthing place, the mother expels the sack from her womb and runs for her life. Within a few minutes of landing on the ground, the baby genhis chew their way through the sack and swiftly begin eating everything within reach. A single brood can have as many as 200 individuals.

Young genhis look nothing like their parents, instead resembling a furry cross between a bird and a lizard with a toothy mouth taking up almost half their length. Their powerful jaws allow them to chew through anything—flesh, wood, metal, and stone. Fortunately, the pests frequently feast on each other soon after birth, minimizing the potential for ecological devastation. The survivors can destroy acres of land, though as the brood spreads out its impact is reduced. As genhis grow larger, they become less ravenous and more docile, until they reach maturity after about five years. For reasons that still puzzle scholars, most of the survivors are female, and somehow become pregnant very soon after reaching maturity.

Adult Genhis

Challenge: Novice (First Circle)

DEX:	4	**Initiative:**	4	**Unconsciousness:**	23
STR:	7	**Physical Defense:**	6	**Death Rating:**	29
TOU:	6	**Mystic Defense:**	8	**Wound Threshold:**	9
PER:	5	**Social Defense:**	7	**Knockdown:**	9
WIL:	5	**Physical Armor:**	1	**Recovery Tests:**	2
CHA:	4	**Mystic Armor:**	2		

Movement: 12
Actions: 1, Bite: 8 (10)
Loot: Birth sac worth 100 silver pieces (worth Legend Points)

Baby Genhis

Challenge: Novice (Second Circle)

DEX:	8	**Initiative:**	10	**Unconsciousness:**	22
STR:	4	**Physical Defense:**	13	**Death Rating:**	26
TOU:	4	**Mystic Defense:**	7	**Wound Threshold:**	6
PER:	5	**Social Defense:**	6	**Knockdown:**	8
WIL:	7	**Physical Armor:**	0	**Recovery Tests:**	1
CHA:	4	**Mystic Armor:**	3		

Movement: 16
Actions: 2; Bite 11 (9)
Powers:
Resist Pain (2)

Globberog

The globberog is a curious and repulsive creature. The actual creature is little more than a lump of quivering meat about the size of a cow, but it exudes sticky ooze that it uses to glue all manner of detritus and trash to itself as a shell to protect its body. The materials in a globberog's shell can range from bits of wood, stone, and metal, to the bodies and bones of those unfortunate enough to fall afoul of it. As the shell grows over the course of a creature's life, it can become amazingly thick and strong.

In addition to exuding the gluey ooze from its skin, the globberog can also spit this substance at a victim. The ooze sticks the target in place, giving the creature time to approach and bind the victim into its shell. These trapped victims are the way the globberog feeds. It doesn't have a mouth. Instead, myriad tendrils and veins wind around and through the material in its shell, breaking down any organic matter and carrying nutrients back to the creature. These tendrils also carry the globberog's slime through out the shell, ensuring it remains intact, and leaving a fresh coat of glue on the outer edge to trap more prey.

The only known way to break free of globberog spittle is for direct sunlight to dry out the glue, allowing it to be cracked and broken. While it prefers dark and cool places, the creature is not negatively affected by sunlight, as its continuous production of slime keeps its own shell from drying out.

When a globberog's shell gets so heavy the creature can no longer move, it detaches itself and beings working on a new shell. This process gives birth to several new globberogs. The newborns take shelter under the old shell, until they grow large enough to start building shells of their own.

Depending on the creature's age, the Physical Armor Rating of their shell can be as high as 20 or more. Depending on the materials making up their shell, the creature might also gain bonuses to Mystic Armor, though this is a lot less common.

Because globberog spittle makes almost unbreakable glue, the glands that produce it can fetch a high price in many cities. Of course, killing a globberog without falling prey to it is a difficult proposition, and only the most cautious and experienced adventurers can successfully hunt these creatures.

Challenge: Journeyman (Fifth Circle)

DEX:	5	**Initiative:**	3	**Unconsciousness:**	55
STR:	12	**Physical Defense:**	8	**Death Rating:**	65
TOU:	10	**Mystic Defense:**	14	**Wound Threshold:**	15
PER:	4	**Social Defense:**	12	**Knockdown:**	18
WIL:	8	**Physical Armor:**	8+	**Recovery Tests:**	3
CHA:	6	**Mystic Armor:**	8+		

Movement: 6
Actions: 1; Sticky Spit: 12 (NA)

Powers:
Blood Veins (15): If the globberog attaches a victim to its shell, its feeding tendrils burrow into the victim's skin. Each round, the victim takes Step 15 Damage. No armor protects from this damage.
Hardened Armor
Sticky Body (12): When the globberog comes into contact with another creature or item, it makes a Sticky Body test against the target's Mystic Defense. If successful, the victim becomes Harried, their Movement rate is reduced to 0, and are unable to take any actions that require movement. A stuck victim is Harried. The victim may use a Standard action to break free with a successful Strength (12) test.
Sticky Spit (12): The globberog can spit its glue at a target within 10 yards. As a Standard action, it makes a Sticky Spit test against the victim's Physical Defense. If successful, the victim becomes Harried and is unable to move. The victim can attempt to break free by succeeding at a Strength (12) test.
Special Maneuvers:
Crack the Shell (Opponent)
No-stick Strike (Opponent): The attacker may use two additional successes to prevent their weapon from being stuck in the globberog despite coming into contact with it.
Pry Loose (Opponent, Close Combat)
Loot: Glue glands worth 250 silver pieces (worth Legend Points). Treasure, coins, and other valuables (determined by the gamemaster) stuck to the creature's back, worth at least 1,000 silver pieces.

Goat

Goats are horned herbivores that are often domesticated. Shepherding herdsmen raise them on Barsaive's mountains and hills for milk and meat. Goats are sometimes used by windlings as inexpensive riding mounts.

Goats are suitable as mounts for windlings and as animal companions.

Challenge: Novice (First Circle)

DEX:	6	Initiative:	6	Unconsciousness:	20
STR:	4	Physical Defense:	7	Death Rating:	25
TOU:	5	Mystic Defense:	8	Wound Threshold:	7
PER:	5	Social Defense:	9	Knockdown:	8
WIL:	6	Physical Armor:	1	Recovery Tests:	2
CHA:	4	Mystic Armor:	1		

Movement: 12
Actions: 1; Horns: 10 (8)
Powers:
Enhanced Sense [Hearing] (2)
Enhanced Sense [Smell] (2)

Riding Goat

Some settlements, especially in mountainous or hilly regions, breed large mountain goats and train them as mounts to take advantage of their natural dexterity in steep and rocky terrain.

Riding goats are suitable as mounts for dwarfs, elves, humans, and windlings, and as animal companions.

Challenge: Novice (First Circle)

DEX:	6	**Initiative:**	6	**Unconsciousness:**	23
STR:	6	**Physical Defense:**	8	**Death Rating:**	29
TOU:	6	**Mystic Defense:**	8	**Wound Threshold:**	9
PER:	5	**Social Defense:**	8	**Knockdown:**	10
WIL:	7	**Physical Armor:**	1	**Recovery Tests:**	2
CHA:	4	**Mystic Armor:**	3		

Movement: 16
Actions: 1; Horns: 10 (12)
Powers:
Enhanced Sense [Hearing] (2)
Enhanced Sense [Smell] (2)

Greater Termite

These enormous insects often reach a size and length Barsaive's largest rats might envy. Like their smaller brethren, colonies of greater termites create towers of mashed tree pulp, but the greater termites' towers often rise more than ten yards into the air and up to five yards across. Greater termites come in many colors, from pasty white to bright red to shiny black. A thick carapace protects them against most predators.

A colony will have three kinds of termites: workers, soldiers, and queens. The workers build the colony's towers, hunt for food, and care for the young. The queen is the mother of the colony, a bloated version of her smaller kindred. Soldiers protect the colony from predators. These termites have powerful pincers, vicious temperaments, and a natural poison that does not kill, but makes its victim writhe on the ground in agony.

Greater termites eat both meat and plants and their powerful jaws allow them to chew an amazing variety of foodstuffs. They also use these fearsome mandibles to bore through any substance in search of food and to make the pulp from which they build their towers.

One mystery about these insects is their apparent ability to communicate silently with each other across great distances. Those foolish enough to attack a termite queen will soon face every soldier in the colony returning from any distance to defend her. Scholars believe them to be under the mental control of the queen, as only an intense mental bond can explain how the soldier immediately knows its queen is under attack. This mental bond also explains the behavior of worker termites. When one finds food, it begins to stuff its jaws, and without moving away from its feast somehow calls its fellow workers. Within minutes, hundreds of other worker termites arrive to help collect the same food supply.

The game statistics provided here reflect a soldier termite, the only kind that fights intruders.

Challenge: Novice (First Circle)

DEX:	6	**Initiative:**	6	**Unconsciousness:**	11
STR:	3	**Physical Defense:**	7	**Death Rating:**	13
TOU:	2	**Mystic Defense:**	7	**Wound Threshold:**	3
PER:	5	**Social Defense:**	6	**Knockdown:**	9
WIL:	3	**Physical Armor:**	5	**Recovery Tests:**	1
CHA:	3	**Mystic Armor:**	2		

Movement: 12 (Climbing 12)
Actions: 1; Bite: 8 (10)
Powers:
Spray Irritant (8): The termite sprays a jet of spit, which causes excruciating pain on a target within 10 yards. As a Standard action, it makes a Spray Irritant test against the target's Physical Defense. For each success, the victim is Harried for 1 round. The victim may make a Willpower (8) test to shake off the effect. The spray loses potency with time, so the Difficulty Number for the Willpower test decreases by 1 each subsequent round.

Special Maneuvers:
Agent Orange (Greater Termite, Bite): The greater termite may spend two additional successes from an Attack test to use Spray Irritant against the opponent as a Free action.
Crack the Shell (Opponent)
Stifle (Opponent): The attacker may use two extra success on an Attack test to prevent the giant termite from using Spray Irritant until the end of the next round. If the attack causes a Wound, the greater termite may not use Spray Irritant until the Wound is healed.
Loot: Pincers worth D6×5 silver pieces each (worth Legend Points).

Griffin

These four-legged creatures combine a lion's body with the head, legs, and wings of a large eagle. Like an eagle, a griffin's front legs are covered in feathers and end in sharp talons; its hind legs resemble those of a lion, covered in soft fur and ending in paws. The griffin stands about four feet tall at the shoulder, is five to six feet long, and has a wingspan averaging eight feet.

Griffins nest in flocks of five to ten adults in mountainous regions, and rarely venture into jungle or forest regions. Griffins seldom attack travelers on foot unless their territory is threatened. They do have a strong taste for horse meat, however, and often will attack mounted travelers and caravans to feed on the horses.

In order for a griffin to be used as a mount, it must be captured young and subjected to extensive and intense training, an expensive proposition. They are difficult to train, but once broken in a tame griffin is an excellent and loyal steed.

Griffins are suitable as mounts for dwarfs, elves, humans, orks, and t'skrang, and as animal companions.

Challenge: Journeyman (Fifth Circle)

DEX:	7	**Initiative:**	11	**Unconsciousness:**	46
STR:	8	**Physical Defense:**	14	**Death Rating:**	53
TOU:	7	**Mystic Defense:**	10	**Wound Threshold:**	10
PER:	5	**Social Defense:**	10	**Knockdown:**	12
WIL:	7	**Physical Armor:**	4	**Recovery Tests:**	2
CHA:	5	**Mystic Armor:**	4		

Movement: 18 (Flying 18)
Actions: 2; Bite: 15 (16), Claws x2: 16 (14)
Powers:
Dive (5)
Enhanced Sense [Hearing] (2)
Enhanced Sense [Sight] (4): Griffins do not suffer penalties from distance to vision-based Awareness tests.
Willful (1)
Swooping Attack: Griffins may split movement (*Player's Guide*, p. 386) without penalty, and does not spend Strain. This ability may not be used if the griffin has a rider.
Special Maneuvers:
Clip the Wing (Opponent)
Loot: Beak and feathers worth 3D6×10 silver pieces (worth Legend Points).

Griffin, Jungle

Brother to the common griffin, the jungle griffin is a creature of even greater grace and beauty. Far larger than common griffins, jungle griffins stand six to seven feet tall at the shoulder, are eight to nine feet long, and have a wingspan of almost fifteen feet. The portion of the creature that resembles an eagle carries much brighter-colored feathers than common griffins—red, yellow, and even green are quite common among jungle griffins. One large horn extends from each side of the jungle griffin's head.

As their name implies, jungle griffins live in or near jungles. The Servos Jungle harbors a few, but most of Barsaive's jungle griffins are found in the Liaj Jungle. Flocks of fifteen to twenty jungle griffins build their nests near clearings in the dense growth, often not far from wide rivers or waterfalls. They appear to love both water and sunlight.

The differences between griffins and jungle griffins go deeper than size or coloring. Of particular interest to Namegivers is this fact: no jungle griffin has ever permitted a Namegiver to sit on its back. More than one Cavalryman or Beastmaster has been killed and eaten after trying to ride a jungle griffin.

Jungle griffins also possess magical abilities common griffins do not. These territorial creatures use their magical abilities to deal with trespassers. Jungle griffins stake out territory surrounding their nests to a distance a Namegiver might walk in an hour, and they can magically sense any Namegivers who enter this region. Two or three griffins seek out the trespassers and attempt to frighten them off.

If that doesn't work, the jungle griffins use a second magical trick. They can send intruders into a trance, and lead the trespassers beyond the borders of their territory. The trance lasts for several minutes after the subjects have departed from the griffins' land. Upon awakening, trespassers have only vague memories of where they were and what happened to them. Most jungle griffins prefer to deal with trespassing Namegivers in this way; they dislike fighting because it endangers their young and taints the air with the smell of blood. However, they will brutally attack any Namegivers who insist upon re-entering their territory too many times.

When forced to engage in combat, jungle griffins attack with their claws, raking with both forepaws. They only use their beaks if necessary, as the beak is more difficult to bring to bear.

While thus far a jungle griffin has not been successfully used as a mount or animal companion, the GM may allow it under suitably legendary circumstances. In that case, they are suitable as mounts for dwarfs, elves, humans, orks, and t'skrang, and as animal companions.

Challenge: Journeyman (Sixth Circle)

DEX:	8	Initiative:	12	Unconsciousness:	51
STR:	9	Physical Defense:	15	Death Rating:	58
TOU:	7	Mystic Defense:	11	Wound Threshold:	10
PER:	6	Social Defense:	15	Knockdown:	13
WIL:	7	Physical Armor:	5	Recovery Tests:	2
CHA:	6	Mystic Defense:	4		

Movement: 14 (Flying 20)
Actions: 2; Bite: 16 (17), Claws x2: 17 (15)
Powers:
Awareness (8): As the skill, *Player's Guide*, p. 129.
Dive (10)
Enhanced Sense [Hearing] (2)
Enhanced Sense [Sight] (2): Jungle griffins do not suffer penalties from distance to vision-based Awareness tests.
Entrancement (15): The griffin can place the target in a peaceful trance. As a Standard action, it makes an Entrancement test against the target's Social Defense. If successful, the victim follows the griffin wherever it leads. This effect fades about ten minutes after the victim leaves the griffins' territory. The victim may break free of the effect by succeeding at a Willpower (13) test.
Frighten (15): As the talent, *Player's Guide*, p. 149, with two differences. First, the effect lasts as long as the target is in the griffin's territory. Second, if the penalty from the power equals or exceeds the target's Willpower Step, the target flees.
Willful (1)
Special Maneuvers:
Clip the Wing (Opponent)
Loot: Beak and feathers worth 5D6×10 silver pieces (worth Legend Points).

Harpy

Harpies are a repulsive cross between bird and human, displaying the worst qualities of both. They have the faces and bodies of hags, covered with grimy matted feathers. Their bird-like feet and short stubby wings are dirt encrusted, their faces are dotted with boils, and their feathers crawl with parasites. Their harsh, shrill voices irritate the ear like the scrape of a sword blade on rocks.

A single harpy poses no danger. Unfortunately, harpies almost always travel in packs, posing a more serious threat. A hunting pack lands in the trees near their chosen victims, at whom they hurl every slur and foul word they know—and they know quite a few. This torrent of abuse angers their opponents and makes them careless in combat. The insults also help the harpies determine the strength of their foe. An enemy who remains calm is most likely too strong for the harpies' taste; whereas one who becomes furious likely has little discipline and so will be easily defeated.

Harpies are cowards by nature and prefer to attack as few opponents as possible, and weak ones, at that. If a pack of harpies decides to attack a group, they usually start by swarming the strongest fighter or group's leader first, and then wheel off to deal with others. They will slash at their victims with taloned feet, or batter them with clubs and other crude weapons. If the battle turns against them, they will retreat to the trees and continue to hurl insults.

The greatest danger posed by harpies, assuming their victims survive an attack, is the threat of disease. These dreadful monsters wallow in their own filth and carry several terrible afflictions to which they are immune but most other living things are not. Often, victims survive an initial harpy attack only to succumb to some debilitating disease within a few hours. If the illness doesn't kill them, the harpies will fall upon their weakened prey and slay him.

Harpy young are born into a world of filth and forced to fend for themselves almost immediately—a harpy feels no familial ties and has no compunction about kicking its offspring away from food. The last to feed on kills, young harpies, when they eat anything at all, feed on a steady diet of rotting meat. Prone to starvation and not yet immune to the diseases rampant in the filth amid which they live, young harpies die at a tremendous rate—though not fast enough to eliminate the species entirely. Harpies appear to have a limited form of intelligence, but they care nothing for the pursuit of knowledge, the study of magic or the arts, or any other thing except their foul kind's survival.

Challenge: Novice (Third Circle)

DEX:	6	**Initiative:**	8	**Unconsciousness:**	30
STR:	4	**Physical Defense:**	10	**Death Rating:**	35
TOU:	5	**Mystic Defense:**	11	**Wound Threshold:**	7
PER:	5	**Social Defense:**	13	**Knockdown:**	6
WIL:	3	**Physical Armor:**	3	**Recovery Tests:**	2
CHA:	6	**Mystic Armor:**	3		

Movement: 10 (Flying 16)
Actions: 1; Claws: 9 (10), Weapon: 11 (by weapon)

Powers:
Disease (10): If the harpy's claws do damage to a target, the victim must resist the effects of a debilitating disease (see **Disease**, p. 186). The disease is Step 10 [Onset: 2 hours, Interval: 4/1 day, Duration: 2 weeks].
Enhanced Sense [Hearing] (2)
Enhanced Sense [Sight] (2)
Taunt (12): As the skill, *Player's Guide*, p. 173.
Special Maneuvers:
Clip the Wing (Opponent)
Curse (Harpy, Taunt): The harpy may spend two additional successes on a Taunt test to curse the target instead of the normal effect. The target receives a -2 penalty to all tests involving a single attribute for one hour per success.
Equipment: Primitive weapons

Hell Hound

Hell hounds are large canines, standing more than four feet high at the shoulder. Their stocky, muscular bodies are covered with short dark-brown fur which seems to absorb the light; indeed, they bear a passing resemblance to gate hounds. The presence of a fire flickering within in its mouth, however, clearly shows the hell hound for what it is. A hell hound's eyes seem to burn; deep within the sockets are twin balls of flame. In complete darkness, the eyes of a hell hound glow like candle flames.

Hell hounds have an impressive magical power: at the height of their power, they can breathe great gouts of flame. Unlike normal fire, this magical flame can briefly burn almost anything, including armor, weapons, rocks, clothing, wood, and flesh. The hell hound's magic flames are not precisely fire as most Namegivers understand it. The flame mixes in the hound's throat with volatile ooze that sticks to the hound's target and burns continuously. One can only put out this burning ooze by completely suffocating it.

Hell hounds travel and hunt in packs so they can surround their prey from all sides. Once the pack has encircled its victim, the pack leader sets the poor wretch afire. If the victim tries to bolt in any direction, the hound nearest him or her coughs up its own stream of fire at the sufferer, forcing the victim to stagger back into the tightening circle of hell hounds. Most victims begin to succumb to the pain and shock of burning flesh within minutes. The smaller the prey, of course, the faster it burns. Hell hounds hunt in this way to ensure only a few pack members use up their fire-breathing power at any given time and to cook their food so as to reduce their chances of eating diseased meat.

More than a few rumors suggest hell hounds were created by dragons as pets. Dragons insist the fact hell hounds breathe fire is a coincidence. A hell hound can be kept as a pet if raised from a pup, and will show amazing loyalty to its master as long as it is not hungry. Those who wish to tame a hell hound would be well advised to feed it often.

Hell hounds are suitable as animal companions.

Challenge: Journeyman (Sixth Circle)

DEX:	6	**Initiative:**	8	**Unconsciousness:**	51
STR:	8	**Physical Defense:**	13	**Death Rating:**	58
TOU:	7	**Mystic Defense:**	14	**Wound Threshold:**	10
PER:	6	**Social Defense:**	11	**Knockdown:**	12
WIL:	6	**Physical Armor:**	6	**Recovery Tests:**	2
CHA:	4	**Mystic Armor:**	6		

Movement: 16
Actions: 2; Bite: 14 (16), Claws x2: 15 (14)
Powers:
Creature Power (15, Fire Breath, Standard)
Fire Breath (15): The hell hound can breathe fire onto a target within 30 yards. It makes a Creature Power test against the target's Mystic Defense. If successful, the target suffers Step 15 Damage from the flames. For each additional success, the flames burn an additional round, doing Step 10 Damage. Mystic Armor protects against this damage. The power can only be used three times per day, and subsequent uses are less potent. The second use has a range of 20 yards and the Creature Power and Damage Steps suffer a -2 penalty. The third use has a range of 10 yards and the Creature Power and Damage Steps suffer a -4 penalty. The power is restored to full potency after one day.
Enhanced Sense [Hearing] (2)
Enhanced Sense [Other] (2): Astral Sight, as the talent, *Player's Guide*, p. 129.
Enhanced Sense [Smell] (2): Tracking
Tracking (8): As the skill, *Player's Guide*, p. 175.
Willful (1)
Special Maneuvers:
Enrage (Opponent)
Fire Fight (Opponent, Steel Thought): An opponent may spend two additional successes from a Steel Thought test against a Creature Power test to evade the attack at the last

minute, redirecting it at a nearby hell hound. This uses the original result against the new target. Knowledge of this special maneuver is rare.

Horse

Horses have recently regained importance in Barsaive. Most of the horses in the region descend from those brought in by the first ork nomad tribes to resettle Barsaive after the Scourge. Ork tribes remain Barsaive's premier source of horses, and ork Cavalrymen take justifiable pride in their tribes' abilities to breed strong, hearty animals.

Draft Horse

Draft horses are used to transport goods across great distances. These animals are often found pulling the carts and wagons of the caravans found on the trade routes of Barsaive.

Draft horses are suitable as mounts for elves, humans, orks, and t'skrang, and as animal companions.

Challenge: Novice (First Circle)

DEX:	4	Initiative:	4	Unconsciousness:	29
STR:	8	Physical Defense:	6	Death Rating:	37
TOU:	8	Mystic Defense:	7	Wound Threshold:	12
PER:	4	Social Defense:	6	Knockdown:	12
WIL:	5	Physical Armor:	2	Recovery Tests:	3
CHA:	4	Mystic Armor:	1		

Movement: 16
Actions: 1; Kick: 7 (14), Trample: 7 (12)
Powers:
Beast of Burden: When used as a mount, the draft horse effectively has 2 less Strength for the purposes of a charging attack.
Enhanced Sense [Hearing] (2)
Enhanced Sense [Smell] (2)
Resist Pain (2)
Special Maneuvers:
Overrun (Draft Horse, Trample)

Granlain

Granlain are unusually large, strong horses that often serve as draft animals. They stand seven feet tall at the shoulder and commonly reach ten feet in length. Granlain are stubborn animals, and trolls are often the only Namegivers strong enough to deal with these massive, willful beasts. Granlain are not common. Wild granlain live only in the plains and foothills near mountainous regions.

Granlain are suitable as mounts for elves, humans, orks, t'skrang, and trolls, and as animal companions.

Challenge: Novice (Second Circle)

DEX:	5	**Initiative:**	5	**Unconsciousness:**	37
STR:	8	**Physical Defense:**	8	**Death Rating:**	46
TOU:	9	**Mystic Defense:**	8	**Wound Threshold:**	13
PER:	4	**Social Defense:**	10	**Knockdown:**	12
WIL:	6	**Physical Armor:**	2	**Recovery Tests:**	3
CHA:	5	**Mystic Armor:**	2		

Movement: 16
Actions: 1; Kick: 8 (15), Trample: 8 (13)
Powers:
Enhanced Sense [Hearing] (2)
Enhanced Sense [Smell] (2)
Resist Pain (2)
Special Maneuvers:
Overrun (Granlain, Trample)

Mule

Mules are the sterile crossbreeds of donkeys and horses. Pack mules are used to transport goods all across Barsaive. Though not as strong as draft horses, they are more sure-footed and travel better on uneven ground. These animals are often found pulling the carts and wagons of caravans traveling through rough terrain.

Mules are stubborn and skittish animals. If startled or attacked the mule's first instinct is to kick up its rear hooves and bolt.

Mules are suitable mounts for dwarfs, elves, humans, orks, and t'skrang, and as animal companions.

Challenge: Novice (First Circle)

DEX:	5	**Initiative:**	5	**Unconsciousness:**	29
STR:	7	**Physical Defense:**	8	**Death Rating:**	37
TOU:	8	**Mystic Defense:**	9	**Wound Threshold:**	12
PER:	5	**Social Defense:**	10	**Knockdown:**	11
WIL:	6	**Physical Armor:**	1	**Recovery Tests:**	3
CHA:	4	**Mystic Armor:**	2		

Movement: 16
Actions: 1; Kick: 7 (11), Trample: 7 (9)
Powers:
Beast of Burden: When used as a mount, the mule effectively has 2 less Strength for the purposes of a charging attack.
Enhanced Sense [Hearing] (2)
Enhanced Sense [Smell] (2)
Special Maneuvers:
Overrun (Mule, Trample)

Pony

A smaller breed of horse used mainly by dwarfs for transportation and war. Many ork, elf, and human children train their horse riding skills on ponies as they grow up. Ponies cannot wear barding or armor.

Ponies are suitable mounts for dwarfs, elves, and humans, and as animal companions.

Challenge: Novice (First Circle)

DEX:	5	Initiative:	7	Unconsciousness:	26
STR:	6	Physical Defense:	9	Death Rating:	33
TOU:	7	Mystic Defense:	8	Wound Threshold:	10
PER:	4	Social Defense:	7	Knockdown:	10
WIL:	5	Physical Armor:	1	Recovery Tests:	2
CHA:	5	Mystic Armor:	1		

Movement: 16
Actions: 1; Kick: 7 (10), Trample: 7 (8)
Powers:
Enhanced Sense [Hearing] (2)
Enhanced Sense [Smell] (2)
Special Maneuvers:
Overrun (Pony, Trample)

Riding Horse

The most common horses used, riding horses make strong mounts, but cannot wear barding or armor.

Riding horses are suitable mounts for elves, humans, orks, and t'skrang, and as animal companions.

Challenge: Novice (First Circle)

DEX:	5	Initiative:	7	Unconsciousness:	29
STR:	7	Physical Defense:	8	Death Rating:	37
TOU:	8	Mystic Defense:	8	Wound Threshold:	12
PER:	4	Social Defense:	8	Knockdown:	11
WIL:	5	Physical Armor:	1	Recovery Tests:	3
CHA:	5	Mystic Armor:	1		

Movement: 20
Actions: 1; Kick: 7 (12), Trample: 7 (10)
Powers:
Enhanced Sense [Hearing] (2)
Enhanced Sense [Smell] (2)
Special Maneuvers:
Overrun (Riding Horse, Trample)

War Horse

Larger and stronger than riding horses, war horses are bred to carry heavy loads while remaining able to canter and gallop. Armies and cavalry units, particularly ork scorcher tribes, often use war horses. War horses may wear barding, which provides the equivalent protection as the type of armor. For example, hardened leather barding provides 5 points of Physical Armor. The mount suffers the appropriate Initaitive Penalty based on the type of armor.

War horses are suitable as mounts for elves, humans, orks, and t'skrang, and as animal companions.

Challenge: Novice (Second Circle)

DEX:	6	Initiative:	8	Unconsciousness:	37
STR:	8	Physical Defense:	9	Death Rating:	46
TOU:	9	Mystic Defense:	9	Wound Threshold:	13
PER:	5	Social Defense:	9	Knockdown:	12
WIL:	7	Physical Armor:	1	Recovery Tests:	3
CHA:	6	Mystic Armor:	3		

Movement: 16
Actions: 1; Kick: 10 (14), Trample: 10 (12)
Powers:
Enhanced Sense [Hearing] (2)
Enhanced Sense [Smell] (2)
Special Maneuvers:
Overrun (War Horse, Trample)

Huttawa

The huttawa's body resembles a large cat, like a lion, but it has an eagle-like head with a large beak and bird-like eyes. Four feet at the shoulder and six feet long, huttawa are a favored mount for dwarf Cavalrymen, and often help pull caravan wagons belonging to dwarf trading companies.

Huttawa are suitable mounts for dwarfs, elves, humans, orks, and t'skrang, and animal companions.

Challenge: Novice (Second Circle)

DEX:	6	Initiative:	8	Unconsciousness:	31
STR:	8	Physical Defense:	9	Death Rating:	38
TOU:	7	Mystic Defense:	8	Wound Threshold:	10
PER:	4	Social Defense:	7	Knockdown:	12
WIL:	6	Physical Armor:	4	Recovery Tests:	2
CHA:	4	Mystic Armor:	3		

Movement: 16
Actions: 1; Beak: 10 (13)
Powers:
Awareness (8): As the skill, *Player's Guide*, p. 129.
Climbing (10): As the skill, *Player's Guide*, p. 134.

Enhanced Sense [Sight] (2)
Great Leap (6)
Resist Pain (2)

Ice Flyer

Ice flyers resemble white, winged baboons, standing roughly six feet tall and weighing up to seven hundred pounds. They often gather in flocks of four to twenty-four individuals; led by one of its members. Some of their feathers gleam as if made of crystal. These feathers stay cold even in tropical heat, allowing the creatures to live in tropical or arid environments.

Ice flyers typically strike from the air, swooping down in a flurry of shrieking and clawing, and then flying out of melee range. The leader of the flock usually stays out of direct combat, preferring to use its powers at range.

Ice flyers are suitable as animal companions.

Challenge: Novice (Fourth Circle)

DEX:	8	**Initiative:**	12	**Unconsciousness:**	38
STR:	5	**Physical Defense:**	14	**Death Rating:**	44
TOU:	6	**Mystic Defense:**	8	**Wound Threshold:**	9
PER:	5	**Social Defense:**	9	**Knockdown:**	7
WIL:	6	**Physical Armor:**	3	**Recovery Tests:**	2
CHA:	5	**Mystic Armor:**	3		

Movement: 10 (Flying 16)
Actions: 1; Claws: 12 (14)
Powers:
Enhanced Sense [Smell] (2)
Howling Challenge (13): The leader of the flock can challenge a target within 50 yards. Using a Standard action, it howls at the target and makes a Howling Challenge test against the target's Social Defense. If successful, the target is compelled to return the challenge, using his Standard action. The victim makes a Charisma test against a Difficulty Number equal to the Howling Challenge test result. If the test is successful the challenge ends. The ice flyer retreats, followed by the rest of his flock. If failed, the ice flyer can continue the challenge, making a new test each round for as long as he wins and uses no other Standard actions.
Ice Shackles (14): The ice flyer can wrap a target within 30 yards in bonds of magical ice. As a Standard action, it makes an Ice Shackles test against the target's Mystic Defense. If successful, the target is incapacitated, unable to take any actions except trying to break free. The shackles last for one round per success. To break free, the target must succeed at a Strength (10) test, which shatters the bonds.
Willful (1)
Special Maneuvers:
Clip the Wing (Opponent)
Rising Morale (Ice Flyer, Howling Challenge): Each additional success gives all other allied ice flyers +1 to their next attack test against allies of the target.
Loot: Ice feathers worth D6×10 silver pieces (worth Legend Points)

Inshalata

The inshalata is a species of giant praying mantis, about seven feet tall from head to tail, which hunts the Servos Jungle. The creature is an exceptionally gifted ambush hunter, striking lightning fast from its position within the foliage of the jungle.

When attacking, an inshalata directs its attacks against a single target. If it defeats this victim, it attempts to carry the body away to its lair, where it will feed.

Tribes in the Servos often use the claws and mandibles of inshalata to craft weapons. The claws are equivalent to swords, while the mandibles are turned into daggers.

Challenge: Journeyman (Sixth Circle)

DEX:	8	**Initiative:**	14	**Unconsciousness:**	57
STR:	9	**Physical Defense:**	13	**Death Rating:**	66
TOU:	9	**Mystic Defense:**	12	**Wound Threshold:**	13
PER:	7	**Social Defense:**	10	**Knockdown:**	13
WIL:	8	**Physical Armor:**	10	**Recovery Tests:**	3
CHA:	4	**Mystic Armor:**	4		

Movement: 16 (Climb 16)
Actions: 3; Bite: 16 (14), Claws x2: 16 (16)
Powers:
Ambush (10)
Enhanced Sense [Sight] (2)
Great Leap (10)
Hardened Armor
Stealthy Stride (14): As the skill, *Player's Guide*, p. 170.
Special Maneuvers:
Crack the Shell (Opponent)
Pry Loose (Opponent, Close Combat)
Squeeze the Life (Inshalata, Claws)
Loot: Claws and mandibles worth D6×10 silver pieces (worth Legend Points).

Jub Jub

Jub jubs are "giant frogs with fangs," as many riverboat captains describe them. The jub jub's name comes from its shockingly loud, rumbling call, which will jolt a Namegiver's bones. A large jub jub can swallow a windling in one gulp. Jub jubs hunt along the banks of the river and prefer to prey on lone individuals.

They attack by leaping long distances and attempting to inject paralyzing venom with their large fangs. If they manage to succeed, they hold on to their prey until it succumbs to the venom and then begin to feed.

Jub jubs are suitable as animal companions.

Challenge: Novice (Third Circle)

DEX:	6	**Initiative:**	10	**Unconsciousness:**	36
STR:	7	**Physical Defense:**	10	**Death Rating:**	43
TOU:	7	**Mystic Defense:**	8	**Wound Threshold:**	10
PER:	4	**Social Defense:**	8	**Knockdown:**	11
WIL:	4	**Physical Armor:**	4	**Recovery Tests:**	2
CHA:	4	**Mystic Armor:**	1		

Movement: 10 (Swim 12)
Actions: 1; Bite: 13 (15, Poison)
Powers:

Aquatic: Jub hubs can breathe underwater.
Battle Shout (8): As the skill *Player's Guide*, p. 131.
Great Leap (10)
Poison (10): If the jub jub causes a Wound with its fangs, the victim must resist the effects of a paralytic poison (see **Poison**, p. 171). The poison is Step 10 [Onset: 3 rounds, Interval: 4/2 rounds, Duration: 30 minutes].

Special Maneuvers:
Grab and Bite (Jub Jub)
Defang (Opponent, Close Combat)
Pounce (Jub Jub)
Pry Loose (Opponent, Close Combat)

Krillra

The female krilworm, or krillra, shares certain features with the male, but in many ways looks quite different. The krilworm, at its largest, measures no longer than a human's hand and foot placed end to end. The krillra, however, often stretches fifteen or more feet. The krillra also has a single, triple-faceted eye. The female's mouth is proportionately smaller than the krilworm's, but on a fifteen-foot-long insect even a small mouth is large enough to tear off a human-or dwarf-sized limb in one bite. Both the krillra and krilworm have black, bat-like wings, though the krillra's span twenty-five feet or better. Like the krilworm's, the krillra's tail is tipped with four squiggling tentacles.

Krillra spend their lives flying over land, rarely touching the ground. They eat birds and other flying things, including an occasional airship crew. In complete and deadly silence, the krillra approaches its prey from the direction of the sun so her quarry cannot see her until it is too late. Once in striking range, the krillra snaps her tail forward and grabs her victim in her loathsome tentacles. Only the largest and strongest creatures can avoid being crushed into a bloody pulp in the krillra's cruel grip—and if she cannot kill by crushing, the krillra simply bites her victim's head in two. Having killed her meal, the krillra holds the corpse in one or two tentacles and uses the remaining ones to tear off succulent bits of mashed, dripping flesh.

To see krillras and krilworms mate is to witness a scene of violence rarely seen in any other of nature's creatures. Once a year, krilworms gather together in enormous swarms and take flight across the countryside, devouring anything in their way. They feed on as many creatures as possible in order to strengthen themselves for their ordeal; the mating ritual will kill the swarm's weakest members. When a single krillra drops down from the sky, the krilworms swarm over her in a violent rush to impregnate her. Not only do the krilworms often kill each other in this frenzy, but the krillra herself kills any krilworm she can reach with her mouth and tentacles. Only the strongest and luckiest krilworms will manage to climb past the krillra's thrashing tail and leave their seed within her.

Once all the krilworms have either mated or died, the krillra flies to the nearest body of water and skims across its surface, depositing her eggs by the thousands. Three months later, the infant krilworms hatch and immediately fly away in a frantic search for food. Both the males and females of this species have a strange affinity for Nethermancers. The krillra also shares the krilworm's preference for underground holes and swampy ground.

Challenge: Journeyman (Seventh Circle)

DEX:	8	**Initiative:**	8	**Unconsciousness:**	71
STR:	14	**Physical Defense:**	12	**Death Rating:**	83
TOU:	12	**Mystic Defense:**	12	**Wound Threshold:**	18
PER:	6	**Social Defense:**	10	**Knockdown:**	14
WIL:	7	**Physical Armor:**	10	**Recovery Tests:**	4
CHA:	2	**Mystic Armor:**	5		

Movement: 4 (Flying 18)
Actions: 4; Bite: 18 (23), Tentacles x4: 18 (21)
Powers:
Affinity for Nethermancers: Krillras have a peculiar affinity for Nethermancers, a feeling often returned by the magicians. Nethermancers gain a +5 bonus to any Charisma-based tests made against a krillra.
Enhanced Sense [Sight]: Low-Light Vision
Willful (1)
Special Maneuvers:
Clip the Wing (Opponent)

Pry Loose (Opponent, Close Combat)
Squeeze the Life (Krillra, Tentacles): Instead of claw damage, the victim takes damage from the tentacles each round.

Krilworm

Krilworms are nocturnal flyers, traveling in swarms ranging from eight to eighty members, and feeding on large insects and small mammals. They have segmented bodies about eighteen inches long, with bat-like wings sprouting near the front. Their needle-like teeth drip a foul-smelling substance many believe to be toxic. Eyeless, they "see" through divination magic organs resembling six open, running sores.

Krilworms generally do not attack larger animal and humanoids, but a swarm of them can cause problems. Fortunately, a determined character can drive them off. Each time a krilworm is killed, the gamemaster rolls a single Willpower (4) test for the rest of the swarm. If successful the swarm stays, otherwise it flees.

Krilworms are suitable as animal companions.

Challenge: Novice (First Circle)

DEX:	7	**Initiative:**	9	**Unconsciousness:**	11
STR:	2	**Physical Defense:**	10	**Death Rating:**	13
TOU:	2	**Mystic Defense:**	10	**Wound Threshold:**	3
PER:	6	**Social Defense:**	6	**Knockdown:**	2
WIL:	7	**Physical Armor:**	2	**Recovery Tests:**	1
CHA:	2	**Mystic Armor:**	3		

Movement: 2 (Flying 14)
Actions: 1; Bite: 12 (7)
Powers:
Affinity for Nethermancers: Krilworms have a peculiar affinity for Nethermancers, a feeling often returned by the magicians. Nethermancers gain a +5 bonus to any Charisma-based tests made against a krilworm.
Enhanced Sense [Other] (4): Krilworms ignore the normal penalties for darkness (*Player's Guide*, p. 386). Instead they make a Perception test with a +4 Step bonus, detecting the presence of all creatures within 30 yards with a Mystic Defense equal to or less than the test result. If the test fails to detect a target, the krilworm suffers the penalty for partial darkness for attacks made against the target.
Special Maneuvers:
Clip the Wing (Opponent)

Kue

The kue resembles a cross between a lizard and a cat, with a reptilian body and feline mannerisms and facial features. Like cats, kue possess excellent night vision, and sometimes serve windling communities as watch animals. A kue has long, slender legs rather than the short squat legs typical of most lizards. They are about two feet tall at the shoulder, three to four feet long, and have horns on their heads and tails.

Kues are native to jungles and forests, and make ideal mounts for the windling Cavalrymen and Warriors who protect windling communities and villages. Kues are generally sold only in larger cities and towns located near jungles.

Kues are suitable as mounts for windlings and animal companions.

Challenge: Novice (First Circle)

DEX:	7	Initiative:	11	Unconsciousness:	17
STR:	4	Physical Defense:	10	Death Rating:	21
TOU:	4	Mystic Defense:	8	Wound Threshold:	6
PER:	5	Social Defense:	7	Knockdown:	8
WIL:	5	Physical Armor:	5	Recovery Tests:	1
CHA:	4	Mystic Armor:	2		

Movement: 16
Actions: 1; Claws: 10 (8), Tail: 9 (9)
Powers:
Climbing (13): As the skill, *Player's Guide*, p. 134.
Enhanced Sense [Hearing] (2)
Enhanced Sense [Sight]: Low-Light Vision
Great Leap (8)
Stealthy Stride (8): As the skill, *Player's Guide*, p. 170.

Leopard

Leopards have yellowish-brown fur, covered with black spots and striations. They are most likely to be encountered in the plains near Barsaive's forests, although snow leopards with white fur and black spots and striations can be encountered in the mountains.

The leopard is a predator. It will attempt to attack lone prey, or single out a target among a group of creatures. If wounded or outnumbered it will attempt to flee.

Leopards are suitable as animal companions.

Challenge: Novice (Third Circle)

DEX:	8	Initiative:	12	Unconsciousness:	33
STR:	7	Physical Defense:	12	Death Rating:	39
TOU:	6	Mystic Defense:	10	Wound Threshold:	9
PER:	6	Social Defense:	9	Knockdown:	11
WIL:	5	Physical Armor:	3	Recovery Tests:	2
CHA:	5	Mystic Armor:	2		

Movement: 18
Actions: 1; Bite: 15 (13), Claws: 15 (12)
Powers:
Ambush (5)
Climbing (12): As the skill, *Player's Guide*, p. 134.
Enhanced Sense [Hearing] (2)
Enhanced Sense [Sight]: Low-Light Vision
Great Leap (8)

Stealthy Stride (12): As the skill, *Player's Guide*, p. 170.
Special Maneuvers:
Pounce (Leopard)

Lion

The lion is a ferocious carnivore, with a yellow-brown coat, a loud roar, and a devastating bite. The males have a long, thick mane, whereas females do not. These animals primarily roam the plains of Barsaive.

Lions are pack predators, singling out chosen prey from a group and running it down or herding it to other members of the pride. If wounded or outnumbered, individuals will usually attempt to flee.

Lions are suitable as animal companions.

Female

Challenge: Novice (Third Circle)

DEX:	7	**Initiative:**	11	**Unconsciousness:**	33
STR:	7	**Physical Defense:**	13	**Death Rating:**	39
TOU:	6	**Mystic Defense:**	10	**Wound Threshold:**	9
PER:	6	**Social Defense:**	9	**Knockdown:**	11
WIL:	6	**Physical Armor:**	3	**Recovery Tests:**	2
CHA:	5	**Mystic Armor:**	2		

Movement: 18
Actions: 1; Bite: 14 (12), Claw: 14 (11)
Powers:
Ambush (5)
Climbing (8): As the skill, *Player's Guide*, p. 134.
Enhanced Sense [Hearing] (2)
Enhanced Sense [Sight]: Low-Light Vision
Great Leap (6)
Stealthy Stride (11): As the skill, *Player's Guide*, p. 170.
Willful (1)
Surprise Strike (5): As the skill, *Player's Guide*, p. 172.
Special Maneuvers:
Pounce (Lion)

Male

Challenge: Novice (Third Circle)

DEX:	6	**Initiative:**	10	**Unconsciousness:**	36
STR:	8	**Physical Defense:**	11	**Death Rating:**	43
TOU:	7	**Mystic Defense:**	9	**Wound Threshold:**	10
PER:	5	**Social Defense:**	10	**Knockdown:**	12
WIL:	6	**Physical Armor:**	4	**Recovery Tests:**	2
CHA:	6	**Mystic Armor:**	2		

Movement: 18
Actions: 1; Bite: 12 (15), Claw: 12 (14)

Powers:
Ambush (5)
Battle Shout (8): As the skill, *Player's Guide*, p. 131.
Climbing (8): As the skill, *Player's Guide*, p. 134.
Enhanced Sense [Hearing] (2)
Enhanced Sense [Sight]: Low-Light Vision
Great Leap (6)
Stealthy Stride (10): As the skill, *Player's Guide*, p. 170.
Surprise Strike (5): As the skill, *Player's Guide*, p. 172.
Willful (1)
Special Maneuvers:
Pounce (Lion)

Lion, Stone

Like the brithan, stone lions are part savage mountain creature and part angry earth elemental. These small, gray mountain lions have fur as hard as rock, along with razor-sharp, crystal-edged claws and teeth which can tear armor as easily as flesh.

Stealthy and patient hunters, stone lions stalk mountain goats and other creatures, and are territorial enough to attack larger animals who intrudes on their hunting grounds, including Namegivers. Most stone lions are solitary, but hunters and travelers have occasionally reported seeing a mated pair.

Crystal raiders sometimes hunt stone lions for their pelts, which can be made into strong and flexible hide armor. Stone lion flesh is tough and unpleasant to eat. Hunting a stone lion is often considered a Rite of Passage for a young crystal raider before he undergoes his Rite of Naming.

Stone lions are suitable as animal companions.

Challenge: Journeyman (Seventh Circle)

DEX:	10	**Initiative:**	12	**Unconsciousness:**	71
STR:	10	**Physical Defense:**	15	**Death Rating:**	83
TOU:	12	**Mystic Defense:**	15	**Wound Threshold:**	18
PER:	6	**Social Defense:**	10	**Knockdown:**	14
WIL:	8	**Physical Armor:**	10	**Recovery Tests:**	4
CHA:	6	**Mystic Armor:**	10		

Movement: 16
Actions: 2; Bite: 16 (18), Claw x2: 16 (18)
Powers:
Ambush (10)
Battle Shout (10): As the skill, *Player's Guide*, p. 131.
Enhanced Sense [Hearing] (2)
Enhanced Sense [Sight]: Low-Light Vision
Great Leap (10)
Willful (2)
Stealthy Stride (15): As the skill, *Player's Guide*, p. 170.
Resist Pain (2)

Special Maneuvers:
Pounce (Stone Lion)
Enrage (Opponent)
Loot: Crystal shards and fragments of Elemental earth worth 3D6×20 silver pieces (worth Legend Points).

Lion, Wood

The wood lion is equally at home in the branches of trees or on the ground. Its fur is dappled like a newborn deer. A full-grown adult is approximately five feet long and weighs about four hundred pounds.

Wood lions usually attack from a concealed position in the undergrowth or from the lower branches of a large tree. Its first attack is an attempt to knock the target to the ground, where it follows up with vicious claw and bite attacks.

Wood lions are suitable as animal companions.

Challenge: Journeyman (Fifth Circle)

DEX:	9	**Initiative:**	13	**Unconsciousness:**	43
STR:	8	**Physical Defense:**	15	**Death Rating:**	49
TOU:	6	**Mystic Defense:**	11	**Wound Threshold:**	9
PER:	6	**Social Defense:**	12	**Knockdown:**	12
WIL:	6	**Physical Armor:**	5	**Recovery Tests:**	2
CHA:	5	**Mystic Armor:**	3		

Movement: 16 (Climbing 12)
Actions: 2; Bite: 18 (14), Claw x2: 18 (13)
Powers:
Ambush (10)
Enhanced Sense [Hearing] (4)
Enhanced Sense [Sight]: Low-Light Vision
Great Leap (10)
Stealthy Stride (17): As the skill, *Player's Guide*, p. 170.
Willful (1)
Special Maneuvers:
Pounce (Wood Lion)
Provoke (Opponent, Close Combat)

Lizard

Lizards of different colors and sizes can be found in almost every corner of Barsaive. Some smaller varieties are often kept as pets by Namegivers. The statistics provided here are for varieties similar to an iguana.

Lizards are suitable as animal companions.

Challenge: Novice (First Circle)

DEX:	6	**Initiative:**	8	**Unconsciousness:**	11	
STR:	2	**Physical Defense:**	10	**Death Rating:**	13	
TOU:	2	**Mystic Defense:**	6	**Wound Threshold:**	3	
PER:	3	**Social Defense:**	6	**Knockdown:**	6	
WIL:	3	**Physical Armor:**	1	**Recovery Tests:** 1		
CHA:	2	**Mystic Armor:**	1			

Movement: 8 (Climbing 8)
Actions: 1; Bite: 10 (5)
Powers:
Awareness (6): As the skill, *Player's Guide*, p. 129.
Enhanced Sense [Smell] (4)
Enhanced Sense [Taste] (4)

Lizard, Ghoul

The ghoul lizard gets its name from its taste for carrion and its unusual appearance—the pale, green-white scales and raised bony ridges around the lizard's eyes and along the top of its snout resemble the upper half of a human skull. Ghoul lizards can grow up to nine feet long, including their long tails. More bony spikes are arranged in three rows down the lizard's back. These spines remain folded flat until the animal is threatened or readies itself to attack.

Though primarily a carrion eater, the ghoul lizard has been known to attack weakened live prey. Though the lizard's claws and teeth are ineffective for this task, its tail is covered with short, bony poisoned spikes that can easily pierce even hard armor.

Ghoul lizards are suitable as animal companions.

Challenge: Novice (Fourth Circle)

DEX:	6	**Initiative:**	8	**Unconsciousness:**	35	
STR:	7	**Physical Defense:**	10	**Death Rating:**	40	
TOU:	5	**Mystic Defense:**	8	**Wound Threshold:**	7	
PER:	5	**Social Defense:**	9	**Knockdown:**	11	
WIL:	9	**Physical Armor:**	5	**Recovery Tests:**	2	
CHA:	5	**Mystic Armor:**	4			

Movement: 10
Actions: 1; Tail: 13 (16, Poison)
Powers:
Climbing (12): As the skill, *Player's Guide*, p. 134.
Enhanced Sense [Smell] (4)
Enhanced Sense [Taste] (4)
Poison (8): If a ghoul lizard causes damage, the target must resist the effects of a damaging poison. The poison is Step 8 [Onset: 1 round, Interval: 1/2 rounds].
Spikes (6, Poison): A character who fails an attack against a ghoul lizard must make a Dexterity (7) test. If failed, the attacker is struck by one of the lizard's spikes, taking

Step 6 damage, reduced by Physical Armor. If the character takes damage, the lizard's poison affects them.

Lizard, Lightning

Lightning lizards are four foot long with three-foot-long tails and weigh roughly two hundred pounds. When dry, their yellow-and-green skin glistens as though oiled. They travel in prides of three to thirteen individuals, and are usually docile unless hungry or provoked. When feeding, they typically eat over one-third of their body weight, then slowly digest the meal over the next 48 hours.

Lightning lizards get their name from their ability to generate electricity, similar to electric eels. They can wrap their bodies in a crackling sheath of lightning, and they use the lightning when hunting prey as well. When attacking with this power, the beast's eyes crackle and spark, and twin bolts of lightning fly at the target.

Lightning lizards are suitable as animal companions.

Challenge: Journeyman (Fifth Circle)

DEX:	7	**Initiative:**	8	**Unconsciousness:**	45
STR:	6	**Physical Defense:**	11	**Death Rating:**	54
TOU:	6	**Mystic Defense:**	14	**Wound Threshold:**	9
PER:	9	**Social Defense:**	9	**Knockdown:**	6
WIL:	9	**Physical Armor:**	7	**Recovery Tests:**	
CHA:	5	**Mystic Armor:**	6		

Movement: 10
Actions: 2; Bite: 10 (14), Claws x2: 12 (10)
Powers:
Climbing (13): As the skill, *Player's Guide*, p. 134.
Crackling Armor (12): As a Simple action, the lightning lizard wraps itself in a protective sheath of electricity. When an attacker hits, lightning arcs to the attacker, causing Step 12 Damage. Physical armor protects against this damage.

Creature Power (14, Twinbolts, Standard)
Enhanced Sense [Smell] (2)
Enhanced Sense [Taste] (2)
Willful (2)
Twinbolts (16): The lightning lizard attacks a target within 50 yards by firing bolts of lightning from its eyes. It makes a Creature Power test against the target's Mystic Defense. If successful, the target suffers Step 16 damage. Physical armor protects against this damage.

Special Maneuvers:
Go For the Eyes! (Opponent): The attacker may use two additional successes on an attack test to inflict Partial Blindness on the lightning lizard until the end of the next round. In addition to the normal penalties, this reduces the Twin Bolts Step by 6. If the damage causes a Wound, the blindness lasts until the Wound is healed.
Grounded Strike (Opponent): The attacker may spend additional successes on an Attack test to reduce the Damage Step of Crackling Armor by 4 for each success.
Loot: Two eyes worth 75 silver pieces each (worth Legend Points).

Lizard, Plague

A plague lizard looks like the twisted offspring of a reptile and a rodent, if one can imagine a lizard-rat measuring nearly 10 feet from snout to tail. Its entire body is covered with boils and welts, each of which carries a different disease. The lizard actually likes contagion, and often seeks out contaminated places where it can browse among filthy sicknesses as a gourmet Namegiver might browse at a banquet. Of course, the unfortunate tendency of most Namegivers to build and live in cities has given the plague lizard any number of such banquets to choose from. Nowhere in the world can a plague lizard find such a delicious variety of diseases as in a city's garbage heaps and overcrowded streets.

Once a plague lizard makes its nest in a garbage heap, Namegivers living nearby start sickening and dying in great numbers. The hallmark of lizard-borne illness is the variety of plagues afflicting the luckless population at once, as well as their virulence. Unless the afflicted have powerful magical and mundane defenses against the lizard's diseases—all of them—death is inevitable. The only way to stop the spread of contagion is to root the lizard out of its nest and kill it, then burn the stinking corpse in a red-hot kiln to destroy all trace of its plagues.

Plague lizards attack opponents with their claws and teeth. Either attack can transmit disease to the unfortunate victim. These beasts have no natural predators; few predators are hardy enough to withstand the diseases a plague lizard carries.

Challenge: Novice (Third Circle)

DEX:	6	**Initiative:**	8	**Unconsciousness:**	39
STR:	6	**Physical Defense:**	10	**Death Rating:**	47
TOU:	8	**Mystic Defense:**	11	**Wound Threshold:**	12
PER:	4	**Social Defense:**	9	**Knockdown:**	10
WIL:	5	**Physical Armor:**	7	**Recovery Tests:**	3
CHA:	3	**Mystic Armor:**	4		

Movement: 8
Actions: 1; Bite: 11 (11), Claws: 11 (8)
Powers:
Climbing (12): As the skill, *Player's Guide*, p. 314.
Disease (10): A victim bitten by a plague lizard is exposed to the virulent disease the beast carries in glands in its mouth. This disease is Step 10 [Onset: 2 rounds, Interval: 6/1 round]. The victim suffers crippling pain and damage while the disease runs its course. The disease is almost invariably fatal to all but the toughest opponents. People unfortunate enough to live near a plague lizard can come down with a wide variety of nasty ailments. See **Disease**, p. 186, for more information.
Enhanced Sense [Smell] (4)
Enhanced Sense [Taste] (4)
Immune to Disease: The plague lizard automatically succeeds at Toughness tests made to resist disease.

Manticore

Long ago, before the Scourge, these terrible creatures were truly noble beings, intelligent and honorable, able to discuss art and nature and other such subjects with ease. As with so many living things in Barsaive, however, the noble manticores were corrupted by the Horrors almost beyond recognition. Those Horrors killed most of the manticores, allowing only those driven mad by their attacks to live. These poor, mad manticores bred and carried on the species throughout the Scourge, passing on their madness to their offspring. Why the Horrors devastated the manticores with such particular ferocity is unknown.

The manticores of this time look the same as their ancestors did—they resemble huge lions with bat-like wings and humanlike faces. Their tails end in spiked balls, which they use to dreadful effect in combat. Most manticores nowadays are dull yellow in color; few of the black, brown, and white manticores remain.

Before the Scourge, manticores only hunted to eat. Those who live in Barsaive these days, however, attack at random. They fly back and forth around their enemy, raking him with their long claws and striking hard with their spiked tails until blood seems to rain down on them. When fighting at close quarters or on the ground, they use their claws to disembowel their foe; if that tactic fails, they knock the enemy to the ground with their spiked tails. If a manticore swings its entire body from side to side, it can hit an opponent standing directly in front of it with its lethal tail. It can even knock over its enemy with its great wings, either by striking with the wings themselves or by creating huge gusts of air sending the foe sprawling backward.

Manticores also cast spells, using their human-like mouths to speak the necessary words as easily as any Namegiver. Some folk find this spellcasting ability terrifying, for good reason.

Challenge: Journeyman (Sixth Circle)

DEX:	7	Initiative:	9	Unconsciousness:	57
STR:	10	Physical Defense:	13	Death Rating:	66
TOU:	9	Mystic Defense:	14	Wound Threshold:	13
PER:	8	Social Defense:	11	Knockdown:	14
WIL:	8	Physical Armor:	8	Recovery Tests:	3
CHA:	7	Mystic Armor:	5		

Movement: 16 (Flying 16)
Actions: 2; Claws: 14 (16), Tail: 14 (20), Wings: 14 (15)
Powers:
Spellcasting (15): As the talent, *Player's Guide*, p. 168.
Spells: Choose up to four spells requiring no threads from any type of magic (Elementalism, Illusionism, Nethermancy, or Wizardry).
Special Maneuvers:
Clip the Wing (Opponent)
Knockout (Manticore, Tail): The manticore may use two additional successes on an Attack test to force the opponent to make a Toughness test against the Damage test result. If the test fails, treat the Damage result as a test against the Toughness result and the target is knocked unconscious for one round per success.
Provoke (Opponent, Close Combat)
Wing Buffet (Manticore, Wings): The manticore may spend an additional success to cause a Knockdown test against the target if the target has a lower Strength Step. The Difficulty Number is the Attack test result.
Loot: Spiked tail worth 5D6 × 10 silver pieces (worth Legend Points).

Molgrim

Most folk who have seen the molgrim and lived to speak of it assume it is not a natural beast, but yet another magically created abomination. They cannot imagine such a creature occurring naturally, as the molgrim combines bits and pieces of many different creatures into a disturbing whole. The beast is about as tall as a large bear, but broader, with a deep and powerful chest. Its back slopes like a toad's, and it has frog-like hind legs with which it can make prodigious leaps. Its forelegs, though smaller, are as strong as a human's arms, and the three fingers on its broad hands are tipped with claws as long and broad as a human's forefinger.

Even though it resembles a large and ugly frog, the molgrim is not an amphibian. Its hide is dry and tough like imperfectly cured leather. Short, thick, oily fur grows from its mottled skin, light gray or tan on the back fading to dark brown or black on the belly. Most of the head looks bear-like, but seems almost too large for its body, and it has beady, red-ringed eyes. In place of a snout, the molgrim has a large beak, wickedly hooked and perfect for tearing flesh

The molgrim is a carnivore, most often found in the foothills of the rugged mountain ranges ringing the Wastes (though any stretch of rough, broken ground will do). It eats bears and mountain sheep most often, as well as anything else wandering into its gaze. Lacking the patience and intelligence to ambush its food, the molgrim prefers to chase down its prey. The creature can leap up significant distances, and run faster than a galloping horse for minutes at a time. Molgrims often capture their prey with one terrifying leap, landing on a victim's back and brutally snapping the spine in half. If a molgrim must give chase to capture its meal, it sets off in pursuit with an ugly, barking cry, only death will end the hunt.

Molgrims are constantly hungry, and during the day they are always either feeding or seeking food. Fiercely territorial, molgrims hunt alone. One of the few things able to distract a molgrim from the chase is the arrival of another molgrim in its hunting grounds. Unless the interloper is a female seeking a mate, the two molgrims will fight. Often these challenges kill both combatants; one gets torn to shreds, and the other dies soon afterward from its wounds. The defender charges the challenger and tries to drive him away. Should this fail, the defender rears up, utters its horrible cry, and leaps at the intruder, slashing with his beak and claws. The challenger often leaps at the same moment, and the two monstrous figures clash in midair, falling to the ground tearing and clawing at each other. If one manages to break free, they repeat this behavior until one loses enough blood to fall unconscious and die at the beak of the other.

The female molgrim always seeks her mate rather than waiting for a male, testing each male she encounters by entering his territory and challenging him. Only if the male survives this vicious challenge does the mating proceed. Because the male molgrim is smaller and weaker than the female, only the strongest males battle their would-be mate to a draw and earn the right to pass on their fitness to a new generation. After mating, the male departs, never to return to the female except by chance. Within six months, the female gives birth to two or three cubs and protects them until they are weaned, a year later. Afterwards, the young molgrims must fend for themselves.

Molgrims are suitable, though strange, as animal companions.

Challenge: Novice (Fourth Circle)

DEX:	7	Initiative:	9	Unconsciousness:	50
STR:	10	Physical Defense:	11	Death Rating:	60
TOU:	10	Mystic Defense:	7	Wound Threshold:	15
PER:	4	Social Defense:	9	Knockdown:	14
WIL:	6	Physical Armor:	8	Recovery Tests:	3
CHA:	5	Mystic Armor:	3		

Movement: 16
Actions: 2; Bite: 12 (14); Claws x2: 12 (12)
Powers:
Climbing (9): As the skill, *Player's Guide*, p. 134.
Great Leap (8)
Resist Pain (2)
Willful (1)
Special Maneuvers:
Enrage (Opponent)
Pounce (Molgrim)
Provoke (Opponent, Close Combat)

Monkey

Monkeys are small arboreal primates who live in the forests and jungles of Barsaive. Many different species exist: baboons, macaques, and mandrills. These animals live in small tribes and are usually peaceful in nature.

Monkeys are suitable as animal companions.

Challenge: Novice (First Circle)

DEX:	7	Initiative:	7	Unconsciousness:	20
STR:	5	Physical Defense:	11	Death Rating:	25
TOU:	5	Mystic Defense:	7	Wound Threshold:	7
PER:	5	Social Defense:	8	Knockdown:	7
WIL:	4	Physical Armor:	1	Recovery Tests:	2
CHA:	5	Mystic Armor:	1		

Movement: 12 (Climb 12)
Actions: 1; Bite: 10 (10)
Powers:
Awareness (7): As the skill, *Player's Guide*, p. 129.
Enhanced Sense [Smell] (2)
Great Leap (8)
Surprise Strike (5): As the skill, *Player's Guide*, p. 172.

Naga

A naga has the body of a snake and the head of a human. The body is roughly the size of a rock python or a sea snake. Coin-sized scales cover it, their color changing to suit the place where the naga lies. As nagas live everywhere, from mountain peaks to misty swamps, differences in color can be huge. Most prefer bare earth and so are dusty brown in color.

A naga's head has the appearance of a human female in the prime of her life, beautiful in face but as bald as an egg. Her eyes are silver-colored, and fine scales cover her skin. Many males of the Namegiver races find nagas' faces irresistible. Even their two-inch fangs don't seem to detract from the nagas' beauty.

Nagas possess an innate magical ability to enthrall almost any male with a single glance. The victim of this power forgets the object of his obsession is a bizarre blend of human and snake. Used in combination with her ability to change the color of her scales to blend with her surroundings, she makes a formidable foe.

A camouflaged naga stealthily approaches her prospective victim, then reveals herself and entrances him in order to lead him to a secluded spot. Once she gets her victim alone, she compels him to lie down so she can feed. Luckily for most Namegivers, the naga has intelligence enough to have developed a conscience. Many nagas no longer kill other intelligent beings, preferring to kill and eat smaller prey like monkeys.

Nagas were not known before the Scourge. Some rumors claim Theran magicians created them as a way to weaken resistance to their rule. The ability of these creatures to thin out the ranks of any army, which might be raised against them, gives some weight to this idea. A few sages speculate the nagas are actually the creation of

Horrors, but their critics point out few if any Horror constructs demonstrate the kind of moral judgment present in the nagas.

Regardless of the truth behind their origin, the nagas have lived more or less peacefully, breeding and raising young (how is unknown, as they all appear to be of one sex) and creating homes in what might almost be called settlements. In general, the best way to avoid being slain by a naga is simply to leave her alone—or be female.

Challenge: Journeyman (Sixth Circle)

DEX:	8	Initiative:	12	Unconsciousness:	60
STR:	10	Physical Defense:	13	Death Rating:	70
TOU:	10	Mystic Defense:	12	Wound Threshold:	15
PER:	8	Social Defense:	15	Knockdown:	Immune
WIL:	8	Physical Armor:	5	Recovery Tests:	3
CHA:	10	Mystic Armor:	5		

Movement: 12
Actions: 2; Bite: 16 (14), Tail: 16 (10)
Powers:
Climbing (10): As the skill, *Player's Guide*, p. 134.
Constrict (10): Grappled opponents take Step 10 Damage each round as long as the grapple is held.
Entrancement (15): The naga can place the target in a peaceful trance. It locks eyes with the target and makes an Entrancement test as a Standard action against the target's Social Defense. If successful, the victim willingly follows the naga wherever it leads for one minute per success. The victim can break free of the effect by succeeding at a Willpower (12) test.
Stealthy Stride (14): As the skill, *Player's Guide*, p. 170.
Special Maneuvers:
Grab and Bite (Naga, Bite)
Pry Loose (Opponent, Close Combat)

Ogre

Ogres are large humanoids, standing between seven and eight feet tall on average, and weighing about 400 pounds. Orks claim they look like overgrown dwarfs, while dwarfs say they resemble large orks. A few have even drawn comparisons to short trolls without horns, but wisely do not do so in the presence of trolls.

Ogres have innate elemental earth magic, and have a strong desire for gold, silver, and other precious metals. They often dig crude mines in search of these materials and may trade for stronger armor and weapons. Ogres normally wield large clubs which they believe are magical weapons, but in truth the club's power comes from the ogre.

Ogres tend to gather in small groups in areas away from settled lands. They are most commonly found in rocky, mountainous areas, but can be found anywhere. While sentient, they are not considered true Namegivers. Most scholars dismiss reports of ogres displaying more advanced magic, though a few do entertain the idea ogres are capable of primitive shamanistic magic, similar to the Cathan tribes in the Servos Jungle.

Challenge: Novice (Fourth Circle)

DEX:	6	Initiative:	5	Unconsciousness:	50
STR:	11	Physical Defense:	10	Death Rating:	60
TOU:	10	Mystic Defense:	7	Wound Threshold:	15
PER:	4	Social Defense:	7	Knockdown:	13
WIL:	6	Physical Armor:	8	Recovery Tests:	3
CHA:	4	Mystic Armor:	3		

Movement: 12
Actions: 1; Club: 12 (21)
Powers:
Detect True Earth: Ogres can sense True Earth, as well as other precious metals and minerals. The ogre knows the location of the largest concentration of appropriate material within 1 mile.
Enhanced Sense [Smell] (2)
Harden Club (5): A club in the hands of an ogre is enhanced by its innate elemental magic, gaining a +5 bonus to damage. This effect fades if the club is out of the ogre's hands for more than one day.
Resist Pain (2)
Special Maneuvers:
Enrage (Opponent)
Provoke (Opponent, Close Combat)
Loot: Ogre club (Size 4, Damage Step 5), hide armor, D6×10 silver pieces.

Ogre Twins

Ogre twins are two identical ogres, only one of whom can inhabit the material plane at a time. The other inhabits a pocket dimension in astral space. Ogre twins are indistinguishable from their single counterparts, unless a character can sense connections between a twin and the astral plane. A character making a successful Astral Sight test against an ogre twin will see a pair of faint white lines trailing from the ogre's head into astral space.

Ogre twins can switch places with a thought. Their physical possessions stay on the material plane; the twin's body appears in the same place and position, even in mid-action. While in their astral pocket, the twin is capable of rapid healing. When a wounded ogre switches places with his unwounded twin, it can appear to outside observers as though wounds are healing instantly.

Like other ogres, ogre twins have innate elemental magic and an affinity for True Earth and other precious metals and minerals. The game statistics provided here are for one twin.

Challenge: Journeyman (Fifth Circle)

DEX:	7	Initiative:	6	Unconsciousness:	55
STR:	11	Physical Defense:	11	Death Rating:	65
TOU:	10	Mystic Defense:	10	Wound Threshold:	15
PER:	5	Social Defense:	9	Knockdown:	13
WIL:	7	Physical Armor:	9	Recovery Tests:	3
CHA:	5	Mystic Armor:	5		

Movement: 12
Actions: 1; Club 13 (21)
Powers:
Detect True Earth: Ogres can sense True Earth, as well as other precious metals and minerals. The ogre knows the location of the largest concentration of appropriate material within 1 mile.
Displace: An ogre can switch places with his twin at any time as a Free action. The magical connection between the two allows one to know what is happening with the other at all times. If one twin is killed, the other appears on the physical plane and attempts to avenge the twin's death.
Enhanced Sense [Smell] (2)
Harden Club (5): A club in the hands of an ogre is enhanced by its innate elemental magic, gaining a +5 bonus to damage. This effect fades if the club is out of the ogre's hands for more than one day.
Regeneration (11): When in its astral pocket, the ogre may make a Regeneration test as a Standard action, immediately healing that much damage. Each twin may use this ability a maximum of four times per day.
Resist Pain (2)

Special Maneuvers:
Enrage (Opponent)
Furious Focus (Opponent): An opponent may spend two additional success from an Attack test on an ogre twin currently under the effects of Enrage or Provoke to prevent them from using their Displace power until the end of the next turn. If the twin on the physical plane is killed, the other will immediately appear as normal.
Provoke (Opponent, Close Combat)

Loot: Ogre club (Size 4, Damage Step 5), hide armor, D6 x10 silver pieces and D4 small gems worth 50-75 silver pieces each.

Pangolus

Some sages claim the pangolus is the ancestor of all the Namegiver races. Others insist the pangolus is actually a degenerate form of Namegiver. The height of a dwarf, the pangolus has the slender body and limbs of a human or an elf. Compared to elves or humans, its arms are longer and its legs shorter in comparison to its height. It also has a useless stump of a tail. Its thin muscles are disproportionately strong, and an average pangolus weighs no more than eighty pounds. The creature's small head has a sharply sloping forehead, leaving relatively little space for a brain, and a pangolus has little more intelligence than a hunting dog.

Pangoli spend much of their time in the branches of large trees, climbing them by means of long hooked claws on their hands and feet. They also use their claws to tear open rotting trunks in search of their favorite food—grubs and other insects. Pangoli also eat tree rats and other small living creatures, as well as leaves and fruit. They stalk and frequently catch nesting birds, including other predators such as owls. On the ground, they dig up small burrowing creatures with their claws—they seem to like star moles and rock squirrels more than anything else. Sometimes they even feed on carrion.

The creatures are swift and dexterous in the treetops—they have no fear of falling and easily leap great distances from one tree to another. Few predators can match a pangolus for climbing speed. They are slow and clumsy on the ground, as their short legs and long arms slow them down to a waddling walk. Only by crouching can they move with any kind of stealth.

Male pangoli are highly territorial. Females are always welcome, but the arrival of another male in a pangolus' territory prompts a threatening display. The pangolus hangs from a large branch and gives a strange, piercing, hooting cry. If the rival does not give ground, the defender starts to charge. If the intruder refuses to flee, the charging pangolus pulls up and hoots again.

If the rival runs from the charge the defending pangolus pursues it and attacks, often killing the unfortunate beast. The only way for an intruder to safely back down from a challenge is to voice its own battle cry and then slowly and deliberately depart. Most challenges end this way, though a few lead to dreadful clawing duels ending only when one pangolus gives up or dies. The beasts cannot distinguish between Namegivers and their fellow pangoli, or between a male and a female Namegiver. Adventurers passing near pangolus territory had best be cautious.

Young pangoli can fend for themselves almost from birth, quite unlike the younglings of Namegiver races. The mother pangolus protects and helps feed her young for almost a year, but the father has nothing to do with mother or offspring after mating.

Challenge: Novice (Third Circle)

DEX:	8	**Initiative:**	9	**Unconsciousness:**	27
STR:	7	**Physical Defense:**	12	**Death Rating:**	31
TOU:	4	**Mystic Defense:**	10	**Wound Threshold:**	6
PER:	4	**Social Defense:**	8	**Knockdown:**	9
WIL:	6	**Physical Armor:**	4	**Recovery Tests:**	1
CHA:	4	**Mystic Armor:**	3		

Movement: 12 (Climb 12)
Actions: 2; Claws: 12 (10)
Powers:
Battle Shout (12): As the skill, *Player's Guide*, p. 131.
Great Leap (10)
Special Maneuvers:
Pry Loose (Opponent, Close Combat)
Squeeze the Life (Pangolus)
Loot: A collection of various shiny objects, worth about 10–15 silver pieces.

Preces

The preces has many different Names. The Name "preces" was bestowed on this creature by the Therans centuries before the Scourge, and the folk of Barsaive's southern regions still call it this. Further north, local people call it "supplicant," to the east, it is called "prayer rabbit," and the few folk along the borders of the Wastes call it "grassfang." To most people, the preces is a legendary beast; few Barsaivians have ever seen a living preces, let alone studied it. Until the past several years, the creature has been rarely encountered outside the Wastes.

The preces is about the size and shape of a large hare, some two feet long. When it sits on its haunches to observe its surroundings, the top of its head reaches as high as a troll's knee. Its fur ranges in color from pale yellow to a rich chestnut brown. While a preces looks and acts much like a rabbit, closer examination reveals the differences. A rabbit's teeth are all the square shape needed to crop and chew grass, whereas a preces also has a set of sharp incisors and eyeteeth. When extended, these fangs show their tips below the creature's lips.

The beast's forelegs are also unusual, longer than its hind legs when fully extended. These legs are usually bent, like a Namegiver holding his arms bent at the elbow, palms together so his fingers are in front of his face as if in prayer. The preces holds its forelimbs in a similar pose, its "elbows" bent so its "forearms" and "upper arms" are close together. When the creature moves its elbows, not its front paws, touch the ground.

Some folk hunt preces for food and for their soft pelts, but the swift-moving creatures have an uncanny ability to sense approaching danger. Often, they dash to the safety of their burrows before their would-be hunters even see them.

Most of the year, the preces is as placid and calm as the rabbit it resembles. It lives peacefully in groups of up to twenty, grazing on wildflowers and fleeing from the smallest threat. For a single month, however, as the days shorten and the harvest approaches, the preces enters its mating season and becomes a crazed carnivore. Males and females both refuse grass and flowers in favor of warm bleeding flesh, and the males battle each other ferociously as the females look on. They tear each other to shreds, continuing to fight long after any other creature would have collapsed from shock, pain, and blood loss.

A preces in the grip of mating frenzy will attack anything it sees regardless of size. A preces attacks with blinding swiftness, flinging itself at its target and extending its forelimbs to catch its prey in a deadly grip. The beast is far stronger than a creature its size would appear, and its small furry feet are tipped with needle-sharp, hooked claws. On the insides of its forearms, usually hidden by its soft pelt, are half a dozen barbs, all tipped with a terrible poison. A single preces in heat can badly maul or kill an unwary Namegiver, except possibly a troll or obsidiman. Though male preces in a frenzy hunt alone, females often hunt in groups of six or more.

Preces are suitable as animal companions.

Challenge: Novice (Second Circle)

DEX:	8	**Initiative:**	9	**Unconsciousness:**	22
STR:	4	**Physical Defense:**	12	**Death Rating:**	26
TOU:	4	**Mystic Defense:**	7	**Wound Threshold:**	6
PER:	4	**Social Defense:**	6	**Knockdown:**	6
WIL:	5	**Physical Armor:**	1	**Recovery Tests:**	1
CHA:	3	**Mystic Armor:**	1		

Movement: 18
Actions: 2; Bite: 12 (8), Barbs x2: 12 (7, Poison)
Powers:
Enhanced Sense [Hearing] (2)
Enhanced Sense [Smell] (2)
Poison (8): A victim hit by the barbs on the inside of a preces' forearms is exposed to the damaging poison. The poison is Step 8 [Onset: 1 round, Interval: 5/1 round]. The pain caused by the poison also applies a -1 penalty to the victim's tests.
Great Leap (6)
Special Maneuvers:
Defang (Opponent)

Prisma

Of all the flying creatures native to Barsaive, the prisma is one of the most beautiful. Its four colorful wings reflect and refract the sunlight, breaking it into ever-shifting rainbows and spears of multicolored light. Despite its resemblance to a dragonfly, the prisma is a warm-blooded creature with a skeleton rather than a carapace. Its body is about forty feet long and its wingspan almost fifty feet. Each of its four legs ends in a single curved claw the length of a human's forearm. They have eight eyes spaced evenly around a spherical head, giving them an incredible field of vision. They feed through a beak set in the underside of their body, hunting smaller flying creatures as prey. Given their size, smaller includes anything up to a large eagle.

The prisma is a fast and maneuverable flyer. It loves the thin, cold air hundreds or even thousands of feet above ice capped mountains. Adult prisma rarely descend nearer to the ground than four or five thousand feet, finding the thicker and more humid air distasteful. Indeed, a prisma rarely sets foot on the ground, and then only on the highest and most isolated peaks. As a result, few have seen an adult prisma up close.

Prisma live short lives, four or five years at the most. Soon after maturity, adults mate and the female gives birth to a clutch of five or six live offspring, which the mother deposits in the rugged ground of a high mountain pass. These larval prisma are about the size of a large cat, and bear little resemblance to their adult form. Slimy black skin covers their broad, flat bodies, four legs end in sharp claws, and the mouth on the underside sports a pair of large fangs resembling an insect's mandibles. The young are aggressive hunters; easily capable of killing adult mountain sheep or any other unfortunate living things they come across. Feeding voraciously, they triple in size in a month, and after a year are fifteen feet in length.

After another year or two of feeding, the young find a large cave, preferring one with a bear or similar inhabitant to provide a last snack before settling down for sleep. The young prisma hibernates for six months or so and undergoes a dramatic change. When it awakes it possesses its adult form and takes to the air.

The following game statistics are for an adult and a larval prisma.

Adult

Challenge: Journeyman (Fifth Circle)

DEX:	7	**Initiative:**	11	**Unconsciousness:**	52
STR:	9	**Physical Defense:**	15	**Death Rating:**	61
TOU:	9	**Mystic Defense:**	11	**Wound Threshold:**	13
PER:	3	**Social Defense:**	10	**Knockdown:**	9
WIL:	6	**Physical Armor:**	8	**Recovery Tests:**	3
CHA:	6	**Mystic Armor:**	3		

Movement: 8 (Flying 16)
Actions: 2; Bite: 16 (17), Claws: x4 16 (15)
Powers:
Enhanced Sense [Sight] (2)
Special Maneuvers:
Clip the Wing (Opponent)
Loot: Wings worth 2,000 silver pieces, or 5,000 silver pieces if retrieved immediately after death (worth Legend Points).

Larva
Challenge: Novice (First Circle)

DEX:	7	Initiative:	7	Unconsciousness:	14
STR:	3	Physical Defense:	9	Death Rating:	17
TOU:	3	Mystic Defense:	7	Wound Threshold:	4
PER:	3	Social Defense:	6	Knockdown:	Immune
WIL:	6	Physical Armor:	5	Recovery Tests:	1
CHA:	6	Mystic Armor:	3		

Movement: 10
Actions: 1; Bite: 12 (8)
Powers:
Enhanced Sense [Sight] (2)

Rat, Leech

The leech rat looks like an ordinary rat, except it has six legs and a much shorter tail. Most have brown fur, but black and white ones have been reported. The leech rat has especially long claws for its size, perfect for climbing, and a somewhat larger mouth than one might expect. At the base of its tail lie two scent glands, which it uses to control larger animals.

The first gland produces a soothing scent pacifying the creature chosen by the leech rat as its mount. The leech rat climbs on the somnolent creature's back, sits on its shoulder, and grips firmly with its claws. Small glands just above each of the claws produce a mild painkiller so the host creature does not feel its rider and attempt to throw off the rat.

The second scent gland sends the leech rat's mount into a frenzy, during which it tries to kill anything in its path. When a creature is under the influence of this scent, killing it is often the only way to stop it. Once the mount has slain every potential predator in sight (or they have all sensibly fled), the leech rat once more exudes the soothing scent to calm the mount. Then it carefully climbs down and feasts on the carcasses of the slain.

To ensure an ample food supply—and to protect themselves from predators with a taste for rats—the leech rat chooses its mount for strength and ferocity. If a mounted leech rat encounters a creature stronger than the one it is riding, it sprays its soothing scent in the air in hopes of ensnaring the other creature and changing mounts. It does not limit itself to dumb beasts, either; there are many tales of powerful Warriors acquiring a leech rat before battling some fierce creature.

Magicians and alchemists will pay a high price for the rat's scent glands, and healers prize the tranquilizing effects the glands can induce. Getting the glands is a risky proposition, as the leech rat may be riding anything from a lion to a brithan to a chimera, and so an adventurer in search of one must defend against all the powers of the leech rat's host creature. When removing the glands from a dead rat, a character must handle them with great care, otherwise the glands will burst and spray their contents all over the place, paralyzing those nearby or driving them into a killing madness.

Challenge: Novice (First Circle)

DEX:	6	Initiative:	7	Unconsciousness:	8
STR:	1	Physical Defense:	10	Death Rating:	9
TOU:	1	Mystic Defense:	8	Wound Threshold:	3
PER:	4	Social Defense:	6	Knockdown:	5
WIL:	6	Physical Armor:	0	Recovery Tests:	1
CHA:	6	Mystic Armor:	3		

Movement: 6
Actions: 1; Bite: 9 (5); Claws: 9 (4)
Powers:
Awareness (6): As the skill, *Player's Guide*, p. 129.
Climbing (8): As the skill, *Player's Guide*, p. 134.
Enhanced Sense [Smell] (2)
Enraging Scent (12): The leech rat drives its host into a killing rage. As a Standard action, it makes an Enraging Scent test against the target's Mystic Defense. If successful, the victim is driven into a killing rage for one round per success. The target immediately attacks the closest living creature, friend or foe. The effect can be shaken off if the victim succeeds at a Willpower (12) test. During this time, the victim must use the Aggressive Attack combat option, but it costs no strain, and gains Resist Pain 2.
Hard to Hit: Hitting a leech rat riding a host requires a Called Shot (*Player's Guide*, p. 384).
Pacify (12): The rat attempts to pacify a victim. As a Standard action, it makes a Pacify test against the target's Mystic Defense. If successful, the victim is pacified for one minute per success, allowing the rat to climb onto the chosen host. The effect can be shaken off if the victim succeeds at a Willpower (12) test.
Loot: Scent glands worth 200 silver pieces each (worth Legend Points).

Relan

The parasite called the relan is incredibly dangerous, simply because it often hides inside a familiar and harmless being. The relan cannot eat on its own, but must use the digestive tract of a larger, more complex creature to process food. It accomplishes this by burrowing into a deceased creature and reanimating it. Therefore, any creature—or Namegiver—may be controlled by a relan (especially if the person or creature in question may have died recently).

As long as the relan is concerned only with making its host eat, there is little danger to fear from it, but if confronted, the host may become a powerful threat. A relan can send powerful venom through the host body causing irreparable damage, but until then gives the host immense strength and endurance. The relan then uses its host to fight its opponent or else makes the body flee to wherever the beast can find a new host.

In appearance, the relan is a squat worm, rarely growing longer than twelve inches. Six small black eyes and other sense organs dot its tiny head. Each of its six legs ends in small, sharp claws used by the relan to burrow into its host. On its underside is a small, thin tube which it extends into its host's intestines. The relan nestles at the base of the corpse's spine, from which it can control all parts of the body. Using its magic, it reanimates the corpse enough to get it moving, and sends the dead thing in search of food.

As the animated corpse eats, the relan siphons off what it wishes through its feeding tube. In choosing its host, the relan prefers as recent a death as possible and an intact body, so the reanimated host will be in fine working order. A powerful physique is an advantage, so the worm will not be forced to change hosts too often. If a relan must change hosts, it can survive on its own internal stores of food for about a week. Afterwards, the creature begins to starve. Before the Scourge, relans mostly used to haunt battlefields, where an endless supply of food lay on the ground for their taking, but they can be found anywhere they might be able to secure a host.

The relan as a species has developed some skill at controlling their hosts. In the past they could only use their hosts for the rudimentary task of eating. Over time, the creatures learned to make the host body walk, run, and perform more complicated physical acts. It even learned to slow down—perhaps even to halt—the decomposition of dead flesh. With these abilities, relans can almost blend in with society. The flaw that gives away the presence of a relan is difficulty speaking, and poor understanding of Namegiver culture, standing out as unusual behavior.

There are legends of a distant land where the inhabitants see relans as the Passions in physical form. They leave their dead where relans can easily find them, and even breed the creatures. They believe if they can't bring their loved ones back from the grave, the walking corpse is an acceptable substitute.

A relan is not capable of attacking on its own; it relies on its host. The game statistics provided here are for the creature if it is caught outside a host. Otherwise, use the appropriate physical game statistics based on the host.

Challenge: Novice (First Circle)

DEX:	4	Initiative:	4	Unconsciousness:	8
STR:	1	Physical Defense:	6	Death Rating:	9
TOU:	1	Mystic Defense:	12	Wound Threshold:	3
PER:	8	Social Defense:	8	Knockdown:	5
WIL:	8	Physical Armor:	0	Recovery Tests:	1
CHA:	3	Mystic Armor:	4		

Movement: 6
Actions: 1; Claws: 6 (4), as host
Powers:

Control Corpse: The relan can animate the corpse of a dead creature or Namegiver, though the power only works on those dead less than two days. While the relan is able to slow decomposition, it cannot hold it off entirely, and the corpse becomes useless after about 4 weeks. While it is in possession of a body, substitute the hosts' physical statistics for the relan's. Any damage done to the host in combat does not carry over to the relan. If possessing a Namegiver, observers may make an Awareness test against the relan's Social Defense to notice something is wrong. The observer must achieve a number of successes based on how well they knew the individual in life. A casual acquaintance might need three successes, while a close friend or family member might only need one.

Corpse Venom: The relan can flood the host body with a concoction providing great strength and stamina. This power increases the host's Strength and Toughness Steps by +8 (including appropriate Damage Steps), and adds +20 to the host's Death Rating. Unfortunately, the venom takes a severe toll, causing the body to decompose within two hours, forcing the relan to find a new body.

Enhanced Sense [Sight] (2)
Enhanced Sense [Smell] (2)
Loot: Host's possessions, if any.

Rhinoceros

The rhinoceros is a large, thick-skinned mammal bearing up to two horns on its snout. They live on the plains, feeding on tall grasses and plants. Rhinos are known for their bad tempers and will typically charge intruders if they get too close, attempting to gore their foes on their horns. Typically, a rhinoceros directs its first attack at the nearest character or animal posing a threat.

Rhinoceroses are suitable as mounts for dwarfs, elves, humans, orks, t'skrang, and trolls, and as animal companions.

Challenge: Novice (Fourth Circle)

DEX:	5	Initiative:	5	Unconsciousness:	53
STR:	11	Physical Defense:	7	Death Rating:	64
TOU:	11	Mystic Defense:	7	Wound Threshold:	16
PER:	4	Social Defense:	10	Knockdown:	15
WIL:	6	Physical Armor:	7	Recovery Tests:	4
CHA:	4	Mystic Armor:	4		

Movement: 16
Actions: 1; Horn: 12 (20), Trample: 12 (18)
Powers:
Charge (5)
Enhanced Sense [Hearing] (2)
Enhanced Sense [Smell] (2)
Resist Pain (2)
Willful (1)
Special Maneuvers:
Overrun (Rhinoceros, Trample)
Provoke (Opponent, Close Combat)

Rockworm

These elemental creatures resemble giant worms ten to fifteen feet long, covered with a rocky hide of overlapping plates. They burrow through the hardest rock and stone like dirt, consuming elemental earth and other minerals to sustain themselves. Though mindless, they are fiercely territorial and will attack any other creature intruding on their territory; miners and prospectors are among their most numerous victims.

Though prospecting around rockworm territory is often dangerous, it can be profitable as well, as the worms tend to lair in areas with high concentrations of elemental earth. Such concentrations usually indicate nearby veins of living crystal or orichalcum, which can net a lucky prospector even more money. Some prospectors and miners follow the signs of rockworm tunnels to find these rich deposits, keeping close watch for an attack by the worms.

A rock worm typically attacks by bursting out from under the ground without warning, biting at the target with its large maw. Its jaws are lined with jagged pieces of crystal and can cause serious damage. Its tough, stony hide makes it difficult to hurt. If seriously wounded, rockworms retreat by burrowing back under ground.

Challenge: Journeyman (Sixth Circle)

DEX:	7	**Initiative:**	7	**Unconsciousness:**	63
STR:	11	**Physical Defense:**	11	**Death Rating:**	74
TOU:	11	**Mystic Defense:**	12	**Wound Threshold:**	16
PER:	5	**Social Defense:**	11	**Knockdown:**	Immune
WIL:	8	**Physical Armor:**	10	**Recovery Tests:**	4
CHA:	6	**Mystic Armor:**	6		

Movement: 10 (Burrow 10)
Actions: 2; Bite: 15 (20), Slam: 15 (20)
Powers:
Ambush (10)
Awareness (10): As the skill, *Player's Guide*, p. 129.
Enhanced Sense [Touch] (4): The rockworm may make Awareness tests against anything touching the ground within 100 yards.
Hardened Armor

Resist Pain (2)
Stealthy Stride (11): As the skill, *Player's Guide*, p. 170.
Special Maneuvers:
Crack the Shell (Opponent)
Provoke (Opponent, Close Combat)
Loot: Gems and crystals worth 5D6×10 silver pieces (worth Legend Points).

Rockworm, Greater

These elemental creatures are a larger version of normal rockworms, but are twenty five feet or more in length, covered with a rocky hide of overlapping plates, embedded with shards of living crystal. The creatures are so large they are unable to sneak up on victims the way their smaller brethren do, but as they burrow through the earth, the friction causes significant heat to build up on their hide.

Challenge: Journeyman (Eighth Circle)

DEX:	5	**Initiative:**	5	**Unconsciousness:**	100
STR:	20	**Physical Defense:**	11	**Death Rating:**	120
TOU:	20	**Mystic Defense:**	12	**Wound Threshold:**	30
PER:	5	**Social Defense:**	11	**Knockdown:**	Immune
WIL:	8	**Physical Armor:**	18	**Recovery Tests:**	4
CHA:	6	**Mystic Armor:**	10		

Movement: 14 (Burrow 14)
Actions: 2; Bite: 18 (25), Slam: 18 (25)
Powers:
Awareness (10): As the skill, *Player's Guide*, p. 129.
Burning Aura (10): The greater rockworm radiates heat. All creatures within 6 yards suffer Step 10 fire damage. Physical armor protects against this damage. Clothing, paper, and other easily flammable objects usually burst into flame when exposed to this power.
Enhanced Sense [Touch] (4): The greater rockworm may make Awareness tests against anything touching the ground within 100 yards.
Hardened Armor
Resist Pain (2)
Special Maneuvers:
Crack the Shell (Opponent)
Provoke (Opponent, Close Combat)
Loot: Gems and crystals worth 5D6×25 silver pieces, Living Crystal worth 5d10x50 silver pieces, additional to 2d6 kernels of elemental earth (worth Legend Points).

Sand Lobster

Sand lobsters like to bury themselves in the sandy banks of the lower Coil River and wait for approaching prey. When a creature or Namegiver walks above a sand lobster, the animal springs out of the ground and grabs at its victim with its claws. Most varieties of sand lobster are small, and their claws inflict no more than painful pinches.

The meat of these smaller specimens is a prized delicacy in Urupa and increasingly popular elsewhere along the river. However, those seeking to cash in on this growing food craze should keep in mind some sand lobster varieties grow to the size of a horse and possess enough strength to crush a troll. The statistics provided here are for a larger specimen.

Sand lobsters are suitable as animal companions.

Challenge: Journeyman (Sixth Circle)

DEX:	7	Initiative:	7	Unconsciousness:	72
STR:	14	Physical Defense:	10	Death Rating:	86
TOU:	14	Mystic Defense:	11	Wound Threshold:	21
PER:	4	Social Defense:	10	Knockdown:	20
WIL:	7	Physical Armor:	16	Recovery Tests:	5
CHA:	3	Mystic Armor:	9		

Movement: 12 (Burrow 8)
Actions: 2; Pincers x2: 14 (16)
Powers:
Ambush (10)
Hardened Armor
Stealthy Stride (11): As the skill, *Player's Guide*, p. 170.
Special Maneuvers:
Crack the Shell (Opponent)

Saural

The saural is a strange creature, resembling a cross between a frog and lizard. Grayish-green and about four feet long, the saural has gills at the base of its thick neck allowing it to breathe in the water as well as on land. Thick, armor-like scales protect it against most natural predators. Its most powerful defense is the burning acid covering its entire body. While the acid looks like sticky slime at a distance, it is not so harmless.

Whatever surface the saural sits on, a cloud of steam rises around it as its natural acid eats through whatever it touches. Often, a saural will spend so much time on a rock its acid eats all the way through. The melted rocks look as if they were as soft as river clay and some huge artist's hand pushed the saurals into the rock to form the impressions.

Obviously, touching a saural is a foolish act, but would-be heroes can come into contact with the acid through no fault of their own. The creature can spit acid more than thirty feet. By instinct, it aims for the eyes whenever it can. If they are lucky, the victim of such an attack is only blinded for life, though strong healing magic can restore the mess that was once his eyes. If the victim is unlucky, the acid eats through the front of his skull, dissolving his brain within minutes. Fortunately, drawing a pair of large and menacing eyes on some other surface or object can fool the saural. The saural will instinctively aim its caustic spit at those eyes instead of yours.

Scholars have questioned why saurals don't melt themselves with their slime. The beast appears to have a protective layer of liquid underneath the acid that neutralizes the burning effect. This also allows saurals to mate; both males and females exude the protective substance so they do not harm each other. An infant saural exudes no acid at all, lest it burn itself out of its eggshell prematurely. When it grows large enough to fend for itself it develops the necessary organs to produce the acidic slime.

The organs that produce the acid and its antidote are in high demand from alchemists and adventurers. Alchemists find the acid extremely useful in their experiments, and adventurers use the antidote to protect themselves against all manner of irritants. Some adventurers also carry samples of the acid in magically treated glass vials in order to melt away locks or similar hindrances. This carries some risk if the vial breaks.

Saurals are suitable, if exceptionally dangerous, as animal companions.

Challenge: Journeyman (Sixth Circle)

DEX:	7	Initiative:	9	Unconsciousness:	48
STR:	6	Physical Defense:	13	Death Rating:	54
TOU:	6	Mystic Defense:	10	Wound Threshold:	9
PER:	5	Social Defense:	10	Knockdown:	10
WIL:	6	Physical Armor:	8	Recovery Tests:	2
CHA:	6	Mystic Armor:	5		

Movement: 10 (Swimming 10)
Actions: 2; Bite: 14 (14)
Powers:
Acid Armor (16): Adult saurals constantly drip acid. Anyone who touches the creature takes Step 16 Damage from acid burns. The acid damages inanimate objects as well.
Acid Breath (19): The saural can spit its acid at targets within 12 yards. It makes a Creature Power test against the target's Mystic Defense. If successful, the target takes Step 19 Damage. The acid does damage for four rounds, though the Damage Step is reduced by one each subsequent round.
Aquatic: Saurals can breathe underwater
Creature Power (16, Acid Breath, Standard)
Destroy Armor: Physical Armor protects against the saural's acid damage, but is damaged in return. Each time the armor reduces damage from saural acid, its Physical Armor is reduced by 1 until repaired (*Player's Guide*, p. 415). Living crystal, blood pebble, and other forms of crystal armor are immune to the acid damage. If the Physical Armor is reduced to 0, the armor is destroyed. Thread items are never destroyed by this effect.
Special Maneuvers:
Block the Stream (Opponent): The attacker may use two additional successes to attack the saural's acid producing gland in its mouth. This prevents it from using its Acid Breath power until the end of the next round. Each additional success used in this fashion extends the duration by one round.
Go For the Eyes! (Saural, Creature Power): The saural may spend two additional successes from a Creature Power test to spit acid in the target's eyes. The target is blinded until the end of the next round. If the damage causes a Wound, the target is blinded until the Wound is healed.

Precise Strike (Opponent): The attacker may use two additional successes to prevent being affected by acid due to their attack, despite coming into contact with the saural.
Loot: Acid-creating and acid-neutralizing organs worth 200 silver pieces each (worth Legend Points).

Shadowmant

Shadowmants resemble flying stingrays with an eight-foot wingspan and five foot long tail. The creature is black with a dark grey underside, and its tail ends in a crystalline stinger. It has two eyes on its front edge, and a small mouth lined with rows of tiny, needle-sharp teeth is on its underside. Shadowmants are nocturnal creatures, spending daylight hours underground.

Shadowmants attack by stinging their prey with their tail. The stinger contains venom strong enough to kill a troll in a few moments. Once the victim is dead, the shadowmant feeds. Alchemists prize shadowmant stingers, using them to brew magical potions.

Challenge: Journeyman (Fifth Circle)

DEX:	6	**Initiative:**	10	**Unconsciousness:**	43
STR:	5	**Physical Defense:**	11	**Death Rating:**	49
TOU:	6	**Mystic Defense:**	13	**Wound Threshold:**	9
PER:	7	**Social Defense:**	11	**Knockdown:**	5
WIL:	6	**Physical Armor:**	4	**Recovery Tests:**	2
CHA:	6	**Mystic Armor:**	6		

Movement: 4 (Flying 16)
Actions: 2; Bite: 15 (13), Stinger: 15 (15)
Powers:
Ambush (10)
Enhanced Sense [Sight]: Low-Light Vision
Willful (2)
Poison (10): If the shadowmant causes damage with its stinger, the victim must resist the effects of a damaging poison (see **Poison**, p. 171). The poison is Step 10 [Onset: Instant, Interval: 10/1 round].
Stealthy Stride (18): As the skill, *Player's Guide*, p. 170.
Special Maneuvers:
Defang (Opponent)
Poison Stinger (Shadowmant, Stinger): The shadowmant may spend an additional success from an Attack test to inflict Poison on the target.
Loot: Stinger worth D10×10 silver pieces (worth Legend Points).

Skeorx

The skeorx is one of the most brutal and dangerous beasts in Barsaive. A skeorx is a four-legged creature with a tiger-like head, commonly eight feet long from snout to tail, but some grow as long as fifteen feet. Their bodies are covered with short fur of a drab, brownish-green shade that blends well with the dark jungle undergrowth.

On each of the skeorx's feet are huge claws and it has a snakelike tail from which row upon row of razor-sharp bones extend. When fighting smaller creatures, the skeorx rarely brings its tail into play; however, when attacking creatures larger than itself, it attempts to wrap the tail around its opponent's neck. Such a grip gives the skeorx a stable position from which to rake its claws across its enemy's flesh—and if the victim attempts to shake the skeorx free, it will cut its own throat. The skeorx is always ravenous, almost always feeding. If it is not hunched over a fresh kill, gorging noisily, it is hunting for something else to kill.

No one should ever go near a mother skeorx and her young. A mother skeorx will so eagerly charge forward to destroy any threat to her babes she often tramples the infants themselves without noticing. The young have developed an interesting habit to ensure their survival—if they spy a creature which the mother might see as a threat to them, they dash away in a direction perpendicular to the creature in question. If they cannot dodge their mother's charge, the young skeorxes flatten themselves to the ground in the hope their mother will miss them.

There are rumors skeorxes can even resist the magical abilities of Beastmasters. Explorers with such abilities should therefore be wary—their talents will probably not save them from this ravening beast.

Skeorx are suitable as animal companions.

Challenge: Journeyman (Seventh Circle)

DEX:	13	**Initiative:**	20	**Unconsciousness:**	59
STR:	13	**Physical Defense:**	16	**Death Rating:**	67
TOU:	8	**Mystic Defense:**	13	**Wound Threshold:**	12
PER:	8	**Social Defense:**	12	**Knockdown:**	17
WIL:	8	**Physical Armor:**	7	**Recovery Tests:**	3
CHA:	6	**Mystic Armor:**	4		

Movement: 20
Actions: 3; Bite: 20 (21), Claws: x2: 21 (20), Tail: 20 (19)
Powers:
Ambush (10)
Battle Shout (15): As the skill, *Player's Guide*, p. 131.
Climbing (17): As the skill, *Player's Guide*, p. 134.
Enhanced Sense [Hearing] (4)
Enhanced Sense [Sight]: Low-Light Vision
Great Leap (16)
Willful (2)
Stealthy Stride (21): As the skill, *Player's Guide*, p. 170.
Special Maneuvers:
Enrage (Opponent)
Jagged Tail (Skeorx, Tail): The skeorx may use two additional successes on an Attack test to automatically grapple the target. Tail damage may be dealt automatically each subsequent round to the target. Any attempts by the victim to break free cause Step 10 damage. Physical Armor protects against this damage, as normal.
Pounce (Skeorx, Bite or Claw attacks only)

Provoke (Opponent, Close Combat)
Pry Loose (Opponent, Close Combat)

Snake

Snakes are reptiles found in many different environments in Barsaive, from grasslands to jungles. Some are venomous, while other constrict their prey. In addition to varieties similar to cobras, asps, and anacondas, more exotic and magical varieties can be found in Barsaive.

Porcupine Snake

These enormous snakes can grow up to sixty feet long and more than a foot in diameter. They are thick-bodied, weighing several hundred pounds. They are semi-aquatic and feed primarily on fish, turtles, beavers and other snakes, but will gladly eat pigs, chickens, and anything up to human size. They are a muddy brown-green with intricate black swirled markings on their backs and yellow undersides.

Porcupine snakes are normally lazy and good-natured (for snakes), allowing curious onlookers within about ten feet before they strike a defensive and threatening posture of puffing up their bodies and hissing. This defensive posture reveals how the snake got its name; three-inch long quills emerge from beneath its scales.

They feed at relatively long intervals and are only dangerous when actively threatened or very hungry. The snake is a constrictor, wrapping around its prey and crushing it to death. The quills dig into the victim, causing additional damage and making it hard to escape the snake's grasp. The quills are often used to fashion darts for blowguns.

Porcupine snakes are suitable as animal companions.

Challenge: Novice (Fourth Circle)

DEX:	7	**Initiative:**	8	**Unconsciousness:**	47
STR:	9	**Physical Defense:**	11	**Death Rating:**	56
TOU:	9	**Mystic Defense:**	6	**Wound Threshold:**	13
PER:	3	**Social Defense:**	9	**Knockdown:**	Immune
WIL:	6	**Physical Armor:**	5	**Recovery Tests:**	3
CHA:	4	**Mystic Armor:**	3		

Movement: 8 (Swim 12)
Actions: 1; Bite: 13 (13), Tail: 9 (13)
Powers:
Climbing (9): As the skill, *Player's Guide*, p. 134.
Constrict (10): Grappled opponents take Step 10 Damage each round as long as the grapple is held.
Enhanced Sense [Sight]: Heat Sight
Enhanced Sense [Smell] (4)
Enhanced Sense [Taste] (4)
Quills: If injured or frightened, the porcupine snake may inflate its body, exposing its quills. This increases the damage from Constrict to Step 25.

Semi-Aquatic: The porcupine snake can hold its breath for 30 minutes before drowning.
Stealthy Stride (7): As the skill, *Player's Guide*, p. 170.
Special Maneuvers:
Bite and Hold (Porcupine Snake, Bite): The porcupine snake may spend an additional success from an Attack test to automatically grapple an opponent. Grappled opponents automatically take bite damage each round.
Pry Loose (Opponent, Close Combat)
Loot: Quills worth 100 silver pieces (worth Legend Points).

Sea Snake

A sea snake is often as long as 10 feet, covered in luminescent blue-green scales that glimmer like jewels in the sun. Its jaws can unhinge to swallow prey much larger than the width of its head. Just behind its jaws lie the sea snake's gills, with which it breathes water as easily as air. The beast can flatten its body and race through water at incredible speeds. When the creature leaves the water, it resumes a rounder shape and slithers up onto the land. Unlike other serpents, the sea snake is warm-blooded.

Sea snakes can eat anything. Though it prefers red meat, this beast will feed on rodents, birds, mollusks, fruit, or tree bark. Some believe it will eat anything it can get its mouth around if it's hungry enough. Sea snakes are vicious, often taking on creatures much larger than themselves. In the water, the sea snake out-swims its prey and then swallows as much of it whole as possible. It will sometimes leap out of the water and knock its victim under the surface, where it can easily swallow its catch. It has even been known to knock sailors overboard this way.

Sea snakes are suitable as animal companions.

Challenge: Novice (Second Circle)

DEX:	8	Initiative:	8	Unconsciousness:	22
STR:	6	Physical Defense:	11	Death Rating:	26
TOU:	4	Mystic Defense:	7	Wound Threshold:	6
PER:	4	Social Defense:	8	Knockdown:	Immune
WIL:	6	Physical Armor:	3	Recovery Tests:	1
CHA:	4	Mystic Armor:	2		

Movement: 6 (Swim 12)
Actions: 1; Bite: 12 (12)
Powers:
Climbing (10): As the skill *Player's Guide*, p. 134.
Enhanced Sense [Sight]: Heat Sight
Enhanced Sense [Smell] (4)
Enhanced Sense [Taste] (4)
Special Maneuvers:
Grab and Bite (Sea Snake)
Pry Loose (Opponent, Close Combat)

Troll Snake

This massive snake is a non-venomous constrictor, with a heavily ridged head, resembling troll horns. These creatures are found in the Twilight Peaks of Barsaive. After biting, it attempts to wrap around the victim and squeeze.

Troll snakes are suitable as animal companions.

Challenge: Journeyman (Fifth Circle)

DEX:	6	Initiative:	6	Unconsciousness:	55
STR:	10	Physical Defense:	13	Death Rating:	65
TOU:	10	Mystic Defense:	9	Wound Threshold:	15
PER:	5	Social Defense:	11	Knockdown:	Immune
WIL:	6	Physical Armor:	8	Recovery Tests:	3
CHA:	4	Mystic Armor:	4		

Movement: 6
Actions: 1; Bite: 16 (19)
Powers:
Climbing (8): As the skill, *Player's Guide*, p. 134.
Constrict (15): Grappled opponents take Step 15 Damage each round as long as the grapple is held.
Enhanced Sense [Sight]: Heat Sight
Enhanced Sense [Smell] (4)
Enhanced Sense [Taste] (4)
Stealthy Stride (8): As the skill, *Player's Guide*, p. 170.
Special Maneuvers:
Grab and Bite (Troll Snake)
Pry Loose (Opponent, Close Combat)

Venomous Snake

This represents venomous species, such as asps, black adders, cobras, and the like. They are found all over Barsaive, but most of them live in forests and jungles.

Snakes are extremely variable in appearance, size, and lethality. Some species will have a higher Dexterity Step, others may be more venomous, or may be semi-aquatic. The statistics provided here are for an arboreal, venomous variety.

Snakes are suitable as animal companions.

Challenge: Novice (First Circle)

DEX:	6	Initiative:	8	Unconsciousness:	14
STR:	3	Physical Defense:	9	Death Rating:	17
TOU:	3	Mystic Defense:	6	Wound Threshold:	4
PER:	4	Social Defense:	6	Knockdown:	Immune
WIL:	5	Physical Armor:	1	Recovery Tests:	1
CHA:	4	Mystic Armor:	1		

Movement: 6
Actions: 1; Bite: 10 (7, Poison)
Powers:
Awareness (7): As the skill, *Player's Guide*, p. 129.
Climbing (8): As the skill, *Player's Guide*, p. 134.
Enhanced Sense [Sight]: Heat Sight
Enhanced Sense [Smell] (2)
Enhanced Sense [Taste] (2)
Poison (6): If a snake's bite causes damage, the victim must resist a damaging poison (see **Poison**, p. 171). The poison is Step 6 [Onset: 1 round, Interval : 5/1 round].
Stealthy Stride (8): As the skill, *Player's Guide*, p. 170.

Snow Badger

The snow badger can only be found in Barsaive's tallest mountains, where snow falls deep and lingers throughout the year. Long ago, when large portions of Barsaive lay under a white blanket for months at a time, snow badgers were numerous and fat. With a temperate climate and growing warmer, many believe before long the snow badger may disappear altogether.

The snow badger resembles its mundane brethren, though it is somewhat larger. Its pelt is almost entirely white, crossed with a few darker stripes. The badger's coloring allows it to blend perfectly with the shadows on the snowy landscape; often, the only clue to a snow badger's presence is its squeal of alarm. Its short muzzle hides small sharp teeth, though its bite does painful damage. A snow badger also has short, sharp claws on its back feet and long, curving front claws which can burrow into the earth as easily as they dig into an unlucky predator's flesh.

The snow badger's real weapon is its ability to give off waves of biting cold. The creature can lower the temperature so far the skin of most Namegivers will freeze, and fingers and toes grow brittle with frostbite and fall off. Most adventurers don't prepare for such extreme concentrated cold and will quickly succumb to it unless they kill the creature or flee. When the beast begins to draw in the cold, blue-white lines form in the snow in a wheel-spoke pattern around the creature, extending in all directions for several hundred feet. It looks as if the badger is drawing in lightning from the snowdrifts—the lines seem to crackle and snap with power.

In many troll communities of Barsaive's mountain ranges, the pelts of snow badgers are highly prized. Obtaining a pelt requires great stealth and cunning and has become even more difficult as the population of snow badgers has dwindled. As a result, they confer great status on their wearers; chieftains and Warriors often wear them as ceremonial dress. Some legends claim a snow badger pelt confers the creature's power on its wearer, but it seems improbable the dried pelt of a living creature would retain any of the creature's magical powers.

Merchants claiming to sell snow badger pelts can be found in many marketplaces in Barsaive, but almost all of these are mundane badger pelts dyed white.

Snow badgers mate for life. They mate during the spring and usually have litters of six to eight dark-gray or black cubs. For the first half year of their lives, young snow badgers do not leave the hidden burrow dug by their parents—their dark coloring, though useless in the snow, perfectly hides them from snooping predators in the darkness of their holes. Many of these burrows are large enough to admit a human and extend downward for several feet, though they are only about three feet across. Of course, the parents are never far off—any predator who tries to crawl inside the burrow will face a couple of angry adult badgers within seconds.

Snow badgers are suitable as animal companions.

Challenge: Journeyman (Fifth Circle)

DEX:	6	Initiative:	6	Unconsciousness:	43
STR:	5	Physical Defense:	10	Death Rating:	49
TOU:	6	Mystic Defense:	12	Wound Threshold:	9
PER:	6	Social Defense:	12	Knockdown:	9
WIL:	8	Physical Armor:	5	Recovery Tests:	2
CHA:	6	Mystic Armor:	6		

Movement: 8 (Burrow 6)
Actions: 2; Bite: 14 (14), Claws x2: 14 (12)
Powers:
Climbing (8): As the skill, *Player's Guide*, p. 134.
Enhanced Sense [Smell] (4)
Freezing Aura (14): As a Standard action, the snow badger can give off an aura of freezing cold in a 10-yard radius, dealing Damage Step 14. Normal armor does not protect against this damage, but at gamemaster's discretion appropriate clothing may offer some protection. This power may only be used once per turn.
Immune to Cold: The snow badger suffers no damage from mundane cold attacks, and gains +20 Physical and Mystic Armor against magical or elemental cold.
Willful (1)
Special Maneuvers:
Provoke (Opponent, Close Combat)
Loot: Pelt worth 100 silver pieces (worth Legend Points)

Spider

Spiders can be found across Barsaive. The vast majority are harmless to Namegivers, but some giant varieties may pose a hazard to unwary travelers.

Giant Trapdoor Spider

The giant trapdoor spider is smaller than its arboreal cousins, and has adopted a different tactic to catch its prey. Rather than spinning a web, the giant trapdoor spider finds an empty animal burrow and lines the interior with webs. It then crafts a cover of sticks, leaves, and rocks, using its webbing as glue to hold it all together. The spider places the cover over the burrow's entrance and hides beneath it, ready to spring out and attack any victim who falls into its trap.

Challenge: Novice (Fourth Circle)

DEX:	7	Initiative:	11	Unconsciousness:	38
STR:	6	Physical Defense:	12	Death Rating:	44
TOU:	6	Mystic Defense:	9	Wound Threshold:	9
PER:	6	Social Defense:	11	Knockdown:	14
WIL:	8	Physical Armor:	5	Recovery Tests:	2
CHA:	4	Mystic Armor:	3		

Movement: 16 (Climb 16)
Actions: 1; Bite: 12 (13)
Powers:
Ambush (5)
Burrow Trap: The spider's burrow may be noticed on a successful Awareness (10) test. Characters with Wilderness Survival, Creature Lore, or similar skills may use those skills in place of the Awareness test. If the test fails, the character does not notice the trapdoor and will be surprised when the spider attacks. He may also fall into the burrow unless he makes a successful Dexterity (9) test.
Poison (12): If the spider's bite causes damage, the victim must resist the effects of a paralytic poison (see **Poison**, p. 171). The poison is Step 12 [Onset: 1 round, Interval: 4/1 round, Duration: 15 minutes].
Stealthy Stride (10): As the skill, *Player's Guide*, p. 170.
Web: A victim who succumbs to the paralyzing effect of the spider's venom is wrapped in the webs lining the creature's burrow. To escape, the victim must succeed at a Strength (12) test. If they were holding a small (Size 1 or 2) weapon when they were webbed, they may add the weapons' Damage Step to the Strength test.
Loot: Lair may contain items and small valuables from previous victims.

Giant Weaver Spider

The giant weaver spiders of the Servos Jungle can grow as large as six to seven feet across, with dripping fangs the size of daggers. Giant weaver spiders can be very dangerous. If a victim falls unconscious as a result of the spider's venom, the spider begins to wrap the prey in a thick cocoon of webs to be eaten at leisure. If the victim wakes up he may free himself, but this does not happen often.

Challenge: Novice (Fourth Circle)

DEX:	7	Initiative:	11	Unconsciousness:	41
STR:	5	Physical Defense:	10	Death Rating:	48
TOU:	7	Mystic Defense:	12	Wound Threshold:	10
PER:	5	Social Defense:	12	Knockdown:	13
WIL:	8	Physical Armor:	4	Recovery Tests:	2
CHA:	5	Mystic Armor:	5		

Movement: 16 (Climb 16)
Actions: 1; Bite: 12 (10)
Powers:
Creature Power (12, Spit Venom, Standard)
Enhanced Sense [Touch] (4)

Poison (10): If the spider's bite does damage to a target, the target must resist the effects of a paralytic poison (see **Poison**, p. 171). The poison is Step 10 [Onset: 1 round, Interval: 5/1 round, Duration: 15 minutes].

Spit Venom (10): The spider can spit venom at a target within 10 yards. It makes a Creature Power test against the target's Mystic Defense. If successful, the target takes Step 10 Damage, reduced by Mystic Armor.

Stealthy Stride (9): As the skill, *Player's Guide*, p. 170.

Web Trap: Giant spider webs are strong enough to entangle Namegivers. Noticing a web requires a successful Awareness (9) test. If a character becomes stuck in a spider's web, he must succeed at a Strength (12) test to break free. If the character was carrying a small (Size 1 or 2) bladed weapon at the time he was trapped, he may add the weapon's Damage Step as a bonus to the Strength test.

Stajian

Stajian are large, bison-like animals often used as mounts by ork tribes. They stand 6 feet at the shoulder, are less massive than a thundra beast, but faster and stronger than a horse. Their broad hooves allow them to traverse mountains and swamps with ease. Stajian live wild on the plains of Barsaive. They eat anything from grass to tree limbs and usually congregate in herds of five to ten females and young, and one to six males. They are rare to encounter in most other places.

Stajian are ornery, and wild stajian frequently fight for dominance in the herd. Even domesticated stajian continue this behavior, and so the animals must be watched carefully. Some ork cavalry use this behavior to their advantage, training their mount to strike out at opposing mounts or Namegivers without direction from its rider.

Stajian are suitable as mounts for elves, humans, orks, t'skrang, and trolls, and as animal companions.

Challenge: Novice (Third Circle)

DEX:	5	**Initiative:**	7	**Unconsciousness:**	45
STR:	10	**Physical Defense:**	9	**Death Rating:**	55
TOU:	10	**Mystic Defense:**	9	**Wound Threshold:**	15
PER:	5	**Social Defense:**	10	**Knockdown:**	14
WIL:	6	**Physical Armor:**	5	**Recovery Tests:**	3
CHA:	4	**Mystic Armor:**	2		

Movement: 20
Actions: 1; Horns: 11 (16), Trample: 11 (14)
Powers:
Charge (5)
Enhanced Sense [Hearing] (2)
Enhanced Sense [Smell] (2)
Resist Pain (2)
Special Maneuvers:
Enrage (Opponent)
Provoke (Opponent, Close Combat)
Overrun (Stajian, Trample)

Stinger

Small and rodent-like, the stinger is about four feet long, though much of its body hunches over its hind legs, making it appear smaller. Vicious barbs flank its narrow head. The beast has two short front legs with sharp claws, which it uses to dig tunnels, climb walls, and attack prey. The creature's body tapers into a sturdy tail, also tipped with a sharp barb.

Stingers tend to gather in swarms of fifteen to twenty, preferring natural caves and abandoned kaers. Unlike many creatures, these beasts do not shy away from Horror-taint; more than a few swarms roam the Badlands in search of food. Stingers use their front claws to dig long, intricate tunnels through the soil that makes up their homes. They are also amazingly swift—faster than almost any other land-bound creature in Barsaive.

Stingers will eat any type of living animal, from small rats and mice to thundra beasts and elephants. The stinger can easily bring down larger beasts because its poison is unbelievably potent. Stingers attack in swarms from all directions at once, dashing by their prey and raking it with their curved front claws. As the creature passes by, it also strikes with its tail stinger, injecting the victim with venom that eats away at the prey's flesh. When fighting smaller prey, the stinger will grab on with its front claws and use its head stingers to inject their venom.

Alchemists and magicians greatly prize stinger venom. Many an adventurer has met his death attempting to harvest it from a stinger swarm.

Stingers are suitable as animal companions.

Challenge: Novice (Fourth Circle)

DEX:	9	**Initiative:**	13	**Unconsciousness:**	32
STR:	5	**Physical Defense:**	14	**Death Rating:**	36
TOU:	4	**Mystic Defense:**	12	**Wound Threshold:**	6
PER:	6	**Social Defense:**	10	**Knockdown:**	7
WIL:	6	**Physical Armor:**	2	**Recovery Tests:**	1
CHA:	5	**Mystic Armor:**	1		

Movement: 22 (Burrow 8)
Actions: 2; Claw x2: 14 (8), Tail Stinger: 14 (10, Poison), Head Stinger: 14 (9, Poison)
Powers:
Climbing (14): As the skill, *Player's Guide*, p. 134.
Enhanced Sense [Smell] (4)
Poison (12): If a stinger causes a Wound with its tail or head stinger, the victim must resist the effects of a damaging poison (see **Poison**, p. 171). The poison is Step 12 [Onset: 1 round, Interval: 3/1 round].
Willful (1)
Special Maneuvers:
Defang (Opponent)
Loot: Stingers and poison sacs worth 2D10×10 silver pieces (worth Legend Points).

Storm Crow

Storm crows are often mistaken for the larger and more aggressive blood ravens, and are commonly found in the same areas. Despite the similarity, the two species are natural enemies. Storm crows will go out of their way to attack blood ravens, protecting the other animals in the process.

Storm crows can often be seen cavorting in the rain and wind when storms pass over the Blood Wood, when other birds would seek shelter. Their kinship with storms gives these birds a dramatic magical power they can employ in combat. When diving toward a target, their talons glow blue and launch a lightning bolt at their target.

This same kinship makes the creatures capricious and volatile. While some have had success with a storm crow as a companion or familiar, they do not take well to training or domestication.

Storm crows are suitable as animal companions.

Challenge: Novice (Fourth Circle)

DEX:	7	Initiative:	13	Unconsciousness:	32
STR:	3	Physical Defense:	13	Death Rating:	36
TOU:	4	Mystic Defense:	11	Wound Threshold:	6
PER:	7	Social Defense:	12	Knockdown:	3
WIL:	7	Physical Armor:	2	Recovery Tests:	1
CHA:	5	Mystic Armor:	4		

Movement: 2 (Flying 20)
Actions: 1; Claws: 14 (10)
Powers:
Creature Power (14, Lightning, Standard)
Enhanced Sense [Sight] (2)
Lightning (14): When attacking, a storm crow may strike a target within 10 yards with a bolt of lightning. It makes a Creature Power test against the target's Mystic Defense. If successful, the target takes Step 14 damage. Physical Armor protects against this damage. This power may only be used once per day, except during a storm, when it can be used every other round.
Willful (1)
Special Maneuvers:
Chain Lightning (Storm Crow, Creature Power): The storm crow may spend additional successes to target additional opponents. The original Creature Power result is used against these opponents. Additional successes resulting from this special maneuver may not be applied to this special maneuver.
Clip the Wing (Opponent)
Loot: Silver talons worth 20–25 silver pieces (worth Legend Points).

Thunderbird

Thunderbirds are enormous birds with wingspans up to twenty feet across. They resemble eagles, with gray and blue feathers. Their feathers often crackle with static electricity. They can usually only be found in the highest peaks, hunting the other animals living in the mountains. Their elemental affinity draws them to places rich in true air, and the animals sometimes cause problems for those seeking to mine the element.

Thunderbirds are suitable as animal companions.

Challenge: Journeyman (Seventh Circle)

DEX:	8	Initiative:	14	Unconsciousness:	71
STR:	10	Physical Defense:	14	Death Rating:	83
TOU:	12	Mystic Defense:	16	Wound Threshold:	18
PER:	8	Social Defense:	12	Knockdown:	10
WIL:	8	Physical Armor:	7	Recovery Tests:	4
CHA:	6	Mystic Armor:	8		

Movement: 4 (Flying 20)
Actions: 2; Bite: 17 (21), Claws x2: 18 (20)

Powers:

Crackling Armor (12): As a Simple action, the thunderbird wraps itself in a protective sheath of electricity. When an attacker hits, lightning arcs to the attacker, causing Step 12 Damage. Physical armor protects against this damage.
Dive (10)
Enhanced Sense [Sight] (6)
Immune to Electricity: The thunderbird suffers no damage from mundane electricity attacks, and gains +20 Physical and Mystic Armor against magical or elemental electricity.
Willful (2)
Swooping Attack: The thunderbird may split movement (*Player's Guide*, p. 386) without penalty, and does not spend Strain..

Special Maneuvers:

Clip the Wing (Opponent)
Enrage (Opponent)
Grounded Strike (Opponent): The attacker may spend additonal successes from an Attack test to reduce the Damage Step of Crackling Armor by 4 for each success.
Provoke (Opponent, Close Combat)

Thundra Beast

This large, four-legged animal looks like a cross between a rhinoceros and a dinosaur, with a tough, rock-like skin covering its entire body. Thundra beasts stand seven feet tall at the shoulder, are ten to twelve feet long, and weigh about five thousand pounds. Each thundra beast has a large horn in the center of its forehead, which it uses to attack opponents.

Ork scorcher groups frequently ride thundra beasts. Thundra beasts are rarely encountered in the wild. Thundra beasts usually attack by charging their target and goring with their horns or trampling with their hooves.

Thundra beasts are suitable as mounts for dwarfs, elves, humans, obsidimen, orks, t'skrang, and trolls, and as animal companions.

Challenge: Journeyman (Fifth Circle)

DEX:	6	**Initiative:**	8	**Unconsciousness:**	61
STR:	11	**Physical Defense:**	12	**Death Rating:**	73
TOU:	12	**Mystic Defense:**	11	**Wound Threshold:**	18
PER:	5	**Social Defense:**	10	**Knockdown:**	15
WIL:	8	**Physical Armor:**	9	**Recovery Tests:**	4
CHA:	5	**Mystic Armor:**	6		

Movement: 16
Actions: 1; Horn: 14 (20), Trample: 14 (18)
Powers:
Charge (10)
Enhanced Sense [Hearing] (2)
Enhanced Sense [Smell] (2)
Resist Pain (2)
Willful (1)
Special Maneuvers:
Enrage (Opponent)
Overrun (Thundra Beast, Trample)
Provoke (Opponent, Close Combat)

Tiger

Tigers are large carnivorous cats found in Barsaive's jungles and plains. Their fur is usually yellow or gold in color, with black stripes. Some rare specimens have black stripes against a white background. Barsaivian tigers are large, often reaching more than three feet at the shoulder, and the largest reaching over eleven feet in length.

Challenge: Novice (Fourth Circle)

DEX:	7	**Initiative:**	11	**Unconsciousness:**	41
STR:	9	**Physical Defense:**	13	**Death Rating:**	48
TOU:	7	**Mystic Defense:**	10	**Wound Threshold:**	10
PER:	6	**Social Defense:**	10	**Knockdown:**	13
WIL:	6	**Physical Armor:**	5	**Recovery Tests:**	2
CHA:	5	**Mystic Armor:**	3		

Movement: 18
Actions: 1; Bite: 14 (14), Claws: 14 (13)
Powers:
Ambush (5)
Battle Shout (7): As the skill, *Player's Guide*, p. 131.
Climbing (11): As the skill, *Player's Guide*, p. 134.
Enhanced Sense [Hearing] (2)
Enhanced Sense [Sight]: Low-Light Vision
Great Leap (10)
Stealthy Stride (11): As the skill, *Player's Guide*, p. 170.
Willful (1)
Special Maneuvers:
Pounce (Tiger)
Provoke (Opponent, Close Combat)

Troajin

Troajin are large felines native to jungle and mountain country. The average troajin stands approximately three feet at the shoulder and has a five-foot body with a three-foot tail. Their fur is often tawny brown with darker stripes, with grey or yellowish variations being common.

Wild troajin are fiercely territorial and defend themselves with sharp claws and teeth. They are a social species, roaming their territory in small packs usually consisting of one or two adult males with half a dozen adult females. This social behavior makes them a popular companion for Beastmaster adepts, and their smaller size makes them a popular choice as a mount for dwarf Cavalrymen.

Troajin are suitable as mounts for dwarfs and as animal companions.

Challenge: Novice (Second Circle)

DEX:	7	**Initiative:**	9	**Unconsciousness:**	28
STR:	7	**Physical Defense:**	11	**Death Rating:**	34
TOU:	6	**Mystic Defense:**	9	**Wound Threshold:**	9
PER:	5	**Social Defense:**	7	**Knockdown:**	11
WIL:	5	**Physical Armor:**	3	**Recovery Tests:**	2
CHA:	4	**Mystic Armor:**	1		

Movement: 16
Actions: 1; Claws: 11 (12)
Powers:
Ambush (5)
Climbing (11): As the skill, *Player's Guide*, p. 134.
Enhanced Sense [Hearing] (2)
Enhanced Sense [Sight]: Low-Light Vision
Great Leap (8)
Stealthy Stride (11): As the skill, *Player's Guide*, p. 170.
Special Maneuvers:
Pounce (Troajin)

Unicorn

The Scourge wiped out many of Barsaive's wondrous beasts and transformed others nearly beyond recognition. The latter fate befell the unicorn, though somehow it was improved rather than corrupted. Before the Scourge, the unicorn was one of Barsaive's most feared predators. The mere sight of the beasts, with their matted fur and blood-encrusted horns, struck fear in the hearts of most Namegivers.

Unlike most predators, the unicorns seemed to enjoy killing for its own sake. These unicorns hunted in packs and showed an uncanny intelligence allowing them to take on larger and more powerful creatures. They often hunted thundra beasts, manticores, and even an occasional dragon, surrounding their prey and wearing it down with sheer numbers. Some unicorns would lie in wait along footpaths and trade roads, where they would ambush small bands of travelers, then feast on their flesh. These unicorns became a special danger, for once they tasted the flesh of Namegivers, they often forsook other prey. These herds took to raiding villages, attacking under the cover of darkness and using their terrible horns and sharp hooves to devastate all in their paths.

Inexplicably, the Scourge changed the unicorn from vicious creatures with a taste for Namegiver flesh to gentle beasts of great beauty. Unicorns have become solitary herbivores. Though unicorns look like large horses with horns on their heads, they are not docile as farm animals. While gentler than they were, a unicorn still loves its freedom and will resist someone trying to capture them.

Most unicorns are pure white, though there are spotted and even black ones. The unicorn's horn is two to three feet long and according to legend can kill a Horror with one blow. While the horn's power may be exaggerated, it can certainly cause a vicious wound—even plunging through bone if the beast is galloping fast enough when it strikes.

Whether or not it can kill Horrors, a fresh unicorn horn possesses a remarkable sensitivity to poisons. When touched to any substance even the least bit venomous—or at least poisonous enough to harm the unicorn—the horn changes color. The darker it turns, the more dangerous the poison. Also, a tiny sprinkling of powdered unicorn horn can neutralize any poison, no matter how potent. This makes unicorn horn a highly prized material by alchemists, magicians, or rulers who might have cause to fear assassination by poison.

While few in number, some pre-Scourge unicorns still exist in isolated pockets. Unfortunately, they resemble their more placid brethren, and those who would hunt the beasts should be cautious when approaching them until they are sure they have properly identified which variety they are dealing with.

Stories of cavalry mounted on unicorns have filtered into Barsaive from other lands, but the truth of these tales remains unconfirmed.

Unicorns are suitable as mounts for elves, humans, orks, and t'skrang, and as animal companions.

Challenge: Journeyman (Seventh Circle)

DEX:	8	Initiative:	10	Unconsciousness:	62
STR:	10	Physical Defense:	14	Death Rating:	71
TOU:	9	Mystic Defense:	15	Wound Threshold:	13
PER:	7	Social Defense:	16	Knockdown:	14
WIL:	7	Physical Armor:	5	Recovery Tests:	3
CHA:	10	Mystic Armor:	8		

Movement: 20
Actions: 2; Horn: 16 (20), Trample: 16 (18)
Powers:
Blood Rage: This power is only possessed by the pre-Scourge variety of unicorn. If the unicorn deals a Wound to an opponent, it becomes consumed with blood lust. It gains an additional attack per round, and a +4 bonus to Attack and Damage tests until killed or driven off.
Calm Others (11): This power is only possessed by the post-Scourge variety of unicorn. It makes a Calm Others test as a Standard action, comparing the result against the Social Defense of each target within 10 yards. If the test is successful, any magical or mundane fear is dispelled, and the target is calmed for one minute per success, losing the desire to take any action that would harm another. The target may shake off this effect with a Willpower (11) test.
Charge (10)
Detect Poison (20): A unicorn's horn can detect poison if the horn is immersed in the substance being tested. A Detect Poison test is made against the Step Number for the poison. If successful, the horn changes color. The darker the color, the more dangerous the poison. Depending on the nature and concentration of the poison, the color change can take up to ten minutes. This power remains even if the horn is removed from the unicorn. If powdered horn is introduced to the poison, a successful test neutralizes the poison completely.
Enhanced Sense [Hearing] (2)
Enhanced Sense [Smell] (2)
Fury (2): Pre-Scourge unicorn only.
Resist Pain (2): Post-Scourge unicorn only.
Willful (1)
Special Maneuvers:
Enrage (Opponent): This may only be used against pre-Scourge unicorns and will cause Blood Rage.
Overrun (Unicorn, Trample)
Provoke (Opponent, Close Combat)
Loot: Horn worth at least 2,000 silver pieces (worth Legend Points).

Velos

The velos inhabit the darkest interior of the Servos Jungle. At first sight, the creature's reptilian features and long tail can easily cause the viewer to confuse them for a large t'skrang. Unlike t'skrang, velos are taller than the average obsidiman and possess long teeth and sharp claws.

Long considered mythical, the existence of the velos was confirmed by agents of House K'tenshin. First reports made them out as savage beasts, because they hunted down and ate many of the early K'tenshin explorers. More recent evidence indicates they may be Namegivers closely related to the primitive t'skrang of the Servos Jungle. While some velos fight with teeth and claws, most wield primitive spears and carry shields. As yet, nobody has successfully communicated with them to determine how intelligent or sophisticated they might be.

Challenge: Journeyman (Sixth Circle)

DEX:	8	**Initiative:**	7	**Unconsciousness:**	60
STR:	13	**Physical Defense:**	15	**Death Rating:**	70
TOU:	10	**Mystic Defense:**	12	**Wound Threshold:**	15
PER:	7	**Social Defense:**	12	**Knockdown:**	15
WIL:	8	**Physical Armor:**	10	**Recovery Tests:**	3
CHA:	7	**Mystic Armor:**	5		

Movement: 14 (Swimming 8)
Actions: 2; Claws: 15 (14), Spear: 15 (18)
Powers:
Ambush (10)
Climbing (14): As the skill, *Player's Guide*, p. 134.
Resist Pain (2)
Stealthy Stride (14): As the skill, *Player's Guide*, p. 170.
Special Maneuvers:
Provoke (Opponent, Close Combat)
Equipment: Footman's Shield (+2 Physical Defense, -1 Initiative), Spear (Damage Step 5, Size 4)
Loot: Villages contain feathers, furs, and handicrafts worth 200–300 silver pieces (worth Legend Points).

Volus

The volus averages fifteen feet long and resembles a cross between a lizard and a large badger. Its body is covered with tough, chitinous plates of varied hues and sizes. The huge claws on its front feet are far larger than its rear claws, and its head resembles the bowl of a thick shovel. It uses its strangely shaped head and large front claws to dig vast tunnels beneath the earth in search of food.

The volus can smell magic as a dog follows a scent, and it uses this ability to find food. When the volus detects the presence of nearby magic, it digs through the earth until it is directly beneath the source. The volus then collapses the earth beneath its victim, trapping and suffocating the victim underground. The volus rarely fails to catch a meal this way, as six feet of earth above the victim's head will kill it as surely as claws and teeth. Few Namegivers can dig half as well as the volus, so travelers beware this beast. One indication of a volus' hunting ground is the presence of several sinkholes in a given area. One safeguard against it is to stand on solid rock, as the volus cannot dig through stone.

The volus' ability is highly refined. It can sense any use of magic, no matter how small. Even the feeble magical aura given off by enchanted items acts as a beacon for the volus. If a great deal of magic is being used, several voluses might converge on the user from a wide range. A Wizard once botched a powerful magical experiment and blew the top of his house off. Half a day later, thirty voluses arrived and proceeded to drag the house under the ground. Scholars speculate the volus developed its unique ability over time as the rise of the world's magical aura created many creatures with innate magical powers. All of these the volus can sense, stalk, and eat.

The volus is a territorial beast, preferring to mark out its own hunting grounds. These hunting grounds may be any region where a good deal of magic is used—towns and villages with too many adepts often fall prey to volus infestations. They also hunt on the high roads of Barsaive, especially in recent years, as more and more of the magically adept travel on those roads in search of adventure. A party of adepts is an invitation to dine to any number of voluses, depending on how many of the creatures' hunting grounds they pass on their journey.

Not surprisingly, magicians and alchemists prize a volus's magic-sensing organ. The little gland forms a small hard lump at the base of the neck, and can be removed with a sharp knife. It is, however, extremely delicate—one touch of the blade on the gland itself will ruin it. To prevent decay, it has to be placed in a magical container or preserved with a spell. Carefully preserved, the organ will retain its magic-sensing abilities indefinitely. The volus can also be trained to act as a sort of hunting dog for magical threats (including Horrors), convenient for helping travelers avoid such perils. To train a volus, of course, first requires catching one—and once it is trained, its master should keep it well fed.

Volus are suitable as animal companions.

Challenge: Journeyman (Eighth Circle)

DEX:	7	**Initiative:**	7	**Unconsciousness:**	76
STR:	10	**Physical Defense:**	12	**Death Rating:**	88
TOU:	12	**Mystic Defense:**	18	**Wound Threshold:**	18
PER:	8	**Social Defense:**	15	**Knockdown:**	14
WIL:	8	**Physical Armor:**	12	**Recovery Tests:**	4
CHA:	6	**Mystic Armor:**	10		

Movement: 12 (Burrow 6)
Actions: 2; Bite: 18 (18), Claws x2: 18 (23)
Powers:
Ambush (10)
Climbing (13): As the skill, *Player's Guide*, p. 134.
Enhanced Sense [Other] (6): The volus can sense the presence of magic within ten miles. The creature makes a Perception test with a +6 Step bonus against a Difficulty Number based on the type of magic being used, as shown on the Magic Use table. If successful, the creature senses the magic and is table to track it as long as it remains in range. Because of the prevalence of magic in the world, the creature can often sense multiple magical sources, and generally prefers to go after the strongest source.

Magic Use Table	
Magic Type	*Difficulty*
Raw Magic Spell	4
Creature Power	9
Talent or Adept Power	11
Magic Item	12
Matrix or Grimoire Spell	14

Willful (2)
Special Maneuvers:
Desensitize (Opponent): The attacker may spend two additional successes on an attack test to remove the Enhanced Sense power and Wound the volus. The volus cannot use its Enhanced Sense until the Wound is healed.
Loot: Magic-sensing organ worth 300 silver pieces (worth Legend Points).

Water Strider

Water striders are one of the many varieties of giant insects living on the Serpent River. These large beetles have bodies about the size of a human's head and legs extending three to five feet in every direction. The creatures' long legs enable them to actually walk on the surface of the water as if it were land. Water striders avoid contact with swimmers and other aquatic life forms whenever possible.

While not dangerous, water striders present a considerable nuisance to riverboat crews because they often climb the sides of riverboats and raid the ship's stores for food. The ravenous creatures can consume a month's worth of provisions in just a few short hours, leaving the crew to go hungry. Boatmen consider it bad luck for a water strider to cross the path of their vessels.

Challenge: Novice (Second Circle)
DEX:	7	**Initiative:**	9	**Unconsciousness:**	19
STR:	2	**Physical Defense:**	10	**Death Rating:**	22
TOU:	3	**Mystic Defense:**	8	**Wound Threshold:**	4
PER:	5	**Social Defense:**	10	**Knockdown:**	8
WIL:	6	**Physical Armor:**	4	**Recovery Tests:**	1
CHA:	4	**Mystic Armor:**	3		

Movement: 14 (Climbing 14)
Actions: 1; Bite: 11 (8)

Powers:
Resist Pain (2)

Will o' the Wisp

The will o' the wisp began as something useful, but as with so many things the Scourge twisted them into something dangerous. Created by magicians in the distant past, the little creature feeds on the ambient magic in its environment, a process generating light. With one of these little creatures beside him, a magician never needed to carry a candle or torch and had his hands free to open doors, read and write books, cast spells, and so on.

Never able to stop once they had created a good thing, many magicians began to experiment with the wisps and created new varieties. One could remember simple instructions and guide people from one place to another. Others gave off sound or heat instead of light. Soon, too many varieties of wisps existed for any one person to remember.

During the Scourge, most wisps were abandoned outside the kaers, where the Horrors slew and ate them. Some wisps managed to hide from the Horrors, and thus survived and bred. After five centuries of existence as wild creatures, most wisps have become just that: utterly feral, and often twisted by the Horrors as well. They only dimly remember their ancient purpose and perform those tasks in a twisted mockery of them

The most dangerous wisps are those meant to paralyze, harm, or even kill those who entered their master's home without permission. The Horrors kept these wisps alive whenever they found them but drove them insane. These wisps often treat all of Barsaive as their master's home and attack any Namegiver they come across. Almost as dangerous are the ones called magic twisters; these wisps can drastically change the effects of any spells cast within the area of their light. Sometimes they reduce the effects to almost nothing, other times they boost a spell's power so it flies out of the caster's control.

A very few wisps are sane and still remember their original purpose. Tales abound of some, created as guides, leading people to the remains of their master's home where forgotten treasures can be found. Of course, and equal number of cautionary tales are told where the wisp leads the erstwhile treasure seeker to his death, with a moral about hard work being the true path to riches.

What makes the will o' the wisp particularly hazardous to adventurers is the similarity of their appearance and the vast difference in what they can do. All wisps emit an unearthly green light, but one can't tell by looking which wisp is a helpful guide, which a harmless light-giver, and which an murderous defender of Barsaive. In addition, because wisps have bred and multiplied on their own for centuries, varieties may exist their creators never envisioned. In short, any wisp may be able to do just about anything you can imagine—and perhaps a few things no one deemed possible.

All wisps give off a pale green light equivalent to a lantern. Some wisps can dim or even extinguish the light.

EARTHDAWN

Challenge: Novice (Fourth Circle)

DEX:	8	Initiative:	12	Unconsciousness:	29
STR:	1	Physical Defense:	14	Death Rating:	32
TOU:	3	Mystic Defense:	14	Wound Threshold:	4
PER:	8	Social Defense:	12	Knockdown:	Immune
WIL:	8	Physical Armor:	1	Recovery Tests:	1
CHA:	8	Mystic Armor:	5		

Movement: Flying 16
Actions: 1; Spells
Powers:
Spellcasting (14): As the talent, *Player's Guide*, p. 168.
Thread Weaving (14): As the talent, *Player's Guide*, p. 174. Wisps have the appropriate type of Thread Weaving based on the spells it knows.
Spells: Varies. Spells commonly used include: Mind Dagger, Spirit Grip. Wisps can have spells available to any magician Discipline. They do not use spell matrices; the spells are considered innate powers, though the wisp still needs to weave threads if the spell requires it. The gamemaster should feel free to adapt other powers or abilities for use by wisps, even bending the rules as necessary to suit the needs of the encounter.

Witherfang

Although found elsewhere in Barsaive, witherfangs are native to the Blood Wood and can be identified by their thick bodies and flared, cobra-like hoods. Most are a dull gray-green, though the coloring of individual snakes may vary depending on their habitat. Witherfangs often match the colors of their surroundings, and possess a form of natural camouflage.

Witherfangs are named for the powerful poison transmitted through the stinger at the ends of their tails. The poison can wither a victim's limb until it is virtually useless. The witherfang's other unique characteristic is its large number of teeth, which it uses to hold victims immobile while it administers its poisonous sting.

Witherfangs are suitable as animal companions.

Challenge: Journeyman (Sixth Circle)

DEX:	8	Initiative:	10	Unconsciousness:	48
STR:	6	Physical Defense:	15	Death Rating:	54
TOU:	6	Mystic Defense:	12	Wound Threshold:	9
PER:	4	Social Defense:	13	Knockdown:	Immune
WIL:	6	Physical Armor:	6	Recovery Tests:	2
CHA:	4	Mystic Armor:	6		

Movement: 8
Actions: 2; Bite: 16 (15); Tail: 16 (16)
Powers:
Awareness (7): As the skill, *Player's Guide*, p. 129.
Enhanced Sense [Sight]: Heat Sight
Enhanced Sense [Smell] (4)
Enhanced Sense [Taste] (4)

354

Poison (16): The poison is Step 16 [Onset: 1 round, Interval: 4/2 rounds] (see **Poison**, p. 171). Unlike most debilitating poisons, witherfang venom and has an effect similar to the Wither Limb spell (*Player's Guide*, p. 333). The penalty from the poison only affects tests made with the affected limb. The effect lasts until reversed with powerful magic like Reverse Withering (*Player's Guide*, p. 333).
Willful (2)
Stealthy Stride (16): As the skill, *Player's Guide*, p. 170.
Special Maneuvers:
Grab and Bite (Witherfang, Bite)
Poison Stinger (Witherfang, Tail): The witherfang may spend an additional success from an Attack test to inflict Poison on the target.
Pry Loose (Opponent, Close Combat)

Wolf

Related to domestic dogs, wolves are wild, fierce carnivores that travel in packs and maneuver to outflank and harass their intended prey before attacking in force. Wolves can be encountered anywhere in Barsaive, but have a preference for mountainous terrain.

Packs often number ten to twenty members, led by an alpha pair. Wolves are one of the few predators who hate and even hunt Horrors.

These statistics represent regular wolf pack members.

Wolves are suitable as animal companions

Challenge: Novice (Second Circle)

DEX:	6	**Initiative:**	8	**Unconsciousness:**	28
STR:	6	**Physical Defense:**	10	**Death Rating:**	34
TOU:	6	**Mystic Defense:**	8	**Wound Threshold:**	9
PER:	5	**Social Defense:**	9	**Knockdown:**	10
WIL:	4	**Physical Armor:**	3	**Recovery Tests:**	2
CHA:	4	**Mystic Armor:**	2		

Movement: 1
Actions: 1; Bite: 10 (12)
Powers:
Enhanced Sense [Hearing] (2)
Enhanced Sense [Smell] (2): Tracking
Surprise Strike (5): As the skill, *Player's Guide*, p. 172.
Tracking (9): As the skill, *Player's Guide*, p. 175.
Special Maneuvers:
Hamstring (Wolf)
Loot: Skin worth 5d10 silver pieces.

Alpha Wolf

These statistics represent a more powerful and intelligent wolf, which often leads a pack.

Alpha wolves are suitable as animal companions.

Challenge: Novice (Third Circle)

DEX:	6	**Initiative:**	10	**Unconsciousness:**	36
STR:	7	**Physical Defense:**	11	**Death Rating:**	43
TOU:	7	**Mystic Defense:**	10	**Wound Threshold:**	10
PER:	6	**Social Defense:**	10	**Knockdown:**	11
WIL:	4	**Physical Armor:**	4	**Recovery Tests:**	2
CHA:	5	**Mystic Armor:**	2		

Movement: 16
Actions: 1; Bite: 12 (14)
Powers:
Enhanced Sense [Hearing] (2)
Enhanced Sense [Smell] (2): Tracking
Surprise Strike (5): As the skill, *Player's Guide*, p. 172.
Tracking (10): As the skill, *Player's Guide*, p. 175.
Special Maneuvers:
Hamstring (Alpha Wolf)
Opening (Alpha Wolf): The alpha wolf may spend additional successes from an Attack test on an opponent suffering from Hamstring to give all other wolves a +1 bonus per success spent to Attack tests against the opponent until the end of the next round.
Loot: Skin worth 5d10 silver pieces.

Ethandrille

Once the ethandrille was a creature with a place in the life of the Universe, a proud beast who roamed the wilds of Wyrm Wood. They preyed on the smaller animals of the forests and even occasionally took on larger prey. When the blood elves used their terrible magic to transform the Wood, they not only corrupted themselves, they also corrupted the innocent living things around them.

Before the corruption of the Wood, ethandrilles were a kind of wolf only a little larger than big dogs, covered in brown and gray fur to better hide in the forest. The wretched creatures still look somewhat the same as their forerunners once did, but now thorns pierce the thin skin around their mouths. Where their pelts are too thick for the thorns to penetrate it stretches their fur in a horrible manner. The poor beasts look tortured, as indeed they are.

Like the blood elves, ethandrilles are in constant agony from the thorns and are immune to the pain-causing powers of the Horrors. The Ritual of Thorns also made the ethandrilles larger, fiercer, and enhanced their already keen tracking abilities. The magic also gave them the ability to discharge a mighty bolt of lightning at an opponent before engaging in combat.

The blood elves have domesticated the once-proud ethandrille, using the beasts as draft animals, pets, and more. The elves use ethandrilles to ferry supplies and food from tree to tree, stand guard throughout the forest, and drive intruders back across the wood's borders.

Ethandrille are suitable as animal companions, though will not leave Blood Wood for extended periods of time.

Challenge: Journeyman (Fifth Circle)

DEX:	7	**Initiative:**	9	**Unconsciousness:**	46
STR:	7	**Physical Defense:**	11	**Death Rating:**	53
TOU:	7	**Mystic Defense:**	12	**Wound Threshold:**	10
PER:	6	**Social Defense:**	11	**Knockdown:**	11
WIL:	6	**Physical Armor:**	4	**Recovery Tests:**	2
CHA:	4	**Mystic Armor:**	6		

Movement: 16
Actions: 2; Bite x2: 14 (15)
Powers:
Creature Power (12, Lightning Strike, Standard)
Enhanced Sense [Hearing] (2)
Enhanced Sense [Other] (6): An ethandrille can locate intruders into their territory. As a free action it makes a Perception test with a +4 Step bonus, and detects the presence of all targets within 20 yards with a Mystic Defense equal to or less than the test result.
Enhanced Sense [Smell] (2): Tracking
Lightning Strike (13): Before it attacks physically, an ethandrille often fires a bolt of lightning at its target. It makes a Creature Power test against the target's Mystic Defense. If successful, the target suffers Step 13 Damage (reduced by Mystic Armor), and suffers a -1 Action test penalty per success on the Creature Power test until the end of the next round.
Surprise Strike (10): As the skill, *Player's Guide*, p. 172.
Tracking (12): As the skill, *Player's Guide*, p. 175.
Willful (1)
Special Maneuvers:
Hamstring (Ethandrille, Bite)

Storm Wolf

The storm wolf is a handsome animal, larger and stronger than a normal wolf with silver-grey fur. An excellent hunter, they travel in packs of eight to twenty-four animals. They are not aggressive towards Namegivers, and will only attack if desperately hungry, or if they sense evil coming from the traveling party.

Storm wolves possess a pure, elemental spirit that can detect the taint commonly associated with undead beings. The wolves often go out of their way to destroy such creatures; legends tell of hunts spanning hundreds of leagues. Other tales tell of storm wolves leading travelers to sites of the undead they wish to see destroyed. A pack of storm wolves is able to call up a storm, and use its elemental power to enhance and strengthen their own abilities.

Despite the beauty of storm wolf pelts, they are not in high demand and hard to find in most markets in Barsaive. Storm wolves can also sense when a Namegiver has hunted or killed a storm wolf for its hide, and will actively hunt them. In addition, many Elementalists revere storm wolves as a manifestation of the ideal relationship between our world and the elemental planes, opposing those who would hunt the beasts for their pelts.

Storm wolves are suitable as animal companions.

Challenge: Journeyman (Fifth Circle)

DEX:	7	Initiative:	11	Unconsciousness:	46
STR:	7	Physical Defense:	12	Death Rating:	53
TOU:	7	Mystic Defense:	11	Wound Threshold:	10
PER:	6	Social Defense:	10	Knockdown:	11
WIL:	5	Physical Armor:	6	Recovery Tests:	2
CHA:	6	Mystic Armor:	4		

Movement: 18
Actions: 2; Bite x2: 14 (18)
Powers:
Enhanced Sense [Hearing] (2)
Enhanced Sense [Other] (6): The storm wolf can tell if undead are in the area. it makes a Perception test with a +6 Step bonus, detecting the presence of all undead creatures within one mile with a Mystic Defense less than or equal to the test result.
Enhanced Sense [Smell] (2): Tracking
Healing Rain (10): When under the effect of Storm Call, storm wolves may heal themselves during combat. This works like the Fireblood talent (*Player's Guide*, p. 146), and may be used twice per day. The leader of a storm wolf pack may transfer this power to an injured character by placing his head in the character's lap.
Storm Call (15): A pack of storm wolves is able to call up a storm. The pack gives an eerie, whistling howl and the leader makes a Storm Call (20) test, with a +2 bonus for each additional member of the pack. If successful, the storm forms in 1D6 rounds, and lasts one hour, unless the pack leader disperses it first (which it can do at will). While the storm is in effect, all members of the pack gain a +2 bonus to their Attack and Damage tests, while their opponent's suffer a -2 penalty.
Surprise Strike (10): As the skill, *Player's Guide*, p. 172.
Tracking (12): As the skill, *Player's Guide*, p. 175.
Willful (1)

Special Maneuvers:
Hamstring (Storm Wolf)
Loot: Pelt worth 75 silver pieces (worth Legend Points).

Zoak

The zoak looks like a cross between a large bird and a bat, with feathers on its body and head and a leathery neck, wings, and tail. The creature's feathered legs each end in four eagle-like talons. Zoaks measure roughly four feet from beak to tail-tip. Their necks are long and flexible, similar in appearance to the crakbill's, but with vertebrae instead of muscle.

The animals are native to forests and jungles across Barsaive. While they can be difficult to train, they make a popular companion for Beastmasters, and are especially favored by windling Cavalrymen. They are rarely offered for sale outside of windling communities.

Zoaks are suitable as mounts for windlings and as animal companions.

Challenge: Novice (Second Circle)

DEX:	6	Initiative:	8	Unconsciousness:	22
STR:	4	Physical Defense:	10	Death Rating:	26
TOU:	4	Mystic Defense:	9	Wound Threshold:	6
PER:	6	Social Defense:	9	Knockdown:	4
WIL:	6	Physical Armor:	2	Recovery Tests:	1
CHA:	5	Mystic Armor:	3		

Movement: 4 (Flying 18)
Actions: 1; Bite: 12 (8), Claws: 12 (6)
Powers:
Enhanced Sense [Sight] (2)
Willful (1)
Special Maneuvers:
Clip the Wing (Opponent)

EARTHDAWN

SPIRITS

Icy bag of dirt and water, no concern have I for seeking. Know the embrace of Mother Flame!
• Last words heard by Ottu Stibonas, self-proclaimed Master of Elements •

Spirits are beings native to the realms of astral space known collectively as the netherworlds. While Horrors are also native to some dark and distant corner of these realms, most scholars classify them as entities distinct from spirits. While Horrors desire to cross into our world to wreak havoc, other spirits generally have more a neutral relationship with the physical realm and its inhabitants.

While Elementalists and Nethermancers have spent centuries studying and interacting with spirits, little is truly known about the nature of these beings. Their motivations almost always seem strange or puzzling to Namegivers, and even broad generalizations will encounter exceptions.

This chapter provides an overview of the different types of spirits inhabiting the world of **Earthdawn** and suggestions for using spirits in your adventures and campaigns. It also provides rules for spirit powers and game statistics for when your player characters inevitably interact with these strange and fascinating beings.

ON ALLY SPIRITS

Excerpt from "A Primer on the Variety of Astral Life" by Restan Blacktongue

Despite centuries of study by followers of the Nethermancer Discipline, there is still much we do not know about the native inhabitants of the astral realms, commonly referred to as 'ally spirits'. Why they were given this title is unclear, but it is thought our Discipline came to be through interaction with spirits who shared an interest in the affairs of Namegivers.

Ally spirits are perhaps the most diverse type of astral life and it is easier to describe what they are not, rather than try and define what they are. Ally spirits are not tied to an elemental plane, nor are they invae spirits or their darker cousins, Horrors, who have a predatory nature toward Namegivers.

Broadly defined, ally spirits are those spirits that arise from, or are related to, Namegivers. They are generally divided into two kinds.

Spirits of Deceased Namegivers

The first kind is the one most commonly associated with Nethermancers in the popular perception: spirits of the dead, or 'ghosts'. A Namegiver who has unfinished business may be able to resist the pull of Death's Domain and remain in our world, albeit in astral form. They retain their knowledge and memory and, in the case of adepts, may even have access to the magic they practiced in life.

It is even possible for those with knowledge of the appropriate rituals to call spirits from Death's clutches. This is most commonly exemplified by the Ghost Master Ritual, where an adept calls upon a deceased master of his Discipline for training. Indeed, this ritual was developed by Nethermancers to keep knowledge from being lost when a master crossed and eventually spread to other Disciplines.

Despite popular perception, these spirits are less common than one might expect. While Death's binding has weakened its grip on Namegiver spirits, few have the strength of will or desire to return to the limitations of the physical realm.

> Restan is blinded by his training, which takes it on faith 'ghosts' are spirits of deceased Namegivers. There are other schools of thought on the matter.
>
> The first posits ghosts are the result of strong magic leaving an impression on the fabric of astral space, like a kind of True Pattern. This is supported by the fact nearly all naturally occurring ghosts have some kind of notable event tied to their creation—the 'unfinished business' he mentions—or had significant magical power. Another fact supporting this idea is the need to know a Ghost Master's Name when summoning them. As even the most thickheaded student of magic knows, Names are the key piece of magical knowledge associated with a True Pattern.
>
> Another hypothesis is ghosts are an astral entity merely taking on the appearance of a deceased Namegiver for some inscrutable purpose. This idea has many disturbing implications.
>
> —*Niruuna, Sister of the Circle Path*

Native Astral Beings

The other type of ally spirit, and the type most commonly encountered by those who deal with such things, are beings native to astral space; a kind of astral 'flora and fauna' that have some kinship with Namegiver society.

As I mentioned previously, this kinship is what defines these beings as ally spirits. Some express their individuality through association with an emotional or cultural more, such as knowledge or love. Some develop an affiliation with a particular location, these so-called "hearth spirits" watch over a town or village. Many tales of helpful sprites or faeries can almost certainly trace their origins back to an ally spirit, and there were multiple kaers aided by ally spirits during the Scourge.

While many of these beings are benign and express some interest in positive relations with Namegivers, they are just as often capricious and overlook more prosaic concerns. Their favor must be carefully managed, and those who would deal with them had best treat them with respect and caution.

Finally, just as there are benign ally spirits, there are those which are indifferent, if not actively malevolent. Ally spirits frequently take on or reflect the object or idea they are associated with—the nature of a graveyard spirit, for example, is apt to result in an unsettling experience for those not prepared. In addition, many spirits suffered at the hands of the Horrors, being driven mad or broken in ways that reflect the twisted nature of the astral space they inhabit. Some cunning Horrors like to present themselves as ally spirits and lead the careless summoner astray.

> This notion of ally spirits representing or being tied to Namegiver culture is one I haven't encountered before. This raises interesting questions with regard to the Passions, which also reflect aspects of Namegiver society.
> —Derrat of Yistaine

ON ELEMENTAL SPIRITS

From a letter to Firal from Jinday the Red

Your mam told me what happened by the river. Looks like you share the family gifts. I promised your da I would take you as apprentice if it came to that, and I'll honor that promise. I have some things to do first and likely won't be back until spring, but until we start your training, I'll send you some letters and give you things to think about.

First and perhaps most important lesson: be careful dealing with spirits. I've seen too many Elementalists—experienced ones at that—treat elementals like they're people, and it almost always ends badly. Of course, there's just as many who put too much weight on a spirit's elemental nature, thinking all fire elementals act a certain way, or earth spirits are all slow, strong, and dull.

Trust me, after dealing with an avalanche spirit, slow is not the word that'll come to mind.

It's about balance. Not just the balance of the elements in nature, but the balance between expectation and experience. 'Tis true spirits carry some aspect of their elemental nature, but just by looking you can see the many ways an element can be. Like people, they can show many different faces.

Think about the fishpond near your house and then think about the Serpent River. Both are water, but they are as different as two orks, one raised in the city and the other in the saddle. Assuming they are the same is just inviting trouble.

There are some things you can safely guess about elementals. First, they tend not to like our world that much, seeing as it's made up of all the elements. It can be tough to make them stick around. They also generally want to see more of their element spread, and the cannier ones can often get a careless summoner into trouble by throwing things out of kilter.

As you're just coming into your powers, no doubt you'll draw spirits like a moth to flame. Not sure why, but elementals love novices. Probably because a novice is more likely to think they're getting the better end of a deal when the opposite is true. Just take care and get used to their different natures by talking with them.

There's quite a bit more, but if there's one thing I've learned in my years of bringing up novices, it's lecturing don't hold a candle to experience. There'll be plenty of time for lecturing, but it can wait until next I see you.

Until then, mind your mam, pay attention, and try not to make any deals.

ON THE INVAE

From the traveling journal of Tomas Runecarver

After some research I learned the strange insect-like creatures were invae, astral beings some associate with Horrors, as they were a harbinger of the Scourge. As the mana level rises, the barriers between our realm and the deep netherworlds weaken. This is what allows the Horrors to cross, but they are not the only astral entity that does so.

Like the Horrors, invae come from an unknown corner of astral space. Unlike Horrors, they do not feed on the pain and suffering of Namegivers. Since the summoning and banishing magic of the Elementalist and Nethermancer Disciplines can affect them (with difficulty), they are considered spirits, but distinct from the more common ally and elemental types.

Invae are only concerned with Namegivers as a means to cross into our world and expand their population. Admittedly, this puts them into conflict with Namegivers, and for practical purposes the invae are as bad as their more malevolent astral kin.

They've appeared in Barsaive in the past, most famously during the Invae Burnings, when it was discovered they had infiltrated and corrupted an organization devoted to the Passion Chorrolis. The ability of these spirits to hide their presence caused a panic in southwestern Barsaive, resulting in widespread destruction.

There are apparently two different forms invae can take. The more common ones resemble Namegivers with insect-like features: faceted eyes, patches of chitinous skin, mandibles, or the like. Some of these features can be subtle, and hidden without much difficulty. Those with more blatant deformities often hide themselves under large cloaks or similar concealing clothing.

The second type of invae—much more rare—resembles the insects of our world, but on a larger scale. I found a journal from an expedition into an invae hive in Scytha that described beetles ranging in size from a large dog to a draft horse.

In order to cross into our realm, an invae spirit needs a host body. The spirit enters the victim and over the course of the next few days transforms and takes over the body. Nothing remains of the victim's original personality. In some cases the spirit has access to the host's memories—though any magical abilities like talents or spell casting are lost.

Once a hive has established a foothold, it spreads its influence by summoning more of their kind to bond with folk abducted from nearby communities. As more Namegivers are turned, more powerful invae can be summoned and bonded.

The documents we recovered in the mine explained the presence of the invae. The Hooded Ones were exploring the ways an invae spirit controls and supplants the host's will, though to what purpose is unclear. Aside from secrecy, the Hooded Ones did not behave like a typical invae cult. There was a purpose to their research and they took care to keep the hive from getting out of control.

Given the history of invae in Barsaive, the presence of a 'controlled' hive below Thurdane is troubling. There isn't any evidence the Hooded Ones used the invae to gain influence in the Kingdom, but I shudder to think what might have happened if we had not thwarted their plans.

ON TASKED SPIRITS

From "Allies and Elementals" by Anselm the Graceful

Many students of the astral realms think of a third category of spirit: the tasked spirit. Unlike more free-willed elemental and ally spirits, a tasked spirit is one brought into our world through the use of a spell or magical talent for a particular purpose, for example, the 'orbiting spy' used by Nethermancers and Scouts.

There is some debate about the true nature of tasked spirits. Are they brought into being by the adept, a bit of astral energy given form while the magic of the spell or talent lasts? Are they instead independent beings, like other spirits, and the magic is a finely tuned summoning ritual which doesn't allow flexibility, like more traditional practices?

These debates, fortunately, are limited to the halls of academia and rarely impact the practices of those whose magic uses tasked spirits.

> 'Tasked' spirits are better called 'slave' spirits! They are given no chance to refuse and no way to negotiate for their service. The sooner their use is ended, the better!
> —*Krylak the Fervent, Beloved of Lochost*

USING SPIRITS IN ADVENTURES AND CAMPAIGNS

In the **Earthdawn** game, the Elementalist and Nethermancer Disciplines have several talents that interact with spirits. Even if you do not have these Disciplines in your player character group, your players will encounter gamemaster characters who follow these Disciplines. Spirits are a fact of life in Barsaive and it is worth giving some thought to how you will use them in your campaign.

Like Namegivers, each spirit is a unique individual with its own attitude and personality. They have thoughts, motivations, and emotions. However, because they are not native to the physical realm, their goals and behavior can seem bizarre and nonsensical.

Most spirits prefer to remain in astral space, manifesting only when necessary. A spirit in astral space cannot usually affect the physical world, and characters in the physical world cannot usually affect a spirit in astral space (for more information see **Astral and Physical Forms**, p. 206 in the *Player's Guide*). Once a spirit is physically manifest, it can affect characters and physical objects, and be affected itself.

Motivations, Attitudes, and Personality

Spirits possess personalities as distinct as any person. Some like to interact with Namegivers and even enjoy being summoned, while others resent being called and asked (or forced) to perform tasks for beings too limited to solve problems on their own. They can be shy or gregarious, placid or excitable, foolish or wise, or any combination. In general, the more powerful the spirit, the more complex its personality.

A weak spirit typically will have one or two strongly defined personality traits, often related to the type of spirit it is. For example, a weak zephyr elemental might be flighty and easily distracted, while a low powered graveyard spirit could be subdued and morose. More powerful spirits will still display aspects of their nature, but they will often show a greater range, and in some cases it may be very difficult to distinguish a powerful spirit from a Namegiver.

Adepts are advised to treat spirits—especially more powerful ones—with respect and caution. Spirits do not have a natural lifespan; they have a long memory and some display patience even dragons would envy. A wronged spirit will often find a way to return ill treatment. This long lifespan also means spirits can learn a great many things. Scholars have been known to seek out spirits to gain insight into the nature of magic, and spirits of deceased Namegivers can provide histories that would otherwise be lost to the Scourge.

STRENGTH RATINGS

A spirit's power is measured by its **Strength Rating**. The higher a spirit's Strength Rating, the more powerful it is in relation to other spirits, and the more powers at its disposal. Please note a spirit's Strength Rating is different from its Strength Attribute.

As a spirit's Strength Rating increases, its game statistics also increase. More information on this relationship is provided later in this chapter, under **Spirit Descriptions**, p. 375. Since a spirit's Strength Rating affects its Mystic Defense, summoning or otherwise affecting a spirit with a high Strength Rating can be difficult.

A spirit's Strength Rating increases as it ages; the older the spirit, the higher its rating can be. A spirit's age is no guarantee of a particular rating, however: a 400 year old spirit might have a Strength Rating of 5, while a 250 year old spirit might have a rating of 7.

The main reason for this is because of the other way a spirit's Strength Rating can increase. When a spirit is summoned, the summoner uses magic to connect to the spirit's pattern. As with any interaction between magic and patterns, this can cause the spirit's pattern to grow or change. Over time, this can increase the spirit's power and its Strength Rating. This can work in the spirit's favor, as a more powerful spirit is more difficult to summon and control.

As with many things relating to magical interaction, there is no hard and fast rule to determine when a spirit's Strength Rating increases. Therefore, this is left to the gamemaster's discretion. Here are a few guidelines, however: if a summoner repeatedly calls an unwilling spirit, the spirit's resistance to the call makes it more likely its Strength Rating will increase. Perhaps if the Summoning test fails, or does not achieve multiple successes, the spirit's Strength Rating increases.

On the other hand, some summoners develop relationships with particular spirits, calling them again and again. If the spirit is not Named (see **Named Spirits**, below), then the summoner might Name the spirit, which reinforces its pattern and can result in a higher Strength Rating. It is also possible sacrifices of magical energy (in the form of Legend Points or Karma) might enhance the spirit's power.

Great Form Spirits

Spirits with Strength Ratings of 13 and greater are considered **great form spirits**, and are almost always Named (see below). Few characters have the ability to summon such powerful beings and even fewer try to do so. Magicians who attempt to control great form spirits typically use ritual magic, often enhanced with pattern magic to gain more power over their target.

Challenge Values for Spirits

The incredible diversity of spirits, and the large number of potential powers they can display, make it difficult to give firm guidelines about a spirit's equivalent challenge value. Using a spirit's Strength Rating as the equivalent Circle can provide a reasonable starting point, but many factors can make a spirit more or less challenging. Look at the guidelines provided under Balancing Encounters (p. 246) to determine whether a spirit used as an encounter or opponent is a suitable challenge for your group.

NAMED SPIRITS

Some spirits are Named; such spirits are usually powerful beings, with Strength Ratings of 8 or more. In addition, having a Name grants them additional defenses against summoning and control. A summoner will not usually call up a Named spirit by accident. When attempting to summon or control a Named spirit, an additional success is required on all relevant tests.

If the summoner knows the spirit's Name, this restriction does not apply. Named spirits guard their Names jealously, and their true Name is often different from the one by which they are commonly known. If the summoner does not know the spirit's Name, a pattern item can be used. Unfortunately, finding a spirit's pattern item is often more difficult than learning its Name. A Named spirit cannot be forced to reveal its Name except under very unusual circumstances, usually involving Warden or Master level magic.

As previously mentioned, some summoners like to build positive relationships with particular spirits and will sometimes Name a spirit in order to strengthen the relationship. Generally, this is only done if the spirit has a Friendly Attitude or better (see **Gamemaster Character Attitudes**, p. 142), and typically increases the spirit's Strength Rating.

Any spirit can be Named (unless it already has one), but Naming a spirit who does not have a positive attitude towards the summoner carries a certain amount of risk. The Name gives the summoner power over the spirit, but the spirit will resent the increased control, and will likely begin working against the summoner, perhaps even trying to kill the character who knows its Name so it can be free from future tasks.

Ally Spirits and Names

Most assume Named ally spirits will be spirits of deceased Namegivers, but they are actually less common than people think. While their Names might be the easiest to learn, these spirits are often powerful and best dealt with by specialized magic like the Ritual of the Ghost Master.

It is possible for a Nethermancer to call up a Namegiver spirit without a Name—or at least an ally spirit who resembles a Namegiver in all appearances—but these shades are generally weaker, and do not express the depth of personality or knowledge of a full-fledged Namegiver spirit.

Other types of ally spirits can have Names, often the result of Naming by a previous summoner. The difficulties of learning the Name are similar to those for Named elemental spirits. If the Nethermancer is the type to develop a positive relationship with the spirit, the spirit might share its Name if its attitude becomes Loyal or better.

Elemental Spirits and Names

Many elemental spirits have Names, especially those with higher Strength Ratings. In most cases, an Elementalist can learn a spirit's Name by developing a good relationship with the spirit, generally requiring an attitude of Loyal or better.

As with ally spirits, many Named elemental spirits first received their Name from a friendly Elementalist. These Names can sometimes be found in old writings and grimoires, though this information is often a closely guarded secret as the Name could allow a summoner's rivals the ability to subvert his ally.

Invae Spirits and Names

According to the limited information known about these mysterious beings, invae spirits are rarely Named. The only examples of Named invae spirits are their "queens", powerful invae who appear to lead a hive.

SPIRIT POWERS

Spirits possess powers unique to spirits, as may also possess talents and spells available to adepts. The spirit descriptions later in this chapter list some of the powers common to these different spirits. The higher a spirit's Strength Rating, the more powers it has, and the more effective those powers become. Unless a power's description states otherwise, any type of spirit may possess the power.

The list of powers provided here is not comprehensive. Gamemasters should feel free to create additional powers for their games. Additionally, the provided restrictions are suggestions – spirits, particularly Named spirits, can break the "rules" assigned to them by Namegivers who do not fully understand their nature.

Game Terms

As with all powers and abilities in **Earthdawn**, spirits use a Step Number to make tests with their powers. These Step Numbers are usually based on one of the spirit's Attributes and add the spirit's Strength Rating (abbreviated "SR"). If a power's description does not provide a Step Number formula, the power has a specific effect that does not require a test.

Spirit powers use the same action types as talents, as noted in each entry.

Adaptability
Step: NA   **Action:** Free

Water spirits only. This power allows a spirit to increase one of their characteristics by +3. The following characteristics may be affected: Initiative, Physical Defense, Mystic Defense, Social Defense, Physical Armor, Mystic Armor, Wound Threshold, Unarmed Attack, and Unarmed Damage. This must be used prior to initiative each round and may be changed at the beginning of each round.

Aid Summoner
Step: CHA+SR   **Action:** Standard

This power allows a spirit to increase its summoner's magical abilities for the duration of a summoning. The spirit merges with the summoner, and makes an Aid Summoner test against the summoner's Mystic Defense. Each success grants the summoner a +1 bonus to talent tests. The summoner may only apply this bonus to one test per round, and takes 1 Strain each time they do so. While this power is in effect, the summoner takes on some superficial characteristics of the spirit that is aiding him. For example, his eyes glowing with a preternatural light, skin taking on a stony appearance, or hair growing small flowers.

Astral Portal
Step: WIL+SR   **Action:** Standard

Ally spirits only. Minimum SR 9. The spirit creates a portal allowing entry into astral space. The spirit makes an Astral Portal test against a DN of 6+the modifier for astral corruption (*Player's Guide*, p. 209). The portal remains open for 1 minute per success. The portal is two-way, allowing entry into and exit from astral space.

Confusion
Step: WIL+SR   **Action:** Standard

Ally spirits only. The spirit temporarily confuses a target by passing some of its own energy through him. The spirit makes a Confusion test against the Mystic Defense of a target within SR x 10 yards. For each success, the target suffers a –1 penalty to his Perception and Willpower tests, including talents and abilities based on those Attributes. The effect lasts for a number of minutes equal to the spirit's Strength Rating.

Curse
Step: WIL+SR   **Action:** Standard

Ally spirits only. The spirit curses a target. It makes a Curse test against the Mystic Defense of a target within SR x 10 yards. If successful, the target suffers a -2 penalty to one Attribute Step for one hour per success. The penalty affects all tests based on that Attribute. The spirit or its summoner chooses the affected Attribute. A target can only be affected by one use of this power at a time.

Destroy Weapon
Step: SR   **Action:** NA

Fire spirits only, requires Elemental Aura: The fire spirit's elemental aura also damages non-magical wooden or metal weapons which strike the spirit, unless the weapon is somehow fireproofed. Wooden weapons have their Damage Step reduced by the spirit's Strength Rating. Metal weapons have their Damage Step reduced by the amount the spirit's Strength Rating exceeds their Damage Step. For example, a normal broadsword (Step 5) suffers no ill effect from fire elementals up to Strength Rating 5.

Bonuses provided by the Forge Weapon talent (*Player's Guide*, p. 148) count towards the weapon's Damage Step for the purposes of this comparison. For example, a metal broadsword that has a +2 bonus from Forge Blade suffers no effects from fire elementals up to Strength Rating 7.

The effects of this power are cumulative, but damaged weapons may be repaired (*Player's Guide*, p. 411). If a weapon's Damage Step is reduced to 0, it is destroyed.

Detect True Element
Step: SR   **Action:** Standard

Elemental spirits only. This power enables an elemental spirit to detect the presence of True Elements, but only of the same type. For example, an air spirit could detect True Air by using this power, but not any other True Element. The spirit can detect any presence of the True Element within a number of miles equal to its Strength Rating.

Because Elementalists generally hope to locate True Elements for their own use, elemental spirits do not like using this power for their summoners. Any attempt to do so requires a Contest of Wills (*Player's Guide*, p. 368). If the summoner wins, the spirit leads the summoner to the nearest source of the relevant True Element within range. Elemental spirits will never aid a summoner in gathering True Elements, only in finding their location. Even a Contest of Wills cannot coerce a spirit to violate this principle.

Elemental Aura
Step: SR **Action:** NA

Elemental spirits only. Manifest elemental spirits with this power are surrounded by a damaging aura of their element. Air spirits may be surrounded by crackling lightning, fire by intense heat, while a water spirit may be surrounded by intense cold. All beings within 4 yards of the spirit suffer damage equal to the spirit's Strength Rating each round. Physical Armor protects against this damage.

Engulf
Step: STR+SR **Action:** Free

Elemental spirits only. The spirit surrounds a victim with its element, causing damage. The elemental must be physically manifest to use this power. This power allows the elemental to spend an additional success on an Attack test to automatically grapple the target. Once the victim is grappled, he is engulfed by the appropriate element and takes damage equal to the result of the Engulf test. The effect lasts until the grapple ends, and can be broken.

Air: The spirit makes the air unbreatheable. The victim can hold his breath (see p. 169), but begins to take damage if he falls unconscious. Mystic Armor protects against this damage.

Earth: The target suffers damage from the crushing weight. Physical Armor protects against this damage.

Fire: The target is covered in fire and starts to burn. Physical Armor protects against this damage.

Water: The spirit is capable of exerting great pressure on engulfed victims. Physical Armor protects against this damage and victims might also drown (see p. 168).

Wood: The target is covered in thorny vines that pierce his skin. Physical Armor protects against this damage.

Enhance Summoner
Step: CHA+SR **Action:** Standard

The spirit is able to provide a significant increase to its summoner's magical ability, but only for a short time. The spirit merges with the summoner, and makes an Enhance Summoner test agains the summoner's Mystic Defense. Each success allows the summoner to add the spirit's Strength Rating to one talent test. When using this bonus, the summoner takes strain equal to the spirit's Strength Rating to reflect the difficulty inherent in channeling the spirit's energy. If multiple uses are available, each bonus may be applied to a different test, but only one test per round. The effect lasts until the summoning ends, or all uses of this power have been exhausted. While the power is in effect, the summoner takes on some superficial characteristics of the spirit, which are exaggerated when applying the bonus to a talent. For example, hair drifting as in a breeze, giving off streams of smoke, or movements becoming more fluid and graceful.

Enrage Element
Step: WIL+SR **Action:** Standard

Elemental spirits only. The spirit creates a tumultuous whirlwind of its element. For example, an earth elemental creates a small storm of flying rocks. The tempest covers an area with a radius of the spirit's Strength Rating in yards, centered on the spirit. The spirit makes an Enrage Element test to determine how much damage suffered by targets within the affected area, and may sustain the effect by using a Standard Action each round. Physical Armor protects against this damage. All targets within the area of effect are considered Harried (*Player's Guide*, p.388).

Find
Step: PER+SR **Action:** Standard

The spirit traces an item to its origin. For example, if a spirit has a lock of hair, it can locate the hair's owner. If it has a piece of a wall, it can locate the building from which the piece came. Elemental spirits with this power can only use it on items that are connected with their element.

The target must be within SR x 10 miles to be affected by this power. The spirit makes a Find test against the target's Mystic Defense. If successful, the spirit is able to locate the target, but the search takes one hour per 10 miles to the target. If the summoning duration ends before the spirit can find the target and report back, the spirit often departs.

Hardened Armor
Step: NA **Action:** NA

Earth, invae, and wood spirits only. Additional successes from Attack tests deal one less damage per success against an elemental with this power. Typically, this means instead of +2 damage per additional success, the attacker only gets +1 damage per additional success.

Insubstantial
Step: NA **Action:** NA

Air, ally, fire, and water spirits only. Attacking a manifested spirit with this power using physical weapons (such as a sword or a bow) is very difficult. Attacks with such items require an additional success, unless the attack has an area of effect.

Invisibility
Step: DEX+SR   **Action:** NA

Air, ally, and water spirits only. These spirits may become invisible to mundane sight at will. The spirit makes an Invisibility test, the result of which is the Difficulty Number for any attempts to detect the elemental. The spirit may be seen normally with Astral Sight.

Karma
Step: SR   **Action:** NA

The spirit has the ability to use Karma. The spirit has a pool of SR x 4 Karma points, and may spend Karma on any test it performs. Each point allows the spirit to roll dice equal to its Karma Step and add them to the test result.

Manifest
Step: N/A   **Action:** Standard

The spirit can manifest in the physical realm. It takes a Standard Action for the spirit to enter the physical realm, or to return to astral space. Remember that to affect the physical realm, the spirit must be manifest.

Manipulate Element
Step: WIL+SR   **Action:** Standard

Elemental spirits only. The spirit can change the basic structure of any object composed of the spirit's native element. For example, a water elemental could turn a pool into solid ice. The gamemaster determines the specific effects of each use of the Manipulate Element power, but the radius of the affected area cannot exceed the spirit's Strength Rating in yards. The effect lasts for a number of minutes equal to the spirit's Manipulate Element test result.

Poison
Step: SR   **Action:** N/A

Ally, invae, and wood spirits only. The spirit's attacks inflict poison. It is assumed any unarmed attacks benefit from this power, though other powers may benefit as noted. The most common poison causes damage, though some spirits may have debilitating or paralytic poison instead.

Remove Element
Step: WIL+SR   **Action:** Standard

Elemental spirits only. The spirit can remove any trace of its native element from an area. For example, an earth spirit could use the power to damage a building by removing the dirt around one or more of the building's supporting walls. The radius of the area affected cannot exceed the spirit's Strength Rating in yards. The spirit makes a Remove Element test against the target's Mystic Defense. This power cannot be used on anything with a true pattern.

Share Knowledge
Step: PER+SR   **Action:** Standard

Elemental spirits only. The spirit learns general information about recent activity in, on, or near its native element. For example, a breeze may carry snippets of conversation to an air spirit. The spirit makes a Share Knowledge (6) test. Each success allows the spirit to learn about events in the previous hour (so three successes allows a spirit to learn about events within the past three hours). The gamemaster determines exactly how much information the elemental learns.

Soothe
Step: CHA+SR   **Action:** Standard

Elemental spirits only. The spirit produces soothing sounds or smells that cause its target to relax, such as a cool breeze, the sound of leaves rustling in the wind, or the sound of a crackling fire. The spirit makes a Soothe test against the target's Social Defense. Each success grants the target gains a +1 bonus to his next Recovery test.

Spear
Step: STR+SR   **Action:** Standard

Elemental spirits only. The spirit forms a spear from its elemental essence to damage a target. For example, a water elemental might throw a spear in the form of an icicle, while a fire elemental might throw a bolt of flame. The spirit makes a Spellcasting test against the Mystic Defense of a target within SR x 10 yards. If successful, the spirit makes a Spear test to determine how much damage the target takes, reduced by Physical Armor. If the target suffers damage, an additional effect occurs based on elemental type:

Air: The target must make a Knockdown test against the damage dealt.
Earth: The target is slowed. Their movement rate is lowered by 2 yards per success on the Spellcasting test.
Fire: The spear does +2 Damage per success on the Spellcasting test.
Water: The spirit may choose one of the bonus effects from another element type.
Wood: The target is harried (*Player's Guide*, p. 388) for 1 round per success on the Spellcasting test.

Spells
Step: Special   **Action:** NA

Ally and elemental spirits only. The spirit knows spells. Elemental spirits may only cast spells of their native elements. Ally spirits can generally cast spells from one Discipline, though some powerful ally spirits can cast spells from two or more Disciplines. The spirit's Strength Rating determines the maximum spell Circle it may know. Thus, a Strength 6 ally spirit could know any spell up to Sixth Circle. Spirits typically know a number of spells equal to their Strength Rating. This power may be selected more than once to learn additional spells. Spirits may not know or cast summoning or binding spells.

The normal requirements for weaving threads apply (spirits use their Spellcasting Step to weave any necessary threads), but spirits do not need spell matrices or suffer negative effects from casting raw magic. Spirits can weave additional threads using their Strength Rating for Circle in the casting discipline. Elemental spirits automatically weave these additional threads for free without requiring any additional threads to be woven.

Talents
Step: Special   **Action:** Special (see text)

Some spirits have powers based on adept talents. Refer to the Talents chapter of the *Player's Guide* for a description of the talent in question. Spirits suffer Strain for using talents if indicated in the talent description. In place of the talent rank, use the spirit's Strength Rating.

Temperature
Step: WIL+SR   **Action:** Standard

Air, fire, and water spirits only. The spirit can alter the temperature in an area with a radius up to its Strength Rating in yards. The spirit raises or lowers the temperature enough to cause discomfort or otherwise distract characters within the area of effect, but not enough to cause damage. The spirit makes a Temperature test, comparing it to the Mystic Defense of each character in the area of effect. Each success causes affected targets to suffer a -1 penalty to their Perception and Willpower based tests. The effect lasts for a number of minutes equal to the spirit's Strength Rating.

SPIRIT DESCRIPTIONS

The following descriptions are organized by spirit type. The provided game statistics follow the guidelines for creatures (see p. 252). Most of the examples below include simple formulas to calculate a spirit's game statistics. The spirit's Strength Rating appears abbreviated as 'SR'. For example, air spirits with a Strength Rating of 5-8 are listed with a Social Defense of 6+SR. A Strength Rating 5 air spirit would have a Social Defense of 11 (6+5).

The provided statistics are guidelines and serve to form a general baseline for spirits of that type. Since each spirit is a unique entity, the gamemaster should feel free to modify these values to suit the needs of his game. The powers listed for a spirit are only the most common examples. The listed powers are the powers every spirit of the type automatically receives. In general, spirits will have an additional power for every two points of Strength Rating. A list of suggested powers is provided for common powers for each spirit type.

In addition to the general game statistics provided for each type of spirit, some concrete examples are provided to give some insight into how spirits can be used in your game.

Spirits and Damage

A spirit's 'body' is made up of astral essence bound into a pattern that defines the spirit's nature and powers. When a spirit suffers damage, this essence is disrupted. Spirits can suffer Wounds, which represent significant harm to its binding essence. Spirits do not sleep, and so cannot be knocked unconscious. When a spirit suffers damage in excess of its Death Rating, it is destroyed. Spirits have a sense of self, and thus a desire for self-preservation. A spirit in danger of being destroyed is likely to flee by withdrawing to astral space where most Namegivers will have a hard time affecting it.

Great Form Spirits

Each great form spirit is a powerful, unique entity. They are difficult to summon and control, and are only rarely encountered. The guidelines provided here are not intended to handle these beings, but they can serve as a starting point to create even more powerful spirits. The appearance of these entities in a game should be a significant event rather than a casual encounter, and it is better to create these beings from scratch rather than fill in numbers from a template.

ALLY SPIRITS

There are a wide variety of ally spirits, and general statements about them end up vague by necessity. Some ally spirits resemble the ghosts or spirits of Namegivers, while others are beings that may relate to some aspect of Namegiver culture or emotion. Some connect to aspects of the world not traditionally associated with an elemental spirit, or are strange fauna of the astral realms with no discernible connection to anything understood by Namegivers.

Even more than the examples for elemental spirits, the game statistics provided here are guidelines. The gamemaster should determine the exact powers and spells of a particular ally spirit to suit the nature of the spirit and the needs of his game. The Ally Spirit Powers Table provides recommendations for minimum Strength Ratings of different ally spirit powers.

Ally Spirit Powers Table

Spirit Power	Minimum SR
Confusion, Talents	1
Find, Curse	5
Astral Portal	9

Some spirit types provide modifications to the baseline game statistics provided. These should be applied as-is, and do not modify any derived characteristics. For example, a change in a spirit's Dexterity does not automatically change their Physical Defense.

Strength Rating 1-4

DEX:	5	Initiative:	4+SR	Unconsciousness:	NA
STR:	5	Physical Defense:	7+SR	Death:	30
TOU:	5	Mystic Defense:	8+SR	Wound:	8
PER:	5	Social Defense:	8+SR	Knockdown:	5
WIL:	5	Physical Armor:	4	Recovery Tests:	2
CHA:	5	Mystic Armor:	3+SR		
Move:	12				

Actions: 1; Unarmed 5+SR (5)
Powers: Astral Sight, Manifest, Power, Spellcasting

Strength Rating 5-8

DEX:	9	Initiative:	4+SR	Unconsciousness:	NA
STR:	9	Physical Defense:	8+SR	Death:	54
TOU:	9	Mystic Defense:	9+SR	Wound:	14
PER:	9	Social Defense:	9+SR	Knockdown:	9
WIL:	9	Physical Armor:	6	Recovery Tests:	4
CHA:	9	Mystic Armor:	3+SR		

Move: 12
Actions: 2; Unarmed 6+SR (9)
Powers: Astral Sight, Manifest, Power, Spellcasting

Strength Rating 9-12

DEX:	13	Initiative:	4+SR	Unconsciousness:	NA
STR:	13	Physical Defense:	11+SR	Death:	78
TOU:	13	Mystic Defense:	12+SR	Wound:	19
PER:	13	Social Defense:	12+SR	Knockdown:	13
WIL:	13	Physical Armor:	10	Recovery Tests:	6
CHA:	13	Mystic Armor:	3+SR		

Move: 12
Actions: 3; Unarmed 9+SR (13)
Powers: Astral Sight, Manifest, Power, Spellcasting

Bone Spirits (Sample Ally Spirit Type)

It is very rare to encounter a bone spirit which is not tasked through the Bone Circle spell. When so tasked, they are extremely territorial and almost animalistic. Otherwise, they tend to be reclusive, quiet, and reluctant to leave the area in which they have made their home. Typical areas where bone spirits call home include old battlefields, crypts, and graveyards. It is quite uncommon to find bone spirits in a broken kaer and the bone spirits residing within are likely quite mad.

When tasked, bone spirits are not particularly creative and will apply the most direct solution to any problem. Their form varies, though typically contains bones, ragged cloth, and chains. A common form is at least the upper torso of a Namegiver wrapped in loose chains and black, ragged robes. It isn't known for certain if a tasked bone spirit will take the same form as one which is simply summoned.

When summoned through means other than the Bone Circle spell, the offerings in which bone spirits are most interested are the stories of the place they inhabit and of the remains which reside there as well.

Listed below are the average changes from a typical ally spirit and suggested powers. The list of suggested powers includes all available selections when a bone spirit is summoned through the Bone Circle spell (*Player's Guide*, p. 318). This list supersedes the list provided in the spell description.

DEX:	+1	Initiative:	+1	Unconsciousness:	NA
STR:	+1	Physical Defense:	+1	Death:	+0
TOU:	+0	Mystic Defense:	-1	Wound:	+0
PER:	+0	Social Defense:	-2	Knockdown:	+1
WIL:	+0	Physical Armor:	+1	Recovery Tests:	+0
CHA:	-2	Mystic Armor:	-1		
Move:	+0				

Actions: +0; Unarmed +1 (+1)

Suggested Powers: Aid Summoner, Astral Interference, Awareness, Banish, Confusion, Curse, Enhance Summoner, Frighten, Invisibility, Lifesight, Surprise Strike, True Sight

City Spirits (Sample Ally Spirit Type)

This is possibly the most diverse group of ally spirits and some Nethermancers argue against it as a category. The arguments against using this grouping is based around the variety of forms and functions these spirits perform. However, there are enough commonalities for it to be useful for taxonomy.

City spirits generally love to be around Namegivers, a feeling which is not always mutual, and are never found outside of dense urban centers of their own volition. In fact, when summoned to even a hamlet, these spirits can become intractable, verging on catatonic. They feel little attachment to particular Namegivers, though may connect with a specific city or neighborhood, or even a type of district found within cities.

They are generally non-confrontational spirits and prone to enjoying company and games. Many affect the customs and mannerisms of their favorite time period within their favorite city, which may make dealing with the spirit difficult depending on just how obscure it is. These preferences can easily change between summonings for these mercurial spirits.

City spirits have a variety of preferred forms, but favor Namegivers, animals, and animated objects. Their Namegiver forms may reflect a single style, or an amalgam regions and times (often a clue to what form of etiquette to use), while the animals are always what will commonly be found in their location with features which mark them as clearly unnatural. They will never, however, take the form of an insect.

Listed below are the average changes from a typical ally spirit and suggested powers.

DEX:	+0	Initiative:	+0	Unconsciousness:	NA
STR:	-1	Physical Defense:	+0	Death:	+0
TOU:	+0	Mystic Defense:	+1	Wound:	+0
PER:	+1	Social Defense:	+1	Knockdown:	+0
WIL:	-1	Physical Armor:	+0	Recovery Tests:	+0
CHA:	+1	Mystic Armor:	+0		
Move:	+0				

Actions: +0; Unarmed -1 (-1)

Suggested Powers: Aid Summoner, Confusion, Curse, Lifesight, Empathic Sense, Enhance Summoner, Find, Talents (typically related to evasion or interaction)

Dodger (Sample Named Ally Spirit)

Dodger is a Strength Rating 6 Named city spirit that favors the ghettos of Barsavian cities, especially those primarily populated by orks, to whom it has a particular fondness. It loves to collect things, whether information or small objects, and will respond well to any such offerings.

This city spirit prefers the form of ork children dressed in the local style, though it doesn't seem to understand the concept of gender very well. Dodger will also adopt the current local lower class customs of whatever city it is currently located, even if it just arrived - it seems to have a perfect knowledge of such things.

Dealing with this spirit is relatively simple, though it refuses to engage in any kind of violence. Even a successful contest of wills will only lead to it finding some way to get out of it, making all such attempts useless at best and only earning the enmity of the spirit. It will, however, happily share information and even items from its collection if given something of at least equal value in return.

DEX:	10	Initiative:	11	Unconsciousness:	NA
STR:	8	Physical Defense:	16	Death:	54
TOU:	9	Mystic Defense:	16	Wound:	14
PER:	10	Social Defense:	15	Knockdown:	9
WIL:	8	Physical Armor:	6	Recovery Tests:	4
CHA:	9	Mystic Armor:	8		

Move: 16
Actions: 2; Unarmed 12 (8)
Powers: Astral Sight (16), Confusion (14), Find (16), Karma (6, 24), Invisibility (16), Manifest, Spellcasting (16)

Greyswain (Sample Named Ally Spirit)

Greyswain is a Strength Rating 10 guardian spirit which was once popular with various elf summoners prior to the Scourge. Since the reNaming of Blood Wood, the guardian spirit refuses to deal with blood elves and has been affected by what can only be termed melancholy.

When summoned, Greyswain is polite to a fault and affects a speech pattern popular in the court of Dalia. The spirit is reluctant to become embroiled in the conflicts between Namegivers, though can be swayed to give aid and protection to an underdog in desperate need. Against Horrors and their kind, Greyswain is quite willing to negotiate favorable terms and may go above the terms of the agreement if the spirit feels the service is a noble one. The offerings Greyswain prefers above all others are finely crafted works of art which are weapons or symbolic of warfare, for example a beautifully wrought piece from a game of strategy.

Greyswain takes the form of a tall warrior with a winged great helm, wrapped in impossibly fine plate and chain. Prior to the Scourge, the spirit's armor was described as gleaming silver, but now is tarnished. Greyswain fights with a variety of melee weapons, but favors the sword and lance.

DEX:	14	**Initiative:**	15	**Unconsciousness:**	NA
STR:	14	**Physical Defense:**	24	**Death:**	78
TOU:	13	**Mystic Defense:**	24	**Wound:**	22
PER:	12	**Social Defense:**	23	**Knockdown:**	16
WIL:	12	**Physical Armor:**	16	**Recovery Tests:**	6
CHA:	15	**Mystic Armor:**	12		
Move:	14				

Actions: 3; Unarmed: 21 (14), Sword: 23 (25), Lance: 22 (26)
Powers: Aid Summoner (25), Astral Sight (22), Crushing Blow (24), Karma (10, 40), Lion Heart (22), Manifest, Spellcasting (22)

Guardian Spirit (Sample Ally Spirit Type)

Guardians are a diverse group of spirits coming in a wide variety of forms, though they are most commonly found in the shape of creatures commonly associated with protection and fighting prowess, and occasionally humanoids. Despite their aggressive appearance, not all guardian spirits are inclined to direct confrontation. Many prefer to provide assistance and support to their summoner, though some are more than willing to directly engage in combat. The main commonality is all guardian spirits have some capacity and stomach for combat.

Just as they are diverse in appearance, they are diverse in temperament, motivations, and desires. These spirits tend to be direct, but may just as well follow complex rules of etiquette or speak entirely in riddles and questions. Despite in complications in communication, guardian spirits are naturally inclined to service and will serve out their agreement the letter if not also the spirit.

Listed below are the average changes from a typical ally spirit and suggested powers.

DEX:	+1	Initiative:	+1	Unconsciousness:	NA
STR:	+1	Physical Defense:	+1	Death:	+0
TOU:	+0	Mystic Defense:	+0	Wound:	+2
PER:	-1	Social Defense:	-1	Knockdown:	+3
WIL:	-1	Physical Armor:	+1	Recovery Tests:	+0
CHA:	+1	Mystic Armor:	-1		
Move:	+0				

Actions: +0; Unarmed +2 (+3)

Suggested Powers: Aid Summoner, Enhance Summoner, Karma, Lifesight, Talents (typically related to combat and protection)

Powers

Improved Characteristics: Guardian spirits have improved characteristics over other, typical ally spirits. To compensate for this, they do not receive the extra power to select as other ally spirits. They only gain powers at even Strength Ratings as is typical of all spirits.

Hearth Spirit (Sample Ally Spirit Type)

Hearth spirits are common throughout Barsaive and gravitate towards communities, particularly smaller, close-knit communities. Some travel from home to home, while others reside in only one and have seen generations of Namegivers within their walls. Their primary interest is the home in which they reside and the people within said home are secondary. In particular, they appreciate cleanliness and good repair, though a happy and caring family will also keep them in good spirits.

Some hearth spirits can become twisted through events and their protective nature becomes possessive and violent. They begin to see anything outside of their narrow view of acceptable as a slight and take escalating measures against the offender. This can take the form of a door being left open (or being closed), or even a crooked picture being straightened, all meet reprisal from the angered spirit.

Dealing with hearth spirits is simple to the point where even non-adepts can earn their favor. Their preferred offerings are handmade objects and foodstuffs. Families which leave these things for them over time will be rewarded in kind with various services. It bears to mention, things which they take to be offerings may not have been intended as such. For example, a sock left on the floor may have been seen a gift by the hearth spirit. They are quite willing to provide aid and comfort when summoned, but loathe to engage in destructive acts.

Listed below are the average changes from a typical ally spirit and suggested powers.

DEX:	+0	Initiative:	+0	Unconsciousness:	NA
STR:	+0	Physical Defense:	+0	Death:	+0
TOU:	+0	Mystic Defense:	+0	Wound:	+0
PER:	+0	Social Defense:	+0	Knockdown:	+0
WIL:	+0	Physical Armor:	+0	Recovery Tests:	+0
CHA:	+0	Mystic Armor:	+0		
Move:	+0				

Actions: +0; Unarmed +0 (0)
Suggested Powers: Aid Summoner, Confusion, Craftsman, Curse, Empathic Sense, Enhance Summoner, Lifesight, Talents (typically related to healing and protection)

Muse (Sample Ally Spirit)

These ally spirits are particularly popular with artists, artisans, and craftsmen of all stripes. There is considerable disagreement among scholars as to where they fit within ally spirit classifications. Guidance spirit is a popular grouping, though refuted by the behaviors of muses, which fly in the face of typical behavior. City spirit is also widely supported given their attachment to population centers, however muses have been encountered by lone summoners away from anyone else, seeking to create. Others still believe a category of creation spirits should exist for them, though others will demand dwarfs stop with this obsessive need to fit everything into tidy boxes for examination.

When they first appear, their form is a simple but beautiful shape of light and sound. Those watching it move cannot help but feel some epiphany just at the edge of their comprehension. Once they have begun aiding someone in their task, their shape becomes ever more complex as it progresses to completion. Within the colors, lines, and sounds can be found exactly what is needed to further the creation. It can be an addictive feeling for those who have experienced it and some refer to it as being "taken by the muse".

Dealing with a muse depends on the nature of the task. They are willing to help with any creation, from a song to a thread weapon, so long as there is only one person involved. Anything which stretches beyond a sole vision and one person quickly loses their assistance. Services which require direct action on the spirit's part will require a contest of wills and result in a sullen spirit which is virtually useless.

Their personality is whatever the creator needs for their project, though it will be consistent throughout the service. This can be a harsh taskmaster, a thoughtful sounding board for ideas, or a constant companion. In return for their assistance, they will request some specific additions to the project to be named at the right time. These never betray the intent, but can have an impact on the finished product. It is not unheard of for muses to recognize the work of other muses with artists who frequently use these spirits in their work.

Statistics are provided for a Strength Rating 5 muse, but other variants are possible.

DEX:	10	**Initiative:**	9	**Unconsciousness:**	NA
STR:	4	**Physical Defense:**	16	**Death:**	54
TOU:	8	**Mystic Defense:**	14	**Wound:**	14
PER:	10	**Social Defense:**	14	**Knockdown:**	4
WIL:	10	**Physical Armor:**	6	**Recovery Tests:**	4
CHA:	12	**Mystic Armor:**	9		

Move: 14 (flying)
Actions: 1; Unarmed 9 (7)
Powers: Aid Summoner (17), Astral Sight (15), Enhance Summoner (17), Karma (5, 20), Manifest

ELEMENTAL SPIRITS

Air Spirits

Air spirits embody elemental air. Air spirits tend to be perceptive and possess better mental acuity than most other elemental spirits. Generally good-natured, but when angered a carefree breeze can become a vicious storm. Of all the elemental spirits, air spirits are the most willing to accept summoning and are the first elemental spirits with which most novice Elementalists will interact.

Air spirits frequently enjoy the material plane and the company of Namegivers. They prefer to be outdoors, or at least in a location near the open sky, becoming uncomfortable in enclosed places—especially deep underground.

A manifest air spirit may take many forms. Air elementals have been known to manifest as a whirlwind, or gentle breeze. Others resemble fog or clouds. Air elementals often assume humanoid faces that appear as wispy, changing visages floating in the midst of their bodies.

Strength Rating 1-4

DEX:	7	**Initiative:**	7+SR	**Unconsciousness:**	NA
STR:	3	**Physical Defense:**	9+SR	**Death:**	24
TOU:	4	**Mystic Defense:**	7+SR	**Wound:**	6
PER:	6	**Social Defense:**	5+SR	**Knockdown:**	Immune
WIL:	5	**Physical Armor:**	2	**Recovery Tests:**	2
CHA:	4	**Mystic Armor:**	1+SR		

Move: 16 (flying)
Actions: 1; Attack 7+SR (5)
Powers: Astral Sight, Insubstantial, Manifest, Power (generally Invisibility), Spellcasting

Suggested Powers: Aid Summoner, Find, Enhance Summoner, Invisibility, Karma, Share Knowledge, Spear, Spells, Temperature

Strength Rating 5-8

DEX:	11	Initiative:	7+SR	Unconsciousness:	NA
STR:	7	Physical Defense:	10+SR	Death:	48
TOU:	8	Mystic Defense:	8+SR	Wound:	12
PER:	10	Social Defense:	6+SR	Knockdown:	Immune
WIL:	9	Physical Armor:	4	Recovery Tests:	4
CHA:	8	Mystic Armor:	1+SR		

Move: 18 (flying)
Actions: 2; Attack 7+SR (4+SR)
Powers: Astral Sight, Insubstantial, Manifest, Power (generally Invisibility), Spellcasting
Suggested Powers: Aid Summoner, Find, Enhance Summoner, Invisibility, Karma, Share Knowledge, Spear, Spells, Temperature

Strength Rating 9-12

DEX:	15	Initiative:	7+SR	Unconsciousness:	NA
STR:	11	Physical Defense:	12+SR	Death:	72
TOU:	12	Mystic Defense:	10+SR	Wound:	18
PER:	14	Social Defense:	8+SR	Knockdown:	Immune
WIL:	13	Physical Armor:	7	Recovery Tests:	6
CHA:	12	Mystic Armor:	1+SR		

Move: 20 (flying)
Actions: 3, Attack 10+SR (4+SR)
Powers: Astral Sight, Insubstantial, Manifest, Power (generally Invisibility), Spellcasting
Suggested Powers: Aid Summoner, Find, Enhance Summoner, Invisibility, Karma, Share Knowledge, Spear, Spells, Temperature
Powers
Vulnerability to Earth: Attacks with the earth keyword against air spirits ignore any protection provided by armor.

Gargan (Sample Named Air Spirit)

Gargan is a Strength Rating 10 Named air spirit who once spent centuries bound to a thread item before escaping. During this time of forced servitude, it has learned a great deal about Namegivers and to hate them. While Gargan does its best to conceal this attitude, it cannot hide the sense of contempt it feels for those of the physical plane. The spirit's appearance reflects its poisonous mind: noxious green fumes forming an enormous troll with grasping claws and dirty yellow eyes.

Interacting with Gargan is notoriously difficult. The spirit is aggressive and manipulative, and will change its attitude and tactics in conversation at a moment's notice to further its own ends. The spirit's primary drive is to punish (or kill if possible) Namegivers, especially those with the ability to summon spirits. Towards these ends,

Gargan is involved in a variety of different plots to manipulate Namegivers against each other and generally make life worse overall. The spirit does have a particular interest in thread items with bound spirits and has gone to considerable lengths in the past to acquire such items.

Gargan is most often summoned by unscrupulous adepts who care little for innocent bystanders as a means to kill their enemies, those who require information at any cost, or have been misled. However, these very same summoners often regret the decision to ask for aid as Gargan has a long memory and will seek revenge on those who impose their will on the spirit.

DEX:	15	**Initiative:**	17	**Unconsciousness:**	NA
STR:	11	**Physical Defense:**	22	**Death:**	72
TOU:	12	**Mystic Defense:**	20	**Wound:**	18
PER:	14	**Social Defense:**	18	**Knockdown:**	Immune
WIL:	13	**Physical Armor:**	7	**Recovery Tests:**	6
CHA:	12	**Mystic Armor:**	11		

Move: 20 (flying)
Actions: 3; Unarmed 20 (14, Poison)
Powers: Astral Sight (24), Elemental Aura (10, Poison), Engulf (21), Enrage Element (23), Insubstantial, Karma (10, 40), Poison (10), Spear (21, Poison), Spellcasting (24)
Poison (10): Characters damaged by Gargan's Spear power are affected by a damaging Step 10 poison [Onset: instant, Interval 5/1 round].
Vulnerability to Earth: Attacks with the earth keyword against air spirits ignore any protection provided by armor.

Mistral (Sample Air Spirit)

Mistrals, also called storm spirits by some, embody the rash furious nature of air. They assume the form of a large pegasus, 12 feet tall at the shoulder. Their body is violently swirling grey winds with crackling eyes of blue lightning.

They have a relatively harsh view of the physical plane and do not like being there any more than required. Mistrals have two primary drives: to become stronger and to return to their elemental home. Due to the former, these spirits are more combat capable than most air spirits and can be quite dangerous when provoked.

Successful bargaining with a Mistral almost invariably involves providing the spirit with the means to become more powerful. Despite their tempestuous nature, long-lasting bonds can be forged and with them by those who are respectful and continue to invest in the spirit.

Statistics are provided for a Strength Rating 8 mistral, but other variants are possible.

DEX:	11	Initiative:	15	Unconsciousness:	NA
STR:	7	Physical Defense:	18	Death:	48
TOU:	8	Mystic Defense:	16	Wound:	12
PER:	10	Social Defense:	14	Knockdown:	Immune
WIL:	9	Physical Armor:	4	Recovery Tests:	4
CHA:	8	Mystic Armor:	9		

Move: 18 (flying)
Actions: 2; Unarmed 15 (12)
Powers: Astral Sight (18), Elemental Aura (8), Engulf (15), Insubstantial, Invisibility (19), Karma (8, 32), Manifest, Spear (15), Spellcasting (18)
Vulnerability to Earth: Attacks with the earth keyword against air spirits ignore any protection provided by armor.

Sylph (Sample Air Spirit)

Sylphs are one of the most common spirits to be summoned. They are masters of air and when manifested in their natural form, they are completely invisible to the naked eye (but not astral sensing). In contrast, when viewed astrally, they appear as a floating, perfect sphere of about 2 feet in diameter. They are capable of radically altering this form when they desire, however, and often appear as androgynous, semi-transparent pale blue humanoids of any Namegiver type.

They are curious by nature and enjoy interaction with Namegivers on this plane of existence. As such, they are quite knowledgeable and understand several languages, though their own speech is imperceptible to the common Namegiver. They are relatively easy to bargain with and usually will be content with opportunities to interact with large numbers of people or guidance in learning a new language. The spirits are most often summoned as scouts or spies to gather intelligence but have a number of other potential uses.

Statistics are provided for a Strength Rating 5 sylph, but other variants are possible.

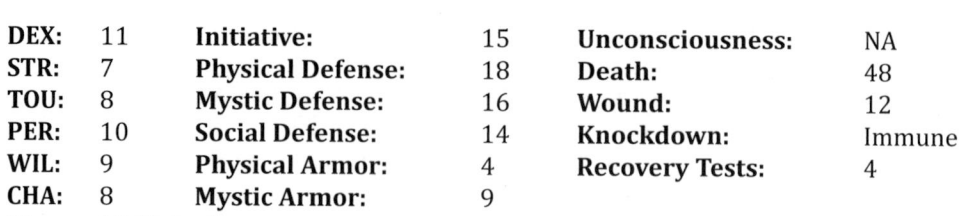

DEX:	11	Initiative:	12	Unconsciousness:	NA
STR:	7	Physical Defense:	15	Death:	48
TOU:	8	Mystic Defense:	13	Wound:	12
PER:	10	Social Defense:	11	Knockdown:	Immune
WIL:	9	Physical Armor:	4	Recovery Tests:	4
CHA:	8	Mystic Armor:	6		

Move: 18 (flying)
Actions: 2; Unarmed 12 (9)
Powers: Aid Summoner (13), Astral Sight (15), Insubstantial, Invisibility (16), Spellcasting (15)
Vulnerability to Earth: Attacks with the earth keyword against air spirits ignore any protection provided by armor.
Spells: Air Armor, Fingers of Wind, Slow Weapon, Winds of Deflection, Air Blast

Earth Spirits

The element of earth is the foundation of the physical world, known for its reliability. Earth spirits often embody this nature, tending to be patient and calm. They take their time, speaking slowly and are deliberate in thought and deed. This placid exterior can lead some to treat earth spirits as dull and unemotional. The wise summoner, however, knows the sturdiness of rock can shift, resulting in an avalanche. Once an earth spirit has set on a course of action, it is very difficult to sway them from their course.

Earth spirits do not typically like being called to the material plane, much preferring their native realm. Some find the open sky troubling and weaker spirits might even display behavior resembling agoraphobia. They are more comfortable in underground environments, like caverns and mines, and are also uncomfortable around larger bodies of water. When manifest, an earth spirit will most often appear within an existing outcropping of rock or dirt, shaping it into a vaguely humanoid face to communicate.

Strength Rating 1-4

DEX:	3	Initiative:	2	Unconsciousness:	NA
STR:	6	Physical Defense:	6	Death:	42
TOU:	7	Mystic Defense:	9+SR	Wound:	11
PER:	4	Social Defense:	6	Knockdown:	6+SR
WIL:	6	Physical Armor:	5+SR	Recovery Tests:	3
CHA:	4	Mystic Armor:	4+SR		

Move: 10
Actions: 1; Unarmed 6+SR (9+SR)
Powers: Astral Sight, Manifest, Spellcasting
Suggested Powers: Aid Summoner, Engulf, Enhance Summoner, Enrage Element, Find, Hardened Armor, Karma, Manipulate Element, Remove Element, Spear, Spells

Strength Rating 5-8

DEX:	7	Initiative:	6	Unconsciousness:	NA
STR:	10	Physical Defense:	8	Death:	66
TOU:	11	Mystic Defense:	10+SR	Wound:	17
PER:	8	Social Defense:	5+SR	Knockdown:	10+SR
WIL:	10	Physical Armor:	6+SR	Recovery Tests:	5
CHA:	8	Mystic Armor:	4+SR		

Move: 10
Actions: 2; Unarmed 7+SR (10+SR)
Powers: Astral Sight, Manifest, Spellcasting
Suggested Powers: Aid Summoner, Engulf, Enhance Summoner, Enrage Element, Find, Hardened Armor, Karma, Manipulate Element, Remove Element, Spear, Spells

Strength Rating 9-12

DEX:	11	Initiative:	10	Unconsciousness:	NA
STR:	14	Physical Defense:	14	Death:	90
TOU:	15	Mystic Defense:	13+SR	Wound:	23
PER:	12	Social Defense:	8+SR	Knockdown:	14+SR
WIL:	14	Physical Armor:	8+SR	Recovery Tests:	7
CHA:	12	Mystic Armor:	4+SR		
Move:	10				

Actions: 2; Unarmed 9+SR (15+SR)
Powers: Astral Sight, Manifest, Spellcasting
Suggested Powers: Aid Summoner, Engulf, Enhance Summoner, Enrage Element, Find, Hardened Armor, Karma, Manipulate Element, Remove Element, Spear, Spells

Powers

Earth Movement: Earth elementals can move freely through dirt, earth, and stone at their normal movement rate, with only a slight disturbance on the surface if they are nearby.

Manifestation Restriction: Earth elementals require the presence of earth to manifest. This requirement can present a problem when the elemental attempts to manifest aboard a ship, on the upper floor of a wooden building, or under other special circumstances. Earth elementals may manifest as pools of mud, large rocks, clods of dirt, or in many other forms.

Vulnerability to Wood: Wood-based attacks against earth spirits ignore any protection provided by armor.

Ethrys (Sample Named Earth Spirit)

Commonly seen on the material plane, Ethrys is a Strength Rating 8 earth spirit that takes the form of a hulking wolf with weathered features of ashen stone and often mistaken for a statue when at rest. Ethrys is unique among elementals and earth spirits in particular as it has developed a good understanding of Namegivers and feels an intense emotional connection with the physical plane.

As is characteristic of earth spirits, Ethrys is physically strong and determined. However, its demeanor could not be more different from its appearance: caring and loyal, Ethrys craves meaningful relationships with others. The spirit can often be found serving as a companion of its own accord, or seeking someone it deems worthy. All those who Ethrys has seen fit to accompany have accomplished great deeds and been acclaimed as compassionate heroes.

Ethrys will do almost anything for the person chosen to be its companion and rarely asks for anything in return, content with kind words, attention, and determined actions from its companion. However, the spirit has a strong sense of justice and will never allow harm to come to an obvious innocent. This is one of the few actions that will cause this spirit to turn its back on its companion.

Summoning Ethrys can be a risky proposition despite its relative good nature. First, it does not like to be interrupted and finds most summoners and their activities to be unworthy of its time. However, those who have summoned it to aid in a task of which it approves will be hard pressed to find a better ally in their cause. Beyond the cause itself, True earth and Karma are the best offerings to make to this spirit.

DEX:	7	Initiative:	7	Unconsciousness:	NA
STR:	10	Physical Defense:	8	Death:	66
TOU:	11	Mystic Defense:	18	Wound:	17
PER:	8	Social Defense:	13	Knockdown:	18
WIL:	10	Physical Armor:	14	Recovery Tests:	5
CHA:	8	Mystic Armor:	12		
Move:	12				

Actions: 2; Unarmed 15 (18)
Powers: Astral Sight (16), Enhance Summoner (16), Engulf (18), Hardened Armor, Karma (8, 32), Manipulate Element (18), Manifest, Spellcasting (16)
Earth Movement: Earth elementals can move freely through dirt, earth, and stone at their normal movement rate, with only a slight disturbance on the surface if they are nearby.
Manifestation Restriction: Earth elementals require the presence of earth to manifest. This requirement can present a problem when the elemental attempts to manifest aboard a ship, on the upper floor of a wooden building, or under other special circumstances. Earth elementals may manifest as pools of mud, large rocks, clods of dirt, or in many other forms.
Vulnerability to Wood: Wood-based attacks against earth spirits ignore any protection provided by armor.

Gnome (Sample Earth Spirit)

These earth spirits take the form of dwarf-sized humanoids made of dark brown clay and with eyes of beautifully cut precious and semi-precious stones. Their features are exaggerated, crude approximations of those of other Namegivers.

Gnomes are considered by many Elementalists to be the most helpful of the earth spirits. They are extremely reliable, a great source of knowledge, and have the ability to craft small items out of their element. However, these spirits are not without their idiosyncrasies.

Verging on emotionless, they have difficulty empathizing with Namegivers. Emotions are nearly a foreign concept to them and they do not expect or see the purpose of politeness or civility. Due to this, they can be difficult during negotiations. Gnomes find pleasantries tiresome and when dealing with them it is advisable to keep sentences concise and stick to observable facts. They do not like observations, complimentary or otherwise, not based on evidence and take great pains to point out the flaws in another's argument. The gnome will eventually lose respect for someone who continues to make non-factual statements and stop paying attention. If this occurs, negotiations will become increasingly difficult as the gnome has lost interest in the proceedings.

Gnomes perform their tasks to the letter of the negotiation, and require detail and specifics in the description. If the spirit is provided with what it considers adequate instruction, the efforts they will make to complete the task goes beyond any other spirit. The task seems to become their entire reason for being. Though they do not seek loopholes, if the description lacks clarity in their mind's eye, these spirits will execute the task to the best of their understanding and fill in the missing details with their alien perspective.

They will patiently wait for tasks, rarely becoming bored, but do not like to be interrupted and will cease working until left alone. Far from appreciating it, these spirits have a grudging respect for those who defeat them in a contest of wills and it does not affect their behavior as much as other elementals. They can still become stubborn and unhelpful, but they accept this is the way of things and do not dwell on it.

Statistics are provided for a Strength Rating 5 gnome, but other variants are possible.

DEX:	7	Initiative:	7	Unconsciousness:	NA
STR:	10	Physical Defense:	8	Death:	66
TOU:	11	Mystic Defense:	15	Wound:	17
PER:	8	Social Defense:	10	Knockdown:	15
WIL:	10	Physical Armor:	11	Recovery Tests:	5
CHA:	8	Mystic Armor:	9		
Move:	10				

Actions: 2; Unarmed 12 (15)
Powers: Aid Summoner (13), Astral Sight (13), Craftsman (13), Spellcasting (13)
Earth Movement: Earth elementals can move freely through dirt, earth, and stone at their normal movement rate, with only a slight disturbance on the surface if they are nearby.
Manifestation Restriction: Earth elementals require the presence of earth to manifest. This requirement can present a problem when the elemental attempts to manifest aboard a ship, on the upper floor of a wooden building, or under other special circumstances. Earth elementals may manifest as pools of mud, large rocks, clods of dirt, or in many other forms.
Vulnerability to Wood: Wood-based attacks against earth spirits ignore any protection provided by armor.
Spells: Earth Darts, Crunch Climb, Purify Earth, Uneven Ground, Shattering Stone

Hasapik (Sample Earth Spirit)

This spirit is a terrifying sight; manifesting as a floating sphere of shifting and swirling blades and saws. From this mass of vicious mass of metal, six flexible appendages can extend which end in a variety of different extremities designed to cause gruesome injury to the target. Their voices are equally unpleasant, sounding like grinding and grating metal, ever changing in pitch and volume—it is truly a disturbing sound.

Hasapiks are methodical, disciplined, and fearless. They feel no sense of regret or revelry in their actions, and an unflinching belief in progress. A belief that requires destruction to make way such progress. These spirits believe themselves to be the perfect vehicle for this and a necessary element in the evolution of the world.

Although they are relatively easy to deal with, caution is advised when asking them to perform a task. This is because, like an avalanche, once set in motion they are almost impossible to halt. The summoner must be absolutely certain he wants the desired goal as a hasapik will not cease until the task is complete. Since they are almost exclusively summoned to destroy, this means completely gone.

These spirits have an obsessive interest in collecting small items and will often ask the summoner for something to complete their collections. Most often this will be a precious stone, metal of some type, or things which cannot be found on their elemental plane - particularly intricate things crafted from metal, such as scissors.

Statistics are provided for a Strength Rating 10 hasapik, but other variants are possible.

DEX:	11	**Initiative:**	11	**Unconsciousness:**	NA
STR:	14	**Physical Defense:**	16	**Death:**	90
TOU:	15	**Mystic Defense:**	23	**Wound:**	23
PER:	12	**Social Defense:**	18	**Knockdown:**	24
WIL:	14	**Physical Armor:**	20	**Recovery Tests:**	7
CHA:	12	**Mystic Armor:**	14		

Move: 10 (flying)
Actions: 3; Unarmed 19 (25)
Powers: Astral Sight (22), Engulf (24), Elemental Aura (10), Manifest, Spear (24), Spellcasting (22)
Vulnerability to Wood: Wood-based attacks against earth spirits ignore any protection provided by armor.

Fire Spirits

Fire is the element that clears away the old to make room for new growth. While a vital part of the natural order, it is unpredictable and often uncontrollable. Fire elementals, as the embodiment of True Fire, display many of these traits. They are frequently temperamental and volatile, shifting quickly from friendly to angry in a moment, and back again. Fire spirits often pursue tasks with great energy and force.

Fire spirits manifest from a source of heat or flame. While they usually take on a vaguely humanoid form, their shape often changes shape depending on the being's mood. As long as a source of fire or heat is present, they have little concern about where they manifest.

Strength Rating 1-4

DEX:	6	Initiative:	6+SR	Unconsciousness:	NA
STR:	5	Physical Defense:	9+SR	Death:	30
TOU:	5	Mystic Defense:	7+SR	Wound:	8
PER:	4	Social Defense:	7	Knockdown:	Immune
WIL:	6	Physical Armor:	4	Recovery Tests:	2
CHA:	4	Mystic Armor:	1+SR		
Move:	12				

Actions: 1; Unarmed 8+SR (8+SR)
Powers: Astral Sight, Manifest, Power (generally Elemental Aura), Spellcasting, Suggested Powers: Aid Summoner, Destroy Weapon, Elemental Aura, Engulf, Enhance Summoner, Enrage Element, Karma, Manipulate Element, Spear, Spells, Temperature

Strength Rating 5-8

DEX:	10	Initiative:	6+SR	Unconsciousness:	NA
STR:	9	Physical Defense:	10+SR	Death:	54
TOU:	9	Mystic Defense:	8+SR	Wound:	14
PER:	8	Social Defense:	6+SR	Knockdown:	Immune
WIL:	10	Physical Armor:	6	Recovery Tests:	4
CHA:	8	Mystic Armor:	1+SR		
Move:	12				

Actions: 2; Unarmed 9+SR (9+SR)
Powers: Astral Sight, Manifest, Power (generally Elemental Aura), Spellcasting, Suggested Powers: Aid Summoner, Destroy Weapon, Elemental Aura, Engulf, Enhance Summoner, Enrage Element, Karma, Manipulate Element, Spear, Spells, Temperature

Strength Rating 9-12

DEX:	14	Initiative:	6+SR	Unconsciousness:	NA
STR:	13	Physical Defense:	12+SR	Death:	78
TOU:	13	Mystic Defense:	10+SR	Wound:	19
PER:	12	Social Defense:	8+SR	Knockdown:	Immune
WIL:	14	Physical Armor:	9	Recovery Tests:	6
CHA:	12	Mystic Armor:	1+SR		
Move:	12				

Actions: 3; Unarmed 11+SR (11+SR)
Powers: Astral Sight, Manifest, Power (generally Elemental Aura), Spellcasting
Suggested Powers: Aid Summoner, Destroy Weapon, Elemental Aura, Engulf, Enhance Summoner, Enrage Element, Karma, Manipulate Element, Spear, Spells, Temperature
Powers

Manifestation Restriction: Fire elementals can only manifest from a source of fire. The size of the source can limit the manifest Strength Rating of the elemental, even if the spirit is more powerful. Torches and other small flames may only spawn fire elementals of Strength Ratings 1 to 4. Only campfires and larger sources can produce a fire elemental of Strength Rating 5 or higher.

Vulnerability to Water: Water-based attacks against fire spirits ignore any protection provided by armor.

Agni (Sample Named Fire Spirit)

Agni is Strength Rating 10 and is considered to be a strange fire spirit among those familiar with it. When summoned, Agni takes the form of an obsidiman burning like molten rock. This is but the beginning of the traits that make Agni strange among its kind.

While lacking the patience of an earth spirit, Agni is remarkably placid for its kind - more than willing to sit in quiet deliberation before making a decision. Dealing with Agni is an exercise in curious manners, which are equally likely to be from a long forgotten nation state as they are to be from contemporary Urupan fishmongers. Despite this, or perhaps because of it, Agni is very forgiving with regard to these ceremonies and shows a wry sense of humor. However, anyone who can seamlessly follow will earn a great deal of respect from this powerful spirit

However, if Agni is interrupted or feels slighted, its body glows brighter and can become enraged at a moment's notice. In combat, Agni is a terror, particularly if possessed by a frenzy.

Agni has a burning passion for knowledge and will rarely accept anything else for its service. It treasures secrets of all kinds, but particularly those of a magical in nature. Due to this, Agni possesses a great deal of knowledge and can be convinced to part with it in trade. The acquisition of learning seems to be this spirit's sole motivation and will stop at little if there is something in particular it wishes to learn.

The curious nature of Agni has led to a hypothesis regarding its origins. The thesis is Agni was once an earth elemental, but through some artifice was reNamed and turned into a fire elemental. If this is true, it would explain a lot, but also show just how little is understood about the nature of spirits.

DEX:	14	**Initiative:**	13	**Unconsciousness:**	NA
STR:	13	**Physical Defense:**	22	**Death:**	78
TOU:	13	**Mystic Defense:**	23	**Wound:**	20
PER:	12	**Social Defense:**	17	**Knockdown:**	24
WIL:	14	**Physical Armor:**	12	**Recovery Tests:**	6
CHA:	12	**Mystic Armor:**	11		
Move:	12				

Actions: 3; Unarmed 20 (24)
Powers: Astral Sight (22), Engulf (23), Find (22), Hardened Armor, Manifest, Share Knowledge (22), Spear (23), Spellcasting (22)
Find: Agni may use the Find power with both earth and fire elements.
Manifestation Restriction: Fire elementals can only manifest from a source of fire. The size of the source can limit the manifest Strength Rating of the elemental, even if the spirit is more powerful. Torches and other small flames may only spawn fire

elementals of Strength Ratings 1 to 4. Only campfires and larger sources can produce a fire elemental of Strength Rating 5 or higher.
Share Knowledge: Agni may use the Share Knowledge power with both earth and fire elements.
Vulnerability to Water: Water-based attacks against fire spirits ignore any protection provided by armor.

Ignis (Sample Fire Spirit)

An ignis is widely considered to be one of the most dangerous varieties of spirits. Their favored form is a hulking humanoid of flame with coal black eyes and a gaping maw. When speaking, their mouth yawns open, but does not move further. Words emanate from the black chasm, a voice of barely contained rage.

Dealing with these spirits can be difficult and most are summoned for violence; they delight in such things. Responsible Elementalists always pass on a warning to their students: once their duties have been fulfilled, an ignis is just a likely to turn on the summoner as it is to return to the astral plane. It is always good to have the Banish talent when an ignis is around.

The preferred offering for an ignis is a sacrifice from the summoner. Whether in the form of blood or Karma, they want a piece of the adept. A lesser offering is the flesh of another creature, the fresher the better, still alive being the best.

Statistics are provided for a Strength Rating 8 ignis, but other variants are possible.

DEX:	10	**Initiative:**	14	**Unconsciousness:**	NA
STR:	8	**Physical Defense:**	18	**Death:**	48
TOU:	8	**Mystic Defense:**	16	**Wound:**	12
PER:	8	**Social Defense:**	13	**Knockdown:**	Immune
WIL:	10	**Physical Armor:**	4	**Recovery Tests:**	4
CHA:	8	**Mystic Armor:**	9		

Move: 16
Actions: 2; Unarmed 16 (17)
Powers: Astral Sight (16), Elemental Aura (8), Engulf (16), Enrage Element (18), Karma (8, 32), Manifest, Spear (16), Spellcasting (16)
Manifestation Restriction: Fire elementals can only manifest from a source of fire. The size of the source can limit the manifest Strength Rating of the elemental, even if the spirit is more powerful. Torches and other small flames may only spawn fire elementals of Strength Ratings 1 to 4. Only campfires and larger sources can produce a fire elemental of Strength Rating 5 or higher.
Vulnerability to Water: Water-based attacks against fire spirits ignore any protection provided by armor.

Salamander (Sample Fire Spirit)

Salamanders are the archetypal fire spirit to many Elementalists. When they are first summoned, their form stretches from the flame with vague appendages stretching from it - resembling their amphibious namesake. After the summoner politely addresses them, which they must or the salamander will be very offended and negotiations will become difficult, the spirit takes a form similar to them, though lacking much definition.

When dealing with a salamander, it is important to always be polite. They are very easy to offend, though can be quick to forgive if an apology or compensation is quickly offered. The spirit will brush off the incident, so long as the offer is sincere. It is best to be to the point, as their attention can easily wander and boredom will set in. A bored salamander becomes irritable, irrational, and easily offended. Their interests for negotiation can be wide, but they generally seem to enjoy being entertained, whether with genuine, amusing anecdotes, tales of grandeur, or song. It is important there be an origin of truth to this offering, for reasons not well understood.

Salamanders perform their tasks to both the letter and the spirit of the negotiation, but can become sullen and irritable if they go long periods without doing anything. Interaction with Namegivers generally brightens their mood. These spirits take even more poorly to a Contest of Wills than most and will offer only the most literal interpretation of any given instruction when controlled in this way. They are somewhat prickly, but their general good disposition makes them by far the favored fire spirits for most summoners.

Statistics are provided for a Strength Rating 5 salamander, but other variants are possible.

DEX:	10	**Initiative:**	11	**Unconsciousness:**	NA
STR:	8	**Physical Defense:**	15	**Death:**	48
TOU:	8	**Mystic Defense:**	13	**Wound:**	12
PER:	8	**Social Defense:**	10	**Knockdown:**	Immune
WIL:	10	**Physical Armor:**	4	**Recovery Tests:**	4
CHA:	8	**Mystic Armor:**	6		
Move:	16				

Actions: 2; Unarmed 13 (14)
Powers: Aid Summoner (13), Astral Sight (13), Elemental Aura (5), Manifest, Spellcasting (13)
Manifestation Restriction: Fire elementals can only manifest from a source of fire. The size of the source can limit the manifest Strength Rating of the elemental, even if the spirit is more powerful. Torches and other small flames may only spawn fire elementals of Strength Ratings 1 to 4. Only campfires and larger sources can produce a fire elemental of Strength Rating 5 or higher.
Vulnerability to Water: Water-based attacks against fire spirits ignore any protection provided by armor.
Spells: Flame Weapon, Heat Foot, Snuff, Fireball, Heat Armor

Water Spirits

The element of water is fluid, always changing and moving. Water spirits display these traits, moving from experience to experience and adapting to new circumstances easily. They often display a great deal of curiosity, which some attribute to the wide range of forms water spirits take. Water spirits can take on the slow, hard nature of ice, the free-flowing movement of water, and the floating airiness of mist.

Like fire spirits, water spirits frequently change their appearance while physically manifest. First appearing as a bubble of water floating in midair, only to disperse into a fog and then coalesce into a block of ice. Water elementals do not mind being summoned to the material realm.

Strength Rating 1-4

DEX:	7	Initiative:	5+SR	Unconsciousness:	NA
STR:	4	Physical Defense:	7+SR	Death:	24
TOU:	4	Mystic Defense:	7+SR	Wound:	6
PER:	5	Social Defense:	6+SR	Knockdown:	Immune
WIL:	5	Physical Armor:	4	Recovery Tests:	2
CHA:	5	Mystic Armor:	3+SR		
Move:	14				

Actions: 2; Unarmed 7+SR (6)
Powers: Adaptability, Astral Sight, Manifest, Power, Spellcasting
Suggested Powers: Aid Summoner, Engulf, Enhance Summoner, Enrage Element, Find, Karma, Manipulate Element, Remove Element, Share Knowledge, Soothe, Spear, Spells, Temperature

Strength Rating 5-8

DEX:	11	Initiative:	5+SR	Unconsciousness:	NA
STR:	8	Physical Defense:	9+SR	Death:	48
TOU:	8	Mystic Defense:	9+SR	Wound:	12
PER:	9	Social Defense:	8+SR	Knockdown:	Immune
WIL:	9	Physical Armor:	7	Recovery Tests:	4
CHA:	9	Mystic Armor:	3+SR		
Move:	14				

Actions: 2; Unarmed 8+SR (6+SR)
Powers: Adaptability, Astral Sight, Manifest, Power, Spellcasting
Suggested Powers: Aid Summoner, Engulf, Enhance Summoner, Enrage Element, Find, Karma, Manipulate Element, Remove Element, Share Knowledge, Soothe, Spear, Spells, Temperature

Strength Rating 9-12

DEX:	15	Initiative:	5+SR	Unconsciousness:	NA
STR:	12	Physical Defense:	12+SR	Death:	72
TOU:	12	Mystic Defense:	12+SR	Wound:	18
PER:	13	Social Defense:	9+SR	Knockdown:	Immune
WIL:	13	Physical Armor:	12	Recovery Tests:	6
CHA:	13	Mystic Armor:	3+SR		
Move:	14				

Actions: 3; Unarmed 10+SR (7+SR)
Powers: Adaptability, Astral Sight, Manifest, Power, Spellcasting

Suggested Powers: Aid Summoner, Engulf, Enhance Summoner, Enrage Element, Find, Karma, Manipulate Element, Remove Element, Share Knowledge, Soothe, Spear, Spells, Temperature

Powers

Manifestation Restriction: Water elementals can only manifest from a source of water. The size of the water source has no bearing on the Strength Rating of the water elemental that may manifest from it. Even a drop of water is sufficient to spawn the mightiest of water spirits.

Vulnerability to Air: Air-based attacks against water spirits ignore any protection provided by armor.

Water Movement: Water spirits can move on and in the water as easily as on land at full movement rate.

Aquans (Sample Named Water Spirit)

Aquans is a Strength 10 Named water spirit. The background of Aquans is well cataloged compared to most other Named spirits. It was summoned and Named by the Elementalist Jenneth of Urupa. The two bonded and through repeated summonings Jenneth continually invested power in Aquans, in turn increasing its power as a spirit. This relationship deepened over the course of years, but was cut short by a fateful encounter with a Horror. During the battle, Aquans was banished back to the astral plane as Jenneth and companions were slain.

Dealing with Aquans can be a simple matter, or quite difficult, depending on how the desired tasks align with its agenda. Since the death of Jenneth, Aquans has hunted for the pattern and thread items of Jenneth, and the Horror responsible for the Elementalist's death. The spirit will eagerly support any adepts fighting against a Horror and will perform virtually any task for information on the pattern items and Horror. There are even records of the spirit providing unsolicited aid to groups of adepts.

However, if requested to perform tasks not involving these areas, Aquans is intractable at best and can become quite violent. The spirit has become quite mad with grief and is incapable with handling issues outside of its obsession.

Aquans prefers to take a variety of animal forms, rapidly shifting between them as needed for changing circumstances. Once it preferred the form of a smiling blob when with Jenneth, but now is typically seen as a stalking cat of water and ice.

DEX:	15	**Initiative:**	15	**Unconsciousness:**	NA
STR:	12	**Physical Defense:**	22	**Death:**	78
TOU:	12	**Mystic Defense:**	22	**Wound:**	18
PER:	13	**Social Defense:**	21	**Knockdown:**	Immune
WIL:	16	**Physical Armor:**	12	**Recovery Tests:**	6
CHA:	16	**Mystic Armor:**	15		
Move:	16				

Actions: 3; Unarmed 20 (17)

Powers: Adaptability, Cobra Strike (23), Crushing Blow (10), Astral Sight (23),

Enhance Summoner (26), Karma (10, 40), Manifest, Spear (22), Spellcasting (13), Waterfall Slam (10)
Manifestation Restriction: Water elementals can only manifest from a source of water. The size of the water source has no bearing on the Strength Rating of the water elemental that may manifest from it. Even a drop of water is sufficient to spawn the mightiest of water spirits.
Vulnerability to Air: Air-based attacks against water spirits ignore any protection provided by armor.
Water Movement: Water spirits can move on and in the water as easily as on land at full movement rate.

Torrent (Sample Water Spirit)

The presence of a torrent is always accompanied by the nearly deafening sound of rushing water. These spirits appear as a turbulent force of water rushing in upon itself. To communicate, they deftly alter their form to create detailed shapes conveying information to any onlooker successfully using Elemental Tongues to communicate with water spirits.

It is generally assumed there is very little which is subtle about these spirits. Some have theorized torrents put on a significant show of bluster to conceal much of their true demeanor. This theory is thus far only supported by the typically complex nature of water elementals and how simple torrents are portrayed in comparison.

Dealing with a torrent is much like attempting to haggle over the price of a new linen shirt with a hurricane; it's unlikely to be distracted and you're going to get wet. It is well known torrents have an appreciation of fine sculptures in many forms, but above this, they are fond of a lovely song. It is important to note they are quite particular about their music and have no interest in hearing another performance of a song they have already heard, unless it is significantly superior or a new interpretation in some way. When listening, they will calm just enough so the music can be heard over their natural acoustics whereupon the sounds will be swallowed from the air.

Statistics are provided for a Strength Rating 8 torrent, but other variants are possible.

DEX:	11	**Initiative:**	13	**Unconsciousness:**	NA
STR:	8	**Physical Defense:**	17	**Death:**	54
TOU:	8	**Mystic Defense:**	17	**Wound:**	12
PER:	9	**Social Defense:**	16	**Knockdown:**	Immune
WIL:	9	**Physical Armor:**	7	**Recovery Tests:**	4
CHA:	9	**Mystic Armor:**	11		
Move:	14				

Actions: 2; Unarmed 16 (14)
Powers: Adaptability, Astral Sight (17), Engulf (16), Enrage Element (17), Invisibility (17), Karma (8, 32), Manifest, Manipulate Element (17), Spellcasting (17)
Manifestation Restriction: Water elementals can only manifest from a source of water. The size of the water source has no bearing on the Strength Rating of the water

elemental that may manifest from it. Even a drop of water is sufficient to spawn the mightiest of water spirits.
Vulnerability to Air: Air-based attacks against water spirits ignore any protection provided by armor.
Water Movement: Water spirits can move on and in the water as easily as on land at full movement rate.

Undine (Sample Water Spirit)

Undines are a commonly summoned water spirit due to their disposition and versatility. They appear as a current of water that shimmers and moves unnaturally, continually changing shape. It is common for an undine to sculpt their form into reflections of their surroundings, then distorting them until adopting a new shape. When communicating with the summoner, a face will emerge from the surface to converse. Often, it is of the summoner, but can be of anyone nearby. This face too will shift slowly into other Namegivers with accompanying speech patterns.

A conversation or negotiation with an undine is generally punctuated with questions. These can be cutting and insightful to the matter at hand, or seem like non-sequiturs. They are generally amenable to most tasks requested of them, so long as they do not require violence or destruction. During negotiations, the offerings which will have the best result are Karma followed by an object of art created specifically for them.

Statistics are provided for a Strength Rating 5 undine, but other variants are possible.

DEX:	11	**Initiative:**	10	**Unconsciousness:**	NA
STR:	8	**Physical Defense:**	14	**Death:**	54
TOU:	8	**Mystic Defense:**	14	**Wound:**	12
PER:	9	**Social Defense:**	13	**Knockdown:**	Immune
WIL:	9	**Physical Armor:**	7	**Recovery Tests:**	4
CHA:	9	**Mystic Armor:**	8		

Move: 14
Actions: 2; Unarmed 13 (11)
Powers: Adaptability, Aid Summoner (14), Astral Sight (14), Find (14), Manifest, Spellcasting (14)
Manifestation Restriction: Water elementals can only manifest from a source of water. The size of the water source has no bearing on the Strength Rating of the water elemental that may manifest from it. Even a drop of water is sufficient to spawn the mightiest of water spirits.
Vulnerability to Air: Air-based attacks against water spirits ignore any protection provided by armor.
Water Movement: Water spirits can move on and in the water as easily as on land at full movement rate.
Spells: Purify Water, Waterproof, Icy Surface, Ice Mace and Chain, Blizzard Sphere

Wood Spirits

The element of wood holds all other elements together. It sends its roots into the earth, where it draws up water for nourishment. It reaches into the air, drawing strength from the heat of the sun. It also provides fuel for fire, and its remains nourish the soil so new wood can grow.

Wood spirits display this unique harmony in their behavior, with many spirits exhibiting keen insight. Since the nature of wood draws so much of the world into itself, wood spirits are often very knowledgeable, and are consulted for their wisdom. Ancient wood spirits are frequently consulted as oracles, though their sayings can be cryptic and twisting like vines.

Wood spirits are reluctant to manifest, preferring to remain in astral space where their access to the flows of magic and information is greater. They object to being summoned in conditions where another element is strongly dominant, such as underwater, underground, or in the air.

Strength Rating 1-4

DEX:	3	Initiative:	5	Unconsciousness:	NA
STR:	4	Physical Defense:	7	Death:	24
TOU:	4	Mystic Defense:	8+SR	Wound:	6
PER:	5	Social Defense:	7+SR	Knockdown:	4+SR
WIL:	5	Physical Armor:	4+SR	Recovery Tests:	2
CHA:	5	Mystic Armor:	3+SR		
Move:	12				

Actions: 1; Unarmed 7+SR (9)
Powers: Astral Sight, Manifest, Power, Spellcasting
Suggested Powers: Aid Summoner, Enhance Summoner, Find, Karma, Manipulate Element, Share Knowledge, Soothe, Spear, Spells

Strength Rating 5-8

DEX:	7	Initiative:	9	Unconsciousness:	NA
STR:	8	Physical Defense:	10	Death:	48
TOU:	8	Mystic Defense:	9+SR	Wound:	12
PER:	9	Social Defense:	8+SR	Knockdown:	8+SR
WIL:	9	Physical Armor:	5+SR	Recovery Tests:	4
CHA:	9	Mystic Armor:	3+SR		
Move:	12				

Actions: 2; Unarmed 8+SR (7+SR)
Powers: Astral Sight, Manifest, Power, Spellcasting,
Suggested Powers: Aid Summoner, Enhance Summoner, Find, Karma, Manipulate Element, Share Knowledge, Soothe, Spear, Spells

Strength Rating 9-12

DEX:	11	Initiative:	13	Unconsciousness:	NA
STR:	12	Physical Defense:	13	Death:	72
TOU:	12	Mystic Defense:	12+SR	Wound:	18
PER:	13	Social Defense:	11+SR	Knockdown:	12+SR
WIL:	13	Physical Armor:	7+SR	Recovery Tests:	6
CHA:	13	Mystic Armor:	3+SR		
Move:	12				

Actions: 3; Unarmed 10+SR (8+SR)
Powers: Astral Sight, Manifest, Power, Spellcasting
Suggested Powers: Aid Summoner, Enhance Summoner, Find, Karma, Manipulate Element, Share Knowledge, Soothe, Spear, Spells

Powers

Manifestation Restriction: Wood elementals manifest within trees and plants, usually altering the shape of the tree or plant into a humanoid form with bark skin and leafy appendages. The approximate size of a plant determines the maximum Strength Rating of the spirit that can manifest. Strength Rating 1–4 elementals can manifest in smaller plants and bushes, or small trees. Strength Rating 5–8 elementals take the shape of large bushes or medium-sized trees. Strength Rating 9–12 elementals only manifest in large, old trees. Great form wood elementals need a giant and possibly ancient plant to manifest in.

Vulnerability to Fire: Fire-based attacks against wood spirits ignore any protection from armor.

Dryad (Sample Wood Spirit)

Dryads are one of the most common of their kind to be encountered or summoned. This is because they are more willing to manifest than most other wood spirits and are frequently curious about the Namegivers who wander through their woods. They will manifest into trees with faces and watch silently.

Outside of their trees, they prefer feminine forms because they seem to be seen in a less threatening light. Their hair is long and made of leaves from their favored tree and match the season.

When interacting with Namegivers, they are quiet and will listen long past when it would be normal to respond. When they do respond, it is almost always as a question, preferably one provoking a long-winded and winding response. They seem to want little more than to listen and watch.

Negotiating with a dryad can be challenging only in getting them to commit. They are extremely reluctant to cause violence, unless it is in the protection of their trees. The offerings which are most appreciated seem to be new young plants and seeds as well as an extremely long and informative story about the world beyond the forest in which they reside.

Statistics are provided for a Strength Rating 5 dryad, but other variants are possible.

DEX:	7	Initiative:	9	Unconsciousness:	NA
STR:	8	Physical Defense:	10	Death:	48
TOU:	8	Mystic Defense:	14	Wound:	12
PER:	9	Social Defense:	13	Knockdown:	13
WIL:	9	Physical Armor:	10	Recovery Tests:	4
CHA:	9	Mystic Armor:	8		
Move:	12				

Actions: 2; Unarmed 13 (12)

Powers: Aid Summoner (14), Astral Sight (14), Manifest, Soothe (14), Spellcasting (14)

Manifestation Restriction: Wood elementals manifest within trees and plants, usually altering the shape of the tree or plant into a humanoid form with bark skin and leafy appendages. The approximate size of a plant determines the maximum Strength Rating of the spirit that can manifest. Strength Rating 1–4 elementals can manifest in smaller plants and bushes, or small trees. Strength Rating 5–8 elementals take the shape of large bushes or medium-sized trees. Strength Rating 9–12 elementals only manifest in large, old trees. Great form wood elementals need a giant and possibly ancient plant to manifest in.

Vulnerability to Fire: Fire-based attacks against wood spirits ignore any protection from armor.

Spells: Shelter, Shield Willow, Plant Feast, Thrive, Grove Renewal

The Pumpkin King (Sample Named Wood Spirit)

The Pumpkin King, a Strength Rating 12 wood spirit, is a benign and enigmatic spirit, and is not usually encountered through summoning. Instead, groups of adepts will stumble upon an overgrown pumpkin field on a moonlit night. It isn't uncommon for a strange series of events to lead the adepts to that place and time. Once they arrive, there are pumpkins of various shapes and sizes throughout the patch and an enormous, towering pumpkin in the middle.

When a suitable amount of time has passed—The Pumpkin King delights in setting just the right mood—the massive pumpkin will adopt the appearance of a jack-o-lantern with hollow eyes and an enormous rictus grin, all backlit with the warm glow of a fire. Though quite capable of speaking in Namegiver languages, The Pumpkin King prefers to converse in its native elemental tongue. It is very important to always refer to the spirit as "The Pumpkin King" after introductions are made. Failure to do so will result in The Pumpkin King shutting its mouth and waiting until corrections have been made. Repeated errors, or deliberate slights, can result in a variety of punitive measures from The Pumpkin King, generally beginning with benign tricks and ending with the offender trapped in a pumpkin prison. At this point, the only way to free their rude companion is for the others to complete the task and for the prisoner to think about what they did to get there and make amends for their insults.

The Pumpkin King always looks happy and sounds delighted, but other pumpkins will similarly change their appearance and adopt different demeanors as they echo the words of The Pumpkin King. This spirit is prone to grand statements and has a bellowing voice.

What The Pumpkin King's goals and motivations are is a mystery. Those to whom it appears may be in need or they may not, but it always comes with a bargain. The spirit offers something they want, generally information or an item, in exchange for a service. It is never an unfair bargain, but always a challenge. During the course of The Pumpkin King's request, the adepts commonly make a discovery that seems small, but can lead to significant events.

Directly summoning The Pumpkin King is difficult for unknown reasons as the spirit does not always respond. The most common theory for this is The Pumpkin King is not actually its Name, but this is complicated by the fact there are records of The Pumpkin King being summoned with this Name. Though such summonings quickly turn into a typical encounter where The Pumpkin King is making the offers.

DEX:	11	**Initiative:**	13	**Unconsciousness:**	NA
STR:	12	**Physical Defense:**	13	**Death:**	72
TOU:	12	**Mystic Defense:**	26	**Wound:**	18
PER:	15	**Social Defense:**	25	**Knockdown:**	24
WIL:	13	**Physical Armor:**	19	**Recovery Tests:**	6
CHA:	15	**Mystic Armor:**	15		

Move: 16 (flying)
Actions: 3; Unarmed 22 (20)
Powers: Astral Sight (27), Karma (12, 48), Manifest, Manipulate Element (25), Share Knowledge (27), Spellcasting (27), Hard Bargain, Illusory World, Pumpkin Prison

Hard Bargain: Characters which bargain with The Pumpkin King and accept the spirit's terms gain a +2 to all actions which directly support completing the required service. Any character which reneges on any part of the deal is followed by the scent of rotting pumpkins for a year and a day. The degree of the stench indicates the severity of the failure.

Illusory World: Illusion. As a Standard action, the Pumpkin King can create an illusory environment in a 100-yard radius. Any aspects of the environment can be altered, but this power can never be used to cause damage to a target. The Sensing Difficulty is 35.

Pumpkin Prison: The Pumpkin King makes a Spellcasting test against the target's Mystic Defense. If successful, they are trapped within a pumpkin just large enough to fit the target comfortably with a grinning face cut out of it. While inside the pumpkin, the target has a -8 penalty to all Spellcasting and Thread Weaving tests. The pumpkin is treated as a barrier with 20 Physical and Mystic Armor and a Death Rating of 100. The pumpkin will last until The Pumpkin King ends the effect. The Pumpkin King will not negotiate to use this power and cannot be forced to use it.

Vulnerability to Fire: Fire-based attacks against wood spirits ignore any protection from armor.

Spells: All Elementalist wood spells.

Thorn Man (Sample Wood Spirit)

Thorn men are wood spirits summoned by the elves of Blood Wood as protectors of the Wood's borders. These spirits are also used as guards in many villages and settlements within the Wood, including Alachia's palace. Due to the ritual used to summon and bind them into their forms, thorn men are considered tasked spirits.

The spirits resemble vaguely human bundles of thorns, and display only rudimentary intelligence. While some remain active at all times, others are bound to wards and activated when intruders trigger the Blood Wood's magical protections. When this happens, the spirits appear out of the forest growth, and seek to eject intruders, or at detain them until reinforcements arrive.

Statistics are provided for a Strength Rating 3 thorn man, but stronger variants are possible, typically including the Engulf power.

DEX:	5	Initiative:	7	Unconsciousness:	NA
STR:	6	Physical Defense:	9	Death:	36
TOU:	6	Mystic Defense:	10	Wound:	9
PER:	5	Social Defense:	9	Knockdown:	7
WIL:	5	Physical Armor:	5	Recovery Tests:	2
CHA:	5	Mystic Armor:	3		

Move: 12
Actions: 1; Spear 10 (12), Unarmed 10 (9)
Powers: Astral Sight (8), Karma (Step 3, 12 points), Manifest, Manipulate Element (8)
Loot: Thorn man spear

Thorn Man Spear: Many thorn men carry wooden spears with polished stone tips. These spears are magical weapons, given to them by their summoners. When wielded by a thorn man, they gain the benefits of Thread Rank One of the Thorn Man Spear automatically. See p. 237 for more information on these weapons.

Vulnerability to Fire: Fire-based attacks against a thorn man ignore protection from armor.

INVAE SPIRITS

The mysterious spirits known as invae are neither ally nor elemental spirits, and cannot be directly summoned by Nethermancers or Elementalists in the conventional sense. In truth, any adept with the Summon talent can contact an invae spirit; this fact is little known and rarely advertised. What is even less known is sometimes an invae will heed the call of a summons even if it is not directed at them. Invae come from an unknown realm in the netherworlds, one spirits have described as "crowded."

While rare, invae are most often found near large population centers. Some are social and gather in groups and often live in excavated warrens resembling hives or the tunnel complexes of ants and similar insects. Other invae are commonly characterized as "solitary" as a distinction from their social brethren. This is often something of a misnomer and more of an indication their social structures are distinct compared to the social types.

While many mistake them for a variety of Horror, invae do not feed on emotions, or take pleasure in causing pain or suffering to living things. Invae cannot cross into our realm at will, instead needing a host. A hive will frequently abduct members of a nearby community and subject them to a ritual inducing metamorphosis, changing the victim into a hybrid of Namegiver and spirit.

Invae cannot manifest in the physical plane without first being spiritually implanted in a host. Each type of invae handles this process differently, but social invae generally prefer to restrain the host within their hive while the transformation process takes place. There is frequently a period of time where the host must be prepared to accept the larval spirit, but this is not true for all invae.

Only Namegivers make acceptable hosts for invae and the power of the Namegiver indicates the subsequent Strength Rating of the invae spirit. Most hosts are only capable of supporting low Strength Rating (1-4) spirits and end up as hybrids. More powerful hosts (such as adepts) can bring true insect spirits into the world (Strength Rating 5+).

Hybrids are the most common form of invae and appear as Namegivers with insect-like features such as mandibles, chitinous skin, and compound eyes depending on the type. Hybrids are used for menial tasks and are considered to be little better than thugs in the hierarchy of a social hive. Other invae (so-called "true insect spirits") appear as large, spirit versions of their invae type, such as an ant or wasp, though other varieties of insect like termites or mantises have been known to appear. These are considerably more dangerous than their hybrid brethren and some of at least Strength Rating 9 may leave the hive to become queens in their own right.

This transition to queen takes place during a spiritual metamorphosis which causes the invae to lose their ability to manifest in the physical world, but allows them to reproduce by implanting their spiritual larvae into hosts. If a hive is being attacked, it is not uncommon for at least one powerful spirit to escape with a small host and establish a new hive. They will then undergo this process and begin building a new hive.

Hives typically gain a foothold in the physical world through wayward summoners who do not realize what they are dealing with, or think they can gain the upper hand. Invae are willing to use everything at their disposal to perform services for the chance at starting a hive. Many of these dealings go awry before they even begin due to their strange pheromones. Targets affected by them become immediately agreeable and willing to help establish a burgeoning hive. These victims are used to gather more suitable targets, creating a support network of local Namegivers to help establish the hive while remaining undetected.

Spreading and consuming seems to be the ultimate goal of the invae. A key piece of this is manifesting a queen. Once a queen has manifested in the physical world, they can reproduce without hosts. The requirements to manifest a queen are unknown, but almost certainly horrifying in their cost.

A wide variety of invae exist and the description and statistics provided here are for the most common type of social invae.

Ant Spirits

Ant spirits are the most common type of invae and one of the most dangerous. This is due to their ability to adapt to virtually any environment and situation. The typical behavior for a burgeoning ant hive is to consolidate their power in a small area before expanding.

In rural areas they tend towards one very large hive covering a vast territory. Eventually another queen will be produced and a breakaway hive will be established a considerable distance away. However, in urban areas they tend towards multiple small hives. There are frequently hidden passages connecting all of the related hives in an urban area. In the event of discovery, these are used to spread the word to the other hives so they can relocate or defend as necessary.

The general tendency is to build hives underneath existing structures. These spirits prefer to be near their potential hosts, but concealed. Their hives are well organized and patrolled. However, ant spirits do not tend to be aggressive to outsiders and will even allow them into the hive if they remain docile. This, of course, makes it much easier to capture the intruder and prepare them as a host.

Strength Rating 1-4

DEX:	5	Initiative:	5+SR	Unconsciousness:	NA
STR:	5	Physical Defense:	8	Death:	36
TOU:	6	Mystic Defense:	7+SR	Wound:	9
PER:	3	Social Defense:	6+SR	Knockdown:	4+SR
WIL:	4	Physical Armor:	5	Recovery Tests:	4
CHA:	5	Mystic Armor:	2+SR		

Move: 14
Actions: 1; Claws 7+SR (10+SR)
Powers: Climbing, Stealthy Stride, Transform
Suggested Powers: Astral Sight, Karma, Paralytic Poison [Onset 1 round, Interval 3/1 round, Duration SR x 10 min], Pheromones, Surprise Strike

Strength Rating 5-8

DEX:	9	Initiative:	5+SR	Unconsciousness:	NA
STR:	9	Physical Defense:	11	Death:	60
TOU:	10	Mystic Defense:	8+SR	Wound:	15
PER:	7	Social Defense:	6+SR	Knockdown:	8+SR
WIL:	8	Physical Armor:	3+SR	Recovery Tests:	6
CHA:	9	Mystic Armor:	2+SR		

Move: 16 (Climbing 16)
Actions: 2; Claws 9+SR (11+SR)
Powers: Astral Sight, Manifest, Transform
Suggested Powers: Hardened Armor, Karma, Manifest, Paralytic Poison [Onset 1 round, Interval 3/1 round, Duration SR x 10 min], Pheromones, Stealthy Stride

Strength Rating 9-12

DEX:	13	**Initiative:**	5+SR	**Unconsciousness:**	NA
STR:	13	**Physical Defense:**	16	**Death:**	84
TOU:	14	**Mystic Defense:**	11+SR	**Wound:**	21
PER:	11	**Social Defense:**	9+SR	**Knockdown:**	12+SR
WIL:	12	**Physical Armor:**	5+SR	**Recovery Tests:**	8
CHA:	13	**Mystic Armor:**	2+SR		

Move: 16 (Climbing 16)
Actions: 3; Claws 13+SR (15+SR)
Powers: Astral Sight, Manifest, Transform
Suggested Powers: Hardened Armor, Karma, Paralytic Poison [Onset 1 round, Interval 3/1 round, Duration SR x 10 min], Pheromones, Stealthy Stride, Summon
Powers
Pheromones (CHA + SR): This power is used to gather followers for a have while they infiltrate a community. To use the power, the invae makes a Pheromones test against the target's Social Defense as a Standard action. The target does not have to be on the same plane of existence, but must be able to interact with the invae (e.g. actively perceiving them with Astral Sight, interacting with Spirit Talk, etc.). If successful, the target becomes friendly to the invae for one day per success.

Each subsequent application improves the relationship by one more level (e.g. a second use will cause the target to become Loyal for one day per success). After the target's attitude can no longer be improved, the duration begins to extend: weeks, then months, and finally years. If a test fails against a target, it cannot be affected by Pheromones from any invae of the hive again. Targets affected by this power are almost never used as hosts. Instead, they are used to gain access to communities, evade detection, and gather other hosts for the hive.
Summon: Invae queens use this power to summon more of their kind into the world by impregnating a host with a larval invae spirit.
Transform (WIL + SR): The invae permanently manifests in a living host. The host is restrained, usually in a cocoon, and spends time in a coma while the spirit takes over the host from astral space. Over time the host body gains a bizarre insectoid features, often creating gross parodies and abominations in the case of a hybrid. Strength Rating 5 and above invae entirely consume the host when the process is complete and can move between worlds as a true spirit.

Once per day the spirit make a Transform test against the target's Mystic Defense. If successful, one of the host's Attributes is replaced with one of the spirit's. When all of the host's Attributes have been replaced, the transformation is complete and the spirit permanently takes over the body. It is rumored the transformation process can be reversed with powerful healing magic and even a consumed host can be saved.

EARTHDAWN

DRAGONS

While Master Vasdenjas was more forthcoming than most, I imagine the things he did share were meant to distract us from other dragon secrets.
• Tiabdjin the Knower •

Dragons have existed for as long as anyone can remember. Every culture in Barsaive has stories about them. Some of these ancient races teach dragons were the world's first inhabitants, though only dragons themselves can verify this. The truth is dragons are solitary creatures, living alone by choice. The rumors of dragon moots, councils, and cooperation among different dragons will continue to live among the legends of Namegivers.

ON THE NATURE AND WAYS OF DRAGONS

During my time as scribe and attendant to Vasdenjas, also known as the Master of Secrets, he shared a great deal of his knowledge about the history and habitat of Barsaive. Much of this knowledge has been collected in various tomes and is available in the Great Library to those so inclined.

When he learned of the library's collection on the Namegivers, he was shocked to discover dragons had not been included and went on at great length about dragon culture and society. These excerpts are only small part of the knowledge he passed along and I present it here as a way of honoring his memory.

Our Noble Form

We are born with strength and power. A dragon is hatched with claws and sharp teeth, and our hide is tough, able to turn away blows that would kill the fragile newborns of you younger races. While it is true t'skrang are born with scales, they are soft and weak compared to ours.

As we grow, we learn to use our magic to recover from injury—an ability you folk have yet to perfect. Even the least of us can cast a spell to knit flesh and weave bone. This is a skill developed out of necessity, because we are tested by nature in ways the younger races are not.

As we grow, we become strong and powerful, often growing larger than airships. After a few years even the smallest hatchlings are larger than most other Namegivers.

One of the most significant differences between us and the younger races is how we experience magic. We breathe it; see it as you see water in a stream. Magic and astral space flow around us, and we draw into it with great ease. Nothing is more natural than magic for us.

Because of this knowledge of astral currents and energies, we can affect events in ways only dreamed of by other Namegivers. We can manipulate not only our own actions, but the strongest of us can affect other creatures, making them extensions of our will.

> When pressed about whether this power extended to other Namegivers, or was limited to more mundane creatures, Vasdenjas would change the subject. I must say I never felt compelled to do anything against my nature, but given their power, would I have noticed if I had? -- *Tiabdijin*

Our Life Cycle

While we are more powerful than the younger races, we do share some similarities with them. We are born, we grow, we mate, and we raise young.

On Mating

Like the younger races, new life begins with mating. Unlike with most other creatures, female dragons decide when they are ready to reproduce. The process of mating and laying eggs leaves them physically drained, so they seldom mate more than once every century or so.

In the First Rite of Mating, the female finds a desirable male, informs him she has chosen him, and asks him to prove his worthiness. It is possible for him to refuse by performing the Rite of Refusal. Both parties respectfully leave and the female seeks a new mate.

In the Second Rite of Mating, the male describes the valuable traits he would pass on to any offspring. This rite is accompanied by the Dance of Courting, where the male dances to show his worthiness with grace of movement and fine oratory. At this stage it is allowed for the female to express disinterest in the male; some females are quite choosy.

Males can invoke the Ritual of Battle over a female, fighting to see who is the worthiest to mate with her. The ritual isn't always to the death, but sadly can result in such. If the female doesn't prefer the victor, she may refuse him.

Once the female is satisfied and chooses to mate, the Dance of New Life is performed in a secluded location. This ritual lasts many days, starting the cycle that culminates in the female's ability to conceive. Once the mating is done, the Rite of Separation is performed and the male takes his leave. The female lays her eggs, three or four in a normal clutch, and then passes them on to be tended by a proper guardian.

The Care of Eggs

Dragon eggs are cared for by great dragons. Traditionally, a female will come to a great dragon and Petition for Caregiving: humbly asking a great dragon to become the guardian for her eggs. She describes her offspring in the most flattering way, telling the great dragon how they will bring pride and happiness into their life. If the petition is accepted, the female leaves her eggs in the great dragon's care and leaves, likely never to see them again.

After hearing a female's petition, it is possible for the great dragon to refuse the eggs. No reason need be given, the female must move on to another great dragon and petition them. There are many reasons to refuse a clutch: having too many to care for already, having received too many petitions at once, or not being able to devote the time and energy to a clutch of eggs and newborns.

The caretaker takes the eggs and provides them with the warmth and protection they need. Given the way the eggs are cared for, it is rare for a dragon to know which female laid their egg and with which male she mated. In essence, the great dragon overseeing the hatching and raising of our young is viewed as the parent. Dragon 'siblings' come from eggs that hatch within a few years of each other and are raised by the same great dragon.

The Stages of Life

A dragon egg's shell is very strong; not like a delicate bird's egg, or even the eggs of the t'skrang. The shell is tough enough to resist a sword blow; made from the same material as our scales.

When the young dragon is ready to hatch it uses its fiery breath—an ability we possess even in the egg—to weaken the shell from the inside. This can be a delicate process: if the shell doesn't weaken properly, the hatchling cooks itself alive. These eggs, along with any unsuccessfully fertilized, are eaten by the guardian dragon in the Ritual of the Quintessential Feast. The purpose of this is to take the substance of life unfulfilled and gain some small part of the lost uniqueness.

> I was privileged to witness a dragon hatching during my time with Vasdenjas. Curiously, the hatchling did not have forelimbs, only wings and hind legs. It also had a stinger at the end of its tail. Coming across it in the wild, I would have assumed it was a young wyvern.
> -- *Tiabdijin*

After hatching, the sire uses Dragonspeech to greet the hatchling and welcome it to the world. From that moment on, the hatchling knows this dragon as its mentor and protector—and as I mentioned earlier, a parent of sorts.

By the time the hatchling reaches 20 years of age, it can fly, hunt, and has basic survival skills. At this point its sire begins teaching the fundamentals of magic and our history. We also begin instruction on using dragon breath and casting spells. All dragons, from hatching to adult, have these abilities, but it is only under the guidance of their mentor they learn to properly harness these powers.

At roughly fifty years of age, the dragon begins learning the intricacies of dragon society, with its many rites and rituals. They also earn time away from the lair—not far, perhaps no more than a day away by flight. For the most part, these older hatchlings stay with their sire, learning and preparing for the time when they are old enough to leave and become part of dragon society.

By the time they reach 100 to 200 years of age, a dragon is self-reliant and encouraged to learn on their own. As they are not yet adults, they remain in their sire's territory to avoid offending another adult.

At this point, the hatchling becomes a fledgling. Young dragons entering this stage seem to lose their minds. They become feral and seclude themselves in the wilderness of their sire's territory, though some fledglings travel great distances to weather this storm within. It is possible for fledglings to attack adult dragons, but we try to avoid this confrontation. We take many steps to care for our young and we don't wish to hurt them during this stage.

> Because young dragons do not have the physical form we associate with the adults, it is highly probable what we call wyverns are actually dragon 'fledglings'. When pressed, Vasdenjas categorically denied the association, saying it was yet another curious coincidence of nature.
>
> I remain unconvinced. If my ideas are correct, it explains many things about dragon-kind and their secrecy. -- *Tiabdijin*

After several decades, the fledgling travels back to its place of birth and begins the Rite of Change. This is when they truly become an adult in mind and body. The fledgling uses magic to create a cocoon of astral threads, where it sleeps and undergoes a transformation. During this time, the dragon's True Pattern changes and its body takes the adult form with which the younger races are familiar.

With the Rite of Emergence, the fledgling becomes an adult. The dragon is reborn in its true form and takes a Name. After they have become adults, they leave their sire and stake a claim to a new territory. Dragons are very territorial and it is possible for two adults to covet the same territory. They issue the Ritual of Challenge and many young dragons die in this way.

If an adult lives long enough, and accumulates sufficient power and wisdom, it is considered a great dragon. This requires centuries, and most adults do not live long enough to reach these lofty heights. We are the elders of our kind, and it is our privilege and duty to guide our race. Our vast experience and knowledge gives us insight into the march of time none can match.

The Rites of Death

All things born must die. We are no exception. Of all the eggs given to a great dragon, not all will hatch, not all hatchlings will live to be fledglings, and we lose many more as fledglings. Adults can fall prey to Horrors, dragon hunters, or may evenfall victim to poor judgment and die in an accident or other misfortune.

Nothing is more sad and upsetting than the death of a great dragon. When one of us dies, we are remembered with the Rites of Death. First is the Dance for the Fallen, honoring the life, thoughts, feelings, and memories of the fallen dragon. Next comes the Rite of Succession, which determines who shall claim what belonged to the late great dragon. Finally is the Ritual of the Cleansing Fire, where we burn the dragon with our breath until only ashes remain. We come from the earth, and so return to the earth in our death.

> These rituals explain the appearance and behavior of so many dragons in the skies over Sky Point in the days following its collapse at the end of the war.
> -- *Tiabdijin*

Etiquette

We dragons have rituals for everything in our society. From meeting to parting, cooperation and disagreement, mating, birth, death, transformation, communication, and challenge. We perform rituals on every occasion we come in contact with another dragon. They must be performed correctly and with precision, as a reflection of their sire's teachings.

The basic expression of these rites and rituals is in dance and gesture. How we stand and the motion and position of our head, body, wings, and tail express volumes about our mood, intent, and thoughts.

Because we can fly, dancing in the air is the ultimate expression of movement. Dances tell a story: the Dance for the Fallen speaks of the life of the dragon who passed.

There is nothing more beautiful than seeing a dragon dance.

Memory Crystals

You have seen crystals in my lair. Some of these are memory crystals: living crystal imbued with memory, images, and ideas that remain unchanged with the passage of time. Once a memory is stored within, we can use Dragonspeech to retrieve the knowledge.

We tend to use smaller crystals for messages intended for other dragons, or as a small piece of a complex thought. The larger crystals are used to house greater thoughts and images. Some of the largest crystals are the size of a troll.

> If only a fraction of the crystals in Vasdenjas's lair stored dragon knowledge and lore, there was more information contained there than in the Great Library. Even if the knowledge contained in those crystals is now beyond our reach, as a scholar I am comforted by this drive to keep and maintain a record of cultural lore.
> -- *Tiabdijin*

Lairs

Our most important place is our lair. It is our home and we spend much of our time there. Every dragon's lair is different, as the snowflakes falling on the mountain are different.

The most common type of lair is a cave found in the mountains. Because we fly, we like to have our homes be high above the earth, although it is not unheard of to have a lair in the depths of a swamp, or dark forest (though we call them dens).

Mountain caves suit us for many reasons. They are usually dry and comfortably temperate, staying cool during the day and warm during the night. Cave walls, floors, and stones are often worn smooth, so when we lay upon them they are comfortable. An occasional rough outcropping of rocks is wanted for scratching dry and itchy scales.

Having no need for furnishings, we only need enough space for ourselves and our belongings. We eat our prey raw and cast the remains outside the lair to serve as a warning for others not to approach without an invitation. We get water from springs and mountain lakes.

Hoarding

In addition to hunting and conducting business with Namegivers and other dragons, we work on our collections. Because we measure time in centuries, our collections are a reflection of the time we've spent on this world. These items help us tell the story of our lives. Of course we use memory crystals, but there is nothing quite as nice as looking back at a jewel given to you by a grateful human for saving their child.

I don't know what it is about these collections that so fascinate the younger races, but they find great pleasure in stealing from us. And then they think we will not want our things back. Given the way they treat those who take from them, I find this position baffling.

Shal-mora

Another practice that takes up our time is a mindful rest called shal-mora. This period of rest allows us to reflect on the many years we have lived and the things we have done or wish to do. This rest is somewhere between true sleep, which we do perhaps once a month, and deep thinking, which you will find we all do.

When dragons are in their Shal-mora rest, we curl upon the ground and appear as though sleeping. Because of this apparent sleep, the younger races believe we sleep all the time. I have lost count of the foolish adventurers who believed I was sleeping while they invaded my home to steal from my hoard.

The Origin of Dragons

Dragons were the first Namegivers, indeed the first creatures to understand the power of Names. When we appeared, long, long ago, we gave Names to ourselves, separating us from the Nameless and formless mass of the world.

It was a very different world then, a world of darkness, pain, and suffering. Black clouds blotted out the sky and the land was covered in foul mists, the waters dark and bubbling.

It was the Age of the Dark One, the sole creature who lived in the world. It had no Name as we know it, it simply was. A creature of unimaginable foulness and corruption. The Dark One created spawn in its image, called horoi. These creatures of darkness and endless hunger fought battles on the land, under the waves, and in the sky above for their master's amusement. The Dark One reveled in the slaughter and the rivers were filled with the toxic ichor of the slain horoi.

And then the Dark One spawned a horoi unlike the others. It possessed a vital essence no other creature had. Instead of joining in endless battle, this horoi fled to a distant part of the world the Dark One and its minions had not touched. There it Named itself and became Nightslayer, the First Named.

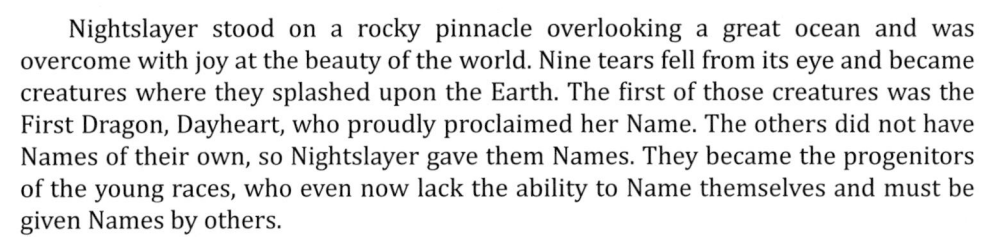

Nightslayer stood on a rocky pinnacle overlooking a great ocean and was overcome with joy at the beauty of the world. Nine tears fell from its eye and became creatures where they splashed upon the Earth. The first of those creatures was the First Dragon, Dayheart, who proudly proclaimed her Name. The others did not have Names of their own, so Nightslayer gave them Names. They became the progenitors of the young races, who even now lack the ability to Name themselves and must be given Names by others.

When the Dark One discovered what Nightslayer had done, it grew furious. It raged and brought forth armies of horoi to kill Nightslayer and its new creations. But the First Named stood against the onslaught. With the power of Naming, it forced the horoi and the Dark One to flee from the world into the depths of the netherworlds.

The Dark One swore, "I will hunt your children for the rest of time. I will slay every last one of them, and my minions will feed on their pain and terror. But I will not give the mercy of death to your favorite—the Dragon, the one you created in your image. As you betrayed me, the children of the Dragon's line will betray you. I will corrupt them, twist their souls, and make them my own. Then I will return and reign over this world."

The Dark One fled, hurling a ball of fire at Nightslayer as it departed. The First Named gathered its children under the protection of its mighty wings. There was a sound like a thousand roars. The earth and sky trembled, and a great cloud filled the sky. When the rumbling stopped, Nightslayer's children lived, but the First Named was no more.

They gathered by its great head and mourned its passing, honoring the sacrifice of Nightslayer so its children might live. Since that earliest time, all dragons are consumed by fire in death, echoing the sacrifice of the First Named for us.

In time, the children of Dayheart, the First Dragon, grew many and strong. They learned the secrets of threads and patterns, and gained wisdom in the ways of the world far beyond the short-lived younger races. They laid the foundations for a civilization that continues to this very day, and we wait and watch for the return of the Dark One, the Great Hunter, Named Verjigorm.

The Passions

You younger races worship the Passions, believing they inspire things like strength, love, and intellect. I find your devotion to these beings—about which you know so little—humorous. We dragons are far more tangible than the ephemeral Passions, and yet you view us with fear. If you knew them as I do, your kind might prefer to come to us for wisdom!

We rely on our own strength and the gifts given to us by nature. We have no need to look up to some higher being to find our place in the world. We know that place and take it with pride. We respect the Passions—as you would respect anyone with power—but we do not worship them.

Dragons in the World

We are the oldest beings in all of living history. We provide a link to the past the younger races have forgotten. We have a greater understanding of the nature of astral space and the weave of fate. We gather knowledge and experiences as a t'skrang child gathers shiny rocks by the river.

We watch you as one would watch children play. You are stubborn. You plot, plan, and struggle. A dwarf lives for decades and thinks himself wise. How much more wisdom does a newly fledged adult dragon have—one who has lived more than twice as long? And yet rarely does one of the younger races seek our guidance.

Some have asked why we aren't more active in the world. If we are so wise, why do we let you folk stumble about so blindly? What a foolish question! You have no doubt seen times when a child rails against their parent, denying the experience and knowledge of a life lived. What then? The parent can either tighten their hold and try to control the life of their offspring, or let the child learn for itself.

We dragons prefer the latter. It is easier, especially with our lifespan in relation to yours. The flame of even an elf's life is a candle's flicker to a dragon. I have seen kingdoms rise and fall in my lifetime. While I have counted members of the younger races as friends, they were—sadly—few and fleeting. The differences between our kinds make such relationships difficult.

Few Namegivers are strong or wise enough to seek a dragon, and few dragons open their lairs to such intrusions. While I appreciate and admire your curiosity and desire to learn and share your knowledge, I find it difficult to truly convey what it is to be a dragon. What can the stream understand of the ocean?

Our Views on Modern Nations

You asked how we see things today, and whom we support. In truth, given how many nations we have seen rise and fall; we don't support any one culture. Our concerns are greater than any one people. This said, here are some thoughts on our relationship with some of the younger powers in Barsaive:

The Kingdom of Throal

In general, the dwarfs of Throal have been good to dragons and respectful when dealing with our kind. They have a healthy recognition for our skills with magic, and scholars like yourself sometimes seek out the more public of our kind for knowledge and guidance.

Indeed, the philosophy expressed within your Council Compact is informed by our own belief that individuals should be free to live as they choose, provided they treat others with respect. We learned long ago diplomacy, rather than physical conflict, is a better way to resolve differences. Fighting wastes energy and often results in a net loss for all involved.

> Given the new ruler in Throal, as well as other changes, it is unclear whether the favorable relationship the kingdom has enjoyed with the Great Dragons will continue. -- *Tiabdijin*

The Blood Wood

In contrast, the elves of the Blood Wood are disrespectful and hateful. They take every opportunity to slander us and have a distrust of us which runs as deep as the roots of their trees. They blame us for the death of their queen Dallia, though if they knew what really happened, they would not judge us so harshly.

Given what they have done to themselves, the Blood Elves shouldn't be so quick to judge other Namegivers.

The Theran Empire

Scholars have long sought to understand the relationship between the Theran Empire and our kind, but as usual you see one tree and claim to know the forest.

Before the Scourge, some of us tried to aid the younger races by sharing knowledge about our lairs. The Therans wanted a monopoly on protection against the Horrors and began a program of persecution and execution against us.

The matter was resolved in the only way they understood. At the time, we thought they had learned their lesson. If they would let us be, we would do the same with them. Of course, given the brief lives of the younger races, those lessons have clearly been forgotten. Once again, the Therans seek to dominate rather than guide, and control rather than teach.

If it becomes necessary, we will educate them again.

> Given Vasdenjas's involvement with the Second Theran War, and the assault on Sky Point, it would seem he felt reeducation was necessary. -- *Tiabdijin*

Iopos

Uhl Denairastas is yet another example of a Namegiver who thinks because he is old, he knows best. His entire clan is caught up with the notion their family has ruled Iopos for centuries, and because of this they have the right to rule all of Barsaive.

This is one case where I will admit our shortcomings—our long view of history can sometimes fail to see a danger right before us. We were not watching them before, but we are watching them now. I have little doubt they will overextend their reach and collapse, like so many other would-be conquerors before them, and their achievements—such as they are—forgotten to history.

Dragon Magic

We have been practicing magic for longer than the younger races have been on this world. Magic is woven into our beings, and is as natural to us as flying or breathing. Over the many years of our race, we have learned much and are masters of magic more than any other living being.

Dragons are born with insights and abilities that would take other Namegivers lifetimes to learn. We are natural wielders of magic, we possess Dragonsight, and we can weave astral space in ways inconceivable to the younger races.

Dragonsight is not unlike windlings' ability to view astral space. We can see the patterns of everything as easily as we can see the physical form of all living things. The disadvantage of this is we can also see the damage done by the Scourge and the taint left by Horrors. Young dragons don't remember a time without the Horrors' marks on the world, but I can and it makes me sad for the world.

From the very earliest times, we understood the importance of Names and patterns, and learned how to use them to our advantage. Weaving connections to True Patterns is an ancient art among my kind.

We use thread magic in much the same way as other Namegivers. We weave threads from our True Pattern to the patterns of other creatures and places to enhance our abilities in dealing with them. It is common for a dragon to weave a thread to its lair.

Dragons can weave threads to other beings, but do so rarely. Given your brief lives, we do not usually concern ourselves with the pattern items of younger races, although many dragons have such pattern items in their hoards. We guard the nature and location of our own pattern items very carefully indeed, as they have great power over us.

Unlike you smaller folk, we do not use the magical devices and equipment that form the basis for so many of your tales and legends. A dragon can weave threads to items of power, but most dragons I know do not bother with such things.

Our intimate knowledge of patterns allows us insight few other Namegivers can match. Adepts have been known to bring thread items to a dragon and ask for aid in deciphering the object's pattern. Doll-Maker—commonly known as Icewing—entertains such requests in exchange for a suitable gift. Personally, I dislike these sorts of visitors to my lair. They are better off learning such things on their own, rather than to look for quick answers from their betters.

Spirits

Despite our intimate knowledge of astral space and the beings living there, dragons do not traffic with spirits in the fashion of your magicians. We have servants enough without the need to surround ourselves with a flock of stubborn and strong-willed spirits, who are often more trouble than they are worth.

This said, we can and do work with spirits. For example, I have called on earth spirits to dig a new tunnel when expanding my lair.

We also have dealings with spirits who are not our servants. Most of them steer well clear of us, as even powerful spirits are wise not to offend a dragon. Dragonsight allows us to see spirits where they would otherwise be invisible, and our powers can easily deal with any spirit who gets out of control.

Blood Magic

We do not use blood magic to empower spells and items. Blood magic of that sort is unnecessary for beings at our level of magical power and sophistication.

Using blood drawn from other creatures for magic is forbidden among dragons. It is a corrupt practice and should not be tolerated. Any power gained is not worth its cost a short way down the path. This is wisdom you younger races would be best to follow.

The only form of blood magic used among my kind is what you call "life magic," a personal sacrifice of some kind to support an act of magic. It is used to create and seal oaths, and to work powerful magic. Dragons can and do use life magic for the creation of blood oaths among us, although such oaths are not taken lightly. A careless oath can bind one for centuries.

Ritual Magic

Until now most of the magic I have described is used by other Namegiver races. We may have more skill and experience, but your most capable magicians can duplicate the feats of magic I have described. However, there is magic we know beyond anything the younger races have ever accomplished.

I speak of ritual magic. These rituals allow us to cooperate magically. Lesser magicians have practices that are a pale echo of this: apprentices lending power to their teachers, servants to their masters. Our rituals allow us to cooperate as peers, performing magic far greater than any one dragon could accomplish on their own.

Our magical rituals can change the face of the world. We can level mountains, flood plains, dry oceans, and sink islands. We can change the course of the heavens, shake the foundations of the earth, and even alter the very course of history. It is the power to speak to the universe and be obeyed; reweaving the most primal patterns of existence into new forms.

It is not a power to be used lightly and at times I question if it is a power anyone should ever have. In the past, this power was used without considering the consequences and terrible mistakes were made. We have since learned restraint and the need to judge every action in light of what might result.

In the centuries your kingdom has existed, no ritual like I describe has been performed. Gathering enough dragons in one place, let alone gaining the cooperation needed to perform such magic, is difficult at best. Any attempts to perform such magic are debated at great length and all participants must agree it is necessary. If we are fortunate and fate is kind, this Age may never see the full power of dragon magic.

> Like so many other things, Vasdenjas refused to elaborate on ritual magic. He anticipated my every question and attempts to learn more were easily deflected. After many fruitless attempts, he shut down my inquiries by stating, "Tiabdjin, you might think my kind fear nothing, and there is nothing we would not attempt. In truth, there are things with which even great dragons do not meddle. Ritual magic is one of them." -- *Tiabdijin*

USING DRAGONS IN ADVENTURES AND CAMPAIGNS

A close look at the abilities and statistics of dragons should reveal one obvious truth: dragons are dangerous! The most basic of dragons is more powerful than most groups of adepts, and a great dragon will dwarf the power of nearly any erstwhile band of heroes. Fortunately, it is rare a group will find themselves the enemy of one or more dragons and is likely they will never face a great dragon directly. Nonetheless, using dragons in adventures is a delicate business.

It requires careful consideration as to which dragon to use, as well as the role the dragon should play in the adventure or campaign. Before we address these issues, we should ask one question. Should dragons be this powerful?

Absolutely.

Dragons are this powerful because they are the oldest and most powerful creatures in the world. Their knowledge of magic is unparalleled. Even the most powerful magicians of the Theran Empire pale in comparison to a dragon's magical ability, and high circle adepts should feel nervous at the thought of confronting them under any circumstance. Gamemasters should exercise great care when using dragons, and ensure they don't become just another monster. Dragons are powerful, intelligent beings with their own desires and goals.

There are two basic approaches to using dragons in **Earthdawn** adventures and campaigns: as allies or as enemies. In either role, dragons function best behind the scenes, spinning plots and pulling the strings of nations and great powers. If he wishes, a great dragon has the power to lay waste to an entire kingdom, but dragons prefer to act indirectly. This fact, along with their nature to act alone, explains why the dragons don't simply descend en masse against the Therans, the Denairastas, or anyone else who offends them. They take a much longer view. After all, what is a century to a being who measures time in millennia?

Dragons as Allies

As previously mentioned, dragons are intelligent Namegivers with their own desires and goals. These goals can sometimes coincide with those of other Namegivers, as demonstrated during Barsaive's struggle against the Theran Empire. These situations allow a gamemaster to introduce dragons as allies or patrons of the player characters.

With their considerable knowledge of magical and mundane matters, a dragon ally can provide important information, magical item Key Knowledge, spells, and much more. Dragons are also known for having great wealth. With a dragon ally, it is possible for adepts to have their adventures paid for, as long as their actions further the dragon's cause.

Of course, dragons are not known for their generosity. They give nothing away unless it benefits them in some way. If a dragon lavishes gifts on the player characters, he will expect their loyalty and service. While beneficial, an alliance with a dragon is likely to be temporary. Once a dragon's objectives have been met, he is likely to cut support.

A typical arrangement might involve the dragon asking the player characters to perform a specific task in exchange for some service or resource the dragon has to offer. For example, adepts might seek out the great dragon Icewing in hopes of learning a Key Knowledge (or some other obscure piece of lore). In return, Icewing asks the adepts to spy and report back to him. Upon completion of their task, Icewing will give the player characters the information they seek.

Gamemasters can also establish more lasting relations between dragons and adepts. A dragon can serve as a patron and mentor for the adepts. In exchange, the adepts serve as the dragon's eyes and hands in Namegiver society. Dragons run whole networks of spies and agents that provide the gamemaster the opportunity to use dragons as patrons.

While dragons usually treat their servants well, they are not bound by the culture and beliefs of other Namegiver races. Dragons are arrogant and often treat other Namegivers as children or pets. It is not uncommon for a dragon to sacrifice agents in pursuit of a particular goal. Adepts chosen for sacrifice will likely not take the same dispassionate view of the situation as their patron. If they survive, they may choose to seek revenge on their former mentor.

Dragons as Enemies

A dragon can be an epic foe for an **Earthdawn** campaign. Dragons are powerful creatures, perhaps the most powerful beings in the world, outside of mighty astral entities such as the Passions and powerful Horrors, such as Verjigorm, the Great Hunter.

Dragons have great physical ability and magical power, and the intelligence to use both well. Fighting a dragon should never be easy; such a battle should be the climax of a long campaign, rather than a simple encounter.

Fortunately, dragons rarely wait around for would-be hunters to come and find them. Most dragons are plotters and schemers. To carry out their plans they operate through complex networks of servants and informants. The nature of dragon culture and custom makes dragons aloof and separate from the day-to-day affairs of other Namegivers.

A dragon villain works best behind the scenes. During their early adventures as low-Circle adepts, the dragon's presence will be virtually unknown as the characters interact with its servants and agents. As the characters gain power and advance in Circle, they will encounter the dragon's more powerful servants and uncover more of its schemes, becoming a thorn in its side. Eventually the adepts may gain enough power to confront the dragon directly and slay it in an epic battle that shakes the earth and is retold in song and story for generations to come. The defeat of a dragon is the stuff of legend.

The power and nature of a dragon creates an interesting dilemma for gamemasters, because a dragon can easily kill all but the most powerful adepts. While character death—especially cheap character death—is generally undesirable, the hazards of facing a dragon should not be downplayed. If the characters escape unscathed every time they encounter a dragon, the significance of dragons becomes diluted. The threat and danger they present to the world becomes less sincere.

So how can a gamemaster use the dragons as enemies, maintaining the threat a dragon represents, but not kill the characters in each adventure? Below are some suggestions for how to resolve this dilemma, while remaining true to the essence of the **Earthdawn** universe.

Dragons should be long-term opponents. Some of the dragon-like creatures included here are suitable for single adventures, but most should be used over an extended campaign in which the characters discover the dragon's plans, encounter its victims, or witness its powers in use. This serves two purposes:

First, the players encounter the dragon indirectly. Over time they learn about its influence and ability. Second, an extended story gives the characters a chance to expand their own power and experience. This makes them more able to face the dragon, or at least with its servants.

A dragon should not be something you battle once and slay. They are very powerful, and only experienced adventurers have a chance at surviving an encounter with a dragon, let alone defeat one. Each dragon presents an opportunity for a unique storyline based on the individual dragon's attitudes and goals. Allowing the characters to learn about, confront, and battle Vestrivan in the course of a single adventure is a waste of a good dragon.

Another idea is characters need not directly confront the dragon at all. Many dragons work through agents, including drakes or other dragons. Some Namegivers might not even be aware they serve a dragon's goals. A series of adventures focusing on disrupting the dragon's plans allows these powerful creatures to be used without risking the lives of the characters, at least too much.

Of course, if a dragon's plans are disrupted too often, it might just focus its attention on the responsible party. This is generally a bad thing and should be used to emphasize the world of **Earthdawn** is dangerous. Even if they survive, the characters should suffer losses of some sort to reinforce the power a dragon represents. It should be a significant event; not simply one of the players needs to make a new character. Don't let the death (or other type of loss) of a character happen for no good reason. The characters in **Earthdawn** are heroes. If they are going to go down, let them go down heroically!

Customizing Dragons

The game statistics provided in this chapter present only a rough guideline for the powers and abilities of dragons and of dragon-like creatures. The gamemaster should use these as a starting point to customize the powers and abilities of a specific dragon. Dragons are not simple monsters to slay; they are individuals with goals and motivations like any other Namegiver.

Gamemasters should reflect a dragon's individuality by adjusting the abilities, attributes, and Step numbers given in the examples to suit the characteristics of the dragon in question. For example, if a dragon is intended to be larger than average, it might have increased physical attribute Steps, Attack and Damage Steps, and similar characteristics. A dragon said to be skilled at magic would probably have a higher Spellcasting Step. Individuals may also have different levels of power for their dragon abilities, and may have different powers from those provided.

Remember each dragon has a unique appearance, personality, and goals. The gamemaster should consider what sets this dragon apart? What does he want and how does he go about getting it? Like any sapient being, personality and temperament can provide notable insight into the way a dragon will relate to other people.

In the game statistics provided for the four types of dragons described in this chapter, a starting point for customizing them in your game is provided in the Starting Powers line. We then provide a recommendation for the number of Power Ranks a typical adult dragon of that type would have. These points can be spent on existing powers, or to buy ranks in additional powers. If you want to make a dragon that is older or younger than the standard adult, you can increase or decrease the number of rank points provided. Finally, we offer Sample Distribution, an example of a dragon with the suggested rank points spent.

DRAGON POWERS

Dragons have a wide range of magical powers at their command. All dragons have at least some of the powers listed here, and great dragons often have all of these powers (and more) to call upon. As a dragon ages, it develops new powers and improves existing ones, similar to the way an adept modifies their True Pattern to develop new talents and abilities.

Adult dragons have the following powers: Armored Scales, Dragonsight, Dragonspeech, Karma, and spells. They may also possess other powers, such as Disrupt Fate, Dragon Breath, Fear, and Regeneration.

Armored Scales
Step: NA   **Action:** NA

A dragon's armored hide provides great physical and magical protection against attack. Damage resulting from extra successes on attacks is reduced by one per success. For example, under normal circumstances each additional success from an attack with a melee weapon does +2 damage. Against a dragon with Armored Scales, each additional success only does +1 damage. This damage reduction also applies to spells that deal extra damage with additional successes, but not extra damage based on additional threads.

Dispel Magic
Step: Rank+WIL   **Action:** Simple

Because of their innate understanding of magical forces, dragons can disrupt magical effects at will. This power works like the Dispel Magic talent (*Player's Guide*, p. 139), but does not require a Standard action, and has a range of 30 yards.

Additionally, this power can be used to dispel the magical effects of creature powers (including Horror and dragon powers) with a sustained duration. Use the power's Step Number as the Circle on the Dispel Difficulty Table (*Player's Guide*, p. 265) to determine the Difficulty Number for the Dispel Magic test. If a creature power or ability Step Number is higher than 15, add +1 to the Dispel Difficulty for each Step above 15. For example, a power with Step 17 would have a Dispel Difficulty of 27 (25+2).

Disrupt Fate
Step: Rank+WIL   **Action:** Free

This power allows the dragon to alter the fate of other creatures. The dragon spends a Karma Point and then makes a Disrupt Fate test against the Mystic Defense of a target within line of sight. If successful, the target must immediately repeat the most recent test made. The new test result stands and cannot be disrupted a second time.

As long as the dragon has Karma Points available, it may make as many Disrupt Fate tests as there are targets. Spending the Karma Point entitles the dragon to use this ability; the dragon's Karma Step is not added to the test.

Dominate Beast
Step: Rank+WIL   **Action:** Standard

This dragon can control beasts, similar to the Beastmaster talent of the same name (*Player's Guide*, p. 140). The dragon makes a Dominate Beast test against the Mystic Defense of any beasts the dragon wishes to control. If successful, the dragon controls the target creatures for a number of minutes equal to its Dominate Beast Step.

Unlike the Beastmaster talent, the dragon may use this power to dominate multiple creatures at once, but no more than their total Step in Dominate Beast.

An animal under the effect of this power will not take any hostile action against the dragon, and will perform one simple task for the dragon that does not exceed the duration of the power. Attempts to dominate or control a beast under the effect of this power must exceed the dragon's Dominate Beast Step.

Dragon Breath
Step: Rank+15   **Action:** Simple

Dragons are famous, and rightfully feared, for their fiery breath. Every culture has tales of a furious dragon raining destruction down on villages, towns, or cities. Dragon Breath targets everything within a 90-degree arc, using the dragon's mouth as the arc's center. The distance the flame extends is based on how much Strain the dragon is willing to take, as indicated on the Dragon Breath Table.

The dragon makes a Dragon Breath test and compares the result against the Mystic Defense of each target within the area of effect. All affected targets catch fire, taking damage from the flames equal to the test result, reduced by Physical Armor.

Dragon Breath damages and burns items, including armor and weapons. Combustible items are destroyed in short order, while non-combustible items takes damage each round, potentially rendering them useless, though magical items are only affected if the dragon's Dragon Breath test equals or exceeds the item's Mystic Defense. Armor and weapons suffer 2 points of item damage each round they are exposed to the flames, with the losses being spread as evenly as possible among the item's ratings. For example, fernweave armor would lose 1 point each from its Physical and Mystic Armor each round.

If a weapon's Damage Step, a shield's Physical Defense bonus, or suit of armor's Armor ratings are reduced to 0, the item is destroyed. If an item is not completely destroyed, damage may be repaired as normal (*Player's Guide*, p. 411 for damaged weapons, p. 415 for armor and shields).

Dragon Breath Table

Strain	Range
1	10 yards
5	20 yards
15	40 yards
30	60 yards

Dragonsight
Step: Rank+PER   **Action:** Simple

A dragon's affinity with magic gives them the ability to view astral space. Dragonsight is a heightened version of the Astral Sight talent (*Player's Guide*, p. 129), except dragons do not have to spend Strain to use it. The dragon makes a Dragonsight test as an astral sensing test. For more information about the use of astral sensing abilities, see the **Workings of Magic** chapter in the *Player's Guide*, p. 209.

Dragonspeech
Step: Rank+CHA   **Action:** Free (Special, see below)

Dragonspeech is the natural method of communication between dragons. It allows the user to transmit thoughts directly to any being within range. The dragon can also send simple images as well as speech through its mental link. The target hears the dragon as a separate 'voice' in his head and recognizes it as the dragon.

Dragonspeech transcends language, allowing a dragon to communicate with another being whether or not it normally understands the subject's language. The dragon can communicate with spirits and uses this power in place of Spirit Talk or Elemental Tongues for negotiations.

This power also allows a dragon to summon spirits. Unlike Namegiver magicians, dragons may summon any type of spirit. The power otherwise works as described as the Summon talent in the *Player's Guide*, p. 171, including the Action type (i.e. a dragon using Dragonspeech to summon a spirit is a Sustained action, as per the Summon talent).

Fear
Step: Rank + CHA   **Action:** Simple

Dragons project an intimidating, even terrifying presence. Many would-be heroes flee in terror when coming face to face with a dragon. The dragon makes a Fear test and compares the result against the Mystic Defense of all characters within 40 yards. If successful against a given character, the victim will sweat, stammer, and exhibit other signs of fright.

The affected character has a difficult time taking any kind of hostile action against the dragon. Any tests the character makes against the dragon suffer a -2 penalty per success scored on the dragon's Fear test until the next sunrise or sunset (whichever comes first). This power cannot be used against a target again until the duration has expired, even if it was initially ineffective; this does not provide any protection for other targets in the area. This power has no effect on targets that are immune to fear.

Karma Cancel
Step: Rank+WIL   **Action:** Simple (see below)

One of a dragon's subtler but effective powers, Karma Cancel allows a dragon to override another character's use of Karma. The dragon makes a Karma Cancel test against the Mystic Defense of a target character within line of sight. Once this power has been successfully used, the dragon may spend its Karma Points to cancel the target's use of Karma on a test as a Free action until the next sunrise or sunset (whichever comes first).

If a target spends multiple Karma Points on a test (for example, when using the True Shot talent), the dragon must spend the same number of points to cancel them. Karma Cancel does not require an action; a dragon may attempt to cancel an opponent's use of Karma at any time so long as it still has Karma Points to spend.

Karma Points
Step: Special (see text) **Action:** NA

All dragons have the ability to use Karma. The value given in parentheses after the Karma power in the dragon's description indicates the dragon's Karma Step. The dragon has a pool of Karma Points equal to its Karma Step x 4, which it can spend on any test. Unless otherwise noted by a particular power, a dragon may only spend one point of Karma per test.

Lair Sense
Step: Rank+PER **Action:** Free

A dragon's lair is an extension of itself, and it can notice intruders anywhere within its lair. The dragon makes a Lair Sense test against the Mystic Defense of a character who performs a test while in the dragon's lair. If successful, the dragon detects the character and knows his location within the lair. This power can only be used against a given target once every ten minutes.

Dragons often set traps in their lairs to take advantage of this power, forcing characters to beat the traps by performing an action that reveals their presence.

Poison
Step: Rank+TOU **Action:** NA

Dragons with this power are able to damage a victim with poison. If the victim suffers damage from an envenomed attack, they must resist the poison's effects. Some dragons have venomous fangs; others have a stinger on their tail or glands that inject venom with their claws.

The poison is typically a damaging poison as described in the game statistics, but may be of any variety. Some dragons even have a combination of poison types. See **Poison**, p. 171 for more information on the game statistics provided. A single character can only suffer from one use of the Poison power at a time.

Regeneration
Step: Rank+TOU **Action:** Simple

Dragons can easily heal damage done to them. The dragon makes a Regeneration test and reduces its Current Damage by the total. Use of this power costs the dragon a Recovery test and 1 Karma Point (the Karma Point spent does not add to the result of the test). This power may be used to heal a Wound, but if used in this fashion it does not reduce the Current Damage.

Skills
Step: Special (see text) **Action:** Special (see text)

Some Dragons have powers based on skills. Refer to the **Skills** chapter on p. 183 of the *Player's Guide* for a description of each skill and how it works.

Spellcasting
Step: Rank+PER **Action:** Standard

Dragons have an inherent ability to manipulate the energy of astral space, and as a result cast spells. Dragons can use their Spellcasting power to cast any spell as Raw Magic. The dragon doesn't need to know the spell, it simply shapes the astral energy to its will and the spell happens.

Dragons still weave threads to cast spells, using their **Thread Weaving** power (p. 174). Hatchlings need to weave the normal number of threads to cast a spell, adults only need to weave half the normal number of threads (round down), and great dragons do not need to weave threads at all.

Dragons do not use spell matrices, casting all of their spells as raw magic. A dragon casting a spell would still potentially suffer the effects of warping or damage, but their innate power and high magic resistance greatly reduce the effects of tainted astral energy on their spellcasting. Dragons are, however, wise enough to not recklessly cast powerful magic in corrupt areas. While the damage they might suffer is small, the threat posed by a Horror—especially one powerful enough to mark a dragon—gives even these mighty Namegivers pause.

Spells
Step: Special (see text) **Action:** NA

Dragons are natural born spellcasters, with an inherent knowledge of the workings of magic. They do not know spells in the same way as other Namegiver magicians. As described above under Spellcasting the dragon simply shapes astral energy into the desired form. When presented with a dragon's game statistics, this represents the maximum Circle of spell effect the dragon can produce.

Suppress Magic
Step: Rank+WIL **Action:** Standard

Some dragons have developed their ability to shape magic to such a degree they can quash the use of magic by other creatures. The dragon makes a Suppress Magic test against the Mystic Defense of a target within 30 yards. If successful, the dragon reduces the target's use of magical abilities by applying a -2 penalty per success to magical talents, the damage from magical weapons, and any other magic use. When applied to magic armor and weapons, this will not reduce the protection or damage beneath the mundane protection provided; e.g. a threaded troll sword enhanced with Forge Weapon cannot have a Damage Step less than STR + 6 due to this power.

This power lasts until the next sunrise or sunset (whichever comes first) and may only be used against a given target once per day. A dragon can selectively use this ability to suppress a specific type of magic, such as talents, magic items or spells, instead of suppressing all types.

Talents
Step: Special (see text)   **Action:** Special (see text)

Many dragons have powers based on adept talents beyond those described here. Refer to the **Talents** chapter on p.119 of the *Player's Guide* for a description of the talent in question.

Wingbeat
Step: Rank+STR   **Action:** Standard

Dragons with wings can use them to knock over opponents. The power affects all characters in a 10-yard long 90-degree arc in front of the dragon. The dragon makes a Wingbeat test, and all characters within the area of effect must make a Knockdown test against the test result. If a character fails the Knockdown test, they are knocked back a number of yards equal to the amount they failed the test. For example, a character failing the Knockdown test by 8 is knocked back 8 yards.

DRAGONLIKE CREATURES

In addition to the descriptions he provided on the different types of dragons, Master Vasdenjas provided information on some of the dragon-like creatures living in Barsaive. These include drakes (shape-shifting servants of the dragons), hydras, and wyverns. Some of the information below is most intriguing.

Drake

Most great dragons prefer to avoid becoming entangled with the culture of other Namegivers. Unfortunately, there are times we need to interact with the younger races. Our envoys and servants in Namegiver society are the drakes. They serve as our eyes, ears, and hands.

Drakes are not Namegivers. They are made using powerful magic in a complex and lengthy process far beyond the understanding of even the most skilled of your magicians. Indeed, the enchantments are beyond the skills of most adult dragons. Creating the spark of life for a drake requires some sacrifice of life energy from its maker.

Because only the most powerful dragons can create drakes and the process is so involved, drakes are seldom created. Tradition sets limits on the number of drakes a dragon can have and we don't make more than are necessary.

Drakes are like Namegivers in most respects. They eat, sleep, and require air—although their limits are greater than yours as a result of their dragon lineage. They resemble miniature dragons, seven to eight feet in length. Their appearance and coloring reveal the dragon who created them. My own drakes appear as Barsaivian dragons with coloration similar to my own.

Drakes serve as excellent envoys to your society through their ability to assume Namegiver form. Drakes can take the form of any race save windlings (too small to imitate) and obsidimen (a mix of flesh and elemental earth). This allows them to interact with you and move through Namegiver society without provoking the fear and distrust generally reserved for my kind.

When in Namegiver form, a drake loses its dragon-like physical abilities, though its magical powers remain. It is otherwise indistinguishable from other Namegivers. Like their kin, drakes have a gift for magic and most follow a magical Discipline, using those abilities in Namegiver form.

Another gift of their dragon heritage is an extended lifespan. Drakes can live for centuries, but their lives are finite. Whether killed in battle or reaching the end of their natural life, upon death the drake decays more rapidly than natural creatures, returning to the base matter from which they are formed

Game Statistics

Challenge: Warden (Ninth Circle)

DEX:	12	**Initiative:**	14	**Unconsciousness:**	81
STR:	13	**Physical Defense:**	15	**Death Rating:**	102
TOU:	12	**Mystic Defense:**	16	**Wound Threshold:**	18
PER:	13	**Social Defense:**	16	**Knockdown:**	17
WIL:	13	**Physical Armor:**	10	**Recovery Tests:**	4
CHA:	12	**Mystic Armor:**	8	**Karma:**	8 (32)

Movement: 14 (Flying 20)
Actions: 3 (1 in Namegiver form); Bite: 18 (22), Claw x2: 18 (21)
Powers: Armored Scales, Dragonsight (16), Dragonspeech (16), Resist Pain (2)
Additional Powers (Choose Two): Dragon Breath (17), Dispel Magic (17), Disrupt

Fate (17), Karma Cancel (17), Poison (15), Regeneration (15), and Suppress Magic (17)
Spells: By Discipline

Shapeshifting: Drakes can freely change between Namegiver and dragon forms, taking a Standard action to change.

In Namegiver form drakes can follow Disciplines and learn talents and skills like any other Namegiver. A typical drake will be at least Journeyman tier in their chosen Discipline. Older and more powerful drakes are more likely to follow multiple Disciplines. Magicians are common, as it is easy to conceal the use of dragon-like powers as spells. Beastmaster, Scout, Swordmaster, Thief, and Warrior Disciplines are also commonly followed. A drake's talents and Discipline abilities only function when in Namegiver form.

When in Namegiver form, a drake's true nature can be detected by someone who examines the drake's pattern in astral space (see Astral Sensing, *Player's Guide* p. 209). The viewer must score three successes on an Astral Sight test against the drake's Mystic Defense; otherwise they see an astral pattern of the drake's Namegiver form.

Drakes have powers like their dragon masters, but while in Namegiver form can only use Dispel Magic, Dragonsight, Regeneration, and Suppress Magic. When a drake switches form, their clothing and equipment vanishes into an astral pocket. The equipment returns when the drake returns to Namegiver form.

Equipment: Varies by Namegiver form
Loot: Scales and blood worth D6×50 silver pieces (counts as treasure worth Legend Points)

Drake, Lesser

There also exists the lesser or "false" drakes, most commonly seen in Blood Wood, though they can be found outside it as well. They are drakes, make no mistake, they just lack the shapeshifting ability. Their only form is a small dragon. They are not as intelligent or capable as the true drakes, but they are still dangerous opponents with more than enough magical power to cause problems for adventurers who encounter them.

> If these creatures are drakes, this means a dragon created them. When I asked Vasdenjas why they were created without the ability to change shape, he deflected the question; only saying their creator prefers servants who lack the 'weakness' of Namegiver form. He refused to identify their creator, or why he had such an interest in the Blood Wood.
>
> Vasdenjas would often close off avenues of inquiry in this manner—often saying 'he had already revealed too much'. To this day, I think he enjoyed teasing me with hints of knowledge he would then refuse to divulge. -- *Tiabdijin*

Game Statistics
Challenge: Journeyman (Eighth Circle)

DEX:	12	Initiative:	14	Unconsciousness:	76
STR:	13	Physical Defense:	15	Death Rating:	96
TOU:	12	Mystical Defense:	14	Wound Threshold:	18
PER:	10	Social Defense:	14	Knockdown:	17
WIL:	10	Physical Armor:	10	Recovery Tests:	4
CHA:	10	Mystic Armor:	6	Karma:	8 (32)

Movement: 14 (Flying 20)
Actions: 3; Bite: 18 (22), Claws x2: 18 (21)
Powers: Armored Scales, Dragon Breath (17), Dragonsight (13), Dragonspeech (13), Poison (15) [Damaging, Onset: Instant, Interval: 1/10 rounds, Duration: Until healed], Resist Pain (2)
Dragon Breath: A lesser drake's Dragon Breath power produces a thin stream of fiery breath that can strike only one target at a time.
Loot: Scales and blood worth D6×50 silver pieces (counts as treasure worth Legend Points)

Hydra

The story of the hydra is a tragic one, and while my fellows will not be pleased I am revealing this information, I think it is too important to keep hidden.

Shortly before the Scourge there lived a great dragon Named Thermail. She had only recently become a great dragon and had mated one last time before ascending to that noble status. As she was a great dragon, Thermail chose to raise her clutch herself rather than foster the eggs with another dragon. There was some concern with her decision, as no dragon since All-Wings herself had cared for her own young. Since Thermail was a great dragon, however, she had the right to serve as guardian.

Thermail was a very public dragon. She enjoyed the company of the younger races. Her wisdom and advice were legendary, and would often entertain guests in her lair where they would have long conversations about philosophy, art, and the intricacies of magic. She was most hospitable to her guests, and it was through her hospitality she was betrayed.

Thermail stopped receiving visitors when her eggs were ready to hatch; she would not allow other Namegivers to see her hatchlings. Unfortunately, a magician of her acquaintance, who had spent much time in her lair, managed to sneak past many of the lair's defenses and stole away seven of her ten hatchlings.

Using powerful magic the magician merged the seven hatchlings into a single creature, the first hydra. This unnatural beast had seven heads sprouting from a single monstrous and twisted body. Somehow he managed to produce a second creature from the first and mated them. Now the beasts can found across Barsaive.

Thermail went mad with grief and searched the lands of Barsaive, destroying towns and cities, killing any who tried to stop her. Sadly, she never found culprit—and his (or her) identity remains unknown to this day. In her grief, Thermail impaled herself on the pinnacle of a mountain, now Named Wyrmspire in her honor.

Hydras are hideous monstrosities, roughly forty feet in length. The magical process that created them gives them sporadic dragon abilities. Some have dragon breath, while others are venomous or are able to strike terror into their prey. No two have the same abilities, and it is impossible to tell in advance what an individual hydra might be capable of. The only positive things I have to say are their inability to fly keeps them from ranging far, their bestial intelligence means they are unable to cast spells, and their lack of subtlety means they can be easily found out if they threaten civilized areas.

If you encounter a hydra, or learn where one might be lairing, please notify any nearby dragons. We do everything we can to eliminate this tragic mistake from the land. While they are not dragons, we feel a responsibility to them, as they did not ask to be created, or choose their terrible existence.

Game Statistics
Challenge: Warden (Tenth Circle)

DEX:	9	**Initiative:**	11	**Unconsciousness:**	136
STR:	22	**Physical Defense:**	13	**Death Rating:**	168
TOU:	22	**Mystic Defense:**	17	**Wound Threshold:**	33
PER:	8	**Social Defense:**	15	**Knockdown:**	26
WIL:	10	**Physical Armor:**	15	**Recovery Tests:**	7
CHA:	8	**Mystic Armor:**	8	**Karma:**	6 (24)

Movement: 16

Actions: 5; Bite x7: 22 (27), Claws x2: 22 (25)
Powers: Dragonsight (15), Fear (18), Fury (2), Regeneration (25)
Additional Power (Choose One): Dispel Magic (25), Dragon Breath (25), Karma Cancel (25), Poison (25), and Suppress Magic (25)
Hydra Armor: Hydra armor, like dragon hide, is extremely tough, reducing the bonus damage from extra successes against the hydra by one per success. However, unlike the Armored Scales ability, hydra armor does not offer increased resistance to spell damage.
Special Maneuvers:
Grab and Bite (Hydra, Bite)
Enrage (Opponent)
Provoke (Opponent, Close Combat)
Too. Many. Heads. (Opponent): The attacker may use two additional successes to target a weak point on one of the heads. If the attack causes a Wound, the head is disabled or severed and the hydra loses one action per round. This effect is cumulative, but cannot reduce a hydra below 1 action per round. Healing the Wound caused by the attack will restore the head.
Loot: Up to 10,000 silver pieces worth of treasure hidden in its lair (counts as treasure worth Legend Points)

Wyverns

Wyverns resemble small dragons, but as I have explained in the past, they are not dragons. They are not even Namegivers. They are savage, mindless beasts driven by instinct. That they resemble dragons is nothing more than the universe's cruel joke called coincidence.

Wyverns grow as large as thirty feet from head to tail, with two powerful hind legs, as well as two wings. They have no forelimbs, instead their wings are tipped with claws which allow them to climb trees and scale cliffs—though their ability to fly means climbing isn't strictly necessary. The claws also serve as a way for the wyvern to grasp their prey while they tear at it with their mouth full of sharp teeth.

As if their sharp claws and teeth were not enough, they have another potent weapon. Their tail ends in a barbed stinger, which contains deadly venom. A wyvern often stings its prey and attacks while the victim is suffering the effects.

Just because a wyvern is not intelligent, they should not be underestimated. They possess a bestial cunning that makes them one of the more dangerous predators to be found in Barsaive. They are excellent at using terrain to their advantage, preferring remote, isolated areas for their homes. They are generally territorial, though groups of wyverns have been known to bring down larger prey—even careless dragons—through tenacity and superior numbers.

> Given his tendency to talk for hours about the mating and life habits of any number of creatures, Vasdenjas was uncharacteristically reticent when it came to describing the wyvern's life cycle. To the best of my knowledge no Namegiver has reported seeing eggs or young, and all recorded wyvern corpses died through violence—none of old age or similar natural causes.
>
> Despite his insistence to the contrary, the evidence indicates wyverns are dragons during their feral, adolescent phase. Even if wyverns are a distinct creature, the physical resemblance and behavior lines up too closely to be a simple coincidence.
>
> To this day, I do not understand my late master's secrecy in this matter.
> -- Tiabdjin

Game Statistics
Challenge: Journeyman (Eighth Circle)

DEX:	11	**Initiative:**	13	**Unconsciousness:**	92
STR:	15	**Physical Defense:**	15	**Death Rating:**	112
TOU:	12	**Mystic Defense:**	13	**Wound Threshold:**	18
PER:	6	**Social Defense:**	12	**Knockdown:**	13
WIL:	7	**Physical Armor:**	10	**Recovery Tests:**	4
CHA:	5	**Mystic Armor:**	5	**Karma:**	8 (32)

Movement: 14 (Climbing 10, Flying 22)
Actions: 3; Bite: 19 (23), Claws x2: 20 (22), Tail: 20 (24)
Powers: Poison (16) [Damaging, Onset: Instant, Interval: 1/5 rounds, Duration: Until healed]
Special Maneuvers:
Clip the Wing (Opponent)
Loot: Hide and tail worth D8 x 50 silver pieces (counts as treasure worth Legend Points).

DRAGONS

Dragon-kind is as diverse as the younger races are. Just as individuals of the younger races have different colors and textures of hair and skin, as well as various body shapes and facial features, we dragons have our own distinguishing features.

Broadly speaking, dragons can be divided into four main groups. You smaller folk have your own Names for these groups, and I will use those for convenience—our own categorization describes these groups in relation to four elements. Given the propensity for your kind to categorize things to the smallest degree, you would likely consider each of type of dragon to be a separate race, like the differences between elves, orks, and dwarfs result in different races. Do not be misled—we are all dragons, tracing our line back to the earliest days of Nightslayer and Dayheart.

Common Dragons

I, along with my other brethren in Barsaive—save Root Protector, who your people call Earthroot—am what most people conjure in their mind with the word dragon, and so are called 'common' dragons. As if something so magnificent could be considered common! I understand the intention is not to belittle us with this label; after all, we are the most common type of dragon a resident of Barsaive is likely to see. Therefore, I view the appellation with some humor. Be warned, however, most dragons (especially younger ones) are likely to take offense, and it is wise to not use this title to their face.

Perhaps, in the interest of interspecies understanding, you might persuade your scholars to adopt a less insulting descriptor. Among dragon-kind, we are known as Dragons of the Earth. We are solid, sharp, strong, and filled with wisdom deep as the roots of a mountain. This may cause some confusion, however, with those who deal with elemental spirits and other residents of those netherworlds. In the distant land of Cathay we are known as 'western' dragons, given we hail from lands to the west of that locale. I think 'western' dragon is probably best to use, and would encourage you to start doing so.

We all have long, powerful bodies with both front and hind legs in addition to a pair of wings. Our heads are large and rest atop a long, powerful neck. Some of us have horns on our head, or even a spiky 'ruff' of sorts, similar to a lion's mane or the scruff of fur and skin behind a wolf's head. It even serves a similar purpose, providing protection from attacks against the vulnerable parts on the back of the neck. Many of us also have a ridge of horns running down our spine and the length of our tail, which is long and muscled. Our bodies average about sixty feet in length, with another fifty to sixty feet of tail, and our wings can span a hundred feet on average.

Other than these broad similarities, quite a bit of variation can be found. Our scales vary in color from black, deep blue, emerald green, reddish brown, golden orange, pale silver, and beyond. Most dragons tend toward a single color, with lighter tones on the underside, though there have been instances of dragons with patterns of stripes or spots.

Another source of variety is our horns, at least for those of us who have them. A few individuals have small horns—barely larger than nubs, really. Others have great, curling horns like a mountain ram. Many females consider horns to be a male's more attractive physical quality.

And then, of course, like any Namegiver, we come in a diverse variety of sizes and shapes. Some are larger than average while others are smaller. The shape of our wings can distinguish individuals. Admittedly, the differences that seem obvious to us are not so clear to the younger races, but I heard some of your scholars tell dragons apart solely by color! You may as well tell obsidimen apart by the color of their skin.

Game Statistics
Challenge: Master (Thirteenth Circle)

DEX:	16	Initiative:	20	Unconsciousness:	172
STR:	26	Physical Defense:	21	Death Rating:	212
TOU:	27	Mystic Defense:	22	Wound Threshold:	40
PER:	17	Social Defense:	22	Knockdown:	30
WIL:	18	Physical Armor:	30	Recovery Tests:	9
CHA:	15	Mystic Armor:	10	Karma:	10 (40)

Movement: 16 (Flying 24)

Actions: 4; Bite: 25 (35), Claws: x4 26 (34), Horns: 25 (34), Tail: 25 (34)
Starting Powers: Armored Scales, Dragonsight (21), Dragonspeech (19), Resist Pain (2), Spellcasting (21), Spells (6th Circle in one discipline), Wingbeat (30)
Power Ranks: 60 Ranks – these ranks may be placed into existing or new powers and talents; additional circles of spells may be taken at 1 rank each (up to 13th circle).
Sample Distribution: Armored Scales, Disrupt Fate (25), Dragon Breath (25), Dragonsight (22), Dragonspeech (22), Fear (25), Lair Sense (27), Poison (28), Regeneration (31), Spellcasting (25), Suppress Magic (25), Wingbeat (30), Spells (9th Circle in one discipline)
Special Maneuvers:
Clip the Wing (Opponent)
Grab and Bite (Common Dragon, Claws)
Horn Sweep (Common Dragon, Horns): The common dragon may spend additional successes from an Attack test using its horns to throw its elephant-sized or smaller opponent. Each success spent in this way throws the opponent 2 yards and the opponent treats this distance as falling (see **Falling Damage**, p. 167). Note: not all common dragons have horns, or horns that can be used as weapons.
Tail Sweep (Common Dragon, Tail): The common dragon may spend additional successes from an Attack test using its tail to throw its elephant-sized or smaller opponent. Each success spent in this way throws the opponent 2 yards and the opponent treats this distance as falling (see **Falling Damage**, p. 167).
Loot: Magical items and a hoard of coins and gems worth about 300,000 silver pieces (counts as treasure worth Legend Points)

Leviathans

As the western dragons are the Dragons of the Earth, the Leviathans are the Dragons of the Water. Dayheart, the First Dragon, laid eight eggs, four male and four female, and gave each pair right of rulership over part of the world. My ancestors were given the earth, and the leviathans were granted the seas. The sea dragons hunt whales and giant squid as their prey, and few can challenge them as lords of the waters.

Their existence under the waves has shaped the leviathan form. They are smaller than my kind, about half our length, and their bodies are much more slender. Their scales are smaller and seem to shimmer, even when out of the water. They tend towards blue and green coloration, though I have known individuals with black scales, and one with scales like mother-of-pearl.

Leviathans have no wings, and their limbs are much shorter—almost resembling clawed fins. Granted, these limbs are still strong enough to tear apart a ship, but they lack the dexterity present in western dragons. Though they prefer not to, leviathans can fly for a short time using their innate magical ability, appearing to 'swim' through the air. They can breathe air as easily as water, and while greatly hampered when on the ground because of their short limbs, they would still pose a formidable challenge to erstwhile hunters.

The snout of a leviathan is longer than a western dragon, but equally filled with sharp teeth. They can easily swallow entire schools of fish, and the larger ones can swallow a small fishing boat whole. Their bite is their strongest weapon, much stronger than their claws, and they often use their tails to deal powerful blows. Some leviathans even have stingers on their tails to deliver powerful venom not unlike the kind we have as hatchlings.

There are a few leviathans living in the Aras Sea, but its limited space is not well suited to maintaining a large population, and the great dragons (rather great leviathans) maintain strict control over the mating of the leviathan population in the Aras. They are much more numerous in the Selestrean Sea to the southwest of Barsaive, and the Sea of Storms off the coasts of Indrisa. There are rumors of leviathans in the Serpent River lakes, but they have never been confirmed and I highly doubt their veracity. While large enough to support a leviathan, it would be very difficult for one to lair in those places without being noticed.

Leviathans have a life cycle similar to western dragons. The eggs are cared for and raised by the great leviathans where they are taught the ways and traditions of dragon-kind. They undergo a period of feral adolescence—the time when most sea-going Namegivers will encounter a leviathan—and reach full maturity after spending some time in an astral cocoon in the depths of the sea.

Unlike western dragons, leviathans tend to have little to do with the younger races. Their homes in the depths of the sea are ill suited to your kind, and they have little interest in the history or affairs of surface dwellers. Indeed, leviathans are perhaps the most hidebound of the dragons, as they have not been exposed to the ways of the younger races.

Leviathan culture is generally insular and they only contact and deal with the rest of dragon-kind when they must. To my recollection, this has only happened once and it was long before the Scourge. Their lairs deep beneath the waves allow them a degree of isolation some of my western kin envy, where they study magic and spend a great deal of time in shal-mora uninterrupted.

Despite this preference for solitude and disdain of the company of other Namegivers, there are individual leviathans who are bit more public. One great leviathan of my acquaintance, known as Wavedancer, lairs near the city of Urupa on the Aras Sea. On a few rare occasions since the Scourge, she has invited visitors to her lair (likely only one of several she has) to a small festival of sorts. The gathering lasts up to a week, with Wavedancer inviting Troubadours to perform for her and her other guests. Displays of skill and strength are performed as well. Some suggest Wavedancer uses these gatherings to find individuals suited to act as her agents on land. If these suppositions are true, it may indicate an end to the isolation of the leviathans of the Aras Sea.

Game Statistics
Challenge: Master (Thirteenth Circle)

DEX:	18	**Initiative:**	22	**Unconsciousness:**	166
STR:	24	**Physical Defense:**	24	**Death Rating:**	204
TOU:	25	**Mystic Defense:**	24	**Wound Threshold:**	37
PER:	21	**Social Defense:**	17	**Knockdown:**	28
WIL:	20	**Physical Armor:**	28	**Recovery Tests:**	8
CHA:	12	**Mystic Armor:**	12	**Karma:**	10 (40)

Movement: 8 (Flying 20, Swimming 24)
Actions: 4; Bite 23 (30), Claws x2 23 (26), Tail 23 (28)
Starting Powers: Armored Scales, Dragonsight (25), Dragonspeech (16), Regeneration (29), Resist Pain (2), Spellcasting (25), Spells (6th Circle in one discipline)
Constrict (20): Grappled opponents take Step 20 Damage each round as long as the grapple is held.
Power Ranks: 60 Ranks – these ranks may be placed into existing or new powers and talents; additional circles of spells may be taken at 1 rank each (up to 13th circle).
Sample Distribution: Armored Scales, Disrupt Fate (25), Dominate Beast (25), Dragon Breath (25), Dragonsight (25), Dragonspeech (22), Fear (25), Lair Sense (25), Poison (28), Regeneration (29), Spellcasting (25), Spells (9th Circle in one discipline), Stealthy Stride (25)
Special Maneuvers:
Coil (Leviathan): The leviathan may spend an additional success from an Attack test to automatically grapple an opponent. Grappled opponents automatically take bite damage, claw, or tail damage each round.
Loot: Treasure hoard worth up to 100,000 silver pieces (counts as treasure worth Legend Points)

Cathay Dragons

Far to the east of Barsaive, beyond the Aras Sea and the distant land of Indrisa is the land of Cathay. The children of Dayheart who live in this distant land are the Dragons of the Wind. They are known by many titles to the Namegivers in this part of the world, including 'celestial ones,' 'masters of wind and storm,' and 'kings of rain.' Scholars in Barsaive and the Theran Empire call them 'Cathay dragons' after the land where they are most commonly found.

Cathay dragons are similar to leviathans: they have no wings and their body resembles a long serpent. But there the resemblance ends. Where leviathans tend toward darker colors related to the deep waters of their home, Cathay dragons are more brightly colored, with iridescent scales commonly of green and gold, with brilliant crimson and bright blue not being unheard of. They have a fringe of whiskers along their chin and cheeks, and horns like my kind, though the horns sometimes more resemble the antlers of deer and elk.

The limbs of a Cathay dragon are much more developed than a leviathan's. Indeed, of all dragon-kind the Cathay dragon has the greatest natural dexterity. I have seen one hold a delicate vase in its claws without so much as scratching it. They likewise have exceptionally strong senses of smell and sight, even compared to other dragon types.

Like leviathans, Cathay dragons can fly while lacking wings, though they are much more graceful in the air than our aquatic cousins. They tuck their legs up against their body and move in an undulating motion resembling swimming. A Cathay dragon leaping in and out of cloud cover while flying can resemble a dolphin playing in the wake of a riverboat. They are masters of the air, constantly twisting and diving and moving, as opposed to my kind who tends to drift like an eagle or other large bird of prey.

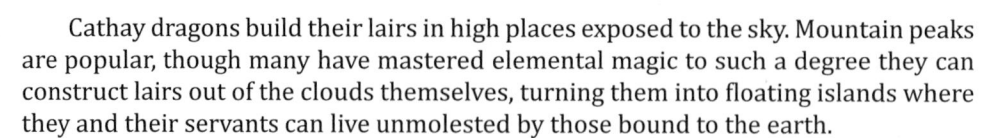

Cathay dragons build their lairs in high places exposed to the sky. Mountain peaks are popular, though many have mastered elemental magic to such a degree they can construct lairs out of the clouds themselves, turning them into floating islands where they and their servants can live unmolested by those bound to the earth.

Of all dragon-kind, Cathay dragons have the closest relationship with Namegivers. The younger races in Cathay view them with reverence, respecting their wisdom, age, and power. In some respects, they are viewed in much the same way folk in Barsaive honor the Passions. Serving a Cathay dragon is seen as a position of great honor, and the Dragons of the Wind never lack for willing servants. Indeed, many of the legendary heroes in the eastern lands have ties to Cathay dragons or were taught by them.

There is a tradition in Cathay for dragons to adopt Namegivers as children, raise and educate them, then send them back as leaders and teachers. The title 'Son (or Daughter) of a Dragon' is not uncommon among the noble houses and heroes of Cathay.

Cathay dragons have great appreciation for beauty and works of art of all kinds. They often act as patrons to notable artists and a Cathay dragon's collection is a thing to behold! Their palaces and lairs are often designed to highlight and organize their collection, and many of them enjoying showing off pieces of their trove to visitors who display suitable deference.

Interestingly, despite their close relationship with Namegivers in the east, Cathay dragons are perhaps even more dedicated to protocol and tradition than others of my kind. Our rites and rituals developed over the millennia as a way of ensuring interactions between dragons would remain polite and not trigger our predatory nature. Cathay dragons expect this level of civility and etiquette not only from other dragons, but any Namegivers with which they interact. If you ever have the opportunity to speak with a Dragon of the Wind, be on your best behavior!

As I mentioned before, Cathay dragons are tremendously skilled in elemental magic, and a great many develop ability in illusion as well, both to enhance the beauty of their lairs and hide places they wish to keep secret. They also deal more freely with spirits than other types of dragon-kind, commonly using elementals—especially air and water spirits—as spies, guards, and servants. I suspect elementals help build and maintain the more elaborate lairs used by Cathay dragons.

One final issue I will address, because I have little doubt the readers of this work will ask the question: Cathay dragons do practice slavery. Unlike the Theran Empire, however, Cathay dragons do not raid villages and steal folk away from their homes. Their slaves are usually thieves or brigands who sought to rob the dragon's home, or otherwise stole something of value belonging to the dragon. Rather than killing them outright (which they would certainly have a right to do), they are put to use as servants, treated kindly and kept well. If they please their masters they may earn their freedom, leaving older—but wiser for the experience.

Game Statistics
Challenge: Master (Thirteenth Circle)

DEX:	20	Initiative:	24	Unconsciousness:	148
STR:	19	Physical Defense:	26	Death Rating:	180
TOU:	19	Mystic Defense:	26	Wound Threshold:	28
PER:	24	Social Defense:	23	Knockdown:	23
WIL:	22	Physical Armor:	20	Recovery Tests:	6
CHA:	16	Mystic Armor:	13	Karma:	10 (40)

Movement: 16, Flying 26
Actions: 4; Bite 23 (30), Claws x4 23 (26)
Starting Powers: Armored Scales, Dragonsight (28), Dragonspeech (20), Resist Pain (2), Spellcasting (28), Spells (10th Circle in one discipline)
Constrict (15): Grappled opponents take Step 15 Damage each round as long as the grapple is held.
Power Ranks: 60 Ranks – these ranks may be placed into existing or new powers and talents; additional circles of spells may be taken at 1 rank each (up to 13th circle).
Sample Distribution: Armored Scales, Dispel Magic (28), Disrupt Fate (28), Dragon Breath (25), Dragonsight (30), Dragonspeech (25), Fear (20), Lair Sense (27), Regeneration (23), Spellcasting (30), Spells (11th Circle in two disciplines), Suppress Magic (28)
Special Maneuvers:
Grab and Bite (Cathay Dragon, Claws)
Loot: Scrolls, books, gems, artwork, and precious metals worth around 300,000 silver pieces. This counts as treasure worth Legend Points.

Feathered Dragons

Another pair of Dayheart's children became the brightly colored Dragons of Fire, called feathered dragons by Theran scholars. They are the rarest dragons in this part of the world as they choose to live in the hot, tropical lands of the distant south, and are most common across the great western ocean near Araucania, where they are called Quetzal. No feathered dragons make their home in Barsaive, and I have only met two in all my years. Your kind is unlikely to encounter one unless you travel very far from home.

Feathered dragons are in some ways the least dragon-like of our kind, at least in appearance. They are long and sinuous, looking in some ways like a large serpent. They have a pair of large wings, and only one pair of limbs—resembling hatchlings in that way. Their most distinguishing characteristic gives them their name: they are covered in brightly colored feathers along their entire body, including a ruff around their head and another tuft of feathers at the end of their tail. These feathers are largest on the wings and much smaller along the body, most commonly colored in bright greens and blues, but purple, crimson, yellow, and other bright colors are common, especially as patterns and highlights on the larger feathers.

They have sharp fangs and a stinger on their tail, which are all venomous. They often coil around their prey to bite and stab with their tail, sometimes choosing to squeeze the life out of their prey like a constrictor snake. They are smaller than western dragons, which suit them well in the close quarters of the jungles where they live. They love the warmth of the sun and can often be found basking in the treetops.

Feathered dragons go through the same stages of life as other dragons, with no significant differences worth noting. They resemble other dragons as well in the sense they maintain lairs, usually in the deep jungle or in caves and grottos near waterfalls. They gather mementos and treasures over the course of their life, and master the intricacies of magic, especially magic relating to plants, as well as a remarkable affinity for illusion.

Unlike my kind, feathered dragons tend to be shy and conceal themselves from strangers. Rather than challenge an interloper to their domain, a feathered dragon will discreetly observe them to determine their intent before taking action. They will frequently use illusion magic and other abilities to mislead and distract, rather than attack.

Feathered dragons have a mischievous sense of humor and it is common for Namegivers who live near their domains to be the subject of elaborate deceptions and pranks, often intended to warn the curious away from the dragon's domain without causing undue harm. Feathered dragons have even been known to aid members of the younger races who get lost in their jungle domain, using illusion magic and other subtle abilities to lead them to safety, sometimes without the subject being aware of the dragon's presence.

Despite this somewhat benevolent approach to relationships with other Namegivers, feathered dragons generally have little to do with the younger races. The native inhabitants of the lands where the feathered dragons live often consider them to be little more than exceptionally large, dangerous creatures. Unlike western or

Cathay dragons, there is little in the way of cultural tradition of the feathered dragons being keepers of knowledge and wisdom.

The most notable way the feathered dragons differ from other types is through significant use of blood magic. They understand the fire that flows through the veins of dragon-kind—and to a lesser degree, other creatures—and use this power to heal the damage done by the Scourge, making the land fertile again.

Unfortunately, this use of magic has caused a rift between feathered dragons. Some are strongly opposed to death magic—blood magic used solely for power—suggesting it partakes of the power of the Horrors, and sustains the Horrors remaining in the world. While they recognize the ability of life magic to heal and restore the land in the wake of the Scourge, they believe the first inevitably leads to the second.

The other group views all forms of blood magic, whether life magic or death magic, as tools. The intent and objective of the one using a tool determines moral weight, not the tool itself. If any beings are wise enough to use blood magic safely, it is dragons. Frankly, I am dismayed some among my kind fail to learn from history.

Most disturbing is the tendency of some in this latter faction to encourage the use of blood magic, teaching it to Namegivers living near them. This is sure to end in disaster of some sort, as while it is possible for a dragon to be cautious in the use of such power, the younger races are much more likely to go astray. The elves of Blood Wood are ample enough evidence!

This philosophical argument has grown to the point where we have heard reports of feathered dragons attacking each other over this matter. I hope the feathered dragons come to their senses and resolve this issue in the manner fitting our ancient traditions instead of simply spilling blood.

Game Statistics
Challenge: Master (Thirteenth Circle)

DEX:	19	Initiative:	23	Unconsciousness:	160
STR:	23	Physical Defense:	25	Death Rating:	196
TOU:	23	Mystic Defense:	25	Wound Threshold:	34
PER:	23	Social Defense:	18	Knockdown:	27
WIL:	19	Physical Armor:	26	Recovery Tests:	8
CHA:	13	Mystic Armor:	11	Karma:	10 (40)

Movement: 14, Flying 24
Actions: 4; Bite 23 (30), Claws x4 23 (28)
Starting Powers: Armored Scales, Dragonsight (27), Dragonspeech (17), Poison (27), Resist Pain (2), Spellcasting (27), Spells (6th Circle in one discipline)
Constrict (20): Grappled opponents take Step 20 Damage each round as long as the grapple is held.
Power Ranks: 60 Ranks – these ranks may be placed into existing or new powers and talents; additional circles of spells may be taken at 1 rank each (up to 13th circle).
Sample Distribution: Armored Scales, Disrupt Fate (25), Dominate Beast (23), Dragon Breath (25), Dragonsight (27), Dragonspeech (25), Fear (23), Lair Sense (25), Poison (31), Regeneration (27), Spellcasting (28), Spells (10th Circle in one discipline), Suppress Magic (24), Wingbeat (25)

Special Maneuvers:
Grab and Bite (Feathered Dragon, Bite)
Clip the Wing (Opponent)
Loot: Magical items and a hoard of precious metals and gems worth around 300,000 silver pieces (counts as treasure worth Legend Points)

SAMPLE DRAGONS

Asante

While substantially older than her mate Nightsky (see p.447), Asante's age of 800 years is still very young by dragon standards. In contrast to Nightsky, Asante's coloration is an unusual creamy white, with a much darker tint on her horns and claws. Among dragons she is considered exceptionally beautiful.

Asante's main flaw is her youth leaves her naïve and unwilling to recognize the power dragon blood gives her over weaker races. Indeed, her fondness for the Young Races became a weakness, which was exploited by cunning Namegivers in her youth, and later forced her into dissension with her elders. Over the years, she has become more self-righteous in her attitudes, and thus still vulnerable to manipulation.

In addition to her naiveté, Asante does not have the vast resources possessed by many other dragons, even those of her age. Much of her wealth has gone to aiding and supporting Namegivers in need—mostly victims of Horrors—and she rarely sees a return on her investments. Her preoccupation with Namegiver affairs has replaced drives common in other dragons, specifically the hoarding of wealth, and accumulation of influence and power. Her attention is devoted to more ephemeral things and she is thus unlikely to be suspicious of well-laid plans.

Challenge: Master (Thirteenth Circle)

DEX:	16	**Initiative:**	20	**Unconsciousness:**	169
STR:	25	**Physical Defense:**	20	**Death Rating:**	208
TOU:	26	**Mystic Defense:**	21	**Wound Threshold:**	39
PER:	16	**Social Defense:**	24	**Knockdown:**	29
WIL:	16	**Physical Armor:**	30	**Recovery Tests:**	9
CHA:	19	**Mystic Armor:**	11	**Karma:**	10 (40)

Movement: 16 (24 Flying)
Actions: 4; Bite: 25 (34), Claws x4: 26 (33)
Powers: Armored Scales, Diplomacy (23), Disrupt Fate (24), Dragon Breath (21), Dragonsight (21), Dragonspeech (23), Fear (29), First Impression (23), Lair Sense (21), Regeneration (30), Resist Pain (2), Spellcasting (25), Suppress Magic (22), Wingbeat (30)
Spells: Elementalism, Wizardry (both at Seventh Circle)
Special Maneuvers:
Clip the Wing (Opponent)
Grab and Bite (Asante, Claws)
Horn Sweep (Asante, Horns): Asante may spend additional successes from an Attack test using her horns to throw her elephant-sized or smaller opponent. Each success

spent in this way throws the opponent 2 yards and the opponent treats this distance as falling (see **Falling Damage**, p. 167).

Tail Sweep (Asante, Tail): Asante may spend additional successes from an Attack test using her tail to throw her elephant-sized or smaller opponent. Each success spent in this way throws the opponent 2 yards and the opponent treats this distance as falling (see **Falling Damage**, p. 167).

Loot: Magical items and a hoard of coins and gems worth about 150,000 silver pieces (counts as treasure worth Legend Points)

Charcoalgrin

The dragon Charcoalgrin is known to anyone who has traveled to Parlainth and Haven in search of adventure and fortune. She is the most powerful creature living in the ruins, except perhaps for Horrors not yet discovered in the catacombs' depths.

Charcoalgrin's story begins before the Scourge, when she was but barely an adult, and when the glorious city of Parlainth had been completed and its wizards and scholars were looking for ways to defend it from the Horrors. Like Mountainshadow, Charcoalgrin was intrigued by the Young Races, and studied the residents of Parlainth at a distance from her lair in the nearby Caucavic Mountains. But where Mountainshadow is wise and maintains discretion in his studies, Charcoalgrin fell victim to the innocence of her youth and grew fascinated by the Namegivers who created the city.

In defiance of dragon traditions concerning contact with the Theran Empire—in particular magicians of the Theran Empire—Charcoalgrin sought out contact with the magicians of Parlainth and willingly taught them mysteries as yet undiscovered by their superiors in Thera.

One Theran Wizard in particular fascinated the dragon. This human Wizard, Named Eyripemes, was among the magicians leading the city's efforts to protect itself from the coming Scourge. Over time, Charcoalgrin took a liking to this human and revealed to him the secret to hiding Parlainth from the Horrors, a spell taught to her by her sire, one which had not been cast since the previous age of magic. She shared with Eyripemes not only this ancient spell, but also the location of a pocket of astral space, a separate reality of sorts where Parlainth could escape to during the Scourge, sealing itself off from the coming Horrors.

Charcoalgrin also instructed the city's magicians and builders in the creation of vessels that would allow them to move about in this astral pocket if needed. These vessels would allow the Theran magicians of Parlainth to explore regions of astral space unknown to any Namegivers save the dragons. The vessels resembled small stone airships, much smaller than vedettes, capable of carrying only a handful of passengers. Parlainth's magicians were able to build only a small number of these, less than two dozen, before they were forced to enact the spell sending Parlainth from this world to the next.

Eyripemes was delighted, not only because he now had a way to protect his beloved city, but also because he now had access to magic more ancient than anyone had ever imagined. The human devoted his life to Charcoalgrin, and would do anything she said in return for another nugget of wisdom. As a gift for Eyripemes' devotion,

Charcoalgrin transformed the wizard, giving him the shape shifting ability of drakes, allowing him to take dragon form, and thus greatly extending his life. The relationship between the two strengthened, as often happens between teacher and student, and Charcoalgrin grew quite fond of Eyripemes, right up until Parlainth's disappearance. The day Parlainth vanished was indeed one of the saddest of Charcoalgrin's life.

Not even Charcoalgrin was immune to the spell the Therans used to cover their tracks into astral space. She, like all other Namegivers, forgot about the city the moment it vanished. The years of the Scourge went by and finally the Long Night had ended. The Namegivers emerged from their kaers, and the dragons once again flew in the skies. Charcoalgrin was among them, but was never as animated or clever as she had been before. Parlainth returned and with it returned Charcoalgrin's memories of Parlainth and Eyripemes. Along with this returned much of her former enthusiasm and energy. She immediately flew to the city, only to discover it in ruins, a shattered version of its former self. Rather than going back to her lair in the Caucavic Mountains, Charcoalgrin remained in the ruins, sequestering herself in what remained of the Imperial Palace, claiming the entire northern quarter of the city as her own.

Along with the return of her memories of Parlainth and Eyripemes came memories of the magical astral vessels she had told the magicians to build. She sought out these vessels in the city, hoping they might hold the secret of Parlainth's fall. She was able to find only a handful among the ruins, while a few others remained hidden deep in the undercity, crushed under the weight of tons of stone and rubble. After an exhaustive search, she returned to her lair in the Vaults of Parlainth, convinced a number of vessels had in fact been jettisoned from Parlainth into astral space. The notion some of Parlainth's Namegivers, perhaps Eyripemes, had escaped the Horror-ravaged city in one of these vessels plagued Charcoalgrin's mind. As stragglers and criminals came to Parlainth, she exerted her particularly powerful personality and created from them a devoted army that now exists only to find clues of these missing vessels. Even more interesting is the evidence Charcoalgrin is in fact searching for clues on how to return the city of Parlainth to its other reality, so she can continue her search for Eyripemes.

Like most of her kind, Charcoalgrin is arrogant to a fault. By sequestering herself in the moldering ruins of Parlainth, the dragon has assured she will forever be the biggest fish in a very small pond. Other dragons view her as little more than an eccentric, content to play with the Young Races and creatures that gather beneath her tattered wings. Her servants are suspicious and thorough, and go to great lengths to ensure there is no way to gather information about her from sources other than herself. Charcoalgrin is always prepared to speak at great length on any topic one could name. Her favorite topic, naturally, is herself. Those who have gone to Charcoalgrin in search of information usually get it, but risk their lives when they show the faintest hint of boredom at her pedantic delivery.

Challenge: Master (Thirteenth Circle)

DEX:	15	**Initiative:**	20	**Unconsciousness:**	166
STR:	24	**Physical Defense:**	20	**Death Rating:**	204
TOU:	25	**Mystic Defense:**	23	**Wound Threshold:**	37
PER:	19	**Social Defense:**	17	**Knockdown:**	28
WIL:	22	**Physical Armor:**	30	**Recovery Tests:**	8
CHA:	14	**Mystic Armor:**	17	**Karma:**	10 (40)

Movement: 16 (Flying 24)
Actions: 4; Bite: 23 (32), Claws x4: 23: 30
Powers: Armored Scales, Dispel Magic (24), Disrupt Fate (29), Dragon Breath (22), Dragonsight (24), Dragonspeech (20), Fear (25), Lair Sense (21), Poison (27), Regeneration (29), Resist Pain (2), Spellcasting (30), Suppress Magic (27), Wingbeat (28)
Spells: Nethermancy, Wizardry (both at Thirteenth Circle)
Special Maneuvers:
Clip the Wing (Opponent)
Grab and Bite (Charcoalgrin, Claws)
Tail Sweep (Charcoalgrin, Tail): Charcoalgrin may spend additional successes from an Attack test using her tail to throw her elephant-sized or smaller opponent. Each success spent in this way throws the opponent 2 yards and the opponent treats this distance as falling (see **Falling Damage**, p. 167).
Loot: Magical items and a hoard of coins and gems worth about 450,000 silver pieces (counts as treasure worth Legend Points)

Nightsky

Nightsky is the youngest adult dragon in Barsaive today, having emerged from his astral cocoon just two years before Throal sealed itself from the world. Nightsky was the last of Usun's hatchlings to emerge before the Scourge. His few brothers and sisters who remained in their cocoons after that year were destroyed by astral Horrors.

Physically, Nightsky is very large for a dragon of his young age, nearly seventy-five feet long. He is jet black in color with flecks of silver on the tips of his scales and horns. This coloration gives the effect of stars on a moonless night, a key factor in his choosing his Name. His natural coloration also led Nightsky to favor nocturnal hunting, and on clear starlit nights, he moves all but undetected through the region of the Caucavic Mountains he and **Asante** (p.444) claim as their lair.

Nightsky awoke from his cocoon impatient and eager to take on the world, as young whelps usually are. He entered adulthood just as the Scourge began in earnest, and did not have time to construct a proper dragon lair, so he was forced to seek shelter with another dragon. Having arrived too late to remain with his sire Usun, he was fortunate enough to find shelter under the Throal Mountains, where Earthroot took him in. His impatience made the time of hiding particularly long and torturous, preventing him from entering the shal-mora as most dragons did during the Long Night. Eventually he could wait no more and left his shelter soon after the Scourge had ended, being one of the first Namegivers to look upon the Scourge-ravaged landscape

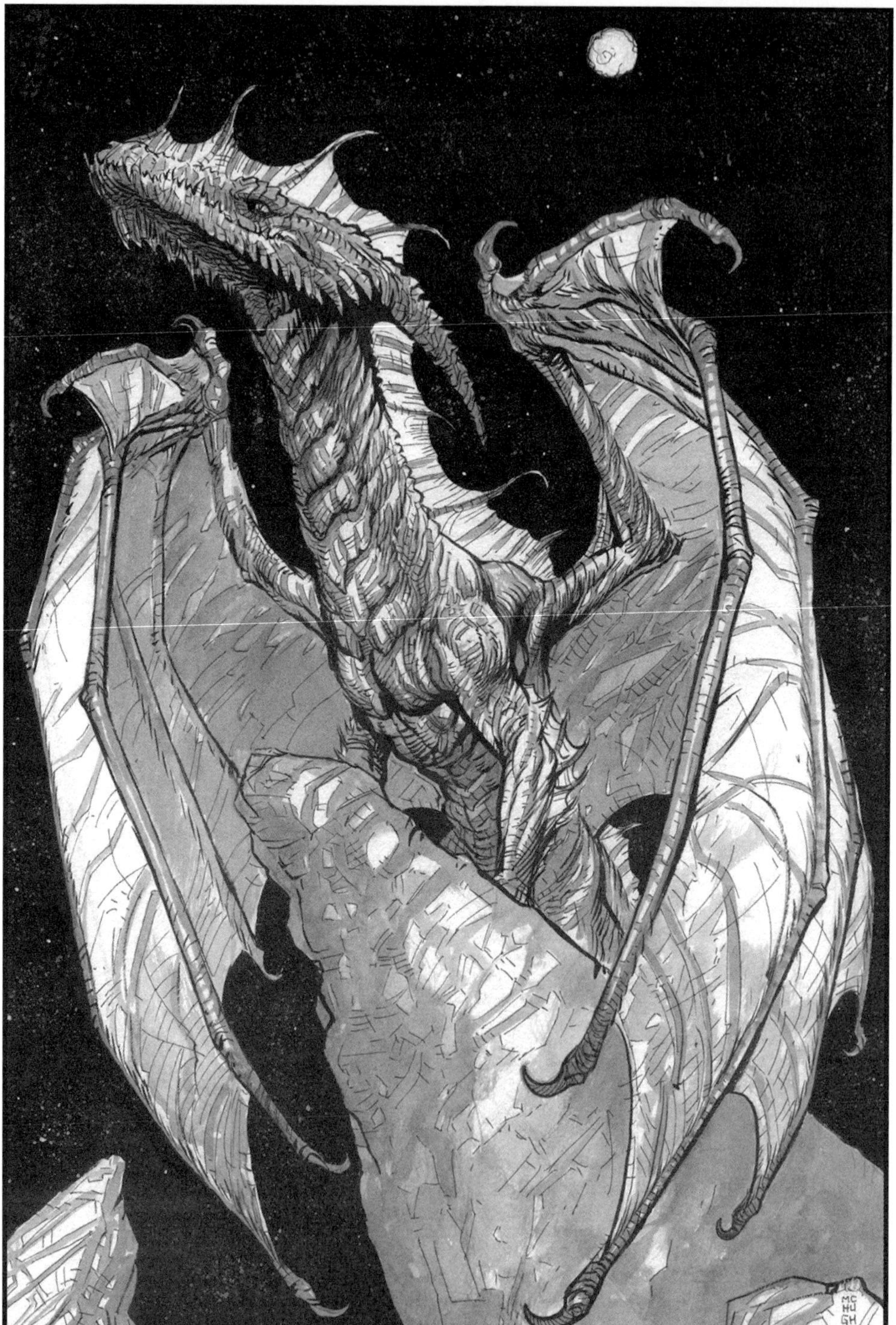
MC
HU
GH

of Barsaive. Even for a dragon this act was a foolish risk, as many powerful Horrors still roamed the world. Though Nightsky would surely deny it, it was fortune rather than physical prowess that kept him alive.

Challenge: Master (Thirteenth Circle)

DEX:	17	**Initiative:**	21	**Unconsciousness:**	172
STR:	27	**Physical Defense:**	23	**Death Rating:**	212
TOU:	27	**Mystic Defense:**	22	**Wound Threshold:**	40
PER:	17	**Social Defense:**	17	**Knockdown:**	31
WIL:	16	**Physical Armor:**	31	**Recovery Tests:**	9
CHA:	14	**Mystic Armor:**	9	**Karma:**	10(40)

Movement: 16 (Flying 24)
Actions: 4; Bite: 26 (37), Claws x4: 27 (36), Horns: 26 (36), Tail: 26 (36)
Powers: Armored Scales, Disrupt Fate (24), Dragon Breath (25), Dragonsight (21), Dragonspeech (18), Fear (26), Lair Sense (21), Poison (29), Regeneration (31), Resist Pain (5), Spellcasting (23), Stealthy Stride (24), Suppress Magic (22), Wingbeat (31)
Spells: Elementalism (Ninth Circle)
Special Maneuvers:
Clip the Wing (Opponent)
Grab and Bite (Nightsky, Claws)
Horn Sweep (Nightsky, Horns): Nightsky may spend additional successes from an Attack test using his horns to throw his elephant-sized or smaller opponent. Each success spent in this way throws the opponent 2 yards and the opponent treats this distance as falling (see **Falling Damage**, p. 167).
Tail Sweep (Nightsky, Tail): Nightsky may spend additional successes from an Attack test using his tail to throw his elephant-sized or smaller opponent. Each success spent in this way throws the opponent 2 yards and the opponent treats this distance as falling (see **Falling Damage**, p. 167).
Loot: Magical items and a hoard of coins and gems worth about 150,000 silver pieces (counts as treasure worth Legend Points)

EARTHDAWN

HORRORS

It came in the night. Its whispers promised me wealth. Fame. Power over those who had insulted and offended me. Passions forgive me, I listened.
• From 'The Testimony of Amnarath' •

The lands of Barsaive stand as they are today because of the Horrors. Knowledge of their coming led to the founding of the Theran Empire and centuries of preparation for their arrival. The legacy of the Scourge continues to this day, decades after most of the Horrors vanished to whatever dark dimension spawned them.

Despite the influence of the Horrors on the land and people of Barsaive, little is actually known about them. The true nature of the Horrors, where they come from, and why they behave as they do are difficult questions to answer. Those who seek answers to these questions put themselves in great danger. Sages and scholars have developed a few theories based on records from those who have shared their experiences with these mysterious and powerful beings, but there are many topics where this information is incomplete or riddled with conjecture.

ON THE STUDY OF THE HORRORS

An excerpt from the journals of Iyva Nassamir

There are those who say studying the astral entities we call Horrors is too risky. They say these beings are too powerful and horrifying for our minds to bear. There are stories told about heroes who have drawn the attention of a Horror merely by mentioning its Name. Fears abound that the knowledge itself can corrupt the unwary scholar.

I do not deny the dangers involved in study involving these mysterious and powerful entities, but ignorance will not save lives. My father was a Warrior adept, and he impressed on me the need for knowledge. To win a war, you must understand the enemy and learn his weaknesses. If we wish to protect people from the Horrors and perhaps one day defeat them for good, we must learn all we can about them. I understand I put my life and soul in danger with this work, but so does the adept who descends into a haunted kaer with sword in hand.

The Nature of Horrors

It is difficult, at best, to make any broadly applicable statements about the Horrors. The only thing they have in common is the need to feed, but what they feed on and the way they approach feeding varies between individuals. Some feed on living matter in much the same way as Namegivers. Others can sustain themselves on stone, metal, and other such materials. The most powerful ones apparently thrive on the life energy of Namegivers, represented by our emotions and sanity.

Even the most basic of Horrors, those who feed on living flesh, often do so in the most disturbing and painful way possible, intent on creating the greatest amount of psychic distress in the victim.

Intent is an odd turn of phrase when it comes to these beings. Certainly there are intelligent and crafty Horrors who spend years grooming a victim, drawing out the feast of fear, guilt, and emotional pain for their own pleasure. What about more basic Horrors? The gnashers and other apparently mindless beasts that exist simply to consume? What intent is to be found there?

And why is it Horrors universally generate and feed on negative emotions like jealousy or hatred instead of positive ones such as pride or joy? Some believe this points to a weakness; somehow these positive emotions hold the key to understanding and perhaps truly defeating the Horrors. I remain unconvinced. There are no reliable reports of a Horror being driven away by the power of love. If these theorists are right, I fear it points to a fundamental weakness in the Namegiver condition: we are so easily tempted to embrace our darker natures.

There are those who believe trying to understand the nature of the Horrors is folly, speaking of them instead as part of the natural order. Our negative view of them is shaped solely by the way they prey on us, much as the rabbit fears the fox. While I must admit this idea holds some merit, it is a rather fatalistic philosophy, and abandons the gifts of reason and scholarship we have been granted by the Passions.

Other than the knowledge that Horrors—at least in the general sense—feed on negative emotional energy, very few facts can be applied to all of the creatures. No two are the same, although some broad categories have been proposed, often dividing Horrors into groups based on appearance, feeding methods, and the like. But even within a particular category there can be significant variation between individuals, and it cannot be taken for granted the powers and abilities displayed by one specimen can be applied to all others of that type.

Naturally, this poses some challenge to those who end up facing a Horror.

On Different Types of Horrors

Broadly speaking, there are three generally accepted categories of Horror. The first are physical in nature. They have a physical body that can be hurt with weapons and spells (though not always easily), and they can be thwarted by sufficiently strong walls. This type is thankfully the most common. By all appearances, the Horror is killed when the physical body is destroyed.

The second category is that of astral-natured Horrors. These exist solely in the astral plane and are more difficult to deal with, as they can only be affected by spells and magical powers which can target their insubstantial nature. Magical wards can protect against this type of Horror, but they are difficult to detect and can covertly infiltrate and gradually corrupt a community without any becoming aware.

The third and perhaps most terrifying Horrors are the dual-natured type. These have a physical form and an astral form. Destruction of one does not mean destruction of the other. Some can operate the two bodies independently, and nearly all of these Horrors can recreate their physical or astral form after it is destroyed, provided the other form remains.

There are many tales of heroes who believed they had destroyed a Horror, only to later find their celebration was premature. Some of these types of Horrors plot elaborate schemes where they deceive adepts into destroying their physical body, only to slowly corrupt them and all they hold dear through their astral form. Fortunately, this variety of Horror appears to be rare.

On the Horror Mark

The most feared and powerful power Horrors can possess is the ability to mark a chosen target. Nearly all intelligent Horrors display this power, but it does not work the same way from individual to individual.

Horror marks usually allow the Horror to keep track of their victim across great distances and even communicate with them at will (though obviously not all Horrors do so). In many cases, the mark allows the Horror to use its powers against the victim without needing to be present. Some theorists suggest this ability involves the Horror tying a thread to the pattern of the victim. While the behavior of some Horrors (and their marks) support this notion, it is far from consistent and little real research has been done on the subject.

It should be made clear that detecting a mark is no easy task. Indeed, no truly reliable method of determining whether an individual is marked is known. Some legendary adepts are rumored to have had the ability, and of course there are countless tales of magical items, rituals, or locations that can provide this knowledge, but are either unconfirmed or impractical.

Indeed, the belief one can prove they are free of Horror taint by demonstrating artistic ability or other craft is steeped in folklore. I realize this is a controversial position, and certainly those who have been driven to madness by a Horror's torment often display this lack of artistic focus. However, I have been unable to find any legitimate study of this phenomenon. Like so many other aspects of Horror scholarship, information is scant and frustratingly vague.

The few brave souls who have studied this power have learned a few details. First, it would appear a mark can be maintained for some time without the victim being aware of the mark. The Swordmaster Arric the Stout, for example, carried the mark of the Horror Granox the Devourer for seven years before he learned of it. Fortunately that tale has a happy ending, as Arric was able—with the assistance of his companions—to track the Horror back to its lair and slay it.

The only reliable way to remove a mark is to kill the Horror in question, or at the very least banish or contain it so it cannot exert its influence. Of course this is easier said than done. Horrors are powerful opponents, and the ones able to exert power and influence through their marks frequently make it difficult to track them down.

Horror Curses

In the same way a Horror can mark an individual, many of them can also mark locations and objects. These places and items are usually referred to as 'cursed' and provide another way for a Horror to extend its power and influence to the unsuspecting.

Items affected by a curse of this sort come in all manner of shapes and sizes. A Horror that prefers a subtle approach might curse seemingly mundane items. Another might curse a magic item, granting it additional power leading its owner down a dark path, or even corrupt the user into a servant of the Horror. Some items are crafted from the remains of a slain Horror and the creature's foul influence can extend even beyond its death.

Cursed places are often the result of a Horror making its lair in a particular location, or a place where a Horror exerted influence over a town or village for an extended period of time. Travelers who visit these places can expose themselves to the Horror's influence, or suffer other ill effects. In some cases these locations are the result of residents making an ill-advised deal with a Horror.

One tale tells of a village affected by a painful wasting disease, and a Horror offered to cure them. The villagers accepted, only to find their survival depended on them offering hospitality to travelers, then betraying and sacrificing them to the Horror to maintain their life.

A Horror-cursed place or item often behaves much like a mark, allowing the Horror to exert its influence or use its powers on those in the area, or those in contact with (or vicinity of) the item. In general, a Horror's ability to extend its power through the curse is limited, but as with so many other things, when it comes to Horrors, nothing is certain.

USING HORRORS IN ADVENTURES AND CAMPAIGNS

Looking at the game statistics and abilities included in this chapter should reinforce how dangerous Horrors are. These beings possess significant power and are dedicated to using that power to further horrible and evil things. They manipulate people into harming their friends and family, and can even drive entire communities to kill themselves. They feed on flesh, as well as negative emotions, and torture people for nourishment.

This combination of power and drive to perpetuate atrocities makes using Horrors in a game a difficult balancing act. Should they be this powerful? Absolutely. If they were not as powerful as they are, there would have been no need for the effort to hide from them for centuries. The Horrors were responsible for the untold amounts of death and destruction, laying waste to nations. Reducing the impact or effect of these actions cheapens the price people paid for their safety.

Introducing any powerful Horrors included here may result in the death or corruption of one or more player characters. In the dangerous world of **Earthdawn**, this should be a possibility. The loss of a character is generally not desirable, but it can serve to underscore the danger posed by these entities. Downplaying the danger or allowing the characters to escape an encounter with a Horror unscathed reduces the impact of these beings on the setting.

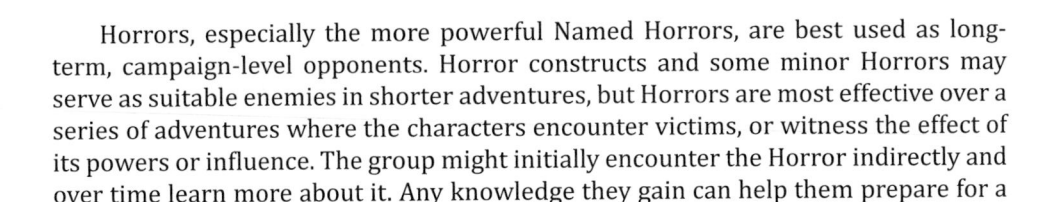

Horrors, especially the more powerful Named Horrors, are best used as long-term, campaign-level opponents. Horror constructs and some minor Horrors may serve as suitable enemies in shorter adventures, but Horrors are most effective over a series of adventures where the characters encounter victims, or witness the effect of its powers or influence. The group might initially encounter the Horror indirectly and over time learn more about it. Any knowledge they gain can help them prepare for a more direct confrontation with the Horror.

Horrors often work through agents. Some are voluntary, others coerced. Some have cults of willing followers seeking to further the influence and goals of their dark master. Other Horrors might influence people by threatening their friends and family. As demonstrated by the elves of Blood Wood, some Namegivers will go to great lengths to protect themselves or their loved ones.

Indeed, adventures featuring a Horror might not end with the characters coming face to face with the Horror. Simply disrupting a Horror's plans, or freeing an area of its influence could be considered a victory. The adepts should count themselves lucky for avoiding a direct confrontation! Of course, if they cause the Horror too much trouble, they are bound to draw its attention.

The more player characters deal with the Horrors, even indirectly, the more likely they are to suffer some kind of loss. Try make these losses part of the story and significant events in the campaign. Make it mean more than a player needing to make up a new character.

One last word of advice: don't make the Horrors invincible. One of the themes of **Earthdawn** is the battle against the Horrors and the attempt to rebuild the world after the Scourge. If making the Horrors too easy cheapens their impact on the setting, making them too hard can destroy all hope of victory. Characters dealing with a Horror, or suspecting Horror involvement, should proceed with caution, taking every opportunity to learn what they can about the opponent they might face. Victory should be possible, but difficult, while heroes who stumble blindly into a Horror's lair deserve their fate.

HORROR POWERS

Nearly all Horrors display powerful magical abilities. The nature of their powers is varied. Some might channel magical energy in the same way adepts power their talents and spells, while other powers are more like the abilities displayed by magical creatures, dragons, or spirits.

The powers listed here are those most commonly known and documented, but this list is far from exhaustive. Not every Horror possesses every power listed here, and there may be Horrors who have abilities not listed, or vary from the descriptions provided in one way or another.

The rules provided here represent a starting point. Just as there are many different varieties of Horror, their powers can be equally varied, and gamemasters are encouraged to modify or adapt these powers to suit the needs of the story. Altering a Horror's powers may make it more powerful, but can also make them less so. Some Horror powers can be deadly, and scaling back on them in some manner might give player characters more of a fighting chance against these dangerous opponents.

The easiest way to modify Horror powers is by increasing or decreasing its range or duration. If the standard version of a power requires the Horror to be able to see the target, perhaps it can use the power on a victim it has marked (allowing it to "see" the character through the mark).

Another way to modify powers is to change the actual effect. This is more common when dealing with unique, Named Horrors, as it helps make the creature distinct and can add flavor to adventures that involve it. Perhaps instead of a single test to mark a victim, the Horror must convince the character to accept its aid in order to be marked, and then the Horror sets up situations where the potential victim is faced with a choice between accepting the entity's help, or letting an innocent suffer needlessly.

Be careful when modifying powers to make them more powerful. Many of them are dangerous enough as written and can result in character death if not used carefully. For instance, Damage Shift can turn a group's physical prowess back on them. Some powers can even prevent characters from taking action against the Horror at all. Terror, for example, can effectively incapacitate an entire group of adepts.

When dealing with powers like this, use the guidelines from the Creatures chapter about balancing encounters, starting on page 246, to judge the effect the power will have on your group. If the Step number of a Horror's power is much higher than the Defense Ratings of the player characters, it is likely to cause problems. It might make sense to reduce the numbers involved, perhaps to only one or two Steps higher than the relevant Defense Ratings, in order to give them more of a fighting chance. Another option is to downplay particular powers, rather than bringing them to bear every round. It's not much fun to have your character rendered impotent and ground into the dirt. Subtlety can be a useful tool when playing the role of a Horror.

Of course, if you want to impress your players with the power a Horror can bring to bear, having it paralyze the group with fear, toss out a devastating (but non-fatal) attack or two, and then walk away will certainly do the trick. Remember, Horrors, especially the more powerful ones, feed on negative emotions like pain, fear, and doubt. Leaving a group of adepts alive, but broken and questioning their abilities, might be too much of a treat to pass up.

Corruption

Some Horror powers, and exposure to extremely Horror-tainted or corrupted locations, can give a character Corruption Points. These represent how much Horror influence and astral pollution is affecting a character. As a character gains Corruption Points, they begin to show signs of their deteriorating condition. These signs will be different for each character, but are frequently related to their particular weaknesses. Examples include signs of emaciation, persistent illness, poor impulse control, or even bizarre or unsettling habits. The more Corruption Points a victim accumulates, the more pronounced these symptoms become.

When introducing Corruption into the game, the gamemaster should secretly choose a Corruption Value. A recommended benchmark is between 10 and 15; the higher the value, the longer the process of corruption will take. A character with any Corruption Points is considered tainted, and one who has equal or more points than the Corruption Value is considered corrupted.

In general, characters with five or fewer Corruption Points do not show any obvious signs of their tainted status, though a well-trained or experienced observer may notice subtle clues. With more than five points, the character begins to show more obvious signs of their increasing decline. At more than ten points, even if they are not corrupted yet, they are walking the razor's edge of sanity and/or health and are likely to have difficulty interacting with society.

Tainted victims can be treated by magic, like the powers possessed by some questors of Garlen. Victims are unlikely to be treated if there is any suspicion they are still under the influence of a Horror. If a victim has been corrupted, powerful magic like the intercession of a Passion or legendary magical artifact can restore them, but even then they will likely bear the mental or physical scars of their ordeal.

Until a character has accumulated enough Corruption Points, there is no defined mechanical effect. Once a character has become corrupted, however, any subsequent Corruption Points result in the victim being modified as by a single success on a Forge Construct test (p. 461). If the Corruption Point comes from a Horror, the modification is at the Horror's discretion. If from another source, such as a heavily corrupted environment, the change should be related to the source.

Rather than provide players with their Corruption Point total, gamemasters should use description and roleplay to indicate something is not right and how far along the character might be. Horrors should remain dangerous and enigmatic opponents. Providing detail can lessen that impact, and even give players the opportunity to game the system.

It is strongly recommended that Corruption be used to advance and enhance the campaign, not as a club to beat your players. The mechanical impact of Corruption is minimal for a reason: if it doesn't suit your campaign style or theme, it can be downplayed or even ignored. In this case, powers that use Corruption should probably be avoided.

Finally, a character succumbing to Corruption doesn't mean their story is over. While it may be difficult for a corrupted character to function in society, the quest for redemption can make for a suitably epic campaign arc.

Game Terms

As with all powers and abilities in **Earthdawn**, Horrors use Step Numbers to make tests with their powers. If a power's description does not provide a Step Number, the power probably has an effect that does not require a test.

Some powers require the Horror to use a Standard action. These are noted with the word "Standard" in the "Action:" notation. Other powers are noted by the word "Simple" or "Free" in the "Action:" notation. These powers are usually an effect resulting from another test. For more information on different action types, see the *Player's Guide*, page 373.

Abbreviated versions of these powers are included in each entry in this chapter for ease of reference. Gamemasters should familiarize themselves with the full text of each power and use the abbreviated entry to speed up conflicts.

Animate Dead
Action: Standard

This power allows a Horror to animate the corpse of a dead Namegiver, resulting in the creation of a cadaver man, ghoul, or other undead construct (the type of undead will depend on the Horror). The Horror touches the victim and makes an Animate Dead test against the target's Mystic Defense, using the Mystic Defense the target had while alive. If successful, the victim is raised. Not all Horrors are required to touch the victim to make use of this power. The Horror may have a number of individual undead under their control up to their Animate Dead Step. If the Horror is within Animate Dead Step miles of the undead, it can telepathically control the undead, issuing commands as a Simple action. Otherwise the undead acts on its own.

Astral Camouflage
Action: Standard

This power allows a Horror to hide its presence in astral space. The Horror increases the Difficulty number for Perception, Astral Sight, or similar tests to notice the Horror by the Astral Camouflage Step. This power lasts until the Horror takes an action that reveals its presence.

Aura of Awe
Action: Standard

This power allows a Horror to influence the attitude of characters towards it. The Horror makes an Aura of Awe test and compares it to the Social Defense of each character within Aura of Awe Step x 4 yards. If successful the target adopts a Neutral stance towards the Horror. For each additional success, the target's attitude improves one degree to a maximum of Awestruck (see p. 142 for more information on Attitudes).

The effects of this power last until the next sunrise, but can be extended by the Horror with additional uses of the power. When a player character is affected by this power, the gamemaster should secretly instruct the player to behave appropriately, and may overrule decisions that run counter to the effects of this power.

The effects of this power end if the Horror directly or obviously harms the target.

Corrupt Compromise
Action: Standard

This power intertwines the Horror mark on a victim in a complex fashion, creating an astral tumor on the victim's pattern. The Horror spends one Karma Point and suggests a course of action to a victim they have marked, offering a bonus to one of the character's traits or abilities. If the victim follows the course of action in spirit, not just letter, the victim gains a Corruption Point, but the bonus becomes permanent, acting like a thread tied to a pattern item (*Player's Guide*, p. 226). Bonuses from this power apply to any circumstance, except actions against the marking Horror.

If the marked victim does not follow the course of action with all sincerity, the marking Horror gains a bonus to one of its own traits or powers. These bonuses apply only against the victim.

This power demonstrates the potential folly of striking a deal with a Horror. Resisting makes the Horror more powerful against the victim, making it easier for the Horror to carry out threats, or making it harder for the character to defeat. On the other hand, attempts to use the Horror's power to good ends results in long-term corruption.

The Horror can provide bonuses to a number of traits or powers equal to their Corrupt Compromise Step, and the maximum bonus to each individual trait is also equal to that Step. Bonuses can be provided to any trait or ability that can be increased by thread magic. A Horror's powers count as talents for this purpose.

Some powerful Horrors have the ability to use their trait bonuses against any target to whom the victim has a thread attached (such as through a pattern item), or even those with whom they share a Pattern (such as a group pattern or Blood Sworn).

Corrupt Karma
Action: Standard

This power allows the Horror to override another character's use of Karma. The Horror makes a Corrupt Karma test against the target's Mystic Defense. Each success allows the Horror to prevent the target's use of Karma on one test as a Free action. The target's Karma Point is spent, but does not provide any additional dice to the test result.

Corrupt Reality
Action: Standard

This power allows a Horror to distort the fabric of reality, affecting the area around a victim it has previously marked. The Horror uses these effects to alarm and torment the victim and those in his vicinity. This will isolate the victim, as other people will avoid his company to escape the strange events.

The Horror spends a Karma Point and makes a Corrupt Reality test and compares it to the Mystic Defense of each character the Horror wishes to affect. If successful, the target suffers a -1 penalty to Mystic and Social Defense for each success.

The Horror can selectively affect any characters within Corrupt Reality Step x 2 yards of the marked victim. The penalties fade at the rate of 1 per day; subsequent uses of this power stack with the previously accrued penalties.

Typical manifestations include spoiling food and drink, changes in temperature, eerie sounds, mundane objects transforming into slime-covered parodies, or any number of other strange or surreal manifestations. These effects last for a number of rounds up to the Corrupt Reality Step, and cannot be dispelled or disbelieved, though the Horror may end them earlier if desired

An object transformed by this power returns to normal after the duration ends, with no trace of the change or permanent ill effect. This power cannot cause damage to living beings, though the fear and mental stress resulting from extended exposure to this ability may cause a victim or those near him to lash out and harm themselves or others.

Cursed Luck

Action: Free

This power allows a Horror to inflict bad luck on a target. The Horror makes a Cursed Luck test against the Mystic Defense of a target within line of sight. Each success reduces the result of one die rolled on a test to 1. The highest die values are affected first, and all reductions are done before any potential bonus dice are rolled. This power may be used once per round.

Mica is attacking a Horror with his Melee Weapons talent, which is at Step 15/D12+2D6. The Horror uses its Cursed Luck power on the unfortunate Swordmaster, and rolls an 18 against Mica's Mystic Defense of 11, scoring two successes, meaning two dice will be reduced to 1.

On his Melee Weapons test, Mica's player rolls a 5 on the D12, a 6 on one D6, and a 2 on the other D6. The 6 and the 5 are each reduced to a result of 1 (canceling the bonus die that would have resulted from the 6 on the D6) and the final test result is 4.

The gamemaster is encouraged to describe the way the bad luck manifests and affects the result of the test. If the Horror scores more successes than the character is rolling dice, the attempt automatically fails and at gamemaster's discretion may result in additional misfortune that inflicts a penalty on the character's next related test, or require their next Standard action to overcome.

Damage Shift

Action: Simple

This power allows the Horror to shift damage it has taken to another character within line of sight. The Horror makes a Horror Power test against the victim's Mystic Defense. If successful, it can transfer an amount of current damage from itself to the victim, up to a maximum equal to the result of a Damage Shift test. This power does not transfer Wounds, but the damage dealt from the transfer may cause a Wound to the victim.

Disease
Action: N/A

This power allows the Horror to infect a victim with a disease. No test is required; the victim is infected if the Horror causes damage with a physical attack, or otherwise succeeds at infecting the victim based on the rules provided in the Horror's description.

The Step Number indicates the Difficulty Number for tests made to resist the effects of the disease, as well as attempts to diagnose or treat the illness. Additional details about the disease are provided in the Horror's game statistics. See **Disease**, p. 186, for more information on diseases and how they work.

Displace
Action: Standard

This power allows a Horror to cross between the physical and astral realms. No test is required, but the Horror must use a Standard action to cross between realms. If a single-natured Horror with this power crosses into astral space, its body disappears from the physical.

Disrupt Magic
Action: Standard

This power allows a Horror to end sustained magical effects. It works like the **Dispel Magic** talent (*Player's Guide*, p. 139) with a range of Disrupt Magic Step x 2 yards, but does not cost strain and can be used against any magical effect with an extended duration. The Horror makes a Disrupt Magic test against the effect's Dispel Difficulty.

For effects not the result of talents or spells, use the power's Step Number as the Circle on the Dispel Difficulty Table (*Player's Guide*, p. 265) to determine the Difficulty Number. If a creature power or ability Step Number is higher than 15, add +1 to the Dispel Difficulty for each Step above 15. For example, a power with Step 17 would have a Dispel Difficulty of 27 (25+2).

Forge Construct
Action: Sustained

This power allows a Horror to create constructs from other life forms including mundane animals, magical creatures, and Namegivers, even inanimate objects. If a Horror uses this power on a living Namegiver, it often leaves some portion of the victim's mind intact and aware of his fate.

To use this power on a living target, the Horror must first successfully mark the victim. The Horror spends 5 Karma Points to infuse the target with the Horror's twisted magical essence to begin the change. This Karma only powers the ability; it does not add dice to the test. The Horror makes a Forge Construct test against the target's Mystic Defense. Each success allows the Horror to change one of the target's attributes by one Step or grants the construct a power or special ability. The Horror can make multiple tests, but must wait a minimum of one day before making a new test. Some Horrors intentionally draw out the transformation in order to prolong the suffering of a victim aware of what is happening to them. The Horror only needs to spend the 5 Karma to initiate the process, Karma is not required to fuel subsequent tests.

Living victims can resist the process. For each Forge Construct test, the victim may make a Willpower test and substitute it for their Mystic Defense if the result is higher.

Once the Horror has made all the desired changes to the victim, it ends the process by making a final Horror Mark test to form a link between itself and the construct. If successful, the transformation is complete and the construct is under the control of the Horror who created it. Many Horrors will create a construct and set it loose to roam Barsaive causing pain and destruction on behalf of its master.

Some dual-natured Horrors use this ability to create a new body if their current one is destroyed, and this power is sometimes built into cursed items that transform the user into a construct.

Forge Trap

Action: Standard

This power allows the Horror to alter the nature of a stone, metal, or earthen passage to become a trap or contain one. The Horror makes a Forge Trap test, and distributes the points from the test among the trap's game statistics. See **Traps**, p. 179 for more information on traps.

Horrors have the ability to feed off the pain created by the trap and use the Harvest Energy power to gain Karma from any character injured by the trap.

Harvest Energy

Action: Free

This power allows Horrors to regain Karma by feeding off their preferred nourishment. This is most commonly negative emotion, but other preferred meals exist. If a character is in the grip of strong negative emotions like hate, fear, jealousy, or pain (such as from suffering a Wound) the Horror can make a Harvest Energy test against the victim's Social Defense. Each success restores one point of Karma to the Horror.

Some Horrors have preferred sources of nourishment, and gain an additional point of Karma even if the test is a failure.

Horrors with the ability to create constructs or undead may feed through any construct or undead under their control.

Horror Power

Action: Varies (typically Standard)

This ability is used in conjunction with other powers, typically against one of the target's Defense Ratings. The description will note the power or powers with which it is associated and the appropriate action type.

Horror Mark

Action: Standard

This power allows a Horror to mark victims and items, linking the Horror and a target within line of sight. The Horror makes a Horror Mark test against the target's Mystic Defense. If successful, the Horror places its mark on the target, concealed within their True Pattern. The mark links the Horror and the target over significant distances. This allows the Horror to keep track of its chosen victim, communicate with them, and in some cases even use its powers on the victim outside of their normal range.

In general, if the Horror is within 10 miles of the victim it may use any of its powers on or through the victim with no restriction. Up to 100 miles the Horror may use powers that do not directly cause damage, and communication is possible up to 1,000 miles. A Horror mark typically lasts until the Horror dies. Some marks last only for a year and a day, though a Horror can extend the duration with a new Horror Mark test against the victim, typically there is no range limit for this renewal.

Unique Horror Marks

The guidelines here outline the basic effects and most common manifestation of this power. It is not uncommon, however, for major Horrors to have variations of this power that demonstrate the entity's strengths, weaknesses, and tactics. The game information for some Horrors (especially Named Horrors) will often include rules on how the particular Horror's mark differs from normal.

Gamemasters are encouraged to modify the nature and behavior of Horror marks to suit the needs of the story and the individual Horror. Horror marks should be mysterious and terrifying, and the information about them within the setting should be unreliable.

Effects of Horror Marks

A Horror mark should have an impact on the marked character, as well as the adventure or campaign. It can serve as a story element, allowing the gamemaster a way to bring a Horror into an adventure without it necessarily making an appearance in the flesh.

Most people in Barsaive are aware that a Horror mark is a dangerous thing. If it becomes known that a character is marked, they will face difficulties when dealing with other Namegivers. Common folk are liable to avoid the character, and be willing to let them die rather than risk exposure to a Horror. There are countless superstitions surrounding Horror marks, and given the many different ways this power can work, some of them might even be true.

Detecting Horror Marks

A mark does not necessarily make itself known. There is no specific physical trace unless a particular variant of mark does so, and even the astral indications of a mark are deeply buried in a victim's pattern and difficult to detect.

To detect a Horror mark using astral sensing, the sensing character must make a test against the Mystic Defense of the Horror that left the mark, with a number additional successes equal to the level of astral corruption (safe = 1 additional success, open = 2 additional successes, etc.). If successful, the mark can be seen as a small stain on the victim's pattern, and detailed examination might reveal clues that may point to the identity of the Horror that owns the mark. For example, the mark of the Horror Aazhvat Many-Eyes might appear as an unblinking eye.

Despite the popular belief a character under the influence of a Horror is unable to create works of art, this method of detecting Horror marks is unreliable at best. While there are Horrors whose influence can result in the corruption of artisan skills, this belief is largely the result of centuries of legend and superstition.

Horror Marks and Raw Magic

If a magician is desperate enough to cast raw magic, they may find themselves Horror marked. While the rules for casting raw magic provided on pages 261-262 of the *Player's Guide* offer values for the Horror Mark test, the gamemaster should feel free to substitute the Horror Mark Step if he has a particular Horror in mind.

In many cases, the Horror mark may be unplanned. This gives the gamemaster an opportunity to introduce a Horror at a later point in the campaign. Just because a Horror has marked a victim does not mean the Horror will start tormenting the victim right away. Horrors can be patient and wily. It could be weeks or months before the mark comes into play. The magician might even believe he has avoided attracting a Horror's attention.

The dangers of raw magic are well known in Barsaive, and careless magicians will gain a reputation. Their disregard for the safety of themselves and others will eventually result in a Horror mark. Do not allow a player character to avoid the consequences of raw magic casting because bringing a Horror into the game wasn't planned.

Horror Marked Items and Places

It is possible for items and places to be Horror marked as well. As previously mentioned, these are usually called cursed items or places. In general, a mark on an item or place works the same way as a Horror mark on an individual, but offer some small degree of protection as the Horror can only work indirectly. Any tests the Horror makes through a cursed item or place require an additional success.

Given the many different ways Horror marks can work, it is possible a Horror might have a mark that works through an item to invoke a particular effect. For example, a cursed item slowly turns its user into a construct, or allows the Horror to use its Cursed Luck power without penalty when the item is being used.

Horror Thread

Action: Standard

This power eventually allows a Horror direct control of a chosen victim. A Horror may only use this power on a victim it has previously marked. It may then spend 5 Karma Points and make a Horror Thread test against the target's Mystic Defense. The Karma spent only powers the ability; it does not add dice to the test. If successful, the Horror weaves a thread connecting its pattern to the victim's.

Once per month, the Horror uses the woven thread to try and learn Pattern Knowledge about the victim. It spends a Karma Point and makes a Horror Thread test against the victim's Mystic Defense. As with the initial Karma spent to weave the thread, this Karma point does not add dice to the test. If successful, the Horror learns a piece of Pattern Knowledge and may weave a new thread to the victim, which costs an additional 5 Karma points.

Each woven thread grants the Horror a +1 bonus to any tests it makes against the victim, and the Horror also has full access to the target's thoughts and memories, allowing it more freedom to taunt and torment the victim.

Once the Horror's bonus from woven threads equals the victim's Willpower Step, the Horror can take control of the victim's body and use their abilities as its own. For example, the Horror could force a Beastmaster to attack his allies with Claw Frenzy. The Horror uses the appropriate Step Numbers for the victim's talents, spells, and other abilities, and may spend the victim's Karma points on them if applicable. The Horror may also use its own powers through the victim. While in the case of some abilities the control may not be obvious, the victim can sense the intrusion.

Karma Boost
Action: Free

This power allows the Horror to tempt a Horror marked victim in need. The marked victim may be unaware of the source of this power. This is particularly true for victims who do not yet realize they have been Horror marked, the character just finds reserves of powers they didn't previously have.

At the marking Horror's discretion, the marked victim may spend an additional Karma Point on any test on which they could normally spend Karma. This Karma point comes from the marking Horror's Karma pool and their Karma Step. Each time the marked victim uses this power, they gain a Corruption Point. See **Corruption**, p. 456, for information on Corruption ranks.

Karma Drain
Action: Standard

This power allows a Horror to drain Karma points from a victim it has marked. The Horror makes a Karma Drain test against the victim's Mystic Defense. Each success transfers one Karma point from the victim to the Horror. The victim must have Karma points available. Once the Horror has failed a Karma Drain test against a victim, it must wait until the next day to attempt another Karma Drain test against that victim.

Karma Points
Action: NA

Nearly all Horrors, and some Horror constructs, have Karma Points they may spend on any test, though they may only spend one point on any given test. Horrors and their ilk do not naturally replenish Karma Points like dragons, Namegivers, and spirits. Instead they use the Harvest Energy power, and some Horrors may have other avenues as well. Horrors have a Karma Pool of their Karma Step x 4, while Horror constructs and undead with Karma generally have their Karma Step x 2.

Poison
Action: NA

This power allows a Horror to poison a victim after dealing damage with claws, teeth, or stinger. No test is required. The Rank is the poison's Step Number. Additional details about the poison are provided in the Horror's game statistics. See **Poison**, p. 171, for more information on poisons and how they work.

Skills
Action: Varies

Some Horrors have powers based on skills. For more information on the listed skill, refer to the *Player's Guide*, starting on page 183.

Skin Shift
Action: Simple

This power allows a Horror to mutilate a target's body. The Horror touches the target and makes a Horror Power test against the target's Mystic Defense. If successful, the Horror makes a Skin Shift test to determine damage. No armor reduces this damage. The victim's skin tears loose from the muscle below, twisting and turning around his body. Each success on the Horror Power test inflicts one Wound on the victim in addition to the damage from the Skin Shift test.

Spells

Many Horrors know how to cast spells. Horrors do not use Spell Matrices, as they suffer no ill effects from using Raw Magic. Horrors must still weave threads, but use their Spellcasting ability instead of traditional Thread Weaving talents. When casting spells, Horrors do not need to perform any of the actions required in a spell's description to cast the spell. Horrors rarely learn spells affecting undead or astral entities like spirits and Horrors.

Suppress Mark
Action: Standard

This power allows a Horror to hide its mark deep within a victim's pattern. The Horror increases the Difficulty to detect the mark by the Suppress Mark Step. While this power is in effect, the Horror is not able to use the mark to affect the victim.

Talents

Some Horrors have powers based on talents. For more information on a listed talent, refer to the *Player's Guide*, starting on page 119.

Terror
Action: Standard

This power allows a Horror to paralyze its victims with fear. The Horror makes a Terror test and compares the result to the Mystic Defense of each character within 20 yards. Each character suffers a -1 penalty to Action tests for each success on the Terror test.

As a Simple action at the beginning of an affected character's turn, they may make a Willpower test against the Terror Step. This test is optional, with each success reducing the penalty by 1. If the penalty ever reaches 0, the effects of this power wear off. If the Willpower test is unsuccessful, the penalty increases by -1.

If the penalty is ever greater than the character's Willpower step, the character is unable to take any actions against the Horror. The character may still make Willpower tests to try and resist the effect, and at gamemaster discretion may use defensive abilities (such as Avoid Blow). Most characters in this state are panic-stricken, and will behave accordingly: fleeing, collapsing into the fetal position, or standing quivering helplessly.

Unnatural Life

Action: Standard

This power allows a Horror to grant a dead character the gift of life. This power can only be used on characters dead for less than a year and a day. The Horror touches the corpse and makes an Unnatural Life test against the Mystic Defense the victim had while alive. If successful, the character is brought back to life. This costs the Horror 1 point of Blood Magic, which cannot be healed until the victim is killed.

While not as dreadful to behold as a cadaver man or ghoul, any decay or damage to the corpse remains. Other than the potentially horrific appearance, the revived character functions as he did in life with all talents and abilities intact. The character's personality and memories are also restored.

Victims of this power are difficult to destroy. They may make a Recovery test at any time as a Simple action, and have unlimited Recovery tests available. The Horror may end the effect of this power at any time, and often uses this to coerce the victim into serving it in some capacity.

HORROR CONSTRUCTS

Constructs are the tools and servants of the Horrors. They are often created from the flesh and bones of a Horror's victims, and can vary as widely as the Horrors themselves. The following only represent a fraction of the possible Horror constructs that can be found in Barsaive.

Horror Constructs are not affected by talents, spells, or abilities that target creatures or animals.

Black Mantis

The black mantis is a 9-foot tall insect with a thick, black carapace. It has eight legs, each ending with a vicious barbed spike. It uses these to spear and tear pieces of flesh from its prey, on which it feeds. The barbs also help it easily climb rough surfaces.

The black mantis was first discovered in the ruins of Talon Kaer, a windling refuge in the Thunder Mountains. Scholars believe it was created from the inshalata, a species of giant predatory insect in the Servos Jungle. Whatever its origins, these constructs have since been sighted in other parts of Barsaive.

Challenge: Journeyman (Eighth Circle)

DEX:	10	Initiative:	16	Unconsciousness:	70
STR:	13	Physical Defense:	14	Death Rating:	88
TOU:	10	Mystic Defense:	14	Wound Threshold:	15
PER:	9	Social Defense:	10	Knockdown:	17
WIL:	8	Physical Armor:	12	Recovery Tests:	3
CHA:	4	Mystic Armor:	6	Karma:	4 (8)

Move: 18 (Climbing 18)
Actions: 4; Bite: 20 (20), Claw x4: 20 (22)
Powers:
Ambush (10)
Enhanced Senses [Sight] (2)
Great Leap (10): As the creature power, p. 251.
Hardened Armor
Harvest Energy (20, Free): The black mantis can gain one Karma per success on a Harvest Energy test against the victim's Social Defense.
Stealthy Stride (20): As the skill, *Player's Guide*, p. 170.
Special Maneuvers:
Crack the Shell (Opponent)
Pry Loose (Opponent, Close Combat)
Squeeze the Life (Black Mantis)
Loot: Claws and mandibles worth a total of 2d6 x 10 silver pieces and eggs worth 150 silver pieces each (worth Legend Points).

Bone Shambler

The bone shambler is an undead construct made from the bones of multiple victims of Horrors. They move and attack by rolling. The bones and bits of armor that make up their body create a disturbing clicking sound that echoes through the hallways of breached kaers.

Many times these constructs will have bits of gold or silver jewelry as part of their body.

Challenge: Journeyman (Seventh Circle)

DEX:	6	Initiative:	6	Unconsciousness:	NA
STR:	13	Physical Defense:	12	Death Rating:	108
TOU:	13	Mystic Defense:	14	Wound Threshold:	19
PER:	4	Social Defense:	11	Knockdown:	15
WIL:	7	Physical Armor:	10	Recovery Tests:	4
CHA:	2	Mystic Armor:	7	Karma:	4 (8)

Movement: 14
Actions: 2; Spikes: 22 (22), Trample: 20 (24)
Powers:
Harvest Energy (18, Free)
Resist Pain (2)
Immune to Fear

Special Maneuvers:
Overrun (Bone Shambler, Trample)
Overwhelm (Bone Shambler, Overrun): After the bone shambler uses the Overrun special maneuver, it may continue its movement and take additional actions without the penalties for splitting movement.
Momentum Killer (Opponent): If the target of an Overrun special maneuver makes a successful Knockdown test against the attack, they may choose to suffer Damage Step 10, reduced by Physical Armor. Taking this damage will immediately stop the bone shambler's movement and automatically cause knockdown. The bone shambler may not use Overwhelm.
Loot: Valuables worth 2d10 x 10 silver pieces attached to the bone shambler's body (worth Legend Points).

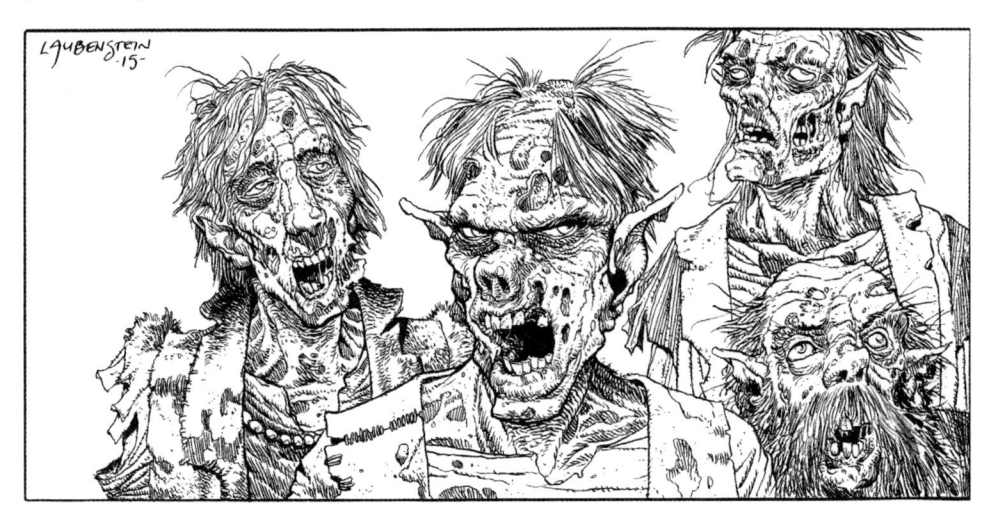

Cadaver Men

These undead constructs are one of the more commonly known and disturbing undead minions of the Horrors. When animated, they retain some semblance of their original intelligence and personality. They are aware of their undead state, but capable of only feeling pain. As a result, many cadaver men are driven insane.

In some cases, cadaver men are capable of interacting with the living, though unsurprisingly this can be an unsettling experience. The most famous of these is Twiceborn, the t'skrang cadaver man and self-styled queen controlling the Eastern Catacombs in the ruins of Parlainth.

Cadaver men have been known to eat the flesh of the living, but despite popular belief do not need to do so to survive. The game statistics provided here assume a human cadaver man, and vary from individual to individual. Cadaver men that were adepts or magicians do not retain any of the magical abilities they possessed in life, though they may remember knowledge or other lore. It is not uncommon for cadaver men to be wearing armor and gain the appropriate benefits and drawbacks from doing so.

Challenge: Novice (Third Circle)

DEX:	5	Initiative:	5	Unconsciousness:	NA
STR:	6	Physical Defense:	9	Death Rating:	52
TOU:	7	Mystic Defense:	9	Wound Threshold:	10
PER:	5	Social Defense:	8	Knockdown:	8
WIL:	6	Physical Armor:	0	Recovery Tests:	2
CHA:	4	Mystic Armor:	3		

Movement: 10
Actions: 1; Claws: 10 (12)
Powers:
Fury (4)
Immune to Fear: Fear effects trigger Rage.
Rage: When a cadaver man experiences any significant pain, such as being affected by the Pain spell or receiving a Wound, they fly into a manic fury. When enraged, a cadaver man makes 3 additional attacks each round and does not suffer the negative effects of Wounds (they still benefit from powers such as Fury). The Aggressive Attack combat option is often used. This effect lasts for 10 rounds, or until the source of the pain is killed. If a cadaver man cannot determine who caused the pain, he will attack and kill the nearest living creature.
Special Maneuvers:
Enrage (Opponent) Using this maneuver on a cadaver man triggers Rage.
Misdirect (Opponent, Close Combat): The attacker may spend two additional successes against a cadaver man affected by the Rage power to direct the cadaver man at a specific target. This may not be used to direct the cadaver man against its allies. If there are multiple instances of this special maneuver or Provoke, only the most recent has any effect.
Provoke (Opponent, Close Combat): This maneuver only costs one extra success if the cadaver man is affected by the Rage power.

Falsemen

Falsemen are servants created from different materials and used by the Theran magicians that used to inhabit Parlainth. Originally intended to carry out tasks deemed too sensitive for slaves, these artificial beings became a status symbol in the former capitol. Some magicians earned great wealth constructing falsemen, sometimes making them out of impractical materials.

Falsemen are created through a high Circle magical ritual. In general, they lack an independent consciousness and simply respond to the commands from their owner. Many of these constructs were made with a unique token that granted the bearer control of the falseman, though unfortunately many of these tokens have been lost or destroyed by the Horrors during the Scourge.

Most of the falsemen encountered in Parlainth and other ruins in Barsaive have been corrupted or altered by the Horrors, and granted rudimentary intelligence. They have a mind of their own, after a fashion, and that mind has been shaped by the Horror. Many of them have been given aggressive instincts, while others may have been granted a sadistic love of torture and extensive knowledge of different techniques. Some have even developed a level of self-awareness greater than the Horrors intended, but their behavior can seem alien and insane in civilized society.

It is possible for a Horror-corrupted falseman to have a small pool of Karma Points, granted to them by their master. These constructs are especially dangerous, as they often share the same Karma Step as the Horror that made them, and can use the points on any test they perform.

While it is possible for a character that has the appropriate knowledge to try and gain control of a corrupted falseman, doing so can pose significant danger. The falseman could bear the mark of the Horror that altered it, bringing the character to the Horror's attention and exposing him to its power in a way similar to a Horror cursed item.

The game statistics provided here are for the most common types of falsemen found in Barsaive.

Strawman

These falsemen are constructed from wood and straw. As a result, they are not especially durable, and few of the original strawmen from Parlainth remain to this day. Unfortunately, it was easy for the Horrors to learn the secret of their construction and made hundreds of their own to infest the ruins of the city.

Challenge: Novice (First Circle)

DEX:	5	**Initiative:**	5	**Unconsciousness:**	NA
STR:	5	**Physical Defense:**	7	**Death Rating:**	27
TOU:	5	**Mystic Defense:**	8	**Wound Threshold:**	8
PER:	6	**Social Defense:**	8	**Knockdown:**	5
WIL:	6	**Physical Armor:**	0	**Recovery Tests:**	2
CHA:	6	**Mystic Armor:**	2		

Movement: 10
Actions: 1; Unarmed: 9 (9)
Powers:
Immune to Fear
Resist Pain (4)
Vulnerability to Fire: Fire-based attacks against the strawman ignore any protection provided by armor. Additionally, any fire-based attacks will set the strawman alight, causing Damage Step 6 each round.
Special Maneuvers:
Pushover (Opponent, Close Combat): The opponent may spend an additional success to cause a Knockdown test against the strawman if it has a lower Strength Step. The Difficulty Number is the Attack test result.

Waxman

These constructs performed menial labor in sensitive areas of Parlainth, and are generally humanoid in shape. They are much less common than other falsemen because they are only slightly more durable than strawmen, and the Horrors did not create more during the Scourge.

Challenge: Novice (Second Circle)

DEX:	6	Initiative:	6	Unconsciousness:	NA
STR:	7	Physical Defense:	9	Death Rating:	40
TOU:	6	Mystic Defense:	9	Wound Threshold:	9
PER:	6	Social Defense:	10	Knockdown:	9
WIL:	6	Physical Armor:	3	Recovery Tests:	2
CHA:	7	Mystic Armor:	3		

Movement: 10
Actions: 1; Unarmed: 10 (10)
Powers:
Immune to Fear
Resist Pain (4)
Vulnerability to Fire: Fire-based attacks against the waxman ignore any protection provided by armor. If the fire-based attack causes the waxman a Wound, they are Harried until the Wound has healed.

Stoneman

These constructs were built as guards for areas vulnerable to sabotage, and all have a stone weapon that was part of their construction. While the Horrors did not make any new ones during the Scourge, stonemen are durable enough that many of them survived the Scourge. Unfortunately, most of them are now corrupted or tainted by the Horrors and pose a danger to careless explorers.

Challenge: Journeyman (Fifth Circle)

DEX:	6	Initiative:	6	Unconsciousness:	NA
STR:	10	Physical Defense:	8	Death Rating:	80
TOU:	10	Mystic Defense:	12	Wound Threshold:	15
PER:	8	Social Defense:	12	Knockdown:	12
WIL:	10	Physical Armor:	9	Recovery Tests:	3
CHA:	6	Mystic Armor:	8		

Movement: 10
Actions: 2; Unarmed: 12 (16)
Powers:
Awareness (13): As the skill, *Player's Guide*, p. 129.
Hardened Armor
Immune to Fear
Resist Pain (4)
Special Maneuvers:
Earth-Shattering Headache (Stoneman, Unarmed): The stoneman may spend two additional successes on an Attack test to strike their target on the top of their head, causing him to be Harried until the end of the next round.
Slowpoke (Opponent, Close Combat): If the opponent has sufficient movement, he may spend one additional success on an Attack test to quickly move behind the stoneman before they can react. The stoneman is blindsided against the opponent until the end of the round.

EARTHDAWN

Steelman

Even more rare and durable than stonemen, these constructs served a similar purpose to their counterparts. Like stonemen, they were well made and often serve as impressive art objects in their own right. Due to the complexity of their construction and enchantment, they took to the rudimentary sentience granted by the Horrors better than other falsemen, and are more cunning and dangerous foes as a result.

Challenge: Journeyman (Eighth Circle)

DEX:	8	Initiative:	8	Unconsciousness:	NA
STR:	12	Physical Defense:	11	Death Rating:	112
TOU:	12	Mystic Defense:	15	Wound Threshold:	18
PER:	10	Social Defense:	15	Knockdown:	14
WIL:	12	Physical Armor:	14	Recovery Tests:	4
CHA:	6	Mystic Armor:	10		

Movement: 10
Actions: 2; Unarmed: 18 (24)
Powers:
Awareness (16): As the skill, *Player's Guide*, p. 129.
Hardened Armor
Immune to Fear
Resist Pain (4)

Special Maneuvers:
Earth-Shattering Headache (Steelman, Unarmed): The steelman may spend two additional successes on an Attack test to strike their target on the top of their head, causing him to be Harried until the end of the next round.

Ghoul

Ghouls are another undead construct of the Horrors. Unlike cadaver men, they do not retain any trace of the sentience or personality they may have possessed in life. They gather and travel in packs, and feed on the flesh and organs of the living or recently dead. A typical pack of ghouls will number up to twenty or so individuals, and will often lurk along trade routes and similar places near inhabited areas where they can ambush their victims.

In the early days after the Scourge, there were reports of large packs of ghouls, sometimes with as many as a hundred or more members. Fortunately, groups of this size are rare in more recent times.

Challenge: Novice (Second Circle)

DEX:	5	Initiative:	7	Unconsciousness:	32
STR:	6	Physical Defense:	9	Death Rating:	40
TOU:	6	Mystic Defense:	8	Wound Threshold:	9
PER:	5	Social Defense:	7	Knockdown:	8
WIL:	5	Physical Armor:	3	Recovery Tests:	2
CHA:	3	Mystic Armor:	2		

Movement: 10

Actions: 1; Claws: 10 (11, Poison)
Powers:
Awareness (8): As the skill, *Player's Guide*, p. 129.
Poison (10, Cacofian): If the ghoul's claws do damage to a target, the target must resist the effects of a damaging poison (see **Poison**, p. 171). The poison is Step 10 damaging [Onset: Instant, Interval: 6/1 round, Duration: Until healed]. The poison stops progressing if the ghoul is killed.
Stealthy Stride (8): As the skill, *Player's Guide*, p. 170.
Vulnerability to Sunlight: When exposed to direct sunlight, all attacks against the ghoul ignore any protection provided by armor.
Special Maneuvers:
Enrage (Opponent)
Provoke (Opponent, Close Combat)
Loot: 3D6 silver pieces, taken from tombs and victims.

Ghoul Leader

These statistics represent a more powerful and intelligent ghoul, which leads their pack.

Challenge: Novice (Third Circle)

DEX:	6	Initiative:	9	Unconsciousness:	42
STR:	7	Physical Defense:	10	Death Rating:	52
TOU:	7	Mystic Defense:	9	Wound Threshold:	10
PER:	6	Social Defense:	9	Knockdown:	9
WIL:	6	Physical Armor:	4	Recovery Tests:	2
CHA:	5	Mystic Armor:	3		

Movement: 10
Actions: 1; Claws: 12 (13, Poison)
Powers:
Awareness (9): As the skill, *Player's Guide*, p. 129.
Poison (10, Cacofian): If the ghoul's claws do damage to a target, the target must resist the effects of a damaging poison (see **Poison**, p. 171). The poison is Step 10 damaging [Onset: Instant, Interval: 6/1 round, Duration: Until healed]. The poison stops progressing if the ghouls is killed.
Stealthy Stride (9): As the skill, *Player's Guide*, p. 170.
Vulnerability to Sunlight: When exposed to direct sunlight, all attacks against the ghoul ignore any protection provided by armor.
Special Maneuvers:
Enrage (Opponent)
Opening (Ghoul Leader): The ghoul leader may spend additional successes from an Attack test against an opponent affected by Poison to give other ghouls a +1 to Attack tests against the opponent until the end of the next round.
Provoke (Opponent, Close Combat)
Loot: Ghoul leaders often carry jewelry worth D8 x 25 silver pieces (worth Legend Points).

Jehuthra

These dangerous constructs are seven-foot long spider beings with ten-foot legs and bristly bodies. Rather than a traditional spider's head, they have the head and face of a Name-giver, deformed and bulging. While their eyes are vacant and they no longer retain any degree of sentience, they do have considerable cunning.

Jehuthra can most commonly be found in forests and jungles where their webbing can blend in with the natural environment. They can be found anywhere, however, and feed on whatever they can catch. They dislike direct confrontation, preferring to ambush their prey, and use their magical abilities to that end. An outmatched jehuthra will flee rather than fight, though it may retreat to set a trap that favors them.

Challenge: Journeyman (Fifth Circle)

DEX:	7	Initiative:	7	Unconsciousness:	56
STR:	7	Physical Defense:	12	Death Rating:	68
TOU:	7	Mystic Defense:	14	Wound Threshold:	10
PER:	10	Social Defense:	8	Knockdown:	13
WIL:	9	Physical Armor:	7	Recovery Tests:	2
CHA:	5	Mystic Armor:	4	Karma:	4 (8)

Movement: 16 (Climbing 16)
Actions: 2; Bite: 12 (16), Claws x2: 14 (16)
Powers:
Ambush (5)
Frost Web (16, Standard): Water – Cold. The jehuthra rubs its thorax, points at a target within 40 yards, and makes a Horror Power test against the target's Mystic Defense. If successful, the target is entangled in an extremely cold icy, barbed web. The jehuthra makes a Frost Web test for damage against the target each round, Physical Armor protects against this damage. The web holds the victim fast, causing damage and reducing his Movement Rate to 0 for one round per success on the Horror Power test, unless he makes a successful Strength (12) test as a Standard action.
Harvest Energy (18, Free): The jehuthra can gain one Karma per success on a Harvest Energy test against the victim's Social Defense.
Horror Power (14, Frost Web, Standard)
Iron Web (16, Standard): Earth – Metal. The jehuthra traces a pattern upon its thorax web and makes an Iron Web test against the highest Mystic Defense among all targets within a 10-yard radius. If successful, a 6-yard tall and 10-yard radius enclosed maze is created, consisting of eight independent paths leading to the maze's center. The Iron Web isolates each character onto one of eight paths. If there are more than eight characters, they are distributed as evenly as possible. The paths lead only to the center of the maze and do not intersect.

Characters moving faster than a slow walk (4 yards per round) must pass a Dexterity (6) test or suffer Step 8 (Physical) damage. Additional successes on the Iron Web test increase the Difficulty of the Dexterity test and Damage step on a failure by +2. Iron Web lasts 10 rounds.

The jehuthra is aware of all targets within its Iron Web and typically does not wait in the center. Instead, it will either escape, or scurry down one of the paths to attack an isolated character. Its movement is unaffected by Iron Web and may cancel Iron Web on its turn at will.

Stealthy Stride (12): As the skill, *Player's Guide*, p. 170.

Special Maneuvers:

Thorax Strike (Opponent): The opponent can spend two additional successes from an Attack test to prevent a jehuthra from using Frost Web or Iron Web until the end of the next round. If the damage causes a Wound, the jehuthra may not use Frost Web or Iron Web until the Wound is healed.

Frostbite (Jehuthra, Horror Power): The jehuthra can spend three additional successes from a Horror Power test for Frost Web to ignore the target's Physical Armor for the duration of the power.

Twisted Metal (Jehuthra, Close Combat): The jehuthra can spend two additional successes from a close combat Attack test against a target within its Iron Web power to manipulate the metal and automatically grapple the target with the twisting barbs.

Attempts to escape are made against the Iron Web Step.

Step into My Parlor (Jehuthra, Close Combat): The jehuthra's opponents are considered to be surprised against close combat attacks while within its Iron Web as it can move easily and freely in the confines. If the jehuthra suffers from penalties (such as Harried or from Taunt) it cannot use this special maneuver.

Loot: Thorax web worth D12 x 10 silver pieces (worth Legend Points).

Plague

Among the many Horror constructs documented since the days before the Scourge, perhaps none are as potentially devastating as plagues. These constructs were first documented in southwest Barsaive just before the Scourge, spreading their infections in the remains of the Kingdoms of Landis and Cara Fahd. It was only through quarantine measures that the illness was contained to that area.

Plagues most commonly appear as tall, gaunt humanoids with wispy hair and splotchy, discolored blisters covering their body. They are usually clad in filthy rags and reek of decay and illness. Despite their haggard appearance, these constructs are physically tough and able to move quickly when necessary.

The disease spread by plagues is highly contagious and a Namegiver infected with the disease may infect others, even after death. These characteristics led to the plague spreading throughout Barsaive, and the decimation of entire kaers and towns. As a result the practice of burning corpses is still employed by Namegivers throughout Barsaive to prevent the creation of disease-carrying cadaver men.

Challenge: Journeyman (Fifth Circle)

DEX:	10	**Initiative:**	13	**Unconsciousness:**	65
STR:	8	**Physical Defense:**	13	**Death Rating:**	80
TOU:	10	**Mystic Defense:**	13	**Wound Threshold:**	15
PER:	9	**Social Defense:**	9	**Knockdown:**	10
WIL:	9	**Physical Armor:**	6	**Recovery Tests:**	3
CHA:	3	**Mystic Armor:**	6	**Karma:**	4 (8)

Movement: 14

Actions: 2; Unarmed x2: 14 (13)
Powers:

Cause Plague (14, Standard): The plague can target any Namegivers within 20 yards with this power by making a Cause Plague test against their Mystic Defense. If successful, the Namegiver is affected by the Disease power. This power may only be used against a specific target once per day.

Disease (14): The disease is Step 10 debilitating (deadly) [Onset: 3-5 days, Interval: Chronic/3 days, Duration: Chronic]. Within the first few days of infection, victims experience red speckles or rashes on their throats and chests. A few days later the victim suffers dizziness, nausea, body aches, and a relentless dry cough. Within two weeks, fever leaves the victim bed ridden and death becomes inevitable. This disease creates a bond between the plague and the victim similar to a Horror Mark, enabling the plague to monitor the victim's location, as well as his physical and emotional state, and feed upon his suffering.

The disease can spread through skin-to-skin contact with victims, and even remains in a victim's corpse long after death. The only reliable cure for the disease is to slay the plague that caused the disease. If this happens, any victims gain a +6 bonus to tests to resist the disease.

Harvest Energy (18, Free): The plague can gain one Karma per success on a Harvest Energy test against the victim's Social Defense.

Resist Pain (2)

Spellcasting (14): As the talent, *Player's Guide*, p. 168.

Spells (Player's Guide): Trust (p. 299), Innocent Activity (p. 300), Mind Fog (p. 301), Clarion Call (p. 304), Notice Not (p. 305), and others as necessary.

Special Maneuvers:

Plague Bearer (Plague, Unarmed): The plague may spend two successes on an Attack test to make a Cause Plague test against the target as a Free action.

Cleanse the Taint (Opponent, Fire-Based): The opponent may spend two additional successes on a fire-based Attack or Spellcasting test to prevent the plague from using Cause Plague until the end of the next round.

Qural'lotectica

The Horror construct known as the qural'lotectica is greatly feared among the Cathan tribesmen of the Servos Jungle, as well as other communities that live near forests and jungles. The construct, often called a qural for short, consists of a bulbous central body with several tentacles. Each tentacle ends in a sharp, hollow claw.

The qural hides in the trees along a forest or jungle path, draping its tentacles to resemble branches or vines blocking the way. When a victim passes by, the tentacles pierce the body and inject a paralytic poison. The qural then feeds by draining the victim's blood through the tentacles, changing to a deep crimson color. The drained, emaciated husk remains as a sign of the construct's presence.

While these constructs are most commonly encountered in forests and jungles, they have been found in abandoned kaers, and even cities and towns where they can mask their presence among trash and overgrowth.

Challenge: Journeyman (Sixth Circle)

DEX:	8	**Initiative:**	8	**Unconsciousness:**	72
STR:	9	**Physical Defense:**	13	**Death Rating:**	90
TOU:	10	**Mystic Defense:**	15	**Wound Threshold:**	15
PER:	8	**Social Defense:**	8	**Knockdown:**	13
WIL:	8	**Physical Armor:**	4	**Recovery Tests:**	3
CHA:	3	**Mystic Armor:**	6		

Movement: 4 (Climbing 4)
Actions: 4; Tentacles: 16 (16)
Powers:
Ambush (10)
Blood Veins (15): If the qural grapples a victim, the hollow claw attached to its tentacle burrows into the victim's skin. Each round, the victim takes Step 15 Damage from blood loss. No armor protects from this damage.
Poison (20, Paralysis): If the qural grapples a victim, the hollow claw delivers a Step 20 paralytic venom [Onset: Instant, Interval: 10/1 round, Duration: 1 hour].
Stealthy Stride (14): As the skill, *Player's Guide*, p. 170.
Vulnerability to Fire: Fire-based attacks against the qural ignore any protection provided by armor.
Special Maneuvers:
Sever Tentacle (Opponent): The attacker may spend two additional successes on an attack test to destroy one of the qural's tentacles, freeing a grappled victim.
Pry Loose (Opponent, Close Combat)
Tangle (Qural'lotectica, Tentacle): The qural may spend one additional success on an Attack test to immediately grab and grapple the target with a tentacle.

Spectral Dancer

This undead construct is typically created from individuals who possessed considerable charm and charisma. They appear as a ghostly image of the body they had in life. The dancer's spirit has been severed from its body, trapped in astral space and with almost no ability to sense the living world.

The spirit occasionally gets impressions from the physical plane, but finds it difficult to reach across the veil and communicate with those on the other side. Its isolation typically drives it to the edge of madness, and it feels a burning need to make contact with another being. Unfortunately, it can only speak in garbled howls, and also lacks the ability to read, write, or otherwise communicate.

Challenge: Novice (Fourth Circle)

DEX:	10	Initiative:	10	Unconsciousness:	NA
STR:	6	Physical Defense:	13	Death Rating:	60
TOU:	7	Mystic Defense:	13	Wound Threshold:	10
PER:	9	Social Defense:	10	Knockdown:	8
WIL:	9	Physical Armor:	3	Recovery Tests:	2
CHA:	9	Mystic Armor:	5		

Movement: 12 (Flying 12)
Actions: 1; Claws: 13 (11)
Powers:
Insubstantial: Attacks with physical items (such as a sword or a bow) require an additional success, unless the attack has an area of effect.
Resist Pain (4)
Spectral Dance (Sustained): Desperate to communicate, a spectral dancer approaches a character and gestures for him to join her dance. If the character turns down the "invitation", the spectral dancer attacks with a desperate fury.

A character may join in the dance, but this carries its own danger. The character and the dancer remain locked in the dance until either the character dies or manages to assuage the dancer's terrible loneliness for a brief moment. Once joined, the character must see the dance through to its conclusion. Each round the dancing character suffers damage with a Step equal to the number of rounds the dance has lasted +3. No armor protects against this damage.

While the dance is in progress, attacks from other characters against the dancer disrupt the dance and the dancer casts Spirit Grip on the offending character as a Free action.

During any round of the dance, the character can try to make contact with the dancer in order to ease its loneliness. The character makes a Charisma test against the spectral dancer's Social Defense; at the gamemaster's discretion, the character may use a Charisma-based talent or skill for the test. To ease the spirit's loneliness and escape its clutches, the character must accumulate six total successes. As the dance nears its end, the character often sees or relives the dancer's memories.
Once the character achieves six successes, the spectral dancer's motions slow then stop. The dancer thanks the character for giving it brief companionship then fades away.
Spellcasting (13): As the talent, *Player's Guide*, p. 168.
Spells (Player's Guide): Spirit Dart (p. 322), Spirit Grip (p. 322)
Special Maneuvers:
Killer Moves (Spectral Dancer, Claws): The spectral dancer may spend two additional

successes on an Attack test to make a second attack with their claws against the same opponent. This special maneuver may only be used once per turn.
Spectral Empathy (Opponent, Spectral Dance): A character locked in the Spectral Dance may spend three additional successes on a single Charisma test to establish a connection with the spectral dancer and end the dance.

Stormwraith

The stormwraith is the result of a Horror corrupting an air elemental. They live near high mountains and are usually encountered in storms, attacking airships and generally causing havoc in shipping lanes. They resemble a dark, vaguely humanoid cloud with glowing blue eyes. They are intelligent, and often work in groups to cause greater damage.

Challenge: Journeyman (Fifth Circle)

DEX:	10	**Initiative:**	12	**Unconsciousness:**	NA
STR:	7	**Physical Defense:**	14	**Death Rating:**	72
TOU:	8	**Mystic Defense:**	13	**Wound Threshold:**	12
PER:	10	**Social Defense:**	8	**Knockdown:**	7
WIL:	9	**Physical Armor:**	5	**Recovery Tests:**	3
CHA:	6	**Mystic Armor:**	6		

Movement: 14 (Flying)
Actions: 2; Unarmed: 14 (14)
Powers:
Insubstantial: Attacks with physical items (such as a sword or a bow) require an additional success, unless the attack has an area of effect.
Invulnerable to Electric: The stormwraith suffers no damage from mundane electric attacks, and gains +20 to Physical and Mystic Armor against magical electric attacks.
Resist Pain (4)
Shock (12, Free): Air – Electric. The stormwraith makes a Shock test as a damage test against a grappled opponent. Physical Armor protects against this damage.
Spear (14, Standard): The stormwraith forms a spear of blue lightning to damage a target by making a Spellcasting test against the Mystic Defense of a target within 50 yards. If successful, the stormwraith makes a Spear test to determine how much damage the target takes. The target must make a Knockdown test against the damage dealt.
Spellcasting (14): As the talent, *Player's Guide*, p. 168.
Spells (Player's Guide): Lightning Bolt (p. 278), Air Blast (p. 280)
Vulnerability to Earth: Attacks with the earth keyword against the stormwraith ignore any protection provided by armor.
Special Maneuvers:
Engulf (Stormwraith, Unarmed): The stormwraith may spend an additional success on an Attack test to automatically grapple the target. Once the victim is grappled, he is engulfed by lightning and takes damage equal to the result of the Shock test. The effect lasts until the grapple ends, and can be broken.
Loot: Kernels of elemental air worth 2d6 x 20 silver pieces (worth Legend Points).

MINOR HORRORS

Calling any Horror minor is asking for trouble. The term is used by some scholars only to distinguish particular types of Horror from their more powerful, Named counterparts, which are referred to as "major" Horrors. Even a minor Horror has the potential to destroy many lives. Adventurers who want to keep their hides and souls intact would do well to remember this.

Minor Horrors are further divided into several different categories like bloatforms, wormskulls, or gnashers. This section provides some general information about these and other types. As discussed earlier in this chapter, the information provided here is a starting point and the gamemaster is encouraged to modify the Horrors from this baseline to suit the needs of the campaign.

Baggi

Baggi are most commonly found in the northern forests of Barsaive near Blood Wood and Parlainth. They most closely resemble obese gorillas with no fur and oily black skin. Their heads are comparatively small atop their wide shoulders, with a pair of large, pale pink eyes and a mouth that seems locked in a vicious, vacuous smile. Their long arms end with vicious claws capable of disemboweling someone with a single swipe.

Baggi do not have a skeleton. They can stiffen parts of their bodies to move and attack, but are otherwise a mostly amorphous blob of flesh. They are excellent climbers and often travel in small groups of three to eight individuals. They hide in the higher branches of trees, then swing down to strike their prey by surprise. They often tear apart their prey with their claws, but they can also stretch their mouths to absurd sizes and swallow a Namegiver whole, suffocating them within their bulk.

A tale from the early days of the Scourge describes a band of elves from Wyrm Wood encountering a Baggi. The Horror devoured one of the group, and his fellows pursued the monster for nearly an hour. During this time, they could see their companion struggling within the Horror's body, fighting to escape.

The baggi climbed a tree, the hunters spent all their arrows firing at it, and the monster took great pleasure in forcing any who climbed after it to retreat. To destroy the Horror, the hunters set the tree on fire. It didn't make any effort to flee, just sat on a branch as the flames grew closer, calling out with a sound that resembled a hooting, mocking laugh.

Challenge: Journeyman (Sixth Circle)

DEX:	8	Initiative:	8	Unconsciousness:	84
STR:	15	Physical Defense:	15	Death Rating:	104
TOU:	14	Mystic Defense:	13	Wound Threshold:	21
PER:	7	Social Defense:	10	Knockdown:	17
WIL:	10	Physical Armor:	9	Recovery Tests:	5
CHA:	5	Mystic Armor:	7	Karma:	4 (16)

Movement: 12 (Climbing 12)
Actions: 2; Claws: 18 (22)

Powers:
Awareness (15): As the talent, *Player's Guide*, p. 129.
Fury (2)
Great Leap (14)
Harvest Energy (20, Free): The baggi can gain one Karma per success on a Harvest Energy test against the victim's Social Defense. If the harvested emotion is frustration or helplessness, the baggi gains an additional point of Karma, and gains a point even if the test is a failure.
Immune to Fear
Karma Void: Whenever an opponent spends Karma against the baggi, he must spend an additional Karma point for each Karma point initially spent. This additional Karma cost does not generate any benefit.

Special Maneuvers:
Devour (Baggi, Close Combat): The baggi may spend two additional successes on an Attack test to immediately grab and swallow the target. Once swallowed the victim is subject to damage from the baggi's digestive fluids and takes Step 3 damage (no armor protects) every round. While inside of the baggi, the target is too constrained to attack effectively with anything larger than a Size 1 weapon. The baggi's interior has no Physical Armor.
Disembowel (Opponent, Edged Weapon): The opponent may spend two successes on an Attack test with an edged weapon for the purpose of attempting to free a character that has been devoured. If the attack causes a Wound, the baggi's stomach is cut open and the devoured character may attempt to escape on their turn. If the attack does not cause a Wound, this special maneuver has no effect.
Pounce (Baggi)

Bloatform

This category of Horror best resembles floating slugs, jellyfish, or bloated and deformed corpses. They frequently have tentacles, and what facial features they do have are often deformed and in seemingly random places on their body. Many scholars consider this category a bit of a catchall based on general appearance and behavior, as bloatforms display a wide variety of powers and personality in addition to their diverse physical forms.

These Horrors rarely kill their victims directly, preferring instead to drive them to madness, murder, and suicide. They take great pleasure in extended torment, and often insinuate themselves into a community, manipulating people into turning on each other. They also tend to be chatty, speaking with their victims through a Horror mark, twisting the knife in conversations that justify the actions taken while at the same time enhancing the feelings of guilt.

Challenge: Journeyman (Eighth Circle)

DEX:	8	Initiative:	8	Unconsciousness:	101
STR:	10	Physical Defense:	14	Death Rating:	124
TOU:	15	Mystic Defense:	18	Wound Threshold:	22
PER:	13	Social Defense:	16	Knockdown:	10
WIL:	16	Physical Armor:	10	Recovery Tests:	5
CHA:	10	Mystic Armor:	10	Karma:	10 (40)

Movement: 8
Actions: 2; Tentacles: 22 (18)
Powers:
Corrupt Compromise (8, Standard): For 1 Karma, the bloatform may suggest a course of action to a marked victim.
Harvest Energy (24, Free): The boatform gains one Karma per success on a Harvest Energy test agains the victim's Social Defense. If the harvested emotion is fear or guilt, the bloatform gains an additional point of Karma, and gains a point even if the test is a failure.
Horror Mark (22, Standard): In addition to the normal effects, the victim of the bloatform's Horror Mark gains a Corruption Point upon receiving the mark.
Resist Pain (2)
Spellcasting (22): As the talent, *Player's Guide*, p. 168.
Spells (Player's Guide): (These are typical spells to choose from) Astral Sense (p. 342), Divine Aura (p. 343), Flame Flash (p. 344), Mage Armor (p. 344), Mind Dagger (p. 345), Astral Shield (p. 346), Crushing Will (p. 347), Astral Targeting (p. 348), Aura Strike (p. 349), Binding Threads (p. 351), Mystic Shock (p. 354), Slow (p. 355), Razor Orb (p. 357), Sleep (p. 358), Confusing Weave (p. 358), Dislodge Spell (p. 359), Hypervelocity (p. 359), Mystic Net (p. 360)
Terror (18, Standard): For each success on the Terror test, victims suffer a -1 penalty to all their tests.

Additional Powers (Choose Three):
Corrupt Karma (22, Standard), Corrupt Reality (22, Standard), Displace (Standard), Forge Construct (22, Sustained), Horror Thread (22, Standard), Karma Boost (Free), Karma Drain (22, Standard), Unnatural Life (22, Standard)

Special Maneuvers:
Terrifying Power (Bloatform): The bloatform may spend two additional successes on an Action test to affect the target with Terror as a Free action.

Crystal Entity

Crystal entities are a type of astral Horror that drops into the physical plane. They inhabit an object or structure at least the size of a large chest. The entity transforms the object or building to resemble glass or quartz with an eerie yet beautiful glow emanating from it.

Crystal entities cannot move, and can only attack and defend themselves with spells. They also possess a terrifying ability that allows them to alter the bones and joints of a victim, forming crystal spikes that pierce the skin from the inside and causing significant pain. When damaged, the crystal structure of the Horror cracks and oozes an oily fluid. Some of this fluid congeals into kernels of elemental earth, which can be harvested after the entity is destroyed.

These Horrors typically mark a target and communicate with telepathic whispers, offering assistance through use of their Karma Boost power. They often present themselves as benevolent elemental spirits, and their assistance starts off innocuously enough. Over time however, they will begin to induce paranoia, leading their victim to believe their friends and neighbors wish to take the entity for themselves, and push their victim to abduct, torment, or kill in defense of their patron.

Some tales tell of these Horrors working their way through entire communities. After marking another victim, they ask for help escaping their tormentor and the cycle starts all over again.

Challenge: Journeyman (Sixth Circle)

DEX:	NA	Initiative:	7	Unconsciousness:	66
STR:	NA	Physical Defense:	9	Death Rating:	80
TOU:	8	Mystic Defense:	15	Wound Threshold:	12
PER:	10	Social Defense:	12	Knockdown:	NA
WIL:	9	Physical Armor:	10	Recovery Tests:	3
CHA:	7	Mystic Armor:	10	Karma:	10 (40)

Movement: NA
Actions: 2
Powers:

Awareness (16): As the talent (*Player's Guide*, p. 129). A crystal entity cannot be Blindsided by any opponent of which it is aware.

Death Spikes (16, Standard): The entity makes a Horror Power test against the Mystic Defense of a target within 100 yards. If successful, the Horror alters the joints and bones of the victim, forming crystalline spikes that pierce the skin from the inside out. This inflicts damage equal to the result of a Death Spikes test (+2 per success on the Horror Power test); no armor protects against this damage. This power automatically causes 1 Wound and can cause an additional Wound from damage. The spikes remain for one day and Wounds caused by them cannot be healed while they last. If Suppress Curse (or a similar effect) is used, the Wound can be healed and if so the spikes will not return after the suppressing effect ends.

Harvest Energy (18, Free): The crystal entity gains one Karma per success on a Harvest Energy test against the victim's Social Defense. If the harvested emotion is pain or trauma, the crystal entity gains an additional point of Karma, and gains a point even if the test is a failure.

Horror Mark (16, Standard): In addition to the normal effects, marked characters tend to find themselves unconsciously fascinated by order and precision, while frustrated by chaos and disorder. The longer the victim bears the mark, the more pronounced this effect.

Horror Power (16, Death Spikes, Standard)
Immune to Fear

Karma Boost (Free): The crystal entity can offer the victim Karma Points in exchange for Corruption.
Resist Pain (4)
Spellcasting (16): As the talent, *Player's Guide*, p. 168.
Spells (Player's Guide): (These are typical spells to choose from) Astral Sense (p. 342), Mind Dagger p. 345), Baseline Subtraction (p. 347), Crushing Will (p. 347), Astral Targeting (p. 348), Aura Strike (p. 349), Binding Threads (p. 351), Mystic Shock (p. 354), Sever Talent (p. 354), Slow (p. 355), Razor Orb (p. 357), Sleep (p. 358)
Additional Powers (Choose Two):
Aura of Awe (12, Standard), Animate Dead (16), Astral Interference (16), Disrupt Magic (16), Forge Construct (16, Sustained), Suppress Mark (10, Standard), Unnatural Life (16, Standard)
Special Maneuvers:
Shatter (Opponent, Blunt Weapon): Opponents attacking the crystal entity with a blunt weapon gain an additional success on a successful Attack test.
Loot: Coagulated blood worth d6 x 100 silver pieces in elemental earth (worth Legend Points).

Deceiver

As the name implies, deceivers are Horrors specializing in illusion and deception. They don't appear to have a natural form, as even in death their appearance is masked. One Illusionist claimed to have pierced their disguise with his True Sight, and described the deceiver as vaguely humanoid, about four feet tall, and covered entirely in gray lumpy skin that resembles exposed brain. Whether this description is accurate or merely another layer of deception is unknown.

Deceivers typically travel in small bands of 3 to 5 individuals. They scan potential victims from a distance using their magical abilities and then create illusions meant to appeal to the victim's most noble instincts. Once lured in, the victim is ambushed.

These Horrors savor the shock and betrayal felt by their victims, and appear to focus their attention on those who act selflessly. In many cases, the victim will be left injured but alive. Some speculate the deceivers seek to inspire distrust, so the next time the victim feels charitable or noble they deny that impulse and be plagued with self-doubt.

In combat deceivers use their empathic powers and mastery of illusion to take the form of their opponent's loved ones. This tactic can be unsettling, providing even more pleasure to the Horror. While it can be emotionally difficult to fight them, they are not physically powerful opponents and actually slain fairly easily. Killing one, however, provokes a final emotional blow: the Horror transforms into a copy of the slayer as a child. After defeating a deceiver, some heroes have needed to face down a mob of angry townsfolk convinced they have apprehended a child-killer.

Challenge: Journeyman (Seventh Circle)

DEX:	9	Initiative:	9	Unconsciousness:	64
STR:	6	Physical Defense:	11	Death Rating:	76
TOU:	5	Mystic Defense:	18	Wound Threshold:	7
PER:	11	Social Defense:	18	Knockdown:	8
WIL:	9	Physical Armor:	3	Recovery Tests:	2
CHA:	12	Mystic Armor:	7	Karma:	7 (28)

Movement: 12
Actions: 2; Unarmed: 14 (14)
Powers:

Ambush (10)

Cursed Luck (18, Free): Each success on a Cursed Luck test against the target's Mystic Defense allows the deceiver to reduce the result of one die on a test to 1.

Damage Shift (16, Simple): On a successful Horror Power test, the deceiver can transfer damage to an opponent up to the result of a Damage Shift test.

Death Curse (Free): If killed, the deceiver transforms into a replica of its opponent as a child. The deceiver actually becomes a dead child of the relevant Namegiver race, matching its opponent at that age down to the last freckle. Against opponents who do not have a childhood per se, it will reflect the equivalent, even if it is their current form. Some deceivers have been known take the form of their opponent's child, for those who have one.

Empathy Net: The deceiver selects a location it believes will attract the right kind of victim and performs a brief ritual during which it dashes out the brain of a living creature against a rock and spends a Karma Point. After this gruesome rite, the deceiver is made aware of the presence of all Namegivers within 500 yards and its mind is filled with images from these Namegivers' minds. From this information, the deceiver can determine situations most likely trigger a self-sacrificing response from the targets, what their past and present loved ones look like, among other details.

False Form (20, Standard): Illusion. The deceiver can mimic anything it sees in an Empathy Net scan. If the deceiver attempts to assume the form of an opponent's loved one, it makes a False Form test against the victim's Mystic Defense. If successful, the victim suffers a -2 penalty per success to all Action tests for a number of rounds

486

equal to the difference between the rest result and the victim's Mystic Defense. When the effect wears off, the deceiver can attempt to adopt the form of yet another loved one. If the deceiver changes its shape while any opponents watch, the victim gains a +5 bonus to Sensing tests against this power.

Harvest Energy (20, Free): The deceiver gains one Karma per success on a Harvest Energy test against the victim's Social Defense. If the harvested emotion is distrust or self-loathing, the deceiver gains an additional point of Karma, and gains a point even if the test is a failure.

Horror Power (18, Damage Shift, Simple)

Resist Pain (2)

Spellcasting (18): As the talent, *Player's Guide*, p. 168.

Spells (Player's Guide): (These are typical spells to choose from) Ephemeral Bolt (p. 296), True Ephemeral Bolt (p. 298), Trust (p. 299), Unseen Voices (p.299), Blindness (p. 299), Displace Image (p. 300), Innocent Activity (p. 300), Mind Fog (p. 301), Phantom Flame (p. 301), Blinding Glare (p. 302), Nobody Here (p. 303), Notice Not (p. 305), Phantom Lightning (p. 306), Stop Right There (p. 306), Suffocation (p. 306), Phantom Fireball (p. 308), Illusory Missiles (p. 311), Memory Scribe (p. 311), True Missiles (p. 312), Vertigo (p. 314)

Thought Mirror (8, Standard): Illusion. This power allows the deceiver to use images gleaned from Empathy Net to create a complex illusion that appeals to the victim's sense of heroism. Examples include a mother and baby trapped in a burning building, a drowning child being swept down a river, or a kitten being stalked by a rabid dog. The illusion covers an area up to Thought Mirror Step x 5 square yards. The illusion has a Sensing Difficulty of 42.

Additional Powers (Choose Two):
Animate Dead (18, Standard), Astral Camouflage (10, Standard), Corrupt Karma (18, Standard)

Despairthought

This Horror resembles a giant white maggot or larva and can range in size from a large dog to a thundra beast. It has multiple pale, sightless eyes and a large, lamprey-like mouth filled with large teeth. It scuttles around on multiple stubby arms.

While it can be a formidable foe in combat, the despairthought prefers to use psychic attacks from a distance. They often hide in ruins or caverns and send an astral projection out in search of victims. While not truly dual-natured, it is capable of focusing on both the physical and astral planes at the same time.

The astral form takes on the appearance of a pale ghost or vague shadow. It often seeks out families with young children, especially those with cruel or fearful parents. It tells the family that it will kill them all unless they help the creature by giving it one of the family members. Despite its threat, the Horror is unable to do any harm through its astral form.

If the family believes the bluff, the Horror describes a simple ritual that must be performed on the chosen victim. This ritual allows the despairthought to mark the victim, forging a bond that lasts until either the victim or the Horror is killed.

Once marked, the victim is unable to speak. The Horror torments the victim with bleak, cynical notions, driving the victim to depression. Coupled with the betrayal of their family and the isolation resulting from an inability to speak, the victim is crushed with hopelessness and frequently driven to suicide.

Challenge: Journeyman (Fifth Circle)

DEX:	5	Initiative:	5	Unconsciousness:	71
STR:	11	Physical Defense:	9	Death Rating:	88
TOU:	12	Mystic Defense:	15	Wound Threshold:	18
PER:	8	Social Defense:	13	Knockdown:	15
WIL:	12	Physical Armor:	8	Recovery Tests:	4
CHA:	8	Mystic Armor:	11	Karma:	8 (32)

Movement: 14
Actions: 2; Bite: 14 (15)
Powers:
Astral Projection (Standard): The despairthought can project itself into the astral realm, perceiving both the astral and physical realms at the same time. It can communicate with those in the physical world by manifesting, though it has no substance. This power has no duration or range limitations.

Commit Suicide (14, Sustained): The despairthought can render a marked victim suicidal. Once a year, the despairthought can attempt to force the victim to commit suicide. The Horror makes three Commit Suicide tests against the victim's Social Defense, while the victim makes three Willpower tests against the Horror's Social Defense. If the Horror's successes exceed the victim's for all three of the sets, the victim commits suicide within 24 hours. The Horror usually does not invoke this power for at least a full year after invading the victim, preferring to wallow in the pain it can cause the victim during that time.

Harvest Energy (16, Free): The despairthought gains one Karma per success on a Harvest Energy test against the victim's Social Defense. If the harvested emotion is despair or hopelessness, they gain an additional point of Karma, and gains a point even if the test is a failure.

Horror Mark (14): In addition to the normal applications of this power, the Horror can mark a victim at any distance if it convinces a loved one to perform a ritual that gives the Horror access to the victim.

Thoughts of Despair (14, Free): The Horror constantly feeds its marked victim bleak ideas, cynical notions, and hopeless views of the world. Once a day, the despairthought can make a Thoughts of Despair test against the victim's Social Defense. This test is usually made when the victim is in danger. If successful, the victim can take no action of any kind. He cannot fall to the floor, take shelter, or do anything potentially useful. Most despairthoughts affect the victim this way to get the victim killed, though some despairthoughts simply enjoy causing the victim inconvenience, embarrassment, or trouble. The power lasts a number of rounds equal to the difference between the victim's Social Defense and the Thoughts of Despair result (minimum 1 round).

Tormenting Voice (14, Free): When the marked victim tries to speak, the creature takes control, making horrible sounds and grunts issue forth instead of words. The victim often spasms and loses control of his body, and his noises torment those who hear them.

The victim can resist with a successful Willpower test against the despairthought's Tormenting Voice Step. Otherwise, the despairthought makes a Tormenting Voice test and compares the result to each listener's Social Defense. If successful, the listener is automatically Knocked Down, clutching at his head. His consciousness drowns in agony for all the painful actions, large or small, he has ever committed against anyone. Some listeners cry, howl, or roll back and forth on the floor in agonizing pain. Listeners may attempt to resist the effects each round by making a Willpower test against the despairthought's Tormenting Voice Step. If successful, they are not affected by this power until the victim speaks again.

While the effect lasts, the speaker may attempt a new Willpower test each round to regain some control of their voice. If successful, the effects end as long as they do not attempt to speak for the next hour.

Additional Powers (Choose One):
Corrupt Karma (14, Standard), Corrupt Reality (14, Standard), Forge Construct (14, Sustained), Suppress Mark (10, Standard)

Special Maneuvers:
Slowpoke (Opponent, Close Combat): If the opponent has sufficient movement, he may spend one additional success on an Attack test to quickly move behind the despairthought before it can react. The despairthought is Blindsided against the opponent until the end of the round.

Doppler

Dopplers are a curious and bizarre Horror. They appear as normal Namegivers aside from a two-foot stinger that can emerge from some part of their body (most commonly the upper arm or hip). This stinger is used to expand the Horror's influence.

Whenever a doppler kills a Namegiver, it uses the stinger to draw blood from the corpse. The stinger then detaches from the body and gets buried or hidden in a secluded spot. Over the next few weeks the stinger grows into a duplicate of the slain character, including the talents and abilities the victim possessed.

Dopplers infiltrate a community and gradually take over. As they replace individuals, those who are untouched develop feelings of uncertainty and paranoia. They recognize something is wrong, but find it hard to put their finger on it. The Horrors are particularly interested in taking over those in authority, and using that position to manipulate events on a large scale.

Because of their appearance and ability to duplicate Namegivers, dopplers can wear armor and fight with normal weapons. They can also cause damage with their stingers, but only do so if exposed.

Challenge: Novice (Fourth Circle)

DEX:	8	Initiative:	8	Unconsciousness:	55
STR:	7	Physical Defense:	11	Death Rating:	68
TOU:	9	Mystic Defense:	11	Wound Threshold:	13
PER:	8	Social Defense:	13	Knockdown:	9
WIL:	9	Physical Armor:	4	Recovery Tests:	3
CHA:	7	Mystic Armor:	6	Karma:	5 (20)

Movement: 12
Actions: 2; Doppler Sting: 14 (16), Unarmed: 14 (11)
Powers:
Astral Camouflage (10, Standard)
Corrupt Karma (14, Standard)
Doppler Sting (16): A doppler can cause damage with its stinger, but only does so when its nature has been exposed. After detaching the stinger to create a new doppler, a new stinger grows in a matter of days.
Harvest Energy (16, Free): The doppler gains one Karma per success on a Harvest Energy test against the victim's Social Defense. If the harvested emotion is paranoia, the doppler gains an additional point of Karma, and gains a point even if the test is a failure.
Spells: As victim if known.
Talents: As victim if known.
Special Maneuvers:
You Won't Be Needing That (Opponent): If the doppler has used its Doppler Sting during this combat, the opponent may spend two successes on an Attack test to cut the appendage off of the Horror. The stinger will grow back as if the doppler had planted it.

Dread Iota

The smallest Horror known to scholars, the dread iota is invisible to the naked eye. It is most commonly found in water, but can also be ingested through contaminated food or drink. Despite their size, these Horrors are intelligent and able to exert a cruel influence on their victims.

Masses of dread iotas can be found infesting streams, ponds, and even rainclouds in locations that still bear the worst memories of the Scourge. Travelers in corrupted lands like the Wastes or Badlands must be careful when trying live off the land or risk infection. There are tales where a Questor has been able to cleanse a victim of these Horrors, but in many cases the victim wastes away and dies before treatment.

A dread iota is unable to affect a victim until it is ingested. Unfortunately, infection is possible by many different means: drinking tainted water, eating an animal infected by the Horrors, even contact with blood or other bodily fluids. Once inside the victim, the dread iota will mark the victim and use its powers to influence the victim to help it reproduce and spread.

As the victim succumbs to the infection, the Horror offers to use its Karma Tap ability to reward hosts with boosts to their Toughness tests. It may seem like the victim is not getting more ill, but it is only a matter of time before they succumb and die. Then the Horrors will animate the corpse and go looking for new victims to infect.

The late Yamonis IV of Throal, a scholar of some repute, wrote in his journals about a device that combined a number of lenses to magnify tiny objects. He used this device to examine some water infected with dread iotas and sketched his observations. The pictures depict them as humanoid with scaly skin and large heads, malevolently grinning.

Challenge: Journeyman (Fifth Circle)

DEX:	NA	**Initiative:**	NA	**Unconsciousness:**	NA
STR:	NA	**Physical Defense:**	NA	**Death Rating:**	NA
TOU:	NA	**Mystic Defense:**	13	**Wound Threshold:**	NA
PER:	8	**Social Defense:**	8	**Knockdown:**	NA
WIL:	8	**Physical Armor:**	NA	**Recovery Tests:**	NA
CHA:	3	**Mystic Armor:**	8	**Karma:**	4 (16)

Movement: NA
Actions: 2
Powers:

Animate Dead (16, Standard): The dread iota can create ghouls with a successful Animate Dead test against the victim's Mystic Defense. Unlike other Horrors that can create undead, a dread iota can only animate a corpse it inhabits.

Degeneration: The presence of this parasitic Horror causes tissue degeneration and eventual death. Infected victims must make a Toughness test each week against a Difficulty Number equal to the number of weeks they have been infected. Each time this test fails, the victim loses 1 point from each of their Attribute values. The victim dies when any Attribute value, other than Charisma, reaches zero. The Attribute value loss is permanent, barring legendary or powerful magic, such as the intercession of a Passion.

Harvest Energy (18, Free): The dread iota gains one Karma per success on a Harvest Energy test against the victim's Social Defense. If the harvested emotion is despair, they gain an additional point of Karma, and gains a point even if the test is a failure.

Immune to Fear

Spellcasting (16): As the talent, *Player's Guide*, p. 168.

Spells (Player's Guide): Astral Spear (p. 317), Ethereal Darkness (p. 319), Spirit Dart (p. 322), Shadow's Whisper (p. 324), Pain (p. 327)

Gharmek

These Horrors feed on feelings of revulsion and disgust. Physically weaker than many Horrors, they lurk in burrows and tunnels near graveyards, catacombs, and other places where large numbers of dead can be found. They use their powers to animate the corpses, and feed off the negative feelings the walking dead create in the living. They are especially fond of the feelings that come from a living person seeing the animated corpse of someone they know and cared for in life.

Gharmek resemble a disgusting hybrid of worm and reptile. Their bodies are fat and resemble maggots, covered in scaly hide pocked with oozing sores and scabby growths. They have a sharp, bony beak that extends back into a frill covering their head and neck. When lodged in its burrow, this is the only part of the Horror visible and protects the rest of its body.

It is possible to converse with gharmek, though they often do their best to turn the conversation to the finer details of decomposition and similar processes in order to evoke the feelings of revulsion and disgust they crave. These Horrors are surprisingly cowardly, often willing to cut deals in order to ensure their survival. Of course, those who strike deals with Horrors should remember these beings are likely to renege on an agreement as soon as it suits them.

Challenge: Journeyman (Fifth Circle)

DEX:	5	Initiative:	5	Unconsciousness:	68
STR:	7	Physical Defense:	8	Death Rating:	84
TOU:	11	Mystic Defense:	13	Wound Threshold:	16
PER:	9	Social Defense:	12	Knockdown:	NA
WIL:	13	Physical Armor:	10	Recovery Tests:	4
CHA:	7	Mystic Armor:	9	Karma:	6 (24)

Movement: 8 (Burrowing 8)
Actions: 2; Bite: 14 (14)
Powers:
Animate Dead (20, Standard): The gharmek can create a cadaver man with a successful Animate Dead test against the victim's Mystic Defense.
Damage Shift (14, Simple): On a successful Horror Power test against a target's Mystic Defense, the gharmek can transfer damage to the target, up to the result of a Damage Shift test.
Harvest Energy (16, Free): The gharmek gains one Karma per success on a Harvest Energy test against the victim's Social Defense. If the harvested emotion is disgust or fear, it gains an additional point of Karma, and gains a point even if the test is a failure.
Horror Mark (12, Standard): The gharmek can use its Animate Dead power on any character it had marked before death.
Horror Power (14, Damage Shift, Simple)
Additional Powers (Choose One):
Corrupt Reality (14, Standard), Terror (12, Standard), Unnatural Life (18, Standard)
Special Maneuvers:
Slowpoke (Opponent, Close Combat): If the opponent has sufficient movement, he may spend one additional success on an Attack test to quickly move behind the gharmek before it can react. The gharmek is considered Blindsided against the opponent until the end of the round.
Soft Underbelly (Opponent): If the gharmek is exposed, the attacker may spend two additional successes on an Attack test to ignore its Physical Armor for this attack. Pulling a gharmek from its burrow requires a character to succeed at an opposed Strength test.

Gnasher

Gnashers are the most basic type of Horror. During the Scourge, thousands of these mindless drones roamed the world, devouring anything they encountered and leaving devastation in their wake. While they prefer Namegiver flesh, they will eat any living thing and even consume stone and similar inanimate objects if there is nothing else to sustain them.

Gnashers do not appear to possess anything more than a bestial intellect and desire to consume. They show no sign of pleasure at the pain and suffering they cause, and do not display any of the powers common to other types of Horrors. They travel in packs as large as several dozen, and the sounds of their feasting can often be heard from some distance away.

These Horrors vary widely in appearance, and typically range in size from a large dog to a horse. Some are reptilian, others mammalian, hybrid forms have been seen as well as ones that do not resemble any kind of natural creature. The only consistent feature is a large set of jaws filled with dozens (if not hundreds) of sharp teeth.

Driven by little more than their insatiable hunger, gnashers have no sense of self-preservation, attacking until destroyed. They never flee or retreat, even in the face of overwhelming odds.

Scholars that have had the chance to examine the remains of slain gnashers have found the creatures do not possess the same sort of life processes as animals native to the material plane. The most popular theory is that these Horrors convert their food directly into mystical energy, which is then expelled into astral space. This may be the source of much astral taint, even in areas that did not see activity by more powerful Horrors.

Challenge: Novice (Fourth Circle)

DEX:	6	Initiative:	8	Unconsciousness:	46
STR:	10	Physical Defense:	13	Death Rating:	56
TOU:	6	Mystic Defense:	11	Wound Threshold:	9
PER:	4	Social Defense:	10	Knockdown:	12
WIL:	8	Physical Armor:	6	Recovery Tests:	2
CHA:	3	Mystic Armor:	5	Karma:	4 (16)

Movement: 12
Actions: 1; Bite: 14 (16)
Powers:
Awareness (10): As the talent, *Player's Guide*, p. 129.
Great Leap (10): As the creature power, p. 251.
Harvest Energy (16, Free): Gnashers can only use this power to regain Karma when feasting on living flesh. If it is a Namegiver they have killed, the gnasher gains an additional point of Karma, and gains a point even if the test is a failure.
Immune to Fear
Special Maneuvers:
Enrage (Opponent)
Provoke (Opponent, Close Combat)
Pounce (Gnasher)

Kreescra

This stealthy Horror inspires nightmares in their victims and feeds off the pain and fear they generate. They are small, standing about three feet tall on average. Their bodies are parodies of humanoid form, with twisted limbs and faces that look like they are about to slide off their lumpy head. Despite their appearance they are rather agile and difficult to catch or strike.

While the kreescra does not cause any direct harm, night after night of nightmares and disturbed slumber can take its toll. Victims of a kreescra grow increasingly tired and irritable, and often grow ill from the lack of sleep. Adventurers are particularly susceptible to the influence of this Horror, as it can take much longer for their injuries to heal, and an exhausted adept is more likely to make a mistake that could prove fatal.

Challenge: Novice (Fourth Circle)

DEX:	9	**Initiative:**	9	**Unconsciousness:**	55
STR:	7	**Physical Defense:**	13	**Death Rating:**	68
TOU:	9	**Mystic Defense:**	11	**Wound Threshold:**	13
PER:	9	**Social Defense:**	10	**Knockdown:**	12
WIL:	9	**Physical Armor:**	5	**Recovery Tests:**	3
CHA:	5	**Mystic Armor:**	5	**Karma:**	5 (20)

Movement: 12
Actions: 2; Unarmed: 13 (13)
Powers:

Astral Camouflage (10, Standard): The kreescra can hide its presence in astral space, increasing the Difficulty Number to detect or notice it by 10.

Cursed Luck (13, Free): Each success on a Cursed Luck test against the target's Mystic Defense allows the kreescra to reduce the result of one die on a test to 1.

Displace (Standard): The kreescra can cross between the physical and astral realms.

Harvest Energy (15, Free): The kreescra gains one Karma per success on a Harvest Energy test against the victim's Social Defense. If the harvested emotion is exhaustion, frustration, or stress, they gain an additional point of Karma, and gains a point even if the test is a failure.

Haunting Nightmares (14, Sustained): Kreescra find wounded individuals who are deep in slumber and place their hands on the victim's head, then make a Horror Power test against the victim's Mystic Defense. If successful, nightmares and horrible events from the victim's past overwhelm the dreamer and disrupt his sleep. The victim does not wake from these terrors; he stays asleep, sweating, and tossing and turning. The kreescra can reactivate this power at a range of up to 100 yards, keeping the victim under its influence for at least one hour each night. During the day, the kreescra trails him, keeping out of sight and only using its powers while the victim slumbers.

During the horrible nightmares, the victim makes a Willpower test against the Kreescra's Willpower Step. If the Willpower test fails, the victim recovers no Recovery tests the next day despite his full night's sleep. For every continuous week that the kreescra haunts the victim, whether or not it successfully keeps the victim from making daily Recovery tests, reduce the victim's Toughness value by 1. If the value drops to 0, the victim dies.

If possible, the kreescra stays with the same victim until the victim dies, slowly killing him with nightmares, the effects of unhealed injuries, and slowly withering. If the victim achieves four successes on one of his Willpower tests against the kreescra, he has forced the Horror from his mind. Once a victim has forced the kreescra from his mind, the creature seeks out another victim. The victim's Toughness will return at the rate of one point per week of good rest.

Horror Power (14, Haunting Nightmares, Sustained)

Stealthy Stride (14): As the talent, *Player's Guide*, p. 170.

Tracking (14): As the talent, *Player's Guide*, p. 175. The kreescra may track a target through astral space.

Mindslug

Like gnashers, mindslugs are another type of simple Horror. These mindless entities are typically about six inches long, glossy black in color, and lack obvious sensory organs. They move around similar to a centipede on small tentacles, each tentacle covered with multiple small hooks. They are often found in small groups of three to five individuals.

Mindslugs feed off the pain caused by their attacks on a victim. The Horror hides in dark places and attack the victim while they rest. It pierces the victim's skull and crawls into the brain and begins to feed. The only way to stop this is to remove the slug.

The mindslug's body is slippery, and the hooks that line its tentacles are used to grip the victim's skull.

Challenge: Novice (Third Circle)

DEX:	6	Initiative:	6	Unconsciousness:	39
STR:	6	Physical Defense:	8	Death Rating:	48
TOU:	6	Mystic Defense:	13	Wound Threshold:	9
PER:	7	Social Defense:	8	Knockdown:	8
WIL:	10	Physical Armor:	4	Recovery Tests:	2
CHA:	6	Mystic Armor:	6	Karma:	5 (20)

Movement: 10
Actions: 1; Tentacle: 11 (12)
Powers:
Ambush (10)
Corrupt Karma (13, Standard): Each success on a Corrupt Karma test against the target's Mystic Defense allows the mindslug to cancel the use of Karma on one test.
Cursed Luck (13, Free): Each success on a Cursed Luck test against the victim's Mystic Defense allows the mindslug to reduce the result of one die on a test to 1.
Gain Surprise (11, Standard): Illusion. The mindslug makes a Gain Surprise test against the Mystic Defense of each target who can detect its presence. If successful, the target can no longer detect the mindslug and is surprised if they are attacked. The Sensing Difficulty is equal to the Gain Surprise result.
Harvest Energy (13, Free): The mindlsug gains one Karma per success on a Harvest Energy test against the victim's Social Defense. If the harvested emotion is pain, the mindslug gains an additional point of Karma, and gains a point even if the test is a failure.
Immune to Fear

Special Maneuvers:
Burrow (Mindslug, Tentacle): The mindslug may spend two additional successes on an Attack test to burrow into its target. Tentacle damage is automatically dealt each subsequent round and armor does not protect against this damage.
Painful Extraction (Opponent): To remove the mindslug, the opponent must make a Dexterity test against the mindslug's Physical Defense. If successful, the character has gripped the mindslug and must make a Willpower test against the Horror's Willpower Step. If successful, the mindslug is removed, but causes Step 6/D10 Damage and 1 Wound to the victim. The longer the mindslug remains in the victim, the more difficult is becomes to remove. Each additional round the mindslug burrows into the victim's brain, it gains a cumulative +2 bonus to its Physical Defense and the Difficulty Number for the Willpower test to remove it.

Scurrier

These Horrors were first spotted in the ruins of Parlainth after its return. They are still most common in that area, but have since been seen in other ruins. Their appearance is disturbing to most Namegivers. They are small, squat humanoids with long, spindly arms and short legs that manage to carry their bulk with surprising agility. Their skin is covered with patches of bristly, spider-like hair, and their large eyes glow a pale, sickly green. The most unsettling feature is the bits of brain that protrude from holes in their skull.

Scurriers are weak and cowardly by nature, preferring to harm their prey from a distance. They use their abilities to repair and modify traps in the ruins of abandoned kaers, often making the traps less instantly deadly but more painful. When explorers get caught in the traps, the Horrors approach and feed off the victim's pain. While they usually flee when confronted, they can fight viciously when cornered.

Challenge: Novice (Third Circle)

DEX:	9	**Initiative:**	11	**Unconsciousness:**	48
STR:	6	**Physical Defense:**	13	**Death Rating:**	60
TOU:	9	**Mystic Defense:**	13	**Wound Threshold:**	13
PER:	9	**Social Defense:**	7	**Knockdown:**	8
WIL:	9	**Physical Armor:**	6	**Recovery Tests:**	3
CHA:	4	**Mystic Armor:**	4	**Karma:**	4 (16)

Movement: 14
Actions: 1; Spear: 12 (10)
Powers:
Cursed Luck (11, Free): Each success on a Cursed Luck test against the target's Mystic Defense allows the scurrier to reduce the result of one die on a test to 1.
Forge Trap (10, Standard): The scurrier can create traps, distributing the result of a Forge Trap test among the trap's game characteristics.
Harvest Energy (14, Free): The scurrier gains one Karma per success on a Harvest Energy test against the victim's Social Defense. If the harvested emotion is pain, they gain an additional point of Karma, and gain a point even if the test is a failure.
Repair Trap (12, Standard): The scurrier may repair a trap by making a Repair Trap test against a difficulty number based on the condition of the trap. If only a basic part needs to be repaired or replaced, the Difficulty Number 6. If the trap has degraded to a pile of rust the Difficulty Number might be 23. A trap repaired in this fashion automatically attunes it to the scurrier.

Slipshade

These Horrors are dangerous, but rare. Slipshades appear as a humanoid shape of absolute shadow, about four to six feet tall, and never have a shadow. They have the ability to shift themselves into a flat, nearly two-dimensional shape that easily slides along floors, walls, ceilings, and the gaps between a door and its frame. They attack with their hands, and the wounds they leave resemble mauling by a large carnivore.

Slipshades are generally solitary, and do not cooperate or work with other Horrors. Their goals are mysterious, as they don't seek out intelligent prey, but will attack any living thing that enters their territory. Scholars are unclear how this entity derives nourishment, and information that might help answer these questions is difficult to come by. There have been no reliable reports of a slipshade in many years, leading some to speculate these Horrors may have been forced to retreat to their native plane.

These Horrors display another behavior that runs counter to those commonly displayed by others of their kind. Rather than destroy works of art or other beautiful and well-crafted items, slipshades seem to prize them. Many reports from the early days after the Scourge describe the treasures pried from the lair of a slipshade after slaying it.

Challenge: Journeyman (Seventh Circle)

DEX:	11	Initiative:	13	Unconsciousness:	82
STR:	8	Physical Defense:	17	Death Rating:	100
TOU:	11	Mystic Defense:	16	Wound Threshold:	16
PER:	11	Social Defense:	15	Knockdown:	10
WIL:	15	Physical Armor:	11	Recovery Tests:	4
CHA:	8	Mystic Armor:	8	Karma:	7 (28)

Movement: 16
Actions: 2; Unarmed: 20 (18)
Powers:
Ambush (15)
Harvest Energy (22, Free): The slipshade gains one Karma per success on a Harvest Energy test against the victim's Social Defense. If the harvested emotion is fear or paranoia, they gain an additional point of Karma, and gain a point even if the test is a failure.
Immune to Fear
Slip from View (16, Standard): Illusion. The slipshade makes a Slip from View test against the Mystic Defense of each target who can detect its presence. If successful, the target can no longer detect the slipshade and is surprised if they are attacked. The Sensing Difficulty is equal to the Slip from View result. This power may only be used while in two-dimensional form.
Switch Form (Simple): Slipshades can switch from three- to two-dimensional form or vice versa instantaneously, as often as they wish. In two-dimensional form, the slipshade can elongate itself and pass through a crack of any width whatsoever, as long as the opening is at least six inches long. The slipshade can move normally by sliding along a wall, floor, ceiling, or ground. If moving upright across an open area while in two-dimensional form, the slipshade's speed is reduced by half and its movement acquires an eerie, unsteady, undulating quality. Slipshades gain +5 to Stealthy Stride tests and to Physical Defense while in two-dimensional form. Additionally, they cannot attack, but take damage normally. In three-dimensional form, slipshades move normally across open territory, but cannot slide up walls or across ceilings.
Stealthy Stride (16): As the talent, *Player's Guide*, p. 170.
Terror (14, Standard): Each success on a Terror test against a target's Mystic Defense causes a -1 penalty to the target's Action tests.

Special Maneuvers:
Shadow Stake (Opponent): The opponent may spend three additional successes on an Attack test with a weapon which has a True Pattern (if a missile weapon, the projectile must have a True Pattern) to strike where the slipshade's shadow should be located. As long as the weapon remains where it has pinned the slipshade's shadow, the slipshade cannot use the Switch Form power and cannot move more than 50 yards from that point. The slipshade's shadow can be attacked to cause damage to the slipshade, meeting the above requirements.

Slipscream (Slipshade, Unarmed): The slipshade may spend two additional successes on an Attack test against a surprised target to use Terror on the target as a Free action.

Wingflayer

These Horrors are one of the more unusual specimens recorded, and their appearance and abilities initially led many scholars to believe them nothing more than exaggerated windling stories. There are enough independent accounts, however, to prove their existence.

Wingflayers appear as a swirling cloud of tiny metallic shards, each shard no more than about two inches long. The typical specimen is about six feet high and two to three feet wide: about the same space as a human or similar Namegiver. Their fluid nature, however, does allow them to take on different shapes, even expanding to a more diffuse cloud three to four times larger than their standard form. It is also possible for the cloud of slivers to pass through narrow gaps by squeezing through the hole bit by bit.

When resting, the wingflayer settles into a pile of shards about a foot across and an inch or so high. The total weight of the shards is rarely more than about five pounds. Despite what would appear to be a fragile or insubstantial nature, wingflayers are capable of causing significant damage, often leaving their victims as little more than shredded flesh and fractured bone. Armor provides little protection from their onslaught.

Surprisingly, these Horrors can be captured when at rest. If gathered into a small container, the shards are unable to build up the speed necessary to damage their prison, even one made of glass or leather.

It is unclear how much sentience these Horrors possess. They do not appear to communicate, either with Namegivers or other Horrors. There is no clear way for them to sense or consume prey. Many scholars believe these entities are highly magical, sensing their prey through some form of astral perception, and feed by converting the motivating life force of their victims directly into a form they can use.

Despite their fluid and insubstantial nature, weapons do have an effect on these Horrors. It is believed blows from solid objects cause damage to the energy matrix that animates them, though ranged weapons like arrows, darts, or spears often pass through with little effect. It may be the damage is caused not by the weapon itself, but the physical connection to the will driving it.

Challenge: Journeyman (Sixth Circle)

DEX:	13	**Initiative:**	15	**Unconsciousness:**	78
STR:	10	**Physical Defense:**	17	**Death Rating:**	96
TOU:	12	**Mystic Defense:**	11	**Wound Threshold:**	18
PER:	9	**Social Defense:**	13	**Knockdown:**	10
WIL:	12	**Physical Armor:**	10	**Recovery Tests:**	4
CHA:	8	**Mystic Armor:**	6	**Karma:**	7 (28)

Movement: 12 (Flying)
Actions: 4; Slivers: 17 (16)

Powers:
Cursed Luck (17, Free): For each success on a Cursed Luck test, the wingflayer can reduce the result on one die rolled on a test to 1.
Flay Armor: Non-magical armor (with the exception of the natural armor of an obsidiman) will have its Physical and Mystic Armor reduced by -1 each round the wearer is in close combat with the wingflayer. The armor may be destroyed and repaired as normal (see Repairing Damaged Armor, *Player's Guide*, p. 415.
Harvest Energy (19, Free): The wingflayer gains one Karma per success on a Harvest Energy test against the victim's Social Defense. If the harvested emotion is pain, the wingflayer gains an additional point of Karma, and gains a point even if the test is a failure.
Immune to Fear

Special Maneuvers:
Blown Away (Opponent, Air-based Attack): The opponent may spend two additional successes from an air-based (not electricity) Attack or Spellcasting test to scatter the slivers making up the wingflayer. The wingflayer is Harried until the end of the next round as it pulls itself together.
Flay Flesh (Wingflayer, Slivers): The wingflayer may spend additional successes on its Attack test to reduce the target's Wound Threshold by 2 per success. Each success spent in this fashion allows the wingflayer to inflict an additional Wound on the target based on the new Wound Threshold.

A wingflayer spends one additional success from on Flay Flesh against Silar, who has a Wound Threshold of 8. Silar's Wound Threshold is reduced to 6 when determining whether the damage from the attack causes a Wound. If the wingflayer does more than 6 but less than 12 damage, Silar suffers one Wound. If the Horror does 12 damage or more, he suffers 2 Wounds.

Because the winglfayer only spent one extra success from the Attack test, it can only cause one additional Wound, even if it does 18 damage.

Wormskull

These Horrors are a category similar to bloatforms. They can vary significantly in appearance but tend to have a common feature: their heads resemble a skull made of a mass of writhing worms. Their hands and feet often consist of worm-like appendages as well. Size can vary, with most between five and eight feet in height, often resembling a parody of Name-giver form. Their bodies often feature bits of metal that resemble plates of armor.

Wormskulls prefer dry environments. In fact, their presence often removes all moisture within about 1,000 yards of their lair. They are not the most powerful Horrors, but they are intelligent, cruel, and patient. They often organize bands of lesser Horrors (like gnashers) as foot soldiers to support their plans.

Records recovered by adepts exploring the Badlands indicate significant wormskull activity during the Scourge. This could explain how the formerly fertile area was changed to a desert wasteland. The records are incomplete, however, and it is unclear whether it was the work of a single wormskull, or the combined efforts of a group.

Challenge: Journeyman (Eighth Circle)

DEX:	8	Initiative:	10	Unconsciousness:	86
STR:	12	Physical Defense:	16	Death Rating:	104
TOU:	10	Mystic Defense:	18	Wound Threshold:	15
PER:	13	Social Defense:	14	Knockdown:	14
WIL:	11	Physical Armor:	12	Recovery Tests:	3
CHA:	8	Mystic Armor:	10	Karma:	7 (28)

Movement: 10
Actions: 2; Unarmed: 20 (20)
Powers:
Displace (Standard): The wormskull can cross between the physical and astral realms.
Harvest Energy (22, Free): The wormskull gains one Karma per success on a Harvest Energy test against the victim's Social Defense. If the harvested emotion is disgust, fear, or pain, the wormskull gains an additional point of Karma, and gains a point even if the test is a failure.
Horror Mark (18, Standard): In addition to the normal effects, marked characters tend to develop odious personal habits, such as eating disgusting food, or extremely poor personal hygiene. Even if they recognize and make a conscious effort to correct these developments, they will unconsciously slip back into them. The longer the victim bears the mark, the more pronounced these habits become.
Horror Power (20, Skin Shift, Standard)
Immune to Fear
Skin Shift (16, Simple): The wormskull touches the target and makes a Horror Power test against the target's Mystic Defense. If successful, the wormskull makes a Skin Shift test to determine the damage. No armor reduces this damage. Each success on the Horror Power test inflicts one Wound on the target.
Spellcasting (20): As the talent, *Player's Guide*, p. 168.
Spells (Player's Guide): (These are typical spells to choose from) Astral Spear (p. 317), Ethereal Darkness (p. 319), Soul Armor (p. 321), Spirit Dart (p. 322), Spirit Grip (p. 322), Shadow's Whisper (p. 324), Pain (p. 327), Viewpoint (p. 330), Blind (p. 331), Wither Limb (p. 333), Bone Shatter (p. 334), Debilitating Gloom (p. 335), Friendly Darkness (p. 335), Recovery (p. 335), Step Through Shadow (p. 336).
Loot: Metal pieces fused with elemental earth. These pieces are worth (D20 + D8 + D6) x 100 silver pieces (worth Legend Points).
Additional Powers (Choose Two):
Animate Dead (20, Standard), Karma Drain (20, Standard), Terror (16, Standard), Unnatural Life (20, Standard)
Special Maneuvers:
Maggot Assault (Wormskull, Unarmed): The wormskull may spend two additional successes on an Attack test to cover the target in wriggling worms and maggots. The target is Harried until the end of their next turn.

INDEX

A

A Changed World	27
Adding Color	106
Adjusting Difficulty Numbers	161
Adult Genhis	289
Adult Prisma	325
Advanced Rules for Injuries	194
Advanced Techniques	91
Adventure Background	99
Adventure Ideas	109
Adventures And Campaigns	99
A Foundation is Laid	17
Aftermath	38
Agni (Sample Named Fire Spirit)	393
Aid Summoner	369
Airship Travel	130
Air Spirits	383
Ally Spirit Powers Table	376
Ally Spirits	376
Ally Spirits and Names	368
Alpha Wolf	355
Ambush	250
Animal Training and Animal Companions	155
Animate Dead	458
Antidotes and Poultices	174
Ant Spirits	406
An Uncertain Future	39
An Uneasy Peace	29
Ape	254
Aquans (Sample Named Water Spirit)	397
Armored Matrix Object	232
Armored Scales	424
Asante	444
Assigning Legend Awards	119
Assistants	94
Astral Camouflage	458
Astral Portal	370
Atmosphere and Mood	102
Aura of Awe	458
Avoiding Attention	128
Awarding Legend Points	119

B

Baby Genhis	289
Baggi	481
Balancing Encounters	246
Band of the Elements	207
Barrier Rating Table	166
Barriers and Structures	164
Bartertown	53
Basilisk	255
Bat, Messenger	257
Bat, Shrieker	257
Bear	259
Be Aware!	85
Becoming Cursed	185
Be Flexible!	86
Behemoth	260
Behind the Numbers	160
Be Knowledgeable!	86
Be Realistic!	86
Be Tough, But Kind!	87
Bite Attacks	249
Black Brine	175
Black Mantis	467
Black Mercy	175
Blade Trap	181
Bloatform	482
Blood Bee	261
Blood Magic	97, 419
Blood Raven	262
Blood Wood	62
Boar	263
Bog Gob	263

Bone Plague	188	Climbing Difficulty Table	167
Bone Shambler	468	Climbing Gear	167
Bone Spirits (Sample Ally Spirit Type)	377	Climbing in Combat	168
Bracers of Aras	208	Clip the Wing	252
Bracers of Obsidiman Strength	209	Cockatrice	270
Brithan	264	Combat Options for Creatures and Opponents	250

C

Cadaver Men	469	Common Dragons	435
Campaign Elements	112	Communities	111
Campaign Ideas	115	Completing Goals	119
Cara Fahd	63	Complications for Travel and Exploration	134
Caravan Campaign	115	Conflicts and Challenges	103
Cat	265	Conflicts and Obstacles	122
Cathay Dragons	439	Confusion	370
Cave Crab	266	Conquering Jerris	73
Cave-In Trap	181	Conspicuous Smuggler	210
Cave Troll	267	Continuity and Change	114
Chakta Bird	267	Corrupt Compromise	459
Challenges And Obstacles	159	Corruption	456
Challenge Values for Spirits	367	Corrupt Karma	459
Changeling	268	Corrupt Reality	459
Changing the Rules	83	Crack the Shell	252
Chapter 1: Introduction	11	Crakbill	271
Chapter 2: What Has Come Before	15	Creating Campaigns	111
Chapter 3: The Land And Its People	41	Creating Difficulty Numbers	159
Chapter 4: Gamemastering	81	Creating Gamemaster Characters	140
Chapter 5: Adventures And Campaigns	99	Creature Attacks	249
Chapter 6: Exploration And Travel	125	Creature Behavior	248
Chapter 7: Encounters	139	Creature Combat	248
Chapter 8: Challenges And Obstacles	159	Creature Descriptions	254
Chapter 9: Thread Items	197	Creature Entry Format	252
Chapter 10: Creatures	245	Creature Powers	250
Chapter 11: Spirits	361	Creatures	245
Chapter 12: Dragons	409	Creatures and Climbing	168
Chapter 13: Horrors	451	Creatures and Horrors	95
Charcoalgrin	445	Creatures and Interaction Tests	155
Charge	250	Credits	3, 8
Cheetah	270	Crocodile	272
Choosing the Difficulty Number	161	Crojen	273
City Spirits (Sample Ally Spirit Type)	378	Crystal Entity	483
Class Warfare	57	Crystal Raiders	65
Claw and Other Attacks	249	Culture and Tradition	43
Climate and Terrain	41	Curse	370
Climbing	167, 250	Cursed Luck	460
		Curse Effects	186

503

Curses	184	Dragonlike Creatures	429
Curse Table	186	Dragon Magic	418
Customizing Dragons	422	Dragon Powers	424
Customizing Earthdawn	94	Dragons	435
Customizing Legend Awards	123	Dragons as Allies	420
		Dragons as Enemies	421

D

		Dragonsight	425
Damage	172	Dragons in the World	416
Damage Shift	460	Dragonspeech	426
Dart Trap	182	Drake	430
Death	172	Drake, Lesser	431
Death and Earthdawn	87	Drama	91
Death Moth	274	Dread Iota	490
Death's Caress	188	Dreams	91
Debilitation	172	Drowning and Suffocation	168
Deceit	145	Dryad (Sample Wood Spirit)	401
Deceiver	485	Duration	173
Defang	252	Dwarfs	46
Dehydration	194	Dyre	278
Delving Campaign	116		
Demiwraith	276		

E

Denairastas	110	Eagle	279
Designing Thread Items	200	Earth Q'wril	280
Despairthought	487	Earth Spirits	387
Destroy Weapon	370	Echoes of the Empire	65
Detecting Horror Marks	463	Economy of Favors	149
Detection	180	Effect	172, 180
Detect True Element	370	Effects of Horror Marks	463
Difficulty Number Table	160	Elemental Aura	371
Disarm	180	Elemental Long Spear	210
Disease	186, 249, 461	Elemental Spirits	383
Disease Treatments	187	Elemental Spirits and Names	368
Dispel Magic	424	Elephant	281
Displace	461	Elfbane	175
Displays	93	Elves	47
Disrupt Fate	424	Encounters	139
Disrupt Magic	461	Encounters While Traveling	127
Dive	251	Engulf	371
Dodger (Sample Named Ally Spirit)	379	Enhanced Matrix Object	232
Dog	276	Enhanced Sense	251
Dominate Beast	425	Enhance Summoner	371
Doppler	489	Enrage	252
Draft Horse	299	Enrage Element	372
Dragon Breath	425	Espagra	282
Dragon Breath Table	425	Espagra Boots	211

Espagra Saddle	212	**G**	
Ethandrille	356	Game Aids	93
Ethrys (Sample Named Earth Spirit)	388	Gamemaster Character Attitudes	142
Etiquette	413	Gamemaster Character Files	94
Example Diseases	187	Gamemaster Characters	139
Example of Interaction Tests in Play	151	Gamemastering Guidelines	85
Exploration And Travel	125	Gamemaster's Authority	81
Exploration Campaign	116	Game Terms	369, 457
Exploring Kaers and Citadels	110, 131	Gargan (Sample Named Air Spirit)	384
Exploring Legends	110	Gargoyle	286
Explosive Gas Trap	182	Gate Hound	287
Exposure and Frostbite	194	Gathering Magical Treasure	122
Eyebite	176	Genhis	288
		Getting Lost	137
F		Gharmek	491
Faerie Mail	213	Ghoul	473
Failing a Climbing Test	167	Ghoul Leader	474
Falcon	283	Giant Trapdoor Spider	340
Falling Damage	167	Giant Weaver Spider	341
Falling Damage Table	168	Globberog	289
Falsemen	470	Gnasher	493
Fastoon's Very Impressive Staff	214	Gnome (Sample Earth Spirit)	389
Fatigue	193	Goat	291
Fatigue and Injury	192	Goods and Services	97
Favor Payback Table	150	Grab and Bite	252
Favors	148	Granlain	299
Favor Success Table	149	Great Bear	259
Fear	426	Greater Termite	292
Feathered Dragons	442	Great Form Spirits	367
Felux	283	Great Leap	251
Female Lion	309	Greenhouses and Mines	61
Feral Bracers	214	Greeting Rituals	129
Find	372	Greyswain (Sample Named Ally Spirit)	379
Fire	170	Griffin	293
Firebird	285	Griffin, Jungle	294
Fire Damage Table	170	Ground Rules	81
Fireleaf	176	Growing Theran Influence	18
Fire Spirits	391	Guard Dog	277
Fleshing Out the Story	106	Guardian Spirit (Sample Ally Spirit Type)	380
Foreshadowing	91		
Forge Construct	461	**H**	
Forge Trap	462	Hamstring	252
Founding an Empire	20	Handouts	93
Frost Pouch	215	Hardened Armor	251, 372
Fury	251	Harpy	296

505

Harvest Energy	462	Invisibility	373
Hasapik (Sample Earth Spirit)	391	Iopos	70, 417
Haven	70	Item Characteristics	202
Hearth Spirit (Sample Ally Spirit Type)	381	Item Description	201
Heat Exposure	195		
Hell Hound	297	**J**	
Hemlock	176	Jaron and the Sphinx	22
High Altitudes	195	Jehuthra	475
Hoarding	414	Jerris	72
Holding Your Breath	169	Jub Jub	304
Horror Constructs	467		
Horror Curses	185, 454	**K**	
Horrorfever	189	Kaer Campaign	116
Horror Mark	462	Kaer Design	133
Horror Marked Items and Places	464	Kaer Ward	183
Horror Marks and Raw Magic	464	Karma	373
Horror Power	462	Karma Boost	465
Horror Powers	455	Karma Cancel	426
Horrors	109, 157, 451	Karma Drain	465
Horror Theme	104	Karma Points	427, 465
Horror Thread	464	Keesra	176
Horse	299	Key Knowledge	200
How to Use This Book	12	Kickstarter Credits	3
Humans	48	Kranguk's Interjection	217
Hunting Dog	277	Kratas	73
Huttawa	302	Kreescra	494
Hydra	432	Krillra	305
		Krilworm	307
I		K'tenshin After the War	77
Ice Flyer	303	Kue	307
Ignis (Sample Fire Spirit)	394		
Individual Deeds and Roleplaying	123	**L**	
Initiative	180	Laésal	177
Injuries	193	Lairs	413
Inshalata	304	Lair Sense	427
Insight	146	Larva Prisma	326
Insubstantial	372	Legendary Thread Items	205
Integrating New Player Characters	108	Legend Award Table	120
Interaction Success Table	148	Leopard	308
Interaction Tests	144	Leviathans	437
Interval	173	Lightning-Bolt Earring	217
Intimidation	147	Light Source Table	137
Introducing Thread Items	198	Lion	309
Invae Spirits	404	Lion, Stone	310
Invae Spirits and Names	369	Lion, Wood	311

Lizard	311	Naga-Scale Brooch	220
Lizard, Ghoul	312	Name-Day Feasts	44
Lizard, Lightning	313	Named Spirits	367
Lizard, Plague	314	Native Astral Beings	362
Loot	118	Night Pollen	177
Loot Worth Money	118	Nightsky	447
Lung-Rot	189	Nioku's Bow	220

M

O

Magic Use Table	352	Objectives	100, 113
Major Cities and Powers	62	Obsidimen	49
Major Curses	185	Ogre	319
Make it Fun	83	Ogre Twins	320
Making an Impression	144	On Ally Spirits	361
Male Lion	309	On Different Types of Horrors	452
Manifest	373	On Elemental Spirits	363
Manipulate Element	373	On Mating	410
Manticore	315	Onset Time	173
Mantrap	183	On Tasked Spirits	365
Mapping Barsaive	111	On the Horror Mark	453
Maps	93	On the Invae	364
Masterminds and Equalizers	107	On the Namegiver Races	46
Master of the Hall of Records	59	On the Nature and Ways of Dragons	409
Memory Crystals	413	On the Nature of Rules	83
Metal Inquisitor	218	On the Study of the Horrors	451
Methods of Exposure	187	Opposition	101, 113
Military Campaign	117	Oratory Necklace	222
Mindslug	495	Orichalcum Shield	223
Minor Curses	185	Orks	49
Minor Horrors	481	Other Languages	46
Mirror	219	Our Life Cycle	410
Mistakes	84	Our Noble Form	409
Mistral (Sample Air Spirit)	385	Our Views on Modern Nations	416
Modifiers vs. Difficulty Numbers	161	Overland Travel	126
Molgrim	316	Overrun	252
Monkey	318	Overview of Thread Items	197
Motivation	101, 113		
Motivations, Attitudes, and Personality	365	**P**	
Mule	300	Pacing	90
Multiple Actions	248	Padendra	177
Muse (Sample Ally Spirit)	382	Pangolus	321
Mysteries Across the Sea	78	Paralysis	172
		Passions and Questors	110

N

		People and Politics	42
Naga	318	Perception Difficulty Table	162

Perception Modifiers Table	165	Riding Horse	301
Perception Test Modifiers	164	Rites of Protection and Passage	19
Perception Tests	162	Ritual Magic	419
Perception Test Success Levels	163	River Travel	129
Pit Trap	183	Rockworm	330
Plague	476	Rockworm, Greater	331
Player Ideas	97	Roleplaying	89, 144
Play Fair	84		
Plot Synopsis	100		

S

Poison	171, 249, 373, 427, 466	Safe Areas	126
Poison Descriptions	174	Salamander (Sample Fire Spirit)	394
Poison Gas	178	Sample Dragons	444
Poison Ivy	224	Sand Lobster	331
Poison Resistance Tests	171	Saural	332
Poison Table	174	Savage Hides	228
Political Campaign	117	Scurrier	496
Pony	301	Sea Snake	337
Porcupine Snake	336	Secrecy	90
Pounce	252	Secret Doors	171
Preces	323	Secrets of Kratas: Vistrosh and the Songbirds	74
Preparation Time	107	Secrets of the Bloodlores	66
Prisma	324	Secrets of the Blood Wood: Alachia	62
Provoke	252	Secrets of the Blood Wood: Ritual of Thorns	63
Pry Loose	252	Secrets of the Denairastas	71
Purifier	225	Secrets of the Ironmongers	66
		Secrets of Vivane: Koar's Fate	79

Q

		Seekers of the Heart	63
Quaking Fever	189	Selecting Creatures for Encounters	245
Qural'lotectica	478	Setting	95
		Seven League Striders	229

R

		Shadowmant	334
Rapier of Wit	227	Shadowmant Venom	178
Rat, Leech	326	Shal-mora	414
Rebirth of a Nation	32	Share Knowledge	374
Recovering From Poison	173	Share Matrix Object	232
Regeneration	427	Silverback Ape	255
Relan	327	Silvered Shield	230
Remis Berries	178	Simplifying Barriers	166
Remove Element	373	Skeorx	334
Resist Pain	251	Skills	427, 466
Restoration Campaign	117	Skin Shift	466
Result Levels	162	Slipshade	497
Return to the Surface	25	Smiling Death	190
Rhinoceros	329	Smoke	231
Riding Goat	292	Snake	336

508

Snow Badger	339	Talisman Statue	235
Social Interaction	128	Task Difficulty	161
Social Interactions	143	Temperature	375
Soothe	374	Terror	466
Spear	374	The Barons	60
Special Maneuvers	251	The Battle of Prajjor's Field	30
Spectral Dancer	478	The Blood Wood	417
Spellcasting	428	The Books of Harrow	16
Spell Matrix Object	232	The Capture of the Triumph	35
Spells	374, 428, 466	The Care of Eggs	410
Spell Sword	232	The Dragon's Secret War Effort	68
Spider	340	The Fall of Vivane	36
Spike Bomb	233	The Gates of Throal and Grand Bazaar	55
Spike Trap	184	The Great Fire	55
Spirit Descriptions	375	The Halls of Throal	56
Spirit Powers	369	The Harwood Incident	33
Spirits	418	The Horrors	102
Spirits and Damage	375	The importance of the Founding	75
Spirits of Deceased Namegivers	362	The Influence of Thera	43
Squeeze the Life	252	The Influence of Throal	42
Stajian	342	The Inner Cities	59
Standard Matrix Object	232	The Inner Kingdom	58
Starvation	195	The Kingdom of Throal	53, 417
Steelman	473	The Long Night	24
Stenchfoot	190	The Mad Passions	102
Step Number Conversion Table	141	Theme	103
Stinger	343	The Nature of Horrors	452
Stoneman	472	The Origin of Dragons	414
Storm Crow	344	The Passions	415
Storm Wolf	357	The Pumpkin King (Sample Named Wood	
Stormwraith	480	Spirit)	402
Storytelling	89	Therans	109
Strawman	471	The Rites of Death	412
Strength Ratings	366	The Scourge Approaches	22
Subplots	105, 112	The Separation of Shosara	15
Suffocation	169	The Stages of Life	411
Suppress Magic	428	The Tale	92
Suppress Mark	466	The Theran Calendar	44
Survival	134	The Theran Empire	102, 417
Swimming	251	The Theran Return	28
Swooping Attack	251	The Throalic Calendar	44
Sylph (Sample Air Spirit)	386	Thorn Bow	236
		Thorn Man (Sample Wood Spirit)	404

T

Talents	375, 429, 466	Thorn Man Spear	237
		Thread Axe	238

Thread Crystal Ringlet	238
Threaded Instruments	240
Thread Item Characteristics Table	202
Thread Items	207
Thread Rank Properties	202
Thread Sword	239
Thread Wand	239
Thread Warbow	240
Throalic as the Common Tongue	45
Thunderbird	345
Thundra Beast	346
Tiger	346
Tone and Mood	96
Torrent (Sample Water Spirit)	398
Trap Descriptions	181
Traps	179
Travar	74
Traveling	125
Treasure	95, 118
Treasures	111
Trigger	180
Troajin	347
Trolls	50
Troll Snake	338
T'skrang	51
T'skrang Aropagoi	76
T'skrang River Towns	52

U

Underground Travel	131
Undine (Sample Water Spirit)	399
Unicorn	348
Unique Horror Marks	463
Unnatural Life	467
Unrequited Wave	241
Urupa	77
Using Dragons in Adventures and Campaigns	420
Using Horrors in Adventures and Campaigns	454
Using Interaction Tests	150
Using Perception Tests	163
Using Published Adventures	100
Using Spirits in Adventures and Campaigns	365

V

Velos	349
Venomous Snake	338
Visibility	135
Visibility Table	135
Vivane	78
Volus	350

W

Walking Fever	191
War Dog	277
Ward Trap	184
War Helm of Landis	242
War Horse	302
Water Spirits	395
Water Strider	352
Waxman	471
Weather	134
Whadrya Venom	178
When Not to Use the Dice	84
Where People Live	52
Who Can Do It?	160
Wild Animals and Creatures	154
Wilderness	127
Willful	251
Will o' the Wisp	353
Windlings	51
Wingbeat	429
Wingflayer	499
Witherfang	354
Witherfang Venom	179
Wolf	355
Wormskull	500
Worship of the Passions	45
Wyverns	434
Wyvernskin Robe	242

Y

Yellow Jig	192

Z

Zoak	359

Extended Step/Action Dice Table

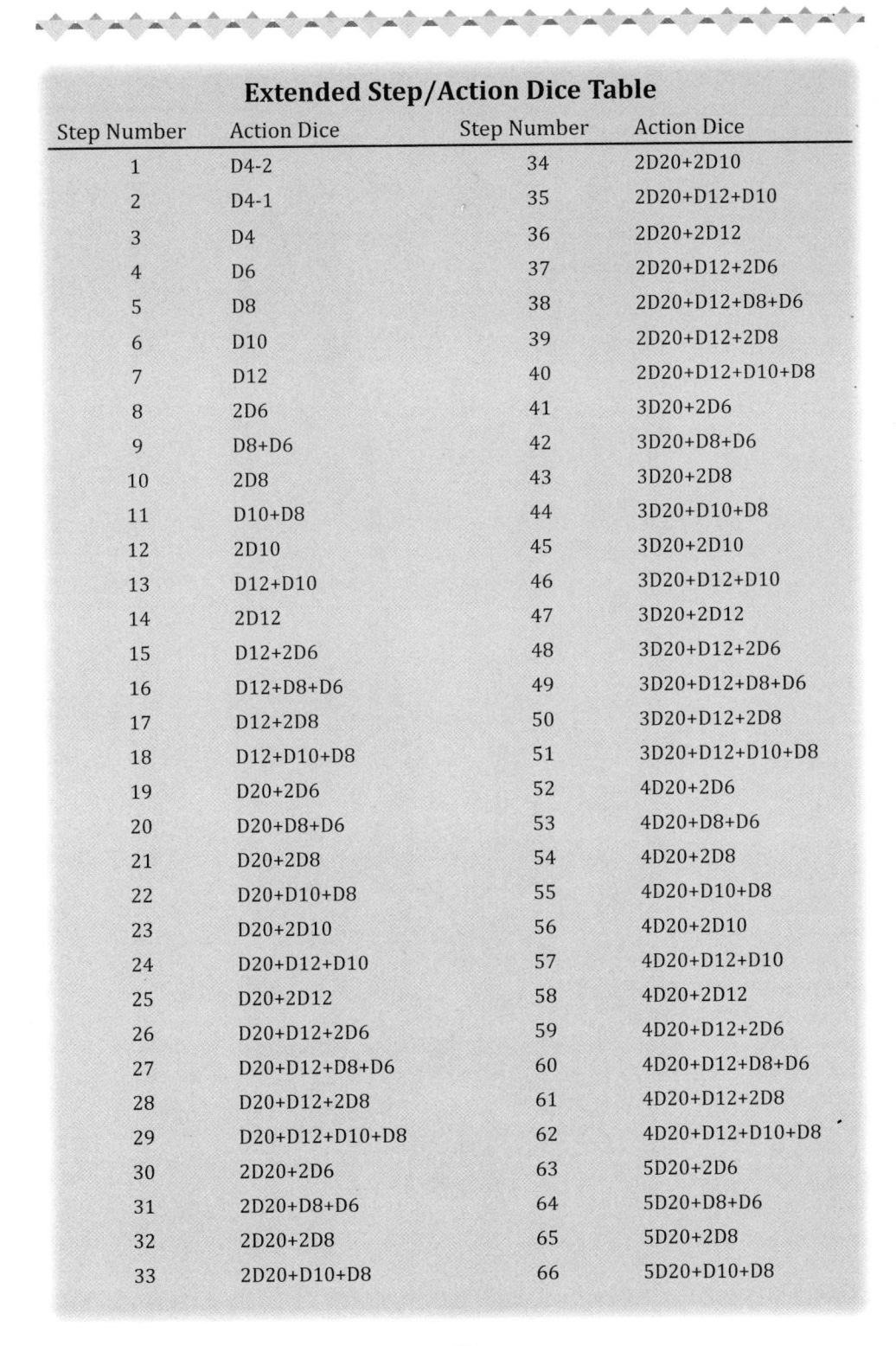

Step Number	Action Dice	Step Number	Action Dice
1	D4-2	34	2D20+2D10
2	D4-1	35	2D20+D12+D10
3	D4	36	2D20+2D12
4	D6	37	2D20+D12+2D6
5	D8	38	2D20+D12+D8+D6
6	D10	39	2D20+D12+2D8
7	D12	40	2D20+D12+D10+D8
8	2D6	41	3D20+2D6
9	D8+D6	42	3D20+D8+D6
10	2D8	43	3D20+2D8
11	D10+D8	44	3D20+D10+D8
12	2D10	45	3D20+2D10
13	D12+D10	46	3D20+D12+D10
14	2D12	47	3D20+2D12
15	D12+2D6	48	3D20+D12+2D6
16	D12+D8+D6	49	3D20+D12+D8+D6
17	D12+2D8	50	3D20+D12+2D8
18	D12+D10+D8	51	3D20+D12+D10+D8
19	D20+2D6	52	4D20+2D6
20	D20+D8+D6	53	4D20+D8+D6
21	D20+2D8	54	4D20+2D8
22	D20+D10+D8	55	4D20+D10+D8
23	D20+2D10	56	4D20+2D10
24	D20+D12+D10	57	4D20+D12+D10
25	D20+2D12	58	4D20+2D12
26	D20+D12+2D6	59	4D20+D12+2D6
27	D20+D12+D8+D6	60	4D20+D12+D8+D6
28	D20+D12+2D8	61	4D20+D12+2D8
29	D20+D12+D10+D8	62	4D20+D12+D10+D8
30	2D20+2D6	63	5D20+2D6
31	2D20+D8+D6	64	5D20+D8+D6
32	2D20+2D8	65	5D20+2D8
33	2D20+D10+D8	66	5D20+D10+D8

EARTHDAWN

2015

FINIS